Praise for Glory

'Many lives were changed irrevocably by the 1915 Battle of Gallipoli. Inspired by her grandfather's experiences, Billington focuses on the battle's impact on a young woman and two soldiers in this heart-wrenching novel of loss, love and survival'

Woman & Home

'Billington vividly creates the doomed [Gallipoli] campaign with its incompetent generals, bullish politicians and sacrificial soldiers . . . a clever, insightful and always readable book'   *The Times*

'Billington's grandfather was killed at Suvla Bay in August 1915, and this piece of family tragedy invests her epic and gripping novel with added poignancy'

Daily Mail

Rachel Billington has written twenty-one novels and eleven books for children, as well as several non-fiction works. She is also a journalist, feature writer and reviewer. She is co-editor of *Inside Time*, the national newspaper for prisoners and a former President of English PEN. She has four children and five grandchildren and lives in London and Dorset.

Also by Rachel Billington

Fiction

ALL THINGS NICE
THE BIG DIPPER
LILACS OUT OF THE DEAD LAND
COCK ROBIN
BEAUTIFUL
A PAINTED DEVIL
A WOMAN'S AGE
OCCASION OF SIN
THE GARISH DAY
LOVING ATTITUDES
THEO AND MATILDA
BODILY HARM
MAGIC AND FATE
PERFECT HAPPINESS
TIGER SKY
A WOMAN'S LIFE
THE SPACE BETWEEN
ONE SUMMER
LIES & LOYALTIES
THE MISSING BOY
MARIA AND THE ADMIRAL

For Children

ROSANNA AND THE WIZARD-ROBOT
THE FIRST CHRISTMAS
STAR TIME
THE FIRST EASTER
THE FIRST MIRACLES
THE LIFE OF JESUS
THE LIFE OF SAINT FRANCIS
FAR OUT!
THERE'S MORE TO LIFE
POPPY'S HERO
POPPY'S ANGEL

Non-Fiction

THE FAMILY YEAR
THE GREAT UMBILICAL
CHAPTERS OF GOLD

Rachel Billington

Glory

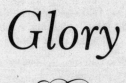

A Story of Gallipoli

'Their glory shall not be blotted out'

An Orion paperback

First published in Great Britain in 2015
by Orion Books,
This paperback edition published in 2015
by Orion Books,
an imprint of The Orion Publishing Group Ltd
Carmelite House, 50 Victoria Embankment,
London EC4Y 0DZ

An Hachette UK Company

1 3 5 7 9 10 8 6 4 2

A CIP catalogue record for this book
is available from the British Library.

ISBN 978-1-4091-4882-1

Typeset at The Spartan Press Ltd,
Lymington, Hants

Printed and bound by the CPI Group (UK) Ltd,
Croydon, CR0 4YY

The Orion Publishing Group's policy is to use papers that
are natural, renewable and recyclable products and
made from wood grown in sustainable forests. The logging
and manufacturing processes are expected to conform to
the environmental regulations of the country of origin.

www.orionbooks.co.uk

For my grandfather, Brigadier-General Thomas,
Earl of Longford who was killed at Suvla Bay on
August 21st 1915 and for all the men who
fought at Gallipoli

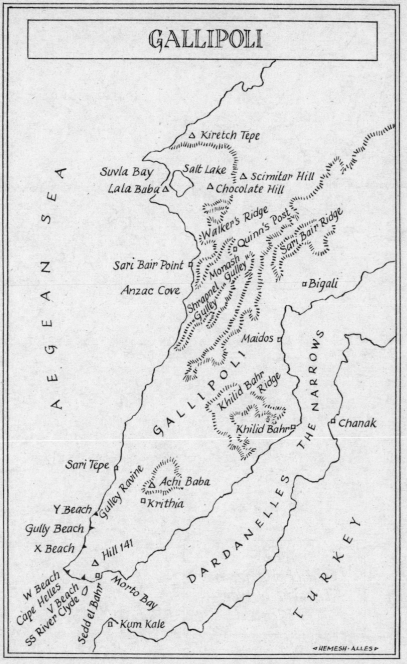

ITALY

GREECE

Salonika

Skyros

MEDITERRANEAN

Athens

SICILY

Gozo MALTA
Valletta

The
Mediterranean
Theatre of War
1915

NORTH AFR

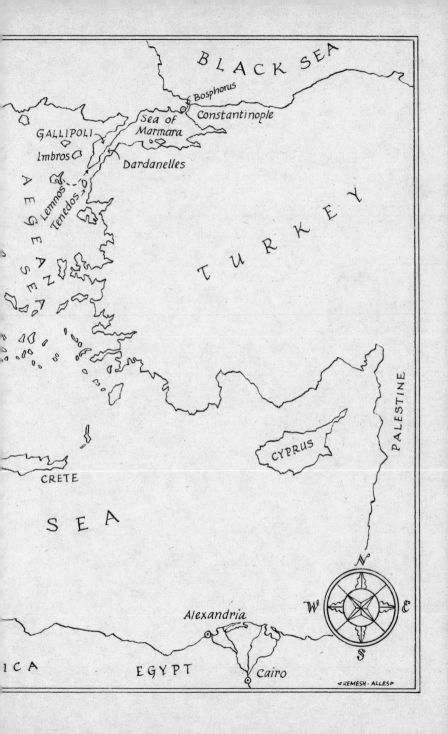

PART ONE

April 1915

✧

'Before us lies an adventure unprecedented in modern war.
Together with our comrades of the fleet we are about to force
a landing upon an open beach in face of positions which have
been vaunted by our enemies as impregnable.

The landings will be made good by the help of God and the
navy; the positions will be stormed, and the war brought one
step nearer to a glorious close.'

General Sir Ian Hamilton
(Commander in Chief of the Mediterranean Expeditionary Force)
– Special order to troops issued on 21st April 1915

One

The sky is an intense shimmering blue. The sea glows turquoise. The bay is a gentle curve, a mixture of shingle and sand. Above, a rim of hills encircles it. At the beginning of the day there was a large fort at the southern end; now it is in ruins, the falling stones still puffing out dust into the hot air, the dried grasses smouldering. The whole area is a battlefield. The ripples at the edge of the sea gradually turn blood-red.

Arthur is clinging to a single line of music. It is a solo cello and he plays it over and over in his head. Now he can't stop it if he wanted to. He had heard it at a concert before his regiment left Egypt for Gallipoli. He can't remember the composer or the soloist. The truth is he can remember nothing of the past apart from these deeply vibrating chords. The present wipes out everything.

For several hours he has stood on a ship watching young men killed in the most gruesome and detailed way. Bullet, shell and shrapnel crack open water and men alike. One spurts in glittering fountains, the other with dark blood which gradually dissolves into the water. Barbed wire, cruel as a crown of thorns, pierces the bodies of the men, dead or alive. The few who struggle to the beach, jump or twist or sprawl as they fall, lying in ugly inhuman postures.

SS *River Clyde,* on which Arthur stands, is insecurely moored against a small pier made of stone and rubble. She is an unwieldy vessel, more hulk than ship, an old collier, originally used for bringing mules from North Africa. There are no plans for her to move again. Embarkation holes – sally ports – have been cut in the side. She was supposed to be a secret weapon, a nautical Trojan horse that burst open unexpectedly, but the Turks were ready on the hill.

Men, packed tight in narrow lighters rowed by sailors, had

3

come in beside them, to be mowed down even before they left the boats. Now the boats rock gently with their cargo of dead. Very occasionally, an arm or a leg moves before a shot stills it. The drowned men, pulled down by seventy pounds of equipment as they dipped to avoid the fire, now float too, mostly face down. This is a mercy for the watchers.

Below Arthur, the soldiers in the *River Clyde* are still moving out: a short journey from darkness to light, from light to the darkness of death. Sometimes their officers need to urge them on but mostly they go out without hesitation.

Soon it will be Arthur's turn. If he lets go of the line of cello – it must be Bach – he will be able to hear again, for all the horror he sees is in dumb show, like a silent film with accompanying music. If he could think, which he can't, he would suspect that his deafness is not just a shocked refusal to hear the tortured and torturing sounds of death – the shrieks, the moans, the imploring sobs, he is close enough to hear it all – but the effect of the earlier shelling from the great battleships behind him. Out of that magnificent but useless roaring which had demolished the fort but little else, had emerged the cello.

Arthur tightens his webbing and checks the pistol at his hip. Briefly he regrets that officers don't carry rifles with their sharp bayonets. As if that could save him! He must go below and find his men.

It seems hard to die so young.

Sylvia carried a basket chair on to the lawn. It was the first halfway decent spring day. At first, she set it down under a tulip tree whose pale leaves were just uncurling, until, annoyed by the insistent cheeping of a blackbird, she picked it up again and marched it to the centre of the grass. But when she sat down, a wind, twisting through the pine trees on the edge of the lawn, blew sharp whips of hair against her face. It was enough to make her move again.

'What *are* you doing?'

Sylvia looked round as her sister, swinging a rather warped tennis racquet, came out of the veranda doors behind her.

'Nothing. Go away, Gussie.'

'I intend to. Reggie is coming over to improve my backhand.' Gussie made a sweeping motion with her racquet and laughed.

'I don't know how you can be interested in dreary Reggie or dreary tennis!' exclaimed Sylvia spitefully. Then, suddenly languid, she collapsed into the chair. It had been like this ever since Arthur had left in January. One minute she was filled with restless energy, the next with a lassitude so great it was a struggle to lift her head. Neither mood helped with her task, which was to study for the Lady Margaret Hall Oxford exam. Her failure was all the more dispiriting because it had been enormously difficult to get her parents' permission to take the exam. 'No woman in our family has ever been mistaken for a bluestocking,' her mother had declared acidly.

It was Arthur, clever, charming, now absent Arthur, who had done the persuading. 'I have always imagined an educated wife,' he had told Sylvia's father over port one evening, although this was Arthur's own account of the conversation so perhaps not to be trusted. 'Sylvia's brain has the potential to transform from jellyfish into dolphin. But only with the proper attention.'

Arthur was no catch in her mother's terms but her father, a retired colonel who had fought in Africa and India, liked his quickness and determination. Since there was no son to receive the proper attention, his eldest daughter was allowed to take the spot. After all, as Arthur had also said to Sylvia's mother, 'Women are not fully part of the university since most dons feel just like you.'

Then the war came and soon there was no Arthur as guide and inspiration. In a gesture of foolhardy pride, she had chosen to read Classics. The dreary Reggie's father, a scholarly vicar, taught her Greek – she had already taught herself Latin because whatever her mother said, she was clever as well as ambitious. If only Arthur had been in England, visiting with his university friends and talking so hard that she could feel her mind sharpening and expanding!

But Arthur's voice was confined to his letters. He had been writing often, describing the Sphinx by moonlight, but nothing since he had announced that his regiment was leaving Cairo. It had seemed a good thing since, even through a veil of classical allusions, she had received intimations of licentious temptations. 'The brothels are more prominent than the mosques.' Not that she wished to limit his experiences, even if she was his fiancée.

They had agreed that a man must be free. A woman must be free too. There were more important things in the world than personal behaviour. Socialism, for example.

Under the burden of socialism, Sylvia slipped further down in her chair. When Arthur and his friends talked about socialism, it seemed wildly exciting, even within reach. But when she thought about it afterwards, her mind became bogged down in images of her mother (daughter of an earl) attempting to treat Cook (red-faced, illiterate, bad-tempered) as an equal rather than a servant. Impossible! She suspected this was the jellyfish side of her brain.

Sylvia shut her eyes. Let the pile of books which she had meant to study lie unopened on the other side of the veranda doors. Just for five minutes she would wallow in self-pity. Why had war come to spoil everything? And why did the young have to fight it? Arthur wasn't a soldier. He was an intellectual. Yet he had gone off willingly before he was called. It was her father, the soldier, now with the Territorial Army, who talked about duty, sometimes glory, but more often duty. To Sylvia, glory didn't seem to mix with socialism yet she suspected glory was in Arthur's thinking somewhere. Look how he and his friends admired Rupert Brooke's poetry. *Blow out, you bugles, over the rich Dead! / There's none of these so lonely and poor or old / But, dying, has made us rarer gifts than gold.* She supposed if you weren't a pacifist, you simply had to make going to war just a little bit heroic.

From the end of the garden, she heard a faraway male cry of 'Well done!'

Brushing a tear from her eye, Sylvia jumped up and strode purposefully towards her books.

Fred crouches in the lee of a small rise at the right-hand southerly corner of the beach. He estimates there is less than six feet of turf and sandy earth to protect him from the Turkish guns. Around him are crowded dozens of men, none speaking a word. They are the lucky survivors. But for how long? Through the loud thud of his heart, which at least partially masks the noise of the gunfire all around, he hopes there are no officers.

When he'd been tipped off the lighter into the water and found the sea jumping with bullets like salmon on a run and the bodies slumping on every side – which is not even to mention the underwater spikes of barbed wire and the fact he couldn't swim – he'd made a quick decision. Off went his pack, his rifle, his ammunition. Only thing he kept was his flask of water. Long hot days at haymaking time had given him a respect for drinking water. Not the salty sort.

He isn't ashamed of the decision. What good is a dead Frederick M. Chaffey to the British Army? And here he is alive, isn't he, ready to give Johnny Turk a jab in the guts if he gets half a chance. But he'd suffered through enough training to know an officer might not look at it like that. Or worse still, the sergeant: 'Cradle your rifle like a bleeding baby!'

Without moving his head, Fred glances at his neighbour. Bad idea. Dead as a rat in a trap and not so pretty. It gives him an opportunity all the same. His arm moves as silently as a snake until it has reached the man's rifle lying by his side. Then it retreats with the gun. That poor bugger has no more use for it. Now for the man's pack. Not so easy to get that off his shoulders as he's half lying on it.

'Hey!' The soldier in front kicks out protesting as Fred nudges his leg. Immediately, a bullet whizzes their way.

'Wouldn't do that,' advises Fred under his breath.

The soldier is groaning and blood seeps out of his boot.

Fred decides he can't do much more till darkness comes – quite a few more hours, he reckons by the heat of the sun. He lies down as comfortably as he can and tries to conjure up an even worse situation where things had come out all right in the end. Up against the magistrates for poaching when they'd taken pity on a poor orphan boy and let him off. That had been a good one. Kissing Mary on Christmas Eve when her father had whacked him with a spade and then come out and said sorry when Mary had cried for him. That was another good one. Buying Lil a hat for church with his first earnings. That had been a day! But then Lil was as good as he was bad. No one ever had a sister like her.

Almost happy, Fred pictures his elder sister who'd brought him up when their parents died. She would be glad he'd cut loose from his pack and got ashore. She'd promised to write to him and she would, first time she had a moment, or even if she didn't have a moment.

It is two nights since Fred has slept but he is young, with a country boy's acceptance of what can't be changed. Hand under one cheek, he falls into a dream-filled doze.

Two

The commanding officer, Lieutenant Colonel Harrington, had given the order: no more men to leave the *Clyde* until nightfall.

Arthur, whose company was next to go, looked at his watch: 9.45 a.m. 'Stand the men down, Sergeant.'

'Sir.' A salute with no sign of emotion. All the slaughter on V Beach had taken place in three hours. He tried to remember the briefing that had told him when protecting darkness would come. Seven? Eight? The adrenalin pumped so hard that it flooded his brain. His blood was up. Meet blood with blood. Still that cello, but thin and wavering now.

Reprieved! The groans and wails of the wounded outside the ship were fearfully loud and close. So close. *He* was not to face death. Not yet. His mind still tried to count the hours till nightfall. Despite the terror, he'd been proud to be leading out his men and now all that impatient energy had been abruptly cut off. Furiously, he hit the side of the ship with his stick. He *wanted* to be out there, playing his little part in winning the war. Standing here, unwanted, rebuffed, made him feel ashamed, cowardly, a failure. He was alive! With so many dead, he was alive. The men were already unloading their packs, putting down their rifles, taking off their sun helmets. Soon they'd be smoking, chewing on army ration biscuits. They were alive too.

One wounded soldier's voice was tragic, high-pitched as he called for help. He sounded like a child calling for his mother – one of the brave Munsters with his Irish accent. Another, gruffer, merely groaned occasionally but so loud that he sounded as if he was in the ship. The reality was that even if he lay dying a few yards from the sally port he could not be rescued without the risk of instant death by sniper.

Arthur decided he didn't have to stay where he was. His feet, in the boots so carefully oiled by his servant the night before, could move. His whole body was a machine, oiled for efficient action. He was alive. He could leave these brave, staunch men who, like him, had been prepared to die – at the thought of their goodness, shameful tears pressed at his eyelids; he was not himself yet – he could climb upwards, pass hurriedly over the middle deck where there was no protection and onwards to the upper deck where the top brass stood. As a junior officer it was not his place but Lieutenant Colonel Harrington had recognised him as a school contemporary of his son's.

'I'll be on the upper deck, Sergeant Babcock.'

'Sir.' He was an experienced soldier, Babcock. Fought in South Africa. Other places. An old man with a son at the front.

Arthur put his first boot on the iron stair and remembered how, that morning at three o'clock, after being wakened with a cup of tea, he had carefully wound the nine feet of puttee from the top of his boot to his knee. He'd bandaged those puttees like the winding sheets enclosing a dead body. He had been looking to a heroic death as he left the comforts of that earlier ship. Or victory, yes, he had dared to hope for victory. Death or victory. They were marching towards the historic city of Constantinople. In his dreams Arthur imagined a glorious entry to ancient Byzantium, the expulsion of the infidel, the revenge of Christians turned out of the city five hundred years earlier . . .

The *Clyde* had been a shock. The ugliness, the noise, the confusion as the huge ship wheeled round. 'They've got it all wrong,' a major had exclaimed furiously. 'We've got ahead of the tows. Now there'll be the usual muddle.'

That was a shock too. A senior officer with a crown on his cuff should not express such a lack of confidence in the efficiency of the army – although in this case, it was the army combined with the navy. He needed to believe that these men who commanded life and death were superior beings, infallible except, perhaps, when the odds were stacked too severely against them. 'The usual muddle'. It was the 'usual' that disturbed him most. He was the one in a muddle, the new boy who gazed in awed admiration at the prefects above.

An hour later, standing on deck in a hazy golden dawn which

would have been breathtakingly beautiful in any other circumstances, he'd watched that major lead his men out from the ship. He'd lasted only a few seconds before being mown down, his whole head, pipe in mouth, swiped off, while his body stood for a moment before falling into the water where it was soon covered by piles of dead and wounded.

It was then the cello had begun, taut wires running through his brain and playing that single line of music.

Maybe, instead of returning to that unrestricted view, he would find a quiet corner and write to Sylvia. He had her notebook and pencil in his pocket. 'Only for poetry or letters to me,' she'd told him seriously.

But there were no quiet corners. All the time officers of various ranks were passing up or down which, since he was just about the bottom of the pile, meant endless saluting and stepping aside. Or there were lines of men, two thousand of them, their morning resolution exchanged for subdued patience. Only their boots clattered.

'Get a move on, there!' A captain was coming off the middle deck as Arthur arrived at the top of the stairs, blocking the man's descent. Mechanically Arthur raised his arm for a salute. He found himself pushed backwards down the stairway.

The captain pulled him up at the bottom. 'I wouldn't want my death on your conscience.' He smiled so that his blond moustache lifted upward above his white teeth and his blue eyes brightened. He was very handsome and confident. 'You can salute me now, if you must.'

Confused, Arthur did so and the captain returned it formally.

As Arthur turned back to the stairway, he heard the officer's voice again. 'Do you find it hard to be one of the lucky survivors?'

'I don't know, sir.'

'I'm not a real soldier, you know,' continued the captain. 'I'm attached to staff HQ. I'm not going out to be killed like you brave fellows. Unless this whole ship blows up – unlikely as the Turkish shells come in from Asia and the German submarines haven't found us yet – I'm safe. They will find us, of course, but by then I'll be on the lovely island of Imbros or Lemnos. You know what they say: "Imbros, Lemnos and chaos".'

Arthur was encouraged to ask a question. 'I say, what are you doing on this ship?'

'I say indeed!' The officer took a step backwards before giving a bellow of laughter. 'Couldn't stand the strain of not being where the action was. Sitting in that hideous Mudros counting ships into harbour and men into ships. Worse when we moved to HMS *Queen Elizabeth*. Killing Turks from a position of perfect safety.'

Arthur could think of no response to this and watched as the captain turned his back to him, moodily leaning against a wall. He was about to leave when the captain turned back again.

'Ever met an Aussie soldier?' He made himself more comfortable against the wall.

'Saw a few in Cairo, sir.'

'They'd as soon salute a rattlesnake as a British officer. Spent an evening with them once. Ended badly. Never drink with an Aussie.'

'No, sir.'

'They had my trousers off. Humiliating.' The captain grimaced. 'Took my revenge the following night, though. Put on my Arab gear, bit of paint on the face and sidled up to them in the bar. Speaking the local lingo plus a bit of pidgin English, I let them think I was a spy. Swallowed it hook, line and sinker. Such a tale I spun. Their eyes on stalks. One of them went off to get their company commander, another for the military police. Just before they arrived, hey presto, I whipped off my disguise.' He chuckled with satisfaction. 'Had to get out of that bar quick. Aussies don't like being fooled.'

'They were supposed to land on the peninsula at the same time as us, I believe,' said Arthur.

'Great fighters. Just don't try drinking with them. They're landing further up north. With the New Zealand crowd. Hope they have more success than here. Hey, fancy a game of backgammon?'

'I'm afraid I've never played it.' Restlessly, Arthur glanced from side to side but saw nothing to divert him from this man's attention. It had begun to be hot. The fierce spring sun beat on the steel ship, turning it into an oven.

'No? I picked it up out here. Been out East for years. Come on, then. I'll teach you.' Gripping Arthur's arm, he led him briskly along two corridors and down a flight of stairs until they reached a dim corner at the bow of the ship. Here he took his pack off his shoulder and produced a board with triangular markings and a box of round counters.

'They're draught pieces,' commented Arthur, without real interest. As he looked at the captain he realised something about him was familiar. 'I say, you were at Eton!' he exclaimed. 'During my first week I saw you getting into an enormous Daimler. It was the car I looked at but I remember you. Never saw you again.'

'Nor would you,' replied the captain cheerfully as he set out the game. 'That was me, all right, being swept away by our chauffeur in disgrace. Never to return.'

Arthur looked down at the red and white counters laid out in opposing lines and his strong feeling that he didn't want to be sitting here playing some Eastern game with this man grew even stronger. 'What are you doing at staff headquarters?' he asked abruptly.

'Intelligence,' answered the captain, amicably. 'Although I'm more of a glorified translator. Ever been to Constantinople?'

'That's why we're fighting,' said Arthur sourly, 'so that we can all go to Constantinople, Russians included. Russians particularly, since they requested us to go there in the first place. What were you doing in Constantinople?' he added almost rudely. Then, 'I don't think I want to play a game.' He jumped up, knocking the board.

The captain bent and carefully picked up a few pieces that had fallen. 'I'm just as keen for our chaps to win as you are,' he said in a calm voice. 'And probably more useful. But I won't stand the stupidity and pretence. It's not the time for a history lesson, I know, but we didn't have to be fighting the Turks. They liked us. More than the Germans. Till Mr Churchill, our dashing First Lord of the Admiralty, snatched their battleships, paid for by them and built by us.'

Arthur glared down at him. 'The Turks are our enemy and I don't think you should say things like that!' He had stayed on at school as a scholar and enjoyed discussing the merits of Plato's *Republic* over More's *Utopia*.

'You shouldn't take me so seriously.' The captain was using his left hand to play the scarlet and white pieces.

'We're in a serious situation,' hissed Arthur. 'At war! And

you've just come along to see the show as if it was .. as if it were entertainment!'

'I'm sorry.' The captain sighed as if with genuine remorse. 'I guessed you were a kindred spirit, someone I could speak to freely. I get fed up with all the old buffers talking humbug. Most of them haven't seen action since South Africa and half of them are dugouts. Even General Sir Ian Hamilton, our great commander, a charming scholar and poet, is sixty-two. The nearest I get to a youthful point of view is my servant who tells me if I wasn't an earl they'd never have had me in the army.'

'*Are* you an earl?'

'The eldest son of one which, in Hepple's eyes, counts as the same thing. Of course my father might try and disinherit me in favour of one of my younger brothers.' He frowned and with abrupt gestures began to pack away the board and pieces. 'If any of them survive the war.' His voice wore a new grit of bitterness. 'Do *you* have brothers?'

'All I have is my uncle.'

'You're lucky.'

'Thanks!'

The captain stood up. 'I've two brothers at the front in France. At least I did till yesterday. Handed a telegram. The elder, and nicest, I may say, killed. Shot through the head, although they always say that. Family in mourning. Wishing it was *moi*, of course.'

Arthur felt himself blushing. 'No one I know has died yet,' he muttered.

'I'm Rupert Prideaux, incidentally.'

Arthur suspected suddenly that Prideaux needed companionship as much as he did. 'Arthur Lamb,' he said and held out his hand.

Prideaux seemed to hesitate for a moment before holding out his hand too. As they shook, Arthur realised that the hand that gripped him strongly enough had no index finger. Trigger finger, as it was called.

'Not A1,' said Prideaux, watching Arthur. 'Nor a war hero. I was playing with a gun on the grouse moors. I'll tell you what, how about you and I pick up some of those poor wretches screaming for their mamas? More entertainment than backgammon. What do you say?'

Arthur stared. Prideaux's tone was as ironic as ever but his face was grave.

'Do you mean it?'

'Because I'm an intelligence officer with a crippled hand? Of course I mean it. Where's your sense of adventure?'

'I'm a junior officer. Under orders.' Arthur thought of the water outside, of the cool tide rushing from the sea of Marmara, through the Dardanelles into the Aegean, now filled with bloodied arms and legs, staring faces, sharp wire, deadly snipers.

'So you are! I can't think how I failed to notice.' Prideaux turned as if to leave. 'I'll find someone less cabin'd and confined.'

Arthur looked at his watch. It was still only eleven. He'd inherited the watch from his father when the face was huge on his childish wrist. 'No! Wait!' He grabbed Prideaux's arm.

Sylvia was trying to look at the drawing room of Tollorum Manor through Arthur's eyes. It was a way of getting close to him. But she had known this room all her life and although she could describe its components – the two bow windows, thrown out in Victorian times from the Georgian original, the high ceiling with the row of three chandeliers, the many sofas and small attendant tables, the excessively large fireplace put in about 1900, the many dull landscape paintings – she could hardly *see* them, let alone from Arthur's point of view.

Instead, she pictured him upright and true in his new uniform and tried to place him in the room. But she was defeated there too. She supposed it was love that blinded her even to his appearance beyond the most obvious – he might as well be any well turned out young officer, a Madame Tussaud's waxwork.

'Sylvia, dearest, if you have nothing better to do than stand there in a trance, how about accompanying me to see poor Mrs Lovage? She's expecting again, this time with twins, or so she thinks, and of course Mr Lovage was first to join up.'

Sylvia sighed and felt sorry for her mother who disapproved of Mrs Lovage but felt an obligation to help her.

'And then afterwards I shall be joining the Red Cross Committee. We are planning to roll bandages.' Since her daughter still said nothing, she continued, 'Now that the last decent horse has been taken, I'm only left with the pony and trap so everything takes far longer.'

Lady Beatrice Fitzpaine had once been nearly a beauty with her creamy complexion, large blue eyes and golden hair, but she lacked animation and now that she had passed forty, she often wore a fretful look, particularly when Colonel Fitzpaine was away, as he had been a great deal since the start of the war.

'I'm sorry, Mama, but I have two books to read before my next tutorial with Mr Gisburne.'

Her mother did not press her further. Beatrice herself would have preferred to spend the morning reading. 'I think I'll work in my room.' Sylvia picked up her books with determination.

'Don't forget I've invited him to lunch. He is kind to give you so much time.'

Her sister Gussie bullied their mother but Sylvia felt a mixture of sympathy and irritation. It was not Beatrice's fault that she had been educated, or rather not educated, in the way of upper class girls. She had a vaguely ironic way of speaking which suggested she understood the life she led was a little foolish.

Musing upon this, Sylvia wandered up the wide wooden staircase and along the landing with its dark red Turkish carpet. Here she stopped and looked down, then crouched, putting her books aside. A Turkish carpet, made by the same hands that were now trying to kill Arthur.

Sylvia tried to picture a Turkish soldier as she had tried to picture Arthur earlier but she couldn't go much further than a turban, a black bushy moustache and a ferocious scowl. Arthur had told her the Ottoman Empire had recently fought and lost wars; he had given this history of failure as one of the reasons why the Allies – British, French and soldiers from all over the British Empire – would be across the Gallipoli Peninsula in a matter of days.

'Then we'll be on to Byzantium and all the glorious treasures of Asia!' he'd exulted. 'Thank the Lord the navy couldn't do the job on its own or the army would have missed all the fun. Think of the horror! Some ignorant naval rating who's only vaguely heard of Helen as if some queen of his local beauty pageant, digging his fat fingers into the great site of Troy!' Sylvia had smiled. She'd read in *The Times* about the navy's failure to get up the Dardanelles Strait and take Constantinople by sea. That was when the army had been brought in.

Sylvia walked, with head downcast, to her bedroom. On this spring morning it was at its most delightful, the William Morris wallpaper bringing the garden into the room. She supposed it was lucky that Arthur had not been sent to the trenches in France.

She went towards the window. How often had she flung it open and with her heart full of Arthur quoted Keats or Browning! ' "Soft adorings from their loves receive / upon the honey'd middle of the night." ' Of course Arthur did not altogether approve of the Romantics, although she did not see how Rupert Brooke was so different.

'Syl-vi-a! Syl-vi-a!' Papa had once commented that Gussie was like an express train, with the roar of the engine, the hiss of the steam and the inexorable churning of the wheels.

'Come and pl-a-ay with me!' She was getting closer.

Why not run about and hit a ball? Sylvia leant out of the window and yelled in tones not dissimilar to her sister's, 'I'm co-ming dow-wn!'

Fred was wakened, although not fool enough to move, by a particularly desperate shriek. Up to now the wails and groans, the whimpers and moans of the wounded had formed a human background of misery on whom, since he could do nothing to help, he wasted no sympathy. But these yells were a whole new level of protest, as if something had happened to them even worse than lying wounded on the beach unable to move, with Johnny Turk taking a potshot at them on and off.

Curiosity being one of Fred's weaknesses, he attempted to angle his head so he could catch a glimpse of whatever was going on behind him. As he did this, with infinite care so he scarcely appeared to be moving, a voice, recognisably an officer's by its vowels, exclaimed, 'The bloody Aegean's coming in! If that isn't the bloody last straw.'

Fred, who thought the Aegean, like every other sea in the world, had a perfect right, indeed a duty, to obey the laws of time and tide, was intrigued by the sense of outrage in the officer's voice.

So intrigued and, it was true, bored after the hours of lying quiet, that he felt the need to ask, 'Didn't you *expect* it to come in, sir?'

'The Aegean doesn't have a tide, you idiot! Now we'll have to listen to those poor blighters drowning for the rest of the afternoon.'

Since the sea *was* coming in, whatever the officer believed, Fred thought he was less of an idiot than the officer. But he said nothing more. Death was an unpleasant business however it came. Even the rabbits screeched when their end was near and their brain was the size of a cobnut. Quite tasty too, if you were hungry enough. The brain, not the cobnut. Never liked nuts.

Through the chatter of his own brain and the crying of the men, Fred could hear the water now: little, lapping, deadly waves.

More as a dare and a diversion than with any real intention of action, Fred raised his voice again (better than his head). 'How about trying to pull up a few, sir? They're not far away.'

There was a pause during which Fred felt that all the men safely huddled under the bank held their breath, then the officer gave an audible sigh. 'Brave man. 'Fraid I can't be with you. They got me in the legs. Can't stand, d'you see.'

Fred cursed himself. Why hadn't he kept his big mouth shut? He hadn't really planned to risk his life for those bloody old moaners – not till nightfall, anyway.

'I'll come along,' whispered a hoarse voice, further away. 'Can't lie here the live-long day.'

Well, I can, thought Fred. Each of us has only one life. Each to protect his own.

'Me, too,' another voice came, 'although I'm not sure about my arm. Might not be much use.'

Two or three voices joined in a mumble of volunteering.

Soon we'll have a ruddy company, thought Fred, with me in command. 'Can't be more than two or we won't stand a chance. Those snipers have eyes like hawks.'

The owner of the hoarse voice wriggled towards him. He was as young as Fred, carrot-coloured hair.

'You're bloodied,' pointed out Fred.

'Sure, that's barbed wire. Snip it, Sergeant says. Might as well try and snip Cloyne Round Tower with a lady's scissors. 'Tis only scratches all the same.'

Fred didn't know any Irish men but there was no doubting where this man came from. 'Want to risk putting your ma in mourning?'

'Better than lying out in this furnace.'

Indeed his face was the colour of skinned beetroot, which didn't go too well with his hair.

'Let's get the one nearest,' said Fred. 'He's moaning like a girl.'

They both listened. For the last half an hour there'd been very little shooting from any direction. No more men had come ashore for a couple of hours. Perhaps Johnny Turk had taken the chance for a nice cuppa.

The two men twisted round so that they were facing the sea. Carrots did it like he was a country boy too, Fred thought. Hardly a sound, make sure the farmer or gamekeeper hears less than a vole's rustle.

In only a few seconds they'd wormed their way five yards down the beach. It was a relief to be facing the sea and sky after so long staring at a dirty bank without wishing to lift his eyes. Fred was aware of the bow of the *River Clyde* like a dark wall ahead and the pebbly beach almost disappearing under the distorted shapes of human forms.

The softly moaning man turned out to be an officer, curled up on his side like a baby.

'He's a big one,' whispered Carrots nervously.

'Too big, too far gone. Let's try that little one.'

But he was no good either because his littleness was due to the fact that he'd lost all his limbs except for the leg nearest them.

'He's dead,' said Fred hopefully and noticed Carrot's red face was tinged with green.

' 'Ere, you buggers.' The voice, more groan, came from behind or even under the big officer. 'Can't you see what's in front of your eyes?'

'Sheltering, were you?' Fred slithered over and pushed aside the officer's outflung arm and slowly rolled him over. No sudden movement to attract Johnny Turk from his tea break.

'Trapped, wasn't I? Shot in my shoulder and thigh.'

Carrots helped Fred as the man himself began to crawl upwards. 'Didn't plan to drown,' he said as they reached the safety of the bank.

Drown in your own blood more likely, thought Fred, which reminded him of their first plan to rescue the men at risk of drowning.

Pushing himself further into safety, he turned his head. 'Sea's still a long way down,' he said to Carrots who'd followed him.

The officer shot in the legs overheard him. 'You're good fellows, you two.'

There he was, caught out by his own big mouth again. Fred looked at Carrots. 'You're on for it, are you?'

'St Christopher himself couldn't drag them all the way up.'

'Yes. Yes. Just out of the water.' The officer's voice was weaker but no less demanding. 'Drowning's a terrible thing.'

'Holy Mother of God!' exclaimed Carrots staring at the officer. 'He's gone. Speaking one minute, up with the angels the next.'

Fred began to be irritated by the religious turn of events. 'There's not much sign of God on this beach.'

Carrots crossed himself nervously before saying in a voice of wonder and reverence, '*He* is everywhere.' A shot being fired at the same time, he lay flat. So did Fred. A few more shots were fired before it went quiet again.

It was very hot, the sun pounding on their heads. There was a new outbreak of groaning and moaning at the seashore. The dead officer's voice repeated in Fred's head, 'Drowning's a terrible thing.' He'd always been better at action than lying still.

He began crawling down, never rising above feet and ankles. Carrots followed. Fred pictured a slow-worm on stony ground. He'd heard there weren't any snakes in Ireland. He wondered what Carrots pictured. The bleeding heart of Jesus most likely.

Prideaux had got command of a boat and a couple of volunteer seamen. They were only boys, really, dressed in white ducks dyed a khaki colour. They'd expected to row in the lighters with the landing soldiers. Instead, they'd watched their mates being destroyed before being told to sit tight till dark. One, called Blinks, with red spots over his pale face, was certain a special mate of his called Ollie Midge was still alive and could be rescued.

Prideaux and Arthur made their way to the stern of the *Clyde*. It was all very irregular.

20

'You lads, steer the boat,' said Prideaux. 'Can either of you swim?'

Blinks could and Strimmer, the other, insisted he'd hang on tight to the side. They would all be in the water sheltering behind the boat.

'The problem will be getting the wounded in,' said Arthur. It was strangely quiet where they stood at the stern of the *Clyde*. Far out on the shining water he could see the great battleships which had done the initial shelling.

'We are not ambitious,' pronounced Prideaux. 'One saved life is worth the risk.'

Arthur remembered a captain during his training pronouncing over dinner, 'As officers and soldiers we are the property of His Majesty and have a duty to preserve our lives accordingly.' But probably he was joking or drunk or both. Then he wondered if Prideaux planned to give his life as his brother had.

It was hot where they stood, the sun directly overhead. The metal ship, which was partly camouflaged with ochre paint, reflected dully into the blue water. It was a relief not to see the horrible sights at the beach.

'Onward Christian soldiers,' said Prideaux to Arthur and both men climbed down a ladder into the boat, held steady by Blinks while Strimmer looked after the oars.

'I'm glad to be off that ship,' said Arthur as he arrived safely.

'Hell-hole,' agreed Prideaux cheerfully. 'Although we'd have to agree that the thousand poor sods inside are better off than the thousand who went out.' He took off his cap – he was not wearing a pith helmet like most officers – and pushed back his thick hair. Arthur tried not to stare at his hand which looked more obviously mutilated in the sunshine. Half of the next finger was also missing.

They moved slowly forward, edging along by the side of the *Clyde*. Occasionally, a shot was fired ahead, usually single. 'Snipers,' commented Prideaux. 'God forbid there're any in the fort.'

Almost at that moment a volley of shots came from their right where the fort crumbled wearily after the early shelling.

The seamen hesitated but none of the shots came anywhere close. Then they died away.

They were now near the first sally port. Arthur expected a

superior officer to hail them: 'What the fuck do you think you're doing!' Instead a trio of wan soldiers' faces stared curiously.

'Into the bath!' ordered Prideaux and one by one they slipped into the water, kicking out to make the boat move forward.

'Shall we get them off the spit, sir?' whispered Blinks intensely. 'Ollie washed up there, I think.'

'One place is as good as another,' said Prideaux, adding grandly, 'Succour has no limitations of person or place.'

They came to the bow of the *Clyde*. Arthur was aware they must be watched from above but all was silent, apart from the shots that continued randomly as before and the louder, because nearer, cries of the wounded. 'The tide's coming in,' he announced suddenly in a horrified voice. 'The Aegean shouldn't have a tide.'

'The East is an impenetrable mystery,' said Prideaux.

Arthur wanted to say this is Europe, we're on the European side of Turkey, but his mind was diverted by his feet which were touching the bottom and feeling heavy, round shapes that made him stumble. 'A lot of packs dumped,' he said. He must not be treading on corpses.

The spit was ahead, broken rubble and, at an angle, the lighter that had formed a bridge from the ship. All around it men were draped, most, it seemed already dead or at least unable to complain.

Their small boat bumped against the edge. Immediately rifle fire broke out making all four men freeze, but it was far to their left and soon stopped. Sniper fire followed in short bursts, again to their left, although now and again it was close enough for them to see a spout of water as a bullet hit the sea.

'They haven't spotted us, have they, sir?' asked Blinks nervously.

'We'll know it when they do.' Arthur and Prideaux exchanged glances. What were they waiting for?

They left the shelter of the boat and waded towards the spit. A young man lay nearest, one eye open, one closed. Arthur nudged him and he slid downwards, sluicing into the sea. The body of the next man was shattered, thin trickles of blood still wriggling into the water.

'Here.' A quiet voice but alive. Arthur, Prideaux and Blinks heaved at the sodden mass while Strimmer angled the boat. The man seemed intact until he lay sprawled out. 'It's my bleeding foot,' he moaned.

'It was,' commented Arthur under his breath to Prideaux. 'However did he get shot there?'

As Strimmer gave the man water, Arthur and Prideaux uncovered an officer under a pile of bodies. 'Dead?'

'Perhaps we should bring him in?' So they did. He was a major, not the same who had angered Arthur, shot through the chest, the hole washed clean.

'A hero,' said Prideaux.

Arthur looked at him suspiciously but Prideaux was staring down at the man admiringly, even with envy.

'Here's a good one.' Blinks had found a young soldier still clinging to his rifle. His eyes were squeezed shut and he was shivering. Once they'd hauled him into the boat, he opened his eyes and let go of his rifle.

'I was praying, wasn't I. St Jude, patron of lost causes.'

'Irish,' said Strimmer. 'Nothing wrong with him that I can see.'

They got hold of two more men, dragging them awkwardly and trying not to hear all the other wounded calling out but who were too far off to help. Arthur looked up at the other side of the spit and wished he hadn't. There were soldiers tangled in the barbed wire, half in the water, half out, some upside down or held outstretched in the position in which they'd been shot.

'We shouldn't push our luck.' Prideaux stamped himself clear of an entanglement round his legs before knocking away a floating water bottle.

It was as if objects were collecting around them. Concentrating on their task, Arthur had lost his sense of danger, but now they had paused, he listened anxiously. The firing had increased. 'There's someone moving on the beach. Two men, I think.'

'They're dragging the wounded out of the sea. They won't do that for long.' Prideaux turned away. 'We should up sticks.'

As he spoke a machine gun opened fire. Or maybe a volley of rifle fire. Arthur watched as the two men on the beach fell flat, not wounded, he thought. One eased over a discarded pack to protect his head. 'They must have come down from under that bank.'

'They're pinned down now,' said Prideaux over his shoulder. 'Once a sniper finds his mark, he never lets go.'

They reached the boat together and just as they grabbed the side, a bullet, slipping an inch above their bent heads, cracked into the wood. Another followed, hitting in almost exactly the same place. A moment later, Blinks, who had jumped inside the boat and whose head was slightly raised, gave a little gasp and fell backwards.

One of the wounded men also gasped because Blinks had landed on top of him.

Arthur, Prideaux and Strimmer began to drag the boat with desperate energy. It was much harder to get it away than it had been to bring it in.

Then they pushed, half swimming, bullets flying by like vicious birds or ricocheting from the wood or sending splinters twirling like daggers. A dreamlike sense took hold of Arthur and gave him courage. He wished, however, that Blinks's childlike face, a bullet hole neatly through the head, was not directly below him.

Now they were swimming fully, even Strimmer was kicking with his legs as if he'd suddenly learnt how; the boat reached the *Clyde* and moved past the first sally port. Better not to stop. Bullets pursued them. Airborne demons. Perhaps it would be his last memory. He was glad of his helmet. Two pale points glowed either side: Strimmer's round pale face and Prideaux's golden hair. Arthur thought he was a life force. Not like his brother. Good sheep dies. Bad sheep survives.

A shriek as a bullet whacked into soft flesh. One of the wounded but he groaned still, not dead like poor Blinks. The spots were livid on his face like the plague. He'd never found his mate.

As in a dream, one moment they were amidst demons and the next in the calm behind the *Clyde*. One boy dead, one man further wounded.

They slumped over the edge of the boat; sweat and water poured off their bodies.

'Who the hell gave you permission to take that boat?' A naval officer was screaming down at them. Behind him a burly army officer stood watchfully.

Prideaux lifted his head. 'Humanity,' he said, either not able or not wishing to raise his voice.

'What's that, Captain?' began the naval officer at an ever higher pitch of rage. He broke off as the burly soldier tapped him on the shoulder and said something into his ear which caused him to step back and salute.

'Is that you, Prideaux?' the soldier bellowed.

'Yes, sir.' Prideaux's attitude changed – as far as the attitude of an exhausted man clinging to the side of a boat could change. 'We need a medic, sir.' He attempted a salute.

Arthur, who was gradually coming to, realised he was staring up at the famous Lieutenant Colonel Doughty-Wylie.

'Of course you need a medic – one for your stupid head too.'

Things happened very quickly. The boat was pulled in, dead and wounded removed and Prideaux and Arthur led to a cabin, where their packs were brought to them.

'Where are servants when you need them?' grumbled Prideaux, trying to rid himself of his sodden uniform.

'Do you *know* Doughty-Wylie? In person, I mean.' Arthur was awed.

'Both out in the East.' Prideaux was still tugging ineffectually at his breeches. 'He's at staff headquarters. Can't stick being out of the action, either. Not surprised to see him here. Must have come off the *Queen Elizabeth* too. Pull off these, be a good fellow.'

Arthur suddenly realised that the reason Prideaux couldn't get out of his wet clothes was his maimed hand.

There was a knock at the door and a medical officer peered round. 'You two need any attention?'

Arthur answered. 'No, sir. Are they going to survive, sir?'

'Survive? Not much chance for the midshipman with a bullet in his skull but the others should. If the hospital ship doesn't kill them. No one was prepared for the level of casualties.'

'Fuckers!' Prideaux had now managed to strip himself entirely and was towelling himself dry. Arthur noticed that, apart from his middle, he was sunburnt to a dark brown.

'Excuse me?' The lean and intelligent face of the doctor looked comically surprised.

'The Turkish are great fighters, particularly defending their own land. Sir.'

'Quite.' The MO looked at Prideaux curiously. 'It's my business to cure. English and Turk alike. I don't make wars. I don't question them, either.'

'No, sir,' said Arthur as Prideaux said nothing.

Saluting so that even the naked Prideaux jumped to attention, the MO left the cabin.

Prideaux collapsed on to a bunker. 'I wish I was a doctor. It's the only responsible profession.'

'You weren't very polite to him if you think that.'

Prideaux looked interested. 'You think politeness worthwhile, do you?'

'Yes, I do,' said Arthur firmly. 'It upholds order and without order we have chaos.'

'Lemnos, Imbros and chaos, here we come again.' Prideaux was watching his hands as he flexed them rhythmically. 'You don't think politeness disguises chaos?'

'No.' Arthur continued dressing briskly. The warmth of a good deed attempted was spreading through his body along with his clean dryness. 'I have to get to my men.' He thought how lucky he was to be in charge of a brave group of soldiers who were willing to die for their country. He felt more worthy of them now. He could look his sergeant major in the eye. He felt like a man of action. 'I must go to my men,' he repeated.

'How Christ-like!' Prideaux, still seated naked on the bunk, raised his arm as if in blessing.

Hoping to irritate, Arthur saluted smartly and left the cabin.

Fred wasn't surprised to find himself lying in such a hopeless position. Life had always been like this as long as he could remember. He didn't even regret leaving what now seemed a perfectly secure billet under the bank. A man has to get on with things and thumb his nose at danger.

It was a pity about Carrots. Didn't even know his real name. Fred moved his leg slightly and felt the dead weight of his companion fallen half across him. He had felt his living body twitch as the bullets sprayed into him but he hadn't made a sound. Rabbits twitched in just the same way.

'Hey.' He whispered across to the couple of lads they'd pulled out of the approaching waves. 'Good to be alive, eh.'

Grunts came back. So they *were* alive. As a survivor himself, he thought too much emphasis was placed on death. Maybe if you were a king with all the luxuries, it was worth worrying. His ma and pa went with no trouble. Quite relieved they looked when they were gone. It was poor Lil who'd suffered. Better to die in your own bed, true enough, but it was Carrots's ma and pa who'd be sad, his kid brother. A kid brother with orange hair just like him. Better if it was a kid sister.

He'd liked watching those soldiers bringing the boat round for the wounded. They got away too. He admired that. If he'd been able to swim, he might have got across to them, although they'd backed off quickly once the snipers found them.

He might not have been welcomed back on that great beached hulk either. He'd come from Lemnos on the *Prince George*. It had been quite something leaving Mudros harbour with bands playing and flags flying. The ship nearest him had *To Constantinople and the Harems* scrawled in huge letters on its side. Joe Dingle, a mate from Dorset, had read it out to him. It wasn't worth wondering where Joe was now. Joe had told him the names of the other battleships.

As a diversion Fred began to recite them to himself: *Queen Elizabeth*, the big one with fifteen-inch guns, *Inflexible*, *Agamemnon*, *Lord Nelson*, *Queen*, *London*, *Prince of Wales*, *Swiftsure*, *Triumph*, *Albion*, *Majestic*, *Canopus*, *Vengeance*, *Goliath* and their old *Prince George*. He might not be able to read but he had a sharp memory. Once heard, never forgotten. Lil said it was a waste on a boy like him. That was when she was angry he wouldn't learn his letters.

The ship had been well organised, he'd say that. Squares marked off on the deck for the companies to stand. Wooden ladders to get down to the landing boats. Darkness all the way, a last meal, a last smoke. Then they'd sat through the shelling coming off the battleships. A noise like God's thunderbolts. Poor fucking Turkeys, they'd told each other. Not just their feathers will be singed with that lot. Made them feel secure, stupid blighters they were.

So, into the *Clyde* and the land showing up against the rising sun. Light still grey and misty, though. He wouldn't forget that in a hurry either. The last moments of peace. Men holding their breath. Not a cough. Your country needs you! And then out into a different kind of noise because it was coming from the enemy trying to kill you, that is if the sea didn't get you first. That's when he'd cut himself free of his pack.

He'd never thought war would be like this. Not much use, all their training. Being barked at by their sarge, 'Don't stretch the fucking line, you fucking 'orrible bleeding wart!'

From what he'd seen of the land ahead, as he'd struggled onto the beach, he couldn't see much chance of a line of men. Rough hills and gullies, not like a proper battleground. The sarge could go mad but it wouldn't help. Fred smiled to himself. It was lucky he'd learnt to see the funny side.

In the last hour or so he'd felt the sun cool a bit. Being wet helped. The cries of the wounded had just about stopped.

War was just a continuation of his usual life, that was the truth of it. Somehow the idea was comforting. How often had he lain in a ditch waiting to be torn apart by Treadwell's twelve bore! Or if not him, his dogs, or if not the dogs, Major I-was-a-big-shot-in-the-army Beech. Gave the tree a bad name, he did.

Fred shifted slightly and was rewarded by a barrage of shots, merging into machine-gun fire. At first he went rigid assuming it was directed at him before realising it was aimed much further up the beach. Some bold officer trying to break out with his men. Fred wriggled further under the heavy pack and Carrots' corpse.

Three

It was strange seeing the Tollorum stables so empty of horses. Of men, too. Treadwell the gamekeeper, Major Beech who ran one of the farms and Sid Small, the groom, had all gone with her father's yeomanry. Sylvia walked slowly across the cobbled yard. She held *The Times* tucked under her arm. Already some tufts of grass were thrusting up between the stones. All twelve of the stable doors were open except one. The cob used for the trap would soon be turned out into the field, along with two old mares that were no use for anything any more. Looking round, it seemed that the stable yard was as big as the house.

'A sad sight, miss.' A young stable boy, Small's son, had come round the corner. He was dragging a bale of straw which he set down, made as if to sit on it before rethinking.

'Good morning, Perry. At least the Colonel took his hunters.'

'Poor old Queen Mab's sick, with just one vet left for the whole county.' He took a step closer. 'My ma says the colonel is sure to be back for the hunting season.'

'Quite right. The war can't possibly last that long,' said Sylvia brightly before noticing Perry's dejected face. 'What's the matter, now?'

'I'm not eighteen till All Saint's Day, miss.'

'Old enough to fight, you mean.'

'Don't worry, miss. Pip will take my place.'

'How many brothers are you, Perry?'

'Six, miss. My ma wanted a girl that much. She says maybe a change of air will put himself in the girl line. It's the male seed that counts, so they say. But my dad'd have to come back first.'

Sylvia began to think she had been talking long enough to this stable boy. In principle she believed anyone should be allowed to speak their mind but in practice it made her uneasy. Arthur said class divisions would soon be a thing of the past but he hadn't grown up in such a hierarchical set-up.

'Good luck with Queen Mab, Perry.' She heard her voice with surprise. It was exactly like her mother's.

'Thank you, miss.'

Sylvia walked back towards the garden where she found a bench sheltered from the sharp wind, for she had come out without hat or coat.

This reading of *The Times* had become a ritual since the departure of Arthur for the front. Her mother took the paper first, exclaiming with little gasps of horror at the progress of the war, before turning to the *Tatler* and handing *The Times* to Sylvia. Gussie seldom bothered to look at it at.

Sylvia turned immediately to page seven. As usual, there was nothing about Gallipoli. Nevertheless, she read avidly: *Roll of Honour, 98 officers killed and wounded, 720 casualties in the ranks.* Two of Arthur's university friends were in France. After eight months of war in Europe, the casualties seemed to be increasing daily. Following the headlines, she went through as many of the names she could bear, more interested when they were second lieutenants like Arthur and rather skipping over the Indian Forces and the Canadian contingent. By the time she reached the fourth column, *British prisoners of War, Official list from Germany, 540 NCOs and men*, she was less concentrated. Her imagination wandered to the young men mourned by their wives or family.

Suddenly cold, Sylvia set off hurriedly for the next destination. This was a tutorial with the Reverend Euan Gisburne on the subject of duplication among the Greek gods. He lived in a square rectory built a hundred years ago beside the church within the Fitzpaine estate.

Mr Gisburne's housekeeper let in Sylvia, giving an obvious frown at her coatless and, worse still, hatless state. The rector's wife had died giving birth to Reggie, which Sylvia thought likely to be a poor swap, and housewifely tasks were covered by Miss Swithen, the housekeeper, and Gwen, an elder daughter.

'Come in. Come in.' The rector seemed to live in his study. He was knocking out his pipe and the room smelt of tobacco and sweet pine wood.

'Ready for the gods, are you?'

'I suppose so.' Sylvia sat on a chair opposite him.

He sighed. 'I know what you mean. Reggie's been hounding me to pull strings to get him to the front. He doesn't believe I have no strings. The trouble is he's too good in the training camp.'

'At least he's wanted somewhere.'

'Oh dear,' said Mr Gisburne. He looked at his pipe as if he wanted to fill it again which he never did when Sylvia was there. 'This war is very disturbing. I suppose there's no news yet of Gallipoli?'

'The troops have landed,' muttered Sylvia. 'Nothing more.'

'Communication across twelve hundred miles of sea is sure to be slow.'

'But the *casualties*?' It was a childish wail.

'You'll hear about them earlier. A hundred years ago when the Empire was still the dream of a few visionaries, English representatives in Java or Borneo could wait a year for orders. Naturally, they acted without. We are an impatient race.'

Sylvia, feeling herself rebuked by the weight of history, stayed silent.

'Perhaps,' said the vicar after a longish pause, 'this morning we should leave the gods to challenge each other on Mount Olympus.'

'You mean, not have my tutorial,' agreed Sylvia eagerly.

As she left the house, shivering, she decided to visit the church. It was typically Dorset, built of soft-coloured stone with a flat-topped tower. Two old yew trees lowered their branches over the path.

Inside, the general dimness was sprinkled with coloured jewels of light from the stained-glass windows. Memorials to previous Fitzpaines decorated the walls. Sylvia sank thankfully into a wooden pew. Occasionally, Arthur had tested his religious views on her: 'Since the beginning of time, man has felt the need of a higher being or beings. Different cultures have invented different deities. We, in England, being a sensible race, yet with a deep vein of mysticism, chose the God of Christianity and then spent a lot of time lauding man, in the person of Christ, as the true exemplar of proper behaviour. God soon became the old man with the beard, genial or vengeful depending on circumstances. In ancient times they did it better by inventing a god for every occasion.'

Although loving Arthur so much, Sylvia sometimes wondered if she understood him. He seemed to live through words, or perhaps *ideas* would be more accurate. Sometimes when he touched her, it felt as if she was hardly flesh to him. Idly, she considered what it must have been like to lose both parents as a child. She had asked him once or twice but he never answered.

Sylvia lifted her hand into a red blob of light, then into a neighbouring blue spark. A scuffle to her left made her turn her head.

A woman had been kneeling but now rose to her feet. 'Good morning, miss.'

'It's Mrs Chaffey, isn't it?' The woman wore the widow's uniform of black hat and long black coat. She was six inches smaller than Sylvia but there was something determined about her upright posture and firm clasp on her bag.

'Lily Holder for six happy years, miss.'

'I am sorry for your loss, Lily.'

Lily walked down the aisle and Sylvia, overtaken by an urge to do something useful, followed her. The two women stood outside the church.

'I wonder if you are looking for employment,' said Sylvia. 'Perhaps we can find you work at Tollorum?'

'I've two children, miss.'

'You have no family to look after them?' Sylvia glanced away at the freshly green hillsides dotted with sheep.

'No, miss. My younger brother is in the army. In the new war in the East, I think. But I have no news of him.' She gave a tolerant half smile.

'He didn't join the Colonel's regiment, then, like most of the men from hereabout? Of course, they haven't left England yet.'

'Fred's always been his own man, miss,' said Lily. 'He wanted to be with people who *didn't* know him.'

They parted, Lily Holder heading briskly for the village and Sylvia wandering back past the rectory. Perhaps Lily could bring her children to the manor. Sylvia had no interest in children and counted it the best of luck that Gwen Gisburne took on herself any teaching help needed in the village school. She supposed she and Arthur would have children some time. Now and again he referred to how their children would live in a new world where old prejudices would be swept away.

Sylvia frowned. Was *The Times*' casualty list an example of old prejudices being swept away?

Such bitter thoughts made the sight of Gussie a relief. Gussie never asked unanswerable questions and any bitterness was directly targeted against those who were not giving her proper attention. This morning Reggie was in her line of fire.

'He promised! Absolutely promised. Ten o'clock by the tennis court. What a rat! An absolute rat.'

'Hear, hear,' agreed Sylvia.

Gussie ignored her. 'As if his revolting men were as important as me!'

Sylvia tried not to laugh. Instead she pointed out mildly, 'There is a war on.'

'Don't talk to me about this beastly war.' Gussie's angry face crumpled and she looked as if she might burst into tears. 'I think it's all invented by men so they can get away from women and be happy marching about and killing people.'

'Reggie isn't killing anyone.'

'It's even worse. He's training innocent boys to kill while being quite safe himself.' She screwed up her pretty face. 'I wouldn't be surprised to find he was a *coward*!'

Sylvia noted how Reggie's 'revolting men' had transformed into 'innocent boys', Gussie never bothered about consistency but, even so, her wild accusations often chimed with Sylvia's most rebellious thoughts. 'I'm sure Reggie is not a coward,' she said out loud, thinking he would have the show-off's need to shine, particularly when there were other men watching. Arthur was not a coward either but he was not vainglorious, rather wishing to take his place in a patriotic history of great men. This seemed a bloodless description of Arthur's attitude but Sylvia could do no better. It was impossible to imagine her clever, thoughtful lover killing anyone.

'Why are you just standing there?' shouted Gussie suddenly.

'I was thinking of Arthur.' Sylvia watched a mixture of contradictory emotions cross her sister's face: fury that Sylvia had trumped all her childish flouncing with a serious emotion – although Sylvia had not meant to do this – sympathy because, if she did trouble to think of someone else, she had a warm heart, and finally depression – the emotion she most despised – because there was nothing more to say. Now she must face Reggie's departure without even a farewell.

'It's not as if I really like him,' she said glumly.

'It's just that there's no other young man around,' agreed Sylvia. 'We're an unlucky generation.'

Sunset spread over Gallipoli in alarming stripes of scarlet and orange. As the two merged, became purplish and turned to black, a bitter cold replaced the sun's heat.

Just before this process was complete, the lieutenant colonel in charge of the attack on the beach was killed as he crossed the deck of the SS *River Clyde*. His adjutant had been trying to hurry him across the unprotected middle deck. Unfortunately, the colonel became obstinate, paused, and, with upturned face, remarked, 'You'll never see a more magnificent sunset, Guy!'

As he fell at Captain Guy Renton's feet, a voice murmured, '*You* certainly won't.' But it may have been only a whisper in the wind, because all the men gathered, including Captain Prideaux, had dropped to lie prone on the deck.

The news caused little interest among the men, sprawled in what seemed like an endless wait in the bowels of the ship.

'One less officer to lead us,' commented Sergeant Babcock to Arthur. 'He was a fine soldier. Like a rock. If you're not careful, sir, you will be in charge.'

Arthur was amazed to realise his sergeant was making a joke. 'Thank you, Babcock,' he said through gritted teeth. He was just recovering from a bout of cramp which attacked him at times of tension. He didn't attribute it to his errand of mercy but to all the hanging around. It was a humiliating weakness when there were men dying all about him.

'I don't expect you've heard when we're landing, sir?'

'When it's dark,' said Arthur. Babcock knew the position as well as he did.

'Some of the men have already eaten their rations, sir. Lack of sleep makes them think they are hungry. They've missed two nights already.'

'I'll see what I can do.' Arthur made his way along the narrow corridor, trying not to limp too obviously. It was very dimly lit and filled with the smell of men confined closely for many hours. No wonder they were eating their rations. What a way to go to war!

Arthur decided he was looking for Prideaux who, being from headquarters, would be sure to know as much as anyone.

'They're all in there,' indicated a lieutenant younger than Arthur when asked Captain Prideaux's whereabouts. 'We'll be off soon, I shouldn't doubt.'

Arthur peered through the door to a largish room filled with officers, some sitting, some standing, most smoking. He recognised Doughty-Wylie partly by his shiny domed head and Kitchener-style – *Your country needs you* – moustache and partly because he was dominating the room.

'We need to get through the Sedd el Bahr fort on our right. Then on through the village behind it and up to the hill behind that, whatever it's called – 141, I think. We're still miles from Krithia and the dominating hill of Achi Baba which was supposed to be our first day's destination.'

There was a small pause before a lieutenant colonel who Arthur didn't recognise pointed out, 'We've got to get the men and equipment on shore first and sorted out, before we can embark on any sort of advance. If we don't have the beach secured, we're nowhere.'

'What about the wounded?' asked the medical officer Arthur had met earlier.

Doughty-Wylie made an impatient gesture. 'We have to get the men clear of the ships before we can bring anyone in.'

The scene had a theatrical air of actors strutting and fretting over matters that were already out of control. Yet the indomitable will of the principal, Doughty-Wylie, made it clear that something *would* happen. Arthur imagined him going forward, cane raised, never looking behind to see who followed. His heart beat faster as he vowed to be one of those lucky fellows in his wake.

Prideaux turned a little and, seeing Arthur by the door, beckoned him in. The discussion had moved to exceedingly vague reports about what was happening on W, X and Y Beaches and to the Australian and New Zealand forces further up the coast and Arthur shook his head. As he slipped away, the very young lieutenant saluted. 'See you on Gallipoli, sir.' His face had a zealot's bloom.

With the darkness came rain. It sloshed and sluiced and deluged on to the beaches. Fred looked up to the heavens with fury. He felt like jumping up and down in childish protest – which he could do now in perfect safety unless one of the newly arrived officers thought he was mad and shot him like a dog. He wouldn't put it past them. He must remember to tell Lily that God didn't exist on Gallipoli.

Soldiers had been coming ashore from the *Clyde* for over half an hour, stumbling half-heartedly over the rubble of men and equipment strewn in the sea and on the shingle. Shoulders bent against the rain, they said no more than the occasional swear word as barbed wire caught their hands or a wounded man their feet. They were like the dark ghosts of the men who had left a mere twenty-four hours earlier from Imbros amidst flags, bands and cheering. Yet they had not even been in action which he, Frederick M. Chaffey, had, if you counted being fired on by an enemy you couldn't see so couldn't attack, being in action.

Uncomfortable with his own thoughts, Fred set out to find his company. Even if there were none under his particular sheltering bank, there must be survivors somewhere.

'Just attach yourself anywhere,' advised the harassed major whose attention he managed to attract. 'As far as I can see they're all mixed up and it won't get better with two thousand men, guns, ammunition, rations, water, mules and even horses being unloaded without any system on a beach that is hardly the size of a parade ground.'

'Yes, sir.' Fred saluted smartly.

The major looked at him more closely. 'You been here all day?'

'Yes, sir.'

'Good lad.' He paused. 'Tell you what. You seem a wiry fellow. Head off right. There's going to be a show up by the fort at first light. They'll need runners. Good luck.'

'Thank you, sir.' Fred saluted again, then bent to pick up a water bottle to join the one he'd already strung around him. Two columns of men, marching with more energy than any he'd seen so far, brushed past him. They were going to the right. On his other side there was a sudden loud braying as a train of mules nearly ran him down. There must be more ships coming in. He needed to move – he'd seen enough of this beach to last a lifetime.

Coming out of the *Clyde* was a sickening experience. The piles of corpses or men as near dead as made no difference were plastered all around the sally ports so it was impossible not to tread on them. In fact in many areas they were actually being used by the men as bridges to the beach. Arthur knew he could do nothing to stop them. Only the MOs intervened with despair or anger, depending on their natures.

'You're stamping on that soldier's hand and he's alive!' screamed one MO to a woe-begone private. The soldier, intent on keeping his balance, took no notice. But Babcock, who was shepherding the men off, shouted roughly, 'Not even God could save that poor bugger. Lying in water for fifteen hours, he'll be fifty per cent gangrenous already and the other fifty by the time you got him into the hospital ship.'

Arthur left them to it. It was a vile business. Far more men had died since the morning but even so there were too many wounded for the few doctors available, even if they could get them into the *Clyde*. As he came to dry land through the crowds of men and animals, he could see stretcher-bearers wearing their distinctive white armbands with red crosses. They were picking over the bodies for suitable candidates to save. Most often, they moved on.

It was a miserable sight and the rain was beastly – he had not expected that after a perfect cloudless day – but his spirits were not low. He and his men were among those detailed to move towards the fort and, with any luck, carry on as far as Hill 141. Their colonel had gathered a few junior officers together before they left the ship.

'HMS *Albion* will start shelling at five o'clock – it's moving in closer now – and at five thirty hours we'll be off. There'll be a simultaneous attack from the beach. Your job is to keep your men going, and going in the right direction. After a bloody awful first day watching the party, this little scrap gives us a chance to hold up our heads. Any questions?'

He'd obviously been surprised when a stocky little captain shouted out, 'What about Achi Baba, sir? Can we have a go at that bastard?'

Arthur thought it odd that this hill which hardly anyone (including him) had got a look at, had already become the hated target.

'How far do we need to go, sir?' Sergeant Babcock was at Arthur's elbow.

'As far as the outer rim of the old fort. We'll spend what remains of the night there; no fires or smokes. Snipers will be above us.'

It was less than half a mile to their position but such was the confusion that they kept losing soldiers to other companies who crossed their way or sometimes gaining men who had nothing to do with them. Several tried to join them since their whole company and officers seem to have been wiped out or at least were not evident.

'Here's another lost sheep,' announced Babcock disapprovingly. 'He says a major, name unspecified, told him runners would be needed in this direction.'

Arthur tried to make out the figure in the dark: several inches smaller than him, dark-skinned, or perhaps that was dirt; his uniform was so begrimed or bloodied that it was hard to confirm his regiment.

'I don't know that I need a runner.'

'I'm fast, sir. Although my legs are as stiff as wood after lying flat most of the day.'

Arthur became more interested. 'You were under the ridge?'

'Yes, sir. I'm pretty good with a rifle too, sir. Show Johnny Turk a thing or two, if I had a chance.'

'Lieutenant Lamb doesn't want your life story,' growled Babcock.

But Arthur was listening attentively, not to the private's words but the accent. 'You're from the West Country?'

'Yes, sir.'

'He can come with us, Babcock.'

'Sir!' Babcock's emphatic salute suggested disagreement.

Arthur understood that he was trying to pretend that they were part of an organised army rather than a giant muddle. He asked his new recruit, 'What's your name?'

'Chaffey, sir.'

'Right, Chaffey. Stay by me.'

They moved on, stumbled on because once the edge of the

beach had been reached the already uneven surface of the ground became covered with a mixture of rubble and larger chunks of stone. The shells from the Allied ships had pulverised the fort early in the morning before. Arthur glanced at his watch to confirm they were already in a new day.

'Grand place for snipers, sir,' said Chaffey.

Arthur ignored him. Since he'd left behind his servant, he liked having a man at his elbow but he didn't need conversation. As always, Babcock was right: he was a cocky fellow.

'Settle down, settle down,' he told a group of men who filed past him. 'There won't be long to rest.' Although he told them to settle down, his own heart pumped with energy. His job was to lead, to show pluck and daring, to face the enemy's guns with the confidence of the righteous.

Four

Fred was deeply asleep when the crashing began. All around him men jerked up, like startled rabbits. A pale glimmer of light was spreading over the ruins and the rising land behind it. The rain had stopped and the air was probably as fresh as any spring dawn except every sense but hearing was dulled by the massive bombardment.

'She's in close.' A soldier peered apprehensively seawards.

HMS *Albion* was close enough for every belching gun to be clearly visible, and even the officers standing on its deck.

'At least they can see where we are.' It was unnerving being under fire but Fred had been out as a beater often enough to know bullets or shells don't suddenly drop in their trajectory, not unless they're mis-aimed. Johnny Turk was getting it all right.

Shaking himself out, he took a swig of water and went tranquilly to find the lieutenant. He was easy enough to spot, standing on the outer rim of a group of officers being harangued by an officer with a huge moustache who seemed to have no trouble out-bellowing the shells. He was gesticulating as he spoke, waving his arms like a windmill, but the officers seemed to be hanging on his every word. Giving them their orders. Must be someone special. Suddenly the officer swung round.

'You, soldier. What are you?'

There was no one else he could be bellowing at. 'Lieutenant Lamb's runner, sir.' Fred gave his sharpest salute which he reserved for difficult situations.

'Now you're mine. D'you hear?'

'Sir!'

'My runner. Stay by me.' He turned back and looked at his watch. 'Nine minutes to go: get your men up.'

'They're ready, Colonel.' It was Lieutenant Lamb. Oh, how fast he was rising! From lieutenant to colonel's runner in a few hours. His new master was holding up binoculars, striding restlessly a few yards here and a few yards there. It struck Fred that if he stayed by the colonel, he was sure to be up at the front.

'So I've lost you, Chaffey.' The lieutenant stood by him. He was restless too, turning this way and that.

'Doesn't a colonel have his own runner?' asked Fred. Shouting to be heard.

'Colonel Doughty-Wylie is from staff headquarters. He wasn't expecting to fight.' He paused, stared. 'Do you always ask questions of your superior officers?'

'No, sir. Sorry, sir.' But he did. Always, and it always got him into trouble. 'I'd better go to him then, sir.' Another opportunity for his smartest salute.

Fred had just reached Doughty-Wylie's side when silence came so abruptly that it seemed as shocking as the noise before. Suddenly he heard a lark singing. Or was it just his ears buzzing? At least the rain had stopped. For a few seconds it was a beautiful morning, even though smoke was still puffing up from where the shells had landed. Then the colonel and other officers shouted and soldiers rose up from the ground and began a zigzagging dash forward. For a moment Fred lost his bearings like the stupid amateur he was, but the colonel was not far away, clambering over fallen masonry, then running over tufty grass. He didn't even have a gun, just a raised cane in his hand. Some of the men who had been hanging back seemed to take heart and move faster. Fred recognised Lieutenant Lamb urging them on. He realised he'd better speed up himself if he wanted to obey the colonel and stay by him. For an older man, he could certainly move.

A machine gun opened up and bullets began to fly. We've disturbed a bees' nest, thought Fred. If you disturb a bees' nest, you belt off in the other direction. But he continued to go forward, zigzagging and bent double like the others, until he'd caught up with the colonel.

Arthur jumped over the crumbled remains of a wall. He felt the jagged stones through the soles of his boot, his heart pounded, a wave of heat rushed through his head but there was no line of music. This was action as he'd imagined it.

41

'Come on, lads! We're in the fort now.' A bullet rushed by his ear and at his left elbow a man dropped down silently. Doughty-Wylie was still ahead but they were surrounded by broken walls and partially destroyed doorways – perfect hiding places for snipers. The fire came from all around.

A gigantic crash ahead made him hesitate before he recognised it as a shell from the *Albion*.

He paused, and as the noise of the crash settled, he realised there was a difference in the gun fire ahead.

'They've knocked out that machine gun.' Babcock panted up beside him. 'I'm keeping some of the men back until those bleeding snipers—'

Arthur was already hurtling forward before he noticed that Babcock's sentence remained unfinished and that he had fallen. He reached a sheltering wall, turned and saw him trying to crawl, one leg dragging. It was a ghastly sight: the sturdy warrior of many campaigns turned into a smashed animal.

He ran back and, with the help of one of the men – Babcock was built like a tree – he dragged him back to the wall.

'He's dying. The sarge is dying.' The young soldier was gibbering as if the sergeant was his best mate. He'd even dropped his rifle.

Arthur bent down and saw that Babcock's eyes were closed and he'd stopped breathing. He lay in a pool of blood. It shocked him that an old soldier should go so easily.

He straightened and grabbed the young soldier's arm. 'Pull yourself together, man. Find your rifle and follow me.'

As if all he needed was an attachment, the gibbering wreck turned into a soldier, rediscovered his rifle and waited for orders. Arthur picked up three more men and pointed out the remains of a turret they needed to clear. They crouched and went forward. For a moment it was almost like a training exercise, then one of the men let out a high-pitched shriek and fell.

The others carried on and Arthur waved up two more men who were trailing hesitantly behind. They, too, turned into soldiers and followed him. Miraculously, without more loss, they stormed up what was left of some steps and into the round area where a pair of Turkish snipers were halfway to making their exit at the back.

'Bayonets! Get them!' Watching his men go at it like hounds on a fox, Arthur felt the kind of triumphant exhilaration he'd previously known after making a first-rate translation from the Greek. He had won! A brave victory. This part of the fort was cleared.

The men came back to him. They were spattered with blood and panting. Two days and nights of waiting and doubt had been wiped out.

With most of the snipers dead, more men could come up safely. Gathering half a dozen, Arthur pressed on. The Turks amazed him by their sticking power but in the end they were either dead or retreated back into the village.

Arthur stopped to look around and found himself almost face to face with Doughty-Wylie. He was standing on a rampart, dead and dying at his feet, a brilliant blue sky above his head. He wore a staff officer's flat cap and carried a small cane with which he tapped his free hand. Except that he stood, he might have been conducting a meeting on shipboard safety. A flurry of larks spurted up suddenly but his intense calm didn't change.

'You, Lieutenant. Can you climb?' The cane was pointing at Arthur.

'Yes, sir.' He could do anything. Anything at all.

'Take a dozen fit men and climb up the sea-cliff to the eastern edge of the village. We need the enemy surrounded.' He turned to a captain at his side. 'You, Captain, go back to the beach. Check on the advance from there.'

'We've had a report, sir. They're stuck on the barbed wire. Unusually thick, sir.'

'Send them my compliments and tell they'd better become unstuck forthwith or I'll have to tear the wire apart with my own hands and them with it!' He began to move away.

'You, runner.' Suddenly the colonel was looking down at Private Chaffey. 'Join the cliff party and let me know when they're at the top.'

The cliff was high and almost perpendicular. Below was the sea and on the rocks at the foot of the cliff more than one mangled body.

Arthur looked at it assessingly. But Private Chaffey started climbing at once. He was like a crab, scuttling diagonally upwards first in one direction and then another.

'Don't get too far ahead!'

Chaffey turned and looked down. 'Sir?' Arthur realised that, although the man had a rifle, ammunition and water bottles slung about him, he had no pack which at fifty or sixty pounds would have made his progress much harder. Most officers carried them, although no rifle.

Arthur began to climb. Men fanned out beside him. At first it was fairly easy, even, in a strange way, pleasurable. There was a light breeze off the sea, tufts of grass to hold on to and the rocks were more or less stable. But as they went higher, the ground couldn't be trusted and the covering fire from below became less accurate so that a sniper above picked off several men clinging to the cliff side.

Arthur had just paused to wipe the sweat out of his eyes when he heard a shouted warning and, raising his head, saw a large boulder tumbling and bouncing directly towards him.

What a way to die, he thought immediately, for there was no time to avoid its path. He didn't even have time to duck, nor to picture himself a broken corpse on the rocks, only a second to think of Sylvia in her virgin whiteness.

'Close one, sir!' A voice with a Dorset accent congratulated him.

A millisecond before it reached him, the boulder had hit a stone, bounced up and flown over his head. Since there was no cry from below, Arthur assumed it had rushed through the air without touching ground again before it reached the bottom.

He wiped his face again and carried on climbing. But it had become more difficult and his legs and arms shook uncontrollably.

Well, that nearly knocked him off his perch. Didn't even duck. Fred looked at Lieutenant Lamb with satisfaction. Life had taught him that having fate on your side was more important than any amount of ducking. He came down a few yards and gave the lieutenant a pull up. When that boulder bounced over his head and his face had been upturned in wonder, like a man looking at the moon, Fred had felt certain he'd seen him before.

'Thanks.' The officer's fine skin was red as a poppy. Red as the poppies on Achi Baba. Like a song, wasn't it. They really were red. Fred could see them now if he turned his head. Flaunting, that's what they were.

Most of the men were reaching the top of the cliff now. Those who hadn't been knocked off one way or another.

The lieutenant straightened up. He seemed excited but a bit nervy too. Fred had given up nerves as a waste of energy years ago. The men were gathering around, catching their breath from the climb, glancing anxiously at the smashed village ahead of them. Nothing like the odd sniper to keep you on your toes. There went one now. Caught a man square in the middle of his head. Brains flying to the wind. You had to take your hat off to the Turkish marksmen – if you had a hat or head still on your shoulders.

Now that they were moving off again, covering fire for the first who went and everyone feeling better about themselves, he supposed he should report to the colonel soon.

The village was already being fought through when they arrived. Soldiers scurried between fallen masonry like rats in a deserted house. Most had their bayonets fixed but there was still a fair amount of shooting, more random than targeted as far as Fred could tell. It seemed that they had come in at the end of the party.

Ahead of him the lieutenant was bending over two Turkish corpses. Fred wondered why and came closer. He saw the pointed ears of a large black cat. He seemed to be draped over the face of a dead Turk.

'Staying by his master,' the lieutenant said admiringly. Fred could have told him cats aren't sentimental.

The cat screeched and fled.

'Owff.' The lieutenant jumped back.

The cat had been feasting on the brains of his so-called master. I hope that's the last I see of brains this afternoon, thought Fred. Definitely time to report to the colonel.

The sun had risen to its height and begun to drop as the last houses along the single street of the village were reached by the British troops. Some of them stood in walled gardens filled with pomegranate and almond trees.

It was still dangerous to cross the street and men ran across like boys daring each other to cross a busy road. Tiredness and fear were forgotten. When Arthur saw the man beside him blown several yards and land on his back amid a pile of stones and masonry and rubble, he was surprised. He noticed it was that Dorset soldier and went over to him.

'You hurt?'

'Don't know what hit me.' He sat up, feeling his head.

'Nor do I.'

'No blood.'

'You're just dazed.' Arthur moved off. 'Dazed' was lucky.

The village ended in an orchard, whose trees were flowering prettily, and a small pristine cemetery. Soldiers were already gathering there, some lying on the grass, some leaning on their rifles. Wounded men had not yet been collected but stretcher-bearers were beginning to run up. The mood was almost light-hearted. No one was digging graves just here, and everybody knew that, after the disasters of the day before, they were on their way to a victory. Small, maybe, just a bit of land secured, but still a victory.

Doughty-Wylie stood with a major at his elbow. He seemed to have acquired a servant who wheeled about him like a clone. He also had a communications' officer with a telephone linked to heavy black wires. By his gestures and the direction he was facing, Arthur guessed he was calling in shelling on Hill 141. They could see it quite easily, the tangle of barbed wire at the bottom, the trenches encircling it and the flat top. An insignificant mound but the way to the infamous Achi Baba. He could see that quite clearly now, hunched shoulders and a smudge of red on the top.

'You got through.' Captain Prideaux stood at Arthur's elbow. As usual his hat was in his hand so that his blond hair blew about in the breeze.

'Climbing up the cliff was the worst part.' Arthur pictured the great bouncing boulder. For the first time it occurred to him that the boulder had not been hurled by the hand of God but by an enemy who had planned to kill him.

'The men coming up from the beach were hard hit. His Majesty's wire-cutters turned out to be inadequate for Turkish wire. Some Irish giant had to lift out the posts before they could get through. I hear Dick was fuming.'

'Who's Dick?' Arthur noticed that even in the midst of war Prideaux and he seemed to steer an uneven course between liking and antagonism.

'Doughty-Wylie.'

'I thought he was called Charles.'

'Dick to his friends. I told you we knew each other out here.'

Inevitably, both men looked towards the colonel.

'We'll attack as soon as the navy's done their bit.'

Arthur gazed up at the sky. 'I was nearly killed by a boulder bouncing down the cliff.'

'Death by boulder. Not the sort of epitaph Dick would win for himself.' Prideaux smiled and sat down on a gravestone. After a moment Arthur sat down beside him. 'Did you hear how Rupert died?' asked Prideaux.

'Rupert who?'

'Rupert Brooke. Is there more than one Rupert?'

'You're called Rupert, aren't you? I heard he died. Nothing more.' I am insignificant, thought Arthur, the sort of man who is killed by a boulder. For the second time that day, he thought of Sylvia. She did not consider him insignificant. She believed him to be brilliant, original, charming. *Un homme sérieux*. A man with a future.

'The official story is that he died from a mosquito bite on his lip. Actually it was one of those lethal injections against typhoid the medics like giving. Turned septic. He's buried on the Greek island of Skyros without seeing a whisker of the enemy. Makes you think, doesn't it? Hasn't stopped him from becoming a hero of the war. "Think only this of me: / That there's some corner of a foreign land / That is for ever England".'

'Foreign *field*,' corrected Arthur.

Prideaux ignored this. 'Churchill wrote an obituary for him in *The Times*. Who knows? Maybe Skyros will become a place of pilgrimage—'

He was interrupted by a massive naval barrage opening up, the shells falling more or less on the hill ahead. Soon it disappeared from view in huge turrets of smoke.

'I've been ordered back to base,' Prideaux yelled in Arthur's ear. 'Apparently the French are bringing in dozens of prisoners from Kum Kale and they can't find their translator. Probably haven't got one, actually. The French like to pretend there's only one language in the world.'

Arthur was glad to see Prideaux go, sauntering off as if he was walking round his country estate – in what lovely part of England was that? Arthur wondered.

'Sir, sir. It's Corporal Snell, sir.'

Arthur looked at the small man with the round red face who was trying to make himself heard above the noise of the shells. His mouth worked in and out around extremely crooked teeth, one almost at right angles to the others.

'Yes, Snell?' He had replaced Sergeant Babcock and was nervously keen to do well.

'We're in the front line, sir.' Snell was now so close that Arthur could smell his rancid breath. 'There's a Captain Richie joining us. The men don't know him so if you'd come, sir.'

What was it Prideaux had said? *Imbros, Lemnos and chaos.* Who was this new captain? But they had an objective and a leader. Once again Arthur looked towards Doughty-Wylie and, as he watched, the shelling stopped in the abrupt way it always did and the smoke, driven by a stiff breeze, lifted off Hill 141.

Fred fixed his bayonet and prepared to charge. Ahead of him Doughty-Wylie crashed like an elephant through the apple trees, blossom floating down like snow, and on till they were through the graveyard – was that a sign of the cross he made on his chest? It was a wild, joyous rush, that's what it was. Something told them that Johnny Turk wasn't fool enough to stick around in any number. The Turks could retreat, that was the thing. Fred understood that. They could retreat to their own country inland, retreat as often as they liked, and then come back. Fred tried not to think like this in the joyous rush and, even as he yelled, and caught with his bayonet his first real kill (a wounded Johnny T cowering in a trench) his country boy's brain told him that sometimes running away is the best way to make sure you live to fight another day. They, the brave Allies, had nowhere to run to but the sea.

There were a few snipers still, a man at his elbow down and screaming, but soon they were pouring over the trenches and the craters made by the shells. More than a few dead Turks had ended their lives there so they hadn't run as fast as all that.

Then there was a twenty foot deep moat before they could get to the very top.

'Only one way up!' The word was all around. One way up the

hill and the same way down. But that didn't stop them. Some waited their turn but others scrambled up using their mates as ladders.

'There's an old fort at the top!' To conquer a fort on the top of a hill, that felt like something. Men who had lain in a funk of terror and exhaustion for twenty-four hours broke onto Hill 141 like bubbles from a bottle of pop.

And there stood the victor Colonel Doughty-Wylie. Fred, who had lost sight of him in the climb up, admired him all over again. The breeze blew and he still had nothing but a stick in his hand. With eyes that were used to picking out details, Fred noticed that one of his puttees had come unwound. In such a magnificent soldier it seemed significant.

Sniper fire came from where the Turks had retreated. 'There's a communication trench down there!' someone shouted. No one's heading that way while their snipers stay put, thought Fred.

An officer beside the colonel had been opening a map when the sniper fire started. Now he'd dropped down: not hit, just sensible. Everybody else was down too, except the colonel and his adjutant. Who was pulling at his master's arm. The men digging in nearest to the sniper fire dropped their tools and lay flat.

There was another volley of fire. No one was hit. Even from where he was, head in the dirt, Fred could hear the colonel's officers shouting at him, 'Get down, sir! Get down, sir!'

Fred felt a burning rage in his chest. He was obstinate himself but he wasn't a fool! When the bullet came he felt it as if it was in his own head. It was an explosive bullet that took the colonel beneath his eye and the adjutant beside him. Anyone who was looking could see it, and anyone could see it coming.

'My God! He's hit.' It was an intense whisper coming, Fred saw as he turned his head, from Lieutenant Lamb, crouched nearby.

'Bastard!' Fred's disgust spat out the word. Why had the colonel left them? His troops. His troops he'd led valiantly to victory. What for? 'Bastard.' He swore again.

'Without him we'd never have left the beaches.' There was a gulp in the lieutenant's voice as if he was on the edge of tears.

Fred began crawling away. Let the man mourn in peace. Tentatively, he stood up. The sniper or snipers seem to have left. Soldiers were shooting down on them from the edge of the hill as they made their retreat. He thought that there was a gulf between officers and men. No man would ever deliberately stand up in the line of fire.

Ever curious and without any orders from anyone, Fred wandered in the direction of the group round the fallen warrior. The firing died away. His anger had begun to dissipate too in the luminous glow of a perfect evening. The battleships out to sea, silhouetted by the sinking sun, some close in, others far on the horizon, had an innocent toy-like quality. Already a yellow haze was softening the darkness of the sea. Along other beaches there might be men yelling and dying, machine guns pouring out death, bullets and shells tearing off limbs but here it was peaceful. The smell in his nostrils was not of war but of wild thyme and lavender crushed underfoot. If Fred kept his eyes turned up, he could imagine himself on an English hill, waiting for the birds to come home to roost.

'Hey, you? Private. Over here!' An NCO was booming, spoiling the peace.

'Yessir!' Fred ran and saluted.

'Burial party detail. Over by that old fort. On the double.'

Fred went where he pointed. He saw that the group round the colonel's body was moving ahead of him into the fort. Some high-ranking officer who'd newly appeared was giving orders.

But his job was to dig. The NCO followed him and stamped his foot on the spot.

'Here. Make it long and wide and deep. The colonel was a giant of a man.'

So it was *his* grave.

'This is a spade.' The sergeant major, as Fred now saw he was, spoke forcefully and also with reverence.

'A spade, Sarn't Major.'

'But it is not *your* spade.' The sergeant major looked at him suspiciously.

'So when you've finished, give – it – back – to – me.' He spoke with grim emphasis.

Fred didn't blame him. A spade like that was worth ten entrenching tools. All round him men were digging, trying to cut into the hard stony ground with useless bits of steel. They weren't digging graves – with any luck, they weren't digging graves. They were digging trenches. Their beds for the night.

'Not my spade, Sarn't Major. Give it back to you. Sir!' Fred began to dig.

But the sergeant major continued to stand over him. 'You're a filthy-looking bleeder.'

'Sarn't Major.' Fred continued to dig. He didn't mind the insult. It was what he expected from a sergeant major. It was the natural order of things. People in authority shouted and ordered him to do things and he obeyed when it suited him.

'What regiment are you? Your badge should be visible at all times.'

Fred told him, keeping his head resolutely down. Then looked up, 'My whole platoon was wiped out, as far as I can find out. The colonel had me as his runner, Sarn't Major.'

'Lieutenant Colonel Doughty-Wiley, recently deceased, had you as his runner!' The man sounded outraged and as if in emphasis, a trickle of blood emerged from his left ear. It made him look demented. Fred watched the other ear.

'Yessir.'

The sergeant major's face seemed to work through some kind of crisis. Spittle appeared at the corners of his mouth. Fred waited curiously. He wondered if this was shell shock.

'So now you're doing something more useful for him. And when you've finished and *brought back the spade*, I'll find somewhere you can run all you want.'

'Sarn't Major.' Fred went back to digging.

Arthur was trying to write a letter to Sylvia. His brigade had been ordered back in reserve to the now secured beaches and he sat in a dugout facing the sea. He would have preferred to be sleeping since it was the middle of the night and his whole body ached with exhaustion but the dugout belonged to a jovial Captain Entwhistle. He was also loquacious. The joviality and loquacity were so exaggerated at this time of night and in their uncertain situation that Arthur suspected it disguised total funk.

He had not suffered any level of funk himself so it made him feel pleasantly superior but all the same, he wished the man would shut up. He was at it now.

'There you are, old chap, the frogs are coming in. Smell the garlic from here, can't you? Hear they had an easy time of it at that place the other side of the straits.'

'Kum Kale,' muttered Arthur.

'Surely that's some kind of fruit, old boy.' Entwhistle was large and he stood at the door blocking any view Arthur might have had of forces landing.

'Spent a week in Paris last year before I got married. Get it out of my system, you know. Volunteered, of course, first moment. Wife encouraged it. Soldiering family. Not like my own pater. A fine man but no soldier. My wife said, "Eardley, you get in there before my brothers" – good men, her brothers, so that's what I did.'

Arthur tried not to listen but after all, it was Entwhistle's dugout.

'You're writing to your fiancée, are you? I expect she gave you a push in the right direction.'

'Actually, I was keen to join up. Miss Fitzpaine wasn't so sure.'

'Ah.' Entwhistle thought about this before pronouncing, 'Not from a soldiering background.'

'Her father's a brigadier-general. A cavalry officer.'

Entwhistle made no response but Arthur could tell by the stiffness of his back that he had felt the rebuke. Childish glee overcame guilt.

Slowly, Entwhistle turned round again. There was only one small lamp in the dugout but Arthur could see his heavy face was no longer jovial but darkly brooding. 'Hell,' he said simply. 'Hell.' Not waiting for a reaction, he walked out of the dugout.

Arthur sighed but could not really bring himself to care whether Entwhistle threw himself in the sea and drowned where so many had before, or so insulted a French Senegalese soldier that he chopped him up and ate him which was the current rumour about the habits of the latest recruits to the Mediterranean Expeditionary Force.

He looked at his letter to Sylvia in despair. He had never felt their link so stretched, although at Oxford when he had been immersed in Herodotus and Thucydides he had felt distanced from her rich young lady's complacency. Not that she was complacent herself but the life she led was. Can a life be complacent? Anyway he loved Tollorum as much as he loved her . . .

Arthur felt his head jerk and knew he had fallen into a second's blissful sleep. He looked out. Minimum lights were the order in case they gave the big gun from the Asian mainland, already christened Asiatic Annie, a decent target.

He picked up his pen and wrote.

Here I am on Gallipoli. From my dugout I can see the shore covered with soldiers, awake and asleep. Some have just come off ships and look about them, bewildered by all the activity in the almost complete darkness. There are French, Indian, English, Senegalese, Scottish.

Arthur stopped writing. No way the censor would pass that. He took a new page and tried again.

There are lines of mules, barrels of water, a few horses, some of them shires, GS wagons, limbers, Maltese carts, bikes, motorbikes, boxes of beef, jam, bacon, cheese and potatoes, dixies, piles of ammunitions, rifles, guns and large coils of Turkish barbed wire, cut and piled in heaps. Behind my dugout the rising ground is spattered with bits of equipment.

He stopped himself from writing *and bodies of the dead.*

It was shaming that there were still bodies of the dead unburied. Turks most probably. He recalled with disgust the cat that had feasted on the brains of a corpse. It was funny the way it had stuck in his mind when, after all, the man was dead and a Turk.

Did it make a difference he was a Turk? Yes, of course it did. He was the enemy. When Babcock died so suddenly, he'd been eager to kill as many Turks as possible. Not personally, officers didn't do so much of that, but to make sure his men got a few. And they had. He recalled the frenzy of killing in the fort. That's the way it should be, a good memory, unlike the cat.

Just one cat! Arthur threw down his pen and stood up. How could he write to Sylvia with such things in his mind? If he was honest the bloody brain-gorging cat was just a block for all the deaths of good Englishmen, starting with Sergeant Babcock and finishing with Doughty-Wylie.

Arthur took a step towards the darkened doorway; a sack had fallen across it when Entwhistle left. It was supreme heroism of the sort showed by Colonel Doughty-Wylie that proved that humans valued the spirit above all. This was what separated humans from animals! This was why he'd been happy as he ran forward, why he looked forward to the next time he was ordered into attack. This was why he couldn't listen to poor Entwhistle.

Abandoning his letter writing altogether, Arthur rushed out of the dugout.

Five

Temporary Brigadier-General Bingo Fitzpaine – elevated for the war, although still called 'the Colonel' by most at Tollorum – was home from his regiment.

'It will be just the family at dinner tonight,' Beatrice told him almost as soon as he stepped through the door. 'But we will dress up for you as if the King had come to dine.'

The servants, reduced by the war to women and girls, stood in the hall to welcome the Colonel.

'What a good idea, my dear,' he said, beaming.

Gussie came flying down the oak staircase. She stopped in front of her father. 'Oh, Papa. You've got so much thinner and your face is a different colour.'

'Really, Gussie, you're not a schoolgirl any more!' Beatrice had been thinking exactly the same thing. He reminded her of the slim young cavalry officer with his face burned by the South African sun.

'It's all the riding and marching about,' said the Colonel good-humouredly. 'Some of the volunteers don't know the first thing about soldiering.'

'That's what Reggie Gisburne says,' Gussie frowned petulantly, 'but I think men like dressing up and competing with each other.'

'I expect they do.' Her father still smiled, although for a moment Reggie's name, brought so quickly into his homecoming, seemed to surprise him. The servants left in a group, accompanied now by two young men who had returned with the Colonel. The outdoor staff, also supplemented by returning soldiers from the Colonel's yeomanry, retreated through the heavy oak door. A couple of older men remained.

'Where's Sylvia?' asked the Colonel.

'She must have been delayed in the village.' Beatrice looked down anxiously. 'She's very restless and we didn't know exactly when to expect you. It's Arthur being at the front and no news at all.'

'No news at all?'

Beatrice shook her head.

The Colonel turned and called out, 'We'd better get started, Bluck.'

'Yes, sir.' A thin oldish man in heavy tweeds hurried over. 'I didn't bring the dogs over . . .'

'I'll visit them later.' The Colonel began to move away. 'Tell Guppy he can bring the accounts whenever he wants.'

'But you haven't had tea!' Beatrice cried out in distress as if her husband's overlooking tea triggered some deep emotion.

'Have Mrs Hepburn bring it to the study.'

'Mrs Hepburn's gone. I told you.'

'So you did.' The Colonel went away briskly with his arm round Bluck's shoulder.

After he had left, Beatrice stood for a moment longer in the hallway. Usually the old-fashioned furnishings, left over from generations of Fitzpaines, gave her a comfortable feeling of continuity but today she was horrified by the gloom of the pictures, the morbidity of the stuffed heads of horned animals and, in particular, two large classical urns which stood in niches on either side of the door to the dining room.

'What is it, Mama?' Even Gussie noticed her mother's wild gaze.

'Take those urns away!' she cried out suddenly. 'They're dreadful. Dreadful!'

'They look frightfully heavy, Mama.'

Beatrice swung on her daughter. 'And you, you. Do not talk about Reggie Gisburne in that way, as if he's your, your . . .' Without finishing her sentence she moved over to the urn closest to her.

Gussie, who had been reassured by the mention of Reggie which showed normal maternal attitudes, watched her warily.

'Is Papa back? I saw his car.' Sylvia stood at the doorway. She panted as if she'd been running; wisps of hair fluttered round her flushed cheeks.

'Then you know he's here,' muttered Gussie, eyes still on her mother.

Beatrice, apparently not noticing Sylvia's arrival, was pulling at one of the huge urns.

Sylvia stared in amazement. 'What are you doing, Mama? If you're not careful, it will fall.'

'I want it to fall!' With one great jerk, the urn lurched forward and crashed to the stone floor.

All three women gasped, then Beatrice burst into tears.

'She must be ill,' said Gussie in shocked tones. Never, ever, had her shy, correct mother behaved in such a violent, uncontrolled way.

Giving her sister a disparaging look, Sylvia put her arm round her mother and led her into a small sitting room. She lowered her gently into a chair and crouched at her knees.

'What is it, Mama, dearest Mama?' Sylvia felt a surge of love for this thin weeping woman who had just broken a priceless Grecian urn. At least she assumed it was priceless because otherwise it was merely hideous.

'It's your father.' Beatrice's large blue eyes stared up at her daughter's through a glistening film of tears. 'The moment I saw him at the door, I knew that his regiment had been called to the front. He's going away from me. Then I saw those urns as if I'd never seen them before and,' she lowered her voice in horror, 'they're funeral urns!' She stared at Sylvia appealingly. 'Oh, Sylvie, how can I do without your dearest papa!'

All this was so extraordinary that Sylvia could think of nothing to say. Her parents were old, her father nearly fifty. She knew they got on well enough but this was a confession of desperate love. When Arthur had left, she had not wept or wailed, nor thrown china about. She had lain on her bed and read Keats. 'Would you like some tea, Mama?'

Blind eyes stared at her but gradually the grief and tears passed. Beatrice looking vaguely around, as if she was reorienting herself, then straightened her bodice and patted her coil of fair hair into place. 'We must order tea for your father.' Her voice was quite as usual, even to the little sardonic edge. As her mother stood up, determinedly erect, Sylvia wondered how she would react to the sight of the broken urn. But when they reached the hallway, only

57

lit now by a few shafts of the setting sun, there was no sign of any disturbance and the two urns sat as securely as ever in their niches. Beatrice never looked in their direction.

'No sugar on the tray. But a slice of plum cake will do him good.' Beatrice put her foot on the first step of the staircase. She did not look back.

The moment she was out of sight, Sylvia dashed to the fallen, now replaced urn. Close to, it was easy enough to see that someone, presumably Gussie, had positioned it so that the smashed handle and hole were at the back.

By the time dinner was served, it was established in everybody's minds, both family and servants, that this was a last meal. Nothing had yet been said by the Colonel but the seriousness and formality of everyone's behaviour reflected it. Sylvia had chosen to wear a navy silk jacket, inherited from a great-aunt which she usually considered too old-fashioned. So when the Colonel spoke in his easy, affectionate way, it came as a relief.

'My regiment will be sailing from Southampton tomorrow evening. We'll initially go to Cairo where we will be held in reserve. We are part of the Mediterranean Expeditionary Force so Gallipoli is our most likely destination.' He smiled at Sylvia. 'Who knows? I might see Arthur.'

Sylvia tried to smile back but it was a wan attempt, restricted by the stricken face of her mother.

'There is no more I can tell you. In fact I shouldn't have told you so much. Truthfully, I know scarcely more than I read in *The Times* myself.' He paused as if expecting a response but, since no one spoke, he continued in a rather more forceful manner. 'It is a great honour for an old soldier like myself to be asked to fight for his country. The yeomanry I lead are truly the backbone of Dorset: farmers, farriers, solicitors, cowherds, shepherds, hedgers and ditchers. Men from this estate. This house. As you know we are a cavalry regiment and while some have ridden to hounds since they were children, others have only opened the gate to let the hunt pass. But over the past months we have turned into one unit, of which I am proud to be the commander. We are ready to fight!'

Beatrice and Sylvia seemed stunned by this declaration. Gussie, however, clapped her hands and cried, 'Long live the King!'

The Colonel smiled. 'I'm glad you're such a patriot, Gussie.'

'I certainly am, Papa! Why ever do they keep men training for such ages?'

'Without proper training, my dear Gussie, you don't have an army. Discipline doesn't come easily to a delivery boy from Bermondsey or an out of work navvy from Liverpool. Discipline is the first essential in a good army. Without it you'd face the enemy with a rabble who'd run in different directions under an attack.'

'But they're brave, Papa. Nobody's making them volunteer.' Sylvia leant forward, pushing her glass of wine aside.

'Not yet, but if the war continues to go as badly as it is in France, then I foresee conscription. Our army is very small compared to Germany or to the armies of our allies, France and Russia.' He paused, looked round, apparently pleased by the attentive expressions on his daughters' faces. He did not look at his wife. 'Of course they're brave to volunteer but it doesn't mean they'll make good soldiers.'

During this unprecedented talk, Beatrice wore a look of woe. She understood that this was a farewell peroration. He was educating his daughters a little and making it clear to his wife that he believed in what he was doing and, since there was no choice about going to war, she should not be sad.

But Beatrice wanted to be sad. She wanted to weep and smash odious burial urns. So she hardly spoke throughout the meal, except to reprimand Gussie who had absent-mindedly picked off a rose head from the bowl at the centre of the table. Beatrice felt sad for the early spring rose, so brave to face the cold nights.

The Colonel continued to talk. 'There are men training everywhere. All sorts. The footballers' battalion at White City, cooks at Belton Park estate, clerks who have never moved a muscle, men in kilts who know the bagpipes better than the bugle, men learning to dig trenches at Oxford in the shadow of our great universities, Welsh recruits who have never left their valleys, men sticking their bayonets into sacks of straw, a field day in Richmond Park giving the cavalry a chance to gallop. All over the country, Kitchener's army is gathering strength . . .'

Beatrice stood as soon as the cheeseboard had passed. 'Girls, leave your father in peace to smoke a pipe.' She led them to the sitting room and took the same chair where Sylvia had comforted her earlier. A line that Bingo had quoted to her all those years ago when he went to South Africa came into her head: *I could not love thee, Dear, so much, loved I not Honour more.* As a soldier's wife, she had nodded dutifully. 'Sylvia!'

'Yes, Mama.' Sylvia put aside *The Times*.

'Can you find me that book of seventeenth-century poems your father likes? It has a poem called "To Lucasta, Going to the Wars".'

'It's in his study, I think.'

Sylvia went quickly. She was followed by Gussie who announced she was too tired to live. Left alone, Beatrice stared at the dying fire.

With the first happy thought of the day, she recognised how lucky she was that Bingo had not been ordered to France. True, he was sailing out to war, but he and his men and their horses would disembark in Egypt where there was scarcely any fighting.

Sylvia found her father in his study. To be precise, he was in the annexe where he kept his collection of bronzes, a mildly eccentric hobby in a soldier and Master of Fox Hounds.

'Look at this one.' He held up a spiky statuette, quite small. Sylvia peered without much interest.

'It's all arms and legs.' She forbore to say how ugly she thought it.

'Shiva, the Indian Hindu god, made in seven hundred AD. The craftsmanship is splendid. I got it in India long ago, even before I met your mother. It's the foundation of my collection.'

He had scarcely looked at his daughter but now he put down both pipe and statuette and turned to face her. 'If I don't come back, I'd like you and Arthur to have them. Your mother has never admired them. I think she even believes they're ugly but is too polite to say so.'

Sylvia was far too shocked by those matter of fact words, *if I don't come back* to do more than nod.

The Colonel returned to the shelves on which his bronzes were displayed. He picked up a horse, about a foot long with a mane rising over his curved neck like a ruff.

'I can see why you like that,' Sylvia said with more enthusiasm.

'My favourite, from two hundred and fifty BC.' He put it back lovingly.

'You must be glad you can take your horses with you.'

'And Sid Small to look after them. He's worried about the big black. Such a bad-tempered blighter. A week or two in the hold of the ship and he might try and kick his way out.' The Colonel smiled almost as if he relished the idea.

'Papa . . .' Sylvia hesitated. What was it she wanted to say? About her mother? About Arthur? About love? About war? About *not coming back*? About herself? She had always found her father easier to confide in than her mother but now there was too much in her head to start.

'Yes?' As she still didn't speak, he came near and put his hand on her shoulder. 'I think it best if your mother doesn't come to see me off at Southampton. It will be a muddle. I will have duties. It will probably rain. You won't mind staying at home with her?'

Sylvia found she did mind. She wanted to see her father among his men. She wanted to see him till the last possible moment. 'Won't you be sad, all on your own?'

'I shall say my farewells tomorrow morning outside my own house. It will be like all the other times I've gone away and come back. I shall write from the ship.' He paused, before adding, 'Your mother and I have visited Cairo so it will not seem too remote to her. Besides, she will have the running of the house and estate to keep her busy. I couldn't bear her to be too sorrowful.'

'No,' agreed Sylvia. But a fierce thought came into her head: She is not the only one to be pitied; my lover is fighting already and may even at this moment be lying dead or horribly wounded on a wild peninsula which I've never visited and can barely imagine.

'What is it, my dear?' The Colonel looked at her, concerned, but not too much. He trusted her to be sensible.

In order to disguise her panic, Sylvia rushed across the study. She stood at the door. 'Mama will be wondering where we are.' She had quite forgotten her mission to collect the book of poetry.

'Indeed she will.' The Colonel gave his daughter a little hug. 'I am fortunate to have a loving family.' His neatly clipped moustache, nearly grey, twitched a little.

Later that evening, the Colonel had just taken off his shirt in his dressing room when he felt arms round his back. Tender fingers stroked his skin.

'Oh my dearest.' He turned round. Beatrice wore a rose silk wrap. Her thick, fair hair was loose and fell below her shoulders. 'My beautiful girl!' He would have embraced her but she held him away, frowning. Her forefinger pointed to his chest.

Do you remember how I used to make fun of your tattoo? Just a silly fad, I told you, you'll regret it later. But now I'm glad of it.'

'Why's that?' The Colonel smiled at her, then, as she still held him away, squinted down at himself. 'I suppose you thought it vulgar, even though it's my coat of arms and not a mermaid or bearded lady.'

Beatrice remained serious. 'I'm glad because it identifies you. If something dreadful happens, you can never be lost.'

Now the Colonel insisted on holding Beatrice and telling her that he had no intention of being lost. 'Remember, we're travelling to Cairo and there're no battles going on there as far as I know.'

So Beatrice kissed him and told him lovingly that she would let him undress in peace as long as he wasn't too long.

In the night, when he was snoring comfortably on his back, she slipped her hand under his pyjamas and, once she'd found the thickening of the skin which marked the tattoo, she laid her fingers over it. It was an imprint of ownership: you are mine; nothing shall part us.

Fred was huddled under a cape he'd taken from a corpse. It smelt a bit but it was very warm and he was quite comfortable in a little hole he'd carved out for himself above the beach. There were men dug in round him, not in the straight lines they'd been taught but higgledy-piggledy. Above them, garlands of stars entwined in fantastic pattern.

Fred liked sleeping under the night sky but he was uneasy about the day ahead. When he'd taken the spade back to the sergeant major, he'd been held on the spot with an assessing beady-eyed look.

'Did that double quick.'

'Sarn't Major!'

'So what are we going to do about you.' There'd been no question mark at the end of the sentence but Fred had answered anyway.

'I'm a runner, Sarn't Major.'

'I've no doubt that you can run like the proverbial hare but where's your company? You're filthy enough to be taken for a spy.'

'No water to wash.'

'Are you giving me fucking excuses!' This was a bellow.

Fred was becoming bored with the conversation. He hadn't eaten since a dawn breakfast and now the sun was just about down.

'Do you see that major over there?' The sergeant major had pointed his stick at an officer leaning against a wall.

'He was the officer who told me to be a runner last night, sir.'

'What a coincidence!' He drew out the word in mocking tones. 'Major Furlong's joining the Australian lot and he needs a few men around him – Englishmen. I suppose you are English?' This was more mockery.

'Sarn't Major.'

'Seems to me, Chaffey, you're just the man for the job. Awkward, dirty and devious.'

At last it had seemed to be going somewhere.

'Cut back down to the beach now and report to HQ at six o'clock tomorrow morning. I'll inform the major I've found the perfect villain to protect him against the Down Under.'

'Thank you, Sarn't Major.' He'd meant it, sort of. But now, five hours later, lying under the stars, he wasn't so sure. Everyone knew the Australians by repute, even if they'd never met one – which Fred hadn't. His brigade had been shipped straight to Lemnos whereas the Aussies had first been gathered in Egypt. There was a story going the rounds about sentry duty at the camps there:

SENTRY: Halt! Who goes there?
VOICE: Ceylon Planters Rifles.
SENTRY: Pass, friend.
(A little later)
SENTRY: Halt! Who goes there?
VOICE: Auckland Mounted Rifles.
SENTRY: Pass, friend.
(A little later again)
SENTRY: Halt! Who goes there?
VOICE: What the fuck has it got to do with you?
SENTRY: Pass, Australian.

He and his mates had cheered and laughed but he knew, alongside the admiration and jealousy, there were some who disapproved. It wasn't the way you behaved in the British Army, was it? And the Aussies were part of the British Army, weren't they, even if they'd never fought a war?

Fred suspected that they wouldn't like the cut of his jib in Anzac land. The major seemed a mild man, with no air of command. A lot of good it did Colonel Doughty-Wylie when a sniper got a sighting on his air of command.

Eyes closed and, curled deeper into his cape, Fred pictured the colonel's body being lowered into the grave he'd dug. You've got to live. Fred was asleep.

Arthur stumbled about the dark beach, getting in the way of ammunition carts covered in bushes, ambulance carts drawn by six mules, lines of soldiers bent under their packs and cursing their fate in various languages, lines of mules lamenting theirs in loud screeches, armourers, engineers trailing telephone cord, a few rows of conical tents, messy rows of graves.

Eventually, he came to a standstill. Once more he stepped aside to avoid a line of bad-tempered mules.

'I'd sooner stop a bullet than be kicked by one of those.'

Arthur swung round.

'Twigg-Smith. We were at prep together.'

Twigg-Smith. How they'd laughed at his name! Joking that he'd better have added Smith – or Leaf or Trunk. 'Funny place to meet.'

'Wish I could laugh. Thing is, can't stop shaking. It's lack of sleep. My mother programmed me to need eight hours' good kip. She told me I'd fall apart with any less. So here I am falling apart.'

Arthur saw that his companion was not so much shaking as trembling all over. His round face looked like a blancmange under the silvery sky. 'Can I help?'

'I've got to report to a new command in the morning. Mine seems to have disintegrated. Have you seen the two long graves in the old fort? Stretch the length of Regent Street.' He stopped abruptly. 'I must sleep.'

'Just follow me.'

When they arrived at the dugout there was a large mound in the corner from which emerged great despairing snores.

'That's your host, Captain Entwhistle.' Arthur waved his hand. 'I hope he won't disturb you.'

Twigg-Smith was already folding himself on to the floor where he stretched himself out on his back. In a moment his eyes closed, his trembling ceased, and he was asleep.

Arthur, still wide awake, sat himself at a little desk Entwhistle had rigged up. He extracted a letter from his pocket and straightened it carefully.

With sudden energy he realised that there was one person he could and should write to:

Dear Mrs Babcock,
Your husband, Sergeant Babcock, who tragically lost his life while doing his patriotic duty, was a man of great goodness and valour, much looked up to by the men he led. I was with him at the end. He suffered very little . . .

Six

Captain Rupert Prideaux stared crossly at ten so-called Turkish prisoners huddled behind trailing rolls of barbed wire. The light was coming up on V Beach so he couldn't avoid their misery. Having handed themselves into the French on Kum Kale, they were now likely to end their days with a shell from their own side. But that wasn't what was making him angry, it was the impossibility of giving a correct report to HQ of the interviews he'd just conducted with them. For a start, everyone expected him to talk about 'the Turks' whereas in fact they were part of the Ottoman Empire: Turks, Armenians, Greeks, Albanians and Arabs. All had different axes to grind and none knew anything useful about the German command, although many pretended to. '*Zoteri!*' an Albanian called him, begging for water. Rupert had travelled round Albania for several months and had been alternately impressed and terrified. He'd bet this man wouldn't be held prisoner for long.

'Good morning, Prideaux.' Rupert turned back to see the long, handsome face of Lieutenant Lamb. The sight was both welcome and irritating. Here was exactly the sort of highly educated Englishman who relished this hopeless sideshow.

'Where are you off to now?' Lamb was fully kitted up, shoulders bent forward under the weight.

'Heading for Krithia, then Achi Baba.' He gave a smile, only partly ironic.

Both men looked up involuntarily as the first rays of sunshine spiked like a crown above the hills.

'Here's something for you to debate as you go. Do you think the Allies' defeat by the Turks is more likely to, a) keep Bulgaria neutral, b) bring Bulgaria into the war on to the side of Germany? No prizes awarded.'

'We're not defeated!' burst out Lamb.

'Yet.' Rupert knew it was cruel to tease Lamb when he was off to fight.

'With fellows like you at HQ it's not surprising there're problems.' Lamb started to move away.

'Nobody listens to me at HQ so you can relax on that front. I'm as keen on a victory as you but I do know you won't be attacking in a hurry. Give it a week, I'd say. Plenty of time to enjoy the local wildlife; the tortoises are spectacular.'

Lamb hesitated, then pulled something from his pocket. 'I wrote a couple of letters last night. See they go, would you?'

Rupert held out his left hand. 'Good luck.'

'Yes. Good luck to you too. In this place you can as easily get killed standing by the supplies as at the front.'

As if to prove his point there was a sudden huge *whoomf* and a *crump* as a shell landed on the sea's edge, blasting apart a boat. Men, boxes and water sprayed into the air. Stretcher-bearers ran from their stations towards the spot. Soldiers, already climbing up away from the shore, dropped flat.

'They were probably aiming for the battleships,' commented Rupert.

Rupert watched Lamb rejoin his men; he went quickly but not gracefully like an athlete. Rupert glanced down at his hand. He'd once been a very good athlete.

He was still holding the letters: *Miss Sylvia Fitzpaine*. Very nice too. He had some idea the mother was a distant relative of his family. *Mrs Thomas Babcock*. He could guess what that was about. Not so very nice.

Rupert began walking over to where the communication officers were dug in. He needed a lift out to HMS *Arcadian* where headquarters had removed themselves. The air was warming but still fresh. If it hadn't been for that nasty spectacle of the blown-apart boat he'd have looked forward to a spin over the bright waters. Come to think of it, he still did!

Fred stared upwards in astonishment. A strip of shingle rose quickly to sheer cliffs, stretching up as far as he could see, with little moving figures all the way, digging in, trying to make homes. 'What do they think they are? Nesting seabirds?'

Major Furlong, usually a man of few words, seemed equally taken aback. 'I'd heard General Birdwood wanted to take his Australians off and General Hamilton told him to "dig dig dig", but . . .' he muttered before realising his only audience was a private and stopped abruptly. He stared rather vacantly round the beach which was the usual mix of essential activities, at first glance more haphazard than planned.

Fred and Major Furlong had arrived at Anzac Cove by boat an hour earlier. It was the middle of the day, very hot, and some men were bathing naked in the sea. As Fred stared enviously – no one could accuse him of over-cleanliness but three days without a drop of water anywhere but on his face made him feel he'd get on with the skunks.

'*Woof*!' Both men turned as a shell landed in the sea, sending up a vast spray of water. '*Woof*!' Another shell followed. The swimmers jumped like a shoal of fish disturbed by fishermen and, splashing and thrashing, made for the shore. When no more shells came, they turned round nonchalantly enough and waded out into deeper water.

Major Furlong collected himself, cleared his throat and stamped his feet. He was quite old, fifty at least by Fred's reckoning. 'You'd better take a note to General Birdwood. Tell him I've arrived.'

'Yessir. Where is the general, sir?' They had already failed to find him on the beach.

'Can't be too difficult to locate the British commander of the combined Australians and New Zealand forces!' The major was very fair-skinned and when he was cross – usually because he was confused, in Fred's view – his face went a livid puce. 'He likes his headquarters at the front. You heard them say it.' He waved his hand towards the cliffs, which were backed by sharp promontories and deep gulleys. 'Up there.'

Fred stared with sharper eyes – funny how it concentrated the mind when you knew you were actually heading to a place. Now he could see the paths curling round the headlands and making circuitous routes upwards. In some parts soldiers were carrying sandbags or even rocks, presumably to make the route or their strange homes safer.

As he watched, a line of stretcher-bearers came down, hurrying, heads bent. *Snipers*, thought Fred.

'Here you are.' The major handed him a note.

'Yessir!' Fred saluted. No lunch again then. He had got a pack now, picked off a dead man. It didn't do to be sentimental, although he'd handed over some letters and a photo to a corporal. Surprisingly, when he checked, the boots fitted him.

Sighing a bit at the prospect of a hot climb, Fred set off. He came level with the stretchers.

'G'day.' The leading stretcher-bearer halted. 'You're out to catch the sun, are you?'

This was Fred's first Australian and he seemed friendly enough. 'Orders to find General Birdwood.'

'Mate of yours, is he?'

Fred decided to overlook this bit of fun. The wounded man on the stretcher, who had one bandage on his head and another on his upper leg, groaned loudly. 'A message for him from my Major Furlong.'

'If we stand here any longer we'll be taken for a bleeding signpost,' shouted the bearer at the back. Shelling had started on the beach and machine-gun fire further up so he had to raise his voice. The wounded man groaned again.

'Shrapnel Gully.' The first man waved his arm airily to the right. 'He's either there or at Plugge's Plateau.'

'Thanks,' said Fred. They were holding up a whole train of stretchers waiting to come down to the beach so it was no time to ask the best way up to Shrapnel Gulley. He stood back to let the stretchers past. The Australians were mostly big men, the size of British officers but broader across the chest. Many of them wore shorts and broad-brimmed slouch hats.

As soon as Fred started seriously climbing he realised how the land lay. When the path swung east you were in danger from all kinds of fire. When it swung west, you were protected. Bands of soldiers had already started piling sandbags in the worst areas but it seemed the best course was to run head down and hope for the best. He used to think stretcher-bearing was a cushy job but going up and down these paths all day with not even a hand free to take a potshot yourself struck him as near suicide.

Shrapnel Gulley turned out to be an irregular, incomprehensible gorge between two irregular, incomprehensible ridges. Part of it was bare and sandy, part covered with undergrowth which was thick and prickly and tore at his hands. Even then the path twisted and turned upwards, sometimes safe from enemy fire, sometimes unprotected. Men and occasionally mules dragging water tanks, or carts loaded with ammunition or food, were hit constantly. The mules shrieked, the men were silent.

Fred fell in with an Australian lance corporal. He was coming up from the shore laden with water.

'We take turns, at night when we can,' he told Fred. 'Makes a break from sitting in the trenches with your head down or, worse still, digging. I joined the army to escape digging.'

'You on the front line?'

'Even a dingo wouldn't call it a line. We're dug in wherever we got to that first night. Every time we move, Abdul pops us one. I'm Bill.'

'Fred,' said Fred, surprised to find himself clasping hands on the edge of a gorge with fire blasting all around.

They both paused for a moment, preparing for a run across an open piece of track. Scarcely more than two feet across, it linked two ridges within the gulley. Looking up, they could see two higher ridges, curling round on the skyline. Where the ground fell away, the soil and stone was a brilliant yellow glowing in the sun.

'That's where they are, of course. Apart from the snipers – they're everywhere. Probably one behind us now, painted green.' The corporal turned to Fred. 'While I go up and down, I've worked out the whole lot of us, Australians, New Zealanders, the lot, are squatting on less than half an acre of ground. Makes you laugh, doesn't it? And the beach is only three hundred feet wide. I've paced it. Where I come from we think anything less than a thousand acres a chicken run. On here we're not far off headless chickens.' He gave Fred a clap on the shoulder. 'We won't run, though. We won't ever run.'

'Not on your life!' agreed Fred enthusiastically. He liked this big fellow with his flat drawl rising at the end.

As they talked, about half a dozen New Zealanders had piled up behind them. 'Scared of Johnny Turk's bullets?' jeered one.

With a swipe of his huge hand Bill tossed him to the ground, then set off, water bottles swinging, along the path. Knowing it didn't do to go in pairs, Fred waited a moment, time enough for the New Zealander to get to his feet.

70

'Mate of yours, is he?'

'I'm English.' Fred spoke over his shoulder as he set off at a run. No way of knowing the New Zealanders' views of the motherland.

Bill had already moved on by the time he arrived at the other side. Looking into a narrow defile to his right he noticed the water tanker and mules crashed to the bottom. One mule still kicked and screamed. Fred pointed his rifle. The Indians who tended the mules mostly seemed to have survived except for one spreadeagled on a bush like a jacket put out to dry.

Now that he was higher up, the noise of rifle, machine-gun fire and shelling was louder but still without any rhythm. It made everywhere feel unsafe, even crouched where he was under a rocky outcrop. Not too much further up, he could see some dugouts that looked as strong and well set in as if a giant badger had made them. Just the home for a general. Brushing off some thirsty flies who were drinking the sweat off his face, he set off at speed.

Sylvia snatched up *The Times* from its place in the drawing room and dashed out to the bench in the garden. In one second she had learnt the headline on page seven by heart: THE GALLIPOLI LANDING. HARD FIGHTING ON SHORE. VALOUR OF DOMINION TROOPS.

At last! At last! Some news. Even a map. Her eyes fought to keep up with the whirl of her brain. Today was Friday, 7th May but this report, from *A Special Correspondent* had the byline *Dardanelles. 25th April*, two whole weeks earlier. How could there be such a time lag! She began rushing through the headlines scattered over the page. GOOD ORGANISATION, THE CRITICAL PERIOD, HALF HOUR OF SUPPRESSED EXCITEMENT, ENEMY ALARMED, AUSTRALIAN BAYONET WORK, THE FIRST WOUNDED, A FORTUNATE ERROR, then under a new date of 26th April: AN IDEAL COUNTRY FOR IRREGULAR WAR, AUSTRALIANS BLOOD UP (why all this about Australians?), HEIGHTS BOMBARDED, A MAGNIFICENT SCENE.

Sylvia tried now to read the story of what had actually happened but it was written in such highly coloured tones that it seemed no more real than an adventure by H. Rider Haggard. Our boys – who all seemed to be *brave colonials*, unless they were *gallant boat crews* – landed on narrow beaches swept by gunfire but nevertheless scaled *pathless hills, valleys and bluffs* of several hundred feet while the Turks were soon *demoralised* and *the Germans had difficulty in getting them forward to an attack.*

As she became calmer she realised that the report came from a correspondent with the Dominion Troops. So she still knew no more about Arthur's situation.

Flicking the pages, she came across a different kind of headline: MR ASQUITH'S CHEERFUL STATEMENT. Although the prime minister didn't seem to get much respect these days, surely he must know more than anybody. Sylvia saw he had spoken the day before in the Commons, his remarks based on a report issued by the War Office on 1st May which at least made him more up to date than the special correspondent. He had concluded a general report by saying, *The operations are being continued and pressed forward under highly satisfactory conditions.*

Highly satisfactory conditions. Sylvia tried out the phrase on the bright blue sky, then on the pink roses whose sweet scent filled the air. *These* were highly satisfactory conditions, even if the garden was looking rather ragged since three of the four gardeners had gone off to fight. She turned back to the paper. HASTINGS and ST LEONARDS. *Magnificent Esplanades (6 miles), Bright Entertainments, Health and Sunshine, Golf, Bowls, Tennis, Motor and Coaching Trips, Delightful Scenery.*

Were they suggesting these as good opportunities for convalescing soldiers? She imagined a uniformed officer, on crutches or arm in a sling, strolling, pipe in mouth, beside the clock made of flowers, or staring peacefully out to sea. There'd been no time for anyone to come back from Gallipoli yet. It struck Sylvia that the principal reason for her restless grief was the unchanging circumstances of her own life while all else changed around her. Arthur left, her father left, but there she was sitting in a rose garden.

She turned round to look at Tollorum Manor behind her. She had always loved everything about it: the colour of the old stone which combined mellow gold, grey-white and soft brown in perfect harmony, the gabled rise of its two wings, the stone-surrounded windows, some square with Tudor stateliness, a few with more elaborate medieval lines left over from an earlier building. She even loved the large Victorian addition, sympathetic to its upstart inferiority. This was her home, her family's home for centuries. That used to make her proud, but now made her impatient.

Jumping up, Sylvia decided to confront her mother. It was immoral to keep this large house empty, when it would make an excellent hospital. She reached the long beech hedge where the bright new leaves were pushing off the faded old, and paused. If Tollorum became a hospital, she would be committed to staying, assistant lady bountiful to her mother. Yet her aim, since meeting Arthur and his friends, had been to leave her family, not just to marry him but to go to university, make something of herself.

There must be an answer. But when it came, she was amazed by its simplicity: she would go to London and train to be a nurse. Her mother's bachelor brother, the Earl of Deverill, owned a large gloomy house in Mayfair where they always stayed when in town. If her mother complained, she would tell her to hand over Tollorum to the authorities and come and join her.

How proud Arthur would be!

Rupert tried not to look at General Hamilton with too much dislike. As a humble intelligence officer who'd wheedled his way even into that position, he had no right to feel anything but awe and adulation. However, he'd bet half the great man's staff gathered in this very hot and fly-ridden tent felt the same disapproval. There was something about his skinny body and his casual almost girlish stance as if to say 'I don't need to prove I'm tough' that was peculiarly irritating. Then there was his silly voice and his even sillier habit of writing his diary – filled with long Greek quotations – far into the night when any normal soldier should be drinking with his officers. Strange to think he'd once admired him for his erudition. Far worse was his manner of giving commands as if they were invitations, as if gentlemanly politeness was more important to him than firm leadership. Some people liked him for it, but no one Rupert had talked to in the army or the navy thought it was the way to win the war. And now he'd ordered his headquarters to be set up on the least salubrious corner of Lemnos, where the wind blew the bare sandy soil into every corner of every tent and there were no trees and therefore no shade. Apparently, this was to show solidarity with the men at the front. How whimsical! How childish! All it did was reduce the efficiency of his staff who were already falling ill, and made sure the men stayed even longer in their appalling trenches.

These were minor problems compared to Hamilton's fixed conviction that his Mediterranean Expeditionary Force was on target for success. The fact that, after more than a week, the Allies had not yet captured one of their first-day objectives seem to cause him no disquiet and, according to a friend Rupert had made among Hamilton's staff, he sent optimistic messages to London, to his old mentor, Kitchener. Like a schoolboy who wants to please, thought Rupert savagely.

'Captain Prideaux. Captain Prideaux!'

'Sorry, sir. Sand in my ears, sir.' Rupert jumped up from his position near the flap in the tent.

The great men were gathered around a small rickety table where crumbs from an earlier meal had attracted an army of flies, continually swept off by an ADC and continually returning. They were large, black and emitted a revolting buzz. Rupert thought nostalgically of the navy's perfect fad for cleanliness. You could thank the efficiency of German submarines for the HQ's transference from shipboard hygiene to unregenerate land. Lately, too many Allied ships had been sent to a watery grave.

'I understand you know the island of Tenedos well?' A captain began addressing him above the buzzing about a dangerous band of spies of unidentifiable nationality, seen entering the island.

'A delightful place, sir.' Rupert was aware of Hamilton's eyes fixed on him. Why did they bother with such rubbish? There were as many spies in the Levant as there were fools in Parliament or flies in this tent. He batted his hands crossly.

' "*Naturam expellas furca, tamen usque recurret*".' The general looked round complacently before translating with a smile. 'You can drive out nature with a pitchfork but he'll be constantly running back.'

There was a communal shudder in the stuffy tent. Did Hamilton truly believe that quoting Latin tags was the way to impress?

'Continue, Mallory,' advised the general with a slight show of uneasiness.

'Yes, sir. So, Prideaux, find yourself a boat as soon as you can, get off to Tenedos and report back.' He paused. 'We can't have spies knowing our every move.'

Various questions came into Rupert's head, the principal being, What could the spies learn that would be of any use to the enemy? Now that the Allies had gained a foothold on the peninsula, it was perfectly obvious that they would try to move further inland.

'Sir!' Rupert saluted and left the tent. It was just as hot outside. He looked at his watch: mid-afternoon, a time for a siesta under a sheltering vine. Maybe he could get to Tenedos in time to take breakfast under one.

Most of the ships were in Lemnos's principal harbour at Mudros but the fishermen and other men of business, selling Turkish Delight and lethal sherbet drinks, put in at the smaller bays. Better one of them, decided Rupert, than the commandeered trawlers where the captains encouraged their dogs to do their business on the deck.

Rupert watched his servant, Hepple, approach with two horses.

'You're riding, sir?'

'Yes. Get my pack and ride with me. Then you can bring the horses back. I'm taking ship for Tenedos.'

'Yes, sir.' The man's pained expression didn't change. Rupert wondered how it must feel to have not a shred of curiosity about the world. Hepple had confided in him that his only aim in life was to get back to the draper's store where he'd worked since a boy. Yet it was just such narrow-minded men whose patriotism led them to answer Kitchener's call to arms.

Rupert walked over to a newly constructed wooden shed and, in its shade, got out his cigarettes. One of the horses, tethered nearby, tried to follow him. They were convivial, horses, a gift that he, unlike most men, did not possess. He did like women – Rupert puffed on his cigarette – which made Gallipoli, an entirely woman-free zone, deeply unfriendly. There would be women on Tenedos.

Eventually, Hepple arrived with his pack. Sweat rolled off his sad face.

Once on horseback, Rupert's spirits rose immediately. He outrode the flies, outrode the mourning for his dead brother, the idiocies of General Hamilton and even, as his horse hurtled down a steep incline, the images of the shattered fragments of men, as liberally sprinkled across that doomed land beyond the shimmering sea ahead as the stones beneath his horse's hooves.

'Come *on*, Hepple!' He reined in at the bottom of the gully where a green path of thyme and wild rock roses led down to a small bay. His horse stamped and sniffed at the sea.

'What the hell do you mean, man? Some major informs me he's on the beach. Having a nice cup of tea, is he? What do I want with a bloody idiot who sends another bloody idiot to find me! What I need is a regiment up here at the *top* of this gulley, not a damned fool major at the bottom!'

This tirade, only partly comprehensible to Fred owing to the crashing of shells and the fire both from the hidden Turks ahead and their own soldiers dug in all around, didn't surprise him, not least because General Birdwood seemed to be Australian, although a dark European sort of Aussie. Something was buggered.

'I've got a letter, sir.'

An ADC took the letter and glanced at it. He immediately handed it back to Fred. 'Where do you think you are?' He had sharp black eyes, red-veined with exhaustion.

'I don't know, sir.'

'Can't you read?'

'No, sir.'

The ADC flinched, not at this news, Fred presumed, but at the shriek of a shell which seemed to be coming straight for them but at the last minute swerved and landed with a thump in an un-inhabited side of the gulley. Earth and stone exploded downwards but the shell itself was silent.

'A dud,' commented the ADC after peering over the edge. He returned to Fred. 'Your letter's for General Birdwood. He's English. In overall command. You spoke to Colonel Monash. This is his command.'

'Sir.' Fred stared up at the sky, then across the unnavigable stretches of broken ridges and collapsing cliffs. One of the cliffs, he noticed, resembled a face.

'We've christened it the sphinx,' said the ADC. 'Like the one in Cairo.' The realisation came over Fred that if he didn't eat something, he'd faint like a girl. Nothing like making a fool of yourself twice in one day.

'General Birdwood's at Plugge's Plateau. Not so far away.' The ADC waved his hand at a parallel bluff.

'For a crow,' muttered Fred.

The ADC turned to check on his colonel but he was occupied with two officers who seemed to be trying to convince him about something. 'We'll be moving, I expect. The colonel doesn't believe in getting killed unnecessarily.'

Through a haze of tiredness and hunger, Fred wondered why this upstanding officer was being so matey before remembering he was an Aussie. It was true then, Aussies spoke to their men as if they were human.

'Here comes a whopper!'

This time Fred didn't wait for the shell to miss them but flung himself flat. As the ground danced a terrible dance around him, he clung to sharp stalked vegetation as tenaciously as a beetle. It seemed to go on for ever until he heard the earth tumbling over him and the world switched to black.

Arthur was ready for the word to go. Like his men he was crouched forward in the trench.

Every day, the British, with the French to their right, waited for shelling from the navy, and then attacked, as if this time they would reach Achi Baba. The red smudge on its top had now defined itself as scarlet poppies waving defiantly like scarlet flags. Arthur believed they'd get there. Not immediately. They had to take the village of Krithia first and they weren't near it yet. But soon. Soon. His heart thumped, his head emptied and he forgot everything but the mad dash, the yelling of the Turks 'Allah! Allah!' His own men beside him with their bayonets fixed, their grim faces, no longer young, impervious to heat, hunger, death. The same men who'd spent half the night complaining about the infestation of lice, met, unafraid, machine gun and grenade. How he admired them!

At night it was the Turks' turn to attack, flinging themselves in wave after wave on the Allied position as if sheer numbers could push the enemy from their shores. Mowed down by machine-gun fire or hacked to death in desperate hand-to-hand fighting, they died in their hundreds.

Every morning the stretch of no man's land – in this part of Gallipoli hundreds of yards wide – was strewn with the dead and dying of both sides. In only a day or two the corpses became black and bloated, unrecognisable as human beings. The stink rose into the air like palpable slime but the snipers finished off anyone who tried to remove them.

But now they were off again. The shelling over and nothing in Arthur's head but the next attack.

Seven

Sylvia stared at the packet of envelopes in her hand with a stunned expression.

'They won't bite you.' Gussie laughed at her. 'I like your uniform.'

'I'm just tired.' It was true that after scarcely more than a week of early mornings and ten hours' work, she was so exhausted that Arthur's handwriting seemed like hieroglyphics: not quite meaningless but from another world. She and Gussie were standing in a small bare room which was apparently for staff visitors, although she had never heard of anyone having a visit.

'I had a perfectly awful time getting you out here. Are you VADs so important?'

'I was washing bedpans.' Sylvia had energy enough to enjoy Gussie's look of horror. 'It's about discipline. Voluntary Aid Detachment may sound grand but actually we're the lowest of the low. How *did* you get me out, if it comes to that?'

'Easy. I said I had bad news about your fiancé.'

'Oh, Gussie.' Sylvia felt too weak to argue that it seemed to be tempting fate to pretend about Arthur's situation. 'But you were holding his letters.'

'They could have been written before his tragic end. Anyway, I hid them. I can't say the sister was very sympathetic.'

'She's not. I don't think she actually hates us, she just thinks we're too posh to be serious. Apparently, she accused one VAD who'd fallen sick of malingering and kept her in the ward so long that the poor thing died of pneumonia.'

'How frightful!'

'Yes, she is.' Sylvia let out her breath. 'I'll have to go back in a moment.'

'Aren't you going to read the letters? You've been waiting to hear from Arthur for weeks and weeks! That's why I brought them over.'

'I'll put them in my locker and read them later.' Sylvia clasped the letters more closely. 'Has Mama heard from Papa?'

'Oh, yes. From the ship. He seemed very jolly, more concerned about his horses than himself. Mama cried, of course.'

'There *are* submarines to worry about.' Unconsciously, Sylvia stroked the letters, before looking up anxiously. 'I'd better own up to Sister or I'll have to wear a mourning band.'

'Tell her there was a mistake. You know Reggie's finally gone to France and the rector told me that the day after he went, the War Office sent a letter announcing he was missing. Honestly. As if he'd gone missing off the ferry or the train. It turned out to be another R.L.C. Gisburne. Reginald Leopold Cuthbert Gisburne. I can't believe I know a man with such gruesome names. I don't expect the other chap had the same names, just the initials, probably.'

'I've got to go,' said Sylvia abstractedly. 'Give Mama my love, won't you. Don't say anything about the horrible sister or my tiredness.'

'Mother's all right. She's decided to turn over most of the house to recuperating soldiers. She's bustling about. She's got a new servant, well, helper. Some local woman. They're thick as thieves.' Gussie stood up. 'If you're really off, I might as well meet Cousin Evie for tea.'

Sylvia thought how pretty Gussie looked with her perfect pink and white complexion and thick dark hair under her hat trimmed with daisies. 'So that's who's chaperoning you,' she said idly. 'Hard luck.'

'Chaperoning!' Gussie snorted. 'As if I need someone hanging around. You're only two years older and you're doing exactly what you want. On your own.'

Still not quite concentrating – now she wanted to open those letters – Sylvia commented, 'But you're not out yet,' before realising just how ridiculous it sounded. 'I really must go.'

'Me too.' The two girls hugged each other briefly.

The moment Gussie had gone, Sylvia tore open the topmost letter. She would just read the first lines.

My dearest Sylvia,
It feels as if I've been here for my whole life. Yet this is my first
letter. I cannot explain. But don't be concerned; I'm doing what
I came here to do and feel proud to be part of something so
magnificent. If you could only see my men. Time and time again
they obey my whistle and go over the top, even though by now they
know exactly what awaits them. Oh Sylvia, I feel that before I
was a boy and now I'm a man—

'Fitzpaine! What can you be doing!'

Sylvia turned slowly. 'Just coming, Sister.'

'I can't waste my time running after you girls. You may not be aware but men are dying while you moon about.'

'Sorry, Sister.' Owing to my bedpan failures, men will die, thought Sylvia scornfully. Unlike some of the VADs, Sylvia wasn't afraid of the sister. She was worn out but not afraid. She could see that somewhere in this hard-faced little martinet there was a professional woman truly offended by being forced to take on untrained staff. But Sylvia was disgusted by her ugliness, her spitefulness and her way of giving little clicks with her teeth when she was particularly annoyed.

'What's that you're holding?'

'Letters, Sister.' She might as well have said 'hand-grenades.'

'You know the rules, even if you haven't been in a place of work before.' A couple of clicks here.

'Yes, Sister. No personal effects on the hospital premises.'

The sister made up her mind. Sometimes Sylvia was able to admire her energy. She must be fifty, yet kept the same long hours as everyone else and never flagged. 'You must see Matron. That's all there is to it.'

Sylvia's heart sank. 'When, Sister?'

'Now, Fitzpaine.' She paused. Small eyes focused on the letters. 'I understand your fiancé was killed.'

'No, Sister.' A VAD who was moving on to become a nurse had given Sylvia advice. 'Treat Sister as if you were a private and she an officer. Yes, sir, no, sir. Yes, Sister, no Sister. She's not so bad once she sees you're serious.'

'Explain.'

'Yes, Sister.' Sylvia considered. 'My brother died, Sister.' In fact, this was true. A baby born after Gussie had died aged three days.

'I see.'

'These letters are from my fiancé. My sister didn't know the rules about personal effects.'

'You must tell her.' She waved her hand. 'Well, back to the ward, then.'

'Thank you, Sister.'

'And put those letters in your locker.'

'Yes, Sister.'

This putting away of the letters involved them treading the same corridors for several minutes. Just before she turned aside, Sister began to speak again.

Sylvia stopped, braced for further reproof.

'When I grew up, nursing was considered a vocation, not a way of filling in time while your boyfriend isn't there to entertain you. Hurry, now.'

'Yes, Sister.' As she opened her locker, Sylvia thought that Sister's last words could equally well be an apology as a reproof. Yet perhaps she was right. Despite all her own high-flown sense of being a part of the war effort, there was a game-playing side of it. She would always be Sylvia Fitzpaine of Tollorum Manor, fiancée of Arthur Lamb, BA 'Oxon'.

Later, lying on her bed in the hostel, Sylvia read all three letters from Arthur. She supposed it might be the effect of the censor, but instead of bringing Arthur closer, they seemed to make him further away than ever. Tomorrow, when she was less exhausted, she would write to him. Half-asleep, she wondered how much he would want to know about her life as a nurse.

She felt very alone.

'They're calling it the Second Battle of Krithia.'

'How grand, when was the first?' Arthur felt relatively comfortable and able to be ironic. He was in the second line of trenches and Twigg-Smith, to whom he'd donated a night's sleep on the beach, had just appeared with a tin of cake and a bottle of green chartreuse. 'Best thanks I've ever had,' he said.

'Best sleep I've ever had. What happened to the man who snored?'

'Wounded, I heard. Let's hope it was bad enough to keep him out of the war. It didn't suit him.'

'It suits you?'

'I'll tell you when I've drunk that bottle.'

They drank the bottle and ate the cake in a gluttonous, selfish way. The Turks started up some heavy rifle firing, which they usually did after dark, but they took no notice. The smell of war – rotting bodies and shit – happened not to be too bad where they were. The flies had disappeared for the night and a cool dampness rose from the earth. The trench was fairly newly dug and Arthur had made sure it was not based on burial ground. Once he'd caught white maggots wriggling up from under his legs and unearthed a corpse.

'To answer your question, it does not suit but I want to be proud of what I'm doing. I want to distinguish myself. I saw Lieutenant Colonel Doughty-Wylie lead from the front. I'd like to be him.'

'He died, didn't he?'

'Yes, yes.' Arthur seemed impatient at this interruption. The alcohol and cake, the company of someone from his past, even if not a friend, made him talkative. 'My parents left no money when they died, you know. Without my uncle, I'd have been just a destitute orphan.'

'But you were clever.'

'That's the point. That's all I was. A scholarship boy at the top schools but not quite out of the top drawer. No real background. Just clever.'

Twigg-Smith shifted uncomfortably. 'I wouldn't have minded being you.'

Arthur ignored this. 'Meeting Sylvia was a miracle. I'd grown up thinking I'd never be rich enough to marry. But she made me feel anything was possible.' Arthur grabbed Twigg-Smith's arm. 'Do you know the first time I went to Tollorum and met Sylvia's parents and sister it was like the dream I'd had ever since my own parents died.'

'Yet you volunteered and risked everything.'

'Don't you see, I want to be the man Sylvia can be proud of. The whole family can be proud of. Her father's a brigadier-general. Anyway, I'm a classicist. How could I resist fighting in the steps of Achilles and Hector?' Arthur smiled and leant back against the wall of the trench to let a trail of stretchers and wounded go by. Despite his efforts, one caught him a blow on the elbow. 'Damn you,' he said automatically.

'Why aren't you in the communication trench?' grumbled Twigg-Smith.

'It's bloody blocked, isn't it?' This time the bearer gave both men a deliberate knock. Neither responded. Communication trenches got blocked all the time. Sometimes troops of men going in opposite directions got inexorably hooked together, neither able to move until some strong character, less weary than most, forced them apart.

'I don't shake so much now.' Twigg-Smith held up his hand. It was perfectly steady.

'Your mind's told your body to adapt and it has.'

'I don't trust it. There're only two things I trust in the world: mathematics and my mother.'

Arthur laughed. The sound surprised him. He didn't think he'd laughed since he left Cairo.

'Wasn't it your mother who told you you'd die without eight hours' sleep?'

'What a good memory! Mathematics tells me the odds aren't good for taking Gallipoli. I'd say we're 250,000 men short, and rising.'

'It strikes me I'm better off with no trust.'

'You don't trust anyone? Anything?'

The food and alcohol clouded Arthur's thinking. He shut his eyes and saw Sylvia's beautiful face. 'I admire Sylvia,' he said muzzily. 'I worship her. She is everything a girl should be. She thinks me brilliant.' This word definitely did not come out right. 'I picture her in Dorset with her family, surrounded by the green hills and valleys that makes England so, so . . .' He gave up the thought and shut his eyes again.

'. . . worth fighting for.' Twigg-Smith completed the sentence earnestly.

'Is that what I was going to say?' Arthur sat up a bit straighter. 'Yes, I expect it was. When I first came here and understood the horror, I couldn't write to Sylvia. The shock was too great.' He raised his arms above his head before retracting them quickly.

Even in the second line at night you were not safe from snipers. 'Now I tell her about the view from the Chinese-blue waters of the Dardanelles, of the plain of Troy, backed by peak after peak of the mountains of Asia. Mostly, I describe myrtle and rock roses and the delicate petals of the cistus. I don't want her to know what goes on over here.' He stretched and flexed his legs. 'I should be posting sentries.'

Twigg-Smith stood – in the crouch that passed for standing in the trenches. 'We're moving up tomorrow.'

Arthur glanced at the sky. 'You'd better be careful, the moon's still up. Incidentally, how did you get hold of that remarkable bottle and cake?'

Twigg-Smith seemed surprised at the question. 'Mater, of course. On my first day at Oxford there was a Fortnum & Mason hamper waiting in my room.'

'No wonder you trust her.' Arthur smiled. 'I don't think Sylvia's interested in food.'

'Good luck, old chap.' The two men who had never been more than acquaintances at prep school shook hands as warmly as any best friends.

Twigg-Smith looked back as he made his way along the trench, dislodging dozing men, some of whom should have been awake. He took their curses calmly and only cursed back if someone tried to trip him up.

Once or twice he turned his round face up to the stars of which he knew all the names. He hadn't told Lamb that his awe of Lamb's cleverness and good looks at school was what had made him, boring as he knew he was, determined to distinguish himself in some way. He had only discovered his gift for maths at his next school. It had made him very happy to be with Arthur, brothers in arms.

Arthur finished with the sentries who needed more prodding than a mule and came back to the trench. He even had to remind one that he could be court-martialled for sleeping on duty. The trouble was that they never got more than a few hours' sleep at a time so that if not actually under attack, they tended to drop off. He must warn his sergeant to be more vigilant.

It was completely black now but he had a candle which he sheltered conscientiously. His letters to Sylvia were written in a notebook, then torn out and put in an official envelope. Sometimes he left them in the book, finding his own sentiments uplifting to reread. Vaguely, he wondered if he had made a fool of himself in front of Twigg-Smith. But since he didn't really care what the fellow thought, it didn't matter.

Dearest Sylvia,
You will laugh but tonight I confused your face with the moon.
Of course you have a classically oval-shaped face so it is not the
shape but the silvery clarity that reminds me of you. You have
always had that effect on me from the first moment we met. I
still have had no letters from you (or anyone else) but I have no
doubt they will come. This evening a man who had been at my
prep school brought a tin of cake and chartreuse wine. The moon
shone down on us as we ate so you were there too. War is like
that, full of chance meetings with men you don't know and never
see again, either because they move elsewhere or because they get
killed. Usually, you don't know which. I've got used to it now. I
think I am becoming quite a reasonable soldier, although I don't
expect a VC.

Arthur put his pen down and then took it up to scribble out the last line.

How are your parents and Gussie? Has your father been posted
overseas yet? Oh my dearest, dearest beautiful Sylvia . . .

Dawn was infiltrating the trench when Arthur finished his letter. He looked up and saw pale clouds tinged with lilac. It was cold and quiet. Soon the shelling would start from the Allied ships at sea and, after that, the rifle fire would build up, the sun would come up and there would be another noise-filled, fly-ridden hot and dangerous day.

Arthur looked along the trench. Men were occupying themselves in small tasks. Some were stripped while they examined the seams of their shirts for lice. If they found one, they cracked it between their fingers or used candles to burn them out. Some oiled their rifles or soaked biscuits in cold tea or talked softly to their neighbours. Apart from one soldier who flapped his hand and uttered little yelps (Arthur made a note to deal with him), the atmosphere was calm. These men were already survivors, pacing themselves for whatever would come next. The Second Battle for Krithia, apparently.

Eeeh! Whoomph! The first shell of the day shrieked over their heads and landed, judging by the colossal crash, only a short distance ahead of the front-line trenches.

Arthur put away his notebook and searched for his helmet.

Beatrice stopped in the middle of the hallway. Now that there were so few servants in the house, the postman – or rather post*boy*, as he was only twelve years old – brought the letters to the front door where he dumped them with a yell.

'Post!' And sometimes, if he was feeling energetic, 'Post! Post! Post!' This was one of those days.

'I'll get them.' Lily Chaffey, at Beatrice's side, went hurriedly to the door. She knew only too well the importance of a letter or the horror of a telegram.

'Oh, thank you, Lily.' Beatrice watched her small figure step over briskly and throw open the heavy door. She was still surprised by this new person in her life who did everything so quickly and efficiently. Sometimes it made her feel quite slow and stupid. At other times it galvanised her so that she felt a new lightness and determination.

'However did I find you, Lily?' she asked as Lily put the packet of letters in her hand.

'Miss Sylvia, the rector and Dr Horsthrup sent me up, m' lady,' answered Lily seriously. She thought, I am Lily Chaffey again as if I was never married. But that is the way of the war.

'Of course.' Beatrice hurried away without more explanation.

Lily watched her go. She had begun to feel protective of someone who seemed so unfitted to take on the world without a husband. She had all the benefits of the upper classes – no money worries, a grand house, servants (at least until the war) a beautiful garden, land as far as the eye could see – yet there was something childlike about her.

*

Beatrice held three already opened letters in her hand. They were all from Brigadier-General Fitzpaine, the Colonel, Bingo, her dearest husband. Two had been written from the ship. She was conscious of sitting differently as she read, her shoulders dropped, her head higher. Bingo had always had this effect on her from the first moment she had met him at a Scottish house party. 'An insignificant soldier,' was her mother's disparaging comment but she had never wavered.

The Countess of Deverill had lost her own husband to illness when her two children were still young. Far from reducing her, widowhood had provided additional opportunities for her enormous energies. Aside from running the family estates, she had helped found the Victoria League, the Primrose League, the Children's Happy Evenings' Association and was now heavily involved in the Red Cross.

Beatrice thought she'd taken her first free breath when she'd left home and married Bingo.

'He is *my* soldier,' she had told her mother. In the first years of their marriage he'd been away fighting in Africa and only returned home when he was wounded. She should understand how to manage without him. But he had been out of the army for years now and she loved him so much.

My dearest Beatrice, my dearest, sweetest wife,
How I miss you already . . . the ship is sturdy enough and we try
not to think of submarines . . . I have my own little study where
I am writing this . . . there are over two hundred horses aboard,
down in the hold. I went to visit Balaam but he hardly looked
up from his oats, cross with me, probably . . . Today we saw a
Japanese ship with a red sun painted huge on the side. The neutrals
are very keen to be seen to be neutral. Can't blame them . . .

Beatrice turned to the second letter. Now he had something to describe:

This morning we passed Cape Spartel and saw our first glimpses
of Africa. Tangier and Tarifa and magical hours steaming through
the narrow waters with pink and white houses hiding under the
hills. Gibraltar town shimmering and asleep in the noonday sun.

We didn't stop at Malta although some adventurous women rowed out to us with their boats piled up with oranges. One day we'll visit there together and wander up through cobbled streets under verandas decorated with coloured glass.

In the third much longer letter, the Colonel had arrived at Alexandria.

What a performance! We weren't expected so soon, or so they say. We are to go to a camp two miles east of here but the French have only just left it to go to the Dardanelles . . . I feel sorriest for the horses stewing down below. It is hot but there is a breeze if you get out to it. There're some Dorsets on a ship nearby who are going straight out to the front. I'll get more news of the war when I get off this ship but there certainly doesn't seem anything worth celebrating . . no cause for you to worry on my account as it sounds as if we'll be here for months . . .

Beatrice read and reread the letters and then turned to her writing desk.

My dearest Bingo,
I am so glad the dangerous journey is over and you and the horses are in Egypt. I am sure Balaam will forgive you soon. Are the two chestnuts and the bay all right? The camp doesn't sound too welcoming but I expect you'll have a brighter time once you get to Cairo. I have something to tell you too. I never like to do anything without your approval but it suddenly seemed rather urgent. Perhaps because Sylvia has become a VAD in London, I felt I must do something too. So Tollorum will soon be filled with our wounded heroes – officers or men, I've said it doesn't matter, but I rather think we will get officers as more fitting. You may ask, how could I do this when, as you know very well, I am shy of people and new things? It is the war, I suppose.

Reggie was kissing Gussie so hard she could hardly breathe. She pushed him away.

'You're hurting.' She felt her lips and face burning where his bristling moustache scratched. When his thick tongue probed her mouth she was frightened by the feelings it gave her.

Reggie stumbled back. Gussie looked away when she saw the way his trousers stretched out in front. They were alone in the Mayfair house belonging to her uncle and she suddenly understood why girls were expected to have a chaperone.

'You're such a child,' muttered Reggie. His face was red too and his hair, usually brushed smoothly back, had fallen down to his nose. 'How old *are* you?'

'Seventeen. You know how old I am.'

'Oh, God!' He had been breathing heavily but now he took more control of himself. 'Why can't I stick with grown-up women, preferably married?'

'What?' asked Gussie, who couldn't quite believe what she'd heard.

'Nothing. You're sweet. But, as I said, a child. I'm sorry, Gussie. I got carried away.' As he spoke, he moved further and further from her.

With a sense of desperation, Gussie suspected he was going to leave. What would she do, left alone in this gloomy house? If it came to that, what was she ever going to do with the rest of her life? 'I wanted you to kiss me, Reggie. You can kiss me again if you like.'

'That's not a good idea.' Reggie frowned and pushed back his hair. He looked very handsome in his uniform. Gussie tried to tidy her own hair which had half come down at the back. Since arriving in London she'd taken to wearing it up but there was no maid and she was too impatient to do it properly.

'I'm going back to France tomorrow.'

'But you've only just arrived!'

'I'm escorting some fresh troops. I have to go and see my commanding officer now.'

'What am I going to do!' burst out Gussie.

If Reggie had been one of Gussie's family or even known her better than his lusty youth required, he would have recognised this as a regular cry from Gussie since the moment she could speak. As it was, he took her quite seriously. He thought for a moment, then made a step back in her direction. She had sat down on a small chair and was staring dismally at her feet. Waves of dark hair tumbled round. She vaguely reminded him of a painting in his father's house – of a sorrowful Madonna. Unlike most Anglicans, the rector revered the Virgin Mary.

'When we arrive in France, the soldiers, I mean, there're ladies in refreshment areas, serving tea and cakes. They're there at all hours, I'm told. A very jolly lot. Perhaps you can be one of those.'

'Oh, Reggie, of course I can! They sound absolutely top-hole!' Gussie bounced out of her seat, looking so childlike that Reggie added quickly,

'You'd have to lie about your age. They'd never have a seventeen-year-old with all those men around.'

Gussie ignored this. 'I know I can do it! And think, we might meet out there, you on your way to fight . . .' Now she wanted to throw her arms around his neck.

But Reggie was wary. 'I've got to go. Where's your cousin, incidentally? I thought she was only away for half an hour.'

Gussie ignored this too. All her imagination was caught up in this new plan. Let her mother and Sylvia play at nurses, she would go out to France and help the soldiers on the spot. She didn't even protest as Reggie moved out to the hallway and picked up his officer's cap.

'Look after yourself, Gussie.' For a second, a sentimental expression sat uneasily on his face.

'Yes. Yes. And you too, dear Reggie.' They parted without an embrace, both thinking with total self-absorption of the exciting times ahead.

Eight

Like everyone dug in round Quinn's Post, Fred knew they were in for it. Major Furlong was now attached to an Australian Regiment and Fred with him. Fred's burial at the Monash command post had left him with nothing worse than earth in his ears.

Sitting in a trench on top of a gulley with the Turkish trenches twenty yards in front, you got used to sensing change. All the front-line soldiers knew just how the Turkish firing went, shells, rifles and machine guns, so when at about five thirty in the afternoon it more or less stopped and the glorious night – no more flies – fell in near silence, you knew, without any intelligence, something was up.

The truth is everyone knew mostly everything about their enemy. The German officers could see just how the Australian and New Zealand lines were set up at angles so they could enfilade any head-on attack. Yet that's what it seemed they were planning, a massed full-front attack – thousands of men had been seen collecting in different places.

'This is going to be better than a wallaby drive,' boasted the Aussie to Fred's right. He was called Lennie, sturdy and ready to talk.

Fed up with being a runner, Fred had picked up a rifle from a fellow who had no more need. Ammo was less easy but he'd swapped his water bottle for one belt and handed over a stolen flask of whisky for another.

'They won't come till the moon's down,' said Fred.

'Gives you the creeps once the light's gone, imagining all those dark Turks slipping through the undergrowth,' said Lennie.

'Not much undergrowth left,' pointed out Fred. It was true; the daily shelling had taken off almost all the cover. They'd see the Allah boys coming all right, night time or not.

Fred didn't enjoy the waiting but it didn't get his wind up, like it did with some – the city men mostly. He'd get a bit of rest, then at the first sight of the enemy he'd be on that parapet and shooting at them like rabbits at harvest time. He was a good shot too, as good as any soldier from Down Under, he'd bet.

At three a.m., just as Fred had predicted, tens of thousands of Turkish soldiers appeared out of the dark, prepared to roll down the hill and crush an enemy that was less than a third their number.

They attacked in waves, hundreds at a time, but there was no scrub to hide them and the Australians were ready. Rifles and machine guns fired from all angles.

Just as Lennie and his mates had planned, they sat astride the parapets and pumped lead at the running figures. There was no way they could miss them, even if they hadn't been blowing bugles and shouting the usual 'Allah! Allah!' It sounded more desperate than triumphant. Fred fired as fast as he could work the bolt, as fast as his thumbs could click another five rounds into the magazine.

There was no covering fire for the Turks, not even for the front lines, and they fell in heaps.

'Play you again next Saturday!' shouted Lennie. 'Ouch,' he added. The woodwork of their rifles was almost too hot to hold. For a second they paused. Somewhere behind the advancing Turks a band played martial airs.

But it didn't do to pause for a second. The Turks may have been charging hopelessly but sheer numbers pushed them forward whenever the gunfire killing them lessened.

Fred found himself watching two Turks, jumping over the parapets, bayonets glinting, faces distorted with effort. They were followed by two more. Fred didn't hesitate. Nor did the men beside him. But they still had to fix their bayonets, a fiddly business at the best of times. Losing patience, Fred dropped his rifle and grabbed an old hunting knife he'd picked up. This was nasty, bloodthirsty fighting for your life, getting your blade into his flesh before he got his in yours. Two fell, one stabbed through the chest and going down like a stone, the other screaming and clasping his face. But Lennie was down too, holding his leg and the still-standing Turks were slashing wildly.

'Keep shooting!' screamed Fred to the men above. 'We don't want more in here!'

There was no officer telling them what to do and it suddenly struck Fred, even as he pushed a wounded Turk backwards over the parapet, that if this point gave way, it would be like a hole in a dam and a torrent of men would gush through until the line broke.

Stabbing one man, then the other, he didn't feel a bullet in his own arm. At the last moment, one of the Turks dropped his rifle and put his arms in the air. 'Too late, you little fucker.' Fred's knife went right through his stomach. He pulled it out quickly. At that moment he could have faced a hundred Turks but first he needed to get rid of the bodies of three dead or dying ones from the narrow trench.

'Strewth!' Lennie stared up from tending his leg. 'Looking for glory, are you?'

'Glory? What's that?' grunted Fred. 'Can you help me heave this lot over?'

'No chance, mate. Nothing personal.'

There'd been no training about how to get a heavy corpse out of the bottom of a trench. He'd just have to leave them in the hope they were well and truly out of action. Take away their guns as a precaution. It was cold, no sign of dawn, but sweat rolled down inside his coat. Using one of the dead Turks as a mounting block, he climbed back up to the parapet.

The firing from the Aussies was just as heavy but he could see that the enemy was less dense and less determined. He caught a glimpse of a Turkish officer beating the legs of a reluctant soldier with the blade of a sword.

'Losing their taste for a fight!' Fred yelled at the Aussie next to him. He was called William, a ploughman.

'Suicide!' William yelled back while at the same time emptying his clip of the final bullets. 'Hardly a fight,' he added, glancing back.

Fred thought of the Turks in their trench. That had been a fight all right. He took up his rifle and slipped in a clip.

The fighting was over soon after five. An exquisite rosy dawn emerged from streaks of lilac clouds. It lit up no man's land, a monstrous scene of corpses stacked on top of corpses, many of them with their hands on the triggers of guns, mowed down as they advanced.

Officers walked along the trenches, followed by stretcher-bearers and burial parties. They came slowly, hampered by their own tiredness, the soldiers, those no longer on duty, who sprawled about, dazed or asleep, the wounded, the dead, the Turkish prisoners, many crying out for water, the detritus of discarded guns, ammunition, packs, bottles and overcoats pulled off in the heat of battle.

It was a great victory, of course. But there was something unsettling about quite so many dead. Nobody talked much.

'It looks like thousands of men bit the dust.' An officer appeared over the parapet. He was tall and his face was splashed with blood.

Still surrounded by his dead Turks, Fred looked up. 'Careful, sir. Their snipers still haven't let up.' His words were confirmed as two bullets, fired in quick succession, cracked into a water bottle hanging behind them.

'Quite.' The officer crouched lower. He indicated the Turks. 'Bagged these, did you?'

'Yes, sir.'

'Good man.' He was about to move on when he turned back. 'You're not Australian?'

'No, sir. I'm Major Furlong's runner, sir.'

'He let you get up front, did he?' He concentrated more. 'You heard he caught it? Ironic. If you'd been with him you'd probably have caught it too.' The officer who was very young and looked as if he might fall over at the merest push, shut his eyes for a moment.

As Fred thought about 'ironic', a stretcher-bearer edged past him to get to Lennie. 'Here, you. Leg's a mess. Want to roll on and we'll have you sorted in two shakes of a lamb's tail.'

Fred turned round. 'He hasn't been speaking lately.'

'Then he won't be suffering, will he.' The two men pulled Lennie on to the stretcher; the one at the back glanced at Fred.

'You've got blood on your arm.'

'Flesh wound.' Fred found it difficult to be interested in his arm, although it had begun to throb painfully. He noticed, surprised, that he was shivering. Yet the sun was already warming up the trench, warming up the stink. A dead Turk stared at him with one eye, the other dangled on his cheekbone. Fred knew he wasn't right when he had a strong urge to push it back into its socket.

'I'll never get them over the parapet now,' he mumbled.

'What's that?' The officer had got himself together again and was on his way. 'Good luck.' His vague benediction seemed to include the Turks.

'You come along with us, mate.' The stretcher-bearer addressed Fred. 'The dressing station will sort out that arm.'

Relieved to leave the scene of his triumph, Fred tottered after him.

Rupert was feeling full of vim and vigour. He had arrived on the island of Tenedos an hour earlier. His belly was filled with coffee and yoghurt, the air was like champagne and Corporal Sourbutts, leader of his welcoming committee, although suffering from an upset stomach which caused him to dive into the bushes unexpectedly, was about to fill him in on his mission.

'So, who are these spies?' asked Rupert.

'Four of them, sir. We've put them in a house, sir. Under lock and key.'

'A house! That's going it.'

'Considering the circumstances . . .'

Rupert began to be bored. 'What circumstances?'

The corporal rubbed his hands together. 'I thought you knew, sir. The spies are all ladies.' He paused. 'Or at least women.'

Rupert's good humour returned and he burst out laughing. 'Beautiful lady spies. I can't believe my luck!'

'There is supposed to be one that's well-favoured.' He paused doubtfully. 'It's hard to tell.'

Despite the corporal's doubts, Rupert felt that among four ladies of doubtful repute one must be beautiful. Or at least tolerable. *Tolerable* might do.

His escort of Tommies seemed in high spirits too, doubtless as pleased as him to be avoiding Gallipoli. Over and over again they sang the same cheerful words:

Are we downhearted? NO!
Not while Britannia rules the waves NOT LIKELY! (Bellowed)
While we have Jack upon the sea,

And Tommy on the land we need not fret.
It's a long, long way to Tipperary
But we're not downhearted yet.

After a half-hour march along some streets and out the other side, the corporal pointed to a stone house standing in its own walled garden. 'The lieutenant will be waiting for you there.'

'I hope you won't abandon me, Corporal,' said Rupert playfully. 'I might need your soldiers to defend me against four lusty ladies.' He pushed open a broken door and found himself inside a wild garden with great bushes of white roses emerging from the dark greenery.

'Here you are, Captain Prideaux.' A laughing voice spoke from beyond this unlikely paradise.

Why was it, thought Rupert, that war threw you into the company of such ghastly people? 'Good morning, Lieutenant Gaythorne.' Rupert remembered that the last time they'd met, he'd challenged Gaythorne to a duel, although his own mauled hand made it impossible to carry out. Still, the hatred was genuine. Their disagreement had been over a woman whose name and face eluded him.

'So I'm to hand over the gorgeous girls to your tender mercies.' Gaythorne smiled and stroked his moustache.

'Where are they?' Rupert stepped through the doorway – the sun had become very bright and hot, making the house seem dark and dank.

'Can't you hear them?'

Rupert listened. 'That weird moaning?'

'I say, after you've done your stuff, I've got a message for you from HQ.'

Rupert thought that Gaythorne had never brought him luck. It was because of him he'd been thrown out of school.

'Corporal.' Sourbutts had appeared behind them and now produced a large iron key as if he were the gaoler at the Bastille.

The moment the door opened, the moaning and wailing rose to new heights and Rupert found himself surrounded by clawing black-robed figures. He couldn't distinguish their faces in the gloom.

'Shall I lock you in with them, sir?' Sourbutts asked.

'Certainly not. Keep it ajar and stand guard.'

Rupert thought that of all the jobs he'd been asked to do since joining the army, this was the most ridiculous. Middle-eastern spies were a rum lot, not the sort to disappear into the woodwork, but a coven of witches was a step into farce.

'Ladies. Ladies. May I have your attention.' He forced himself to a small window and, backlit, turned to face them. He spoke sternly, like a professor, beginning in English, then moving through French, Greek, Turkish and Albanian, asking them to reveal their nationality.

They stared at him, at last silent. He stared at them. Their faces, at least the part of them uncovered, were now visible. One had a nose like the funnel on an express train, the second a weeping boil on either cheek, the third a grotesque chin bursting above her drapes, the fourth was so thin and toothless that her cheeks were altogether concave.

'Where were you last living?'

A babble broke out in a mixture of languages. Two fell to the floor and, arms outstretched, knelt in supplication. One beat her horrible breast.

Corporal Sourbutts opened the door slightly. 'All right, sir?'

Rupert moved towards him, followed closely by the knee-shuffling supplicants. 'What are they accused of?'

'The lieutenant didn't tell you?'

'No. He did not.'

'Passing secrets, sir. They came from Alexandria but they are not Egyptians. A bit of everything, I'd say.'

'Who accused them?

'The so-called consul, sir. He seems to know them very well, sir. I'd say there's history between them.' The corporal was now shouting to make himself heard above the noise.

'Summon the nameless, so-called consul!'

Sourbutts saluted and withdrew.

Ignoring the women, Rupert leant against the window sill and waited. Obviously, it was some family argument, maybe centuries old. Maybe these hags were sisters, mothers and daughters. Almost certainly someone had stolen something from someone. They were not spies, that was certain.

'*Arrêtez-vous*! Silence!' It was a relief to shout at someone.

Rupert sat in a café at the harbour waiting for a boat. In front of him was a bottle of ouzo and the orders handed him by a smirking Gaythorne. He was to proceed with all speed to the Anzac Corps on Gallipoli. He hadn't even achieved a good night's sleep.

'*Monsieur, monsieur.*' The girl who served at the café stood at his side.

She was extremely pretty with clear creamy skin and luminous dark eyes. Talking in Greek, she indicated the house and pulled gently on his arm. Probably, she was only offering him somewhere to rest out of the sun – it was very hot now – but he followed hopefully.

Fred sat in the dressing station. It was a dugout raised up with sandbags for walls and a tarpaulin for a roof. Outside, stretcher cases minus their stretchers were neatly lined up on the ground. Over them a thick cloud of flies, revoltingly fat and predatory, buzzed continually. Occasionally a hand flapped a few away. An Australian with a head wound who'd been given a swig of water spat out a mouthful of flies.

'Why don't the flies stick to the already dead?' Fred complained.

'Spoilt for choice,' agreed his neighbour, who seemed not to be suffering despite a deep furrow in his scalp. 'They'll be as big as vultures soon.'

'Vultures do a good job,' said Fred. They'd been waiting for the MO for five hours while he attended to the worst cases and Fred was so bored he was even thinking of moving on. Although where would he move on *to*? 'Vultures clean up the countryside; flies just spread disease.'

'You're from the country, are you?' The Aussie leant forward, giving Fred an unsettling view of the hole in his head. 'I'm Charlie Tuck from Melbourne, a big-city boy. Wish I was there now. Want to see a picture of my girl?' Without waiting for agreement, he pulled out a photograph of a pretty round-faced girl holding a baby.

Fred nodded. After five hours side by side with hardly a word, this sudden intimacy was nearly as disturbing as the head wound. Perhaps Charlie Tuck was about to drop dead. 'You're a dad, then.'

'Everyone says that. It's her ma's. She was looking after it when she went to the studio so it ended up in the picture.' Charlie put away the photo lovingly. 'You got a girl?'

'Only a sister. Best girl I could ever have.' Fred was surprised by the sentiment in his voice.

'So what have you two got to show me?' The MO burst in surrounded by a buzzing escort of flies, including those massed over the bloody red on his coat. He looked at Charlie. 'Headache, have you?'

'No, sir.'

'Good fellow. Can't stitch that up. Unconscious, were you?'

Charlie seemed unable to answer this so the MO continued, 'Nothing to be done. Go down to the beach dressing station and wait and see what happens. And don't put on a helmet.' He turned to Fred. 'Arm. Show it to me, man.'

The doctor tapped his foot impatiently while Fred stripped off. Fred suspected he'd fall over with exhaustion if he stopped moving. The wound which Fred hadn't bothered to look at before was a neat hole. Clearly, there'd been a lot of bleeding which had now stopped. He brushed off a dozen bulbous flies.

'Lucky blighter.' The doctor peered for a second. 'In and out. The bullet's missed everything that matters. Left-handed, are you?'

'Yes, sir.'

'Get yourself dressed on the station at the beach, give yourself a day off and then you can be back on duty.'

'Yes, sir.'

The MO took off his cap and wiped sweat and flies off his forehead. 'You're English?' Sharp grey eyes estimated Fred.

'Yes, sir.'

'Which regiment?'

Fred told him and began to explain his present circumstances but the MO interrupted.

'Doesn't do to be separated from your regiment, Private. It's your family. You look after each other. Seen it a thousand times.'

'I was a runner, sir—' began Fred before being once more cut off by the MO who was scribbling a note.

'Here. Take this down to the beach HQ. They'll sort you out. Read it, if you like.'

If I could, thought Fred. 'Thank you, sir.'

But the medical officer was already outside, his long thin back bent over the lines of misery.

The sun was not yet lighting Anzac Cove when Rupert jumped out of a post ship. He'd begun in a fishing boat, enjoyed a few comfortable hours on a destroyer, during which he learnt from the captain (a friend of a friend) that the Second Battle for Krithia had been a failure, before changing into the requisitioned pleasure steamer. He'd found all the naval officers charming – *tant pis* that they hadn't sailed through to Constantinople when they'd had the chance.

Rupert walked along the beach swinging his pack. Soon it would be as bright as a stage, target for shelling in every direction; now the place was a mad rush of activity: men or mules transporting water, ammunition and supplies up to the front, whole companies moving down or up, communication officers running about with boxes trailing wires as if they might actually work and, above all, ranks of the wounded, Allies and Turks, being loaded on to boats. From there they would be taken out to the hospital ship, its illuminated green cross visible across the dark ripple of sea.

'Been a big show, has there?' He stopped a passing officer.

The officer, a young sub lieutenant, stopped and saluted. 'Yes, sir. Turks tried to push us into the sea by sheer numbers. Massacred. Now we've got to deal with their wounded.'

'Mostly Turks?'

'Ten to one, I'd say.'

Rupert disguised a yawn. The officer, a New Zealander, despite a distracting tic in his right eye, seemed up to the mark. He was even clean-shaven at this grisly hour. 'I need to report to HQ and, more important, cadge some breakfast.'

'Follow me, sir.'

Fred stayed beside Charlie Tuck for nearly twenty-four hours until he was carried out to a boat. Half an hour earlier, he'd stopped talking and keeled over. He was still alive, though, and on his way home – if he survived. Fred wondered if he was jealous. But he felt more like a soldier now. Ready to do his duty. So he'd better cut along to HQ and find out where he'd be off to next.

The HQ was a substantial collection of shacks, dug deeply into the cliff, with double walls of sandbags and projecting roofs of tin and tarpaulin. The first light of morning was marked by the first shell of the day. But the HQ was in the most protected end of the beach.

Fred hovered at the entrance.. He held the MO's note in his hand. What if it said, *Arrest this man for desertion*? Panicking, he scrumpled the paper up and threw it away. He might as well report all the same.

Rupert was drinking a cup of coffee laced with brandy from a tin mug. He wasn't particularly surprised that nobody had an idea why he'd been summoned.

'My orders said it was urgent,' he told a harassed New Zealand major.

'Urgent for whom?' the major had replied, reasonably enough. 'Have breakfast and we'll find you something to play with.'

Intelligence officers were never popular, whichever troops you were among.

He noticed a slight wiry soldier hovering outside the entrance; he was extraordinarily dirty with a bandage on one arm. Having nothing better to do, Rupert wandered over. 'Looking for someone?' To his left, the sun was beginning to rise over the hills.

'Sir!' The man saluted smartly, although wincing slightly as he did so. Rupert noticed keen blue eyes assessing him. 'I'm to report. Lost my regiment, sir.'

'Your whole regiment. That takes some doing.'

'Company then,' conceded Fred.

'Don't ask me to find them. I'm an intelligence officer which means I haven't a clue what the army's up to, although I wouldn't think you'd find an English regiment at Anzac.'

'No, sir.' The soldier peered beyond Rupert. 'Then I'd better go inside.'

Rupert finished his coffee regretfully. 'I doubt you'd be welcome. With due respect, they're in a stew about problems wider than one lost soldier. Might not take your entrance in the positive spirit you mean it. Longing to fight shoulder to shoulder with your company, that sort of thing.'

'I see what you mean, sir. Mind if I take off my helmet, sir?'

'Cool your head, before the sun gets up? Sensible man.' Rupert peered forward. 'Wounded badly, are you?'

'No, sir.' He jiggled his arm. 'When I can get someone to do it, I'll have a smaller bandage.'

'So, what are we going to do with you?' said Rupert, thinking at the same time, what was he going to do with himself? Both men glanced into the HQ.

'I know what they should be in a stew about.'

'What?' Rupert was surprised the private dared offer an opinion.

'All those corpses in no man's land. Mostly Turks. Another day in the sun and they'll be stinking mush.'

Rupert winced. 'The Turks can bury their own.'

'We shot them, sir.'

'I suppose we did.'

The sun was rising and men went past them, in and out to HQ. Dismally, Rupert supposed he'd have to make plans to get back to staff headquarters. Even Gallipoli had its attractions when he thought of Lemnos and all those old generals convincing themselves that they were running a successful campaign.

'Captain P-Prideaux!' A second lieutenant with a slight stutter was calling.

'*Morituri te salutant*,' said Rupert, going inside.

Bloody show off, thought Fred, although he'd quite liked him up to then. Not too pompous for a captain. Now what? He put his sun helmet back on and stared out to sea. He thought of Charlie with the hole in his head and hoped he got back to his girl, whoever owned the baby. Maybe the MO was right: he needed to have mates around him. He pictured his company's bloody landing on 25th April. He'd had some mates then.

'Wool-gathering, are you? What's your name, come to that?'

It was the same officer who'd spoken to him before. 'Private Frederick M. Chaffey, sir.' Fred added his number, while staring at the hand holding another cup of coffee; it was short on the finger front.

'Righty-ho, Fred. I've had you attached to me. Not quite sure in what capacity. How about servant?' The officer looked doubtful.

'I was a runner, sir.'

'There you are. So you'll know where we're going. Quinn's Post. They're holding a Turkish officer up there. Don't expect he'll say a thing but it's my job to question him. Got your pack?'

'By the dressing station, sir.' Fred noticed how much more lively the officer was now.

'You'll need that smaller bandage. Get a move on, then. I'll come down to you in five minutes.'

Fred hesitated. 'May I ask *your* name, sir? In case of questions.'

'Captain Rupert Prideaux. Intelligence officer, attached to General Hamilton's staff headquarters, presently assigned to Anzac. And, if that's not enough, tell them I'm Lord Prideaux, heir to the Earl of Filchester.' He gave a sudden hoot of laughter and waved his mug almost in Fred's face.

So that was it, for coffee, read brandy. 'Yes, sir, Captain Lord Prideaux, sir.' Fred set off. Alcohol had never done much for him but he didn't blame the man wanting a bit of Dutch courage before facing that mess at the front.

'And mind the shells!' the captain shouted after him as two landed with great walloping crumps on the edge of the beach.

Nine

Acting Brigadier-General Fitzpaine sat in the British Club in Cairo, a whisky and soda at his elbow. He had spent the day seeing his men into barracks outside Cairo and himself into the National Hotel. So he felt he deserved an evening off. Not that the men had been any problem; they were gung-ho for the city and the pyramids – their camp in the desert outside Alexandria had offered nothing more than flies and sand. It was the horses that had caused trouble – far too fresh. Balaam had even kicked Small, who had handled him since he was born. The challenge was to organise at least three hours' exercise before it got too hot for anything but lizards.

The Colonel (he still thought of himself as that) took a deeper sip of his drink and glanced round the room. The leather sofas, polished tables and prints of hunting and polo could have been in London were it not for the slowly turning fans and the turbaned waiters. He was waiting for Major Whitehead of the Notts who'd already fought on Gallipoli, and Colonel Bentinck of the Leicesters. He hadn't seen them since Africa but Cairo seemed a good place to renew their acquaintance.

The Colonel stood up as a striking figure, with long white moustache and many medals on his chest, entered the room.

'Fitzpaine, old boy! Unchanged, unlike most of us. I see you staring. Yes, may I introduce Verity, Lady Bentinck. Goes with me everywhere, even my club.' He laughed heartily. 'Don't look so upset. Wartime. Rules relaxed. Ladies invited into the sanctum.'

Trying not to appear the dumb fool he felt, the Colonel shook Bentinck's hand and bowed to Verity, Lady Bentinck who wore a beaded silver dress. 'Lady Bentinck. A pleasure.'

'Verity, please.' She had a hard, ugly voice. And it was not a pleasure. He had been looking forward to an old soldier's gossip which would gradually lead into a good talk about their situation here and the likelihood of being summoned to Gallipoli. Besides, the sight of the smart, self-confident Verity made him miss his beautiful, gentle Beatrice more than ever.

'Verity is helping at the hospital,' boomed Bentinck after they'd sat down and ordered drinks.

So she had to be admired for good works too. 'That must be very upsetting,' said the Colonel politely.

'The hospital's on the Nile so the view outside is delightfully romantic.'

Did she really think wounded men were interested in romantic views? 'I expect there is a breeze too.'

'If I'm not in the saddle by six,' interrupted Bentinck, 'I don't stir till night falls.' He looked up. 'Ah, here's Whitehead. Poor fellow. Got a dose of shrapnel in his backside. Doesn't look good, however you play it.'

Verity laughed shrilly and the Colonel remembered he'd always thought Bentinck a conceited ass.

'Good evening, Bentinck, Fitzpaine. Lady Bentinck.' Whitehead also looked askance at the latter which made the Colonel think that there was no wartime relaxation of rules. He waved his hand and ordered another whisky. There was no way he could ask Whitehead about his experiences at Gallipoli with Verity crossing her legs and trying to draw all eyes. Her small mouth was as round and red as a cherry. Polite conversation about amenities in Cairo was only interrupted as they ordered their meal.

At last they went into dinner where their food was already waiting.

'I just heard the Oxfords have lost their adjutant, Bonham-Carter,' said Whitehead who had not addressed a word to Lady Bentinck and seemed determined to prove she wasn't there. 'I liked him so much. I believe you knew his father, Fitzpaine?'

The Colonel remembered a small boy with dark curls. 'Bad luck. Nice family. Have you been out of it long?'

'Three weeks. Can't wait to get back. The devilish problem is lack of ammunition.' Whitehead pushed away his roast beef almost uneaten. The Colonel noticed he was exceedingly thin. 'Apart from lack of men. They say Hamilton doesn't dare push Kitchener for more of either. His protégé, you know.'

'Don't think much of Kitchener myself.' Bentinck crunched on a bone in his quail. 'He was always too fond of listening to every nation's complaints and going against the white man.'

'He looked lovely on the posters,' trilled Verity. All three men, including her doting husband, gazed at her with disdain verging on horror.

For the first time, she lost her confidence and, muttering about powdering her nose, rose and took herself off.

The Colonel breathed a sigh of relief.

'It's tough for her out here,' mumbled Bentinck. 'No friends.'

Whitehead nodded kindly. It had been a sort of apology. 'I gather there's to be a slap-up do on June the fourth.'

'Oh, yes!' Bentinck cheered up and they all watched as cheese soufflés approached across the room. 'There're enough Etonians here to fill a banqueting hall.'

The Colonel tried to bring back the conversation to the war before Lady Bentinck returned. 'I hear the Queen of Greece got hold of some plans about a big Anglo push on the Dardanelles.'

Whitehead smiled. 'And the Rothschilds believe the war will be over by the autumn. There are always rumours.'

The Colonel decided he liked Whitehead. 'I can't see there'll be much use for horses on Gallipoli,' he exclaimed suddenly. It was his biggest worry.

Both men stared without answering before allowing themselves to be deflected by the soufflés, arriving in front of them, an elegant froth of creamy yellow.

'Sauce, sir?' The waiter held up a brimming silver spoon.

Arthur held the parcel reverentially. It was a book, perhaps. Sylvia's handwriting on the wrapping. He had been out of the front line for twenty-four hours. It was midday and he was due back that evening. Meanwhile, he lay under an olive tree – only a little shattered at the top – and tried to ignore the sounds that never properly stopped all over Helles: sniper fire, machine guns and shells. There were a few seconds of total silence when there was no particular push as at present, but they were not worth enjoying, only making the noise worse when it returned. One of his men had brought him the parcel – they liked delivering parcels, a link with home, presumably. Before his arrival, Arthur had been watching a tortoise tethered to a stone. The bit of string was quite long and it seemed perfectly happy with its lot, crawling quietly round before stopping for a little nibble. He had found it a soothing sight. But now he had a parcel. Carefully Arthur took out the book – it was a book – from several layers, including one that was waterproof. It made Arthur happy to think of Sylvia's slender fingers doing up the knots.

He held it up. The light was dappled, the grass turning from green to gold. Few flowers left. The book had a dark blue cover. Oxford blue. He turned to the spine: Homer's *Iliad*. Oh, Sylvia!

Without opening it, Arthur lay back on the grass and recited:

'The lives of mortal men are like the generations of leaves: now the wind scatters the old leaves across the earth, now the living timber bursts with new buds and spring comes round again. And so with men: as one generation comes to life, another dies away.'

He had always loved those lines, said by Hector to his wife Andromache who held their son in his arms. They had seemed both sad and consoling. Now he thought of his love for Sylvia and regretted that their purity and high ideals had kept them away from any more physical contact than a loving kiss.

How beautiful it would be to have a child by her!

Putting the book aside, Arthur shut his eyes. But more words came into his head: *Everything is more beautiful because we are doomed.*

Sylvia and her new friend, Hilda, stood waiting for a tram to take them to hospital. It was six o'clock in the morning and it was raining.

'The Zepps won't be over anyway,' said Hilda, staring up at the overcast sky. 'Question: would you rather have rain or Zepps?'

'It'll be so-called flaming June soon,' grumbled Sylvia.

'I don't think they know about June in south London. And "flaming" is a term of abuse.'

Both girls looked at each other and laughed. Finding a friend had made all the difference to Sylvia's life. Hilda was a stout, no-nonsense girl in her late twenties who came from a manufacturing family in Birmingham. 'This was my one chance to get away,' she had told Sylvia frankly. 'I'm too stupid for further education, too plain to catch a husband and too rich to find work. In fact, every day of the war makes my family richer.'

She had said all this after she'd found Sylvia crying over a letter from Arthur. The nurses' hostel didn't provide places to cry secretly. Through sobs, she'd confided in Hilda that she was only in the hospital because the misery of it all made her feel closer to her fiancé and the misery he was suffering in Gallipoli. 'Not that he writes about that.' More sobs. 'It's as if he's on a walking tour of classical sights. Doesn't he know I read *The Times*?' Lessening sobs. 'Although that talks cheerful rubbish most of the time.'

Becoming close to Hilda taught Sylvia that the sort of high-minded ideals she and Arthur took for granted were seen as rather peculiar in the wider world. Patriotism was fine because it had a practical aim: to defeat the enemy. But there was no use dressing it up. Hilda had never read a poem in her life outside Shakespeare. 'My father approves of Shakespeare,' she'd told Sylvia, 'because he came from the Midlands and understood the dangers of power.'

At last the tram came and the two friends, dark capes dripping, jumped on.

'I'm glad we didn't have to walk.' They often did, on a bright morning choosing the half-hour plod through grimy streets over the fusty heat of the overcrowded tram.

This morning they each hung on to a strap and carried on their conversation. Once arrived at the hospital, the only likely words were, 'Cup of tea now for the house surgeon', or 'Turn the man in bed sixteen.'

'Do you know what I saw in *The Times* yesterday?'

'Oh, no.' Hilda groaned. 'You haven't been at your casualty lists again.'

Sylvia frowned but decided not to be cross. 'Much stranger. It was in the agony column: *Lady, fiancé killed, will gladly marry officer incapacitated by war.*'

'Out of her mind.' Hilda didn't hesitate. 'Men are bad enough with their needs anyway but they do have their uses – for earning money or heaving coal – but if they were incapacitated you'd get all the aggravation and none of the bonuses.'

'Oh, Hilda, you're not so hard-hearted!' Sylvia lurched into her firm friend as the tram stopped abruptly and several bodies fell into her. She righted herself. 'Think of that poor woman. When I read the words "fiancé killed" I thought of the despair that made her want to do something worthwhile in her life. I think it's *noble*.'

'You imagine too much.'

Sylvia could see Hilda was trying to be tactful by not mentioning Arthur. Arthur killed, Arthur maimed. Sometimes she lay awake imagining the best kind of injury. Not his right hand because he needed to write, not his eyes because he needed to read, not his legs because he needed to walk with her through the Dorset meadows, through the bluebell woods with the greenish trunks of beech trees rising above their heads.

'Sylvia. Sylvia! Are you planning to go on to Elephant and Castle?'

Hastily, Sylvia pushed her way through unyielding backs and out on to the pavement. It was still raining.

'You're such a dreamer!'

There was no time for dreaming at the hospital. The first challenge was a cluster of black beetles under the sink. At home Sylvia would have screamed and called for a servant. Instead, she forced herself to stare at them until they scuttled away into a hole. Then she went in search of Bob, an old man who acted as odd-job man round the place. He was bad-tempered with most people but she had discovered he liked toffees which she supplied.

'Can you stop a hole for me, Bob?'

'I can, but will I?' Bob sniffed and scratched his head. He really was a revolting old man.

'Fitzpaine! Nurse! Where are you?'

'It's beetles, Bob. Big black ones,' said Sylvia quickly. 'Under the sink.' She was behind with bedmaking. Behind already and the day had scarcely started. She passed Hilda running, although they were not supposed to run.

'Sister's in a filthy mood. We've had a death.'

'A death!' exclaimed Sylvia, stopping in the empty corridor. They never had deaths in Ward 7.

'There you are, Fitzpaine, lingering again.'

'Sorry, Sister. There were beetles—'

Sister cut her off crossly and, indeed, thought Sylvia, what were beetles compared to a death? And she *had* been lingering. 'The ward is a disgrace. This morning I found a swab under a bed. A *used* swab!' Sister's voice rose to a shrill squeak.

'Sorry, Sister,' repeated Sylvia and decided she dare not ask about the death.

'Hurry. *Hurry!*'

But when she got to the ward, the dead man was still in his bed. She knew him well, always a ghostly presence who'd uttered no more than 'yes' or 'no' since his arrival. He had gone from yellow to grey, from thin to skeleton, without anybody, it seemed, being able to do a thing for him. Nor was he ever visited. Now he was dead. His was the first dead body Sylvia had ever seen.

She stared down, studying his bony head, the hair shaved, making his long nose more prominent, and waited for emotion to surface. Nothing. Nothing at all. There he was. Her first dead body and her heart was moved with neither dread nor pity. Most important, he had nothing whatsoever to do with her nightmares about Arthur. The man who had never been very alive during her experience of him was now a corpse. God rest his soul.

'Fitzpaine!'

'Sorry, Sister,' said Sylvia automatically. She had just learnt something important: a dead body meant very little without love.

Yet despite this calm conviction, Sylvia felt curiously remote for the rest of the day. She needed time to process her thoughts. But there was no time. The result was that she performed every duty more slowly and eventually the exasperated sister sent her to Matron.

'Good afternoon, Nurse. You may sit down.'

Matron, Sister's ultimate threat was, in reality, a large comfortable woman who always had a cup of milky tea and a biscuit at her elbow.

'Thank you, Matron.' Sylvia sank into the chair gratefully.

'It must be hard being on your feet all day when you're so tall and thin. In my day, most nurses were short and strong. I was myself.'

Sylvia could think of nothing to say to this. It had been rumoured that Matron was getting a bit 'eccentric' due to her selfless work and growing age. 'I do my best, Matron.'

'Yes. Yes. You probationer VADs have a difficult time.' She

suddenly leant forward and gave a kind of gleaming smile. 'I believe you have a title.'

'No, Matron.'

'No?'

Matron looked so disappointed that Sylvia added quickly, 'My mother has a title, Matron.'

'She does!' The unlikely smile reappeared. 'I thought I wasn't misinformed.' She leant back in her chair which creaked protestingly. 'Before this great war, I collected reports on London society. Sometimes I even stretched to Ascot. I have twelve full scrapbooks. You'd be surprised at the things that are to be learnt from society's goings-on. Did you know Lady Verena Pope married her stepfather's nephew, Sir William Lysander Hardwick?'

'No, Matron.' Sylvia began to feel sleepy. The room was warm and Matron embarked on a litany of titled names and their 'goings-on'.

She jerked awake as Matron's voice rose in what seemed to be triumph. 'Lady Beatrice Fitzpaine, daughter of the Sixth Earl of Deverill, deceased. How could I be so slow! Oh, the war. The war. Your uncle is the Seventh Earl!'

'Yes, Matron,' agreed Sylvia meekly.

At this happy moment, there was a sharp knock at the door. Sister put her head round. She seemed surprised to see Sylvia still there.

'Yes, Sister?' Matron, who had been lolling rather, sat up straighter.

'The doctor has signed off for the deceased, Matron.'

'Proceed, Sister. I need a moment more with Nurse.'

Sister closed the door, slightly harder than necessary.

'I suppose you mix a great deal in London society?' There was that hopeful smile.

Sylvia racked her brains. 'We sometimes stay with Lord Deverill in Bruton Street.'

'But he is a bachelor, is he not? The line will not continue through him.' Her large face creased anxiously.

'I'm afraid not.' Sylvia put a hand to her cap. She felt, suddenly, as if she might faint. 'Sorry, Matron. I'm not feeling too well.'

'Of course, you're not.' A faraway look came into the pouched eyes. 'You are made for cocktails and organza. Find a nice nursing home in the country, that's what I tell girls like you. You can't make a silk purse out of a sow's ear.'

Sylvia began to feel hysterical, although she didn't know whether she'd laugh or cry. With angry determination, she controlled herself. 'I *will* be a nurse!'

'Yes, yes. Go off now and try to stay awake on the job.' She patted the biscuit tin. 'And eat more, Nurse.'

Later that night, over mugs of Horlicks, Sylvia described to Hilda her interview with Matron.

Hilda laughed so much that she spilled her Horlicks over her dressing gown and there'd been no hot water to wash anything for days. 'You're making it up, surely. Oh, Sylvia, I haven't had such a good laugh for ages. Mind you, she's right. I don't see you ever turning into a nurse. I don't believe you've got a practical bone in your body.'

'But I have. I have!' protested Sylvia. 'It's just the way I was brought up.'

'Look, dear, I was brought up with every comfort, servants doing the dirty work, not grand like you, but just as spoiled. The thing is I have no problem doing what's necessary because I'm not dreaming or reading poetry—'

'I haven't read poetry for ages!'

'You would if you weren't so tired. What about that dead man? I looked and saw a dead man and you mooned over him for ages, doubtless having all sorts of clever thoughts . . .'

'But that's what I decided: he was just a dead body. It's about loving, I thought, and nothing to do with whether the soul is in—'

'There you go! On to the place of the soul in a split second.'

Hilda's pretence horrified face was so comical that Sylvia couldn't help smiling. No, she was not the right person to discuss the soul. She would write to Arthur. 'I wonder if Arthur's received the copy of *The Iliad* I sent him,' she said out loud.

Ten

'Are you telling me you can't read?' Rupert put on the face of a regular captain. 'An important cog in His Majesty's great army and you can't read.'

'And I can't stand on my head, either.' Fred had already discovered that his latest boss preferred a snappy conversation to a respectful one. They were holed up in a second-line trench, and Rupert had been reading an old copy of *The Times* by the last light of the day.

'As a matter of fact, I was a slow reader myself. Luckily, my nanny loved me – I wore dresses and had golden curls to my shoulders. She devised a plan to sort me out. If I can find a pencil and paper, I'll show you.'

While Prideaux scrabbled in his pockets and then his pack, Fred lay back and shut his eyes. It had been a trying two days. First of all there'd been the captured Turkish major. He'd begun silent and dignified but after the captain had gabbled away in Turkish, he'd started gabbling back. It went on for hours and hours, as if it was an old friends' reunion, with much clapping on the back and calls for tea, which Fred was expected to rustle up from somewhere or other.

'Tea and sweetmeats!' The captain had cried out at one point, then become quite sniffy when Fred had produced a tin of bully beef. 'Add some marmalade, if you want it sweet,' he'd advised, 'although the flies will probably get there first.'

Eventually, they'd had to stop because blood was trickling down the major's sleeve. Fred knew the feeling but this chap had never mentioned he was wounded. The captain was sitting cross-legged by now but he'd leapt to his feet and shouted for a medic. Presumably that was the way sons of earls were taught to behave.

Today had been even worse because the captain had got it into his head, following his conversation with the prisoner, that the Turks would give themselves up in droves if an Allied officer stood up waving a white flag and, addressing them in Turkish, told them how they could never win and how well treated they'd be if they gave themselves up.

Amazingly, the colonel in command had agreed to the proposal – Fred was beginning to think the army was composed of madmen. So Captain Prideaux had walked up and down with his little flag and yelled warm invitations to the Turks. The response surprised no one but him: heavy fire directed wherever he popped up. It didn't take long for the Aussies to groan, 'Here he comes! Angel of bleeding death!'

Fred, who had been forced to follow his master, was just as unpopular: 'Get hold of that lunatic, can't you? Or better still, knock him out before I do!'

The miracle was that the captain wasn't killed himself, although of course no one on the Allied side could understand what he was shouting. Maybe he was telling them the Aussies couldn't hit an elephant. After several terrifying hours of this when not one Turk had come over, the captain had given up of his own accord.

'Silly buggers,' he'd told Fred as they were manhandled out of the front line. 'I was giving them a chance to live. But I suppose they prefer the righteous path to heaven. That's the trouble with Muslims. They really do believe in their religion.'

Fred had said nothing. The second line suited him fine, not only because of the captain's dangerous antics, but because the stink coming from no man's land made life at the front unbearable. He didn't blame the Aussies for being in a foul temper. Some of them had wound cloths round their noses but they said it didn't help; the smell clung to you all over. It was three days since the great battle, three days in which the corpses grew black and bloated and the flies, not to mention other marauding creatures, multiplied by the trillion.

'What's the matter with you?' The captain had found an official-looking notebook and a stub of pencil.

'That smell. That rotting flesh smell. Doesn't leave you,' muttered Fred.

'Hmm. Yes. Revolting. Inhuman. Men should be buried.' He held up the pad. 'But reading first before the light goes. Ready.'

'Yessir.' Fred pulled himself up reluctantly.

'Know any letters, do you?'

'Some. Maybe most.'

'As I thought. Now. I'm writing a word. We'll do capitals. Most soldiers don't get much further. G-O-D.' Prideaux wrote with his uninjured left hand. 'You see, God. Might as well start at the top. Now you write it back to front.'

'I thought I was learning to read, not write,' grumbled Fred as he carefully copied *D-O-G*.

'So read it!'

'Dog,' said Fred.

'There you are,' triumphed Prideaux. 'From the top to the bottom. My nurse, like most nurses of the aristocracy, was a genius, of course. Now try the next: P-A-L. Pal. Over to you.'

'L-A-P. Lap,' said Fred.

T-A-B, wrote Prideaux 'Tab.'

B-A-T, wrote Fred, 'Bat.'

As they continued the words – top and pot, mug and gun, mad and dam, sip and pis, 'Missing an s,' commented Prideaux, 'but who cares' – Fred had the weird feeling as the lesson continued that he could already read and write after less than an hour playing a stupid game. It was as if it was all there in his head, waiting to be unlocked. Surreptitiously, he glanced at *The Times*. That brought him down: so many long words. But, if he kept his head, he could read the short ones.

Prideaux yawned, then shut his mouth abruptly. 'You're right. That smell doesn't just get up your nose. Something's got to be done.' He shut the notebook and handed it to Fred. 'For you. *Inshallah*, we'll carry on tomorrow.' Fred saw that the cover had a War Office stamp on it.

'How wide is no man's land?' Prideaux asked.

Fred thought of saying, 'You should know, you've been shouting across it all day,' but instead answered firmly, 'I'm not creeping out to bury them. There're thousands, most of them falling apart by now.'

'Beyond the call of duty. Quite.' Prideaux settled himself more comfortably. 'What we need is an armistice. I'll try and catch the effete General Hamilton in the morning. Not that he's been near a corpse since 1898, decomposing or otherwise. More likely to write an ode than take action. Here, throw me that water bottle, the one with the brandy in it.'

Fred supposed it wasn't just Captain Prideaux who got the idea of an armistice going but he was certainly in the midst of it all. As the Turkish speaker, he was the officer who escorted the Turkish envoy who came over, blindfolded and riding on a mule.

Fred stood outside the tent on the beach where talks were held. The captain began by assuring everyone that General Hamilton was right behind the plan. The colonel present looked doubtful but everyone wanted to get rid of the bodies. Since Prideaux was translating the Turkish point of view there was no problems with getting agreement there.

The rules were to be rigid. No firing from ten o'clock to four o'clock. Burial teams to wear white armbands.

'How can we stop them taking a dekko at our defences?' demanded an unhappy Aussie major. This was a tricky one but before anyone produced the obvious answer – the Allies could equally well look over the Turkish trenches – there was a sudden interruption. A large Australian wearing baggy shorts, boots and nothing else, forced himself past Fred and two on-duty soldiers, before shouting into the hushed tent.

'Have any of you bastards stolen my kettle?'

After he had been removed, unconvinced that colonels can't steal kettles as well as the next man, things proceeded more swiftly. Perhaps they feared more threatening intrusions.

'First sensible decision since we landed on Gallipoli,' commented Prideaux when he returned from escorting the Turkish major back to his own lines. 'Care for a swim?'

'A splash anyway,' agreed Fred, who certainly wasn't going to reveal he couldn't swim. The captain was perfectly capable of giving him a lesson in that too, with the whole of Anzac watching.

'Race you into the water!' shouted Prideaux, stripping off his clothes like a boy on a holiday outing.

'Race the shells more like,' muttered Fred as a big one splashed out to sea. 'I'm going to give my lice a surprise!' he shouted and ran fully dressed straight towards the sea.

'You bloody cheat,' complained Prideaux, dashing quite naked after him.

Glancing over his shoulder, Fred saw the captain's tall, muscled body, mostly burnt brown but startlingly white in the middle, and felt glad he'd kept his own clothes on.

An hour or two after dawn, two lines of soldiers carrying white flags formed up either side of no man's land. Officers of various nationalities, German, Turkish, Australian, New Zealand and British, gathered in agitated knots. This was unusual and no army likes unusual.

Rupert was in the midst of it. He was exhilarated but also disgusted by the smell. Everyone was disgusted. Quite a few had vomited beside thyme bushes not devastated by gun fire. He held to his nose a pad of cotton wool impregnated with disinfectant which a member of the Red Crescent team had given him. Luckily it was a cloudy morning and soon drizzling.

'Let's hope the sun stays hidden,' he said to a Turkish officer, the same who had been the original envoy.

'Allah is merciful.'

A whistle was blown and teams of diggers came from both sides. At this point no man's land was only ten yards wide. In some parts, the corpses formed lumpen hills, each body, or part of body merging together in a single mass. A rat dashed out in front of Rupert. Men began to dig.

An Australian captain came running and tried to begin an argument with a Turkish captain who didn't understand what he was saying. An English colonel and a German colonel, very smartly turned out, joined the young men, while eyeing each other with extravagant *froideur*.

Rupert translated. It was about spying, of course, and taking rifles belonging to the enemy. Everything had to be sorted out calmly. The colonels looked on silently.

The digging soldiers were trying to smoke as they worked. Some offered them to the Turks. But they only frowned on the Germans. One man leaped backwards as the arm he was pulling came off.

A sergeant marched up and saluted. 'We'll have to shovel them into trenches, sir. The ones who've been here longest. Just mush. Can't get a hold of them.'

Mush. The word made Rupert shiver. He remembered Fred had used the same word. 'Appalling,' he muttered after the man had gone.

The Turkish envoy said slowly, 'At such a spectacle even the most gentle must feel savage and the most savage must weep.'

A German officer appeared and spoke accusingly in excellent English. 'Your soldiers are digging trenches towards our lines.'

The English colonel spat out a cigar from his mouth. 'They are digging *graves*. We estimate that up to four thousand of your soldiers need burying. We have probably no more than three hundred dead. We are burying *your* dead.'

The German seemed about to expostulate but then caught his colonel's eye. He said nothing and bowed.

This is the most ghastly, grisly, inhuman day of my life, thought Rupert. All exhilaration had long evaporated. He was called over to adjudicate over an area of land where it had been agreed, because the opportunities for spying were too great, that no one might venture.

He found Fred there. 'Why aren't you with me?'

'Sorry, sir.' The man was too independent to be any kind of soldier but he intrigued Rupert. After three brief lessons, he seemed to be able to read. I can remember anything I've seen once, he'd told Rupert – so that was it. It seemed extraordinary he'd resisted reading for so long.

Padres were saying services all over the place. No imams, though. The Turks didn't seem so worried about giving their dead the last rites.

'You see where that padre is.' Fred pointed further down the line. Rupert saw a tall priest, one arm raised, white chasuble gently billowing. A welcome breeze had risen. 'It's that communication trench which gave so much trouble. They've filled it in with dead bodies. Crafty move.'

Rupert couldn't disagree. He gave Fred a cigarette. In the circumstances it was essential to have at least one cigarette on the go.

'Careful, sir.'

Rupert felt something squashy under his boot and stepped back quickly. Too late, the still recognisable face of a Turk, although flattened to the ground, stared back at him.

'You're wanted!' An Aussie came panting up. He smelled

nearly as bad as the corpses. Rupert bent and picked a branch of rosemary and put it to his nose. It still had a few bright blue flowers. 'What's the problem?'

'A Turkish officer tripped over one of our chap's spades and it's turning nasty.'

Rupert and Fred followed him. Despite the breeze, the grey sky still dripped miserably. The Turkish officer had recovered his dignity when they arrived and stood with his opposite number smoking yet more cigarettes. Two soldiers, a Turk and an Australian, were smiling at each other, swapping words, chocolate, a photograph. Rupert was amazed at this instant friendliness. Tomorrow, or even later that day, they would as easily kill each other.

Fred, who'd been watching too, said, 'It's good to know we're not fighting demons.'

Rupert thought, *Surely it's easier to kill a demon*. But he knew men liked to respect their enemy. The world was mad.

The dragging, the digging, the spying, the praying, to a God (of whatever sort) who didn't seem very present, went on and on. The armistice was to last eight hours and Rupert wondered whether he could last out. Already, his throat felt sore, as if he'd caught an infection. He feared it was in his brain too.

Whoever dreamt up this ridiculous campaign was a murderer. And he knew who it had been. He'd met him several times. The charismatic man with the cigar. Rupert's stomach and mouth and head were filled with bile.

'Anything the matter, sir?'

'Nothing. Nothing. We'd better check along the lines.' If only he'd been able to be a real soldier. For some reason, he remembered that innocent long-faced lieutenant who'd shared that little escapade from the SS *River Clyde*. He would make a good soldier, if he survived. He had a whole body and a belief in a proper moral order. He wouldn't lose faith in the campaign or, at very least, his place in it.

As Rupert peered at trench fortifications, some of them including Turkish corpses, and advised some slackers to get on with their jobs for there was only an hour or two to go, it struck him that he could no longer work at staff headquarters. Not under General Hamilton.

'What is it, sir?' asked Fred again.

'Nothing. Nothing,' repeated Rupert. He'd have to find some reason why he was needed in London. That was the only way out.

Arthur blew his whistle and clawed and scrambled and finally sprang out of the heavily banked trench. He was just ahead of his men but some were faster than him and poised to overtake. There wasn't a shirker among them.

It was exhilarating to be out of the trench, no longer bent double like an animal. There was a freedom in dashing towards danger. It was six thirty a.m., the best part of the day, before the glaring sun took all the freshness out of the air.

'Come on up!' he shouted to the men who were following him. It looked as if they were dancing but it was only their efforts to untangle their feet from the coils of barbed wire. There were one or two corpses, making their own graves in the dusty ground. It was so long since they'd made an attack that his heart thudded louder than his boots on the hard ground. At this point no man's land was several hundred yards wide so, if they were lucky, they could run for a minute or more without attracting enemy fire. Then they were seen.

Oh, the reverberations of earth and sky! The sounds spat and whizzed and blasted and rocketed and echoed. One man fell, then another. There weren't so many of them: forty men and a corporal, all volunteers. Arthur had volunteered to lead them. They were attempting to take a spur to the Turkish trenches, dug by the enemy the previous night. They should have waited for nightfall themselves but it was judged too dangerous to delay. Most carried improvised grenades which were possibly better than nothing, although they had a bad reputation for blowing off the sender's hand.

Arthur did not carry one. Their only chance of success was to take the Turks manning the trench by surprise. Seven o'clock in the morning was habitually a post-breakfast visit to the latrine or a bit of washing and tidying. Both sides knew each other's habits.

But they'd been spotted and there was still a hundred yards to cover. The men ducked and weaved. Corporal Snell of the unfortunate teeth fell like a stone beside Arthur. 'I'll be back!' he shouted. He had no wish to turn round. His high spirits carried him forward. And the first men were throwing their grenades, everybody shooting. Some of the Turks in the spur, still shallow, were only half-dressed, making it obvious that, however hard they were trying to fight now, they had been taken by surprise.

Arthur yelled more – he didn't know what – and smelled the smell of war – and somewhere charcoal burning. Had the Turks been cooking a late breakfast?

Now they were running or dying. Some put their hands up. But they could not stop to take prisoners. This was just a warning: *Your new spur is not safe from us; discontinue its use.*

It was time to abandon ship, checking on their wounded as they ran. The corporal had already been collected and taken back. So had the rest of their wounded. How many? Arthur wondered.

He half fell, half jumped over the trench parapet and lay, gasping at the bottom. Above his head, a gunner fired a shot or two, although he had no target. None of the Turks had been fool enough or prepared enough to follow them. Mission accomplished! After a few seconds he saw that his hands and shirt were criss-crossed with red. He had not felt the barbed wire as it tore at him.

Arthur stood up but kept his head down as his sergeant, who'd stayed behind, came close and saluted.

'Good job, sir.'

'Thank you, Sergeant. How many?'

'Six wounded. None dead.'

'Thank God.'

'Snell is bad but he's tough.'

'Where's he hit?'

'In his head, sir. Caught his eye.'

The pride in a job well done diminished. An officer's job was to look after his men, even his NCOs, who were usually more experienced than him.

'It was a brave deed, sir. Not a peep from that quarter since.' The sergeant was trying to cheer him up, reminding him that this was war. 'The colonel's asked for a report, if you're up to it.'

Arthur felt surprised and not altogether pleased. Did he look so cut up? 'I'll go straight away and visit the wounded later.' He spoke brusquely.

'I'll tell the men.' The sergeant took a step back.

The sun was rising over the bluff to the east. Its rays glittered disapprovingly at all the ugliness in the trench. Arthur rubbed his eyes.

'Do you want your wounds attended to, sir?'

'They're just scratches.' So that was it. He'd already forgotten the blood. He'd wipe it off before he went to give his report. He dismissed an image of himself as the bloodied hero receiving the approbation of his commanding officer. Their success had been more lucky than anything. They'd scarcely been out more than twenty minutes. 'I'll need a clean jacket.' He had a new servant but he was never around when needed.

It was already hot and the flies celebrating a new day when Arthur made his way to the colonel's headquarters. As soon as he left the trenches, he was in countryside, once tenderly farmed with corn, turnips and grassland but now overgrown, trampled down, burnt off and littered with holed water bottles, smashed rifles and torn clothing. That was a desperate sight. Yet now and again, for no obvious reason although maybe because near a redoubt, a little pocket of untouched beauty remained: waves of sunlit barley, gilded whiskers lifting in the breeze, a few remaining poppies with scabious, scarlet and mauve among the gold, wild roses flowering in the dark hedges, even a surviving tree or two. These were not places to linger – too easy for a Turkish sniper to hide among the bushes. But on this morning, Arthur did pause.

He took off his helmet and sniffed the thyme whose scent seemed to permeate the whole peninsula. There was sage and lavender too; spotting a springy tuft under his feet, he bent down and picked a spray. He would save it and perhaps describe this moment to Sylvia. She would not know because he would not tell her that his feelings of pleasure in this scene, in the gold, scarlet and pink, in the blue sky and the perfumes of wild herbs, arose because he was a survivor of a bloody action. Not so bloody for him but bloody to the death for the surprised, still half-dressed Turks in their forward, half-finished trench. Their commanders would have known how vulnerable they were but they were expendable. This was war.

For one day, he and his men had done more than their duty, the endless drab and dangerous duty. *Without a sign, his sword the brave man draws, and asks no omen but his country's cause.*

Taking a deep breath, Arthur put back on his helmet and made his way along the edge of the field. An itch began under his armpit. That servant couldn't kill a louse with a machine gun. Arthur smiled. It had been a wild dash for glory.

PART TWO

June 1915

❧

'The yeomanry never faltered. On they came through the haze of smoke in two formations, columns and extended. Sometimes they broke into a run but they always came on. It is difficult to describe the feelings of pride and sorrow with which we watched this advance in which so many of our friends and relations were playing their part.'

Major Aubrey Herbert describing the
advance at Suvla Bay, August 1915

Eleven

Beatrice stood up from the Colonel's desk and wandered through to the adjoining room where the bronzes were displayed. Today the recuperating officers were arriving. She felt some way to breaking through the pall of grief which had hung over her ever since her dearest Bingo had left.

'Mama!'

Beatrice hadn't heard the door open and whirled round, almost as if frightened. In her hands she held a small bronze statuette of a mythical beast.

'Sylvia! I'm sorry. You're early.' Beatrice stared at her daughter. 'You're so thin and pale.' She put down the bronze almost guiltily.

'For a moment, I thought Papa was here,' said Sylvia, with an expression nearly as startled as her mother's. She did seem to be accusing Beatrice of something.

'You know he's in Cairo!' Beatrice felt she should kiss her daughter, this ghost-like girl that stood in front of her, twisting the string of her little pouch bag. Her hat, with its navy and white plumes, looked too big for her pinched face.

'I'm so tired,' said Sylvia, then added more warmly, 'But I'm very glad to be here. So many changes. Beds in the dining room.'

'And the drawing room,' said Beatrice with a note of pride.

The two women came together and merged briefly in an embrace before moving to the main part of the study. Beatrice, about to sit down once more in the Colonel's chair as she did often to comfort herself, took a different place. 'How are you?'

'I need a wash before lunch.' Sylvia began to unpin her hat. 'The train was full of soldiers. I wished I'd worn my nurse's uniform but they were all very respectful. I shall wear it – I mean uniform – in future. These hats seem so ridiculous in time of war. Although

London – the smart part – is full of women looking just as usual, with flowers and feathers, and parties and theatre.'

Beatrice tried to understand why Sylvia was talking about hats and parties. 'Gussie is here,' she said with unconscious association.

'I'd never expect Gussie to change,' said Sylvia with a tolerant smile. 'That's better.' She wrenched off her hat and held it to her breast. 'I'll come down at the first gong.'

'There're two new girls cooking and no gong . . .' began Beatrice but Sylvia had turned suddenly and left the room.

Oh, the relief of space! The freedom to do whatever she felt like! Sylvia hurried to the hallway and, in a giddy sense of release from hospital rules, the cramped hostel, blackened south London, Zeppelins and overcrowded trams, overcrowded trains and her own ever-churning thoughts, flung her hat away from her. It flew like a discus and landed without any aim on her part on top of an umbrella and stick stand by the door. She laughed delightedly and dashed up the shockingly wide stairway. Reaching the landing, she slowed again to savour the sense of home. Somehow the beds in the drawing room and the dining room, the new young staff of whom she caught glimpses down corridors, made no difference at this moment of return. Besides, her bedroom was altogether unchanged, except that it seemed to have quadrupled in size. She flung herself on her bed. For thirty-six hours she had no responsibilities and need think of nothing, not even Arthur. Her eyes closed.

'Do wake up, Sylvia! Someone was shaking her shoulder. 'I'm having a fearful row with Mama and I need you to stick up for me. You've slept through lunch already and the frightful wounded will be here soon and Mama will be all in a flap.'

Unable to rouse herself from the heavy weight of sleep, Sylvia murmured without opening her eyes, 'Oh, Hilda. Is it time to get up already?'

'Yes, it is,' said Gussie sternly, 'and I'm not Hilda, I'm your sister appealing for help.'

Very slowly, Sylvia sat up but it still took time to focus on Gussie. 'My dear. Sorry.'

'Are you ill or something? Anyway, you've got to come down. I need Mama's permission to work in France welcoming our soldiers with tea and sandwiches, you know the sort of patriotic thing. Cousin Evie told me that Baby Fox-Brown who's fearfully smart and respectable, has been out there for weeks. If Mama won't say yes, I shall do something rash. Go to the bad or something.'

'Just wait a moment.' Sylvia walked over to a stand by the window and poured cool water from a large jug painted with roses into a matching bowl. She sluiced her face and neck until the water ran inside her jacket. The window was open and she breathed in the fragrances of summer: flowers, leaves, damp earth.

Gussie hovered anxiously while she dried herself, but not too thoroughly because she liked the freshness of wet skin.

'Why don't you help out here?' Sylvia asked eventually.

In answer, Gussie burst into angry tears. 'I'd *die* of boredom. Even you won't do that. I'm too young to be incarcerated. It doesn't matter for you. You're engaged already!'

Sylvia turned back to the window. Perhaps at this moment Arthur was lying mortally wounded in what *The Times* called the need to take the enemy positions *Hill by hill, valley by valley, and trench by trench* . . . It took her a moment to see the procession of vehicles coming slowly up the drive.

'There you are!' Gussie cried despairingly from behind her. 'Now it's too late! I'll never get Mama even to listen.' The sisters stood side by side and watched three cars, four ambulances and two large unmarked vans approach the front door. In the distance they could see two pony traps bringing up the rear.

Lady Beatrice and Lily Chaffey, backed by an assortment of female helpers, mostly young, waited at the door. Beatrice had her arms folded across the severe navy coat and skirt she felt suitable for the occasion. Her hat was dark and her shoes black. For the first time since the Colonel had left, she felt calm. Here was a duty she could do which was worthy of him. For a moment she pictured her mother, whose whole life was driven by public duties.

As a much beribboned officer emerged from the first car, Beatrice took three steps forward, 'Major Collier.' She held out her hand. 'Welcome to Tollorum Manor.'

'I must not become drab and worn down,' Sylvia told herself as she lay in her narrow bed in the dreary hostel room. Already, less than a week after her return to London, her visit home seemed like a dream. 'I must remain romantic and silvery like a moon as Arthur thinks of me.' She wanted to smile at this image so far from the truth but exhaustion had fixed her face.

On the bedside lay two letters she had received on her return from the hospital. The first, from Arthur, began, as usual, with natural description:

With summer, the wildflowers have gone and insects have taken their place: tarantulas, centipedes, scorpions, lizards, cicadas . . . Sometimes when I'm only half awake and behind the lines, I imagine I am back in the days when I travelled through Europe and lay down to rest in an olive grove with springy herbs as my mattress and cicadas to chorus me to sleep. But I did not know you then so I have no wish to put the clock back. The fates have given mankind a patient soul. I shall know the whole Iliad *by heart before my return.*

I try and imagine you in a nurse's uniform but can't quite do it. I always think of you as so flowing and soft, not crisp and white with starch and bustle. It is strange seeing not a single woman for so long, not since I left Cairo in April. No one gets leave here, unless they're hit. Nowhere to go, of course, without taking a ship. When I see you first, you must dress in grey or perhaps quietest blue, the colour of first light. I don't altogether like to think of you in London. But perhaps you meet people who can help you understand the war we're fighting here. It feels awfully like a stalemate just at the moment. But I expect more troops will be sent out. Your family is well connected; maybe they can take a wider view . . .

He had not pursued this thought and Sylvia, rather surprised the word 'stalemate' hadn't been censored, passed quickly over it. The idea of her 'well connected' family was utterly alien to her day-to-day activity of alleviating pain in young men, each one of whom had something of Arthur in their eyes.

The second letter was from Gussie who had given up trying to contact her sister any other way.

Oh, Sylvia, I am in London again with dreary old Cousin Evie as chaperone. I think my life is over before it began. Do you

*know it was my eighteenth birthday and no one noticed? Even
Reggie never writes. But today a spark of hope dawned. Uncle
Robert arrived and opened some of his mail that had been sitting
here for ages. One envelope was very stiff and hugely crested so I
watched it closely and it turned out to be an invitation to a grand
fund-raising soirée for our boys-at-the-front at which the prime
minister will be present. All linked to the war loan or something.
Uncle Robert was about to put it in the waste-paper basket when
I snatched it from him and begged that we should go. I threw in
the fact it was my birthday and nobody had even remembered and
Mama had been married at eighteen. Anyway, he remarked coldly
that he believed I was his niece Augusta, not his niece Sylvia
and, if he was to go to this vulgar soirée – filled with politicians
of whom he disapproved not least because they were incapable of
winning a billiard match, let alone a war – which he was not,
then he would take the oldest sister, not the younger sister, who
he believed was not yet out in society. But how can I come out
if I'm kept in! I wailed pathetically and burst out sobbing. This
turned out to be a master stroke. He looked at me with absolute
horror. I suspect he's never seen a woman in tears. I don't expect
Grandmama knows how. He waved his white hands about saying:
'Stop. Stop. My dear child.' He even patted my back. It was like
a spider walking over me so I sobbed a bit more and, to cut a long
story short, he said he would take me but only if you also came as
eldest sister. You will, won't you, dearest, dearest Sylvie? Blood is
thicker than water and you wouldn't want to see me unhappy for
the rest of my life. And if you absolutely loathe it, you can think
of all the money collected for our boys-at-the-front which includes
Arthur . . .*

Sylvia had always disliked the house in Bruton Street, heavily
furnished in the Victorian way and even darker than usual with the
windows muffled in black serge against the threat of Zeppelins.
She had absolutely refused Gussie's plea, truly disgusted at the
thought of a party however good the motive, but fate had decreed
otherwise. One of her fingers became infected and Sister banished
her from the hospital until it was cured. 'Two months and you
pick up an infected finger!' as she'd commented disdainfully.
    So here Sylvia stood in the drawing room of her uncle's house,

dressed in a shimmering lilac gown sent up from the country, with a spray of diamonds at her shoulder and a headdress of lilac and pink feathers on her hair, coiled and piled up by a maid imported for the occasion.

'Where is that sister of yours?' Lord Deverill, Uncle Robert, leant languidly against the mantelpiece, bored even before the evening had started.

'The maid is slow,' answered Sylvia, who assumed her uncle was spoiled by his position as a rich bachelor, living mostly in the imposing house he'd inherited and which was still run by his mother. Sylvia did not approve either of the medals he wore since she knew he'd earned them by waiting on the elderly Queen Victoria rather than through glorious exploits of war. *He's an old drone*, decided Sylvia, without realising that such hostility to her own race was quite a change from her previous unthinking accept-ance.

'I am sorry, Uncle. Truly!' It was quite clear that Gussie, making an entrance in a cloud of pale tulle, was not sorry at all. All the same, Sylvia enjoyed Gussie's childish enthusiasm.

Uncle Robert pulled a large gold watch out of his waistcoat. 'We will be present at this patriotic event for precisely an hour.'

Rupert Prideaux stared at the massed ranks of the English upper classes, sprinkled lightly with some invited more for their pocket book than their ancestry, and wished he hadn't come. On the ship home he had gone down with some fever which he couldn't help feeling was a result of his frightful experiences at the Anzac armistice, and still felt weak. He had been seduced by the idea of hearing a speech from the prime minister who, for the last weeks, had been leading a coalition government. But as yet there were no politicians present that he recognised.

There were some pretty girls but he was hardly in the spirits to chase a skirt. Better to see if he could keep down a glass or three of champagne and pick up with some of his contemporaries – not many there, of course, and all of them in uniform as he was him-self.

'You're Prideaux, Filchester's son, aren't you?'

An elegant, middle-aged man, wearing a cluster of unknown medals, was staring at him through a monocle.

'Yes, sir, Rupert Prideaux.'

'Mmm. Heard you were at Gallipoli.'

'Intelligence officer.' Rupert made his maimed hand obvious on the champagne glass; it saved embarrassment to get it over with straight away.

'Going to win, are we? Now that damned fool Churchill's been chucked out. We spectators only know what we read in *The Times*.'

Behind his unnamed questioner, Rupert noticed, was a very pretty girl, with a slender figure, shiny dark hair and a rosy complexion. She looked about fourteen. Or maybe he was getting older. 'Churchill's still on the Dardanelles Committee, still in the War Cabinet.'

'More's the pity! So what do they think about Kitchener out there?'

'They wish he'd send more troops, sir. Or more ammunition. Preferably both.'

'And General Sir Ian Hamilton? A clever fellow. Terrific dancer.'

Rupert thought it was hard that he should be interrogated like this by some country buffer who admitted *The Times* as his only source of information, when he'd come hoping to pick up some first-hand up-to-date political gossip. Looking at the pretty girl again, he noticed that there was a taller, paler, less focused version beside her. They must be sisters.

'With the help of the navy, General Hamilton has landed his army. His only problem is how to move forward,' said Rupert, congratulating himself on his restraint. The pretty girl took a step forward.

'More interested in my nieces, are you?' The monocle dropped down and swung from its ribbons, the gentleman turned round to the girls.

'Lord Prideaux, may I present Miss Fitzpaine and Miss Augusta Fitzpaine.' Having delivered this introduction, still without identifying himself, Lord Filchester brought his watch half way out of his pocket and tapped it with a meaningful look at his nieces before moving off.

'He's your chaperone, is he?' Now that he had the girls to hand, Rupert felt weary at having to make conversation.

'A very unwilling one,' replied the younger girl, Augusta,

chattily. The elder stared pensively with large grey eyes. She looked as if she might topple over at any moment.

'Would you like a seat, Miss Fitzpaine?' began Rupert, and as he pronounced the words he remembered an envelope given to him in Gallipoli by the serious, long-faced lieutenant. 'I believe we are slightly related,' he said.

'Oh, that's why Uncle Robert palmed us off on you.' Augusta – *Surely more of a Gussie*, thought Rupert – gave a winsome smile. He found himself surprised that such an innocently flirtatious girl still existed. He had spent so little time in London for the last few years that he had somehow imagined all that kind of life had vanished.

'I'm happy standing, thank you.' Miss Fitzpaine – now what was she called? Violet? Pansy? Stella? – seemed only now to have taken in his words. 'But I'd love another lemonade.' She held out her glass.

'Sylvia is a nurse,' offered her sister. 'She's fearfully over-worked.'

Sylvia, then. He wasn't so far out.

'I'm a VAD,' corrected Sylvia. 'Not a proper nurse.'

'Like me. I'm a captain in the army but I've never been near a battle, except by chance. I'm an intelligence officer.'

Rupert took her glass, watched her notice his maimed hand and wondered what to say about Lieutenant Lamb. After all, he was quite likely killed by now. He refilled his own glass, then ordered the lemonade. 'Add some champagne,' he ordered the waiter.

When he returned, the girls were staring towards a dais at the far end of the room. A party of politicians, accompanied by some ladies, had arrived. Herbert Asquith, looking like a country squire, was preparing himself to speak. Surprisingly, Lord Kitchener was not present. Rupert wanted to go closer so that he could be in position to catch Asquith, or if not him, his secretary, Bonham-Carter, who he knew slightly, afterwards. But he decided he must first do his duty by Lieutenant Lamb.

'I was in Gallipoli . . ' he began.

Immediately, Sylvia's whole stance altered and the unfocused air turned to glittering intensity. 'You've met my fiancé, Lieutenant Arthur Lamb?'

This was a quick jump from learning he'd been in Gallipoli,

Rupert thought, but since it was true, and the man perhaps still alive, he answered, one eye on the dais. 'Yes. We were together at the landings on April the twenty-fifth. He was a bit of a hero. Then I saw him on Cape Helles later. In fact, he asked me to see a letter for you was sent. I assume it arrived?' A line was forming on the dais.

'He writes quite often now. I . . .' She put her gloved hand to her cheek which, whether owing to the champagne or mention of her fiancé, was now as pink as her sister's. Rupert saw that, although not girlishly pretty, she was almost beautiful in a fine, angular way. Not his type anyway. He would have said more – why should Lamb not be a hero in his fiancée's eyes – but they were interrupted by the speeches.

Murmuring excuses, Rupert hurried forward.

'War is a time for sacrifice . . . The sacrifice of our young men is the highest price . . . A supreme cause is at stake. We have each and all of us – I do not care who we are or what we are – to respond with whatever we have, with whatever we can give, with whatever we can sacrifice, to the dominating and inexorable call . . .'

No one could say the prime minister lacked the inspiring phrase. He had been forced into a coalition government – Bonar Law, his bitter enemy, stood beside him as the leader of the Conservatives – but he still tried to move the country with his rhetoric.

A burly man sidled up to Rupert and whispered too loudly, 'This is only the dress rehearsal. Next week he's speaking at the Guildhall.'

Rupert recognised him as a journalist he'd drunk with in the past. 'Good evening, Brendan.'

'Nice to see cripples are accepted in the army these days.'

Too late, Rupert remembered the venomous creep he was. He'd already sidled off to pour poison in the next ear.

'The policy of this new coalition government remains what it has been since the first week in August – to pursue this war at any cost to a victorious issue. But the cost is great, not only in lives, that supreme loss, but in money. Last August the national debt stood at £651 million. There are those who believe it will reach £2000 million. But these are depressing figures and this evening I'm here with happier news. Up to Saturday over £1 million had been received by the Post Office for £5 and £25 bonds. In this way the nation shows its will. The people make sacrifices that the war may be fought to a victory. Let you who are here today stand shoulder to shoulder with the man who has never saved more than five pounds in his life and now gives that up to the war loan. To invest in the war loan is to invest in ammunition for our brave soldiers. To invest in the war loan is to invest in the freedom of our great country!'

Rupert stared about him as the grand words rolled round the gilded room, filled with gilded people. He'd never felt more alienated from his class. He assumed Asquith was a clever man. Yet he, too, must bear the weight of Gallipoli. Oratory could not disguise his responsibility for the decision to go forward. He and the rest of his cabinet had allowed and continued to allow men of the Mediterranean Expeditionary Force to deliver 'the ultimate sacrifice' for no possible gain.

Rupert stepped back and to the side of the hall. Even this new way of getting money disgusted him. If Brendan was right, and he was a sharp chap, the prime minister's next step would be to plead for serious money from the city and its financial circles. The war loan was a clever way of dunning the poor. The well-heeled men and women in this room would rather argue about the relative merits of Bonar Law and Asquith than give a penny of their hoarded gold to a coalition government whom they didn't trust for a minute. He'd bet his own parents felt exactly this. What a hopeless mess!

Rupert's dyspeptic view – and he was beginning to feel distinctly ill – was confirmed by the words he overheard from a large lady in a dazzling tiara: 'I shall tell my housekeeper to suggest the servants invest five shillings on pay day.'

'Indeed, servants always have spare money,' nodded a small lady, plumed in vibrant blue. 'They have no responsibility and everything paid for.'

Rupert pushed his way to the door, his earlier urge for political gossip unequal to his irritation and sickness. He looked at his watch. Time for the theatres to come out. Would a dalliance with a girl he'd been told about at the Empire make him feel better or worse?

'You're leaving. I wondered if . . .' Sylvia's grey eyes, brilliant with appeal, stared at him.

'Yes.' She wanted to hear more. It was natural but, as he thought this, he was overcome by an urgent need. 'Excuse me . . .' He dashed past her, threaded his way through wide corridors lined with flunkeys, down a great staircase and at last to the pavement where he vomited all the champagne in a frothy puddle under and over one of the chauffeur-driven cars waiting at the kerb-side.

'Bloody hell!' exclaimed its elderly driver. Feeling instantly better, Rupert looked up. 'It's only a car and not even yours. What about my poor stomach? I'll give you a fiver to take me home. They'll be ages in there yet.'

'Yes, milord,' said the chauffeur, changing his tune with alacrity.

Sylvia and Hilda sat as usual over their Horlicks, both in their dressing gowns, hair plaited down their backs. 'Shall you go?' asked Hilda, looking at the note in her friend's hand.

'Oh, yes!' Sylvia replied warmly. 'It's a strange thing but ever since he spoke of Arthur at that appalling reception, I felt calmer and more confident. He said "he was a bit of a hero" but that wasn't it. I think I'd lost a sense of Arthur's existence, even though he wrote – silly, I know – but Captain Prideaux had met him there.'

Hilda nodded. 'But why do you want to see this Prideaux again when he abandoned you so rudely?'

'The letter explains. He was taken ill that evening and just recovered now. It's only tea at the Ritz. I'm not going to bed with him.' Sylvia blushed at the freedom of her words, making Hilda smile.

'You'll be a woman of the world yet.'

'I just want to hear everything he can tell me about Arthur,' Sylvia insisted seriously. 'I need him to be *real*. Then everything else seems real too.'

This was too much for practical Hilda. 'Whatever could be more real than green pus on the remains of an arm?'

'I can't really explain it. But you have to admit I've been managing better lately. Sister only shouted at me twice the whole of yesterday.'

The two girls smiled at each other and leant closer together. 'That's because you're Matron's pet,' said Hilda, digging Sylvia in the ribs. 'Had any tête-à-têtes recently?'

'Oh, Hilda! You're such a beast!' And like two young children, the girls put down their mugs and started whacking each other with their pillows.

Gussie never knew a man could weigh so much. Reggie was like a huge animal lying on top of her. Men's bones must be heavier or something. Gussie realised these weren't very romantic thoughts but she couldn't stop herself thinking them all the same. She supposed she was frightened about what was happening but, on the other hand, she was very excited and she certainly had no wish to stop it.

Reggie grunted and she felt his fingers grasping at her bottom – through at least two layers of material. He had come to her unexpectedly that afternoon – his job seemed to involve regular visits to London. She was alone, Uncle Robert returned to the comfort of the country, Sylvia back to doing good, Cousin Evie visiting a sick relative and the servants in the basement.

Perhaps Reggie had been drinking because when she flew at him joyfully, he had swung her round and round so that one of her booted feet had knocked off a bowl which had smashed on the parquet floor. He hadn't even noticed.

'Oh, Gussie! Sweetest Gussie!' He had been drinking because his breath smelled when he kissed her.

Very quickly, they'd arrived on the long red sofa and he'd begun to feel her body all over. His face was red, his hair all over his face and he was really more like a big dog than a man. 'Oh, Gussie! Gussie!'

Then he was on top of her, his great unexpected weight pressing down and she couldn't move if she'd wanted to. That was exciting too.

Suddenly she felt his fingers tugging at the string of her drawers. They felt enormously strong, as if they could rip apart all her clothes. He'd lifted her a bit to get more space to manoeuvre.

Surely he would stop now? Surely she would tell him to stop? 'Reggie. Reggie. What are you doing?' Her voice was very weak and he stopped it all together with his mouth, with his tongue.

Now he had rolled off her and pulled up her skirt and her drawers down and then the weight was on her again and something else. She knew exactly what was happening but she felt powerless to stop it, not because he was forcing her – she could have kicked and screamed and got away – but because she wanted him on top of her, inside her. She'd grown up with horses, after all. Once she'd seen an excited stallion.

But why was he taking so long? She was soft and ready and his thing had felt hard and strong.

'Oh, damn it!' Reggie's voice was above her head, above her closed eyes. She opened them a little, then closed them quickly. He had been doing something to his great red thing.

'Oh, Reggie.'

'Damn it to hell!' His full weight fell back on her and she felt herself pierced.

A scream which must have come from her made her ears tingle. She clutched Reggie's thick black hair.

'Oh my God!' There was a loud thump as Reggie rolled off her on to the floor.

Gussie heard his loud breaths gradually slow. Pulling her drawers up and her skirt down she peered over the edge of the sofa. Reggie was lying face down, and unmoving.

Gussie sat up. It hurt a little down there but not much. She looked at Reggie again. Presumably he hadn't died so he must be asleep. She didn't mind. She wanted to savour this moment alone. Her main emotion was satisfaction with a little of triumph thrown in. She thought of Sylvia briefly. How shocked she would be! Not that she'd tell her. This was her secret. Her life.

Heart rate almost back to normal, Gussie sat on the sofa and reordered her hair.

Five minutes later, Reggie turned over and stared at her bemusedly before an expression of horror spread over his face. It made him look quite stupid, Gussie thought. Even more so, when he saw the bit of rubber on the floor and with shaking fingers stuffed it in his pocket at the same time as trying to do up his trousers.

'Yes, it's me. Gussie. And we made love.'

'I'm so . . . sorry. I . . . Unforgivable . . . I . . .'

'Don't you love me?' asked Gussie. He should regain his swagger, she thought. His swagger was the best part of him.

'Of course I do. That's why I would never hurt you.' He ran his fingers through his hair distractedly and was staring at her still with a kind of horror. 'Are you all right? I mean . . .' Once again words failed him.

'Yes,' said Gussie firmly. 'I suppose you'd been drinking. But I don't regret it.'

'Don't regret . . .' Reggie seemed even more stunned. He looked round the over-furnished drawing room wildly before picking up a beaded cushion from the floor and placing it beside Gussie. Gradually, he regained some composure. 'You're honestly all right?'

'I told you. But Cousin Evie will be back any minute.'

Reggie went to an ornate mirror and stared at his face. He seemed to be struggling with a new idea. He turned round and he was straight and soldierly again. 'Naturally I shall ask your father for your hand in marriage.'

Now Gussie looked shocked. 'You can't. He's in Egypt. And he'd never give permission.'

They stared at each other.

'I'm going back to France tomorrow.'

'You might be killed,' said Gussie, and was surprised when Reggie's face expressed some relief at the idea.

'It's so dangerous for an officer in the front line that we don't bother to get to know each other.'

'You're a hero,' said Gussie to cheer him up. It cheered her to think she'd been made love to by a hero.

They both stopped talking as the front doorbell rang and a servant came up from the basement. 'You'll have to go.' For the first time Gussie looked a little scared. 'That'll be Cousin Evie.'

'But how can I leave you . . . My dearest love . . .' He returned quickly to practicalities. 'I'll meet her in the hallway.'

'Tell her you were leaving a note. Notes are awfully respectable.'

'Oh my pretty darling . . .'

'Go!'

'Then adieu!' cried Reggie. He bowed. He kissed her hand. The swagger was back.

'Adieu,' agreed Gussie, and she smiled sweetly so that he would remember her pretty face as he went to war. His whole visit had lasted scarcely fifteen minutes.

Sylvia and Rupert sat at a table in the Palm Court at the Ritz Hotel.

'I'm told this is the only place in London where a young lady can take tea without a chaperone,' said Rupert.

Sylvia looked round at the gilded alcoves with their urns and palms, the ceiling ornamented like a Louis XIV palace, the rows of white tablecloths, gilt chairs and waiters in tails. 'I'm afraid I'm not smart enough,' she said, although it was obvious the idea gave her no pain, maybe even pleased her.

'You look perfect,' said Rupert, also unconvincingly. She was wearing a dark toque that didn't suit her and a long striped coat-jacket that was ridiculously too big.

'I'm not used to going about in London. I more or less live in my uniform.'

'Me too,' smiled Rupert. 'No one wants to be given a white feather.'

For the first time, Sylvia properly registered that he was a remarkably handsome man but it was only a remote recognition. That kind of reaction to a man had disappeared with Arthur's absence and her constant preoccupation with young men's tortured bodies. A few days earlier, the ward had been so busy she'd been entrusted with bathing a young man who had a stomach wound and had lost a leg. She had been far too aware of his suffering to be embarrassed by her first sight of a man's genitals.

'In fact,' she said suddenly, 'it makes me a little uncomfortable to be here in such luxury when our soldiers are having such a miserable time.'

'You shouldn't feel that,' advised Rupert who'd just ordered champagne and smoked salmon sandwiches and was clearly bent on having a good time. 'The men at the front love the idea of life going on as usual back home. You won't help them by suffering. I'm sure Lamb feels just the same.'

Sylvia thought wryly that tea at the Ritz was hardly Arthur's idea of life as usual but she only said shyly, 'I expect you're right. When are you going out again?'

'I'm being sent to Cairo. Someone somewhere believes I understand the Eastern mind.'

'I see.' Sylvia looked and felt disappointed. She knew it was absurd but he had seemed her link with Arthur.

Meanwhile, Rupert wondered what he could tell her of his meeting with her fiancé. He thought back to the SS *River Clyde* and their escapade trying to rescue the wounded but the sheer horror of that time could not be sanitised into something happy and glorious. How do you describe walking over dead and drowned bodies or, worse, only partially dead and drowned?

'Have a glass of champagne. Or there is tea.' He looked at the white pot that had just arrived. 'Probably China.'

'Champagne,' said Sylvia to both their surprise. Rupert waved over a waiter who took the bottle from its ice bucket and poured for both of them. After a sip, she leant forward. 'I believe Arthur enjoys being a soldier. It's very strange. Before he went he talked a lot about death and not at all about soldiering. He's a classicist, you know, and, in that ancient world, death seems to be at the bottom of everything, bad and good. He's not an heroic person, quite a modest person, although he's most frightfully clever, but I think he'd worked up to a feeling that death gave meaning to life. A good death, that is. Now he doesn't talk about death at all. He doesn't talk about soldiering much but between the lines I think it's being a lieutenant in charge of his men that keeps him going.' She stopped, seeming bewildered.

'A lot of soldiers fight for their companions,' said Rupert, rubbing his face.

Sylvia noticed his maimed hand again and felt sorry, imagining a shell or bullet but only for a moment, because she wanted to work out her thoughts about Arthur.

'But Arthur wasn't like that, Captain Prideaux. I mean, not companionable. He was an orphan, brought up by an elderly uncle. He had friends at Oxford, classicists like him, but they talked about subjects, if you know what I mean. Since he went away, he's never asked about any of them and I've seen in *The Times'* lists that two have been killed in France.'

'Perhaps he's found real comradeship for the first time,' suggested Rupert but he wasn't really concentrating. He ate one smoked salmon sandwich then another. He was pleased his appetite had come back – just in time to enjoy Cairo and talk Eastern politics, always an amusing concept. Best of all, he'd be far from the inanities of practical warfare.

'I probably won't understand him when he comes back,' Sylvia said sadly.

Rupert looked at her again. He was surprised by her confidences.

'Lieutenant Lamb believed in victory, or at least he did when I met him. He looked forward to taking back Constantinople and avenging the defeat of the Christians by the infidels in the fifteenth century.'

'Yes, I know. And what do you think?'

This was a facer. With the big eyes staring at him it would be too cruel to give his real view. 'I admire the brave men out there – Turks too – but I can't say the same of their generals.'

'But will we win?'

'If God wills.'

'You don't think so, do you?' Sylvia's voice had become despairing. 'All those young men – Arthur, too, perhaps – giving up their lives – dying – for nothing!' In her emotion, her voice rose to a wail. A waiter who had been approaching retreated hastily.

'I'm just one ill-educated man. Don't believe in my opinion. I left school at sixteen, thrown out, and have been roaming about the world since. It makes me cynical. I should stick to Lamb's point of view. He's much cleverer than me, much more principled.'

'I want to. I want to.' Sylvia put her head in her hands. 'But if Arthur's killed like so many others, I shall have to ask myself these questions. I have to feel it's worthwhile. I think of him every day. Every wounded soldier is him. I'm not such a bad nurse now . . .' Her voice suddenly trailed away.

Having nothing to say of consolation – after all, she had only spoken the truth – Rupert finished his glass of champagne and ate more sandwiches, cucumber this time. Food was expensive at the Ritz and not to be wasted.

The waiter started to bring their champagne out of its bucket and Rupert told him to put it on the table. Sylvia watched vaguely. She straightened up and, taking a handkerchief from her purse, pressed it to her eyes.

'I suppose we just carry on,' she said in a steady voice.

'I believe that's the general view.'

'Thank you for listening to me. You're a kind man.' She even managed a smile.

Rupert thought it was the first time anyone had called him kind. 'There's an awful lot of champagne to drink.' He refilled both their glasses. To his surprise, she drank thirstily.

'I should go. I'm on duty tonight.' She gathered herself together, then hesitated. 'Where did you say you're going?'

'Cairo.'

'My father is out there. He was a cavalry officer in the regular army. Now he's been made a Brigadier-General and commands a yeomanry brigade. They're in reserve. Perhaps you'll come across him. Then you'll have met all the people dearest to me, apart from my mother.'

'Perhaps,' said Rupert.

Catching the inference, Sylvia couldn't blame him. He was a dashing young intelligence officer who would hardly search out an elderly, retired soldier from the shires even if he now had a command. But he *had* been kind to her.

She pulled on her gloves as they crossed the crowded and elegant room. Twice, Captain Prideaux was stopped by young men, one in uniform, one not. Once an older woman wearing a rainbow-coloured cape flapped her napkin at him. He scarcely paused. Sylvia pictured her crisp white uniform waiting at the hospital with a sense of comfort.

Twelve

'I could have you shot for desertion!'

Fred stared with unblinking blue eyes at the Sergeant Major in front of him and thought that maybe he'd made a mistake trying to rejoin his regiment.

'Yes, Sarn't Major!' He was already at attention but he stood even more stiffly. The interview was taking place in a boiling hot tent somewhere on Helles. One way and another, particularly after he'd been arrested, Fred had rather lost his sense of direction.

'Where do you say you last saw your company?'

'April the twenty-fifth. V Beach. Sarn't Major.'

There was a slight change in the Sergeant Major's granite face. Fred knew, because one of the soldiers escorting him had told him, that the Sergeant Major had only arrived from England two weeks ago. Of course this might make him even angrier with a soldier who'd seen hard action.

'You came from Anzac. What were you doing with the Dominion troops?'

'Major Furlong took me, Sarn't Major.'

'So why isn't he vouching for you?'

'Killed in action. May the twenty-fifth.'

'It's June, now. Flaming June!'

'I was then attached to Captain Prideaux, Sarn't Major. An intelligence officer.'

'If there's one thing I hate more than an effing Turk, it's an effing intelligence officer! So what's happened to *him*?'

'Ordered to England.'

The Sergeant Major snorted in disgust.

'Permission to move?'

'I'll teach you to move, you squirm-bag.' Taking this as

permission to move, Fred extracted a piece of folded paper from his jacket pocket and handed it to the sergeant.

'Want me to read your life story now, do you?'

Fred had forgotten the talent sergeants shared for keeping dialogue at a bellow. He wondered if it was inborn or learnt. 'Yessir. Please, Sarn't Major.'

While the Sergeant Major slowly read the paper, holding it at a distance and grunting crossly, Fred looked through the flap of the tent and saw, in the white glare, a group of young officers smoking and talking. He'd always had more luck with officers than NCOs. He seemed to get up the nose of the latter while the others took him as he was. All the officers out there were very thin, like every soldier who'd been out there for a bit, but one was nastily gaunt – dysentery probably. Even the Sergeant Major would lose his flesh in a few weeks.

'I suppose you think this will get you off!' The Sergeant Major's face was even angrier. Maybe Captain Prideaux's idea of writing what he'd called an affidavit wasn't so clever.

The very thin lieutenant looked towards the tent, apparently attracted by the raised voice. He strolled over, followed by a second officer. Fred stared.

'A problem, Sergeant Major?' The first officer put his head in the flap.

'Sir!' The Sergeant Major saluted. The officer saluted back. 'This scruffy fellow says he's part of the regiment but if you ask me he's more of an effing deserter. Excuse my language. Sir!'

The officer peered at Fred who was still stiffly to attention. 'I know you.'

'Yessir. Private F. Chaffey. In April. Up the cliffs I was your runner. Not for long, sir.'

The Sergeant Major gave such an expressive snort that the second officer had to repress a smile.

The first officer tried to remember. Despite his deep sunburn, he had a terrible colour, Fred thought. 'I'm from Dorset, sir.'

'That's enough!' yelled the Sergeant Major.

But the officer held up his hand. 'I remember you now. We fought through the village to Hill 141 where Colonel Doughty-Wylie was killed.' He paused. 'You didn't seem to be part of a company then.'

146

'He says he's been with an intelligence officer. A Captain Prideaux,' bellowed the Sergeant Major, who clearly wasn't enjoying the sympathetic tone of the proceedings. 'And before that with those bloody Anzacs. You can read it for yourself, sir.' He thrust the paper at the lieutenant with the air of a man who was washing his hands of a dirty affair.

The officer read the paper carefully. Then he looked up. 'How long have you been here, Sergeant Major?'

'Sir! Two weeks. Sir!'

'And do you find the army organised?'

'Yes. Sir!'

'So do I, thanks to men like you. But if you'd been here in April you would not have found it well organised. On V Beach only three hundred of the first seven hundred landed made the beach and they were mostly wounded. And from the SS *River Clyde* less than half survived with only a handful of officers. The army was not then what it is now. This soldier is a survivor of one of the most fatal attacks on record. Six VCs were handed out on V Beach alone.'

Oh God, thought Fred, if he makes me out a bloody hero, I might as well shoot myself before the Sergeant Major gets there first.

'In such circumstances, Sergeant Major, I'm sure you will understand that the normal, much to be desired, line of command breaks down. In other words, an inexperienced but resourceful soldier may find himself taking independent decisions.' He stopped and looked interrogatively at the Sergeant Major.

'Yes, Lieutenant Lamb, sir.' The words were strangled at birth.

'So make sure he has a proper uniform and find him a place in my company.' The lieutenant left the tent, knowing that the discipline invested in his rank would make certain that his orders would be carried out.

'Yes, sir!' The Sergeant Major saluted to his back, then yelled, 'Corporal!'

The corporal, a stubby, sweating man appeared. 'Yessir!'

'Take this bleeding apology for a man and try to make him look like a soldier!'

*

It was lucky for Fred that Arthur's company almost immediately became involved in one of the continual small-scale attacks designed to improve the tactical position of the British front line but which invariably provoked a grim Turkish response and little territorial gain on either side.

During this engagement, carried out following a feeble amount of shelling, Fred received a blow on the head which laid him out cold. He was taken down to the beach by a medical orderly. By the time he could walk and see straight, all the rumours were of a really big attack.

When he returned to the trench, prepared for the usual struggle for water and a place for his kit, the complaints about the flies, the lice, the smells, the new recruits who got lost and kicked dust in your face, the latrines where a dog wouldn't defecate, the sun which banged at you like a hammer, the dew which soaked everything at night, he was surprised to find an air of expectation. Nobody knew what or when, but everybody knew it was to be a big job, with proper support from half the guns on Helles and howitzers and mortars from the French.

Out of touch following his injury, Fred chanced on a young private who was keen to share information. He was called Ernie Wilkes and came from the Isle of Wight. 'I'm going to be a teacher,' he told Fred between runs to the latrines – like many of them he had a low-grade dysentery – 'and I'm going to teach my pupils about the real war, not the patriotic stuff, but the things we know: bodies chopped up like meat and left out for the rats. Then they'll become pacifists and if everyone becomes pacifists there'll be no more war.'

'You're not a pacifist?' asked Fred, lying comfortably against the back of their trench and staring up at the night sky. A half-smoked cigarette dangled from his mouth. Soon the misty dew would descend on his face.

'Not yet. But it stands to reason, if every one of us is a pacifist, there's no one to do the killing.'

'So what about this push?'

Ernie answered him with a remarkably clear account of the plan to attack along Gully Spur and capture five Turkish trenches. 'At the same time, we'll push up Gully Ravine and also on Fir Tree

Spur, try to take out the formidable Boomerang Redoubt. You've heard of that place, I expect, taken hundreds of lives.'

'For a pacifist you're fucking well informed,' commented Fred.

'That's my business.' Ernie's sickly, intense face expressed pride. 'I ask. I listen. It's surprising what you can learn if you listen to the officers talking.'

As he carried on, mentioning *our* lack of ammunition and *their* superior bombs, Fred began to wonder if he might like to be a pacifist after the war. He didn't doubt his own bravery, like some men who had to prove it with stupid heroics, so he'd feel fine in himself as a pacifist.

Fred thought of home. It was late June, the corn up high if the weather was right, the pheasants strutting about with their broods, the hedgerows dangling with wild roses, honeysuckle and elderflower. It felt like looking at something down the wrong end of a telescope. When he'd first come out here, there'd been poppies and flax, all sorts of wild flowers, but now everything was trampled, burnt out or dried by the sun.

'I've drawn some maps. Want to see?' Ernie scrabbled at his pack.

'Mind they don't arrest you as a spy,' said Fred. He was beginning to feel sleepy. But Ernie impressed him. He'd bet he knew more than most officers. You didn't have to speak with a plum in your mouth to work out what was going on. 'You'd make a good officer.'

Ernie's sharp little eyes flicked up for a moment, then back to his map. 'You see, what always happens is they enfilade us . . .'

On he went. Fred wondered if he himself would make a good officer. Now he could write, he could send stupid notes with the best of them. As far as he could see, the officers' most important job was encouraging the men. That couldn't be too hard. Doing what the generals and colonels told you to, that was harder.

Fred smiled to himself and yawned. He thought of lighting up another cigarette but decided against it. He'd never really taken to smoking, unlike some men who couldn't think of anything except the next fag. Foxy Ernie was still explaining how everything depended on the firepower before they climbed out of the trenches. In the hazy starlight – could there be rain on the way? – Fred saw the ladders all the way along this trench. Nice one.

He pictured himself clambering up and running . . . what had Ernie said? Eight hundred yards to the Turkish lines. It made your heart skip along, the thought of that. Some of the men, he knew, slumped along like old sacks at the bottom of the trench, were imagining the bullets slamming into their soft flesh: a leg, an arm, chest, vital organs turned to red jelly. Those who had been here a bit had seen it all. They dreaded being hit in their privates most, and their face. Never get a girl with a smashed out eye or nose or mouth.

Funny how he didn't worry about any of that. Most of the officers seemed to take it calmly. Or knew how to hide their jitters. Lieutenant Lamb would be ahead of him as they advanced. He'd changed a bit – even aside from being so skinny – since they'd climbed that cliff together and the lieutenant had narrowly missed being bowled over by a headlong rock. Look how he'd taken on that fat sergeant major.

'It seems like you could run this show,' said Fred.

'I've got an active mind, that's all,' replied Ernie, peering at Fred who had half pulled his helmet over his face. 'If something happens to me, will you tell my family that I was getting on well with soldiering? That I kept myself busy. They'll know what that means.'

Too sleepy to ask what it *did* mean, Fred accepted a piece of paper with an address and settled down to sleep. Just before his mind closed down with his effortless ability to take rest when needed, he pictured foxy Ernie side by side with Lamb, both men dressed in officers' uniform. Why ever not?

Arthur lay in the bottom of a newly captured Turkish trench. He had been fighting all day and now night was upon them and the firing and shouting and screaming was still all around but he could not move a limb. Presumably he was wounded, perhaps dying, perhaps dead. But since he couldn't move, he couldn't do a test.

'Sir, Lieutenant! Are you hit?'

Arthur half opened his eyes. Once again he tried to move; he could feel the dank sweat and blood soaked into his khaki. Dead Turks lay about in blown-apart chunks.

'I don't know. I just can't move.'

'Stretcher-bearer!' the corporal yelled. 'Stretcher-bearer for the lieutenant!'

Arthur shut his eyes again. The evening air was cool on his eyelids.

He felt *The Iliad* near his heart but didn't have the strength to remember a line.

'Fucking hell!' Fred had never been in an attack that went on and on like this one had. And now it was over they were in one of Ernie's gullies and ordered to dispose of the Turkish corpses. Corpses! What a laugh! If you could match up a head, two legs and two arms, then the officer keeping numbers knew where he was. Blown apart, this little lot, where they sat in their dugouts, which were more like shepherds' sheds. There were too many to bury, so they were making fires with the wood from the sheds and throwing on the bits that had once been men.

The eyes of the men working beside him were bloodshot and wild above the bits of cloth wound round their noses and mouths. What a stench! The flames crackled up into the dark sky, throwing up charred or still burning fragments like fireworks, sometimes exploding so that men leapt back. Or maybe that was the explosions of fighting in other gullies. Would the Turks never give up?

Fred hadn't seen Ernie for a while. A man tipped over and disappeared; that was the way it was. But Fred had something invested in Ernie Wilkes. He picked up his rifle where he'd lain it on the ground, bayonet still fixed, blood dried brown, and went looking.

It was the brains that caught his attention. Shining white – like lumps of porridge. Ernie wouldn't have known a thing. His face was like a pale mask in front of them, quite serene. Fred was glad he'd found him and admired his brains in all their glory. He wouldn't forget him. More than half mad and hardly knowing what he was doing, he stood straight and saluted.

'Hey, you crazy fucker!' a corporal shouted at him.

'Saluting a brave officer! Got any problems?' Fred snarled, clutching his rifle and baring his teeth like an animal.

The corporal decided it was not worth the trouble and turned away.

Arthur lay on the ground outside the hospital tent on the beach. Dawn had come and gone and now a fresh sun flickered over the rows of wounded. Some cried for water, some groaned, some babbled crazily but most were quiet.

Not long ago a medical orderly had peered at Arthur but seeing no obvious wound passed on, while noting to his assistant, 'Dysentery. Put him on the list to go off.'

'Dysentery.' So that's all it was, this utter feebleness. Of course he'd known he'd kept nothing inside him for days, even weeks. Shit rolling down his legs. Disgusting. Yet before he collapsed, he had fought all day, without feeling any particular difficulty.

The sun rose in the sky and the flies collected in black swarms. Some men were moved into the tent from which terrible cries could be heard. Some lucky men were carried down to the edge of the sea and loaded into boats, taking them to the hospital ship and thence to Lemnos or Malta or Alexandria. Some were rolled over and removed to burial grounds.

As the heat became more intense, the need for water overrode everything else and Arthur began to feel he had to find the strength to move. He twitched a leg, lifted an arm, bent the other leg. Crawling seemed the best option. Slowly he edged on to his side, but before he could get further, fell back. He tried again.

Every so often there was a huge *whoompf* and crash as Asiatic Annie sent over her daily gifts. No one took any notice except once or twice when she found a human target. Then there was a brief rush to the rescue before normal tasks were resumed.

Unnoticed, Arthur managed to crawl to the sea. The warm waves washed over his feet. His body felt as light as paper.

''E's not dead. His bleeding foot's twitching.'

'What's 'e doing here, then?' Two ambulance men argued over Arthur's body.

'I didn't bring him down!'

'Nor did bleeding I.'

'I brought myself down,' murmured Arthur. One of the men bent over him, good-humouredly.

'Saved us the trouble, have you?'

'I'm on a list.' Arthur screwed up his eyes against the sun reflected off the water. 'Dysentery.'

'There you are. I told you he wasn't dead. Tip him in the boat.'

Arthur lay in the boat with men who smelt of blood and pus and faeces. It was a relief when he became unconscious.

25th June, The National Hotel Cairo
My dearest Beatrice,

Yesterday was the anniversary of my proposal to you. I thought of the garden seat and you in your flannel jacket with the buttons in twos. It is twenty-one years ago but you look no older.

I can't believe I've stayed here two months already, no use to anyone. I can hardly face the wounded men who walk around the zoo like tourists but dressed in pyjamas. I'm fit enough, although the daytime temperature seldom drops below 90°. It's the men who suffer; they're still waiting for their summer kit. Which reminds me, would you send out some light drawers and same socks as I took.

Last night I dined at the club with General Sir J. Maxwell. He entertained me last in Pretoria in 1900. He has still the same smart American wife. I saw him this morning walking in khaki in the funeral procession of the sultan's sister-in-law, surrounded by tarbooshed and frock-coated notables and escorted by Egyptian cavalry and infantry feeling the heat very much, while a Gippy band played Beethoven's funeral march. Afterwards I saw a Gippy officer's charger being ridden home by a white-gowned syce boy who had put on his master's sword with beautiful gold embellishments.

Thanks to the Australians' lack of discipline, the bars, even of clubs, are closed for liquor selling at 10 pm – two nights ago Sir J. Maxwell, whose decree it was, was observed having a whisky and soda at 10.40 but in spite of much prompting, no one dared remind him.

Today I had the brigade out in the desert for a couple of hours. It was a great pleasure to handle them. I galloped them three miles in line – not very fast, with drawn swords, and then when they expected to charge, I slowed them down to a walk and a halt. This was to steady them, usually they are too eager when there is any suspicion of being allowed to charge.

I hear the Berks' wives are rushing out in the middle of September – far too soon, the heat will be not much better till late October. But how I long to have your face beside mine on the pillow. The National Hotel where I am now – cheaper by three shillings a day than Shepheard's – is a grubby old place but if you were to come I might try and find a house outside Cairo.

Oh my dearest wife, how I love to think of you at Tollorum, doing so much good in your own sweet way. I believe it is only your dear mother who made you feel inadequate. I have never felt that about you. I am glad that the village has thrown up such a paragon of virtues as you describe in Lily Chaffey. She sounds like the sort of sergeant major we treasure in the army, although she can never replace the good commanding officer!

I have had letters from both the girls. Gussie's is some madcap scribble about how she wanted to go to France but thinks it might be better to come out to me. Of course she's far too young and irresponsible to do either on her own, even if there weren't submarines to consider. But I'm quite sure you'll share my view and deal with her.

Thank God for Sylvia's good sense, although I hope she doesn't push herself too hard. She writes about an army acquaintance of Lamb's who's coming out here as an intelligence officer. Captain Rupert Prideaux, Filchester's eldest. Got thrown out of Eton, I believe, but perhaps he's settled down. The war changes people in all sorts of ways – mostly for the better – but then I would say that as a soldier.

I wish I knew what was going on in the war. Despite all the generals knocking about here, I only know the gossip or what I read in the papers. Gossip says the Dardanelles still goes badly, and by the wounded we see coming in every week, it must be true. Shells cause the most ghastly wounds. By the time they get men across the 800 miles of sea from Gallipoli, a lot of them are dead anyway.

A Yankee ship is sitting in Alexandria. I wonder if they'll ever get involved. It is very frustrating knowing so little. For the twentieth time since I've been here, it was rumoured that Achi Baba had been taken. You hear more men are needed and yet there are thousands sitting here on their backsides. One rumour is that they can't fit any more on the beaches. If that's true, why don't they try another beach, go up to Bulair, for example? That

journalist, Ashmead-Bartlett who survived being blown up in some
ship or other, put it about that Bulair's the place.

My dearest, did I ever tell you that I prefer it when you wear
shoes to boots? Of such things is my mind filled. I do want you.

Your ever loving husband,
Bingo.

I've forgotten if I wrote that Balaam has disgraced himself on
the polo field – he began kicking out and I dare not risk maiming a
subaltern who cannot remonstrate. So we take long hacks instead.
He shies at every train but rather likes the camels.

Please, darling, don't let your new young parlourmaids touch
the bronzes. I know some of them have survived 2000 years but I'd
rather think of you handling them.

Beatrice stood up and laid the letter carefully on a second growing pile on Bingo's desk. She would handle his bronzes, perhaps
she would even grow to like them, and he would handle his men
as they galloped, swords upraised, across the desert, pulling them
in before a full charge. That would have made him happy. He was
such a good, careful man.

Beatrice smiled at the thought of Balaam liking camels.

'Lady Beatrice?' There was a knock at the door.

'Yes, Lily.'

'The three men are ready to leave. They would like to say thank
you.'

The two women went out to the hall where Mr Gisburne, his
gloomy daughter Gwen, the local doctor, Dr Horsthrup, a tall
seedy-looking man with a red nose and a tic in one eye, two older
nurses, a variety of helpers and several blushing, wriggling maids
were waiting.

'Major Collier sent a message to say he's been delayed,' said
Lily.

The three young officers stood in a group. They were very
young, slim handsome boys whose fresh complexions had been
revived by helping Beatrice in the garden. They had all been
wounded within days of landing in France. One was hit in the
arm, one in the shoulder, one in the thigh. They would rejoin their
regiments immediately and soon be back in France.

'We are so sorry to lose you!' Beatrice went towards them with outstretched arms. The little maids tried to stifle their nervous giggles.

One of the officers shuffled his feet before producing a large bouquet of flowers from behind his back. He held them out awkwardly. 'They're from your garden, of course. But we couldn't think of anything better.'

'Nothing could be better!' said Beatrice, taking the flowers and shaking each soldier's hand in turn. 'The garden will miss you as much as we will.' She thought, *I am a soldier's wife and will not shed a tear. On the other hand I shall forget their names so I cannot look them up on the casualty lists.*

The car that was to take them away was waiting, the driver smoking a cigarette. It was a hot day and the soldiers' faces grew pinker as they carried out their packs. Everyone wanted to help them but knew they must not.

'Lucky to get some petrol,' said the driver, an old soldier who'd taken to wearing his medals, 'or you'd be walking to the station.'

The giggles of the parlourmaids turned to sobs.

Beatrice waved her bouquet at the departing car and several petals floated away. 'They've picked overblown flowers,' she said to Lily. 'They won't last long.'

Lily nodded. 'Dear lads. One of them is an only child and one is the last of three brothers. They're young, they can take what's coming to them. But their poor mothers.'

Beatrice thought, *Bingo's not young.*

Dr Horsthrup and the rector, who'd hovered a little, hoping for a glass of sherry, gave up and walked down the drive together. Gwen Gisburne hurried into the house with the other helpers.

Beatrice and Lily followed them slowly. The sun warmed their backs.

'Those were volunteers,' said Beatrice suddenly. 'But what will it be like when they introduce conscription, as it seems certain they must?'

'I'm sure everyone will do their duty, Milady.'

They stood in the hallway which on this Sunday morning held few shadows. Lily's hand went to her pocket. 'I had something special come today.' She pulled out a regulation army postcard.

'It's from my brother . . . Fred. When he volunteered, he couldn't read or write although he could pretend with the best of them.'

'The army *can* help these young men! Where is he?'

Lily hesitated. 'Gallipoli. He seems to have been there from the first. But of course he can't say much.'

'He is alive, that's the thing.' Gallipoli. Lily's husband had died in France. 'I don't think I remember your brother. Were you close?'

'Chalk and cheese.' Lily smiled. 'I wanted everything to be done as it should and he wanted to break every rule. He couldn't keep still for a second. He was just three when our parents passed on, so I was his mother and what a dance he led me!'

'But you didn't mind?'

'How could I? He was my only living relative and so bright. Even though he couldn't or wouldn't read, by the age of five he could say back to you whole sentences you'd only said once. When I married, my husband tried to take him in hand but no one could keep up with Fred.' Lily looked down at the letter and said slowly, 'I would've been sorry if he'd gone as well as my Sam.'

'Yes. I'm glad for your letter.' Out of the corner of her eye, Beatrice saw Gwen Gisburne hovering. What an annoying woman she was, with her sackcloth looks and ponderous questions. 'Is there a problem, Gwen?'

'I'm afraid the milk's run out again, Lady Beatrice, and six of the men are on milk diets.'

Beatrice sighed. That was the Home Farm getting things wrong again. 'The cows keep getting milked by new girls. None of them stay long. The pay's better in the munitions' factories even if it does turn their skin yellow,' she said patiently. 'But cows don't like change and hold back their milk.'

'So what shall we do about the men?'

'We'll go to another of the estate farms,' said Beatrice firmly. Avoiding Gwen's sour face, she looked out at the bright day. 'I'll get Perry to harness the pony and trap and take a ride round. I can't think what the farmers are doing with their milk that's more important than fattening up our brave soldiers.'

Lily nodded and Beatrice set out briskly across the garden towards the stable yard.

*

Lady Filchester looked sideways at her eldest son. Aslant, askance, thought Rupert. She hadn't looked at him directly since his arrival at their house in Northamptonshire. At first her eyes had seemed to express surprise that he wanted to see his parents, then wonder at his sunburnt skinny appearance, finally settling into a terrible disappointment that he was not his younger brother, George, who lay buried in a grave in France. This, at least, was how Rupert interpreted his mother's sliding eyes. However, since he did not expect warmth from her and felt genuine sympathy for her suffering over the loss of George who had always been her favourite, he was not unduly upset. His father had been welcoming, although pointing out that, since the hunting season was long over and the shooting season not begun, there was nothing to do.

'Are you still hunting and shooting then?' Rupert had asked, genuinely surprised.

His mother had intervened (eyes on a portrait of an eighteenth-century Filchester over Rupert's left shoulder): 'Your father likes to keep up his spirits. Perhaps it is our duty.'

Rupert made no further comment. In the last eight years he'd never stayed longer than a few days and claimed no family rights, except eventually of inheritance, which he could not disavow. He was here for a short period of rest and recuperation – his parents seemed to have hung on to a considerable level of staff – and then he'd be in Egypt, or thereabouts. He was still awaiting a final briefing.

His simple plan was successful until, at breakfast on the second day, Lady Filchester, eyes on the sideboard, announced that they were to have a luncheon party. 'Eddie telephoned to say he's staying in a house party at the Duckworths', and Winston's driving himself and everyone else mad with his disappointments and rage, even though he spends most of the time painting in the garden; Eddie thinks a change of scene might calm things down.'

Rupert's immediate thought was flight. He went up to his room and, without summoning a servant, flung his suitcase on the bed. What fiendish luck that the man he most blamed for the great disaster of Gallipoli should be invited to his home during the short period he was staying there! The fact that he was sacked as first Lord of the Admiralty made him no less guilty. Besides, he still held a place on the War Committee, renamed the Gallipoli Committee.

Rupert sat on his bed. He could not have a row at his sorrowing mother's dining table. Even he couldn't do that.

There was a knock at the door. A boy, about fourteen or fifteen, but swamped in a footman's uniform meant for someone twice his size, put his head round.

'Did you call, my lord?'

'No. But come here a moment.'

The boy, bright-eyed, with pink cheeks, and hair that refused to be watered down, stood inside the door.

'There's no need to look so guilty. How old are you?'

'Sixteen next birthday, my lord.'

'And what are your plans?'

The boy edged away without answering.

'Would you like to be a soldier?'

'Oh, yes, sir!' His whole face flushed scarlet.

'So I thought.' Rupert waved his hand. 'You can go now.' As the door closed, he jumped up and cast away his case. A bold, careless mood took him. That boy's life was in the hands of politicians in London. Why should he run away? At least he had never been a coward. He would collect some dogs as companions, take a long walk in sun-bathed fields and cool woods and return, invigorated, good-tempered, to face whatever challenges luncheon presented.

Champagne was served on the terrace. Numbers had swollen to over twenty since Lady Filchester had prepared for Churchill's ill-humour by diluting the Duckworth house party with several neighbouring families. She also wished for a sizeable barricade between Churchill and her husband who, like most Tories in England, despised the politician, not because of Gallipoli, but because, before the war, he had turned his back on them, and crossed the floor to become a Liberal.

It was not just Rupert who suspected the lunch might produce challenges. But what lunch party of any interest does not? So Lady Filchester told herself, and her husband too: 'Just make sure the champagne is directed at Winston and he'll be as good as gold.'

'I have already warned Pither,' replied Lord Filchester whose dislike of their guest was balanced by his pleasure that his dear wife was entertaining again. It was three months since George's death and she was still swathed in the blackest mourning, including a sagging veil at the back of her hat which made her look like a witch. It had crossed his mind (rather surprising himself at the subtlety of the thought) that maybe Rupert's presence had had a galvanising effect. He was a damned fool, of course, but he looked fine in his uniform – a good show to be in the army at all with his crippled hand – and he *was* the heir. Perhaps his mother wanted to help him by inviting all these bigwigs, even though they were bloody Liberals, with bloody Churchill in semi-disgrace.

So the champagne flowed, the sun blazed down, the ladies opened parasols and chairs were put out for them under the beech trees on the lawn.

'Like a painting *Japonaise*,' commented an artistic neighbour with a quick glance at Churchill. He had *not* come with his easel and oils.

'Bloody neutrals,' said Lord Filchester.

Before lunch, this was the closest they came to talking about the war. Churchill, quaffing champagne as they all were, was remarkably silent.

'He woke late and has not thrown off a headache,' whispered Eddie Marsh to Rupert. Their paths had crossed once in the Riviera and once in London. For some years now he had been Churchill's devoted private secretary, his monocle and high-pitched falsetto disguising a sharp mind.

Rupert nodded and watched Churchill process into the dining room with his tall wife, Clemmie, on one hand and Rupert's mother on the other. Rupert was suffering acutely from the stifling feeling that life in England always gave him. Even though Churchill thought himself abused and derided, he seemed to expect the deference due to a great man and therefore received it. Rupert's own father, however much he hated Churchill's politics, toed the line.

Lunch proceeded, course by course, led in by the ancient butler, Pither, followed by his team of dwarf footmen. Churchill said little, and the conversation skirted warily round the war loan and other non-political subjects. There was a short discussion on the ammunition needed to make another push in France, and just for a moment Churchill raised his head, blue eyes gleaming, as if he might speak, before once more dropping his attention to his food. The word 'Gallipoli' seemed to be banned by common consent.

At last the final course was cleared by the footmen and the ladies were led out of the room by Lady Filchester. A few of the younger men, all in khaki, resolved on a game of croquet with the ladies and departed too. The remaining men clustered together at one end of the long mahogany table. The decanters of port and brandy reflected in circles of ruby and amber. A window had been opened and the faint click of croquet balls plus the occasional sharp trill from a blackbird punctuated desultory conversation. The sunlight had become a mellow golden and a few insects danced in the beams that struck across the table.

A typical summer Sunday afternoon, thought Rupert, and yet we are at war. Spirits dulled by too much wine and food, he could do nothing with the idea. He sank lower in his chair and, holding up his port, turned Churchill's handsome face a glowing red. Then he thought of the men landing on V Beach, the red sea lapping at their death masks.

At last Eddie, in his clever silly voice, said, 'Captain Prideaux came back from Gallipoli recently.' He was addressing Churchill who seemed almost to be dozing. He slowly heaved himself up and fixed his gaze on Rupert.

'I am an intelligence officer.' Rupert feared he sounded defensive.

Churchill put a fleshy hand on the table and leant forward. 'I wanted to go there, myself. Should have been there now. It was all arranged but *they* refused it. Colonel Hankey has gone instead.' Churchill's voice, beginning as a rumble, began to grow. 'It is not over. You know it is not over! Finally three more divisions have been sent out. Never enough, always too late, but I believe we will secure two more. The tug-of-war for men and ammunition is always between East and West. Lord Kitchener, although a great soldier, cannot see that in the East we may win with one decisive victory and alter the whole fate of the war . . .'

Rupert, preparing for the questions he might be asked by Churchill and how he should answer, started as his father rose from his seat and blundered out of the room. Presumably he had decided not to sit through criticism of his hero, Lord Kitchener.

Churchill hardly noticed. 'Victory in the Dardanelles, the

161

occupation of Constantinople is the master key to the whole area. At one stroke, we persuade Bulgaria not to enter the war, and save Serbia.' His face jutted forward in determination. 'The navy must be allowed to try again, the army must be given enough men and ammunition, their commanders must be given proper backing by the politicians. We have always sent two-thirds of what was necessary a month too late . . .'

As Churchill continued, on and on, in rounded sentences of forceful, well-chosen words, Rupert realised that he was to be asked no questions. Here was a man convinced of the rightness of his cause who needed no humble intelligence officer to feed him information from the ground.

Two more men left the room and Rupert had the strange feeling that Churchill wanted to convince him personally. Had some instinct told the politician that this young officer with the crippled hand was no friend? If so, it would have rankled, because Churchill was a hero to most of the gilded officers in the Royal Naval Division and in other well-connected areas.

But now Churchill was distracted from Gallipoli, as he made a bitter attack on the Conservative press led by Beaverbrook and Northcliffe who had orchestrated a national campaign against him. 'No fewer than 2,600 letters accusing me of disloyalty to the country arrived from readers of the *Daily Express*. I entrusted their disposal to the housemaid.'

'It is a disaster,' said Rupert suddenly. Churchill had paused for a moment as a new cigar was lit for him. Wreaths of cigarette and cigar smoke rose upwards and merged with the shafts of sunlight. Rupert continued more loudly. He wanted his words to dissipate the fumes and clouds of Churchill's endless talk.

'It is a disaster, based on a fantasy that we could ever win at Gallipoli. First that a navy alone could take and hold a city, then that an army could run across a peninsula defended by a brave Turkish army under the command of two great leaders, Liman von Sanders and Mustafa Kemal and indeed others, less well known. Our army is led by incompetent, over-optimistic, old generals, pinned down in two main areas. There have been nearly two hundred thousand casualties already and now you want to send in more young men. It is all a dream. A foolish, uninformed dream, based on romantic wish fulfilment. I am going to Egypt now, or perhaps Salonika or wherever I am ordered, and I will find myself an insignificant part of this gigantic mess that has been created in the area and continues to be created, with absolutely no possibility of success.'

The room was silent as Rupert finished. Even the croquet balls and birds could no longer be heard.

Churchill stared at the table, his wide shoulders hunched. The cigar smoked between his fingers. The other men tried to give the impression that they hadn't been listening. Perhaps they hadn't. Only Eddie Marsh waited expectantly.

Rupert stood. He bowed at Churchill. 'With due respect, sir, that is my opinion and I *have* been there.' He moved towards the door. His face had gone very pale and his legs shook.

Churchill said nothing until Rupert was near the end of the room, then he spoke with icy calm. 'You young men can only understand what you see in front of your eyes, the deaths, the suffering, the defeats following the victories. When I was a soldier, when I *fought* in South Africa,' his protuberant blue eyes seemed to search out Rupert's maimed hand, 'I felt the same. That is why I became a politician. It is up to the politician to take the longer view. The sacrifices of our soldiers are great but we suffer too . . .'

It was at this point that Rupert knew he could listen to no more. He had said his piece. Turning the heavy doorknob with some difficulty – doorknobs were always a problem for his hand – he went out. At that moment, he never wanted to enter his parents' house again. He thought that he would rather listen to a cut-throat Albanian holding forth for twenty-four hours on the merits of a Mannlicher M95 rifle over the Mauser M1880 than an English politician clinging to the chimera of victory.

Thirteen

Sylvia read the telegram as slowly as if every letter was a word. ARTHUR SERIOUSLY ILL STOP ON SHIP TO ALEXANDRIA STOP AWAIT FURTHER NEWS STOP. The message had been sent to the hospital by Arthur's uncle. She had imagined this moment so often but not the word 'ill'. What did that mean? Ill as in wounded, therefore ill, or ill as in *disease*? She had never put disease on her list of imagined threats. Now her mind set up a distraught buzzing, as if a hive of angry bees had taken over. It was impossible to think rationally in such a racket.

Things were made worse because she had been on her way to dress a soldier's wound and knew that by delaying she was extending his suffering. Yet even this anxiety, a tiny clear part of her mind told her, was only a tactic to avoid the terrifying word 'seriously'. Seriously as in *dying*? Oh my God. In the middle of the corridor, Sylvia fell on her knees and prayed with such intensity that the bees flew out of her head. An even more terrifying silence followed.

'What *are* you doing?' Hilda came and pulled up her friend.

Unable to speak, Sylvia still clasped the telegram against her breast. Perhaps it was a mistake. She must not show it to anyone, especially not to Hilda. Hilda wouldn't understand that it was a mistake.

'Poor old Captain Whittingham's been waiting for ages.' She stopped and took a closer look at her friend. 'Are you ill?'

The word, applied to herself, suddenly changed its meaning. 'Arthur's ill,' she whispered. 'He's on his way to Egypt.'

Hilda thought for a moment. 'That's not such bad news, is it? It means he's not being shot at, anyway. I'm told those hospital ships are the height of luxury, white sheets changed daily and breakfast of kedgeree and braised kidneys. Here, give me the stuff and I'll do Whittingham while you recover. Nasty things, telegrams. Once you get over the shock, you'll have a reason to rejoice, believe Nurse Hilda.'

Hilda's affectionate, cheerful voice reached Sylvia through a haze but she handed over the ointments and dressing obediently and with a steadier mind watched her friend bustle off. Perhaps the 'seriously' was only a product of her over-fearful imagination. She opened the telegram hopefully. But there it was still. She needed to go away somewhere and think. In a moment the inevitable shout would come from Sister: *Where's Fitzpaine got to? Where is that stupid girl?'*

It was only as she imagined herself answering this summons that she realised that the telegram was itself a summons: she must somehow get permission to go to Egypt and nurse Arthur. It was not only what she wanted to do but also her *duty*. Matron would be on her side. Matron would think it was normal behaviour for the aristocracy. This passionate determination gave her the strength to fold the telegram into her pocket and walk down the corridor.

Gussie gasped and clutched at Reggie's shoulders. Her eyes were squeezed tightly shut but she knew he was smiling. How could anything be more thrilling!

Reggie had taken her for tea at the Ritz but she had only eaten one cucumber sandwich when he'd leant across and told her there was a cab waiting outside and he wanted to show her a surprise. The surprise turned out to be a small, not very clean room in a not very respectable building. She might have objected but immediately the door was shut, he'd started to undress her.

This time he was not drunk and his hands were careful and dextrous.

'My God, Gussie! You're so beautiful!'

Although she shivered a little because the room was quite cold, Gussie knew he was right and she felt proud of her naked body.

He carried her tenderly to the bed and looked down on her. 'I'm the luckiest man alive. You do know I love you and I want you to be my wife.'

She said nothing. In fact she said nothing all along. She wanted his homage, not his love, but she didn't tell him that. She *loved* what he did to her, what he made her feel, even if she did keep her eyes squeezed shut. Most of all, she loved the boldness of their assignation, the breaking of every rule she'd grown up by. But that didn't mean she wanted to *marry* him, Reginald Gisburne, the local rector's son. Truth was, she felt superior to him and nothing could change that.

'Oh my dearest, dearest. If I could only explain how this makes up for the shocking things I have seen. Your youth, your freshness after the cruelties and misery . . .'

Gussie knew he was talking about his experiences of war but she didn't want to hear it. She didn't mind that it assuaged any guilt he might have for *ravishing* a young girl – Gussie had read plenty of romantic novels – but she wanted all his attention concentrated on her. His love-making had been so tender, so *besotted*, although he had, this time with perfect efficiency, fitted a rubber cap over his great thing. A proof of his care and love, he told her in a mumble.

Once it was over, he fell asleep as he had before, just for a few moments, lying beside her. She liked that she had time on her own to enjoy the sense of pride and satisfaction. Also he had turned away from her so she couldn't see his face which, unless she made an effort at seeing the brave officer or the adoring love, sometimes seemed quite silly.

'Where is Cousin Evie today?' said Reggie, waking suddenly with a little snort. 'She's not much of a chaperone.' He sounded disapproving.

'Sylvia told me a girl doesn't need a chaperone at the Ritz, so I told Cousin Evie.'

Reggie frowned at the mention of Sylvia, before asking, 'Any news of Lieutenant Lamb?'

Gussie saw it was the war again and sighed. 'He's ill. On the way to Egypt. Sylvia's dashing out to nurse him.' Gussie shivered and pulled a grubby sheet and blanket over her white body. 'It's not very warm in here.'

'My dearest girl! What a rotter I am.' Reggie's dark eyes glistened with loving concern.

Gussie sat up, pulling the bedclothes with her. She found Reggie least attractive when he was most sentimental. It was his maleness that drew her to him, not his romantic softness. 'Perhaps, just to be sure Evie doesn't suspect anything, we should go back to the Ritz.' This immediately seemed a terrific idea and she was impatient to be gone from the nasty little room.

Reggie, perhaps thinking of his meagre bank balance, was less enthusiastic. 'I hate other men looking at you.'

Gussie laughed. 'As long as I only look at *you*!'

'My dearest, darling . . .' He lunged towards her.

'No, Reggie. No. We must dress if you don't want me to get pneumonia.'

Once more Reggie was penitent and, as Gussie turned to look for her clothes, liberally spread across the room, he dressed in a trice, so that when she turned back and began to sort the bundle, he was already in full uniform, only his bootlaces still to tie. This was maleness indeed. Gussie stared at him admiringly.

'How can you be so quick?'

'Soldiers learn. I expect your father's just as speedy.'

Gussie didn't want to think of her father at that moment. 'I may need help with the buttons.'

'Your buttons,' repeated Reggie, as if in awe of the concept, but Gussie could see that his mind had wandered. She had already put on her drawers and petticoat and now she began to roll on her stockings.

'Are you planning to go to Tollorum?' Reggie's voice had an annoying hesitancy.

'It's my home, of course. But it's so drear. Perhaps I'll take over Sylvia's work at the hospital.'

Reggie didn't respond to this. 'It's just that, censorship and all that, but we chaps know there's a big push coming up – can't tell you where – well . . . if I, well . . . don't come back . . . I wanted to feel you'd be kind to my pater.' Reggie had become red in the face but stared at Gussie earnestly.

'Kind?' Gussie, who was buttoning her skirt, thought that Mr Gisburne was not a kind man. His sermons were distinctly *unkind* and sometimes seemed to be aimed directly at her with words like 'frivolous' or 'privileged' or 'misguided'. 'Surely your sister will look after him?'

'I expect so. But I'm not close to Gwen as I am to you. My dearest, perfect Gussie.' He tried to touch her shoulder but Gussie twitched away.

'Why do we have to talk about such things?' She couldn't deny he was close to her in a way but not, she hoped, in the way he meant. 'I'm not very good with unhappy people. I don't know why. It always seems just too sad. Mama was very sad when Papa left. She cried for ages.'

'Is the Colonel still in Cairo?'

'I suppose so. Having a jolly time with his old army friends. Sometimes Mama reads bits from his letter and he writes to me. And now Sylvia will be there too, and Arthur. Oh, Reggie, do button me up at the back and then let's go to the Ritz or you'll be gone too. Oh, what is the *point* of being sad!'

Since Reggie could see no point in this either, they soon finished their tidying and left the not very respectable building with quick, eager steps.

Heat tore through Arthur's body like an animal clawing at his head, his heart, his entrails. He knew he was on a ship because he could feel the roll but no cooling breezes came to him in his stuffy cabin. The army medical orderlies, young men, poured water inside him and over him but the water inside came out again and the water on his body warmed immediately. He wondered, in a vague, uncaring way, how much a body can stand. Someone, perhaps a doctor, told him in a nagging voice that he probably had enteric fever and flu as well as dysentery. Or perhaps dysentery was the name for all of them.

At Lemnos where the ship put in, he became aware of two new bodies beside him in the cabin. He could hear their voices and one occasionally tried to talk to him. He heard the name Twigg-Smith but it meant nothing to him. His will was utterly sapped and, neither asleep nor awake, he floated, like the ship that carried him over deep and dangerous waters. But neither submarines nor sickness prevailed and, on the fourth day, he opened his eyes to a steady ship and a round face bent over his.

'We're in Egypt, old chap. Just before dawn. They'll be taking us off soon.'

To his surprise, Arthur found he could take this in. 'Thanks.' It was the first word he was conscious of speaking during the whole voyage.

'Good chap. I knew you were on the mend when I heard Greek spouting out from your corner.'

Arthur said nothing more but he recognised the tall soldier with bandages on his head and his arm in a splint as someone he had known in another life.

A procession of ambulances, buses and carts waited on the quayside. Lamps and flares illuminated the darkness but already a silky dawn was rising over the infinite expanse of the desert.

By the time Arthur was stretchered out to an ambulance, colour had been painted into the grey and he shut his eyes against the brightness. When he opened them again, he saw nurses, all in white, their veils flying behind them like angels' wings, poised in welcoming rows. To Arthur's hazy mind, their hands seemed stretched out to guide him through the pearly gates. Except that he also knew he was alive. But where was the noise: hurtling, turning, whistling shells, the screeching mules, yelling men, bullets swarming, the groaning, moaning, swearing, expiring? Where was the stench?

There was noise around him now: thumping, bumping, crashing as the ship unloaded, other sounds as he reached the quayside: rattling wheels, roaring engines, voices shouting a babble of languages. But none of it threatening.

'We're putting you on a train to Cairo,' said a bright woman's voice in his ear. 'Someone has requested you. Aren't you lucky? Much more fun to get better in Cairo than Alexandria. You wouldn't like to take me with you?'

Arthur looked up at the face between the white wings and felt the cobbles rumbling under him. 'Yes,' he said politely.

The girl gave a delighted laugh. 'If only. But I'll look you up if I ever get there.'

The room was endlessly long, seeming longer because of the repetition of narrow beds lined up three deep and the identical square windows now shuttered against the sun. A row of fans fixed to the ceiling moved slowly round but hardly seemed to stir the air. It was the hottest time of the day, rest time for the men and the nurses. In a couple of hours, the shutters would be taken down and a cooler breeze would float in from the Nile. Cries from the men working their boats on the river and the donkey-riding peasants returning to their labours on the rich soil of the banks would enter the room too. Then it was the turn of the visitors, not many, but enough to give the room a slightly festive air.

Arthur had been in the hospital a week and for the last few days had felt well enough to enjoy the tranquil routine. The day before, the doctor, a tetchy Scotsman, had taken his temperature and grumbled to Sister, 'I don't know why they bothered to send him all the way here when we're so short of beds. He could perfectly well have recuperated on one of those nice Greek islands.'

Arthur wondered if the doctor thought he couldn't hear but, on consideration, decided he was right: a Greek island would have done very well – perhaps Skyros where Rupert Brooke lay buried under an olive tree.

On the other hand, then he would have missed the visits from Brigadier-General Fitzpaine who had come every afternoon since his arrival. He always came at precisely five o'clock, perspiring heavily but vigorous and cheerful, and stayed for precisely half an hour. The day before he'd talked with great enthusiasm about a brooch he was having made for his wife's birthday. 'She is such a modest woman, you know. I'm afraid her mother never gave her much chance to flower. Of course I worshipped her the moment I met her.'

Such an intimate conversation would never have happened in Tollorum but Arthur was not particularly surprised and he was glad that his future father-in-law felt so relaxed with him. In a day or two Sylvia would arrive and then everything would change. He could not regret it, he even yearned to see her calm face, but he was frightened at her expectations.

Sometimes he lay awake in the early hours of the morning when a vicious wind had opened a loose shutter and made it bang like a cannon and the room suddenly became restless with men who had memories they could not easily forget, and wondered what Sylvia and he could say to each other. Where was his assumption of a glorious future which had given the lustre, even the substance, to their love affair?

He was comfortable with the Colonel. They were both soldiers. It flattered him that the older man, the professional, admired and was even jealous of his recent experience in the field. Behind all their conversations was the acceptance that Arthur would soon go back to Gallipoli and be with his men again and that the Colonel would, very likely, follow. Where did Sylvia fit into this?

'Good afternoon, Lamb.' Arthur looked up and saw Twigg-Smith looming over him. The shutters were still closed and his face had a greenish tinge in the dim light. He had been sent to another hospital, but, as walking wounded, made unheralded visits.

Arthur pulled himself upright and felt the renewed strength in his arms. 'How did you get by Sister?'

'I'm the sort of person sisters don't bother about.' Twigg-Smith sat on the end of the bed. His expression was unhopeful.

'What's the news of your mother?' enquired Arthur.

'She's on the way.'

'Lord! What a woman!' Arthur vaguely wondered if Mrs Twigg-Smith would arrive on the same ship as Sylvia. 'How's your head?' It had turned out that, although Twigg-Smith's arm was healing well, the small wound in his head disguised a shell fragment still lodged near his brain.

'That's the point. They can't decide whether to operate. The surgeon longs to, of course. High-risk stuff but leaving it there is probably an even greater risk, so he says.' Twigg-Smith paused. 'I was always rather proud of my brain, you know. Once I found mathematics.'

'I'm sorry,' said Arthur.

They both watched as a clutch of buxom nurses, mostly English, swooped along the room, flinging open the shutters.

'The Colonel will be along soon.' Arthur looked with pleasure at the golden light streaming in. A pretty nurse stopped by.

'You should be going for your walk,' she told Arthur, blushing rather.

Twigg-Smith still sat. When the nurse had gone, he leant forward. 'I met a friend of your family's the other day.'

'My family?' Arthur looked surprised. His only family was the elderly banker uncle.

'An intelligence officer. Very handsome and aristocratic but with a maimed hand. He seemed to know you and Miss Fitzpaine. He'd seen her in London, I believe.'

'What's he doing here?' asked Arthur. 'He's called Prideaux. No friend of *my* family's.'

'Captain Prideaux. Yes. I believe he's going to Salonika,

something to do with Serbia. All very hush-hush. Actually, he seemed a bit mad to me. He's got a bee in his bonnet about Winston Churchill.'

'When I met him,' said Arthur, 'he blamed General Hamilton for everything. Personally, since becoming a soldier, I've kept away from politics.'

'I suppose, as an intelligence officer, he can't avoid it. Look, I must be off, but I just wanted to tell you,' Twigg-Smith half rose, before subsiding again in an uncomfortable hunch, 'that I've decided to have the operation tomorrow before my mother arrives. If anything goes wrong I'd like you to tell her, as one who's known me nearly two decades, that I was in good spirits. You know the sort of thing we write to our soldiers' wives.' He gave a smile which came out like a grimace. 'The mater will probably bring out heaps of goodies so you'll certainly benefit.'

Arthur swung his legs out of the bed and placed his long, absurdly white feet on the wooden floor. It seemed a bit thick to take responsibility for this fellow who'd meant nothing to him even when they had been at school together, but there was no help for it. He patted Twigg-Smith on the shoulder. 'I'm sure your op will go well, old boy. But I'll be here for your mother.' It seemed churlish to point out that it was perfectly possible he wouldn't be here but on his way back to Gallipoli.

'Thanks, old chap.'

Arthur stood on the steps of the hospital breathing in the outside world: river marsh smells, bonfires of rubbish, dung, scented herbs, baked earth, drains, sweat from a couple of soldiers lounging nearby. Being Australians, they hadn't bothered to salute him.

A car drew up. The driver, a corporal, opened the door and the Colonel jumped out. He spotted Arthur. 'That's a good sight! How about we take a spin to the pyramids?'

'I prefer horses, of course,' said the Colonel when they were both seated in the back of the car, 'but the corporal's persuaded me we'll lose this tin can if we never use it.' He pulled a piece of paper from his pocket. 'I received a cable from Sylvia's ship today. Should be here in a couple of days, unless they need to make a diversion. Submarines are being a damned nuisance.' He paused as Arthur said nothing, before adding, 'I suppose she's lucky to catch you still here.'

'The medics have given me another couple of weeks.' He made an effort. 'Can't get rid of this feebleness.' He thought that two weeks seemed an age to him; Gallipoli had taught him to live every moment and never look to the future.

'Hmm,' said the Colonel. He put away the note, brought out his pipe from his pocket and lit it. The smell of the tobacco reminded Arthur of Tollorum.

They were travelling along the Nile, the only car in view, but the sandy road was filled with men on donkeys, their panniers overflowing with green feed for their animals, or men walking slowly, mostly barefoot, carrying hooks and rakes, woven baskets or hemp bags. The river itself looked black, scarcely reflecting the evening sky which was changing quickly from golden to scarlet to deep red and navy.

' "The Ploughman homeward plods his weary way / And leaves the world to darkness and to me",' Fitzpaine recited in a sing-song voice.

Arthur glanced at him. He supposed it was a countryman's poetry but it still surprised him. 'How are your horses?' he asked.

The Colonel smiled. 'For a moment I thought you said "bronzes". I found a man in Sharia Wagh-el-Birket who's got a few things up his sleeve.'

'I thought there were only brothels in that part of the city.' So enclosed was Arthur in his sickness that sometimes he had to remind himself that this was the same city where he'd spent several weeks before leaving for Gallipoli.

'Doubtless my man's a pimp too. He was trying to sell me hashish originally. So far I've only seen one piece, Indian, quite late but he's described something that may be pretty good. Natural traders, the Gippos.' He looked at Arthur who was leaning close to the open window and had shut his eyes for a moment.

'All right, old man?'

'Fine. Sorry. I was just remembering a concert I went to here. Cello and piano. Or maybe just cello.'

'Music not much in my line, although there's quite a jolly Gippo army band plays in the Ezbekieh Gardens. If you don't like the music, you can admire the royal palms and the banyans. Or even a dog-faced baboon in tweed trousers.'

'Yes,' agreed Arthur. Maddeningly, he could no longer remember the line of cello that had sustained him during the horrors of his arrival on V Beach. 'I'll be glad to be back with my platoon,' he said suddenly, adding, 'If there're any of them left.'

The Colonel nodded sympathetically. 'The opera house is next to my hotel but I've never been inside. Cairo is one big funfair.' He sighed. 'Every morning I wake up hoping this will be the day my orders arrive.'

'Yes,' repeated Arthur. Now Sylvia was replacing the cello, just as perfect, just as difficult to recall. 'She'll like the gardens,' he said eventually.

'What? Oh, yes. I get my exercise on horseback but she's never been much of a rider.' The Colonel took off his hat and rubbed his head which, so Arthur thought, had become balder since England. 'I find it hard to believe they don't need our two thousand men on Gallipoli, even if we are yeomanry and cavalry. It's not going well out there, you know. You *do* know.'

'Yes, sir,' agreed Arthur.

'The higher up the army you go, the more optimistic they get,' said the Colonel in a fretting voice.

By now they had left behind the outskirts of the city and the great black river had snaked off to the right. Ahead, silhouetted against the sky which still gave off a murky glow, three pyramids seemed to be more like stone-clad animals than man-built monuments.

'Sylvia will like this,' suggested Arthur, although he wasn't liking them himself.

The Colonel peered past the driver. 'Never fails. Different every time you see them. I brought Lady Beatrice here in '08. She said the Sphinx reminded her of Queen Victoria. Of course the great queen hadn't been dead long, her face everywhere. She went to India but never to Egypt. Corporal!' He tapped the driver on the shoulder. 'Stop here. We'll walk a bit. Wait for us at the Mena House.'

Arthur wondered why the Colonel was conducting this tour of ancient Egypt in near darkness when a cold wind was blowing in from the desert and any shadowy, robed figure, of which there were several, might think it profitable to stick a knife into two unguarded English officers. Perhaps he had something serious to say but, since they walked in silence, perhaps he was merely in search of peace.

The Colonel led them right up to the great pyramid, transformed now from animal to giant construct of the gods. As Arthur stared upwards with neither the will nor the strength to do more, he saw a figure slowly descending.

'Damned fool,' commented the Colonel. He turned his attention to his pipe which had gone out – he filled and lit it once more.

From behind the pyramid appeared a syce leading two horses, one presumably belonging to the climber.

Arthur lit a cigarette, coughed and put it out. As the man got lower, jumping down rather awkwardly from stone to stone, he recognised an English officer's uniform. At last the man made a final jump to the bottom, sand puffing up round his boots. He was hatless, strictly against regulations; his yellow hair caught what little light there was. He walked stiffly over to them.

'Harder coming down. I always forget that.'

'Evening, Prideaux.' Arthur wondered if the Colonel would overlook Prideaux's lack of a hat and a salute. He rather hoped not. But the Colonel merely drew on his pipe. When he did look up it was with kindly interest.

'Prideaux, are you? The fellow my daughter spoke of.'

'Brigadier-General Fitzpaine,' introduced Arthur stiffly. The two men shook hands.

'I used to know your father,' said the Colonel.

'I'm sure he'd have sent his regards. I saw him just before I came out.' Prideaux smiled charmingly.

Arthur felt tired by the threats of night, by the sand blowing in the wind, by the great sandcastle in front of him and by the need to converse politely with the two men. Damn and blast Prideaux.

'Miss Fitzpaine wanted to hear all about you,' said Prideaux.

'She'll be here soon.' Arthur pulled up the collar of his jacket. 'She'll see for herself.'

'This poor chap's only just out of hospital. In fact he's still in,' said the Colonel. 'How about coming with us to the Mena House? Shouldn't keep him standing about.' He clapped Prideaux on the

175

shoulder. 'Put him on the horse, why don't you? Save his legs. I always say, never walk when you can ride.'

'Spoken like a true cavalry officer, sir,' said Prideaux. 'I feel like a stretch after that climb. You two take the horses.'

Despite Arthur's protest, he found himself on a horse with the Colonel ahead and, pipe still in his mouth, soon breaking into a canter. Sometimes his future father-in-law seemed like a schoolboy. Arthur managed to rein back his own horse. As he plodded in the darkness, he realised that he was jealous of Prideaux for having seen Sylvia since he had. On the whole this cheered him because his biggest fear, scarcely acknowledged, was that he would not only have nothing to say to Sylvia but no longer love her. The death of love would be a terrible thing, as bad as any of the deaths he'd seen.

Arthur rode so slowly that Prideaux, walking with his syce, caught up with him.

'Sorry you've been ill. What an accursed place Gallipoli is!'

Arthur peered down at Prideaux. 'I wonder if we'll want to go back there when it's all over. Such lovely flowers when we first arrived. Do you remember the poppies on Achi Baba?'

'Don't. Don't!' Prideaux's voice was hoarse. 'I'm trying to avoid the Sphinx because it reminds me of that headland the Australians called by the same name. If I survive, I shan't go back. I might try a new world altogether. I expect I could go to the bad cheerfully enough in the Antipodes.'

'I don't see you in Australia,' said Arthur.

'Why ever not? I liked the men. Maybe New Zealand, then.'

Arthur remembered that one of the irritations of Prideaux was that he was never serious. 'Haven't you got estates to inherit?'

'In England. Oh, yes. Estates to inherit. A title!' His voice sounded so bitter and angry that Arthur pulled up his horse and tried to make out his face in the darkness. 'England's rotten! Rotten! Not the men but the rabble who run it. I don't know how you bear it!' He began to beat up the sand with a cane he held in his left hand.

'I don't know the men who run it,' said Arthur.

'You're lucky.' Prideaux began to walk quickly. Arthur kicked his horse because he didn't want to feel any sympathy with Prideaux.

Neither man said any more, until the bright lights of the Mena House appeared like a ship on a dark sea. Soon they could hear music. Prideaux stopped. 'I don't think I'll come in. Make my apologies. Good luck.'

'What about the other horse?'

'The syce will take it.'

Arthur slipped off his horse and felt his legs buckle as they hit the ground. He didn't feel much like going into the Mena House either. He watched Prideaux mount the other horse and ride away.

Sylvia stood at the rails of the ship as it moved slowly and noisily into Alexandria. The wind dropped, died altogether and she felt an enormous wave of heat engulf her body. She put up her hand and touched with relief her naked neck. Bobbing her hair had been her last and best decision before leaving England. Even Gussie had been shocked, exclaiming, 'What will Arthur think!'

What would Arthur think?

Released from its coiled weight her hair had turned out to be quite curly and looked much fairer than it had before. Staring at the little mirror in her cabin, Sylvia liked the sharp boyish look of herself.

'You'll be able to recognise him soon.' Sylvia turned to the strange swathed figure at her side. This was Mrs Twigg-Smith who wore a hat tied with a long scarf over a long baggy topcoat all in shades of beige. She had informed Sylvia that it was a good colour for repelling heat. Early on in the voyage she had discovered everything about Sylvia, culminating in her joyful announcement that her son and Arthur had been at prep school together.

'There're so very many men in uniform,' said Sylvia with a sense of panic. She had received a telegram on board saying her father planned to meet her. But how would they find each other? Perhaps *he* wouldn't recognise her.

'Oh, look, a camel!' cried Mrs Twigg-Smith. Actually, there was a whole train of camels, their noses lifted disdainfully. The ship suddenly seemed to be coming in faster and Sylvia felt her heart keeping pace with the engine. The harbour was very busy, from small boats, with men selling oranges, to huge steamers, mostly moored but one passed them, its deck crowded with soldiers, singing 'La Marseillaise'.

'French,' said Mrs Twigg-Smith with satisfaction. 'An excellent army and with plenty of guns, I'm told. More than us anyway.' She sighed, and the loose material round her face puffed out. 'If only Roderick wasn't wounded, this could be a magnificent holiday.'

Sylvia stared at her companion. Surely she should not talk like that when there was a war on and young men dying every day, even those French soldiers dressed in blue whom she so admired. But perhaps this was merely a way of keeping calm and carrying on, which Sylvia had not yet mastered.

The journey which had begun in Marseille with a strike and a three-day wait, had tried her patience terribly. When they did set sail, she felt convinced that Arthur was already dead and began to worry, in what even she understood to be a neurotic way, how she would find mourning black in Cairo. In such anxiety she had been easy prey for Mrs Twigg-Smith who held her hand and told her that she was very brave, while trying to play down her own invincible optimism. 'My trunks,' she told Sylvia, 'are filled with the sort of nourishing treats I have been sending to Roderick since he was a child. His father, the late Mr Twigg-Smith, enjoyed them too when he was posted to Russia.'

Sylvia had let the stories, not uninteresting, wash over and had even been glad of Mrs Twigg-Smith for, after all, it meant she did not have to talk to other passengers – two dentists, one clerk and a collection of very young officers. But now they had arrived, she feared Mrs Twigg-Smith would be a liability, and only had room in her anxious mind to feel slightly guilty.

The ship docked to a wild uprising of figures as if an ant hill had been poked, and Sylvia immediately spotted her father. With a huge surge of love, she pronounced 'There he is!' to the hot air, to Mrs Twigg-Smith. There he was, tall, direct, smartly turned out in his summer uniform, with an ADC at his side and a swirl of robed men offering him their services, but kept at a respectful distance – presumably by the ADC.

This ADC, Sylvia noted, was extremely thin, with ears that stuck out on either side of his cap and restless legs like a grass-hopper's.

'Where? Where?' asked Mrs Twigg-Smith.

Sylvia didn't really blame her for latching on. She could join whatever transport her father had provided. Arthur and her son had not only been to the same school but were now both in hospital, she understood, if not the same one. 'There.' She pointed. 'With the stick-like officer beside him.'

The Colonel stared at the ship, now being moored with a lot of hullabaloo, and wondered why he had not allowed Beatrice to make the journey out. The heat, of course, and torpedoes too, were the reasons, but the idea that he might have been looking for her at the rail, instead of Sylvia, made him feel quite sick.

'I haven't seen her yet, sir,' said Arthur, at his side.

'No. Not yet.' He would get over this sense of loss. It struck the Colonel, who was not usually introspective, that perhaps he had not wanted Beatrice with him because it would have meant another farewell with her.

Passengers started coming down the steps angled sideways against the ship.

The Colonel found himself watching an elderly lady, dressed like a beige Bedouin, accompanied by a schoolgirl.

When she reached the bottom of the steps, this schoolgirl crammed on her straw hat and began running in their direction, forcing her way through the crowds.

'Oh lord,' exclaimed the Colonel, 'I think it's Sylvia.'

Arthur took two or three steps backwards.

'Father!' cried Sylvia. She was a child again, leaping into the big soldier-daddy's arms.

Oh, if only it had been Beatrice! The Colonel hugged his daughter and felt how thin she was and smelled strong shampoo on her hair.

'What have you done to your hair?' he said, his deep voice in Sylvia's ears.

She sprang back excitedly, took off her hat and shook her pale hair in the brilliant sun. 'Isn't it wonderful! I gave it to the orphans and widows.' Her voice rang out in its clear English accents. She looked adoringly at her father. It was as if she had lost and found him again.

'I expect it's very modern,' said the Colonel, trying to look at her lovingly but still not quite able to exorcise Beatrice's ghost.

'Oh, yes,' agreed Sylvia, smiling. 'Do we go to Cairo by car or train or camel?'

'But you haven't said hello to Lamb!' Both father and daughter looked shocked.

'How could I—' began Sylvia, before being interrupted by the tall, thin ADC with the sticking-out ears.

'Hello, Sylvia.' He took off his sun helmet and put it under his arm. His hair had been cut inches above his ears. His skin was a yellowish colour and drawn smooth and tight over his face, in particular over his nose, so that it looked as prominent as that dead man Sylvia had considered in the hospital. Her face expressed bewilderment.

'He's not very strong,' said the Colonel. He shifted about them both and looked as if he wanted to run.

'Oh, I am,' said Arthur, prolonging the moment. He thought of the time when Babcock had died and it seemed much like this.

'Arthur.' Sylvia's voice was an appeal, as if everything could be different. It had been a very long voyage and she'd lived in her imagination for months. The sun beat down and the crowds rushed upon them and Arthur wiped his face. It seemed possible that he would faint.

'I was expecting to *nurse* you,' said Sylvia helplessly. 'I can't tell you how difficult it was to get out of the VAD.'

'I'm sorry to disappoint you.' Arthur gave a stiff little smile.

'How stupid I am!' Sylvia put forward her hand as if to take his but then lost her nerve.

'What's this now?' muttered the Colonel.

Relieved, Sylvia looked where he was staring. 'Oh, that's Mrs Twigg-Smith.'

The lady, undaunted, bustled towards them, a large basket over her arm, a guard of porters vying unavailingly for her favour. She planted herself in front of the Colonel and lifted the veil on her hat.

'I'm so very glad to make your acquaintance, General Fitzpaine. Your daughter and I have become great pals over the last days. And this must be Captain Lamb.'

'Lieutenant,' corrected Arthur automatically.

Sylvia, recognising the necessity for social behaviour, smiled as her mother might have done. 'This is Mrs Twigg-Smith. We met on the voyage.'

'She of the chartreuse wine,' said Arthur and gave something between a hiccough and a sob.

Luckily the noise was so loud that no one heard. The Colonel shook Mrs Twigg-Smith's hand kindly. 'How do you do? Looked after my girl, did you?'

Taking Arthur a little aside, Sylvia whispered. 'She's fine really. She says you were at school with her son.'

'Yes, I was.' The heat was mounting. Arthur wiped his face before groaning. 'What can we do?'

'Catch a train, I suppose. What do you mean?' Sylvia was not prepared for this – for many things, but not this preoccupied groaning.

'It's ghastly.' Arthur put his helmet back on.

Sylvia imagined all sorts of things, but really it was beyond her. She frowned into the crowd before absent-mindedly accepting a bottle off a dirty boy in rags who began to shout.

'He's dead,' said Arthur, taking the bottle and giving it back to the boy who continued to shout. 'Captain Twigg-Smith. Her son. Yesterday. Under the surgeon's knife. I didn't know for certain you were with her.'

Meanwhile Mrs Twigg-Smith and the Colonel were making polite conversation, despite the trying surroundings. The Colonel, who knew about poor Twigg-Smith's death, did not feel it his duty to pass on the information. _

Arthur and Sylvia gazed at each other. It was the first time they had done so. Perhaps they could recognise each other and become lovers again. But what were they to do with Mrs Twigg-Smith?

'I will tell her,' said Arthur.

'Poor you,' said Sylvia. 'Did you like him?'

'I scarcely knew him,' said Arthur. 'I think he liked me.' As a soldier, he approached Mrs Twigg-Smith and drew her aside. It was absurd, of course: the milling populace, the sweating faces of every race, the Egyptians, Nubians, Sudanese, Indians, English, Australian, French, Maoris, Sikhs, Gurkhas, New Zealanders, the eager optimistic woman, the sick young soldier with his beautiful fiancée who'd turned into a boy. Arthur said the words of death with feeling; it was his duty. Mrs Twigg-Smith did not weep nor wail, but suddenly became smaller. She lost a foot in a minute,

Sylvia thought, and then they all went off to catch a train where the Colonel's real ADC was waiting to be helpful.

'How dreadful,' said Sylvia when she was close to Arthur for a minute, 'to have to tell her that.'

'It was a shock when I realised who she was. That's all. But we knew she might be on the ship.' Arthur said nothing more but looked at Sylvia calmly and she understood that, in the scheme of things, or the scheme of things that was now his life, telling Mrs Twigg-Smith, a widow, that her only and beloved son was dead, was not so very dreadful.

'I can't believe I'm really here,' said Sylvia.

'You'll believe all right if any more people force their way into this carriage.'

'Oh, Arthur!' Sylvia took his thin hand and squeezed it as if she would pass over all her healthy energy. 'Where's your watch?' she asked suddenly.

'It slipped off my wrist, I suppose,' answered Arthur indifferently. Noticing Sylvia's concerned expression, he remembered that he'd told her once that it had been his father's. 'I always thought I'd be upset if it went but now I find it doesn't bother me.'

Fourteen

Fred was writing a letter to his sister, Lily:

*We are stuck in the same place in the same trenches, doing the
same thing – NOTHING. This is my day – 'stand to' an hour
before dawn at 4.30, then sleep again (if the flies will let you) till
8 o'clock when you get up and make breakfast. The eating is a race
with the flies who love jam. You then try to do nothing comfortably
(not easy with the flies) until 10.20 when the platoon is inspected.
Then you can really get down to doing nothing, apart from a few
more fly-fights over snacks, until 8 p.m. when you watch the stars
coming up before going to sleep.*

Fred put down his pencil. He was pleased with the writing,
although the message was not quite true. Occasionally, his
platoon was sent out under the replacement for Lamb, Lieutenant
Doubtfire, who was still pink-faced and healthy with a girlish,
turned-up nose, to test the Turkish defences. These trenches
snaked their way up and along the contours of Achi Baba, and
beyond that, more fortifications barred the way inland. The Allies
were no closer to reaching Constantinople than they had been
on 25th April, just hotter and sicker – those that weren't dead
or wounded. It had taken Doubtfire some time to recognise the
situation.

He had persuaded his commanding officer that a night reconnaissance would be a good idea. Fred volunteered out of sheer
boredom. Besides, he was one of the fittest men in the company.
Ignoring his fellow soldiers' ribaldry, he had rigged up an eating
net with which he enveloped himself before opening a tin – never
bully beef which he distrusted and was often liquefied to a poisonous soup by the heat. Most of his food he scrounged off officers by

doing them some menial service – he was never proud. Hearing tortoises were a speciality in the French cuisine, he tried for himself. But it was too difficult getting off the shell and it made him unpopular with the other men, some of whom kept tortoises as racehorses – a race could fill hours of time.

The reconnaissance had been a farce, since there was no moon and they could see nothing. But it had felt good to move forward. Doubtfire was disappointed so Fred suggested they had another go with a five o'clock start. 'Dawn is the time, sir. Johnny Turk's still nodding and we might be able to lob in a few bombs.' They'd all become quite expert in making bombs out of tins, gunpowder and a fuse. The trick was getting the fuse short enough to explode in the enemy's face but not so short it blew off your hand before you threw it. If you went the other way and opted for a longer fuse, the chances were the Turk would pick it up and throw it back, although he might blow off his own hand in the process. The dawn raid had been put off when the lieutenant got his first experience of the runs.

Fred picked up the letter. Nothing to suggest danger, yet men still got picked off by snipers or hit by random shelling. Sometimes he remembered Ernie and pictured his clever brains spilled out of his smashed skull. The worst thing was that he had lost the address Ernie had given him so could never contact his family as he'd promised. How carefully Ernie had studied and how well he had understood the business of war! Yet he had been a mere private.

He could tell Lil about his reading. His mates called him the dustbin; anything with words on it was welcome: cake tins, official forms, newspaper, books, whole or torn. He'd had to put a hold on Bibles, though, after he got given ten in a day – dead men, nor some living neither, didn't need Bibles. The long nights and the stars – they were breaking through the darkness at that moment – had taught Fred more respect. He liked the idea of a great all-powerful God looking down on him, even if some of the things he had to see were disgusting. He didn't blame Him for that. Oh, no. The blame must be laid fair and square at the feet of men. You couldn't even blame the Turks because, after all, it was their country being attacked. Who wouldn't defend their own country? They were clean, hard fighters.

The God Fred imagined on Gallipoli was quite different to the one Lily had tried to teach him as a child in Dorset. That was a repressive, carping sort of God that made him instinctively rebellious. Lying in his little corner of the trench, not too uncomfortable with his overcoat over sandbags, he stared out into the great space and imagined a universal being who had created the whole world, man, beast, fish, tree, mountain, sea, and wanted nothing more than perfect harmony.

Words, thought Fred, in some words there is harmony. Harmony, harmony, harmony. That wasn't such a bad word. Harmony. Harmony. Harmony. Shutting his eyes, he drifted off.

'Glad to see you looking so active, old chap! And this young fellow too!'

The important general, a monocle in one eye, and long drooping moustaches, stared approvingly at the Colonel and Arthur who sat on the other side of a table heavy with cut glass and highly polished silver. The Colonel, who had invited to the club this eminent colleague from the Boer War, thought of replying, 'We old soldiers must stick together,' but knew this would not please his guest. Although ten years older, the general had not retired and therefore had proceeded further up the army ladder; he had spent the last decade in an office job in London. For reasons of army protocol, he had been given the responsibility for leading a new front on Gallipoli.

'Thank you, General,' said the Colonel. 'Riding keeps me fit.'

'You cavalry men are all the same. Never happy unless you're on a horse. What are you going to do on Gallipoli, eh? Or are you hoping to fight round here?' Without waiting for an answer, the general, who'd had two whiskies before they sat down, turned to Arthur. 'So you're taking on Fitzpaine's daughter, what? Brave man. But then I hear you are a brave man. Got some news for you.'

Arthur was appalled by the general's confident, hectoring manner. Was this the man who must break the deadlock at Gallipoli? 'Gallipoli is full of brave men,' he said, 'many of them lie under its earth.'

The general looked momentarily nonplussed by this unnecessarily realistic comment before continuing jovially, 'The British Army recognises bravery and I've been given permission to tell you that you will be receiving notification of your commission as a captain.'

An enormous flood of pleasure swept over Arthur, turning his still yellowish face a healthy red. He was surprised and embarrassed that he should care so much and barely managed a muttered 'Thank you, sir.'

'We need you young men. Not usual army material, maybe, but courageous enough to serve your country well. Met a headmaster chappie the other day. Told me what he'd said to his boys: "If a man cannot be useful to his country, he is better dead." Going back soon, are you?'

'Next week, sir. To Helles.'

'Hum. Hum.' He turned to the Colonel. 'And you, dear fellow?'

'I expect that depends on you,' said the Colonel, drily. 'There're thousands of well-trained men waiting here, doing nothing. We've been here for three months.'

'Always the eager soldier.' The general gave another laugh. 'You believe territorials can be well-trained, I surmise?'

The Colonel leant forward intensely and it became clear that he wanted only one thing out of this evening. 'The Second Mounted Division are the true yeoman stock of old England with hearts of oak, every one of them, whether landowner, or groom, bailiff or ploughman, clerk or manager. I've known many in my own brigade since they were boys, trained them myself. They're as good as any fighting force in the army.'

The general leant back in his chair and Arthur found himself hating his patronising, weak face. 'Quite an advocate. Should be in the courts, eh. I expect you've heard the news then?' He half winked at Arthur.

'No, sir.' Young lieutenants on sick leave shouldn't have ears. He had a second release of glowing pride as he remembered he was to be a captain.

'There have been speculations on the reason for your arrival,' said the Colonel, losing none of his intensity.

'Yes, yes. Everyone will know soon enough, although not our enemy, I trust. Ha!'

Arthur suddenly caught an expression of appeal in the bulbous eyes of the general and it struck him with unexpected intuition that the man was frightened of what lay ahead and all his arrogant bombast was actually cover for this. In fact he probably needed a talk with an old soldier colleague.

However they were interrupted by a parade of roast beef and two vegetables borne in by sweating Egyptian waiters in tarbooshes. It was five minutes before the general could begin again.

'Suvla,' he said, puffing out his cheeks so his moustaches flapped. 'Helles and a break-out from Anzac. Those Dominion troops have a reputation for fighting like tigers. But Suvla for me. Know where it is, Lamb?'

'Yes, sir. North. Beyond Anzac but not as far up as Bulair.'

'That's it. The navy chappies are messing about trying to decide where we should land. There's a salt lake somewhere around. Might be dry now. And some useful hills beyond. Not many Turks in the place, although it's always the same with scouts, don't see the enemy till they're staring down the barrel of a gun. Quite a show, whichever way you look at it.' The general, who was now drinking claret, took a deep swig.

Arthur glanced round to check that the waiters were out of earshot. The Colonel also seemed uneasy, although he still pursued his purpose.

'Sounds as if you'll need some fresh men.'

'No doubt. No doubt.' The general winked conspiratorially, causing his monocle to drop, narrowly missing his food and making him look very drunk. 'Funny thing: the navy want to take us generals to check out the shore. On board a frigate or something. But worried that the Turks might get the wind up with a clutch of top brass staring at them through their binoculars! Ha!' The general let rip with a mighty snort. 'Not so wrong, have to admit. So how do you solve it, eh? Dress the generals as sailor boys!' He slapped the table with his hand. 'Never imagined you'd see me in a sailor suit, what!'

While the Colonel and Arthur smiled politely, the general, perhaps aware that he was heading out of control, jerked himself upright and stabbed a finger at Arthur. 'Where's your girl? I like to see a pretty young girl.'

'Miss Fitzpaine has a touch of heatstroke, sir.' This was not true: her father had not invited her to the dinner for reasons Arthur now understood. 'She's dining quietly in her hotel.'

'Pity. Pity.' The general picked up his monocle and slid it into the top pocket of his uniform. 'Ladies don't do well in the heat. Glad you haven't brought out Lady Beatrice, I don't doubt.'

'I didn't expect to be here so long.' The Colonel sighed and pushed away his roast beef, already curling at the edges.

'All waiting comes to an end.' The general also pushed away his plate and sighed.

Arthur thought, *Two tired old men*, and a line from *The Iliad* came into his head: *Without a sign, his sword the brave man draws, and asks no omen but his country's cause.*

He hadn't been planning to see Sylvia this evening but now he had a yearning for a young face, young skin, clear eyes. Since he had met her off the ship they had seen each other only in public, often in crowds. Even when they sat down peacefully in the gardens under a banyan tree, a noisy group of soldiers set up a boxing ring right by them or a street seller with a tower of tarbooshes camped at their feet. When Arthur once expostulated, the tarboosh tower exploded and the wails of their owner were even worse than his pleading.

Arthur felt that his contact with Sylvia was hardly less tenuous than at her arrival. They walked together as ghosts of what they'd been with only the past, which seemed as far away as the moon, to link them. Yet in a week he would be gone, perhaps for ever.

As the old general and the acting brigadier-general moved out of the dining room for coffee and port in the library, Arthur stood determinedly before them.

'If you don't mind, sir, I'd like to check on Sylvia.'

The general, heading for a deep armchair, smiled benignly. 'Off for a night on the town, eh. Well, Captain. When will we three meet again, in the Bard's words? Somewhere beginning with G, what! Need good men. Good luck and good men. What say, Bingo?'

It was the first time the general had used his old colleague's first name and Arthur saw that he was entering a more relaxed state. Trying not to look as if he was fleeing, he put on his cap, saluted and swivelled smartly away.

Sylvia sat in her bedroom writing a letter to Hilda. She had decided it should be bright and informative, a travel guide to lift her friend's spirits from London's wartime grey, from early mornings and rubbing meths into men's buttocks. After all, she had sunshine, free time to explore a frenzied, fascinating city, her dearest father and her beloved Arthur, alive and fairly well. So much to treasure! Yet the letter had a languishing droop which no amount of funny stories about Australian soldiers swimming naked in the Ezbekieh Gardens' lake could disguise.

She gazed dispiritedly at the dark room. The heavy furnishings seemed to soak up the light from her small single lamp and not a hint of fresh air came in through the windows, barred against mosquitoes.

There was a knock at the door.

'Yes?'

Skinny brown fingers proffered a note. Sylvia read it quickly. 'Wait!' She scribbled a note and gave it to the fingers. Her whole expression had changed. She stood with a hand to her breast, gazed round rather wildly, then began to clear away what lay out, which was not much. She stood at the window but there was nothing to see through the mesh.

There was another knock at the door.

'Come in.'

'Did you mean me to come up?' Arthur stood diffidently in the doorway.

'Oh, I'm so fed up with being always surrounded! I thought I'd go mad if I didn't see you on my own. I mean, really on our own.' Sylvia took a few steps towards him. Her short hair fluffed up in the warm heat.

'That's just what I've been thinking!' Arthur flung his cap on the bed. 'And everywhere downstairs was filled with drunken officers. Not that I'm so sober myself. That friend of your father's can certainly put it away. And, Sylvia, I've got something exciting to tell you. Boasting, I'm afraid, but you won't mind.'

'I won't mind anything now we're together!' Sylvia took another step towards him and this time he joined her in the middle of the room and they held each other in an embrace close enough that each could feel the other's pounding heart.

'Oh, my dearest girl.' They broke apart and Arthur went to the chair. 'Come and sit on my lap. I want you wound all round me. Then I'll tell you my news.'

189

Sylvia did as he told her, putting her cheek to his. The dull room transformed itself into a glowing background for their love.

Arthur whispered, his breath tickling Sylvia's ear and lifting light strands of her hair. 'I'm to be a captain. Of course I never would be if so many hadn't died, but I can't help being proud.'

'That's marvellous!' Sylvia hadn't expected this but she was so determined on the course of love and joy that it was easy to celebrate. Shifting her position, she took his face in her hands and kissed him on the lips. Arthur responded with an eager lack of restraint he'd never shown before.

'My darling. My darling.'

Sylvia could taste the drink in his mouth and loved the sensation. His strong fingers began to caress her shoulders and then her breasts. A glorious sense of relief made her push aside his hand so that she could undo the buttons on her blouse. There was still her camisole, straightened tight against her hard nipples. Arthur bent his head down.

Why ever have we waited so long for this, thought Sylvia vaguely. Years and years. 'Darling Arthur.'

He raised his head. 'I love you. I love you. I love you.'

It was impossible that they should not move to the bed, that they should not undress and exclaim with wonder at each other's naked bodies. 'We're both as thin as children,' whispered Sylvia, between kisses.

'Beautiful. Beautiful.'

They fumbled, they explored and, since even Arthur had little experience, neither took the lead. As an act of love it was perfect and they looked with thankfulness at each other's flushed faces. It was the link that, without admitting it, they had been seeking since Sylvia's arrival.

'I'm so glad,' whispered Sylvia. She lay back and put her arms above her head.

'My love is greater than the greatest ocean.' Arthur leant on his elbow and looked at Sylvia and, as he spoke, he thought, Captain Lamb, and smiled. Soon he would be a captain leading his men.

Sylvia saw the smile and smiled too. They both became silent. They'd done so much chattering in the last few days that silence was healing. After a while Sylvia pulled up the sheet and said, 'You'd better go now before my reputation's ruined.'

'Perhaps we should marry here,' suggested Arthur lazily.

'Oh, we couldn't do that to Mother! Or to Gussie. She's banking on a bridesmaid's dress.'

Arthur decided not to say that he wasn't serious. Marriage had very little to do with what was on his mind at the moment. He was trying to understand the implications of the general's garbled hints. It seemed there would be a completely new attack at Suvla Bay. He had seen the place on maps, a wide open bay with the long range of Kiretch Tepe to the left and small hills nearer, as well as several bigger the other side of the salt lake, together forming the Anafarta range. To the right and not so far down the coast were the narrow beaches and rough gullies and ridges that made up the land held by the Anzac forces. It wasn't difficult to guess that the plan would be to break out with these forces and join up with Suvla.

But what about Helles, previously the spearhead of the fighting? Where he was based. It almost made him laugh to think how long they'd fixed their eyes on Achi Baba as the only way through to Constantinople. Was there any chance his regiment could get transferred to Suvla? Almost certainly not. The men were experienced, good fighters, made veterans by the impossible tasks set before them, but they were also sick, utterly worn out. Arthur pictured a young lad called Billy, not yet twenty, who needed help to button his uniform or load his rifle. There were plenty of Billies, young men in old bodies.

He shifted restlessly. If it wasn't for his platoon, he'd see if he could wangle a posting to Suvla. Perhaps the general could fix it. He remembered a rumour circulating among the officers before he'd left Gallipoli.

'There's talk of General Hamilton being sent home,' he said suddenly. 'But I think it's only wishful thinking among some of the officers.'

Sylvia, whose eyes were shut, opened them and looked at him vaguely. 'I think when you leave, I'll stay on and carry on nursing here. It would make me feel useful and closer to you.'

'Yes.' Arthur sat sideways on the bed. It struck him that he would rather Sylvia was in England where he could picture her in all the loveliness and safety of Tollorum. He realised that neither of them had commented on her decision to abandon her studies for Oxford.

'I bumped into Lady Carnarvon the other day and she's desperate for nurses in her hospitals. I am trained, even if I'm not qualified.'

'Yes,' repeated Arthur. He looked at her large eyes gleaming above the white sheet. Slowly he turned and bent down for his clothes.

As if recognising his resistance, Sylvia added. 'There's Father too.'

Arthur paused before buttoning up his trousers. 'He'll be gone soon.'

'Oh!' Sylvia put her hand to her mouth and gasped; she thought of her mother. Somehow her father with his fixed routines, his early morning rides, his attention to his men in their desert barracks, his daily letter writing to Beatrice, his dinners at the club, his kindness and good humour, had come to seem an unchanging part of Cairo. Or Sylvia's Cairo.

'Yes,' said Arthur, finishing dressing in a hurry. 'But it still might be weeks.' To him, weeks were for ever. 'I think that the general's on the job.'

'I'm beginning to hate that general,' said Sylvia without much energy. She was waiting for Arthur to go now. She wanted him to kiss her tenderly and leave.

Arthur gently pushed Sylvia's halo of hair back from her forehead. 'Did I tell you I love your bobbed hair? I'm the luckiest man alive to have a girl like you.'

'I'm so glad.' Sylvia stared at him gravely.

Arthur went to the door before turning for one more look. He was glad he hadn't told her about his medical board the following morning. Peace such as they had shared should never be disturbed.

Fifteen

Gussie lifted the rectory's knocker, a brass fox's head, and let it drop with as loud a bang as possible. She stood under the small portico and felt wild with impatience. She lifted and banged again.

The door sprang open. The vicar, wearing slippers and a shawl round his shoulders as if he was an old widow, peered out. 'Ah, Miss Augusta. Caught in the rain, are you? What rain!' He stared for a moment as if trying to make out the meaning of so much rain, then stood aside to let her in. He led her across the neat hallway to his study.

'The manor is like a mausoleum, except that it holds the living,' said Gussie, crossly. 'If you could call wounded men on their way to death "living". Mama tells me to cheer them up but what do I have to be cheerful about? Anyway, *they* seem perfectly cheerful.'

The rector's bright eyes under bushy eyebrows took in Gussie's disaffected stance. He half smiled. 'I suppose neither of us can make a pot of tea?'

'No,' said Gussie.

'That's what I expected. I *hoped* otherwise but *expected* that would be the case. I am writing my sermon and do not like to be disturbed so I shooed everyone out.'

'*I'm* disturbing you,' pointed out Gussie with more satisfaction in her voice than apology. 'If there wasn't a war on I'd have come out this summer. The season is still on, you know, but Mama won't hear of it with Papa away.'

'Perhaps you can help me with my sermon.'

'Most sermons are too long. That's my view,' said Gussie challengingly, as she took a chair facing the rector.

'You have sat through a good many of my sermons, I suppose. Do you find thirty minutes too long?'

193

Used to the older generation dismissing her views, either with toleration or irritation, Gussie hesitated.

'How many games of tennis could you play in the half-hour?' encouraged the rector.

Gussie blushed. She had liked Reggie on the tennis court. He ran and bounded, his skin flushed and he smelt slightly of sweat. White suited him too. 'That depends how quickly Reggie smashes me.' Now his name was out and she found herself pleased. She gave the vicar a sly look. Would he condemn her to eternal damnation if he knew she and his son were lovers?

'Does he always smash you?'

'He's a man.'

'So true.' The rector sighed. 'A soldier. At war. We must keep all those brave soldiers in our prayers.'

'There's a new big "push" on'. How I hate the word! More long casualty lists in *The Times*, more long faces.' Gussie frowned ferociously. 'I saw Reggie in London,' she added without altogether meaning to. 'He told me to visit you. We had tea at the Ritz. It's quite the place.'

'So I should imagine.' The rector picked up his pipe, then put it down again. 'He has not been down here. But then I have not been up to London.'

'You have your sermons,' said Gussie, flustered. She looked about for help. 'And your books.' Indeed the walls were lined with bookcases.

'When Reggie's dissatisfied with me, he always complains of my books.'

Gussie twined her fingers in her lap. Somewhere along the way, she had lost the upper hand. 'You should write your sermon,' she said with a brisk social manner.

The rector leant forward and patted her hands with his dry fingers. 'Never mind, my dear. You're young and the war will be over in a year or two.'

'The rain's stopped!' Gussie jumped to her feet. What could there be about her that had made this dull village priest pity her? It was almost too much to bear.

The room in which the medical board was carried out was large, brightly lit by electric bulbs as all the blinds were drawn, and very hot. It smelt strongly of disinfectant, and most men, first entering it, naked but holding a bundle of their clothes, made a disgusted face. Some, including Arthur, sneezed.

The three doctors, sweating behind a long wooden desk covered in papers, also sneezed now and again. Orderlies, also sweating and sneezing, escorted the men in and out. None were good specimens of the human race. Many were marked by old wounds or not so old wounds and all were very thin.

The doctors, especially one, wearing little round glasses although he still appeared short-sighted, were, despite their surroundings, trying to do a good, efficient job.

'Lieutenant Arthur Lamb?' He peered worriedly while he read out Arthur's army number, his regiment and other details.

'Yes, sir.' But soon to be 'captain', thought Arthur contentedly.

The doctor sighed with relief from which Arthur gathered that men appearing in front of the board were not always who they were supposed to be. He had already been weighed and examined and he had no doubt he would be passed fit. Even while he answered questions, his mind was picturing his arrival at Helles, passing by the beached hulk of the SS *River Clyde*, through the detritus of the sea and the beach, freshly amazed by the activity of so many men and mules and transports and horses and supplies and guns and boats and remembering again what it was like when Asiatic Annie sent over one of her shells: the warning bugle, the advancing noise, the exploding crash. Perhaps he'd be scared as he hadn't been since the first days. He might be recognised by an officer or man, a slap on the back, a wry 'Welcome home', before he started the climb up to his men, under orders again, giving orders again. The smell of thyme came to him as strongly as if a sprig had been under his nose. It was the smell of death but also the smell of camaraderie and valour.

It seemed to him that Gallipoli was more strongly his fate than anywhere he'd ever been. His first term at Oxford had affected him deeply but there it had been a matter of the imagination: the romance of historic buildings and the magnificence of the classical world. From the start Gallipoli had a powerful physical reality: the brilliant sky and sea, the cliffs and ravines, the distant islands that seemed to come and go according to the light, the spring wonder of the wild flowers before the summer scorched them all

to nothing. Yet this was only a backdrop for the battles that destroyed the beauty and demanded new and ever greater deeds from
its soldiers. Every moment was lived with a passionate intensity.
Each man lived his story to the full.

Vaguely, Arthur watched the doctors conferring.

'Can you run with a pack on your back?'

'Yes, sir.' Arthur thought that very few of the men he'd left
behind on Helles could do that.

'Thank you, Lieutenant.' It was over. He was told to dress and
wait for his papers. But in his imagination he had already gone.
Only the practicalities were necessary: equipping himself properly
with the basics – not for him the first-time officer's trunk – finding a new servant, then saying goodbye to Sylvia. For a flash, he
pictured the boy he'd been on his first day at prep school, waving
goodbye to his mother – it was the last time he'd ever seen her.

It was noon when Arthur came out on the streets, the crowds
thinning a little as the hottest part of the day approached. Another
officer, limping quite heavily, came out with him. 'Cleared, were
you?' he asked.

'Yes. Not you, I suppose?' Arthur only partially attended.

'You bet your life.' The officer, who was very fair with almost
white eyelashes, grinned cheerfully. 'Managed three steps without
limping. What a buzz! Care to celebrate with a beer?'

'As long as it's not at the club.' Arthur didn't want to run the
risk of seeing the Colonel or Sylvia quite yet.

'Not likely! I know a place where you can follow up your beers
with a girl at any time of the day or night.'

Arthur looked at the man, surprised. 'I'll just have the beer.'

'Righty-ho! Now, you young jackals.' The man swiped with
his stick at some boys who'd collected. The smallest, in a tat-
tered striped robe, pretended to be hit, and rolled over and over,
mimicking frightful agony. The officer laughed, 'Clever little
monkeys.' He took a coin from his jacket and threw it at the boy.

Followed by a growing train of excited children, the two men
walked side by side down the main street before turning into an
alleyway, overhung with elaborate wooden balconies and fronted
by decrepit verandas, occasionally decorated by bougainvillea.

'I am the very model of a modern major general,' sang the fair officer.

Behind him the children shrieked an enthusiastic imitation, 'Hamamodanmajoajenera!'

The Colonel was writing once more to Beatrice. He sat at his desk in his large and square hotel room and thought for several minutes without putting pen to paper. He pictured nostalgically his wife in a blue jacket, full skirt and the little buttoned shoes he liked, first at her dressing table in their bedroom, then at the dining-room table after the candles had been lit, then in the garden, walking on the lawn in the early morning when her light footsteps left a trail in the dew. None of these loving images had any effect on his soldierly resolve. He had fought before. It was his duty. Beatrice understood that.

He pulled the notepaper with its picture of the hotel towards him and began to write determinedly.

July 1915 National Hotel Cairo
My dearest wife,
Sylvia, Arthur and I are having some good times together. Sylvia seems to have no problem with the heat which makes me wonder whether I was wrong to stop you coming. My pillow is empty without your face beside me. But I know you are doing so much good at Tollorum and it really does seem as if we'll be moving off soon. I'll write to your brother, too, to let him know, not that he has ever shown any interest in what the army is up to! But he is an earl and earls can sometimes be useful. I managed to entertain my old friend, General Sir Frederick Stopford the other day. He hasn't worn well (don't show this letter to anyone) but seems to have been put in command of some important new 'push' in Gallipoli – can't tell you where or when. I would certainly not have chosen him. He is soft, not what is needed out there, seems like an old man. But the politics of the upper ranks of the army have always put ability low on the agenda. It makes me even more glad that I got out when I did. And my being at Tollorum has given us so many happy years together, my dearest darling Beatrice.

Arthur and Sylvia get on well enough, although it's not as it was in England, I believe. He is much changed, quieter and less 'clever', if you understand what I mean. I expect you do! He is clearly an excellent soldier, which I'm ashamed to admit somewhat surprised me, although, as you know, I've always liked the boy. The general brought the news that he will soon be made a captain. An accolade indeed. Perhaps he will be the first of the family to win a medal. How I would enjoy that!

I think I already told you that Sylvia arrived on the same boat as the mother of one of Arthur's fellow officers, Mrs Twigg-Smith, and we had to break the news that her son had just died under the surgeon's knife. She turns out to be a formidable organiser and is already running a team of young women helpers in the hospitals. She seems to have a direct line to the suppliers of everything from the best sore throat medicine to the best brandy – or perhaps they are the same thing. Sylvia has already mentioned staying on when Arthur returns to Gallipoli, now a matter of days. I hope this won't be too disappointing for you, although you do have Gussie! Dear Gussie. I wonder how her life will turn out. She has a strong enough will to follow any course once she has decided on it. Young women today have many more opportunities than ever before.

'Yes?' The Colonel put down his pen as a servant knocked and came in with a large envelope. 'Put it here.'

He was surprised to see that his fingers trembled as he opened it. He read it quickly, let it lie for a moment, then buckled on his belt, picked up his cap and cane and left the room.

It was four hours before he returned and went to his desk. The electricity was off in the hotel so he lit a small gas lamp. Immediately an insect with transparent whirring wings and long dangling legs threw itself against the shade. He took out his handkerchief, wiped his face and head – the temperature had been constantly over a hundred degrees for the last few days – before sitting quietly.

He thought of the wheat fields at Tollorum and how he'd meant to ask Beatrice about them in every letter and failed. In peacetime they made all the bread for the estate out of their own wheat. It was something he was proud of but he doubted it would happen with the few men left in charge. When he went back, he'd get it going again. He was glad he had his horses with him, although that thought led back to the news he'd just received.

His division, five thousand strong, including the brigade he led and four others, had orders to go as infantry to Gallipoli. Six divisions would be involved in this new attack, under the overall command of General Stopford. This armchair general had already been transported to the Greek island of Imbros where General Hamilton now had his headquarters. It was not yet clear whether his division would be under the command of Peyton, as at present, or taken over by Kenna who led the Notts and Derby Brigade. Of course they had been given no real information about when they would go or where they would fight. Suvla, so firmly indicated by the general at the club dinner, had not even been mentioned.

They were warned to be ready, that was all, and they would be on foot.

Dearest wife, I was interrupted but start again with my heart filled with love of you. It has been confirmed that if and when we go to the Dardanelles we will be on foot. I don't mind walking – you know how happily I stride over the land at Tollorum. Besides, I don't fancy the distances are great, although the deviation and dodging will make it more. Tomorrow, we'll draw infantry packs, in fact the whole equipment. The men are strong enough but quite unused to carrying. No horses are to be taken. We shall leave a good few men, Small included, to look after them, assisted or impeded by syces. I suppose we shall ultimately come back to them. But I don't know. I believe they are soon to be fighting hard on Gallipoli: enormous numbers of K's army are gathering – a Welsh division has arrived at Alexandria but whether for garrison or offence I don't know. If not the latter then Egypt will be left under the protection and at the mercy of the Australians.

I wonder what the use is of being a 'Brigadier-General' when you're told so little. I suppose we might be told something if and when we get on the spot. There's always such a flap on about spies. I suppose that's one of the reasons we're kept in the dark, although you only have to go down to the bazaar to realise the whole Middle East knows what General Hamilton thinks he's kept secret for his nearest and dearest. They'll even give you a date for the big offensive: 6th August – too late for my lot. I think I'll have

'Reserve' tattooed on my chest. It can join my coat of arms. Oh my lovely girl!

Filchester's son was here but has gone off to Salonika to look over things. Maybe I'll end up over there, defending the Greeks against the Bulgarians. Talk is, the latter won't stay neutral much longer. Young Prideaux looked a bit rocky, I thought, although he did say he'd spent a weekend with his parents during home leave. I suppose he gets on well with spies, being pretty dodgy himself.

This is such a long letter but you are my best confidante. My dearest, darling wife, do not worry too much. I may not go for weeks, or never, I may sit on a Greek island in the sun listening to far-off gunfire. You know what a sensible old chap I am, glory days long past. I will get word to you if we really do leave.

Adieu!

Your loving and adoring husband

Bingo

After the Colonel had finished the letter, he sat scowling at it for a moment. He got out his pipe, then put it down and drummed his fingers, one decorated with a gold signet ring. The insect, which had been quiet, rattled its wings against the lamp. They glittered like tinsel. He stared admiringly before cupping his hands and carrying it to the window. He watched as it circled out into the darkness.

It was not true that he felt that his glory days were over. He was fit; even in the prime of life; he commanded a thousand well-trained men who would follow him anywhere. His face flushed and the sweat started again. The unbearable waiting was nearly over.

Sylvia said goodbye to Arthur in Cairo. Her father had taught her to value unemotional farewells. The sight of his still almost emaciated body at the rails of one of those great troop ships was quite definitely to be avoided. At the city's railway station they held hands until the crowds of soldiers forced them apart.

Leaning out of the window of his compartment, Arthur cried out words of Greek. He was gone before Sylvia had recognised and translated them: *The single best augury is to fight for one's country.*

From Alexandria, Arthur sent her a rather wistful telegram telling her that he was staying overnight in a fleapit hotel run by

Algerian gangsters. He would be leaving at dawn in a nearly empty hospital ship on its way back to Imbros. 'Heaven knows when I'll reach Gallipoli but at least I won't be sunk by a submarine. They light up these ships like Christmas trees.'

Arthur had been very busy after he was passed fit and Sylvia had seen little of him – a few meetings in the gardens, a few in the club. He had not asked to visit her again in her room and she had not suggested it. She understood that he was a man girding himself for battle and not for love. Honestly, she was a little relieved. Their love-making had brought them closer and cemented their pledge but she felt no need to repeat it in a hurry.

Her days, both before and after Arthur's departure, were spent at Mrs Twigg-Smith's command who, as it turned out, had been more welcoming than Lady Carnarvon. Remembering the hospital in London, she sometimes thought it was her fate always to be at the beck and call of someone with a stronger will than her own. But, for the time being, while her father was still there, she was glad to have any reason to remain in Egypt.

It was at a dressing station attached to one of the hospitals, four days later, that she spotted Captain Prideaux. It was another desperately hot day; she could feel her cotton dress sticking to her breasts and buttocks and sweat trickling down her back. Sweat was darkening her freshly whitened shoes. She had taken to carrying a parasol as well as wearing a hat so when she first came into the dim, stuffy room, she knew Prideaux wouldn't recognise her. His own appearance was startling. He was unshaven with the beginnings of a darkish beard, his usual golden hair was so grimy that it also looked dark, he was not in uniform, wearing instead a semblance of Greek national dress, and one arm was in a rough sling. He was haranguing a little nurse and, judging from his slurred voice, was quite drunk.

Quelling a strong urge to run before shutting her parasol, Sylvia stepped forward. 'Captain Prideaux. Can I be of help?'

Rupert stared at her out of bloodshot eyes, then swaying slightly declaimed in theatrical manner, ' "What angel wakes me from my flowery bed?" '

'It's Sylvia Fitzpaine,' said Sylvia sternly and moved out of the way of his clutching fingers, although she suspected they probably reached out more for support than with any lecherous intention.

'He's filthy drunk,' whispered the little nurse indignantly.

'What's wrong with your arm?' asked Sylvia, ignoring the girl.

' "A dark night, where owls do fly, where owls do fly, a slash with the sabre . . ." ' This time he really did grab at Sylvia. 'I think I may vomit. Nothing to do with you, of course.'

'I told you so!' said the nurse triumphantly as a ghastly stream spewed over Sylvia.

Somehow both the spewer and the spewed upon found themselves in a small back washroom. Indian boys, the sons of men in the mule corps, cleaned them both up good-humouredly.

'What we need is a change of clothes.'

Sylvia looked up surprised. Captain Prideaux's voice seemed almost normal.

'I owe you an apology. Nothing like getting rid of it all to restore your senses. Always happens.'

Beside them, the Indian boys giggled happily, their clever bright eyes taking in every detail of such an interesting scene.

'Yes, we do. What about your arm?'

'There is that. It needs cleaning and stitching or I'd never have come to this hell-hole.'

'We'll go to the hospital proper. They'll deal with you and I can borrow a nurse's uniform.'

'As long as I can fill up my flask on the way.' Rupert lifted a leather-clad bottle dangling from his waistband and waggled it in Sylvia's face.

Much later, Sylvia thought that it wasn't just the captain who was emotionally disturbed. She, herself, was scarcely coping with all the changes in her once quiet and secure life. However, at the time, she cast herself in the role of Rupert's sensible saviour, rather in the mould of Mrs Twigg-Smith, and quite ignored her own emotional response to the captain's disreputable reappearance in her life. Mrs Twigg-Smith would need no barriers, so Sylvia put none up.

Early in the morning when the sun was only a lilac ribbon in the east, the Colonel ordered his car to take him out to the horse-lines. He was not a sentimental man but it was right and proper to say farewell to his horses and to the men who looked after them.

Sid Small, the groom from Tollorum, opened the door to Balaam's box. The Colonel entered and found the large black

horse still lying down. 'Caught you napping, have I, old fellow?'
Immediately the horse heaved himself up and, baring his teeth,
snickered crossly. Under Small's watchful eyes, the Colonel
patted his firm neck while giving him some oats which the horse
delicately picked off the palm of his hand. He turned to Small.

'He does you proud.'

'Yes, sir. I'm sorry, Colonel.'

'What's that for, old man?'

'That the brigade's walking, sir.'

'Ah, yes. I don't expect the men are too pleased.'

'They don't complain.'

'No. Well, the war doesn't give us too many choices, does it,
Small?'

'No, sir. You can trust the horses to me. To all of us left behind.'

'I know I can.' The Colonel patted Balaam's neck again and
he responded by shoving his nose into his master's shoulder. 'He
hasn't kicked anyone lately then?'

'Currying favour, I'd say.' Both men smiled.

The Colonel left the stable with no more farewells but continued his inspection of as many horses as he had time for. By the
time he left, walking briskly to the car, the sun was already a great
red ball of heat, making the sand shimmer in its rays.

Between five and six when the temperature was cooling a little and
the glare of the sun had softened to a dull haze, Rupert came to
Sylvia's hotel. She descended from her room and found him sitting on the veranda, surrounded by other soldiers and memsahibs
taking tea. Beside him, on a chair, lay a bunch of orange gladioli.

'Hideous, aren't they?'

'You look cleaner anyway.' Sylvia sat down. He had also shaved
off his moustache, and the flowers *were* hideous.

'My heart is still as black.'

'What about your arm? You're still in a sling.'

'Not infected. No chance it will carry me off, sadly. Tea? Or
something stronger? Your hotel doesn't look much but it's got a
good cellar. How about a touch of the Widow to perk you up?'

'Tea for me, please.'

Ignoring this, Prideaux ordered a bottle of Veuve Clicquot.
'You'd never get a European observing Ramadan. On my way

here I passed rows of men waiting for the sundown muezzin. All right for the big chiefs who laze around all day and then guzzle all night. Not so easy for the fellahin up at dawn working in the fields.'

'It must be very hard,' agreed Sylvia who, although she liked the regular wail of the muezzin, had only recently understood about Ramadan. 'Of course you've lived here,' she said, 'so you know how it feels.'

'That's why we're going to lose the campaign at Gallipoli. No one among the politicians, nor even the diplomats, and certainly not the army, have taken the least trouble to understand the Ottoman Empire. We wrote them off as pork-hating wuzzies who bend over to pray just when they're needed and lost all their recent wars. We always thought once we landed we could skip to Constantinople. The truth is, when well led, your Turks are tough fighters, used to hardship and ready to die for their country and for Allah. And the Germans are leading them; Liman von Sanders is a clever soldier, quite apart from their chap, Mustafa Kemal. But try telling that to anyone in power. Even now when we're at the last throw of the dice, Hamilton is still writing optimistic notes to his masters in London.'

Suddenly pausing in this intense diatribe, Prideaux leant closer to Sylvia. 'You realise your father will be offered up on these sacrificial killing grounds?'

Sylvia gazed back. 'Arthur is already there.'

'Oh, yes. Your fiancé.' The captain looked impatient. 'An honourable man. But he has found his destiny. I'm sure he quotes Homer at you. You can't argue with fate.'

'Arthur is a good soldier!' said Sylvia firmly. 'In fact he is to be made up to captain.'

'Congratulations.' Prideaux sank back in his chair. 'Don't worry. I expect I'm jealous. It's no fun being the maimed black sheep of Tory aristocracy to whom no one listens. Think young Ancient Mariner. But to send someone like your father at this late stage! And the men too, all those thousands of brave men.' He interrupted himself as the champagne arrived. 'Thank God. Now we can drown our sorrows.'

Sylvia, who had determined not to drink with some idea of

setting a good example, found herself sipping the golden bubbles with extreme pleasure.

'Incidentally, I like your hair. It makes you look less virtuous.'

Sylvia thought wryly that she *was* less virtuous, if sleeping with Arthur made her so.

'What happened to that pretty sister of yours?'

'Poor Gussie. I'm afraid no one's taking much notice of her.' Sylvia was feeling a delightful sense of relaxation, akin to happiness, as she finished her glass of champagne. She did not object as Prideaux poured her another one, even though she noticed an army wife she vaguely knew eyeing her disapprovingly. 'So what are you doing out here, Captain Prideaux?' she enquired brightly.

'Entertaining you, I hope. I'll tell you a story about spying in Egypt if you promise to call me Rupert – a silly name, I know, but now gilded with the romance of the dead poet.'

'I'd like to hear a spy story, Rupert.' Sylvia watched the bubbles in her glass and folded her hands in her lap expectantly.

'Once upon a time there was a subtle Egyptian nationalist – let's call him Abdul – who decided it wasn't a good idea to be so nationalistic when the British took over running the place. But how to convince them of his changed allegiance? A brilliant plan struck him: he approached a wily Greek – called, let's say, Stavros – and asked him to arrange for guns to be brought into the country. The moment they arrived Abdul planned to reveal this subversive plot to the British, thus proving his own loyalty. All would have been well for Abdul except that Stavros the Greek was more wily than the Egyptian was subtle and Stavros himself went to an English intelligence officer with the news, hoping to be paid both by the Egyptians and the English, which of course meant that the Egyptians, i.e. Abdul, had to own up that the hare had been started running by them. You see the sort of job I have.'

'It does sound quite odd,' conceded Sylvia, smiling, 'but not boring. Can it be dangerous?'

'If you're asking how I got my sabre cut, it was more this,' Rupert lifted the champagne and drained it, 'than my spying activities, although Salonika's a rum old place. It was part of the Ottoman Empire till 1913. Indeed, the aforementioned Mustafa Kemal, who's the Turkish commander beating the hell out of us on Gallipoli, was born there.'

'I wish I were better educated about the world,' sighed Sylvia.

'I'm not well educated, not like your fiancé. I left school at sixteen. Kicked out, actually. I just pick up things on the run.'

'Gussie and I did go to a boarding school for a couple of years but then my grandmother persuaded my mother it wasn't suitable. I can't think why. It was so correct that we had to walk in threes to church in case we became too pally with one girl. Lately, I've been studying with the local rector. Believe it or not, I had ambitions to go to Oxford. Arthur encouraged me. He said he'd always wanted a bluestocking wife.'

'Silly idiot, begging your pardon.' Rupert had not listened to Sylvia very attentively and was now looking restless. 'How about we visit the zoo? Have you noticed how zoos take on national characteristics? In London it's all snakes, watching you out of their little malevolent eyes, ready to strike the moment your back is turned. I do *hate* the English!' He exclaimed this so loudly that several army officers turned with an astonished air.

'Perhaps it *is* time you moved on,' suggested Sylvia, smiling soothingly at the officers.

'The Cairo zoo,' continued Rupert, 'boasts a vast hippopotamus as their star turn. It has a malevolent eye too . . .' Losing his train of thought, he suddenly stood. 'Yes, let's go.' He grimaced at Sylvia. 'Actually, I'm not feeling too well.'

'But I'm wearing my prettiest dress!' Sylvia laughed. Somehow everything seemed amusing: Rupert's hippopotamus, the shocked young officers, the hideous flowers that she would certainly leave behind. It struck her that she hadn't felt so carefree for ages, as if Rupert's frightful behaviour released something held taut whenever she was with Arthur or her father.

'I'll escort you to the door,' she said, 'at a distance.'

At the door, with porters behind and importuning donkey boys, beggars and soldiers on the street, Rupert grabbed her arm. 'I need to lie down. Where's your room?'

'Certainly not my room!'

'It's too dark for the zoo.'

'Surely you're staying somewhere?'

'But how shall I get there?'

'Any one of these boys will take you.' Sylvia thought that this was what a brother must be like. Drunk. Friendly. Ridiculous.

Warm air, scented with dung, herbs, charcoal, and something heavy and sweet which she couldn't identify, came in on waves of dusky evening.

'We could go to the opera,' said Rupert, adding with a giggle, 'Except I hate it nearly as much as I hate the English.'

'You can't be so drunk,' said Sylvia. She supposed she should leave him but her stuffy little room didn't appeal.

'Just walk me back,' said Rupert with a winning smile. 'It's only two streets. And the bougainvillea on the veranda is spectacular. People come to view it from miles around.'

Sylvia laughed and was lost. The hotel where Rupert had a room was small and, in fact, did have spectacular purple bougainvillea decorating the front porch. There was no one in the lobby so at least, thought Sylvia, her reputation was not at risk. The bedroom was small and the moment they entered it, Rupert took off his sling and laid himself full length on the bed.

Realising now was her chance to leave, Sylvia sat down on the only chair. She took off her hat and shook out her hair. She felt peaceful. Outside time. Outside place. She gave quite a jump when Rupert spoke.

'Are you a virgin?'

'That's nothing to do with you!'

'You're not then. That's a relief. I don't like seducing virgins. Some men have quite a thing about it. Not that I could do a thing about you at the moment. I had a few whiskies before we met. To steel me for the occasion. I expect the fiancé's a much better bet, although there is his dysentery to take into account.'

'I don't know what you're rambling on about,' said Sylvia, surprised to find herself hardly disconcerted at all by his remarks. 'I just came with you to see you were all right.'

'So why are you still sitting there?'

'I don't know.' Sylvia smiled. 'You behave so badly it makes me feel free to behave any way I want to. And I feel pleased to be just sitting here.'

'Ah, well. I might as well have a kip then.' Rupert shut his eyes.

Sylvia listened to the noises from the street for a long time, then went to the bathroom. When she came back, Rupert was sitting on the edge of the bed. 'My turn.'

207

She went back to the chair and listened to him urinating, then a tap running.

He came out and stood over her. 'I was feeling quite suicidal, you know.'

'I'm sorry.'

'That's nice.' He went back and sat on the bed. 'Tomorrow I'm off to see Sir John Maxwell with a bit of a briefing and then I'm supposed to report back to Hamilton. But frankly, I can't face it.' He looked at Sylvia. 'Are you sure you aren't up for a bit of farewell love-making? Can't be much, what with my wound etc.'

Sylvia thought she'd already done some farewell love-making and she *loved* Arthur.

'Hang on, I might be on song now.'

'Rupert!' Sylvia exclaimed as she saw that he had opened his trousers and put his hand inside. But her genuine shock was still more filled with amusement than outrage.

'Oh, dear,' said Rupert with a mock mournful face. 'Now you've sent my male member into hiding and he'd only just made his presence felt. I'll tell you what, why don't you undress and let me touch you, on condition that I keep my member out of the whole business.'

Sylvia knew she shouldn't laugh but Rupert's face was so abject that she couldn't resist. Eventually, she managed to say, 'I'm engaged and I love Arthur and now I'm going.' But still she didn't go.

She couldn't really blame the two glasses of champagne for the air of unreality that allowed her to do everything Rupert asked. She knew she didn't love him but she felt as if she needed this evening before she could return to being the good, dreamy Sylvia that everyone, including herself, recognised.

Rupert kept his promise and did not allow his 'male member' to enter her but did things to her body with his hand and his mouth which she could never have imagined. At the end, when she lay utterly languid in his arms, he smoothed her hot cheek and said, 'Well, Miss Fitzpaine, I hope you don't want me to say sorry.'

'Oh, no,' agreed Sylvia. 'I still love Arthur.'

'Ah, the fiancé. We should not forget the fiancé. He's a lucky man. Now we'd both better dress and I'll take you back.'

*

Later, Sylvia dined briefly at the club with her father. He told her about his ADC, Captain Willoughby, who she hadn't met. 'A fine boy,' he said. 'After we've won the war, I'll introduce him to you and Arthur.'

Later still, Sylvia lay in bed and recalled her evening with Rupert. She did not try and deny the extraordinary feelings he had induced in her. Indeed, she relived them, with a delicious thrill, but she could not understand why she felt so little guilt. As she fell deeper asleep, she found Rupert's face gradually changed to Arthur's, accompanied by an unusual sense of happiness.

Sixteen

Arthur had a pleasant cruise back to Gallipoli in his hospital ship, apart from the stink of blood. 'Can't get it out, sir,' said the orderly cheerfully. 'Don't smell it myself any more but you officers always complain. What I say is: be glad it isn't *your* blood.'

The sun shone, the breeze was sweet, and there were half a dozen other officers to keep Arthur company – on the deck in daytime or playing cards below in the evening. They were all recovering from some form of injury or sickness and knew exactly what faced them when they reached their units but none of them seemed a bit worried. On the second morning, when they were sunbathing naked on the front of the ship, a sailor gave the signal for a submarine sighting. None of the men moved. 'Is it a log? Is it a bird?' murmured one. It turned out to be the leg of a mule, the bloated carcass floating legs up.

'A one-legged mule,' commented the same sanguine wit, 'or can't sailors count up to four?' Intimacy with death had taught them to become fatalists. Arthur, whose habit of quoting Homer to himself had become ingrained, tried out, '*I too shall lie in the dust when I am dead, but now let me win noble renown.*' He also had discovered in himself a more sociable aptitude for racing demon. They played every night and Arthur soon was owed huge notional sums by all the players – none of them carried money. 'A reason to live, old chaps,' said Arthur, on their last night together. 'Debts of honour.'

Once they arrived at Imbros, the fun must end. Arthur had never been to the island and looked with interest at its rocky outlines. He wasn't surprised that Homer had placed the great sea god Poseidon's home under the ocean nearby. As the ship manoeuvred closer, not easy since the harbour was busy with vessels of every conceivable size, including ships crammed with new troops, to judge by their cheerful singing of 'Rule Britannia', Arthur pulled out his copy of *The Iliad*. The ship had anchored, still fairly far out, before he found the passage he wanted:

> *In the depths of the sea on the cliff*
> *Between Tenedos and craggy Imbros*
> *There is a cave, wide gaping*
> *Poseidon who made the earth tremble*
> *Stopped the horses there.*

Sylvia would like the quotation, he thought. He would try to write to her that evening wherever he might be. But first there was work to do.

Despite all the multitude of ships, there seemed not one prepared to take a single officer to Helles. After three hours on the harbour front, Arthur discovered that everyone except him was either heading for Anzac Cove or Suvla Bay. Reinforcements had been sent to Helles but that had been two days earlier.

Exhausted and sweating heavily despite his new servant, Private Rendell, who was built like an ox, carrying all his kit, Arthur decided to see if he could find help at headquarters. The tents and small wooden holdings were spread out over a flat plain which gave no shade against the boiling sun nor protection against the wind, the dust and the flies. General Hamilton continued to be infamous among his staff for his choice of unfriendly locations for his headquarters. As always before big new battles, there were high-level meetings in progress everywhere.

As Arthur approached, a brigadier-general left a tent, expostulating loudly to his ADC. 'Don't they understand the first rules of engagement? You can never dislodge an enemy entrenched on higher ground until the artillery's been brought up.'

Arthur recognised the general as a famous VC from South Africa and was surprised to hear him sounding so defeatist. He must have just arrived or he'd know there was never enough artillery and the enemy was always entrenched on higher ground. He presumed he was referring to the new attack on Suvla. None of his business, of course. What *he* needed was a friend who could command transport. As he thought this the general he had met in the Cairo club emerged from the same tent, surrounded by officers.

His hair, before he put his hat on, and his bushy moustache looked very white in the glare. Almost as if with relief, he hailed Arthur in a jovial manner, 'Know you, Lieutenant. Remind me?'

Arthur saluted. 'With Brigadier-General Fitzpaine, sir. In Cairo.'

'Yes. Yes. Not a captain yet, then. So, you're with us on this show?'

'I'm rejoining my unit on Helles, General.'

'That won't do. I'll see what can be managed. Brave fellows like you. That's who we need. With experience too. Nothing against Fitzpaine's yeomanry, but you can't be sure of men who've never faced a bullet.' He turned to one of the officers who Arthur suddenly recognised as the lugubrious Captain Entwhistle who'd once shared his dugout and whose wife had sent him to war.

'See if you can get this chap attached to Brigadier-General Fitzpaine when he arrives.'

Arthur joined Entwhistle in saluting as the general moved on. Entwhistle hung back. His height was accentuated by his thinness and unpressed uniform. 'Thought you'd bought it,' he said gloomily to Arthur.

'Just back from a nice break in Cairo. When did you get on to staff?'

Entwhistle swatted a formation of flies who'd targeted his eyes. 'Wounded in the leg. Malta hospital, back on the job, leg still bad – so staff.'

'They must be proud of you back home,' said Arthur encouragingly. He recalled as if from years ago the night in the dugout when Entwhistle had talked endlessly in long-winded paragraphs about how the ladies expected their men to go to the front. The telegraph-speak he seemed to have adopted was a distinct improvement.

Entwhistle stared at Arthur, his eyes baggy and watery so that Arthur saw why the flies had been attracted. 'Why should you know? Wife killed. Zeppelin. Unlucky.' He paused, allowing Arthur to mutter his shocked sympathies before continuing, 'Do you *want* to leave your regiment?'

'No,' said Arthur. 'Unless . . .' He, too, paused – *now let me win noble renown* . . .

Entwhistle sighed. 'Probably won't happen, anyway. Chaos. Muddle. Confusion.'

Since Entwhistle was about to leave, Arthur raised his voice, 'There is one way you could help.'

'Yes?'

'Transport. I can't get to Helles.'

'I'll try. Send your servant round later.'

Arthur lay in his small bell tent trying to write to Sylvia before the flies, undeterred by his net through which they wriggled like Houdinis, drank the ink. Just before dawn when he'd drifted into a restless sleep, Rendell shouted in his ear, 'Sir! Lieutenant Lamb, sir! There's transport!'

'I can hear you,' grumbled Arthur, before becoming fully awake.

They stumbled down to the harbour where lines of ghostly figures were also making their way. The noise and activity was as great as ever but for an hour or two the air was pure and fresh and the flies left inland.

'It's a yacht called *Medea*,' said Rendell anxiously.

With all the tugs, liners, destroyers, fishing boats, packets, trawlers and lighters, it took them an hour to find it, or rather an irate Australian major found them. 'You're not a bloody Brit lieutenant called Lamb, are you?' In the East the sun began to shoot up scarlet rays like fireworks.

'Yes, sir.'

'Got the bugger!' bellowed the major to another officer on a small pier neither Arthur nor Rendell had noticed. The yacht, judging by its graceful lines, now smirched white, and gold accessories, must once have been the holiday entertainment for a lucky magnate. 'Come along, unless you want us all to be shelled to kingdom come.'

Arthur, with Rendell following, came along as ordered, although it struck him that these men were more likely to be heading to Anzac than Helles. He'd cross that bridge when he got to it.

Apparently, they were giving him a lift, General's orders, but not *their* general, which annoyed these independent fighters at every possible level, so Arthur kept himself out of their way, sat on the deck and tried to find again the calm he'd enjoyed on his voyage from Egypt to Imbros.

As they neared the peninsula, a heavy barrage of naval gunnery from the Allied ships lying along the coasts signalled a new offensive.

The sailors, Greek civilians, suggested this wasn't a healthy place to be but the Australians laughed and answered that they could easily slip in under the fire.

Arthur, the unwanted passenger, watched from the deck while Rendell, confiding he'd always suffered from seasickness in small boats, went below. Arthur wondered how he'd ever persuade the crew to take him on to Helles once they'd survived a landing at Anzac.

'Come on, Lieutenant,' yelled the major above the roar of the guns as they passed the destroyers and continued in, 'I don't know how close they'll get us.'

'I'm going to Helles, sir.'

'Helles?' The major looked startled, then shrugged as if nothing surprised him any more. 'By the sound of it they're already fighting over there. Not sure these buggering Greeks will take you. Good luck to you.'

'Thank you. And to you too, sir,' bellowed Arthur.

The shelling continued while he was still trying to bend the Greeks to his will. Like a policeman, Arthur held one arm directed to the south. His few weeks away from the peninsula had given him a fresh perspective and he was amazed to see how small the distances were. Yet a man fighting at Helles would have no idea what was going on at Anzac because his way was blocked by a multitude of ridges and nullahs, often literally impassable. He assumed the same would apply to Anzac and Suvla. If the present plan really was to link up Anzac with the north, the Allied generals had set themselves a hard task.

'V Beach! Helles!' roared Arthur to the sailors who were as deaf as Odysseus's crew, their ears bound against the siren song. Then the shelling ceased. The airwaves changed and the overwhelming barrage of sound was replaced by the more particular and individual. The Australians had been right: fighting was also going on at Helles; even at this distance he could distinguish between artillery, machine gun and rifle. He couldn't exactly blame the

Greeks for preferring to set their course for a peaceful island. If he wasn't careful, he'd find himself back where he'd started on Imbros.

Gripping the arm of the yacht's skipper, he glanced at the Anzac beach in time to see his Aussie companions scrambling ashore off a small boat.

Newly determined, he realised that bribery was the obvious answer to his problem. But he had no money. 'Rendell!' Rendell was just the sort of careful countryman to have money hoarded away.

It was afternoon before Arthur finally landed on V Beach and trudged along to the headquarters, perched precariously under a north-facing pile of rocks. Nothing much had changed and he had a warm sense of homecoming, inexplicable to any but a soldier.

'You've chosen quite a time to return,' said the major to whom he reported. 'You know we're just starting an advance, although "advance" may be a misnomer. Let's hope not. Between you and me I suspect it's more about a diversion from whatever's going on at Anzac and some new place we don't talk about.' The major took off his cap and wiped his sweating head on which a swarm of huge flies immediately settled. He swore, put his cap back on, swore as a fly buzzed inside and took it off again. 'Johnny Turk's best ally!' He spat one out of his mouth.

'I'm ready for duty, sir.'

'Yes. Of course. Actually the reports have been pretty good. The gunners are full of confidence. Usual casualties. They'll be coming down soon. Head for Krithia and ask around, that's the best directions I can give you. There was a chap, Doubtfire, who took over from you but I rather think he copped it. We both know the form. Good luck. May we meet on the far side of Achi Baba!' He gave a smile hovering between triumphant and ironic.

As Arthur left through a wall of sandbags, closely followed by Rendell with the new boy's look of tremulous excitement, the major shouted, 'Hey, Lamb! Just remembered. There was a telegraph about you. I'll ask about and give it to you when you get back.'

'Thank you, sir.' He turned to Rendell. 'Looks like we're in

215

time to catch the party. Leave the heavy stuff and bring the basics. You've got a rifle, I assume?'

'Yes, sir. Oiled and ready for use.' Rendell had sulked for a while after Arthur had removed all his money but now he seemed ready to go.

Soon the two men were climbing upwards. After half an hour, when they were fully aware of the sounds of fighting ahead although the shellfire had stopped, Arthur shouted, 'Can you smell that?'

'What, sir?' Rendell sniffed, his wide nostrils flaring like a bullock's.

Arthur didn't answer. He was staring at the thick yellow smoke rising ahead that had an acrid smell all of its own. It must have been a fierce bombardment.

'Gunpowder,' said Rendell.

'Yes. Gunpowder and death and thyme.'

'Time, sir?' asked Rendell, curiously.

Again Arthur didn't answer and they moved forward at a faster pace. He wondered about this Doubtfire who'd been leading his platoon in his absence. He wondered how many were still alive. He wondered whether he'd be given a different command altogether. He wondered whether the telegraph that had come for him was notification of his new rank as captain.

Fred sometimes amazed himself. Brought up to believe he was a stupid illiterate, it took some getting used to the fact that on Gallipoli, at least, he got the point of things quicker than anyone. Take this new attack, for example. It kicked off at two twenty p.m. with two hours of shelling, which was supposed to be a surprise to Johnny Turk and knock him off his perch. But it was so little a surprise that Johnny Turk's shells were soon flying over, and what with them bursting over the lines and the Allied efforts mostly going where they were supposed to but often enough falling short (although everyone said the new Australian gunners who'd joined them were the tops), there was enough shrapnel in the air and bouncing off the ground to kill off both armies before they even got out of their trenches.

It was amazing they did get out but they did. Over and over again. Fred was thinking these thoughts as he lay, wounded, with his trousers blown off, in a shell hole in no man's land. They had attacked at ten to three in a hellish fog of smoke, dust and bullets and he had been hit almost immediately. The question was whether he should try to crawl back the forty or fifty yards to the trenches or remain where he was till nightfall. Certainly no one would come and find him.

He'd been hit by a shell splinter in his thigh, tearing down nearly as far as his knee, but since there wasn't much bleeding, he wasn't too worried. On the other hand, crawling wouldn't be much fun.

Men were still advancing over him but there were so many fallen, so much noise and most were so intent on their brave attack with bayonets fixed, that he was as invisible as a lump of earth. *Dust to dust*, thought Fred, which hardly helped his decision-making. The trouble was that because men were still going forward, bullets and bombs were fairly bouncing round him like hail on stony ground. You're so poetic today, he thought. Someone had given him a book of poetry and he enjoyed the words, if left unmoved by most of the sentiments.

'Hey!' A bullet ricocheted off the sun-baked ground and took a divot out of his hand. That decided him. Rolling on to his side, so that his wound was uppermost, he began to inch forward.

Arthur had been directed to go immediately to the right flank. Major Levatt-Hughes, who gave him the order, had just returned from the front; thick dust coated his face and his moustaches bounced all over the place. 'It's the vineyard! We need to take the vineyard!' Arthur felt his heart pound and his body suffused with the urgency of battle. 'You won't recognise many of our men,' continued the major, shouting, although the noise of fighting was not overwhelming where they stood. 'It's the new army being fed in. Glad to see someone like you. Cheers, old chap!'

Thus heartened, Arthur, with Rendell, wide-eyed at his elbow, zigzagged, heads down, in the direction of the vineyard – it seemed nothing had changed. At various points they found handwritten directions to the safest side of the rough path.

At last they broke out of the everlasting scrub and fields churned up by endless fighting and littered with spent bullets, shell fragments and discarded clothing amid the occasional rough grave, marked, perhaps, by a wooden cross.

Almost at once Arthur spotted his company. They were entrenched near some Australian machine-gunners who were blazing away at a massed attack by the Turks at the far end of the vineyard. The vines were so shattered by fire and so trampled that it seemed the fighting had been going on for some time. This enemy advance, although so large, must be just one of many. For a fleeting second, Arthur wondered what was so special about this piece of land, a couple of hundred yards long and about a hundred wide, then his soldier's lust for the fight sent him forward.

Fred was still inching homeward, cursing, as he went, the varied obstacles in his path: the torn-about poles for the vines, the barbed wire, the abandoned rifles, the helmets, the shell fragments, the bombs, some of them unexploded, the corpses and the wounded, the bleeding limbs of the wounded, his own bleeding limbs.

But he was used to fighting his corner and it was only when he was forced into the hard ground by the advancing boots of his own company that he lay still. He was semi-conscious, feeling no pain, and the ear-splitting sounds of battle were reduced to a soothing drone – a bee in summer.

The bottom of the trench was filled with the hand-made bombs that the men had spent long dull days creating. Arthur gathered four or five and searched for his matches. Ahead of him he saw a captain he didn't recognise standing on the parapet and lighting a bomb with his cigarette before running out and hurling it at the enemy. He did this several times, each time laconically returning the cigarette to his mouth.

Arthur laughed with exhilaration. This was the bravery of the true warrior. Running forward, he drew out a match and joined the bold captain.

Dusk, with its subtle tints of mauve and purple, muffled the mass of men tangled in a constantly changing dance of death. Smoke from the Turkish fourteen-inch guns, rolled across the vineyard like a mist, although its acrid smell, mingled with the smell of human blood and entrails expended over the long hot day, gave the air a ghastly texture.

As the last reflections of the sun died away, the gunfire also died down. It was impossible to tell friend from foe. Soldiers drifted back to their trenches, the same trenches they had left, ghosts of the young men they had been a few short weeks ago in England. Even the sturdiest, most experienced fighters tried to hide their trembling hands and quivering lips.

Arthur collapsed in the bottom of the trench. Apart from some abrasions and burns on his hands and bruises from shrapnel on his back, he was unhurt. His ears still rang with the noise of battle so he scarcely heard lesser sounds. Eventually he became aware someone was speaking to him. It was the bold captain. His bloodshot eyes were still excited, his arms gesticulated wildly. Sweat poured off him, although the air had already cooled.

'We could have finished them! One more push! We had them running. Despite their guns. Did you see how our men fought! And those gunners from down under! We could do with more like them. There was a difficult hour or two, I admit it! Must have been ten thousand of them . . .'

Only partly listening, Arthur looked at him sympathetically. He probably hadn't been on Gallipoli long. He was clearly planning to relive the whole day's fighting, adrenalin still firing up his body, unable to unwind.

Arthur was beginning to hear the worst sounds after any big battle: the wounded crying out for help in no man's land. He would never get used to it. But even in this apparent darkness, if anyone tried to rescue them or just take out a water bottle, he would certainly be shot at. He heaved himself up. 'Want to see if we can bring in any wounded?'

Thirst woke Fred from his semi-conscious state. His swollen tongue hung in his parched throat. He was surprised to see it was dark and he felt about carefully in case Lady Luck had placed a water bottle nearby – not that it was likely to be full. They'd been at the front all day. But night gave him hope. His fingers touched something silky and round. He recoiled quickly, imagining it to be an eyeball, until another idea struck him. Yes, there were two more and several others, crushed. Grapes! All afternoon he'd been cursing the vines and now Lady Luck had taught him a lesson. They wouldn't be ripe but a sour grape was as welcome as a pint of ale in the present circumstances. Attention revived, Fred quoted himself a line of poetry that had caught his memory the day before: '*a beaker full of the warm South*'. There was nothing a man couldn't do with a memory like his! That Captain Prideaux had called it 'total recall', 'visual', he'd said.

Uncaring of his thigh, Fred began to crawl more determinedly. Now and again he saw a match struck, although quickly extinguished, which helped show him the way. Other men were doing the same around him, as if the ground had spawned great slithering lizards. The distortions caused by their wounds or by their attempts to protect their wounds, gave them strange humps and crests and angles. Some groaned and occasionally one cried out for help or for water, which was a mistake as their plea was answered by the sharp crack of a bullet. They all knew they must be out of no man's land before dawn if they were to have any chance of survival. Even so, many could not continue. Then they screamed in final protest, uncaring whether the bullet found them. The sound was unearthly and spurred on those around them.

When Fred was still twenty yards from the trench, his leg, quite suddenly as if a switch had turned, began to torment him beyond all limits. Tears ran down his face. He stopped.

A second or an hour later, eyes shut and once again in a semi-conscious state, Fred imagined a stretcher gently lifting him out of his misery. Another second or an hour later, he found himself in a trench with an officer standing over him saying, 'He's one of mine. Name's gone from my mind. The Dorset boy. Turns up in odd places. He is the only one of my lot I've found. Alive, that is.'

Another voice spoke. 'Doesn't look too bad, apart from his leg.'

Fred tried to focus. He recognised the officer who'd claimed him. 'Dorset boy!' Well, it was true enough, if he was more of a man now. The other officer, a bulky chap was moving off, talking about his men. How they loved to talk about their men! Not that he wasn't grateful for their rescue efforts. No sign of a stretcher so they must have lifted him themselves. Lucky not to be killed.

'We'll get you down that trench as soon as I can catch a

stretcher-bearer.' The lieutenant was bending over him with a kindly expression which suddenly changed. 'What's that sticking out of your leg?'

Fred peered but could see nothing. He ran his fingers gently down his wounded thigh. Halfway down, he reached something hard. 'Sorry, sir,' he said as he fainted.

Arthur found he was unwilling to lose this single representative of his platoon. What he needed was a medic. For a flash, in the way he now thought about anything or person who was not part of a soldier's life, he imagined Sylvia bending over the wounded private. It was the Dorset connection.

'Sir!'

Arthur stared round and there was Rendell who he'd quite forgotten for the last hours.

'Glad to see you safe, Rendell.'

'Thank you, sir.' He looked down curiously. 'What's that in his leg?'

'No idea. How about you?'

'If you won't think me making fun, sir, I'd say it looks like a set of false teeth.'

'False teeth!'

'It looks like he's had a bit of an abrasion and then the teeth have got blown into the wound. Got quite a grip on him.'

With a huge effort, Arthur restrained a guffaw of laughter which would certainly have affronted Rendell's serious concern. 'Do you think we dare loosen the grip?'

'He'd certainly be more comfortable without them.'

'Then find my medical pack; we'll give a shot of morphine and have a go. Meanwhile, I'll keep my eye out for a medic.' While he did this, Arthur mused that the clenching teeth must belong to the Allies since he couldn't imagine that the Anatolian peasant who made up a large part of the Ottoman army ran to false teeth. Chaffey, he remembered his name now, had been felled by 'friendly' teeth.

'I found a stray pack, sir,' announced Rendell, returning, 'since yours seems to have gone AWOL.'

'Good man.' The big man had gained initiative since coming

to the front. 'What were you at home, Rendell?' he asked as he injected the morphine.

'Butcher's apprentice, sir.'

'Perfect. Then you're the man to dig out the teeth.'

The next day Arthur went to visit Fred in the dressing station just above the beach. It was the usual frightful scene of horrors, with water the main cry, even for men with wounds you could hide your fist in. Arthur was no longer shocked by the failures of the medical care; it was just another fact of life on Gallipoli.

Fred, tough as ever, was sitting on the ground enjoying a mug of tea. His leg was bandaged from hip to knee. 'Afternoon, sir. How's it going up there?'

'I've been given another platoon of sorts and now we've been pulled back.' Arthur hesitated. It was odd how he talked to Chaffey as if he was one of them.

Fred nodded. 'They'll be at it for days, I shouldn't wonder.'

'Not you, though. How's the leg?'

'The MO was proper impressed when I showed him the teeth. Said I was lucky the owner was a clean fellow. I've kept them. Might come in useful one day. Cost a bomb, a good set like these.' Fred felt in his pack at his feet and produced the teeth which were indeed gleaming white. 'I've polished them up a bit since. The MO said your man did a good job too. Cut them out perfect. Like a surgeon.'

'He's had a bit of practice.'

'Oh, yes?'

'Butcher's apprentice.'

'Might have guessed. Not that he's done me such a service. I'm not even getting a break on one of those cushy islands. They say the wound will be healed before they could find me transport. Still, help me catch up with my reading.'

'Reading?' Arthur stood away a little and looked out to sea. He'd heard that the German submarines were very active and had recently sunk two ships, but there was no sign of lessened Allied activity. The whole area was filled with ships of every size and shape moving in every direction except towards the Dardanelles. He might have been watching a regatta round the Isle of Wight.

Overhead, an aeroplane flew low, the sun flashing off the blades of its propeller.

Then Asiatic Annie sent over a couple of shells and his ears, which had tuned out the continuous sounds of gunfire above where he stood, heard again. He turned back to Fred.

'You deserved a rest.'

'There's only one thing I couldn't have borne: losing my leg. We kill animals, mercy killings true enough, when they're too maimed to look after themselves. Should be the same for humans.'

'You're very certain.' Arthur thought of all the men he'd seen with one leg or one arm or less than that. He'd never felt more than pity, never imagined how they felt.

'Anyway, your leg's withstood its mauling wonderfully.'

'Yes, sir.'

'I'm going down to the beach. Anything you need?'

'I'd be pleased if you could see my letter off.'

Arthur took the letter and climbed down to the beach. He was still not as strong as he would have liked but as he looked at the other men going about their various duties, he realised he was at least in as good nick as most. Even the new recruits quickly acquired a wasted sleepless look, although at the same time the urgency of the present fighting gave them a febrile anxiety which hadn't been there when he'd left.

Rendell had reclaimed their packs and was waiting for him on the beach. His big face was red and peeling from the sun.

'They've found your telegram, sir.'

Arthur strolled over, trying to subdue his warm expectancy. As always after heavy fighting, he had a sense of disengagement with his surroundings that was not unpleasant. It was not unlike the feeling after strenuous physical exercise but with the additional pride of having done well in tough circumstances.

'Oh, yes. Lamb. Glad you made it through. Hot stuff up there by the amount of casualties coming down.' Major Levatt-Hughes shuffled papers for a moment. 'Came in yesterday morning. You've friends in high places. Although the latest news is that General Stopford's being sent home. Tried to command from HMS *Jonquil*. Even had a go at catching up with his beauty sleep, they say.'

'So it's not going well?'

The officer stared at Arthur without answering. 'Anyway,

you're to proceed immediately to Imbros where you'll be given further orders. Here, read for yourself.'

Arthur read. 'But I've just come from Imbros. And I'm being given a new command here.'

The captain shrugged. 'You'll find the transport officer over the other side. He's a man with a megaphone and a permanent frown.'

'We're back to Imbros, sir? Are we, sir?' Rendell didn't try to hide his satisfaction.

'That depends on the transport officer!' replied Arthur angrily.

Seventeen

Rupert Prideaux lay in his bell tent on Imbros swigging brandy from his water bottle. His Greek servant had twice arrived with a bowl of water to shave him, but he had swatted him away.

Suddenly he let out a bellow of laughter. In his ears rang a line from Hamilton's proclamation issued to the army on August 6th, two days earlier. *The faith which is in you will carry you forward . . .* 'Faith!' Rupert pronounced the word out loud with a snort. The man was a dangerous lunatic: what his soldiers needed was ammunition, competent officers, plenty of food. And, on this particular enterprise, plenty of water too. Water was far more important to them than *faith*. They were far too busy to ponder on *faith* – or should be, anyway.

But off the brave soldiers had gone, dropped like parcels on the peninsula of death, and already the reports were coming back of botched plans, orders misunderstood, leadership non-existent. Oh, they'd be heroes. There were always heroes. Far be it for him to knock valiant men going to probable death. Rupert took another deep pull on his brandy. But heroes don't win a war. In fact you could argue they lose it, since they give those idiotic madmen at the top the chance to believe that all would be well.

Yesterday, he'd winkled out the plans for the Anzac campaign. They could only have been conceived by men who'd never tried to cross steep cliffs, spurs and ridges, or find their way among its dry watercourses, creeks, fissures and ravines. And all this was to be done by night when even the guides habitually lost their path. The gallantry of the Australian and New Zealand and Gurkha forces – men so far from home as to make their position the more tragic – could not save them from an impossible task.

They were supposed to take the high point of Lone Pine – perhaps they had done that or would do that – but there were always

225

more heights behind. Then they were to link up across the cliffs and ravines to the soldiers advancing from Suvla Bay, except that the reports coming in suggested that no one much had advanced from the bay. Or not very far anyway.

What folly! What overweening pride and folly! Yet he when he tried to explain things he was considered a joke, a lunatic, out of control. People avoided him. So what else was there for him to do but drink his brain into a numbed stupor?

Throwing down the empty bottle, Rupert stood, although not entirely upright. He needed a piss.

The air was fresher outside. It must be still early. He had lost count of the hours. The long lines of white tents where the departed soldiers had camped stretched out of his view. Their emptiness struck him as infinitely pathetic. How many men would return to them?

He rebuttoned his trousers. He'd see if he could hitch a ride to Suvla and bear them witness.

'Stavros!' He called for his servant. At least he could access an endless supply of brandy.

Beatrice received two letters from Egypt. It was never possible to know which had been sent first, so she opened the thinnest.

It was dated Wednesday, 11th August, 1915. She glanced at *The Times* lying opened on Bingo's desk: 19th August – this letter had come to her quite quickly.

Cairo, 11th August
Dearest wife,
We are leaving very soon – Friday or Saturday. I am very busy with last-minute preparations and then we shall be at sea for a few days. I don't know yet where we will gather – Imbros is the closest island. It is strange to think that you and I have sailed these waters in happier times. Everyone is very cheerful. Except for leaving the horses all would be perfect. I had a wonderful last ride on Balaam. He was very skittish so we had a bit of a charge. Yesterday I said farewell with a handful of oats and he was almost affectionate, most unusual in a horse of his nature. But animals understand more than we ever admit.
I wonder how the dogs are coping in my absence? I've been

meaning to ask. But now they live in the stables, I don't expect
you see them. I hope young Small remembers to worm them. No
news from Arthur, which, one assumes, means good news. There
is already a huge push all along the peninsula. I won't call it do
or die but I'm glad we're part of something big. Filchester's son
turned up again. Sylvia saw him but not me. She said he'd been
wounded though I can't think how since he was on intelligence
work in Salonika. I somehow don't trust him. However, he seems
to have left again. Cairo is emptying fast. We'll be in Alexandria
tomorrow. I trust this won't be my last letter. You know I don't
believe in too many goodbyes. I won't let Sylvia see me off but
she will write to you after I've gone, no doubt. I have regretted
sometimes that I'm part of the Mediterranean Expeditionary Force
when the whole of France is a battlefield and so much closer to
you, my dearest, but now we're actually off, I'm as excited as any
schoolboy soldier at the prospect of the strange land we are going
to and the strange enemy we face.

Well, my dear, we may have luck, we may have glory, we may
have fatigues on the Beach!

Give my love to Gussie and to you, my dearest wife,
From your adoring husband Bingo.

Putting aside the second letter, Beatrice walked over to *The Times*. It was open at page six where news of the fighting was generally recorded. THE NEW GALLIPOLI ATTACK. *Small gain at Suvla*. But when she read further and found a short statement from Sir Ian Hamilton, there was very little about Suvla: *The troops on the left flank made a short advance on the afternoon of the 15th with a view to straightening the line.*

Bingo would have scarcely left harbour by then. Perhaps it would all be over by the time he arrived, although of course she did want him to have glory, but maybe luck even more. Or had he meant that the luck was to bring him glory?

Too restless to read the second letter and too restless to settle to anything else, Beatrice decided to visit the abandoned dogs. It was raining a little so she picked up a heavily belted mackintosh and a wide hat and umbrella from the hallway. Bingo would not have admired the outfit. She tried to make herself smile. The house was very quiet. In the last few days they had had no new patients.

227

It seemed the supply was drying up from France where the men, as far as she understood it, sat in trenches until there was some new horrific push. The casualties in the East mostly went to Malta or Egypt, of course, so it was harder to know what was going on there.

Beatrice walked quickly through the rain, an August thunderstorm which rather suited her mood. The stables were quiet – no animals that she could see, human, horse or dog. Then she heard a noise.

'Gussie!'

'Hello, Mama.' Gussie looked up from the bale of straw where she was sitting reading a letter.

'Whatever are you doing here?'

'I like it. It smells nice and sometimes Sid Small's son, whatever he's called, comes and talks to me.'

'Is that interesting?' Beatrice came in and sat on another bale. With a pang of guilt she realised how seldom she tried to talk to Gussie.

'Depends on the alternatives. Sometimes I take tea with Mr Gisburne. I've found out how to make it.'

'He's a very learned man,' said Beatrice. She looked at the letter Gussie still held. 'I had one from your papa. He says he's leaving Egypt. He sent you his love.'

'He's always leaving, isn't he.' Gussie was scarcely interested. Her eyes dropped to her own letter.

'This time it's true. It's in *The Times* too.'

Gussie held up the letter with a diffident look on her face Beatrice had never seen before. 'Reggie Gisburne's written to me from the front in France somewhere or other. He's been put up for an MC. He rescued a whole lot of wounded men or something.'

Beatrice, who'd been thinking of the Colonel, exclaimed after a beat, 'A Military Cross! You're sure he said that?'

'I know. He must be most frightfully brave. He says it's all the most stupid rot. He did what anyone would have done. He doesn't expect to get it but I think he wants me to be proud of him. That's why he told me.' Gussie's round blue eyes stared up in appeal to her mother just as if she were still eight instead of eighteen. 'Oh, Mama, men are so odd, aren't they? One minute they're like silly boys and then they're doing heroic things which will help win the war. Or I suppose it will. Do you think it's just because they have the opportunities? Or because they're stronger than us? Or because they get things all wrong? And then have to put it right? Oh, Mama, I'm sure we'd never be fighting this war if women were in charge!'

'My darling, my darling Gussie!' With the affection usually reserved for her husband, Beatrice sat beside her daughter and hugged her as hard as she could. 'I'm afraid I've been selfish not thinking how dreary life has been for you. I don't understand anything much better than you, except that sometimes wars have to be fought and men must fight them. Women have an important job too, even if all we're doing is keeping the home fires burning. Soldiers need to know it's all right at home.' She smoothed a couple of dark curls emerging from under Gussie's hat. 'Lily tells me you've been a great help recently.'

'I like Lily,' said Gussie, who suddenly seemed on the verge of tears. 'She's had a horrible life but she never complains. I like her children too.' Gussie stopped abruptly and bent her head down.

'I always forget she has any children. She keeps them so tucked away.' Beatrice watched as Gussie stood up and picked bits of straw from her long woollen jacket. 'Where are you going now?'

'To see the rector.'

'That's kind.'

Both women walked out into the stable yard. 'I hate the emptiness,' said Beatrice. 'Where are the dogs, incidentally?'

'They've been spread around the different farms. Nothing for them hanging around here.' Beatrice felt Gussie was including herself in this indictment.

'Your papa says Small will stay behind in Egypt to help look after the horses. I'd always thought he'd be back in time for the hunting.'

'I read something the other day about a charge on Gallipoli. That must be rubbish, mustn't it?'

'Total rubbish,' said Beatrice sadly. 'There are some horses on the peninsula, I believe, but only to carry messages on the flatter ground or heave around the odd gun. It's mostly mules. Pack animals.'

'It's stopped raining.' Gussie blinked at the sky.

Beatrice watched her walk away, then turned back to the house.

*

The rector welcomed Gussie into his study. Owing to his wife's early death and an inbuilt curiosity into what made humans different one from the other, he was more interested than most men in children and young persons. 'I guess you've heard from Reggie.'

'That's why I came in the morning.' They sat down in their usual places. 'There's something else too.' Gussie suddenly went bright red.

The rector looked away tactfully. Although his sermons were often ferocious, he never liked to embarrass anyone face to face. 'He told you about the MC, I expect?'

'Oh, yes. He must be frightfully brave,' said Gussie, repeating the words she'd already used to her mother.

'Bravery is his strong suit, I'd say,' said the rector meditatively. 'Exemplary gallantry, that's what they give it for. I'm an armchair fighter myself.'

Gussie, whose flush had finally subsided, leant forward. 'Wouldn't you like to be one of those army padres who say prayers on the battlefields? It must be most awfully exciting.'

'I prefer *preaching* about hell fire. But I'm glad for Reggie. God keeps a special place for the noble warrior.'

'Yes. Women don't get a choice.'

The rector leant back in his chair. 'Lily came to see me recently. She hymned your praises. Said you cheered up the men no end.'

'I had to do something.' Gussie picked up a book on the table beside her and held it like a shield. 'Apparently Papa is finally off to Gallipoli.'

'May God be with him.' The rector looked at his guest curiously. What was the 'something else' that was making her so distracted?

'I suppose, being a priest, you come across quite a lot of fallen women?'

'That depends how you define "fallen"?'

'You know, the usual way,' said Gussie impatiently.

'You refer to sins of the flesh,' said the rector, trying not to smile. 'Although even that could include gluttony and all kinds of carnal desires. "God chose us to be holy and without blemish before him..."' He stopped quoting as he saw Gussie's face crumpling miserably. 'What is it, my child? Nothing is as bad as that.'

'It is,' wailed Gussie. 'I'm going to have a baby!' And she bent and hid her face in her hands.

Mr Gisburne sat quite still and upright. He was aware of the clock on the mantel ticking. He remembered the moment his wife had died and he'd heard the clock ticking then. Now he understood why Gussie had made a friend of him. A fallen woman? Miss Augusta Fitzpaine? It was unbelievable such a thing could happen. If only his wife was here. Obviously, it was his fault. He had failed with Reggie. They had never been close. In fact he'd never liked him much. Could this child really love him? He must speak to her. But what to say? Now he did ask God to help him. And God came back with some practical words.

'Reggie will want to marry you, my dear. He will be so proud.'

'As proud as of his MC?'

'Much prouder,' said the rector, gaining conviction. 'A baby is the greatest gift God can give.'

'Is that what you tell all the fallen woman?' Gussie's face was still buried.

'Who else have you confided in?'

'How can I tell Mama when she's so unhappy about Papa? And Sylvia's in Cairo doing good and Cousin Evie would die of horror. I told Lily who thought I could talk to you, like God.'

'Oh, well,' said the rector. 'I'm not sure I could rise to those heights. So Reggie doesn't know?'

'I don't even love him!' exclaimed Gussie with the dedicated air of someone intent on revealing the whole truth.

'You will *love* the baby, I expect.' The rector brought his hands together. 'Would you like me to inform Lady Beatrice?'

'No! No!' Gussie started back wildly. 'I wouldn't have told you if I thought you'd do that.'

'But you will have to see a doctor.'

'Not yet. I am not even sick.'

'You look quite the same,' agreed the rector. Again, he thought of his wife. She had looked quite the same too. It struck him gloomily that the Fitzpaines would be furious with Reggie, and him too. The more he thought, the blacker the picture became until his face was as downcast as Gussie's.

231

'I'm sorry,' said Gussie in a small voice. There was a pause while they stared at each other before Mr Gisburne changed the direction of his gaze to his bookshelves.

'I might lose it,' said Gussie. 'People do.'

'You should not talk like that,' said the rector sternly. 'Reggie must be told immediately. Perhaps he will come to London to collect his award.'

A glimmer of light pierced Gussie's gloom. 'I'd be a war bride like the photographs in the *Tatler*. Soldiers hold swords over the couple.' The light faded. 'But I don't want to marry Reggie. In fact I won't tell him quite yet. Just in case. He should be allowed to enjoy being a war hero, don't you think?'

The rector didn't know what to think and was glad when there was a knock at the door. His housekeeper put her head round the door. 'I didn't know you had a visitor. Mrs Horsthrup has come to discuss hymns with you.'

'I'm just going.' Gussie jumped up, quite shockingly transforming from broken sinner into bright young thing.

Mr Gisburne stared. 'If you must ... Come again soon.'

'Oh, yes!' Gussie bounded out of the room. The front door slammed and the rector saw her pass quickly by the window.

He turned to the sturdy Mrs Horsthrup with relief, although his anxiety left a lingering shadow which Mrs Horsthrup, being the doctor's wife, put down to stomach troubles. It was well known that the poor rector had not been fed properly since his wife died.

Eighteen

The Colonel had never felt so fit, so staunch, so determined in his life – well, not for years anyway. He thanked God for giving him such a chance to pay back for all the good things He had given him. Since eleven o'clock the night before he had lain sleepless on his bunk in the comfortable liner that was taking him to Gallipoli. He had composed a long letter to Beatrice but as he wanted to spare her too much emotion, it went no further than his head. Five minutes ago his servant, Andrews, had informed him that it was three a.m. and they would be anchoring off the coast in an hour or so.

'No submarines, then,' the Colonel had replied encouragingly.

'Not yet, sir.'

The Colonel had smiled into the near darkness and taken the tray of tea and biscuits. Afterwards he would join his staff and officers to check on the men, one thousand of them, yeomanry who had never fought a battle. He allowed himself to think with pride of their lion-hearted resolve, their practicality and humour. Only that afternoon, his ADC – Noel Willoughby, a nice boy – had overheard one man say to another, 'I hear they've been fighting at this new front for two weeks and kept us for the end. Just like the good Lord, the best wine's served up last.'

Another exquisite dawn spread slowly over the bays and cliffs of Gallipoli. Little puffs and twists of mist uncurled from the deepest clefts and disappeared into the slowly brightening sky. The Colonel stood on the top deck waiting for transport. His men were already disembarking into 'beetles', a new form of armoured and motorised lighter which he watched with interest. Not that there seemed much danger on the beach, apart from the occasional shelling. He had forgotten that noise. What a wild sound it was!

Further inland there was the crackle of desultory fire which lit up the darker corners. Nearby, a hospital ship was preparing to leave.

'There's a launch coming now, I think, sir,' said Willoughby, peering through his binoculars.

The Colonel put up his own. 'It looks more like someone bringing orders.' He longed for orders or information of any sort. He swept his binoculars over the land curving round the wide bay. He could now make out the salt lake which was supposed to be dry. To his left, there was a long high ridge and to his right a small hill around which the troops swarmed. Beyond the lake a group of hills gradually revealed themselves, rising to much higher ground on all sides. At that moment he did not even know which land had been taken by the Allies, apart from the fringes of the bay which must be relatively secure for men to be walking around as they were, although as the skies lightened the shelling had increased in volume.

The launch arrived and a young lieutenant (everybody seemed like children to the Colonel) hopped out. He came bounding up to the top deck, saluted smartly. 'All brigade commanders are being invited to a meeting on board the *Jonquil*, sir. Tomorrow nine a.m.'

No hurry, then. Message delivered, the lieutenant seemed about to go, before turning back with a sudden joyful look. 'The 29th are coming from Helles, sir. We're waiting for them.'

'Thank you, Lieutenant.'

So they were bringing along some old hands. The Colonel, who always revered any good soldiers, nevertheless frowned jealously.

'The men will be proud to be fighting alongside them,' said Willoughby. He was a small youth with a surprisingly large gingerish moustache and a lively mind.

'Quite right, Noel. They'll certainly prefer fighting to digging in.' His brief survey of the terrain had already convinced him that all the land beyond the direct hinterland to the beach would be horribly rocky. 'Have you spotted where Karakol Dagh actually is?'

'Yes. It's north from here on a little rise. Don't worry, sir, we're going to build you a dugout fit for a sultan.'

'With entrenching tools?' The Colonel smiled. Many of his officers were the age his son would have been if he'd had one.

Briefly, he considered Lamb. He was a good boy, presumably now on Helles. Probably safer there.

'We're meeting on a ship, then,' he said to Willoughby.

'New style of making war, sir.'

He was right. Until now the Colonel had not properly appreciated that the navy was fighting the war alongside the army, the great guns of the destroyers pointed to the land. He'd *known* about it for months but not felt it in his bones. The navy instead of horses; it was an unsettling sort of swap.

Andrews appeared. 'They're serving a full-scale breakfast below, sir. Linen napkins and silver service,' he added admiringly.

But the Colonel had eaten enough full-scale breakfasts. He shook his head and picked up his binoculars again. As he did so the brilliant curve of the sun rose above the hills, blinding him. He put down the glasses to rub his eyes. At one stroke the delicate flush of dawn had been swept aside by the glare of day.

Arthur, still on Helles, watched the famous 29th Division embarking for Suvla. There were thousands of men, some of whom had fought from the beginning of the campaign. He was envious of their unity and their reputation. As a mere volunteer he could never reach their heights. Nevertheless, they were clearly suffering from the same ills as every other soldier on Helles: dysentery, lice, exhaustion. A new location, with a proper fight, would be a boost to their morale.

Arthur stopped a major who looked less brusque than most. 'Sir!' He gave his sharpest salute. It was the middle of the day and very hot. Everybody ran with sweat. 'I'm commanded to Suvla, sir. The transport officer . . .' He waved his pass.

'Not my business, Lieutenant.' The major looked at him wearily. 'You've been on Gallipoli a while, have you?'

'Yes, sir.'

'Then you know the rules?'

'I think so, sir.' *Rules?*

The major, who was watching his seventy men pass by as he talked, made the shingle jump with his stick. '*No* rules! If you're going to Suvla, get on board but don't ask me to help you. I still like to pretend I'm a soldier not a bus conductor.' His stick shot up suddenly. 'You, man. What's that on your leg?'

A captain stepped forward. 'It's a splint, sir. Broke his leg. But says he can fight, sir.'

'Damn fool! Damn fools both of you. Send him to the medics.'

Arthur left and, immediately spotting the large figure of Rendell, laden with his baggage, led him down to the lighters taking men out to the troop ships. It was a relief to get his steaming boots in the water. He turned his head to stare at the cliffs and headlands. It had felt like coming home when he'd arrived there and now, only a few days later, he was off on a new course.

The Colonel watched his second Gallipoli dawn from the entrance to his dugout. Noel had kept his word and made him a fine structure from stones, sandbags and some strips of sheet metal. He'd finished by hanging a sign by the doorway – *Battle View* – which the Colonel had told him to remove. It was not fitting for a brigadier-general. Later he saw it hanging jauntily outside Willoughby's own quarters. The Colonel remembered he was not commanding officers from the regular army.

Everybody was in good spirits, despite the predicted problems of digging in rock. Several men had been wounded while collecting water from the tanker on the beach but then they'd been directed to a newly discovered well near where they were camped. He'd been told the lack of water, plus the confusion of landing on an unknown shore, had been the principal cause for the failure of the earlier attacks. However, there were also rumours of a prolonged and unnecessary delay after the first landings which had allowed the enemy to gain the advantage. There was even a grim joke going round about a swimming gala for which the prize had been a day sunbathing with the generals on their ships. His old friend, General Stopford, had been sent back to England in disgrace. Now, although things were makeshift – no roads or proper piers – there was a business-like air, or so it seemed to the Colonel.

At seven o'clock he went down to the bay with his staff and joined other brigade commanders waiting to be ferried out to HMS *Jonquil*. They were talking about the various 'small' attacks made the day before.

'The 34th are brave enough but they hardly knew what they were up to or where they were,' said one angry major. 'I'm told the Northumberland's lost nearly all their officers and four hundred men in forty-five minutes.' He jerked his elbow to a further beach. 'They've been loading the wounded all night, even so half of them are left up there.' He jerked his thumb to the hills.

No one wanted to hear this news which sounded almost seditious under the circumstances and there was a concerted move towards the shoreline where several new launches had appeared.

The Colonel found himself seated near a general he knew slightly. 'I hear the 29th are joining us.'

The general sagged in a kindly but not very martial way and remarked without emphasis, 'Only the 87th Brigade has arrived here, I'm told. The 88th is supposedly holding the front line at Helles and no one seems to have an idea about the 86th.' He paused as a shell passed over their boat and landed with a splash in front of them.

'They haven't a clue where they're firing,' commented the general, pulling his moustache. The shell had been damned close.

'I don't suppose you've seen a map, have you?' the Colonel asked, as the boat rocked from the waves made by the shell.

'Map of this place, you mean?' The general gave an ironic smile. 'Yesterday I was handed a map. It showed the whole of the peninsula. No detail at all. Worse than useless. Do or die. Do or die.'

Willoughby, although it was not his place to speak, intervened. 'A chap showed me a map. Very excited he was when he opened it. Turned out to be a map of Norfolk. Every village church and tumulus.'

Since no one else found anything to say about this, silence fell, broken only by the bang of the water against the boat and random but fairly continuous fire from the shore.

Rupert had got himself attached to Ashmead-Bartlett, the journalist who was covering the campaign for *The Times* and other newspapers. His reports, edited by the censors, produced good news stories but out on the peninsula he was famous, or infamous depending on your point of view, for his criticism of General Hamilton's conduct of the war.

They had first met aboard HMS *Minneapolis*, one sultry afternoon when yet another failed attack was being perpetrated at Suvla.

'It's horrible, the way we can watch it all,' Rupert had muttered, clutching his usual water bottle of brandy. He was sitting cross-legged on the deck.

Ashmead-Bartlett, standing above him, put aside his binoculars. 'Clearly you are no newsman. What *are* you, if you don't mind my asking?'

'Ask. Ask. Would that I had an answer.'

'OK. I get the point. An intelligence officer with nothing much to do.' The journalist had laughed. 'Do you speak many languages?'

'So they say.'

'You could be useful.'

'I doubt it.' But Ashmead-Bartlett had recognised a kindred soul for he half longed, half dreaded to be sent home in disgrace. If he no longer had a role to play, as he told Rupert, he could speak out honestly and inform the British people, in which he adamantly included the brave men from down under, what was really happening at Gallipoli.

A few days later, they took a boat together to Imbros where Ashmead-Bartlett wrote up his copy on what had happened to the Anzac attack – although he had not been there himself. When he had finished, they walked to a high rocky place where they could see the coastline of Gallipoli.

Ashmead-Bartlett took up the conversation where they'd left it. 'Must more and more be killed before the politicians are made to understand that we have lost?'

To hear enunciated by someone in a position of power, however thwarted, Rupert's own long-held convictions, was a solace to his solitary misery. 'Isn't it too late now?'

'It's never too late for the men alive and fighting here. It's never too late for the truth. The truth is we must evacuate,' continued the journalist forcefully.

It was the first time Rupert had heard this word used and it shocked even him. He took a swig from his water bottle before deciding to play devil's advocate. 'We are in the middle of huge battles on three fronts. More and more regiments are being poured in. Our army has never been so strong.'

'The Turkish army has grown even stronger. At Suvla they reckon we have fifty thousand men against their seventy five thousand. Also, they have the advantage of the high ground and a proper knowledge of the terrain. You know that.'

For a moment Rupert stared at the sea and sky, both painted in layers of colour as the sinking sun cast its rays. 'And we are led by timid old fools who need their rest in the afternoon.'

'Even Hamilton saw through Stopford,' said Ashmead-Bartlett with no lightening of his mood. 'To be fair, he didn't want him in the first place. You can blame Kitchener for that one. Major General Beauvoir de Lisle's been put in temporary command. Given male life expectancy is fifty-two years, it's bad luck that so many exceptions to the rule have landed up here.' He too stared at the startling rainbow in front of them. 'The beauty of the islands and the peninsula will be here long after we've left.'

'I lived in this part of the world before the war,' said Rupert thoughtfully. 'I always considered myself as a bit of an outcast, a man who couldn't get on with his own race and, although I didn't like to admit it, I assumed that was because they were superior and I was inferior. But I don't believe that any more. Not after what I've seen out here. When I was staying at my parent's house, Churchill came to lunch, a great sackload of self-pity! I've never met a man more absurdly convinced of his absolute knowledge nor more ignorant about Gallipoli. We have no right to win this war. At least not this little bit of it. We are *not* a superior race!'

During this emotional speech, Ashmead-Bartlett shifted uncomfortably. He took off his cap and fanned his face with it. 'I'm just a reporter,' he said eventually. 'I don't have to make grand judgements. You're young.' Then he stopped. He *liked* feeling himself part of a superior race. 'Bad management,' he said, 'that's what I rail against.'

The following morning, 21st August, Ashmead-Bartlett, with Rupert in tow, took a trawler to Suvla. It was ten o'clock when they arrived, after the usual delay in leaving. It was another clear, hot day.

While Ashmead-Bartlett went away to make arrangements, Rupert stood out of range of the shells idly watching the stretcher-bearers bringing the last of the wounded down to the beach. Some of them were clearly shot almost to pieces so that he wondered why they bothered. One officer's face was entirely destroyed apart from one eye and his body looked just about shattered too.

'Has he any hope?' he said to the stretcher-bearer who had laid down the wounded man to wait his turn for a boat.

The man looked at him. 'He's alive, isn't he? That's our orders: bring in the living. What happens afterwards isn't our business.' He turned away and lit a cigarette.

Against Rupert's will, he found himself staring mesmerised at the poor remains of the wounded soldier on the ground. He was young, obviously, a lieutenant. Suddenly he realised that the eye was staring at him and, far far worse, that he recognised him: it was Gaythorne, the smirking Gaythorne, last seen on Tenedos. He also realised that not only was he alive but that he had ears and that, if his eye was open, he probably recognised *him*.

Before Rupert could find any words, he found himself convulsed by tears. They poured down his cheeks, choking his voice. He was crying, he knew, for the past, for the innocence and idiocy of childish enmities. Only a few months ago on Tenedos he had wished the gods to smite this man, when even then war was creating the vilest happenings. He was right to weep. The eye blinked.

Rupert fell to his knees. 'I'm so sorry, Gaythorne. I'm so very sorry. They will get you to the hospital ship . . .' He stopped. What use was a hospital ship?

There was one hand uninjured which he took and held. He felt the slightest of squeezes, then the eye blinked, blinked again and remained closed.

The Colonel was taking his men along the coast to the area behind the hill of Lala Baba where they were to be held in reserve. Again in reserve. No advance of any sort would take place, according to the plan he had been told the day before, until three p.m. This gave his brigade an early morning march, followed by a long hot day waiting.

'Tell those men to keep on their helmets,' he shouted, 'and no, absolutely no, paddling in the sea.' Discipline was essential, particularly when such a vast horde of inexperienced men were gathered in such a small space. He was told the 86th Brigade had finally arrived. He turned to Willoughby. 'I'll tell you what, let's test that lake we've been told is dry. Never believe in hearsay.'

Four men were sent off with a sergeant immediately. The Colonel watched warily. Would the surface hold a thousand marching men who were following behind other thousands? He looked at his watch. Still only ten thirty.

The men returned; like boys playing, they showed off their boots caked with fine white soil. 'It'll hold, sir,' said the sergeant, 'thick crust on the top, soft underneath. Sir!'

'Thank you, Sergeant Pomeroy.' The Colonel looked at him affectionately. He was one of the Dorsets, a gamekeeper from a neighbouring estate. But not the ratty sort, a fair-minded man, married with three children.

He began to walk again. It was difficult to believe that out of this sunny peace, the storm of battle would soon emerge. He turned to Willoughby. 'Make sure the men don't loosen their puttees. It makes them no cooler and they're liable to get hooked up once we're into the prickly scrub.'

'Yes, sir.' The ADC's face was bright with eager excitement.

The salt lake shimmered white in the brilliant light. When – or if – their yeomanry was called out of reserve, they would cross it briskly in loose formation. By the afternoon the sun would be behind them, shining in the enemy's face, shining on their guns. It was the only point that was new about the plans, so that rebarbative major had said at their meeting.

The Colonel screwed up his eyes and stared again at the lake and the hills beyond. He could make out Chocolate Hill where the Allies were ensconced but could see little of the surrounding land, W Hill, Hill 112, Green Hill, Scimitar Hill, Hill 60 – many of them already had names despite only two weeks having passed since the British arrival. Men liked giving names. At Tollorum Home Farm many of the cows were given names. It was strange how one could not see a wink or a blink of the enemy. But out there they were, crouched at the ready in their trenches.

The Colonel's attention was diverted by two figures at some distance from each other crossing the blank whiteness of the lake. He pointed his stick. 'What are those?'

Major Beech answered. Strange to see a man from Tollorum just after it had been in his mind. 'Could be anyone, sir. Going to Chocolate Hill. They're walking apart because the Turk doesn't bother to shoot unless he sees more than one.'

'I might know the soldier at the back.'

'What, sir?' Willoughby came closer. His eyes were sharper than either the major's or the Colonel's.

'Nothing. Nothing.' Once they were behind Lala Baba, they would see very little of what was going on. He must make sure to climb on top of the hill.

Ashmead-Bartlett and Captain Prideaux arrived at Chocolate Hill.

Rupert wiped his face. 'That's the scariest thing I've ever done, including the amnesty at Anzac when no one believed a few white flags would stop an array of cocked rifles.' He thought grimly: But I still had hope then.

'You were *there*, were you?' questioned the journalist with interest.

'From ten a.m. to four p.m. when we let the dogs off the leash.' It no longer seemed important that he'd been central to making it happen.

'Good show.' Ashmead-Bartlett stared upwards anxiously. 'We need to be on top to get the best view, if these soldiers will cooperate.'

The trenches which encircled the front of the hill were stuffed with dirty, unshaven, exhausted men. They became more co-operative when Ashmead-Bartlett produced a camera from his pack. 'I'm a newspaperman,' he announced bracingly. 'Do you want to be famous?' They did, it transpired.

Winding their slow way upwards from the trenches, the two men eventually reached the top of the hill. Rupert gaped. The view from the ship had given him no idea of the extent of the high ground – to the north the long uneven ridge of Kiretch Tepe, some of it now in the hands of the Allies, and to the south the endless ranges and gullies of Anzac, again some of it recently taken by the Allies. Straight ahead were all the hills that had been fought over in the last two weeks. Even if the Allies took them, they soon had to retreat as guns blazed down at them.

'What's going to be different about this afternoon's attack from all the others that have failed?' Rupert grabbed Ashmead-Bartlett's arm.

Ashmead-Bartlett shrugged him off. 'We're not trying to get to the Anafarta Spur any more. Just W Hill and Scimitar Hill and

Hill 60 with any luck.' He pointed to one of the officers. 'Ask him. Perhaps he knows something we don't.'

The officer in question had his arm in a sling and an open cut across his face. Moreover, one of the very random shells that still came over hit a trench at that moment, throwing up a huge waterfall of earth and causing cries of 'Spades! Spades over here!' Followed soon by further cries of 'Stretcher-bearers!'

It was not the moment to ask unanswerable questions.

Arthur, with Rendell at his side, was coming ashore at what he was told by the sailor navigating the lighter was called A Beach at Suvla. 'Most of the new soldiers are held behind Lala Baba.' The three men looked across the rippling blue water to the little hill nearest them.

Arthur thought this wide-open beach was very different from the rest of the coastline. How he longed for a map! It was unfortunate to arrive here with no written orders, not even the telegraph which he'd somehow lost. And he must remember to ask for Brigadier-General Fitzpaine and not 'the Colonel'.

'That's Chocolate Hill.' The sailor pointed. But Arthur could only vaguely see it through the heat haze. 'There're some navy gunners up there.'

He looked at the man – scarcely more than a boy really. It was an odd subservient role the navy played. 'Odd to be a sailor on land.'

'There's a whole naval brigade, sir.' The young sailor had childish blue eyes in a deeply sunburnt face. 'But someone has to face down the submarines, sir.'

'No fun,' said Arthur.

The boy's expression took on a yearning look. 'If we'd been allowed to try again, we'd have got through those blasted Dardanelles.'

'I expect you would.' The boat grounded. No fire, or so little that it counted as none. The soldiers round them pushed their way out, cursing merrily as their boots splashed through the water and sank into the soft sand.

'Like Weymouth Beach, sir.' Rendell took both their packs and swung them on his broad shoulders.

'A damned sight hotter.' Arthur thanked the captain who'd let them hitch a ride and, among hundreds of other arriving troops, set off for Lala Baba.

A worried group of generals stood on the top of Lala Baba, some with binoculars to their eyes, some simply staring, all facing the same direction.

'Every single afternoon, it's been so clear you can pick out each of their guns but now it looks like the Highlands when one of those Scotch mists blank out the whole countryside.'

'It's not as bad as that, General,' ventured one officer. 'Once we're in there fighting it won't make much difference.'

'General Hamilton is adamant we don't put off the attack,' said a second general in a loud, forced voice.

'He came to see for himself. That we should be so honoured,' muttered a captain before moving away down the slope of the hill.

The atmosphere was as uneasy as the weather. It was an hour before the naval bombardment was due to begin. New commanders to the scene, like the Colonel, wanted to be with their men but still felt ignorant of their task and hoped that they might gain some useful information from the old hands. Instead, there seemed to be uncertainty and bad news.

With relief, he turned away. He knew enough to lead his men in the direction of their duty.

'Sir! Brigadier-General Fitzpaine.'

The Colonel looked at the young lieutenant climbing up the tufty grass towards him with a huge fellow carrying his pack behind him. 'Lamb! My dear fellow.' How young he looked, and so thin still. 'I pictured you in Helles.'

'Just arrived, sir. With the 86th. Orders from on high. Your friend, the general, I suppose.'

'Good man. In time for the fun.'

The two men stood talking in the glaring heat which was not diminished, if anything was increased, by the strange mist. They were pleased to see each other, although the Colonel's pleasure was tinged with a sense of responsibility. He could not allow Sylvia's fiancé to be lost when under his care.

'I'll send you over to the London Yeomanry,' he said. He had been told that, once they had crossed the salt lake, they would go to the right of Chocolate Hill, instead of left towards the infamous

Scimitar Hill where he himself would lead the attack. 'They're short of at least one officer. They'll be glad to see you.'

'Thank you, sir.' Arthur thought it was odd that he would not serve directly with the Colonel which was, presumably, the point of him leaving his own regiment. But he said nothing. This was a very superior officer's decision.

Now the Colonel's staff, who had been waiting at the bottom of the hill, came quickly towards him. Willoughby looked at his watch. 'We thought you'd decided to lead us from afar, sir,' he said jokingly.

Arthur was surprised by his familiarity. He waited to be introduced. He felt awkward and then thought how absurd it was to feel awkward at niceties of behaviour when they all might be killed in a few hours.

'You've forgotten we're in reserve again.' The Colonel tapped his ADC with his stick.

'Oh, sir.' Willoughby grimaced.

At two thirty p.m. the great guns from the Allied ships, brought in as close as possible to the shore, began to pound the distant hills. There were spotters on land but the thick mist made it impossible to call in accurate fire. Nevertheless, the colossal noise and the dramatic sight as whole sections of ground were flung into the air, suggested a satisfactory level of destruction.

Rupert, still on top of Chocolate Hill with Ashmead-Bartlett, felt an instinctive urge to crouch down and put his arms over his head. It seemed that being a spectator turned one into a coward and he longed for a mug of brandy. The journalist, wielding his camera, was uncaring of his own safety, muttering now and again, the words lost in the noise, 'Artillery's the only way.'

At three o'clock precisely, the naval guns ceased and almost at once the reverberating silence was filled by the sound of Turkish shells falling on the first line of men advancing across the salt lake towards their positions. From this moment the scene watched by Rupert on the top of Chocolate Hill became more confused. Fighting started in areas to both sides of him and since the hill itself was under fire, usually, but not always, inaccurately, it was no longer a safe place to be. But Rupert, tied to Ashmead-Bartlett who persisted in his fearless stance, stayed put, at one point even having to dig out the reporter when earth from a shell literally buried him and blew off his outer clothes.

In the direction of Scimitar Hill, the battle raged in a smirch of smoke, a pall of smog, a continuous roar of artillery, a rush of men up the hill met by a smash of guns, the fall of men, another rush, another fall. Then came fires, flames leaping up among the scrub, pushing back the attackers below the rim, consuming the fallen.

'They can't do it!' yelled Ashmead-Bartlett at one moment of horrible defeat. Defeat and victory, victory and defeat. Up and down they went and the fires rose and fell until it seemed there could be nothing more to burn. Moving khaki figures disappeared among the charred shrubs.

In the other direction where the men strove to capture W Hill and join the Anzac forces who were supposed to capture Hill 60, scarcely more than a hillock, it was harder to make out the shape of the attack. Hedges, ditches, trees, wide valleys and shallow trenches confused the shape of the battle. Sometimes groups of soldiers emerged from the general disorder, the Allies emerging daringly to attack, their enemy equally fearless in sending them back or dropping them as they ran. It was hard to tell whether any ground was gained on either side, except that W Hill was certainly not taken. Dust rose up and occasionally the shouts or screams of men.

All this time, the Colonel waited behind Lala Baba. Arthur, at another point behind the hill, also waited. The men were seated on the baked earth in low rows. At first they had joked, fidgeted, adjusted their infantry uniform which as cavalry men they were not used to, exchanged cigarettes, complained of the heat. It was nearly two hours since the naval bombardment had begun, followed by over an hour of fighting during which the horse-drawn ambulances had brought back a continual flow of wounded. Even from behind the hill, they could see the smoke from the fires and hear the unending chorus of shells, rifle and artillery fire. Everybody knew without knowing exactly why they knew, although the ambulances were some indication, that things were not going well.

The question was whether the new commander, Major General

Beauvoir de Lisle, would call it a day or order his reserves into one final desperate attack.

'The orders have come,' Willoughby panted as if he'd galloped miles to bring this message, rather than merely passing it up the line.

The Colonel stared at him for a second; the boy rode a horse well. How he'd enjoyed their charges in the desert! He called up his servant, who was not marching with them, and quietly gave him a short letter he'd written to Beatrice and a small Bible that he carried with him but didn't like to take to the front. Then he was ready.

Arthur felt every muscle in his body jumping with the resolution of attack. He was in the first brigade of the reserves to set off. He'd never taken part in a march across open ground before since the nearest to open ground any other part of Gallipoli could provide was a small field or vineyard. The salt lake which they must cross was two miles wide with no cover in any direction. Far from finding the prospect daunting, he felt excited and invigorated. The wait was over, now was the time to go forward. Fleetingly, as always when he thought of Sylvia now, he allowed her face with its halo of pale hair to drift before him for a moment, as a sliver of moon appears before clouds cover it over. She was there. She was his.

The brigade marched to the sound of a single mouth organ played by one of the men. It was a cheerful sound, mundane, English music to give everyone heart. The soldiers were stretched out in long lines across the white heat of the lake. Their boots kicked up dust but they advanced as if they were on a parade ground; regiments followed each other in squadron order, officers marching with men, each squadron in line of troop order at set regular distances. There was no slackening but no dashing either.

After about half an hour, this steadily moving army entered the field of shrapnel put across by the Turks. There was no avoiding it if they were to reach Chocolate Hill. No one faltered, although for most it was their baptism of fire. Soon men began to fall. Still, they marched stolidly on.

Arthur, who had long ago conquered any fear of fire however heavy, marvelled at their fortitude. One man in front of him even bent to pick up a large tortoise who had wandered across his path. Hardly breaking his stride, the soldier scooped it up and carried on with the animal like a breastplate at his chest.

The shrapnel became more vicious; more men toppled, most not making a sound. Lead tore into their heads, their stomachs, their arms, their feet. The men on either side, trained only to carry on forward, left even their best mates for the stretcher-bearers who came behind. Sweat poured off their bodies, soaking their uniforms. Their slippery hands clung to their rifles as if they were protection against the storm.

The Colonel led his brigade out onto the lake. Like all officers free of the burden of a rifle, he swung his arms, one grasping a cane, and held his head high. Noticing Willoughby duck, he shouted across at him in the ringing tones he used when a hound got out of order at a hunt, 'Don't duck, Noel; it does no good and the men don't like it.' If he regretted his tall black horse, there was no sign of it.

He had no time to wonder how Arthur had fared, although glad he had sent him ahead with the London Yeomanry. The shelling was increasing every minute. Men were continually having to alter their stride to avoid the earlier wounded.

As Arthur and the rest of the London Yeomanry neared Chocolate Hill, the order was given to move at the double. This wasn't easy as all their boots were caked with the soft soil under the surface of the lake. It was hard enough to walk, their feet were like lead, their backs ached with the weight of water bottles, ammunition, food. But how they wanted to run and reach the shelter of the hill! Heads down, not because they ducked, but because they needed to push themselves forward like animals straining every muscle, they staggered and panted and, when they had the breath, cursed. But none of them wavered and none of them broke the line.

At last Arthur saw, through the sweat dripping into his eyes, the trenches that encircled the hills, that grew up it like the remains of an ancient fort.

'Come on, men! Keep going forward. We're nearly there!'

Then they were there, pitching in among a jumble of other

soldiers, some waiting to go forward, some just pulled back, many wounded, waiting for nightfall to be transported back across the lake.

'And all this before we fight,' said Arthur as Major Bubby, now his commanding officer, arrived beside him. 'I feel sorry for the new men.'

The major, a small wiry individual with a long beaky nose, wiped his face. 'It will be a relief to see the enemy.' All the dead and wounded had been targeted by invisible guns, entrenched in the surrounding hills and further hidden by the unexpected mist.

Rupert crouched on Chocolate Hill, in an area protected from flying shrapnel and bullets by sandbags, trenches and stone walls. He was watching the soldiers march across the white plain. Their advance seemed endless; they were like figures in a frieze.

'They're dismounted cavalry, you know, this lot. Yeomanry.' A young naval officer who would have been a spotter for the naval guns if he'd been able to see anything or been told where to look, whispered reverently.

'There's no point in whispering,' said Rupert, irritated by this childish awe. Yet he felt it himself, mixed however with a terrible rage that this pointless attack was happening at all. He looked around for Ashmead-Bartlett but he'd gone off somewhere – or perhaps he'd been hit. Nowhere was safe any more. That was some consolation. He turned back to the spotter. 'Cavalry, you say.' Cavalry might mean Brigadier-General Fitzpaine. Very probably meant Fitzpaine. He remembered him the evening they'd met at the pyramids, a bluff, friendly man, nothing unusual for his class. How keen he'd been to get on a horse!

He took another long look at the white expanse, still filled with marching figures. They were the yeomen of old England, descendants of men who had fought at Poitiers, Crécy, Agincourt, striding behind their fox-hunting leaders. They were just the sort of people he'd tried to escape when he fled to the East. But here they were, thousands of miles from pastureland and moors, determined to do their patriotic duty. How could anyone fail to admire them and be moved by their suicidal bravery!

'I only learnt one poem at school that I can still remember,' he shouted to the naval man who was bent over trying to light a cigarette – a slight wind had come up. Looking towards Scimitar Hill, the ultimate destination of the yeomanry going north, he saw that the breeze had fanned the flames which now licked upwards in scarlet tongues.

Since the naval man still took no notice, a crazy notion took hold of him and he scrambled to his feet. Jostling in his head was the tragic pathos of these deluded heroes heading inexorably to their death, the build-up of months of fury and frustration, the sense of his own inability to fight and the horrible death of his old enemy that he had witnessed earlier in the day.

As usual without a helmet, fair hair lifting in the wind, slender frame bowed back, he yelled at a storming rate:

> *Half a league, half a league,*
> *Half a league onward,*
> *All in the Valley of Death*
> *Rode the six hundred . . .*
> *Theirs not to reason why,*
> *Theirs but to do and die;*
> *Into the Valley of Death*
> *Rode the six hundred.*

Around him the mixed fire from machine guns and shells, quite enough to keep men in the trenches, sparked and spat and thudded in war-like chorus. Then a machine gun opened from the south-east.

'Who's that madman?' screamed an officer. 'He'll get us all killed!'

Rupert bellowed even louder and faster:

> *Cannon to right of them,*
> *Cannon to left of them,*
> *Cannon in front of them*
> *Volley'd and thunder'd;*
> *Storm'd at with shot and shell,*
> *Boldly they rode and well,*
> *Into the jaws of Death,*
> *Into the mouth of Hell——*

His head jerked backwards. Slowly, he slithered down to the ground, finally lying flat.

'Damned fool,' muttered the same officer who'd shouted before. 'Get a stretcher-bearer up here.'

Peaceful for the first time in months, Rupert lay unconscious, eyes closed but lips parted as if he was still roaring out his verses.

Nineteen

Thousands of hot and exhausted soldiers jumbled together with men already crouched under the dubious shelter of Chocolate Hill. The wounded, still waiting for horse ambulances, groaned and protested as legs and arms straggled over them. The new arrivals dropped down and lit cigarettes without speaking. The senior officers wiped their faces and went off for a briefing.

The Colonel understood everything. They were being sent off on a lost cause. Probably, most of the officers in command also understood that, although a fair proportion didn't seem to know where they were or where they were heading.

The noise was immense, the heat, despite the sun being still muffled by the freak mist, seemed more suffocating than ever. None of this mattered to the Colonel. Having successfully crossed the dried lake, he would lead his three divisions to the left, to the north, with the aim of taking Scimitar Hill. It was of no importance to him how many times already this small rise of curved land had been taken by the Allies before being lost again. He had a job to do which he intended to execute with patriotic fervour.

'Well, now you have your chance, old boy!' he said to Willoughby who was keeping very close.

'Yes, sir. It's damned real, at last.'

The press of men was so great that it was becoming hard to keep companies intact. Also, the light was beginning to fail. It was obvious that the sooner the attack began the better, although 'better' was an unlikely notion.

'Get the men up!' ordered the Colonel. He thought of nothing but the job ahead and his heart drummed strong and hard. His officers went about their business, the NCOs went about theirs, pulling men when necessary and in half an hour columns of men were forming up and marching off.

At once, the fire they had been under doubled and trebled until the whole air was filled with the shriek and whistle and boom of machine gun, rifle, shrapnel and shell. It was at least half an hour's march to Scimitar Hill and, as they approached, the men were given the order to break ranks and move forward as best they could, using what cover had not been burnt off: ditches, hedges, even the black skeletons of the hard prickly scrub that covered the ground.

Men dropped, men skidded, men flew, men simply crumpled. The Colonel was at their head and all around him his officers chided and encouraged:

'Come on now!'

'Don't look back!'

'Forward to victory!'

On the ground lay the already dead but the attackers went round them, bending their eyes forward. The shouts from the officers lessened as they were picked off, too easily visible. The men carried on, as the ground sloped up, as they lost sight of their friends or saw them toppling over. Shellfire tore them apart.

For a long time the enemy remained invisible, obscured by the mist, by their well dug trenches, by their position on the higher ground, by the thick green scrub around them. But as the yeomanry approached the flat crest of the hill, a yelling force was there to greet them.

'Allah! Allah!'

The Colonel ran forward waving his stick: 'For God and country!'

Enough soldiers followed him to burst through the Turkish defenders and overrun the hill.

Willoughby, shot in the leg, lay on the ground and watched them go.

The firepower was so intense that any undergrowth not yet burned burst into flames. In the great heat, scrub of all different sorts blazed up and caused a new hazard to healthy men and a torturing death to the wounded. Acrid white smoke swirled up into the darkening sky. Painfully, Willoughby began to crawl down the hill. He rested for a moment. Another bullet hit him in the groin.

Behind him the smoke and the flames formed a barrier between him and the men, including the Colonel, who had gone over the top. Whole areas were piled with dead and wounded. Soon some were burned into charred lumps.

At the furthest point towards the Turkish lines, the Colonel lay sprawled out on his face. He was still just alive. As a dark curtain drew over his mind, he thought of his beloved Beatrice. He said a prayer that her grief should not be too great to bear and that she would find happiness again. Too late he wished he had sent to her that emotional message of love written only in his head.

Arthur, with others of the London Brigade, had been directed to the right of Chocolate Hill with the object of taking Hill 112 and eventually linking up with the Anzac forces above.

Immediately, the soldiers in his brigade were broken up in confusion. The ground was treacherous with dried watercourses and separated into sections by thick hedges and brambles, quite apart from the vicious scrub that grew thickly everywhere except in a few untended fields. It was impossible to keep any sort of order or command. Things were made even worse by soldiers from other units who had fought earlier and were now returning, either wounded or because they thought they were being replaced. Units became hopelessly mixed.

All the officers could do was encourage any men they could gather round them – and none of these men had fought before – to group together and take limited objectives in the right direction. Not that they could ever be certain of the right direction. Arthur's months on Helles had taught him a self-sufficiency in battle that few of his fellow officers who had come fresh from England shared. Many of them had travelled straight from the ships that had brought them out to the battlefield. They were not even acclimatised to the heat and a large number were suffering from recent injections against typhoid.

They were not fighting an invisible enemy, although the Turkish snipers performed their usual trick of disappearing in any cover above waist height and delivering precision death. Arthur was used to this brilliant infiltrating but for many soldiers it was unnerving because it was unexpected, almost unearthly.

But the Allies had come prepared to fight and, with all their disadvantages, there were a great many of them.

Turk and Englishman struggled at close hand, with equal determination to give no quarter. Bayonets, fixed permanently to their rifles, sliced through flesh. Sometimes a dagger came out of a sleeve and finished off an unwary soldier. It was a confused slaughter which seemed to have no object but to kill before being killed.

There were lines to be held or taken, saps to be protected, but in the busy killing fields of no man's land, nothing could be certain.

As the murky sun gave way to a dusky twilight, Arthur found himself with Major Bubby and about a dozen men very close to the edge of one of the Turkish trenches.

His heart leapt and pumped new blood through his tired body. The major had seen the trench too and waved them forward. They crouched, each man intensely aware of every movement round them, as well as being determined on the goal ahead. For a moment there was an eerie calm, so that Arthur even imagined he heard a bird singing, then they burst forward, the men shouting, bayonets fixed.

Their speed took them in a few seconds to the trench, their eyes brilliant with triumph, their bodies stretched to the limit.

The screams from the first man alerted them to danger but it was too late to stop their forward motion. Beyond the lip of the deep trench glittered an array of bayonets and knives. They jumped and, as if in a mantrap, they screamed and fell.

Arthur found himself rolled in the bottom of the trench, unhurt. He couldn't see Major Bubby. Around him were three or four of his men who were also unhurt or only slightly hurt. Blood spurted over him and he prepared to die.

A rough hand grabbed hold of his shoulder. A dark face with narrowed eyes stared at him.

'Officer?' The word was just recognisable.

Arthur nodded.

The man shouted commands at his soldiers and bundled Arthur backwards out of the trench. His legs didn't seem to be working but it didn't matter because the Turk who held him dragged him along.

With a feeling of disbelief, Arthur realised that, at this moment at least, he was not going to die: he had been captured. An immense sense of aloneness, followed by utter exhaustion, overwhelmed him.

PART THREE

August 1915

༒

'Please send me as soon as possible your report on the main
issue at The Dardanelles, namely, leaving or staying.'

Telegram from Lord Kitchener
(Secretary of State for War) to General Monro,
received on the island of Imbros, 29th October 1915

Twenty

On 29th August, Beatrice received a telegram from the War Office. She knew instinctively what was inside the envelope and that the date would be for ever fixed in her mind. She didn't open it at once but sat in the Colonel's study where Lily had brought it, and looked out of the window. It was a hard, bright, windy day and a clematis which needed tying back (a stripy purple Viticella) was scratching the glass.

Nobody came near her and she heard none of the usual noises of the house. After a while she picked up from the desk the case containing the brooch Bingo had sent her for her birthday from Cairo. It was stamped with her initials and the date of the Mediterranean Expedition. Lifting the lid, she stared at the diamond star and crescent for several minutes before closing the case again and putting it away in one of the drawers of the desk. Then she opened the envelope.

It took her some time to take in what she was reading: *Wounded ... Missing.* The relief was overwhelming. Jumping up, she flung open the window and drew in great gulps of summer air. Out loud, she told the wisteria, 'He's just wounded so put away your claws and behave yourself!'

She returned to the desk and the telegram which told her that it had happened on 21st August and there were no particulars yet. This was unsettling. Her euphoria began to evaporate. How badly was he wounded? Where was he? Was he in hospital? In Gallipoli? In Egypt? In Malta which they had both liked so much? She knew there were hospitals there. Or was he on some battlefield, some valley, some hilltop? Was he in pain? Did it mean loss of limb, or disfigurement, or perhaps it was so slight a wound he would go back again and fight? Why were there 'no particulars'? Perhaps the worst had happened already and all this talk of 'wounded and missing' was merely a smokescreen to conceal the truth.

Jumping up again, Beatrice ran through to the room where the Colonel's bronzes were displayed and picked up the Etruscan horse. Even though it was small, it was a cool heavyweight in her hands. She ran her fingers along its arched back as she had often seen Bingo do. Her heart rate calmed. Of course the War Office was not lying to her. It would be cruel and pointless. Bingo was wounded and missing. But now the horror of 'missing' struck her all over again. How could they know how he was, if he was missing? Someone had seen him wounded, probably one of his staff, she would find out who, and no more was known. At last she understood what 'no particulars' meant. But it read 'no particulars yet'. The 'yet' was hopeful. They expected more particulars or they wouldn't have written 'yet'.

Beatrice carefully reinstated the horse and returned to sit at the desk. She must think sensibly, without panic. All over the British Isles women were receiving telegrams like this – over the British Empire, indeed – and remained strong. But, Bingo, her dear Colonel, lying injured somewhere, and she could not go to him nor even know where he was or how he felt. It was hard, so hard. She pictured his steady wide-spaced eyes, his short straight nose, his high forehead, higher still since his hair had receded. He would have comforted her. Even now the thought of his face helped. She must remember he was only wounded. *No particulars yet*.

A new idea struck her and she looked round for *The Times*. But all she could find was a map she'd clipped out a few days earlier. The caption to it reported good news:

> The newly landed British forces in Gallipoli pressed forward from Suvla Bay, swept beyond the Salt Lake, captured Elgin Burnu, and formed a long fire lane about two and a half miles inland facing the Anafarta Hills. At the same time the overseas troops pressed forward at Sari Bair, and the lines in this northern zone and at Anzac were joined for a length of twelve miles.

Beatrice put the map close to her eyes and gazed attentively. Perhaps it would tell her where Bingo lay – although of course he had probably been found by now. She put the map aside and took up the telegram again.

There was a light tap at the door. It made no impression on Beatrice. The handle turned and Gussie's head appeared. She wore a hat with white flowers on it and a short pleated jacket.

'Mama.' Gussie hesitated. She felt herself flushing. Everyone in the house knew that a telegram had arrived. She had waited to be summoned. The dread had become greater every moment. 'Are you coming to church?' What a stupid question when her mother sat like a waxwork at her father's desk.

'Oh, darling! Oh, dearest Gussie!' Beatrice held out her arms across the desk.

'Oh, Mama, dear Mama.' Gussie came into the room and stood helplessly. They had been getting on well recently, almost as if her mother knew her news and wanted to be kind. But she didn't know and now it would be even harder to tell her.

'You have come to see the wire I've had from the War Office, I expect. Here, it's in my hand.'

Gussie thought her mother's voice had changed. It had none of the usual distracted quality as if what she was saying was not quite worth anyone's attention. She was exerting self-control, Gussie realised, determined to appear sensible.

'It's not the worst, Gussie. Your father has been wounded. You can read it for yourself.'

So instructed, Gussie took the paper, although continuing to look at her mother who was still speaking. 'It's not very clear, I'm afraid. Perhaps you can make more sense of it. I've been sitting here wondering what it means.'

Now Gussie sat down and read the few words. Beatrice came over and stood beside her.

'What do you think, dearest?' she asked anxiously, but with a practical kind of anxiety.

Gussie's eyes were blurring with tears so she didn't answer.

'I was thinking I might go up to the War Office myself and see if I can find out more. Grandmama has a young friend there, I believe. Even during wartime, the trains will take me there and back in a day. I could catch the nine thirty-four a.m.'

She stopped suddenly, hand to her heart. 'What's that noise?'

'It's the bells, Mama. For church.' Gussie knew her eyes were brimming but she tried to sound as sensible as her mother. 'It's Sunday.'

The two women looked at each other in a new kind of face to face shock, until Beatrice said firmly, 'Of course it's Sunday. Your papa always likes us to attend the morning service so we must not disappoint him.' She took a step or two to the door. 'We must begin as we mean to continue.'

This was too much for poor Gussie who began to weep in earnest.

'Dearest Gussie,' said Beatrice with the look of compassion that her daughter had never seen before. 'You are very young to have to be so brave. Scarcely more than a child, after all. But, if you can bear it, I would like you at my side. We will be late going into church, you see, everyone will turn and I don't want to break down.'

This pathetic plea only made Gussie's tears flow more freely.

Beatrice crouched down beside her and said comfortingly, 'Sssh, dearest. He is just wounded, remember, and the "missing" merely means he hasn't made it on to the army lists yet. You know how the army loves lists but is frightfully bad at them. Besides, all the clever people who might have sorted out things are fighting now. *The Times* is more reliable, but it's Sunday. No *Times* today. So, be a good child, dry your eyes and come with me while I find a hat. I shall wear the one with cornflowers. It was – it is – your papa's favourite.'

Beatrice stood up again and went to the door where she waited expectantly.

With a great effort, Gussie stopped crying and, wiping her eyes, went to join Beatrice. She wanted to match her mother's heroic dignity but surely it was too much to bear; her dear old papa 'missing' – the very word dreadful – a baby growing in her tummy, and Reggie back from the front next week when she must tell him that he was a father. A father in waiting. To her horror, Gussie found herself giving a terrified, explosive giggle.

Beatrice, unhearing, took her arm and together they left the room.

A small procession of recuperating officers and servants, led by Beatrice and Gussie, came out of the wide front door, across the drive and into the garden, the quickest way to the church. They would be late all the same. The vicar would certainly have started his sermon, thought Gussie, feeling glad that he no longer gave the hell-fire variety.

The sun blazed down from a clear blue sky and as Beatrice set a brisk pace, everyone began to sweat and go red in the face. The soldiers dropped back and, when they reached a part shaded by tall azalea bushes, Gussie timidly touched her mother's arm.

'Could we go a little slower, please?'

Beatrice stopped and turned round. 'Oh dear.' She took in the ragged nature of her followers. 'I'd never make a good general. I suppose my feet were keeping pace with my thoughts. I can't tell you how they are racing round. In circles mostly. We must send a wire to Sylvia as soon as possible. Although we could wait until I have further news. I expect she wouldn't want that.' She tried and failed to smile reassuringly at Gussie. 'Are you feeling unwell?'

'A little faint.'

By now everyone had caught up and Beatrice set off again at a calmer pace. 'It's not as if I care whether we're late,' she murmured to Gussie. 'I only care about one thing now. How odd it is that a little bit of paper should entirely change the way one looks at things!'

Fred was dreaming of the hospital ship. A silver sickle moon, almost transparent, hung above it in the black sky. He couldn't see the outlines of the ship which was moored about a mile from shore, but its lights dazzled his eyes and cast multicoloured reflections into the dark sea. At the bow and stern there were two brilliant globes; along its sides strung green lights glittering like emeralds, at its centre flamed the scarlet cross.

'Chaffey!' A hand shook him and handed him a mug of tea.

Fred sat up immediately. 'Thanks, Parky.' In the day the sun was still hot but the nights were cold now which was why he slept restlessly. At some point the army would think about providing blankets. He was lying on a low headland, protected by sandbags. Over them he could see the hospital ship which was exactly as in his dreams, although dawn's approach caused the lights to seem dimmer.

'What's up, today?'

'I don't know why the dysentery chaps come in. They only get sent back up.'

'Makes a break, I suppose.'

'It's not as if we're any safer here.'

'You can be killed anywhere in this bloody place,' agreed Fred.

'You're telling me,' said Parky with feeling. The day before, two medical orderlies had been seriously injured leading a group of wounded to the beach. Parky was a medical orderly himself, a tall gangly youth who had a pronounced lisp owing to his front two teeth projecting over his bottom lip. Everyone except Fred called him 'Bucks' or 'Bunny' and pretended not to understand him. Fred had showed him the teeth in his pack and joked, 'If they'd been yours, they'd never have got them off.' Parky had not laughed much but appreciated Fred's attempt to make light of his affliction. Fred was still off sick but quite often he kept Parky company on his rounds. It was something to do. The doctors found him quite useful too, if he didn't ask too many questions.

Today, when they reached the dressing station, two young officers who had come in for treatment stood discussing life.

'We'll have to do something about that pier,' said one, staring down at the beach. 'Once the autumn gales get going, it'll disappear overnight.'

'Ditto, the breakwaters. Look, that one's already half broken after that smallish storm we had a couple of days ago.'

For a moment they stopped talking as Fred came closer but such was his insignificance in their order of things that they soon started again.

The other officer shook his head. He wore the pinched expression common to everyone who had spent much time on the peninsula. He had one arm in a sling. 'It's not that I think we can't do it, get to Achi Baba and the rest, Constantinople even, but we can't do it as we are. Do you know I've had three machine guns fall apart in the last week? How am I going to replace *those*?'

They were interrupted by a doctor, beckoning them inside the wooden shed where he worked. Fred turned to watch the usual magical sunrise come up over the hills. It amazed him that those officers, despite all their experience of failed attacks, still felt success was possible. At the moment men were digging saps at the front, getting closer and closer to the enemy lines. The trouble was that once they were nearly touching, as he'd been told they were in some cases, then the barrage from the ships couldn't get the Turks in case they got our lot as well.

One way and another, people got injured or killed. He'd be back there soon. He'd never be a shirker, not like that chap yesterday who blew his own foot off.

'Hey, Chaffey!' Parky came up in a hurry. 'They need someone who knows the terrain to guide a walking wounded back from somewhere near the French lines. You up for it?'

There was no doubt Fred knew the terrain: scored, mined, criss-crossed with traps, skilfully concealed barbed wire, new defences, new artillery posts. But with any luck this chap was far away from such nasties, perhaps in what remained of a vineyard or an olive grove. Almost nostalgically, Fred thought back to the early days at Helles. There'd been more proper fighting, certainly, but their spirits had been high. After the disastrous landings were put behind them, they still hoped the army knew what it was doing. On a good day, it had still been an adventure.

'I'll go,' said Fred, fixing his helmet more securely. 'Do my leg good to get a bit of exercise. I'll need two water bottles and basic first aid kit.' As he left, an Allied reconnaissance plane flew overhead. He wouldn't mind being up there, looking down. He used to think that watching the birds flying over but lately he'd seen none. He didn't know the migrating habits of birds in Asia, but he guessed it was the guns that scared them away. At home it would still be too early for any exodus. It felt as if he been away for years, not months. It felt as if he was an entirely different person from that rebellious country boy who'd left but what he was now he couldn't tell.

Fred set off up the track. He was so practised in recognising the distance of enemy fire that he only bothered to duck when it must land within a few yards. Sometimes being on Gallipoli seemed the only world he'd ever known.

Rupert was aware of blackness and a headache that crashed against his skull like a shell from a fifteen-inch gun. It was an unending pounding that made him put up his hands, which met bandages. His whole head including his eyes seemed to be swathed which would explain why he could see nothing but blackness. This might have been a relief – what was there that he wished to see? – but for the endless sound and fury inside and outside his mind.

Unwillingly, he groaned, causing only more agony.

'He is conscious.' A man's voice spoke close by. So he could hear outside his head. This was neither good nor bad, simply a fact of his new existence. He had no doubt everything had changed.

He felt a movement beneath him, a regular swaying motion which, after a few seconds, he realised meant that he was at sea. In a ship. Probably a big ship. These deductions told them that his brain was still working despite the hideous assault of the fifteen-inch guns, and, again, this was neither good nor bad.

'Can you move your hands?' The voice spoke slowly and distinctly as if to a fool.

'I just did.' So he could speak too. Perhaps not so very much had changed. Then why did he feel so certain that nothing would be the same? A new sound joined the pandemonium in his head: a discordant rollicking, ringing and jangling as if all the bells in all the cathedrals in England had decided to practise there.

Rupert groaned again.

A hand touched lightly on the arm. So he could feel as well. 'Can you move your legs?'

He moved them.

'Good. Thank you.'

Something was good. He had been thanked for something. It made him want to laugh except even the thought of such activity set off new gunfire. This time it was accompanied by two or three scarlet flashes of light. It was the darkness that was stifling him and turning his mind inwards. Sweat ran off his body.

He put a hand up to tear away his bandages.

'Sssh.' The man's hand restrained him.

'I want to see!' He thought he had wanted nothing ever again but now he wanted to see. So quickly. 'I want nothing.' He lay back quietly.

'The doctor will come as soon as he can.' The invisible man patted his leg. 'I've sent a message saying you're conscious.'

Curiosity. Could he really be feeling curiosity about this man?

'I'm going to give you an injection.'

But he had lost interest.

'He is conscious.'

Rupert entered the darkness again.

'I am Dr Coutts. You have been unconscious or sedated for some days. We are at sea, going back to England.'

The doctor's weary voice scarcely reached Rupert through the renewed bombardment. He made an effort. 'Take away the bandages.'

'We can't do that yet, I'm afraid.' There was a pause. 'Are you up to hearing about your condition?'

There seemed no answer. Rupert groaned as lightning struck a sensitive part of his brain. His body trembled. The doctor seemed to take this for assent or perhaps he regretted his question. The whole ship was full of wounded.

'You have a bullet or perhaps a piece of shrapnel lodged in your brain. It might be extracted but not on board ship and not by me. You will need a specialist. At the moment it is likely you are blind. You appeared to be blind when we first got hold of you. Perhaps you remember. Hence the bandages. Just a precaution. You can have them off if you like. The nurse will see to it. I'm sorry.'

The doctor went. The doctor's footsteps went. There was the light touch.

'Go away,' said Rupert.

So he was blind. That was why he'd known everything was changed for ever.

The nurse's footsteps went away.

The pain came in waves, the ship rode on waves, time floated or perhaps he floated on time. Sometimes he was on top, a real presence in the darkness. Maybe he couldn't stand it. Maybe he wouldn't be asked to stand it. There were no people anywhere except for the nurse with his light touch.

'Shall I take away the bandages now?'

'What's the point?' *There* was a question. He groaned.

'Shall I give you an injection?'

'Brandy would be better.'

Rupert heard a laugh. Through the violent barrage in his head he heard a small chuckle. If a man could still laugh, if he could make a man laugh, then he didn't know what to think. 'Take off the bandages. Things can't look worse.' Again he heard a little sound. 'Any submarines spotted lately?'

*

Cairo was hotter than ever and the hospitals had suddenly become so overcrowded that some lucky wounded had to be sent on to England, although the conditions they endured lying jammed on the decks side by side, were not likely to improve their health.

Sylvia, not content with 'ladylike' nursing once her father and Arthur had gone, was now working as a nurse. This change, usually a matter of endless interviews with matrons as unfeeling as mountains, was arranged by Mrs Twigg-Smith whose only interest in life since her son's death was to overcome challenges.

'You are a gift to them, dear: calm, trained . . .'

'I'm not really fully trained, Dorothy,' Sylvia had intervened.

'I will see you are placed in recovering surgery,' Mrs Twigg-Smith had riposted confidently. 'You are quite up to that.'

Now Sylvia's life shrank to what she had found so trying in Camberwell: a dawn-to-dusk day of hospital routines. Moreover, she must leave her hotel and join the other nurses in the hostel where they lodged and which carried its own rules and regulations.

But she no longer found it difficult. In fact she found the never-ending work a relief. This was mainly due to something near to a nervous collapse she had suffered after her father had left. In his absence and in the absence of anyone she felt close to. Her behaviour with Captain Prideaux, which she had at first so easily and shamelessly accepted, became a source of misery and self-reproach. She lay in the stuffy heat of her room or walked aimlessly in the noisy shambles of the streets, while her heart hammered home the appalling truth: she had slept with Arthur because she loved him, because they loved each other and because he was going to war, then only a week or two later, she had slept with a stranger who she didn't love, who was an alcoholic, a cynic, a beastly man, and certainly didn't love her. Looking back to their brief coming together in his squalid room (but not as brief as all that) she had to admit that he had not forced her, or even seduced her. If anything she had been the keener while he had been understandably prepared to take what was on offer.

The worst of it, of the whole torturous situation, was the knowledge, if she allowed herself to be honest, which she dreaded but which descended when she lay awake, like a nightmare, unbidden, unstoppable, that she had enjoyed making love – no, *sleeping with* (although she'd never slept) – more with Prideaux than Arthur. This was true, even though he had not tried to satisfy himself but gained all his pleasure apparently in making her sigh and tremble under his touch.

Then she loathed herself, was filled with confusion and spent a sleepless night. Usually, by morning, her exhaustion produced a kind of amnesty between her wavering feelings, where she was certain that she loved Arthur as deeply as she could love anyone and that her behaviour with Prideaux had been the product of hysteria – the hysteria of war, the hysteria of departures into danger. It meant nothing true or lasting and, as such, must be disregarded and eventually forgotten.

Through this process of thought, she looked about for a worthy calling and thankfully handed herself over to the life of nursing. It was a kind of penance but one about which she felt positive and even proud.

When a note had come from Arthur saying he was moving to be with her father – no names of person or place to attract the censor – she was able to feel glad that the two men she loved most on earth were together. She neither knew nor cared about the whereabouts of Captain Prideaux and gradually thought of him less and less.

In fact, she had so little time to herself, sharing a bedroom with a depressed older nurse called Lettice Evercreech who, moreover, snored, that she did not consciously think even about Arthur and the Colonel all that much. It seemed that they had been gone for a very long time, although in her father's case, it was less than three weeks.

She had just washed her hair, a small luxury, and was looking in amazement at the amount of sand in the bottom of the bowl, when Lettice came in with a telegram.

'It looks as if it's from England,' she said, pretending to be casual. Her adenoidal tones didn't disguise her curiosity.

'Thanks. I expect it's Mother trying to persuade me to go home. I'll open it in a moment.'

Disappointed, Lettice left the envelope and went.

Sylvia wrapped her hair in a towel and thanked God yet again that she had kept it short. Half an hour and it would be dry. The telegram didn't worry her. Her mother liked to send one now and again because, as she explained, it helped her to feel more closely in contact than letters which were always so out of date by the time they arrived. A half-written letter lay on Sylvia's bedside table at the moment. Yet again she was trying to make her mother understand why she felt it her duty to stay in Cairo.

This was a good time of the day. The rich glow from the setting sun came in through the square window and varnished the beds and furniture inside. The air was still nicely warm before the surprisingly cold night took over. Sylvia had a rare evening off. She opened the cable.

She sat on the bed. The Colonel wounded and missing. Further information on the way. Wounded. Sylvia knew about wounded. She knew about the wounds that mattered and the ones that healed easily. She'd seen men without features, without eyes, without limbs, without stomachs or sometimes scarcely more than lumps of breathing flesh. She did not want that for her father. Trying to control horrible images, Sylvia moved on to the missing. If he was missing, he was gone, surely that was the sense. Did missing men return? To avoid the vile images returning again but now set on some corpse-strewn battlefield, Sylvia stood up and went to the window. The blood red of the sun now struck a desperate chord.

Running her hands through her wet hair impatiently, she picked up a Panama hat and bag and hurried to the door.

'I'm going to the telegraph office!' she called to Lettice who was sitting reading a magazine on the veranda.

'Shall I come with you?'

'No. No.' Sylvia dashed across the courtyard into the streets. The everlasting hubbub made no impression on her as she pushed her way through steaming bodies, street sellers with heavily spiced food, beggars whining for baksheesh, raucous colonial soldiers, silent merchants smoking their hookahs. Joining the tide, she ran to a tram stop and leapt on board the first one that arrived.

It was almost dark when she arrived at the post office. As everywhere, it was crowded, although very few people seemed to be doing any business. As a European woman, Sylvia was pushed straight up to one of the windows. She began to explain the telegram she wanted to send. Before she had finished, the clerk, a sharp-faced, efficient young man, perhaps of French extraction, interrupted her. 'We have a telegram for Fitzpaine, Miss S. I took it myself.'

Sylvia waited. Vaguely she noticed a British officer with a bandage on his head, staring at her.

The telegram arrived and she opened it immediately. It was from Arthur's uncle. ARTHUR MISSING STOP DO NOT GIVE UP HOPE STOP.

Hope? Behind the window, the efficient clerk was holding up a telegram form but she turned away. She must go out, catch another tram, before she fainted or was sick.

'Can I help you?' It was the staring soldier. Sylvia tried to focus on him. She must remember she was a nurse, although in civvy clothes. He was a major, she could see the crown on his sleeve.

'Do missing men ever come back?' she asked impulsively.

He looked at her warily. His face was gaunt like all the men coming out of Gallipoli, but not haunted like some. It was a sensible face. He spoke seriously. 'Some do. One man in my regiment took three days to crawl back from the front line through a watercourse. Then he was picked up by a stretcher-bearer and his number was incorrectly noted so it was over a week before I found out what had happened to him.'

'Thank you.' Sylvia gave a gasp. She felt as if she'd been holding her breath ever since she'd received this second telegram. There *was* hope then.

'Would you like to join me for a drink? I was on my way to Shepheard's.' He seemed tentative and lonely. 'You do know me. At least, you bandaged my head this morning. I'm Major Guy Rockbourne.' He held out his hand.

As Sylvia said nothing, he added, 'I was hoping to receive a letter from my wife telling me our first child is born but no luck. Separation is hell, isn't it?'

Sylvia went with him. He had brought her hope, after all, and anything was better than the hostel and Lettice. She would spend an hour or two with this modest man, not sharing intimacies but sitting together. Then she would take up whatever her life had become again.

At dawn the following morning, Sylvia wrote a letter to Hilda. She explained the two telegrams coming so close together and realised, as she wrote it, that this was most likely no coincidence because they would have been in the same attack, the very attack that had crammed the Cairo hospital full of wounded. She was sitting on the veranda of the hospital where she had crept silently to avoid poor Lettice. (But it was no good pitying Lettice when her pleading eyes annoyed her to madness. She had been still awake in bed when Sylvia returned from her courteous major. 'Do you want to talk, old girl?' she'd asked. 'No' was the only safe answer.)

Outside in the cool pearly light, with the hostel's wall separating her from the first murmurs of the street, she felt able to command herself, to write to Hilda, to plan the renewed visit to the telegraph office as soon as it was open, and from there to turn up at the hospital as usual. She supposed that she might be in shock that she could do these things, or plan to do them. She did feel strange, as if her centre had been hollowed out, leaving only a fragile casing. Yet, looking down at her letter, she could see no change in her handwriting.

It has just occurred to me, she continued, *that I might make enquiries about Arthur and Papa from my patients. It is better, I think, hearing the news out here – I feel sorry for Mama and Gussie. There are just so many sad stories I see or hear every day and the men are so stoic. I've decided men are much more stoic than women, about the big things anyway. Sometimes they let slip the horrific life they lead on Gallipoli. Dear Mama could have no idea of such misery – I don't even want to describe it to you. It makes me glad that Papa was there for only a few days and it also makes me understand why it was difficult making a real connection with Arthur when he was here – even though I did have some idea what he was going through. He needed to keep his armour bright. But we did, in the end, become close.*

Here, again, Sylvia put down her pen. Was it true what she had just written? Yes, it was. She had given herself to him. The sky above the wall had just changed colour and become a thick unbroken yellow. The sound, too, had risen to the babbling and shouting and occasionally revving of some grand person's car which would build to a crescendo during the day. She looked at her watch: five thirty, time to put on her uniform. *Her* armour.

Mrs Twigg-Smith's face beneath and above its usual veils and drapes wore a ruffled look, even a sense of injury which Sylvia had never seen before.

'My dear girl, this is not good. I have just heard.' She came close to Sylvia who stood on the steps of the hospital. The sun was already blazing down and she could have wished for Mrs Twigg-Smith's veil.

'Do you mean my father being missing?' Sylvia screwed up her eyes, then blinked rapidly.

'Brigadier-General Fitzpaine,' Mrs Twigg-Smith began severely, 'is a man for whom I have deep respect, the true yeoman, salt of old England.'

Sylvia suddenly felt enormously tired; she only just stopped herself yawning. Was this the sort of platitude she would have to put up with? She had thought Mrs Twigg-Smith was more eccentric. 'Yes, yes,' she murmured.

'My point,' said Mrs Twigg-Smith, surprising Sylvia by throwing back her veil,' is that your father's ADC has just come into Cairo. Wounded. Seriously wounded. He was on his way to England – you would have thought Malta would have made more sense if they were to divert – but somehow he was brought here.'

Since Sylvia said nothing, and indeed was trying to stop herself from fainting of which Mrs Twigg-Smith seemed quite unaware. She continued with her more ordinary commanding manner, 'I suggest therefore we talk to him before either the British Army or the grim reaper, equal threats to vulnerable men, whisk him away. He is called Captain Noel Willoughby, shot in his leg and groin or perhaps hip, or perhaps both; in any case his brain should be perfectly functional. He is in St Mary's.' Mrs Twigg-Smith stopped abruptly. 'Are you all right, my dear?'

Sylvia, who had been steeling herself to tell her old travelling companion that Arthur was also missing before this new extraordinary piece of information, now took a deep breath. 'Let us see him, this Willoughby, at once.'

'Exactly my thought. I have already apprised your matron of the situation.'

Despite her anxiety verging on panic, Sylvia found herself thinking that, if Mrs Twigg-Smith was running the British army, there would be more successes than failures.

*

St Mary's was a small hospital for acute surgical cases. The matron there seemed bewildered by her own behaviour in giving anyone permission to visit Captain Willoughby. She was small and anxious and sat behind a desk in a hot cubbyhole of an office, as if for protection.

'He is in great pain, imagined in the case of his leg which they took off before he came here, real enough in his groin. His ship, a transport, was torpedoed and he was picked up and first sent to Malta but for some reason he ended here.' She raised her tired eyes which had been staring at the table. 'Are you sure you can't wait a few days?'

The matron was Scottish and Sylvia found herself listening to the soft Scottish accent instead of what she was saying. Now she roused herself. 'We'll only stay a moment or two.'

'I see you are a nurse yourself,' wavered the matron. 'Well. Just a few minutes then. I'll have a sister take you to him.'

Willoughby's eyes were closed and he lay quite still on the iron bedstead, white sheets raised over his body from the waist down. His colourless face was made more tragic by a large orange moustache.

'Captain Willoughby.' Mrs Twigg-Smith spoke gently but with authority.

He opened his eyes which wore the glazed look of someone whose pain had been made a little more remote by the use of morphine.

'We understand you are Brigadier-General Fitzpaine's ADC. This is Miss Fitzpaine. The general has been listed as wounded, missing, and we believe you will have been the last to see him.'

Willoughby turned his head so that Sylvia was in his eye-line. He cleared his throat and when he spoke, his voice was surprisingly strong. 'He was charging on ahead, leading us all up Scimitar Hill. There had been fires earlier and it was black. The Turks met us on the top, first we'd seen of them. But then I was wounded.' He stopped. His eyes shut for a moment. Sylvia imagined he was fighting waves of pain, or maybe he was just remembering.

'Could you still see Brigadier-General Fitzpaine?' encouraged Mrs Twigg-Smith. 'Did you see him wounded?'

He began to speak more quickly. 'I was on the ground. It was smoky. Noisy. Terrifically noisy. When we were crossing the lake, he'd said to me, "Don't duck, Noel, it does no good and the men don't like it", and I thought of it as I lay there. I've no doubt I'd ducked and caught one while he was going forward like a hero. The bullets might have been hail. With only a stick in his hand, he went right over, out of my sight.' He stopped again.

'Shouldn't we go?' whispered Sylvia. Sweat was pouring off Willoughby's face.

Mrs Twigg-Smith ignored her. 'What happened next?'

Again he made an effort and now his words ran together. Sylvia bent closer. 'I may have been unconscious for a bit. Fires had started and it was dark, although there was still gunfire and the flames lit up things. For a few seconds I really did think I was in hell. I managed to crawl back, a Tommy helped me. We didn't want to be burned alive. Everything is vague after that. I was taken back across the lake in a mule ambulance. I remember that because I thought the jolting would kill me if nothing else. Later I heard the hill was lost again. We could never hold it in daylight.' He looked at Sylvia with bleak, unfocused eyes.

'I'm sorry. I admired the Brigadier-General more than I can say. All day we'd waited for our turn to come, but by the time it did, we knew it was pretty hopeless. But your father was so strong, none of us, not even the Tommies, poor boys, thought of anything but going forward. I've thought of it lots since, lying around as I am; we were young men believing we were invincible. But he was different. He understood the risks. That's true heroism.'

'Thank you.' Sylvia laid her hand on his; the skin was pink and peeling as if with old sunburn. He closed his eyes again and made no sign he felt her touch. Red patches appeared on his cheeks. She thought that he was the last connection to her dear papa because everything he'd said made it clear that he'd died on the battlefield. She wanted to sit there quietly with her hand on poor Willoughby's. How strange it was that the kind, convivial father she knew, a modest man who loved his wife and his daughters, his horses and his land, should end his life in such a dramatic way. It was hard to imagine but she had no doubt it was true. Perhaps she would come to be proud of him, of his bravery, but at the moment, she could only feel the dreadful waste.

'We should go,' said Mrs Twigg-Smith, rising. Reluctantly, Sylvia followed her. 'I'm sorry, my dear,' she said once they were in the corridor. 'I'm afraid there seems little doubt. I can't think what the War Office means by "Missing. Wounded." Best to take it on the chin.'

'Yes,' said Sylvia. 'Thank you.'

'Nor do I think that young man will see many more days.'

'Oh, no!' Sylvia, who had managed to accept the death of her father without collapsing, found herself overwhelmed with sorrow at the idea of Captain Willoughby not making it. Her shoulders heaved and tears ran out of her eyes and down her chin.

'Buck up, old thing.' Mrs Twigg-Smith whose many skills did not include easy sympathy but who was fond of Sylvia, stared at her in dismay.

'It's just that poor boy. Everything he's been through and all the pain and no leg . . .' Sylvia's attempt at an explanation ended in further tears.

'He might be happier d—' began Mrs Twigg-Smith before thinking better of it. 'I don't believe we need to thank Matron. How about a cup of coffee?'

'No. No,' sniffed Sylvia. 'I'll get back to work. They're frightfully short-staffed.'

'That's the girl,' said Mrs Twigg-Smith, surveying the swirling flood of humanity in the street below them like a strong swimmer on a diving board. 'Your dear father would expect no less of you and I might be wrong about young Willoughby. Didn't strike me as a weakling.'

'No,' agreed Sylvia, 'he certainly didn't.' She thought that in happier days his moustache must have been a jolly sight.

It was obvious to her now that she was not going to tell Mrs Twigg-Smith that Arthur was also missing. Later she would send a reply to Arthur's uncle and, her heart quavered, another to her mother.

Just as they were parting, Mrs Twigg-Smith surprised Sylvia by taking her arm. 'You may think I am rather unfeeling but I'd like you to know that my own dear lost boy is always in my thoughts. I have taught myself to be strong, just as you will.'

Sylvia sent a telegram to her mother. SPOKE TO FATHER'S ADC STOP NOT GOOD NEWS STOP. The following morning she received a telegram signed by Gussie. MOTHER IN TOUCH WAR OFFICE STOP CONVINCED HE'S ALIVE STOP PLEASE COME HOME STOP.

Fred had gone down to W Beach because he'd seen the mailboat arriving, a tatty old trawler who believed herself not worth a torpedo. This afternoon the danger came not from torpedoes or shells but a ferocious storm Fred could see chasing along behind. The rumble of thunder and the wild zigzags of lightning mimicked the fighting on land. Although things were quiet just then.

'Take a bet on who wins the race?' he said to the private standing behind him.

'That fishing boat has a charmed life.' The other man smoked his cigarette while looking ruminatively at the massing black clouds. 'I've seen a shell fall fore and aft yet not touch a whisker of her.'

'A direct hit from the lightning?' suggested Fred.

The man, Silas Oakes, a countryman from Cornwall, nodded. 'That would do it.'

Suddenly, much quicker than even they had expected, the squall pounced upon the boat like a toy. It was spun round, tossed into the air, held motionless, then whisked towards a maelstrom of waves.

The men watched silently. 'At least there's no lightning,' said Fred.

At that moment, the sky blazed with silver light, accompanied after a couple of seconds by the crack and roll of thunder. Automatically both men ducked and ran for cover. Out at sea, the boat, which had seemed lost, righted itself and, plunging up and down on the waves like a rocking horse, moved slowly forward. By the time it reached the pier, half washed away, the squall had passed and a brilliant sun sparkled on the water streaming off the boat's deck.

A cheer went up from the soldiers waiting to receive it.

Fred was reading a letter from Lily. Troops were in such short supply that he was back in the front line again. But he'd made himself cosy and was always the first to know about a new enfilade or sniper or threatening mine work. There was no point anybody risking their life unnecessarily. He wasn't much for the underground work himself but some men seemed to take to it like badgers.

The letter was soaking wet. Sent early in September.

Not much good news from here, I'm afraid. The Colonel is reported wounded and missing which everybody except poor Lady Beatrice assumes means he's passed on, God rest his soul, and today we heard Miss Sylvia's fiancé is reported missing too . . .

Fred put down the letter and, carefully cupping his hands, lit a rare cigarette. Even though he'd worked out since they'd started regular letter writing, that Lieutenant Lamb was Sylvia Fitzpaine's fiancé, he'd not found much in their goings-on to interest him. It was sad the lieutenant was missing, of course – he'd got those teeth dug out of his thigh, for one thing – but there wasn't any use for sadness where he was.

The big secret which I'm only telling you because you're in no position to tell anyone else (although I don't mind if you shout it to Johnny Turk!) is that young Miss Augusta has fallen pregnant with Reggie Gisburne's baby, the rector's uppity son. The poor girl doesn't dare tell her ladyship. The only silver lining is the man's just won an MC so maybe him being a war hero will help sugar the pill.

Fred stopped reading again. The closest he'd come to a woman was when the lads had caught a sniper who they'd sworn was a female, Jenny Turk. But when they'd got off the green paint and branches, he'd been as male as the rest of them. In their disappointment, they'd shot him there and then.

Apart from Jenny Turk, they didn't even talk about women any more, unless you counted their mums. If you weren't fighting, you were digging and if you weren't digging, you were in the latrines or scavenging for food which usually sent you back to the latrines. A chaplain had told him that there were hundreds of dysentery cases being taken off the peninsula each week, despite the cooler weather and the departure of the worst of the flies. The chaplain said he must be made of steel to have lasted so long. Well, perhaps he was. All his wounds were as good as new.

Night had fallen while Fred lay reading and thinking, and it was his job to check out a gully which had been giving them a spot of bother. The corporal would come for him in a moment. Warmed you up, didn't it.

Rupert had been told by a nurse – oh, the surprise of a girl's voice! – that the ward he lay in held twenty beds for acute head and eye injuries. He was also told by a doctor that he was on Malta. He had visited the island often in the past; now, in his imagination, it became Prospero's isle filled with magic and fairy voices. After all, they had been shipwrecked.

The hospital ship in which he and many other patients travelled had been torpedoed. The open sea at night, the cries, the panic, the waves had been experienced only through his ears and the feeling of his body. He had not expected to survive. It seemed certain that the grim reaper who had refused to take him when he offered himself on Chocolate Hill, had returned to gather him in. He had prepared himself. He wasn't worth saving.

Maybe his mistake had been to take the war too seriously. Even a peasant soldier from Anatolia or a Tommy from Bermondsey could have told him that.

On this afternoon, his head was blazing with agonising star-bursts as if shells exploded inside his brain. He was also cold and waited for the nurse's footsteps so that he could ask for more bedclothes. Instead he heard the tentative step of a man; he already knew his doctor's brisk stride and this was not it.

'Captain Prideaux?'

It was strange how the habit of looking in the direction of a speaker persisted.

'I wonder if you'd mind asking the nurse to bring me another blanket.'

'It *is* cold here. I'll do it straight away.' The footsteps went. Rupert's greatest worry was that one of his parents – or a relative dispatched to represent them, came to find him, to take him 'home'. Home! Luckily, his manner of arrival at Malta would probably confuse things for a time. Perhaps he would die before they arrived. The specialist had declined to operate, saying that the shell fragment had most probably severed the optic cord but somehow missed anything more serious. On the other hand, so he gave Rupert to understand, it could move, which would not be a good thing. 'I'm sorry,' he'd said, as they all did. Sometimes he wondered if they'd be so kind if he told them the circumstances of his wounding.

Soldiers who shot themselves in the foot were executed for their pains. He, of course, had been seeking suicide with honour. Ironically, his failure seemed to have ended the wish or at least any action towards it. Sharp knives were safe with him.

'Thank you.' A blanket was laid across his bed and he heard a chair being scraped up.

'It must have been nerve-racking for you when the torpedo hit,' said the voice.

'Ah,' Rupert sighed as the pain suddenly lessened. 'The torpedo didn't worry me. I was helpless and in darkness already.'

'You were carried to a lifeboat?'

'The sailors were very kind. The cold was intense. I feel sad about so many good men lost but we must expect no better during a war.' Rupert thought that he heard the man sit up straighter. 'Who are you? Are you a priest?'

There was a small gasp. 'How do you know?'

'When the hospital ship sank, I knew it by the indrawn breaths of the men in the lifeboat around me. I "saw" it going down. Are you young? I can't tell that.'

'No. I'm forty. I'm Maltese, although I was educated in England. My name is Father Lombardi.'

'The main thing is you're not against death.'

'I'm sorry?'

'You think death is a gateway to somewhere better. If you've lived your life properly, that is. Do you believe in hell?'

'I believe there is a hell,' said the voice carefully, 'but I'm not sure if anyone's in it.'

'That's very wishy-washy of you.' As Rupert spoke it was as if the letters W and S set up a tsunami in his head and the new pain flooded out everything. He groaned. He cried out. He didn't hear the priest leaving. But he was still alive, he knew that.

Twenty-One

Arthur sat behind the Turkish lines. His arms were tied behind his back. There was a German officer who spoke good English. 'You're out of the war now,' he said. His neat moustache twitched disparagingly.

It had been raining and the ground on which Arthur sat, once a field, was soft and muddy. He was no longer anywhere near the fighting and the only sound was the occasional truck, the whinny of a horse, and the birds, black as crows, wheeling above their heads. It seemed as if he had been either sitting or walking for days and days. Now this officer planted himself above him.

'Where did you learn your English?' Arthur roused himself to ask a question which only marginally interested him.

'That is not the point.'

'No. But since I'm out of the war, which you've been kind enough to mention, you might as well tell me.'

'Charterhouse and Oxford,' said the officer, relenting, although he still dominated the skyline. There were pine trees behind him, dark and dripping.

'Are you my interrogator?'

'I am not your official interrogator.' He looked down and frowned. 'The Turks will treat you well because you are an officer.'

It was true that recently no one had shown him any violence. At the beginning it had not been so easy. Twice, Turkish soldiers moving to the front had tried to attack him, one levelling his rifle, but at that point the officer was still with him and had beat each of them off quite brutally with his sword. When the officer had left he had received a blow on his head which may have been the reason his grip of time was vague. His present guard, two very young soldiers, scarcely ever looked at him, although once they'd

281

fed him a bunch of grapes – perhaps as a joke. How greedily he'd eaten them! 'There were three or four men captured with me.'

'They are not so kind to the men. There is nothing we can do. Now I shall go. Later I may bring you a book.'

Arthur had a sudden panic. 'Where will I be taken?' he shouted.

The German didn't turn round. Why should he know the answer? He was only trying to be kind. But he didn't return with a book.

Some hours later Arthur was moved again. It was evening, the birds had disappeared. Soon the long cold darkness would come again. His stomach had begun to play up but when he asked to stop, his guards shouted '*Yok*,' which he guessed meant no. He hated the idea of days in soiled breeches but they seemed to know when he was at the last point of agony and came over to untie his hands. They stood near him smoking pungent cigarettes. They would have been more caring if they'd been leading an animal. By their ragged clothing, hardly uniform at all, he guessed they were peasants, brought in as support, and not yet trained to fight.

His thoughts, chasing wildly at first, had now settled into one constant preoccupation. How was it he had never considered the possibility of capture? And what would it mean? From the beginning, even before he volunteered, death had been a fate he understood, the fine death described by Homer. With university friends – a life that seemed irretrievably far away – he had discussed, with excitement and solemnity mixed, the concept that death, always a heroic death, gave meaning to life. As he crossed that white salt lake, only a few days earlier which now seemed an eternity, he had still believed it. Perhaps he believed it now. If one of those *yok*king peasants stuck a knife into him, would his life make more sense? It certainly would be easier. Of course his months on Gallipoli had shown him that death was not the only kind of heroism; he had seen wounds that were worse than any torture man could devise, sometimes borne with fortitude, sometimes provoking an abject cringing cowardice which made other men turn away. But surely death remained the greatest sacrifice?

So where, in all this, was captivity? He had not asked for it. He had not surrendered. He had not laid down his arms nor put up his hands. He had been taken. Snatched. Abducted. If a soldier can be abducted. He'd had no choice in the matter. Did that make things better? But what did he mean by 'better'? More honourable? Yes, more honourable. But soldiers, even great soldiers were captured, usually surrendering so that their men should not be killed. But his capture had been too quick for any of that.

The reality was that he had, in one instant, become a prisoner of war and he must learn to live with it. The German officer who had spoken to him saw him in that light, out of the fighting, a non-combatant, a non-person, a nuisance. His Turkish guards looked at him in the same way, except they probably thought he was lucky to be alive. It must have been arrogance that had made him believe, if he thought of captivity at all, that it happened to other people.

It was raining again, bitterly cold. Arthur massaged his leg. The cramp which had assailed him on his landing on Gallipoli and left him alone since, had recently returned in a random vice-like grip. He lifted his head and saw through the water running down his face – he had lost his helmet in the trench – lights ahead. Soon he saw a couple of round white tents and a small group of wooden buildings. To his left there were moving shapes which might be horses or mules. It seemed this was some kind of destination.

His guards, throwing away cigarettes, pushed him towards the first tent. Arthur had a hallucinatory sense of entering a child's story-book world. What would be the other side of the closed flap? A candlelit feast with veiled dancing girls? Again, he shook the water from his eyes. A horse whinnied. A winged horse, perhaps. He imagined a black-bearded, turbaned tyrant, cringing slaves…

'Welcome old boy. Major Bubby thought you'd been taken. Then, when you didn't turn up, we feared the worst. You can't trust the Turks not to stick in a bayonet if the mood takes them. Come in. Come in.'

Blinking idiotically, Arthur surveyed a group of British officers seated close together on the floor. The one who had spoken, who was still speaking in a cheerful matter-of-fact tone, was a captain. He had a rough bandage round his head that gave him a piratical air although his face was thoroughly English with a large brown moustache.

'Thank you. I…' Arthur hesitated, looked round at the expectant faces. Their pleasure in seeing him was so obvious that he suddenly felt moved. During his days alone, he had not thought there would be others like him; he had felt utterly solitary as if he must face all the implications of his situation inside his own brain. But here he was being welcomed by a band of brothers. He realised he had begun to shake as if the shock was too much. He must have taken a step backwards because there were loud '*Yok*'s from behind. The sound was almost reassuring, as if he'd adapted to one situation and feared the change to another.

'Take off your jacket, Lamb. You're soaking.' A younger man stood up and put a hand on his arm. 'You are Lieutenant Lamb, aren't you? The Major thought so. He's not well, incidentally. Been driven off to hospital somewhere, poor chap. Turkish hospitals, if you know what I mean. I'm sure we can rustle up a blanket.'

'You're very kind.' Ashamed that they should see him trembling, Arthur slowly took off his jacket. He could hardly recall the face of Major Bubby who had so briefly commanded him. A rough grey blanket was placed round his shoulders and he was invited to take a place in the group on the ground.

'Warmer like this,' explained the captain who seemed to be their leader. He gripped an empty pipe between his teeth. 'Like sheep on a hillside, minus the woolly coats, more's the pity. Hot enough in the day, as you know well enough. We'll dry out your jacket then. I won't bother you with introductions yet. We'll have food, if you can call it that, any time soon. Perk you up a bit.'

Arthur wanted to perk up in the face of such sympathy but simply did not have the strength. Shoulders bent, he sat silently with his dirty sunburned hands on his knees. After a while a Turk brought them in a big bowl of bread, followed by another man carrying a tray with mugs of steaming tea. Arthur took the tea gratefully but refused the bread.

The food was eaten in silence. When it was finished, despite Arthur's continued lack of perkiness, the captain began his introductions: 'I'm Captain Paul Lipcock, of the 6th Battalion, East Yorkshire, taken at Suvla, like you, although earlier in the month. These two young 'uns are lieutenants in the Royal Navy – they start them in the cradle there – Lieutenants Alan Trebble and Aidan Standley.' The captain gave the two men a wink. 'Submarine men, which must be the reason they've got the best manners of the lot of us. Picked up on one of their secret missions.' The two young men with narrow, grave faces, both with beards, nodded at Arthur. A wry thought occurred to him: the notification of his promotion to captain would never find him now.

'Have you been interrogated yet?' It was Trebble speaking, or maybe Standley. He had long dark eyes which with his untrimmed beard gave him a Christ-like air.

'A German officer dropped by but he didn't ask me anything. He'd been educated at Oxford.'

'That's the Turks' problem: not enough interpreters. You may avoid it altogether. They're hot on the French. Broussac here's taken off all the time.'

Arthur looked across and saw a wavy-haired boy with naive blue eyes – not the usual image of a French officer. 'I don't know what they think we can tell them.'

'It's all part of the game, I suppose.' Trebble (as Arthur had decided he was) seemed undisturbed by the idea, then looked concerned. 'Are you all right?'

Arthur realised he must have grimaced at one of the increasingly sharp pains in his stomach. 'It's nothing. I may need the latrine.'

'Hole.' Trebble smiled nicely.

'Is there any way of getting letters out?' This idea which he had never contemplated while on his own struck suddenly with great force.

'Lipcock managed it once but lately things have been getting more difficult. It seems we're off to Anatolia shortly. With any luck beginning our journey by sea or it'll be a long run. One of the Turkish officers worked in a hotel in Constantinople and had English friends. He appears now and again and gives us snippets of information. Cigarettes, if we're lucky. The truth is we're in their hands.'

Yes, that was the truth. All the same he'd see if he could talk to Lipcock about getting a letter or telegram off. He tried to remember what he'd been taught about the rights of prisoners of war; letters had to be part of it.

'Were you at German headquarters when you met your officer?' Trebble asked.

'I don't think so. It's all rather vague, actually. I got a bit of a bash on my head. A Turkish soldier whose blood was up; I'd lost my helmet earlier.'

'It's amazing any of us survived.' Trebble leant closer. 'Major

Bubby was taken to General Liman von Sanders himself. Some of the men too. He was quite kind apparently, gave them some money. Do you know what von Sanders said?' He was almost whispering now. 'Lipcock doesn't like it but the major's not a liar.'

'I should think not,' agreed Arthur who was seriously near to visiting the 'hole'.

' "Why did General Hamilton send a handful of men to attack the great hill that commands all my position? Did he think I could be so blind as not to defend it against even a much stronger force?" The poor old major got quite upset by his words, repeating them to anyone who'd listen. Made him sick, or sicker anyway, poor chap.'

'I'm sorry.' Arthur scrambled to his feet and made for the flap. The guard led him to the hole without protest. Afterwards, he stood for a moment and looked up at the sky, encrusted with sparkling stars. He recognised Orion, the Southern Cross. As a prisoner, he might need to treasure the freedom of the skies. He thought of his old platoon in the trenches at Helles and of the men he hardly knew at Suvla. Then, at last, he thought of Sylvia and promised himself to try as hard as he could to get a message to her.

Beatrice travelled up to London with Gussie. They were in first class, of course, but unfortunately the swaying of the train affected Gussie adversely and she spent a lot of the journey rushing to the toilet. The first time she muttered to her mother, 'Tummy's a bit upset.'

Beatrice patted her hand sympathetically. 'It's all such a dreadful shock.'

Gussie thought despairingly, We're so close now but I still can't tell her. Her mother's eyes were made huge by dark circles and her face was as pale as a ghost's. She hadn't eaten since the news of the Colonel and probably not slept either.

On one visit along the corridor, Gussie pulled down a window and let the wind cool her skin. They stopped at a station where soldiers, laden with bags, surged forward. She recoiled but they didn't come into first class.

Then at Basingstoke two officers got into their carriage. They were young and respectfully requested permission to join the ladies. There were no Ladies Only carriages on the train so

Beatrice nodded graciously but she held up *The Times* to avoid any attempts at conversation.

Gussie sat down beside her to show support. Although her mother's brave self-control continued, Gussie knew that she had received a letter from the Colonel that morning, posted on 20th August. She had found her mother standing in the middle of the hall apparently unable to move. Luckily Lily had appeared and gently led her into the study.

'I've read it,' she'd said, looking up with blind eyes. 'It's very short. He wrote that they landed on the eighteenth and that the beach was under fire but not much harm done.' She'd paused for what seemed like ages, then murmured, 'I shall have to write to him, of course. But it's very horrid not knowing if he's still alive – although I'm sure he is – or in great pain or where he is – or even back in danger again.'

'Oh, Mama!' Gussie had cried out, unable to bear the misery any more.

The appeal seemed to bring Beatrice back to herself. She had put her arm round Gussie and said almost bracingly, 'Today we go up to London. It will be good to take action.'

So there they were, sitting in the train, pretending to the two officers that everything was calm and ordinary. But then nothing could ever be calm and ordinary in a war. These bright young men might well be dead or frightfully wounded in a few weeks and she herself, an eighteen-year-old unmarried girl, was going to have a baby. It would never have happened without the war which had taken away all the fun in her life. Despairingly, Gussie reminded herself that she didn't even *like* Reggie – hero or no hero.

Suddenly, Beatrice who had continued holding up *The Times* while turning the pages in an unconvincing way, dropped the paper in her lap. It slithered to the floor and one of the officers hurried to pick it up. Since her mother didn't seem to want it back, Gussie took it.

'Thank you.' She smiled at him but not in the pretty way she would have in the past.

'There's a report,' whispered Beatrice in an agonised voice. 'Read it for me.'

Gussie knew now to turn to page seven where she immediately saw the headline: YEOMANRY IN GALLIPOLI followed by

GLORIOUS BAPTISM OF FIRE and OVER THE CREST OF
THE HILLS. Reading further she caught the line: *The feature
of this action was a brilliant charge by a dismounted Division of
Yeomanry.*

'Oh Mama,' she gulped out, her tears always so ready now.
'They did a brilliant charge.'

'That would please your papa.' Whispering, Beatrice bent towards Gussie. 'Who's written it?'

'E. Ashmead-Bartlett. From Alexandria.'

'Alexandria. Isn't Sylvia in Alexandria?'

'No, Mama. Cairo.' They were still whispering and the officers
were trying to look as deaf and unknowing as possible.

Glancing at them briefly, Beatrice gripped her daughter's wrist.
'Read some more.'

'Out loud, Mama?' asked Gussie, surprised.

'No. No. Just tell me a little.'

So Gussie read the report to herself and then she had to press the
tears back into her eyes with her handkerchief and she didn't feel
sick any longer, just shocked and very cold so that she trembled.
She didn't see how anyone could survive the things described:

> The rifle fire was deafening, and I do not think I have
> ever heard such a din as that produced by ships' guns,
> field pieces, bursting shells, and thousands of rifles on
> any battlefield before... A great solid mass of khaki, with
> bayonets glistening amidst the smoke and dust, seemed
> to emerge from the burnt scrub and surge towards the
> trenches on top... It was now almost dark, and the attack
> seemed to hang fire, when suddenly the Yeomanry leapt
> to their feet and as a single man charged right up the
> hill. They were met by a withering fire... but nothing
> could stop them. They charged at amazing speed without
> a single halt from the bottom to the top, losing many
> men, and many of their chosen leaders... It was a
> stirring sight watched by thousands in the ever-gathering
> gloom... From a thousand lips a shout went up that the
> hill was won. But night was now rapidly falling, the
> figures became blurred, then lost all shape, and finally
> disappeared from view. The battlefield had disappeared

completely, and as one left Chocolate Hill one looked back on a vista of rolling clouds of smoke and huge fires, from the midst of which the incessant roar of the rifle fire never for a moment ceased. This was ominous... all through the night the battle raged incessantly, and when morning broke the hill was no longer in our possession.

It took Gussie a long time to read the article and by the end she could hardly believe she had read it correctly. Had this drawn-out horror really been for nothing? The hill won but lost again?

Meanwhile Beatrice sat patiently waiting, hands tight together in her lap. At Woking two more officers entered their compartment and they were squeezed closer together.

'It was a great victory, Mama,' whispered Gussie. 'They were so brave. They charged up a hill and won it.' She began folding away the paper quickly. Perhaps she could lose it somewhere on the way to the War Office.

'I am glad,' said Beatrice. 'I expected no less of your father. He is a good, kind man but he is also a courageous soldier.' She sighed, but not in anguish. 'I truly am hopeful that we will get more news from Major Bingley, Grandmama's friend, at the War Office.'

Unfortunately, Major Bingley had been called away and they were received by a young Lieutenant Knott who was very obviously struggling with a false leg. Gussie, who for the last days had constantly been on the edge of hysteria, had to stifle giggles when he tripped against a chair and, blushing hugely, only managed to right himself by grabbing the desk. The inkpot danced dangerously.

Beatrice didn't seem to notice. They all seated themselves without further mishap. Behind the lieutenant's head hung a portrait of a red-coated general who glared at them ferociously.

'Major Bingley made a few notes before he left, Lady Beatrice,' began Knott, still blushing. 'I'm afraid they are not very helpful.' He looked up as if hoping he need go no further.

'Yes?' encouraged Beatrice.

'Well, I'm afraid there's no more official news. Brigadier-General Fitzpaine is still listed as wounded and missing. We, are, however, continuing to make enquiries...'

'There was a sighting in a hospital in Alexandria,' Beatrice interrupted him.

Gussie looked at her mother with surprise; nothing had been said about this. She felt the inappropriate hilarity change into a sagging despair. How could that be true?

Obviously nonplussed, the lieutenant shifted his paper around. 'Major Bingley didn't know about any sighting,' he said. 'Perhaps, Lady Beatrice, you could give me the name of your informant and I could check—'

Beatrice interrupted him again. 'It's probably not true. The woman is frightfully unreliable and she was reporting from someone her son had spoken to. But it's a sign, isn't it, that soldiers do turn up if they're wounded or shocked? It's a sign we should carry on.'

'Yes, indeed. And we mean to. Major Bingley told me to tell you that most firmly.' His face was pale now and very earnest.

'I was wondering,' said Beatrice, 'whether it's worth writing to hospitals in Turkey. Men do get captured. I think we could involve the American Embassy in the search.'

Knott looked flustered again and Gussie started to feel really sorry for him. 'Yes. I'm sure that could do no harm . . .'

'If you could get me a list. There must be a great many.'

Gussie began to fear she might be sick again and found herself eyeing the large waste-paper basket as a handy receptacle. 'I'm afraid I'm not feeling well, Mama.'

'Oh, dear Gussie. I'm so sorry.' She turned to the lieutenant. 'Is there a ladies room . . . ?'

'Down the corridor. I . . .' He began to heave himself up again and Gussie thought, Oh no, I shall have to follow him down endless corridors and he will be in pain and embarrassed. And poor poor Mama and Papa! Why is everything so dreadful? She glanced towards her mother and caught her eye.

Beatrice stood up. 'You've been so kind, lieutenant. I think what my daughter needs is fresh air. Please give Major Bingley my regards and inform him that I'll look forward to any further information. I appreciate my husband is only one of the many officers and men missing in the action in which he took part.'

'Lady Beatrice . . .' The lieutenant stopped whatever he was going to say and began blushing again and Gussie wondered how ever he could have led his men into battle. Then she thought, But he is probably a war hero, like Reggie, like my father – what do I know how men behave on the battlefield?

An even younger soldier was summoned from outside the door to take them downstairs.

As they stood waiting for their cab to take them back to the station, Beatrice looked up at the skies which were heavy and grey and murmured, 'It's lucky Winston Churchill wasn't in evidence or I'd have throttled him with my bare hands.'

'What, Mama?'

Beatrice drew on her gloves slowly. 'I told Grandmama I wouldn't enter a drawing room if I knew Churchill was present and she said she'd wouldn't either. But I don't believe her. She's far too worldly.' She turned to Gussie. 'Are you feeling better now, dear?'

'Yes, thank you, Mama.' She thought if she was ever going to confess her situation it would be in a place like this, the middle of a powerful city, crowded with other people's lives. What was one more silly girl to the mass of people rushing by, on foot, in horse-drawn carriages and motors, stuffed in the massive buildings all around?

'Mama?'

'Yes, dear.'

'I think it's beginning to rain.'

They sat on the train again and, for some reason Gussie couldn't understand, her mother seemed cheered by their visit. 'That unfortunate young man was on our side, I think. He will keep the important Major Bingley up to the mark. I have another plan too. I've had several letters in the last day or two from wives of other officers in your father's regiment who are also posted missing. I shall draw them all together and see if I can help them. What is that saying, "United in victory." After all, I could not use Grandmama's contacts just for Papa. It would be selfish and unchristian.'

The only good point, as Gussie saw it, about her mother's ever-elaborate plans and strategies was that she failed to ask for *The Times*, which Gussie had dropped in the gutter on their arrival in London.

Sylvia knew she must do two things: go back to England to be with her mother, and tell her mother that Arthur was also missing – that is, if she hadn't already read it in *The Times*. But as the days passed, she did neither. Instead she spent longer and longer in the hospital, her whole self concentrated on doing the things that could make a wounded man's life more comfortable. The great heat continued and she was so thin that, if she caught sight of herself in the mirror, she quickly looked away.

Now and again she allowed herself the relaxation of gin fizzes in Shepheard's Hotel. She put pink salve on her lips and rouge on her cheeks and soon found herself surrounded by officers of various nationalities, most of them recovering from wounds and waiting for their next posting. Despite constant propositions, she was never tempted to repeat her experiences of sexual relations and none of them attracted her romantically, although she felt immense sympathy for them. They, like her, were in a kind of perpetual shock, living in a hiatus which gave everything a sense of unreality.

Strangely, her most tranquil moments were sitting at the bedside of her father's ADC, Noel Willoughby, now dying, as Mrs Twigg-Smith had predicted, slowly and in great agony. At first he had tried conscientiously to tell her more about her father's last hours but in truth there was no more he could add. The Colonel had disappeared up Scimitar Hill and the whole place was consumed by smoke and flames. Few emerged. Willoughby had been one of the 'lucky' ones who'd fallen earlier.

'You can't describe hell,' Sylvia told him one evening. 'It's not possible and it does neither of us any good.'

After that he talked to her about his five younger sisters. He loved the five-year-old particularly, called Millie, short for Amelia. 'She jumps up on me and rides me like a horse, with her little legs clasped tight round me.' Sylvia promised to visit Millie when she was back in England but suspected she would not be able to bear it. Lately he had been in too much pain to talk at all so Sylvia read to him. She prayed he would be released soon but then she thought he was her last contact with her father. One evening, he suddenly whispered, 'I was only there three days,' so that she knew he was thinking about Gallipoli. Another evening, in an even weaker voice, he said, 'I can't believe men are still out there.'

As Sylvia left, the anxious Scottish matron who had become her friend, said, 'I hope you've said your goodbyes, dear.'

'Every time I come,' answered Sylvia simply.

On her next visit, Willoughby's bed was filled by another patient.

It was only after his death that she wondered why she hadn't asked about Arthur. It was true that his uncle had been unclear where Arthur was fighting when he became 'missing'. He had not been with his own regiment, it seemed, but probably at Suvla. Recently, an officer in Shepheard's had mentioned a friend who had become a prisoner of war. Sylvia knew that was the hope that her mother clung to for the Colonel. But for Sylvia the whole idea seemed unreal, almost absurd and when the other – admittedly rather drunken – officers laughed off the notion, she put it out of her mind. She didn't know what had happened to Arthur and she tried hard not to think about it. One day she would get another telegram from his uncle.

Sylvia did write to Hilda whenever she had time, although she knew only a handful of letters were likely to make their way through the increasingly dangerous seas. Then a letter came from Hilda:

I'm so very excited, my dearest friend. The powers that be have decided that there is such an acute shortage of nurses on Malta that they'll have to risk losing some of us valuable commodity to alien torpedoes and they've asked for volunteers. As you can imagine I was first in line and we're leaving in two days' time!

Sylvia looked at the date of the letter and saw it had taken over two weeks to reach her. Hilda might have arrived on Malta already – or be at the bottom of the sea. Sylvia chided herself; she must not become bitter. Hilda sounded so thrilled to be on the move. On the other hand, *her* father was still alive and managing his profitable business in Birmingham and she had no fiancé to lose. Sylvia sighed, then picked up the letter again and found herself catching some of her friend's cheerful spirit. *They say Malta is all golden stone walls and blue seas and exotic birds and dazzling flowers – not so much at this time of year, I suppose – certainly a long way from Camberwell . . .*

If only Hilda was coming to Egypt! Lettice, with her self-pity and snoring for Britain, was no substitute. It was interesting that they were so desperate for nurses on Malta. Sylvia, lolling on her bed, suddenly sat up straighter. Now that Willoughby had died, there was nothing to keep her in Cairo. Her shoulders sank. How could she possibly explain to her mother a move away from Egypt but not to England?

At this point, Lettice, who'd been dozing, woke up with her usual snort. 'Time to go?' They were on night shift.

'Not yet,' said Sylvia. 'Another hour of beauty sleep,' she added, in what she hoped was a kind voice but feared otherwise. Oh, to be joking about with Hilda!

The 'good' Turkish officer came to see the POWs early in the morning. His English was poor but Arthur gave him Sylvia's name and the name of the hospital in Cairo where she worked.

'There are Turkish prisoners there.' Arthur tried an appeal.

The officer had brought with him some friends who peered into the tent with great curiosity and satisfaction. Arthur guessed he'd have to get used to such humiliations; at least they were not dragged through the streets in chains, as they might have been in classical times. Captain Lipcock, however, became momentarily angry and had to be restrained by his colleagues. It seemed that he had been promised orderlies – one way of providing security for a few men – but none had been forthcoming. The officers were forbidden to see the men, which gave a sense of foreboding for their future treatment. Trebble had caught sight of a group being marched away, many of them without boots or proper clothing.

Arthur was still feeling unwell, with a burning flush or an icy grip, and found it hard to keep a constant grasp on reality. The two young naval officers, who had been captured straight off their submarine, and were therefore fit in the way none of the soldiers were, took him under their wing.

They marched, when they were ordered to march, on either side of him, half carrying him if his weakness or cramp was too bad. After many hours they arrived at some kind of dock where they were led into a torpedo boat. The Christ-like Trebble announced cheerily, 'No more walking for a bit, unless it's on water.'

An interpreter whose face, to Arthur's bloodshot eyes, resembled Bluebeard's, overheard Trebble's comment.

'I may warn you that danger lies in the hearts of your compatriots. For they will seek out this poor boat and hurl it to your Davy Jones' locker. Lucky it is for you that night has tipped over and your navy's aim is not so good.'

Later, when they were squeezed into hot and filthy quarters, Standley, more liable to depression than his friend, commented, 'This rickety old tub doesn't need the British Navy to sink it. Did you see the state of the screw?'

Arthur, feeling too wretched to rise to contemplate a new sort of death, sank into a black sleep that alternated with unconsciousness.

He awoke to find the boat moored to a quay. Trebble gave him a hand up as the interpreter began to address, even exhort them. Dawn rising over the water showed him to be a cheerful little gnome of a man, not at all the Bluebeard of Arthur's imagination.

'We are now at the famed city of Constantinople, you may be lucky enough to see the dome of the great Blue Mosque. You are taken to the Ministry of War in carriages. You see that well we treat the British officer.'

'Like bully beef in a tin,' whispered Trebble.

'Not exactly how we planned to visit the city,' added Standley dourly.

Arthur remembered a ship he'd seen at Mudros with a white-painted slogan on its hull: *To Constantinople and the harems*. He remembered the young seaman at Suvla who assured him the navy would have got through the Dardanelles if they'd been allowed to carry on.

'You perking up, old chap?' The captain had come to check on his sick.

The streets were still mostly empty, the shops shuttered, heavy doors closed and bolted. There seemed no hints of war or emergency and yet they had been told that the city had emptied in frantic flight as the Allied army approached.

Eventually, they were led through an archway into a courtyard and up to a large blue room with a tiled floor. It was empty apart from some benches and a few mats. Arthur began to feel the truth of the notion that a human's capacity for adapting to his circumstances was his main distinguishing feature from an animal. He sat down on a bench and thought he could be almost happy if brought a cup of tea and something to read.

An hour later a very grand personage appeared, laden with gold braid, and asked them, through the interpreter, whether there was anything they wished for.

After deliberating, Captain Lipcock gave a list which the interpreter noted down. It was long, for the grand personage had encouraged a sense of limitless possibilities. It included such items as blankets, soap, plates, mugs, toothbrushes, books, clothes, paper and pens. The captain then paused before saying with great emphasis, 'But first of all we must be permitted to see our men.'

There was a pause while the interpreter summed up the prisoners' needs in a sentence, then the great personage smiled, spoke, and the interpreter pronounced that the items would be with them in an hour, perhaps.

Two hours passed. The sun rose and the room became stuffy. Looking out of the small window, Arthur saw that on the other side of the courtyard there was a row of barred windows as if on a prison. As he watched, a skeletal hand appeared, accompanied by moans.

'It's like a set for *Fidelio*,' he said to Trebble who was standing behind him.

'I suppose there're some people worse off than us.'

Arthur pondered whether Beethoven had made captivity heroic 'I think I could manage with a pencil. I'd write riddles in Greek.'

'They'd have you shot as a spy. There are *real* prisons in Constantinople.' He nodded across to the bars. 'Not like that. Below ground.'

Another hour passed, Arthur was taken to 'the hole', and recited Homer to himself in defiance. He felt his spirit was returning.

The muezzin called for midday and half an hour later, the interpreter returned. Behind him walked guards with tea, cakes and fruits. He smiled.

Captain Lipcock faced him squarely. He looked less piratical because he had taken off his bandage, revealing a deep cut. He said in a loud voice, 'We thank you for this food but our most important request is to see our men.'

The interpreter remained cheerful. He waved to a guard who was carrying a brown paper bag. 'Toothbrushes!' he exclaimed, extracting one, like a conjuror pleased with his trick.

For a moment, Arthur thought the captain was defeated but he had underestimated their leader. He bellowed, 'We must be allowed to see our men. It is our duty and our right!'

The interpreter's smile faded and he looked sadly at the toothbrushes. Arthur imagined it would not have been easy to procure them. Then the interpreter brightened and waved another guard forward. 'I have, for you, chessmen so that your hours may pass in happiness.'

This was imaginative, thought Arthur as a board and gracefully carved chess pieces were set out on one of the benches. Captain Lipcock remained unpersuaded. 'There is talk that our men are being held underground, ill fed and ill-treated. This is not following the rules of all civilised countries.'

'You are right, Captain. Everything must be done, according to the rule. It is the sign of a civilisation.' He gave a bow. 'Thank you.'

'And now all he has to do is go,' muttered Standley, and indeed the interpreter went.

Arthur wondered if there were the makings of a life here, a study of the confrontation between West and partially Westernised East. He wasn't fool enough to think Turkey didn't have a share of educated men but it seemed unlikely that such people would oversee their captivity. It would be the ordinary Turks, their wishes channelled through an interpreter, although they would be fortunate to have one as amiable as the present man. He found himself remembering Prideaux, that aristocratic black sheep who seemed to have as much if not more sympathy with the Turk, the Greek or the Albanian than he did for his own countrymen. He had the air of a man set to wander the globe.

'One must keep trying,' the captain said, a little defensively, and everyone nodded. There was a right and wrong to their behaviour, even if they were captives and most decisions taken out of their hands.

The following morning was an example of the limits to be

endured. After an evening spent eating, brushing their teeth and playing chess (most knew the game and the rest were taught) a night spent fighting off the voracious insects that emerged from the blue walls, they were marched off to a square. It already seemed wonderful to escape their room. At the square they were instructed to march round and round while being filmed by a large movie camera. The captain was suffering from a sudden high fever and had been left behind, his place being taken by the French soldier, Broussac.

'We are not circus animals,' he pronounced courteously.

'You are distinguished officers,' agreed the interpreter. And around they went. And around and around, twice, three, four times till the midday sun became wearisome. There was no wish to torture them, Arthur decided, but merely a desire to add numbers to their captives since, on film at least, one Allied officer must, to a Turk, look very like another.

The local populace watched with some interest, although that was probably for the camera, and no apparent animosity.

Arthur tried to imagine such a scene at Piccadilly Circus and decided that the appearance of the enemy would certainly produce booing and catcalls. But then, in England, they did not parade their prisoners.

Twenty-Two

Reggie Gisburne MC, or very nearly – he was to receive the medal from the King the following day – had arrived at the vicarage. There was patriotic bunting along the driveway and at the station a small crowd had collected to cheer him. For such a small village to possess a hero was exciting indeed. Even Beatrice noted it and said to Gussie over lunch (on their laps in the small sitting room because there'd been a new influx of walking wounded patients), 'We must call on the Gisburnes to offer our congratulations. Let us go at five and then they'll need to provide neither tea nor sherry.'

Gussie's smoked haddock seemed to look at her with vengeful eyes. 'I've promised to go along earlier,' she said brightly, 'but I'll wait for you to come and then you will have to stay an even shorter time.' As she spoke, she saw this was the wrong approach for she must encourage her mother to appreciate the Gisburnes. Mustn't she? It was true she had promised Mr Gisburne to visit at four which was why she was wearing her prettiest pink linen dress. It was pre-war, cut with a generous amount of cloth that hid any thickening in her waistline. She didn't think Reggie would mind any enlargement of her bosom. A vision of his naked body on top of hers made her give a little shudder. How exciting it had been! Perhaps everything would be all right and she'd find she loved him now he was famous. After all, judging by the casualty lists in *The Times*, there would hardly be any young men left after the war.

'Are you all right, dear?' said Beatrice.

'Just a little hot.' She was blushing at the shame of such low and petty thoughts when both her father and Arthur were missing. War demanded so much good behaviour and she was still not quite in the way of it.

*

'Welcome, my dear.' The rector opened the door to Gussie. 'The returning hero is in the drawing room. He is much looking forward to your visit.' As Gussie came in and he saw more clearly her miserable face, he added with gravity, 'May God bless you both.'

The handle to the drawing-room door seemed very big. At last Gussie managed to turn it – and there was Reggie standing in full uniform against the fireplace. He stared at her greedily.

'I wanted to let you come in so that I could just look at you. Oh, Gussie, how can you be so glorious?'

Gussie's head whirled. She had forgotten how much he adored her, the effect it had on her. She was so hot she might faint. Actually, it might be a relief to faint. 'You're wounded,' she stammered.

Reggie put his hand up to his forehead where there was a dressing. 'Just a scratch. So annoying but it bleeds when they take it off.'

'And your hand?' There was a bandage on his left hand.

'That's nothing too. Oh, dear, wonderful Gussie, I am so proud you've come to see me. When they told me I was to be honoured, all I thought was that it might make me a little more worthy of you.'

Gussie, hands and legs trembling, desperately wanted to collapse in a chair but knew that once she sat, she'd never have the courage to speak. Faced with the bodily presence of Reggie, his desirous admiration coupled with his warrior's wounds, she realised that he was a far more powerful personality than she had ever credited. The knowledge confused her even more.

'Oh, Reggie . . .' She could get no further.

'I should have said at once – the colonel and Lieutenant Lamb.' He frowned in an attempt to dim his good spirits. 'I'm so awfully sorry. Such a terrible time for your family! If there is anything I can do . . .' So far Reggie had kept his arms rigidly at his sides as if controlling the temptation to touch Gussie. But now he took a step forward and held out his right hand.

This was too much for Gussie who, uttering a little cry, burst into tumultuous sobs.

'Gussie. My dearest. What is it?' One arm round her shoulder, he led her to a chair and sat her down. He knelt in front of her anxiously.

Even through her tears, Gussie noted that he had adopted the right position for the next part of their reunion.

'I'm going to have a baby,' she sobbed.

'What? What!' Reggie seemed bewildered.

'Your baby! Our baby!' Suddenly impatient, Gussie shouted out the words with an air of accusation. She didn't mean it; she was more impressed by him than she'd ever been but it seemed so unfair that he was handsome – he was handsome in a soldierly way – and triumphant – while she was . . . what was she? A harlot!

Reggie breathed deeply, almost snorted. He knelt still. His plummy eyes looked at Gussie in wonder. 'You are carrying our baby.' He spoke slowly with a gulp or even a sob in his voice. 'I know I should be sorry and I am most awfully sorry that I was such a beast. But, Gussie, I so adored you, that's my only excuse. And now you've told me the most wonderful thing in the whole world has happened. If you could understand what I've seen at the front over the last few months . . . but I don't want you ever to understand . . . you would know the idea of a baby and a baby with you . . . oh, Gussie. It is too much, much too much. I always thought of you as my wife but now you will be, we will be joined for ever!'

Gussie stopped crying and let him take her hands. She felt a mixture of contradictory emotions, in which relief and fear predominated. Then an entirely new sensation took hold of her. She found herself smiling wildly. 'Oh, Reggie, the baby's moving. I can feel it. It's fluttering angels' wings. I'm sure I can feel it.' Falling forward into Reggie's strong arms, she gave herself up to the thrill of pure joy. 'You know, Reggie, I do love you.' She breathed the words in his warm ear. 'I thought I didn't because you were . . . well, anyway . . . but . . .'

'Of course you love me. I always knew that.' Reggie's hot breath batted her in passion. 'Do you know I am a hundred, no a thousand, a million times happier than the happiest fellow in the world?'

Uncaring of who might come in, the two throbbing bodies entwined in a passionate embrace. Gussie's hat fell off backwards, followed by a shower of hairpins.

Eventually, Reggie extricated himself a little and whispered urgently, 'We won't have one baby, we'll have two, three, four. Perhaps a dozen.'

To Gussie, the dark clouds of the last weeks swept away by Reggie's ardour, this seemed an entirely delightful prospect. The two lovers righted themselves, sat a little apart, while managing to stare confidently into each other's eyes.

It was only three quarters of an hour later when Lady Beatrice was announced, that Gussie's rosy glow dissipated.

Beatrice had spent the afternoon in the Colonel's study as was her usual habit. But whereas in the past she had read and reread her husband's letters or caressed his bronzes, now she sat at the telephone and made calls with a notebook at her elbow. She wrote endless letters too, because many of the officers' wives or mothers from her husband's regiment, also missing, did not yet have telephones. In her distress, it was as if her mother's forceful spirit, previously so inimical to her, had come as support. Sometimes, with heart-stopping sadness, she thought how proud Bingo would have been – would be – of her. He always said that she under-valued herself. She had become the spearhead of women searching for information about their missing relatives.

With such preoccupations filling her mind, it took Beatrice a moment to adjust to the sight facing her in Mr Gisburne's study: the words *radiant youth* came into her head. Gussie in her pink dress, with flushed face, stood holding hands, yes, holding hands with Reggie Gisburne, who was like a poster for the perfect officer, upright, glowing with fitness and the consciousness of success. His two white bandages only increased this impression. Beatrice was confused and said nothing.

'We're engaged, Mama! Reggie and I are engaged!'

Gussie's breathless words only increased Beatrice's bafflement. Sylvia and Arthur were engaged. She had not been in favour of it because he had no family to speak of and only a small allowance from his uncle but Bingo had persuaded her he had 'prospects'. She had to admit he was very well educated. She glanced at Captain Gisburne again; his face was so red, his expression ridiculous, she turned back to Gussie. 'You'll have to get your father's permission, of course,' she said calmly.

It was an automatic response, a normal response in abnormal

times. Beatrice saw Gussie looking at her with horror and sat down in the nearest armchair. She understood what she'd just said made no sense but she didn't feel like saying anything else. Really, there was nothing else to be said. She took her handbag from her arm and placed it on her lap.

The door opened and the vicar came in. He held a decanter of sherry in his hand as if a defensive weapon. The small room seemed very full. Shocked into statues by Beatrice's reaction, Reggie and Gussie still stood, hands joined.

'I see the young people have made their announcement.' The rector addressed Beatrice but his tones would have been more suitable for a sermon on the mercy of God.

'Yes. Yes.' Beatrice hardly seemed aware.

'We are very happy,' said Reggie, hopefully. 'In these terrible times . . .' He paused. They all saw tears sliding out of Beatrice's eyes.

'Oh, Mama!' Gussie sprang across the room. She hugged her mother as if *she* was the child. 'Dearest Mama, please don't.'

Beatrice seemed to become aware of her tears for the first time. She brushed them away with her still-gloved hand. 'It's all over. Everything's gone.' Her despair had a tinge of defiance.

'No. No. It is *good* news, really it is.' With all the determination of youth, Gussie looked closely into her mother's pale face. 'I didn't think so at first but now I know. Reggie is such a hero and we have a glorious future. Papa would be so proud. And there's something else even more extraordinary. I'm going to have a baby. A real life baby! You're going to be a grandmama!'

Reggie gave an audible gasp. The vicar put down the decanter on a marble table with a click.

Beatrice gently stroked her daughter's cheek. 'I see.' She glanced at Reggie, then quickly away again. 'How stupid of me not to have realised. My poor Gussie.'

'No, Mama.' Gussie crouched back on her heels and said with the conviction of someone who had always thought motherhood her first ambition, 'I am not poor. I am happy. Reggie and I will be married. Here at the vicarage. His soldiers will hold crossed swords to make an arch. You will come and Sylvia and Papa and Arthur will be there if possible and next year there'll be a baby.'

She stopped, breathing passionately, as if she, too, might burst into tears.

Reggie who had, perhaps wisely, spoken little up to this point, now said gravely, 'I count myself the most fortunate of human beings.'

His strong masculine voice seemed to affect Beatrice. She held herself straighter while Gussie scrambled to her feet and sat down on a chair. 'I was unprepared,' said Beatrice.

The rector put his fingertips together. 'The ways of God are often called mysterious.'

'That is true.' Beatrice flashed him a look, if not of dislike, then of distaste, before adding, 'Yet the mysterious ways of men on occasion outdo the deity's.' The rector bowed. He was prepared to be whipping boy, although his eyes slid longingly to the decanter of sherry.

'The wedding should be soon, I surmise.' Beatrice took in Gussie's prettiness, her swelling bosom, her glistening skin. 'It will be hard to hold a marriage without the Colonel.' She sighed, then carefully took off first one glove and then the other. 'But we are certainly not in mourning and my daughter's future must be assured. Mr Gisburne, I see you have sherry there. Perhaps we should have glasses to go with it.'

Gussie smiled at her mother tenderly. How brave she was! How generous! How could she ever have thought it would be otherwise!

Rupert was escorted to some kind of courtyard. 'Where are we?' That was a question he liked to ask. It gave pleasure to his nurses who enjoyed describing things for him.

How could a piece of metal in his head change his nature? He had been arrogant, headstrong, led by his desires. Now he was the humblest of God's creatures: grateful to those who looked after him, thankful for the times when the pain was less devastating, like this afternoon, when he could enjoy the warmth of sunshine on his skin.

'We are on a terrace, Captain Prideaux.' This was a female nurse, Nurse Riley, who had a charming Irish accent. 'We are looking directly back to Valletta town. If only you could see the blue of the sea and sky, the gold of the walls!'

He felt a particular affection for the soldier of the Ottoman

Empire who had aimed for his head, assuming, of course, it wasn't a random shot which would be just as likely but less dignified. 'I can, I can,' said Rupert to console her. He never asked, however, about the progress of the war. If other patients began a conversation – about replacement troops at Helles or an Anzac breakthrough to some ridge or other – he turned on his side and covered his head with his arms. 'What is that bird I can hear singing?'

There was a pause. 'To be honest with you, Captain, I'm not very well up with foreign birds.'

Rupert smiled. How was it that he'd never noticed how many people were filled with the milk of human kindness? 'Do you think it could be a sparrow, Nurse Riley? Sparrows go all over the world, I believe. Although they are usually in groups.'

'The thing is, I can't see it, although that probably wouldn't help. There now. It's flown away and I only caught a glimpse of a brown tail.'

Again Rupert felt the need to comfort her. 'Then it was a sparrow. What else can you see?'

'There's a very big ship coming in.' Her voice rose. 'Painted over with that camouflage stuff. Oh, that's exciting for sure! We're expecting some new nurses all the way from England. Perhaps they're on board.'

As if the mention of England was its cue, a vibration began inside Rupert's head which was usually the sign that an attack was on the way. But he wanted to continue this conversation. Its innocence soothed the soul he was only just discovering. 'I think the sparrow came here on that ship,' he said. 'Boarded at Southampton and come over the seas to us.'

'That must be it!' Her voice was further away and he imagined her leaning over the balustrade, eagerly peering across the blue water to see any sign of white-clad nurses.

'Aahh.' He gave a small exclamation. The vibration had started to roll and form into waves and now was joined by a sharp ticking.

'Nurse Riley!' The matron's voice came like a boom and a crash. 'How long have you had Captain Prideaux out here? You know he's not allowed more than five minutes in the sun.' Her voice changed direction towards Rupert. 'Look, he's all huddled and trembling. You'd better get the chair. He'll never walk in that state.'

Rupert wanted to defend her but his teeth were chattering as lightning drove into his skull. He tried to hold out his hand but even that was beyond him.

'He'll need the morphine, poor man. What the good God sees fit to impose on his creatures!'

Rupert wished he could reassure her that he needed no pity but it was impossible to do more than gasp and grimace.

Hilda stared up from the rocking boat at the great golden walls of this historic island and felt a keen joy. She knew this was inappropriate during a dreadful war but, being a practical woman, gave herself the leeway of truth. The journey to Malta had been arduous – most of the nurses had succumbed to a nasty infection (probably due to the filthy condition of the ship which had not been cleaned since carrying the sick) and Hilda, remaining healthy, had been constrained to nurse them. But her sense of adventure had sustained her, even when their sister ship, going ahead, met a torpedo. (They had been too far away to help.) She had never even thought she would escape the monotony of her spinster's life to the extent of reaching a golden city, built, so she had read, by the Knights of Malta in the sixteenth and seventeenth centuries. 'Forgive me, Lord,' she prayed, as the brilliant blue water splashed over her less than sparkling uniform, 'but I've never been so happy!'

Beatrice sent a cable to Sylvia: GUSSIE TO MARRY CAPTAIN REGGIE GISBURNE MC IN OCTOBER STOP PLEASE RETURN STOP.

Sylvia, whose sense of dislocation from the normal had convinced her there could be no more surprises, was very surprised, not least because her mother had put in 'captain' and 'MC'. She understood it was a kindly plea on Reggie's behalf, mitigating circumstances, but the annoying rector's son was incapable, surely, of changing his colours – or his class. She suspected at once what would have been unthinkable a few months earlier: Gussie was pregnant.

Sylvia stood in the post office which was even more crowded than usual owing to a fierce thunderstorm which had raced in a black cloud out of the desert and was now battering the building. Even the elements were out of joint.

'Not bad news, I hope?' Lettice had come with her, hoping in vain for a letter from what Sylvia estimated to be an imaginary sweetheart, a manager on the railways in Leeds.

'No. Happy news. My sister is to marry Captain Reggie Gisburne MC.'

'Your *younger* sister,' replied Lettice, pityingly.

Yes, thought Sylvia, I shall have to leave Egypt. Arthur, if he was to reappear, which she believed and disbelieved by turns, would be as likely to turn up wounded in England as anywhere else. Lately, the stream of wounded to Cairo had lessened to a trickle, indicating there had been no new offences on Gallipoli. The hospitals were still full with old cases but there was not the same sense of emergency. No one would miss her, not even Mrs Twigg-Smith who had told her, on their last meeting, that her duty was to her mother.

'This place smells.' Thrusting her way through hot bodies, Sylvia reached the doorway where she stood watching sheets of unseasonable silver rain falling out of a black sky. But what ever would she do in England?

Lettice joined her. 'Phew!' she exclaimed, 'it's like the end of the world. I don't know how we'll get to the hospital.'

'Of course, I'll have to go home for the wedding. I'll try and find a ship for Malta as a first step.'

'Ugh. Oh how filthy.' Both girls, in their spotless white uniforms, watched as a torrent of waste materials, including excrement from every kind of animal, not excluding human, swept down the street reaching almost to the step on which they stood.

'I wonder where Arthur is now!' exclaimed Sylvia. She thought she had trained herself not to wonder, and certainly not to wonder out loud to the infuriating Lettice.

'Only our Maker knows that,' intoned Lettice with a mixture of sympathy and complacency.

Shall I push her? thought Sylvia and imagined her friend's round face submerged under excrement like an Ophelia for our times. Yes, she must leave as soon as possible before she went entirely mad.

*

Hilda still felt as if she were on holiday. In front of her was the most elegant building she had ever seen, two vast colonnaded wings and at the centre a third structure which housed, so Nurse Riley was telling her, a chapel and administrative offices. This was the hospital where she was to work, a ferry ride across the bay from Valletta.

'It's a pity you've come when the weather's breaking, although it's been terribly hot – up in the nineties weeks on end.'

Hilda didn't care that the weather was breaking. It had rained in the night but now it was heartbreakingly clear and hot, and she didn't think she'd have coped well with very high temperatures.

'We do have fans, although the electricity is unreliable. Often a breeze comes off the sea. The men never complain. They've been through so much that being allowed to lie quietly on a bed is like a miracle. Sometimes I have to go away and weep.'

'Yes. I was nursing in South London,' said Hilda in the tones of someone who didn't need to go away and weep. But she liked the little Irish nurse who'd volunteered to show her round. She was hardly more than five foot tall but filled with energy. At the start of the war she and her parents, a doctor and a nurse, had been visiting relatives on the island and, when the wounded began arriving, they had stayed to help.

'You should see the wild flowers in spring.' Riley looked disappointedly at the expanse of burnt earth that stretched on either side of the hospital which was perched on a promontory above the sea. 'Would you like to meet Matron first or go straight to the wards?'

'Oh, the wards, please.' They smiled at each other.

Rupert heard two sets of rubber-soled nurses' shoes approaching. The pain was not bad but his brain seemed to be having trouble holding on to the reality of the world around him. He would not have been sure, for example, whether it was night or day. The sound of slightly squeaky rubber on stone was reassuring, therefore, even if it did not answer the question.

'Captain Prideaux!'

Carefully, Rupert eased himself upright. He had learnt to outwit the tigerish pounce of the pain with slow, cautious movements. 'Good morning, Riley. Or is it afternoon, or evening?'

'Right first time. But what a storm in the night! You were lucky not to be out on the verandas. Some of the men got soaked. Major Samways said he needed his cap to bail with.'

'Major Samways is a wit. I think he likes you, Riley.'

The nurse giggled. 'But here, I've brought a new nurse for you, fresh from England, on that ship we saw, well, I saw yesterday.'

'Good morning, Captain.'

Rupert felt a firm hand take his and shake it with a quiet movement. The voice was several tones deeper than Riley's with an accent he couldn't place. 'Where are you from?' he asked.

'Birmingham. My family is in manufacturing.'

Not his sort of England then and thank God for that – she could have been a spy sent by his family.

'I've been working in a hospital in South London. So it's very exciting to be out here.'

Exciting? Not the way most people described their reaction to rows and rows of wounded men. She was confident, he realised, unafraid to speak her mind but not charming and silly, he felt, like Riley.

They had said goodbye and moved on while he was thinking like this so he continued to recall women he'd known and was quite surprised to realise that the last woman he'd had was Sylvia Fitzpaine. Well, not exactly had. That had been an unlikely event altogether: he had been wounded and she was more or less a virgin. Probably, he had behaved badly, but she had been keen for it and he had been crazy with the horror of the war. Had her priggish lieutenant survived? Rupert wondered. It was unlikely. Then he stopped thinking because the war was off-limits and fell into a kind of wary doze that passed for sleep.

In the afternoon Hilda came back with a wheelchair to take Rupert to the terrace. She looked down on him. With his eyes closed, masking the blank stare, he was very beautiful, his nose and mouth like a Greek statue. The fair hair was already growing back over the shaved area. The doctor had informed her that any sudden movement was likely to be fatal for him and that he would die very soon in any case.

Rupert opened his eyes and Hilda said, 'I think you knew a fellow nurse of mine, Sylvia Fitzpaine.' She was surprised by his smile.

'Not very well,' he said. 'Did her fiancé survive?'

'He's missing.'

'Have you come to take me outside?'

'If you would like.' Hilda decided to drop the subject of Sylvia. That smile had unnerved her. A very beautiful young man was dangerous, even though sightless. Hilda realised she was glad that he could not see her homely face and figure.

The day after Sylvia left for Malta and England, a letter came for her. Lettice studied its foreign franking and felt a duty to open it. Hands shaking at her daring, she found a knife and slit the flimsy envelope:

My dearest Sylvia,

I so hope this letter will get through to you all right. I am afraid my campaigning is over for the present as I am a prisoner with the Turks. I am being treated with kindness and courtesy by all ranks. I cannot tell you about how it happened now and I expect you will hear something of the action. Perhaps your father has written to you. We were together at the beginning but separated on the advance. I fear the regiment suffered rather heavily but I could only see what was going on round me pretty close, and my impressions are rather confused. I only hope we did our best to achieve what was asked of us.

I must not tax the patience of any censor by writing too much. This is not coming by the regular channels as we are at present on wanderings through this huge country. I will let you know when we have a settled address so that you may write.

Oh, my dearest girl, you will understand my emotions on finding myself in this situation. It is not what I envisaged when I joined the army. But I do not want you to be unhappy on my behalf. What we cannot change, we must endure. If there is one thing I miss it is reading material so be sure you will have an address as soon as I have it. Marmalade and cake come next after books.

I dream of you, my own extraordinary Sylvia, as a beggar dreams of a gold coin, a drowning man of a lifeboat, a frightened child of morning, a thirsty man of a pool of clear water. We are kept apart now by time and space but our hearts and bodies are for ever joined.

Arthur.

Lettice, sweating rather because the small nurses' room in the hospital was stuffy and because she always sweated when she was moved, put down the letter and wiped away a tear. How she would like to be the one to answer it! Of course she would post it on immediately. How happy Sylvia would be that her fiancé was alive. Lettice had never met him nor seen a photograph but her imagination pictured the most romantic of profiles.

Three days later she was just about to forward the letter which, placed under her pillow, seemed to sustain her for the difficult day ahead, when a second letter arrived. This had been sent a mere ten days ago. Having opened the first, it seemed only natural to open the second. In front of Lettice's misty eyes, her name slipped over Sylvia's.

Dearest Lettice,

I hope you received my last letter. I am in Stamboul, as my companions call it, although I believe not for long. We have just moved from a kind of prison, although we were not exactly imprisoned, to a house overlooking a garden and then the Bosporus. It is distant but I stare at it often, not just because of the splendour of satin water and gilded sky but because its existence is the cause of our campaign. I say no more.

Things are a little easier here since the American Embassy has taken our welfare in hand. Yesterday they came with underclothes and pyjamas. Long may they remain neutral! The Turks give us a floor to sleep on but everything else we must find. We are told the Red Cross will become involved soon. We play auction bridge and chess. Sometimes we are taken to walk in a garden overlooking the Bosporus and the Golden Horn.

We are allowed one letter a week. My uncle will want to write sometimes, although of course I do not know whether any letters will arrive. They should be addressed to me stating my regiment, rank and that I'm a prisoner of war in Angora, Turkey. We are moving eventually to a camp at the foot of a great mountain – or so rumour has it. My dearest, oh my dearest, as the days pass, our time together in Cairo becomes more and more glorious. I'll say no more.

Arthur.

Lettice was in such a dream herself that she didn't hear Mrs Twigg-Smith who seemed to be everywhere at once, come into the room.

'What is it, dear? Have you had bad news?'

Lettice, red-eyed and red-faced, could think of no lie to cover the truth. 'It's a letter for Sylvia from her fiancé. He is a prisoner of war.'

'Excellent! What excellent tidings. And you thought it right to open it. Sylvia will be pleased – about Lieutenant Lamb being alive, not you opening it. Hand it to me, dear, and I'll see it goes off to the right place. I believe there is a ship due in a couple of days.'

So that there should be no confusion, Mrs Twigg-Smith held out her hand and Lettice, in her shame, failed to confess there had been an earlier letter.

'Perhaps I did wrong,' she murmured, and thought that she would treasure the first letter for ever.

Twenty-Three

Charing Cross station at six in the morning was a dark and doleful place. Too many soldiers had said goodbye there and never come back. Some pigeons, disturbed in the smoky glass roof, fluttered and banged together crossly.

General Sir Charles Monro and his chief of staff Major General Arthur Lynden-Bell were in not much better humour. They were sitting in the first class carriage of a train waiting to leave. They were accompanied by their servants who stank appallingly of stale beer. It was clear they had celebrated their departure for Gallipoli all night – forgivable, but hard to endure.

Monro tried to take his mind off such minor examples of the active soldier's habits by reading a note he had received from General Sir Charles Caldwell, the director of military operations:

> *Ian Hamilton's failure was to my mind to a large extent*
> *due to his disinclination to tell Lord Kitchener unpleasant*
> *things . . . I would urge on you not to hesitate before telling*
> *unpleasant truths in your wires to K. Especially I would keep*
> *on about the troops being so very short of establishment and*
> *the discouragement which this causes them—*

'General!' Monro looked up in time to see a handsome pink face with dishevelled fair hair appear at the window.

Lynden-Bell jumped up as a bundle of papers flew in and landed with a thump on the floor.

A voice shouted, 'Don't forget, if you evacuate it will be the biggest disaster since Corunna!'

One of the servants picked up the bundle, the train started with a lurch and the face disappeared.

'Was that Churchill?' asked Monro.

'Seems like the sort of silly ass thing he might do,' replied Lynden-Bell.

'Got to admire his tenacity.' Neither men made any attempt to look at the papers.

'Have you heard the news?' Fred shook the shoulder of a man buried under a blanket and a torn overcoat. 'Come on, Joe, you've got to hear this.'

Joe Dingle, Fred's old mate from Dorset who he'd assumed dead long ago, had recently returned to his regiment and Fred liked to keep him in the picture, whether he wanted it or not.

One eye opened. 'We've been given bleeding roast potatoes, otherwise you can bugger off.'

'General Hamilton's been kicked out, packed his bags and left already, and General Monro's on the way. Those that rule our life from afar have finally seen the light.'

'I don't know about the light,' grumbled Joe, 'it's the cold that's getting to me, it makes my wound ache, and there's nothing one general or another can do about that.'

Fred sat back on his heels. He looked up at the sky where the first star blinked in the gathering night. It was already cold but at least it wasn't raining. 'Do you want to stay on this bit of blasted land for ever?'

'Why don't you make yourself useful and brew up some tea?'

Both men suddenly rolled forward under the front wall of their bunker as the ping of bullets hit the sandbags, turning now and again into a crack like a whiplash when they hit a stone.

'Bugger me,' muttered Joe, head well down. 'I don't know why they bother. You'd think they'd want a decent night's sleep.'

'What must it be like,' murmured Fred, 'sitting up there on Achi Baba or even on Khilid Bahr, looking down on us poor mortals?'

'Khilid Bahr nothing. Those bullets are coming from yards away. You read too many books, that's your trouble.'

'Knowledge is power.'

'Bugger off.'

Sometimes the firing, desultory and pointless, went on all night so men couldn't even get to the latrines without risking their lives. Even in the cooler weather, half of them still had dysentery. It didn't raise a laugh any more when someone copped it on his naked bum.

'They've obviously got more ammo than us,' said Fred, after a pause. It rankled with all of them how short they were kept of bullets and how seldom shells or machine-gun fire went over from their side. Even the French who'd always been better armed, lay low most of the time. Also, Fred had discovered that ten thousand of the frogs had gone off to Salonika to defend Serbia against some new enemy.

Fred found out these things, usually when he was on some sort of reconnaissance mission with an officer, but he didn't bother to tell Joe. World politics was never likely to be his thing.

'I'll make that tea now.' The bullets hadn't stopped entirely but the news about Hamilton and Monro had made Fred restless. Expert at creating a fire unseen by either the enemy or his corporal, he shook some tea into a can and added water from his flask. He thought that the next morning he'd find some pretext for being sent down to the beach. It was being stuck for days in a hole on the edge of a gulley that got to you. It was only the books that stopped him turning into a caveman, talking in grunts like Joe and the rest of them. They still got killed too. Only two days ago an experienced captain who'd been wounded twice already but always came back got shelled in his own trenches while he was sorting out a couple of earlier wounded. Caught it in his pelvis and liver. Carried off to the hospital ship and another ghost for Gallipoli.

A cold wind was blowing from the east but Fred wasn't afraid of that. Once he'd finished his tea, he picked up a heap of old puttees and began winding them round his head and neck – like an Egyptian mummy, he was, in more ways than one since he'd taken them off the legs of dead men. The smell was disgusting but worth it for the warmth. He'd seen a dozen Turkish prisoners recently, shivering with the cold and only wearing rags. Both sides the same.

He'd written a bit about it to Lil but she'd said it arrived with more black ink than words. She'd been worried he was up to something. She didn't realise what a good chap he'd become. Sometimes he'd caught himself wondering if he'd stay in the army after the war, make a real go of it, become an NCO with medals and a loud voice. Trouble was there were always orders to be obeyed, unless you were the commander-in-chief and then there were politicians. Besides, he'd probably got a bit of a wrong idea about the army, being on Gallipoli where he'd always found room to do his own sort of manoeuvring. Perhaps he should have stayed with the Aussies when he'd had the chance. They weren't big on obedience either. Too late now. They were all dug in and nowhere to go.

The small vessel carrying the second letter addressed to Sylvia and opened by Lettice arrived at Malta ahead of the large vessel transporting its proper recipient. This time, Hilda picked the letter up and, assessing at once its potential importance (and having no temptation to open what was clearly not hers) took it across to Valletta on the ferry where she planned to wait for her friend's disembarkation. The rigours of Camberwell had thrown them into quick and easy intimacy, but Hilda calculated that they had spent less time together than the time which had passed since Sylvia had bobbed her hair and taken off to nurse her sick fiancé. Their letters, however interrupted by torpedoes or pressure of work, had been a continuing bond. Now there was this other letter.

Sylvia did not wave when she saw Hilda standing all on her own on the quayside, nor did she look admiringly at the golden city. The moment her ship had left Alexandria, booming and whistling as if there was something to celebrate, she became overwhelmed by depression. The ship was, after all, going to England and even if she was making a stop in Malta that must be her ultimate destination. She felt that she had finally said goodbye to her father and probably to Arthur too – she felt disloyal in her leaving, although she knew that was absurd – and all that awaited her was her sad, too-hopeful mother and Gussie. She certainly did not wish to think about Gussie's wedding.

'Sylvia! Sylvia!'

Hilda, wearing nurse's uniform, was waving so hard that it reached even through Sylvia's misery. On board ship there had been a group of young officers, cured of their wounds and now being sent to France. They had tried to woo her with their cocktails and laughter but she could not bring herself to join in and she knew they thought her cold and standoffish. To her their laughter sounded tragic and their cocktails made her queasy without lifting her spirits.

'Oh, Hilda. It is kind of you to meet me!' In her friend's embrace, Sylvia felt her heart warm a little.

'I make every excuse to see the island, you dear old thing.' Hilda took a step back to look at her better. 'You seem a bit cut up. Bad journey?'

'No. No.'

Since Sylvia said no more, Hilda carried on. 'I've got a pass from the hospital for the afternoon and I thought we might explore Valletta a little since we're over here. I've bribed a porter to take your cases up to Bighi – that's the hospital where I work on the other side of the harbour. Are you game?'

'If you like,' replied Sylvia indifferently before noticing her friend's disappointment. She added, with an attempt at enthusiasm, 'What a good idea! I need to stretch my legs.'

Hilda, letter in her sensible canvas bag, decided that her plan to take Sylvia to Valletta's most famous café and there hand her the letter was a good one. A public place would give her time to take in whatever the news might be. Good or bad, she would be forced to preserve an appearance of calm. Hilda believed in self-control.

The sun was warm as the two friends started up a long flight of stone steps towards the centre of the city. A brisk wind made the ends of Hilda's cape flap and Sylvia held on her hat.

'The wind might be the *Siroca* which they call Xaroco here,' said Hilda who was beginning to be nervous and found facts comforting. 'It often blows in October, I'm told. I hope not because when it gets up to 70 mph it drives everyone mad.'

Sylvia stopped and Hilda was struck by how very thin she'd become, almost gaunt. 'Is it much further?'

'One more flight and then we're on level ground. The café's opposite the cathedral.' Hilda had also thought that Sylvia might want to visit the cathedral after reading the letter. Now she wondered whether the whole idea was a mistake or self-indulgence because she herself so longed to come to town. 'There's very little privacy at the hospital.' She thought the street they were in very attractive: the tall stone houses were decorated with balconies, constructed of elegantly carved wood, many of them with shutters still closed against the sun. Every few houses there was a church, to St Anthony, St Peter who was supposed to have been shipwrecked here, to the Virgin Mary and St Ann. She thought of telling Sylvia this but was put off by her blank face.

Instead, out of the blue, quite unplanned, she started talking about Captain Prideaux. 'You know how one never nurses anyone one knows? Well, at the moment, I'm looking after someone *you* know: Captain Prideaux. I think you had tea with him in the Ritz once. Such a shame, poor man.'

'What's wrong with him?' Sylvia stopped again and stared at her friend with wide open eyes. Around them, the streets, only sloping gently now, were filling with people amongst which priests and nuns were prominent. One bell began to toll, then another.

'He was blinded, I'm afraid. I'm sorry. I didn't mean to startle you but it's just that we've become friends. I mean, we talk.'

'About me?' Sylvia started walking again.

'Oh, no. Never about you!' Hilda looked shocked. It was true that she and Captain Prideaux got on well together but why was she telling this to Sylvia, upsetting Sylvia, it seemed, when that letter was in her pocket?

'The cathedral's just ahead. You can see the dome,' she cried. It was obvious now that everybody was hurrying to an early evening service. 'And here's the Jubilee Café.'

Sylvia instantly felt comfortable in the café. It was lined with panelled wood, paintings and mirrors and lit by three chandeliers. She put her hand across the table to reach Hilda's.

'I know I'm odd. Sorry. I'll be better soon, I expect I've been alone too much. I think Captain Prideaux is . . .' She paused. What was he? 'It's terrible that he's blind. If you don't mind, I'd prefer not to see him.'

'He won't expect it,' said Hilda but her face gave away that she had told Prideaux of Sylvia's arrival.

Very good coffee was served in small white cups. 'What luxury!' said Sylvia. She smiled at Hilda. 'To be drinking coffee with a friend.'

'Yes. Amid so much unhappiness.' Hilda's hand slid into her bag. She felt as if she was reaching for a pistol, surprising herself with this unusual sense of drama – there was enough in the reality, surely. She noticed that the café was nearly empty and suspected that this would all change when the worshippers came out of the church.

She laid the envelope, small and grey, on the table.

'What's this?' asked Sylvia, putting down her coffee cup.

'It's for you. It was forwarded from Cairo. I thought you would want to read it straight away.'

Hilda's flushed and agitated face made Sylvia inwardly tremble but she still did not pick up the envelope. 'What do you think it is? Do you think it's important?'

'I think so. You see it's come from Turkey.'

'Turkey.' At last Sylvia reached across the table and now her hand shook too. 'I'm not sure I'm up to this,' she murmured.

'I know. Would you like me to leave?'

Sylvia didn't answer; all her concentration was centred on the envelope. She picked up a pearl-handled knife that had come with her patisserie and very carefully slit open the envelope. 'Do people die of fright?' she said, almost whimsically.

Hilda watched her friend but said nothing. You could not share moments like this.

Sylvia read the letter very slowly. It was obvious to Hilda that she was reading and rereading. At one point she put her hand to her heart. It was an unconscious gesture, like a dancer expressing love.

A waiter came to ask their needs and Hilda waved him away. He turned and went over to close the door more securely against the wind. Late sun streaked through the windows and turned the chandeliers into glittering showers of colour. Hilda took out a handkerchief and patted her face.

'It's extraordinary!' Eyes still on the letter, Sylvia spoke with a voice of wonder. 'It's from Arthur. I suppose you guessed. He's a prisoner of war. Who could have expected such a thing? Such an extraordinary thing.' She looked up. 'He's alive, Hilda. This is his own handwriting. I can hardly believe it. I don't know what to do.'

Since Sylvia seemed expectant, Hilda asked, 'Where is he, dear?'

'Constantinople. He calls it Stamboul. Do you think he's all right?'

'What does he say?'

'He says everyone is kind and courteous. But that can't mean the Turks, can it? He doesn't write anything bad. He describes walks in a garden and looking at the Bosphorus.' Sylvia began reading the letter again almost with an expression of despair. 'How can one know if it's *true*? Maybe it's all a lie and he is badly wounded, beaten, tortured.'

'I shouldn't think so. There are international rules, you know.'

'Of course. How silly of me. I'm just so *thrown*. Perhaps Papa will reappear too. No. No. That's silly too. His ADC described the horror . . . Oh my poor mama . . . I feel as if everything's rolling beneath me, Hilda . . . I think I'll just be quiet for a little while.' Sylvia laid down the letter and, sitting back in her chair, shut her eyes.

Hilda hesitated and then signalled to the waiter. 'Two glasses of red wine, please,' adding in case he didn't understand, '*Vino tinto, vin rouge*.'

The wine came and Hilda took a sip. The bells were ringing again.

Sylvia opened her eyes and seeing the wine, took a thirsty gulp. 'Yes. He's alive. We should celebrate that. Missing, now found. I can't get much further than that. I can't work out what it *means*. Not beyond that.'

'I don't think you have to just now, dear,' said Hilda.

'He came into my life and gave everything a meaning. I couldn't believe he wanted me. He and his friends were so *clever*. I used to just listen. But I told you all this in Camberwell.'

'Yes,' said Hilda. From where she was sitting she could see people beginning to come out of the cathedral. It had not been a long service. Several of the women wore black mantillas that fluttered in the wind.

'But then the war came.' Sylvia looked in surprise at her empty glass. 'Do you think it would be wrong to have another glass of wine?'

'Of course not. I'm wearing nurse's uniform which makes us respectable. Anyway, we're about to be invaded by joyful worshippers so we'll need something to fortify us.'

'Funny how happy one feels coming out of church,' said Sylvia absent-mindedly. 'I can never decide if it's God's good effect or the relief of escape.' She picked up the letter again.

Men streamed into the café, talking loudly. Old women hung onto young women's arms. The wind tore at the white tablecloths, before everything settled again.

'You see the thing is, Hilda, I thought Arthur was dead. I was facing up to what life would be without him. Or trying to . . . Or at least I knew I was going to have to. Now he's alive but not coming home.'

'You don't have to think through everything just now,' advised Hilda, as she had before. She had to raise her voice above the chatter.

'No. He writes the American Embassy provided underclothes and pyjamas. You never think of such things being unavailable. On the other hand he wouldn't have had them at the front. Or perhaps he did, just didn't mention it. There were other more important things.'

'Like death,' agreed Hilda.

'It's all very strange. Here, you read the letter.'

Hilda took the flimsy bit of paper although she'd have preferred not to. She read it quickly. 'It is strange. You're quite right.' She handed back the letter.

'It's a new Arthur. First there was the clever student, then the warrior, now the prisoner of war.' Sylvia looked into her once more empty glass.

'Well, I suppose you've changed too.' Hilda decided she wouldn't offer Sylvia more wine. 'Why don't you eat your patis-serie?'

'In case I get drunk? I don't eat much any more. Somehow I can't. You do believe that I'm glad Arthur's alive?'

'Oh, yes!' Hilda was astounded at the question.

'The trouble is, he might rather be dead. He and his friends talked a lot about death. They were really rather keen on the idea.'

'Talking is one thing, being is another.'

'He was fearfully brave. Do you get the feeling he is among a group of officers?'

'I should think so.'

'The army mattered to him. I could hardly believe it at first.

321

He'll like being with other soldiers. Now I'm talking too much. Would you like to go?'

'No,' lied Hilda, who hoped to get into the cathedral before it was dark. Captain Prideaux had told her about a famous Caravaggio there.

'I'm afraid I've had no one to talk to for so long and you're paying the price. I feel quite odd, light-headed, but also very anxious. But we just carry on, don't we? The point is which direction to carry on in.' Sylvia gave a wild laugh, causing the family at the next table to look up reprovingly. 'Once at home, you see, I won't be able to nurse, in fact I don't want to. I'll be back with my mother, just as I was before Arthur came into my life. Except that he'll be far away in Turkey. I suppose it's wrong to think of myself.'

'Oh, no,' said Hilda helplessly. 'We must all do that.'

'Not women. I mean without the war, you'd never have escaped. I'm beginning to believe that Gussie may have made just the right decision to marry the ghastly Reggie. A pity she had to sleep with him first. She'll get enough of that after the wedding. And a baby at the age of eighteen! No. Perhaps she's in the usual trap prepared for women. I slept with Arthur in Cairo, you know. He was over the moon but . . .' She stopped.

Hilda, who had been eyeing their neighbour and hoping they didn't speak English, began to think they had spent enough time in the café.

'I'm sorry.' Sylvia saw her friend's face. 'Have I embarrassed you? Or even shocked you?'

'No. no. Wartime rules seem different from peacetime. I say, you wouldn't like to walk across to the cathedral, would you?'

'You are a dear!' Sylvia stretched her hand to Hilda as she had at the beginning. 'I hardly know what I've been saying. Let's go and light a candle for Arthur. Remind me, when I witter on, I only need to say one thing: Arthur's alive.'

The two friends, one thin and tall, one short and sturdy, walked arm in arm across the square and were engulfed in the shadow cast by the cathedral.

Inside, they whispered in hushed awe at the baroque elaboration of the high altar, the side chapels and ceiling. They knelt together and Sylvia prayed for Arthur. Hilda prayed for Captain Prideaux.

'There's an amazing Caravaggio,' whispered Hilda. So they found the sacristy and stared at a vast and lifelike painting of St John the Baptist's head being cut off.

'It's very gruesome, isn't it? Look at the tendons in his neck.'

'And what a trollop Salome seems!'

'I suppose she was.'

As they turned to go, a dark priest with a beard arrived and began to harangue them in Maltese. Then he switched to Latin. Sylvia and Hilda hurried away.

'Why didn't your nurse's uniform save us?' asked Sylvia when they reached the square.

'Perhaps he was just being friendly,' suggested Hilda and they both began to giggle.

Worried that ferries might stop when darkness fell, Hilda rushed them through the streets, back down the flights of stone steps.

When they were safely aboard the last ferry and the lights of Valletta were shining out of the darkness behind them, Sylvia said, 'I think the secret of happiness is to take yourself seriously. Men seem to achieve it naturally. So that's my resolution. I shall be loyal to Arthur in every way but I shall also take myself seriously.'

Hilda said nothing. The engine was noisy and the wind, still blowing, caused the boat to bump against the waves. She was surprised at Sylvia's words because she had never seemed very independent. She, herself, had been the one who had struck out on her own, first going south to London, now to Malta. Yet when she came to think about it, her happiness depended more and more on a few words spoken by a blind aristocrat who scarcely knew she existed. Nothing was certain.

Sylvia decided to return to England as soon as another ship showed up. Meanwhile, she helped in the hospital.

One afternoon when there was a lull, she suddenly asked Hilda to take her to meet Rupert. Instinctively, Hilda felt jealous which she knew was ridiculous.

'We can take him out to the terrace,' she offered.

'Can't he walk?'

'Yes. It's just to guide him and to see he doesn't get into difficulties.'

'Of course.'

The *Siroca* or Xaroco or something else had moved on, streaming away over the sea, leaving behind a period of warm, calm days. Rupert was sitting in a chair with a book of Braille on his lap; it was the Bible and, although he had not yet learned to use it, he assured Hilda he liked its presence.

'I've brought you a visitor,' announced Hilda.

Rupert had already looked up at the sound of two sets of approaching feet. It was afternoon and on either side of him, men dozed. There were a few flies but nothing much else moved.

Sylvia hesitated. After all, she was not prepared for the jutting bones and dead staring eyes. His long feet were in strange, rather Moorish slippers. She fixed on those.

'It's Sylvia Fitzpaine, Captain Prideaux. I'm passing through Malta on my way to England.'

'As one does,' said Rupert. 'How kind of you to call.'

His voice was quite normal, although softer, and still with that irony which Sylvia had found infuriating and, perhaps, attractive.

'Shall we go out to the terrace?' suggested Hilda. She fiddled around with the bedclothes.

'I'm having a good day,' volunteered Rupert and smiled (just as if he could see, thought Sylvia) first at Hilda and then at herself. The smile, gentle and almost sweet was quite new and unexpected.

They walked out slowly; Rupert refused help and carefully negotiated his way through the beds.

'I'm not ill, you know,' he said when they arrived outside where a few chairs were placed. 'I just have a bullet in my brain – or have they decided it's a piece of shrapnel? Nurse Horridge will tell you. You'd think the X-ray could tell the difference. The effect is the same.'

'I'm sorry,' said Sylvia.

He turned his face to her but said nothing.

Hilda stood. 'You're shivering. I'll get you a blanket.'

'Do you think she's left us alone on purpose?' asked Rupert when she'd gone. 'Women are always trying to please.'

'You *are* shivering,' pointed out Sylvia. 'Why would she think we wanted to be alone?' A hot blush spread over her face and neck and she was glad Rupert couldn't see it.

'Why indeed? I know I have a small place in your life but you have an important place in mine.'

Sylvia looked a question before remembering she must speak. 'Why is that?'

'You're the last woman I shall ever make love to. They tell me any exertion will be fatal. To be honest I am keeping the option up my sleeve. Should I wish to exit this life, I can think of worse ways to go.'

'Yes,' agreed Sylvia, willing away her blush. Hilda had eyes.

'Talking of which, is your fiancé still with us?'

'Not dead,' said Sylvia, 'but not with us. He's a prisoner of war. I've just heard from him.'

'I liked him, you know. Although why should you know, con-sidering my behaviour – *our* behaviour, actually. He was a good man and a good soldier.'

'Is,' said Sylvia, 'not was.'

'Is a prisoner of war still a soldier? Is a blind man still a soldier?'

'Yes,' said Sylvia firmly.

'I suspect I was jealous of Lieutenant Lamb,' said Rupert, the irony suddenly leaving his voice. 'He knew what he was up to, your fiancé, or he thought he did which comes to the same thing. I sometimes wonder if I could have been a Lieutenant Lamb if I'd had the proper complement of fingers. I suspect not. I was a terrible tearaway even in the nursery, I'm told.'

Sylvia looked round. The view across the water towards Valletta was dazzling. It seemed that Arthur's re-emergence had dispelled the muffling depression and made her interested in her surround-ings again.

'I'm sorry. I'm talking too much. It never used to be my prob-lem. I'm glad you've visited me.'

Sylvia was surprised that he could tell her attention had wavered. 'Hilda is devoted to you,' she said. She paused. 'You won't tell her about, about us?'

'Hilda? Is that Nurse Horridge's name? I might have guessed.' He smiled, not unkindly.

'She is clever and good.'

'And plain?'

Sylvia said nothing.

'It's strange how you can tell a plain woman even when you

can't see them. It must be the way they behave, their tone of voice – although Nurse Horridge has a nice voice – a lack of expectation, of flirtation. For example, I'm certain Nurse Riley who also looks after me is a very pretty young woman.'

'The Irish nurse?' asked Sylvia.

'Am I right?'

'She has blue eyes, reddish curls that tend to escape from her cap and a trim waist.'

'Exactly! You see what philosophical thoughts I have time for now. But I won't tell Nurse Hilda our shameful secret.'

'Thank you.' Sylvia felt her unseen blush arising again. She was not sure she wanted him to think it shameful.

'Hilda says you won't talk about the war,' she said quickly.

'Do you find that surprising?'

'It's all anyone thinks of.' Sylvia paused. She was thinking of her father.

As if reading her mind, Rupert leant forward a little. 'I haven't asked about your father. I was there, you know, when those heroic fellows, your father included, your fiancé included, walked across the dry salt lake into the valley of death – except it was up into the hills.'

'He was reported wounded and missing – that's still the official news. My poor mother believes he'll turn up in some Turkish hospital, having lost his memory. But I spoke to his ADC in a hospital in Cairo and he believes he died. So do I.'

Rupert nodded. 'I'm surprised anyone survived. I was on the top of Chocolate Hill, named, fancifully, for the colour of the earth, and I watched the whole vile debacle until finally it drove me mad. There was a journalist with me – I hope he wrote about it. The men were being sent on a suicidal mission. Quite point-less too. As I said, it drove me mad so I jumped up and spouted poetry. I was fairly potty already and it seemed the only sort of protest I could make. Pretty pathetic really when you think of heroes like your fiancé and your father.' He paused. 'I'd like to have been a journalist.'

Sylvia stood up and went to him. She put her hand over his which was cold despite the sun.

'I admired your father. I lent him my horse once, by the

pyramids at Giza. How happy he was, cantering off! I think he had the gift of happiness.'

'Yes. I don't know how my mother, how all of us, will manage without him.' Sylvia looked down and found tears in her eyes, although who they were for she couldn't tell. 'Am I tiring you?'

'When the pain leaves me it is like a miracle. I expect Nurse Horridge will come in a moment and chase you away.'

'Would you like me to make contact with your family?'

'Could you face it? They're quite dreadful, you know. Last time I was there, that shit Churchill came to lunch. Much worse than a shit, of course. Not that I blame only him for this blithering arsehole of a Mediterranean Expedition! Hamilton, Kitchener, Fisher, Asquith! All of them . . .'

Sylvia saw red spots appear on the sharp points of Rupert's cheekbones. They spread in dangerous blotches down his face and neck. 'Don't,' she said. She picked up his hand again and squeezed it. He was taut and trembling with rage. Gradually, he relaxed.

'You see why I don't speak of the war.' He reflected. 'In fact, I thought I'd come to terms with it but I see I haven't quite. But all those men, all those good, happy men.'

'Please!'

'No. They can't have all been good and happy. One mustn't sentimentalise.' He put his head on the side like an animal cocking his ear. 'Do I hear the steps of my guardian angel?'

Sylvia dropped his hand and looked up. Hilda was coming towards them, her steps less confident than usual.

Sylvia waved. 'Where have you been?'

'Emptying bedpans, that sort of fun thing.'

The two women stood looking down at Rupert. Hilda frowned anxiously. 'I'm afraid I've worn out your Captain Prideaux,' said Sylvia.

'It is just possible,' said Rupert, standing up but facing to neither woman, 'that the navy could have got through the Dardanelles, braving mines, machine-gun fire, etc, etc. But then what? If they arrived at Constantinople where were the plans to take them on to the next stage? Where was the *army*?'

As he stopped speaking with an expression of despair, Hilda

stepped forward and took his arm. 'I think we'll go in now,' she said and cast a look of reproach at Sylvia.

'I'm sorry,' murmured Sylvia. She didn't follow them but stayed outside, watching how the lowering sun made the city float on a yellow haze. She thought of the darkly painted Caravaggio with only St John the Baptist's bleeding head and Salome's lovely face shining out of the canvas. She thought that Salome might be the face of war demanding the sacrifice of heroes or saints.

Then she went inside and gave Hilda a hug.

A few days later, without seeing Rupert again, Sylvia walked down to catch the ferry to Valletta, the start of her journey back to England. Hilda, snatching time from her duties, came with her.

'Prideaux dictated a letter for you to take.' She handed over the envelope. 'He says it's for his father who can't help being what he is.'

'That's noble of Captain Prideaux.'

'It is, actually, because his real belief is that far too many people among the upper classes in England enjoy being what they shouldn't be. But you know that.'

Sylvia glanced at her friend. 'You won't leave him, will you?'

'Not unless he kicks me out.'

'You'd better watch Nurse Riley then.'

At the ferry, several soldiers on crutches were gathered to watch the action.

'You taking the ship out there, miss?' one of them asked Sylvia politely. Her cases had already been brought down and she stood among them.

'I hope so.'

'To Blighty, I expect.' The man nodded to himself. He was young, a private. Balancing on his remaining leg, he produced an envelope. 'Would you post this, if you please?'

Sylvia took the envelope. 'You'll be back yourself soon.'

'So they say. Part of me, at least.'

'I've got to go.' Hilda took Sylvia's arm. For reasons neither of them could define – perhaps just sadness of the wounded homesick men – they felt as if they would never meet again. They hugged. Hilda walked swiftly up the hill and Sylvia climbed into the small ferryboat. It bounced about on the grey, choppy water. She wasn't wearing her nurse's uniform and felt exposed. The wounded men watched her jealously.

Arthur's *alive*, she told herself and gave a little wave to the Tommies. Most of them waved back.

Twenty-Four

A black cloud followed the boat that brought General Monro
to Helles. Blue sky surrounded the cloud which gave it the
odd appearance of a canopy, a funereal canopy, perhaps.

'I'm told the weather will hold till January,' said the general to
his chief of staff, 'but I don't believe a word of it.'

No one disagreed. He had already been to Suvla and Anzac.
The speed of Monro's inspection of Gallipoli, his questioning
of corps and divisional commanders, had stunned everyone on
the peninsula. Gallipoli had evolved its own way of doing things,
sometimes brilliant, often a desperate muddle, usually inexplicable except to those who were engaged in them. This whirlwind
inspection shook them.

The new arrivals were equally shaken by what they found.
When Monro had inspected staff headquarters, passing between
the lines of men, he had said in an aside to Major General Lynden-
Bell, 'Have you ever met such a down and out lot of fellows in
your life?' Lynden-Bell agreed he hadn't, and noted the comment
in his journal. Both of them knew about the letter written by an
Australian journalist, Keith Murdoch, which had made its way to
the Prime Minister and the cabinet. They had assumed its high-
coloured, vehement criticism of the handling of the campaign a
gross exaggeration. Now they were not so sure.

On the battlefronts, Monro was equally appalled by the conditions which men and officers were enduring. It seemed that
General Sir Charles Monro was the new eye anticipated hopefully
by Fred.

None of the other men took much interest, there were always
rumours. But Fred persuaded his sergeant, who was going to the
beach, that he should accompany him and so was able to see for
himself the way the wind was blowing.

'He means business, this new chap,' he told Joe Dingle who showed his usual scorn for the information Fred brought him.

'Are you saying you scrounged nothing from the beach?'

Fred continued, undeterred. 'You should have seen the way he came off that sunk destroyer they're using as a pier. Johnny Turk had better look out for this one.'

'You're not saying we're in for an attack?'

'I'm not saying that. I'm no keener on getting killed than you are. I just don't fancy sitting here for the rest of my life.'

Fred gave up trying to interest Joe, but later that night when he was on sentry duty, slapping his sides to keep himself warm, he tried to imagine the outcome of the general's visit. He could hardly fail to see that a mere fringe of the coastline had been secured and that beaches and entrenchments were always overlooked by Johnny Turk and his artillery. Whereas the poor old Tommies, not forgetting the French and Anzacs, had to deal with the weather, sickness and exhaustion and almost no artillery to support them, even if they could get into a decent position.

In this humble private's view, thought Fred, loosing off a few rounds from his rifle in retaliation to the same from Johnny Turk, evacuation was the only answer.

Yet in the days that followed, Fred found himself made depressed and uneasy by his conclusion. Pulled back for a brief rest in a tent encampment besides the stumps of olive trees, he spent time mournfully visiting the ever-growing crop of wooden crosses – men were still dying daily, mostly by unseen shells or artillery. He felt leaving them would be a desertion and his usual energy and curiosity left him. Now he felt both that he had been on Gallipoli too long, a lifetime, and that he could never leave it.

He wrote to Lily,

You wouldn't believe how old your baby brother feels sometimes, like my shoulders are bowed by the weight of all the vile things I've seen, and by the souls of the thousands of good English men lying under Turkish soil. If I do get home, I doubt you'll even recognise me as the same cheeky chap that left. Do you remember how I bagged that big pheasant for my last supper and how angry you were? I don't think I'd have the heart to kill a rabbit now.

Fred put aside the letter then and two nights later, back in the trenches, added, 'Despite the above, I am keeping well as I trust you are too.'

Then came the news that the great general, Field Marshal Lord Horatio Herbert Kitchener, Secretary of State for War and whose face (on a poster) had persuaded many of the Tommies to join up, was himself on Gallipoli. Even Joe Dingle dug out an old camera he'd removed from an officer's corpse and announced he was ready to take a photo of the general, for Margie, his sweetheart.

'Why do you think you'll get anywhere near him?' protested Fred. 'And why ever should that old box work? It took the same shell and weight of rubble that killed Doubtfire and he was a whole lot bigger.'

'That's a sturdy camera,' insisted Joe. 'Why else would it survive?'

Surprisingly, both Joe and Fred got near enough to touch the famous general because he was led through their trench one sunny morning. They even had their photograph taken with him, but by the official photographer.

'We'll be famous!' exulted Joe to anybody who'd listen.

'In your grave,' said Fred, but he thought, First Monro and now Kitchener, they've got to sort something out.

'Dearest Gussie, I've never seen you look more lovely!' Sylvia was taken aback by the sheer animal vitality of her sister. She wore a long white satin gown – their mother's, expanded at waist and hips.

This was all part of the compromise between the quiet wedding ordained by Lady Beatrice and the splendid celebration envisioned by Gussie. The county would not be invited, her ladyship's mother would be persuaded to stay away. Lily's children could hold the train, there would be enough soldiers to hold the swords, the recuperating Tollorum wounded would fill some pews, the vicarage some others and a few chosen from the village – Dr and Mrs Horsthrup, Mr Block, the estate manager, the old schoolmaster, Mr Badger. Afterwards there would be sandwiches at the manor.

Gussie was posing in front of her bedroom mirror, trying to decide whether to carry a bunch of pale chrysanthemums or a white prayer book. 'The chrysanthemums are so funereal and the prayer book a little too holy, given my situation.' Gussie looked at herself critically. 'Switch on the light, Syl, dear. It's such a dark morning.'

Sylvia obliged and watched her sister's skin and eyes glow even brighter. 'Why don't I pick some autumn leaves? It would be very stylish and trail down your front, if that's what you're worried about.'

'You are a darling!' Gussie had been in affectionate good humour ever since Sylvia had returned. Now she hugged her sister. 'How I wish we were having a double wedding! But it will happen. We just have to wait for this horrid war to be over. Do pick me some leaves. I'd love that.'

It was odd to be patronised by Gussie, Sylvia thought as she wandered into the garden. She didn't particularly mind, glad at this point, that anyone could find confidence and happiness.

She stood with her scissors and looked up at the leaves of the tulip tree. She'd known it all her life. The leaves had been golden when she'd arrived home but now they were bronze. Soon they'd turn brown and drop to the ground. So much was inevitable and she couldn't tell whether that was a comfort or a heavy weight. The war would end some time and quite probably Arthur would return. But the idea of their marriage seemed quite fantastical.

She turned her back on the tree and went to a young copper beech whose leaves clung on tenaciously. She cut three slim branches and thought how charming they'd look dangling over Gussie's fecund stomach.

Beatrice went to the War Office again, this time in the company of her formidable mother, the Countess of Deverill, who had the confidence of Mrs Twigg-Smith with the addition of ruthless aristocratic charm.

On this occasion they were shown into a large office dominated by a gigantic painting of the Battle of Trafalgar and a smaller portrait of the Duke of Wellington. Major Bingley was there to welcome them.

'I do apologise, Lady Deverill, for missing you on your last visit.'

'I was not with my daughter on that occasion.'

'Of course.' The major regrouped. 'The prime minister sends his best wishes.'

Lady Deverill bowed graciously.

Beatrice, lingering a pace behind, felt like a child again and recalled, with a twist to her heart, the joy of escaping her mother when she set up home with Bingo. She did not, in fact, want her powerful mama's help because she felt competent to do everything necessary but it seemed to be a quid pro quo for her mother's banishment from Gussie's wedding. On the other hand, despite all her efforts over the last weeks, she had discovered nothing more about Bingo's circumstances. At this point her mind hastily veered away from a conversation dear Sylvia had tried to have with her about a meeting with Bingo's ADC. After all, the man had been dying and poor Sylvia had just heard about dear Arthur . . .

The two ladies, their wide hats almost touching, sat upright on their seats, while Major Bingley studied some papers.

Beatrice couldn't help feeling sympathy as the stalwart middle-aged soldier was reduced to a nervous schoolboy.

'What I was trying to say so clumsily, Your Ladyship, was that the general's valiant spirit took him to the furthest point of the attack and that thereafter the Allies withdrew, at no point regaining the position. So if – hum – your son-in-law, your husband – hum – fell, he could not have been found.'

'Why, then, was he declared "wounded, missing"?' demanded the countess.

'There is an accepted formula, Your Ladyship,' began the major, glancing uncomfortably in Beatrice's direction.

'My dear man, we are not here for formulas,' interrupted the countess once more, but this time before she could finish there was a knock at the door.

'Come in,' said Major Bingley promptly and with obvious relief.

Beatrice felt relieved too as the one-legged Lieutenant Knott edged through the door. This duel between the poor Major Bingley and her mother was getting them nowhere and trampled on her own sensitivities.

The lieutenant shook hands, apologised for intruding and handed the major a note which he read. He, too, apologised and the lieutenant left. Beatrice thought that since she had last seen him, he had learnt to walk more adroitly, and she began to count the weeks. Her heart became heavier.

'What is the situation on Gallipoli?' The countess tried a new tack. 'Are we anywhere near winning? General Hamilton is telling all sorts of stories round town. Insists he was on the verge of a breakthrough and just required another regiment or so. But most people I talk to seem to take the opposite view. Is it true Lord Kitchener's been out there?'

The major, flustered, admitted that Kitchener had been out to the peninsula. 'He likes to judge things for himself, I understand.'

'And what has he judged?'

'Oh. Hum. The state of – er – things.'

'You cannot speak. But I can. The soldiers will be brought home or sent to some other godforsaken place – have you ever been to the East? I have – and the grieving wives like my daughter here will hear no more of their husbands, until they have no tears left for weeping. After a year they will be told, cruelly, without information, "You are a widow"!'

'Mother!' protested Beatrice.

'Warfare is a beastly business,' said the poor major, blinking rapidly. 'My own father—'

'I do not wish to know about your father. I'm sure he is an honourable man, just not relevant in this instance. Please give my compliments to the prime minister and Lord Kitchener and say they should run their army more carefully and with proper attention to detail. If they did, they might have more successes.'

It was a final note and a small part of Beatrice admired her mother. Yet the brutality of the picture she painted had brought a hot flush to Beatrice's pale face. Even so, she was not prepared for her mother's comment as they sat in the back of her chauffeur-driven car.

'You may have to accept the facts, my poor child. At least I can do no more. We see widows all around. What fortitude! What dignity! War is a time to carry on. Although Gussie has chosen an impossible husband, at least he is recognised as an exceptional soldier and now that she is having a baby, herself scarcely out of the nursery, you will have your hands full. My advice is to feel content with your twenty-five years of marriage and look ahead. You are still young. I myself lost your dear father when I was at an even earlier age. There are many years to enjoy and to carry out your duties.'

That evening, Beatrice noted the date, *23rd November, 1915* in her occasional diary, and wrote, *Mama cannot understand how I feel or she would never have spoken to me in that way. It was as if Bingo's disappearance from my life was of no consequence or no more than the loss of a housekeeper or maid. I'm afraid she has no deep feelings and I will attempt to avoid her.*

Fred, Joe and two other Tommies were rebuilding an officer's dugout on a ridge fairly near a wide dry gulley one afternoon in late November. Fred felt uneasy and repeatedly looked up at the sky. 'I don't like it,' he muttered. It had been a bright morning but the steadily rising wind had switched to the north-east and the temperature plummeted.

'I don't know why you're worried,' said Joe, 'the squalls always come in from the south-west.'

All the men liked the job – something that had a bit of a point to it – and wanted to finish it properly, and it was true that the damage had been done by vicious wind and rain from the south-west. Yet Fred felt something new and ominous in the air; it was like when he sensed Johnny Turk was about to attack and he'd always been right about that. Further down the ridge he could see a round-tented encampment and men urgently banging in the guy ropes.

The major whose dugout it was came over and stood behind him.

'You a countryman?'

'Yessir,' said Fred, saluting. It was odd that an officer would address him like that.

'This wind is a new one.' He glanced at the rest of the men. 'See if you can get the roof up before we're all blown away.'

Fred was about to repeat 'Yessir' when a great crack made both him and the major spin round, prepared either to return fire or lie flat. But it wasn't an attack, from any human enemy, at least. Everyone gaped upwards and saw the sky above the hills split open in a jagged flaming tear. Lightning slashed down and as they cowered, thunder roared over the land.

'It's enough to make you believe in God,' shouted Fred who thought he'd seen every fearful thing on offer over the last months and who did, in fact, believe in God.

Lightning, thunder and now the wind roared and hurtled. There was another small crack but this time nearer at hand, as the metal sheeting the men had been trying to hammer into a roof wrenched itself free, flew through a Tommy in its way and sailed out across the gulley.

The man shrieked; he seemed to be sliced in half but there could be no use in calling for a medic. The sounds of nature outdid even the most fearsome barrage.

'Think of it,' yelled the major who seemed to have elected Fred his friend. 'I shall have to write to his parents, dear Mrs Woolley, your son suffered death by sheet metal.'

Fred, scarcely hearing, said nothing; they needed shelter. Racing towards them, across the ridge and the bump of Achi Baba, was an army of black clouds.

'Get in!' bellowed the major.

The rain reached them as they lay below the sandbags, almost on top of each other, weighting themselves to the ground. It fell in solid walls of water so that in just a few moments men were more afraid of drowning than anything else. It rushed at them so fast that if they didn't hang on to something, they were in danger of being swept into the gulley.

Fred pictured the soldiers perched precariously on trenches along the front line. They would flood in minutes and the men washed out like rats in a drain. He had come from there that morning and his kit was still there; he imagined his precious books sodden and dashed about the hillside.

The intensity of the water made it difficult to breathe. When Fred was about five, he had fallen into the River Stour. How the water had swirled above his head, filled his nose and mouth, stopped his breath! He'd shut his eyes so he was blind too. It was only a thick tree root growing down from the bank, which had saved him then. Once he found it, he'd clung on for dear life.

That's what he was doing now, Fred realised, hanging on to a tree stump with no idea how he'd got there. Water cascaded over his head and shoulders. He looked down and saw the gulley below him. In just a few minutes it had become the channel for a violent torrent. And the rain still came. The thunder rolled and the lightning split the increasing darkness. He tried to see the encampment below but either it was hidden by the blackness and rain or it had been swept away.

'Joe!' Fred called. Stupid to think Joe could hear him in all this mayhem. Well, he certainly wasn't going to let go of this kindly stump to find him. Let's hope its roots held. Things were whirling past him all the time, sandbags, boots, rifles, packs, no bodies, thank God, and stones, some of them, like the couple tearing past right now, big enough to smash his skull. Lucky he'd got his helmet firmly attached. He'd learnt that trick early on.

He'd been reading the Bible lately. The Old Testament really knew about things that could destroy a man: *plagues and scourges*. Look at poor old Job, the righteous man who'd had all his ten children killed by a mighty wind, plus five hundred oxen and five hundred donkeys carried off by the Sabeans, whoever they might be, followed by boils so painful he scraped at his skin with broken pottery. No fun being Job but, brave man, he still didn't deny God.

As the wind and rain continued to pour over him, Fred eased his arms slightly and changed the position of his legs. It caused him to see the major's upturned face behind. There was a great gash across his forehead through which the white bone showed. The rain had washed away any sign of blood. Fred didn't even know his name. But then how many names could he put to the faces of the dead he'd seen on Gallipoli? He only remembered Ernie Wilkes because he'd taught him the power of learning and because he'd been so shocked by the sight of his clever brains poured over the ground.

To distract himself, Fred went over the ten plagues of Egypt in his head. Number one: blood, which meant blood in the Nile and all the fish dead; number two: frogs; three: lice – Lice, ruler of the world, thought Fred, before bringing himself back; he had to keep a grip, and not just on the stump. Four: flies or wild animals; would tortoises count? Five: pestilence. Six: boils, back to Job again. Seven: hail or a great storm – no comment. Eight: locusts, covering the sky in a giant shadow. Worse than number nine: darkness, so heavy they could feel it. Darkness without wind and rain sounded quite pleasant to him. Somewhere a man was screaming even louder than the wail of the wind. Number ten didn't worry him either: death of the first-born; he'd be lucky if he ever got to that point. Gallipoli was one way of keeping the population down. Added to France and all the other campaigns he didn't know about. There'd be girls for the taking if you did survive. It was a wonder God hadn't put in war as one of the plagues.

His arms were sore, tired and cold. Whoever thought to put a dugout on the edge of a ravine was a fool. But then whoever thought to bring thousands of men to a Turkish peninsula and leave them there till winter was a fool. Probably a whole tribe of fools. Like the ancient Egyptians. Pity God hadn't struck them down.

Anger was the best source of heat in the world. It was weeks since the Lord High Kitchener had come: he'd been sure Kitchener would see them out of such a joke but here they still were. Probably the politicians were taking a bit of time off on their grouse moors. Made your blood boil. That's right: blood, boil.

The wind seemed to be letting up a bit but the rain was still sluicing. He could hear the water rushing down the gulley now. Straight out to sea, no doubt. Someone crawled by him. Or maybe it was a corpse floating. Fred tried to stop him heading to the gulley with one arm but couldn't hold him. He was still wearing summer kit, poor fellow. Maybe he'd float all the way down and end up in a nice big hospital ship.

Perhaps he'd got it wrong and he'd placed himself in the path of a river. The dead major had been swept down a while ago and if he didn't make a move soon, he'd be too weak for a choice. Life or death? He'd faced that every day. Suddenly, he wanted to let go. He imagined himself jumping and leaping down the flow of water, like a great fish plunging into the sea.

'Hey, you! Private!' Someone was shouting in his ear.

'I'm not deaf, am I,' grumbled Fred. A huge man in a British Warm stood over him. He towered above the flood like a god.

'Grab on to me. Pretend I'm a fucking tree if it helps.'

Fred wanted to obey but his arms were locked and numb. The giant lifted him off the stump and carried him like a child. They splashed along as if they were fording puddles in an English country lane. In the darkness Fred noticed the man's RAMC armband.

'I've been picking men up from all over the place,' said the giant conversationally. 'Not at first, even my eighteen stone couldn't withstand the deluge, but the last half-hour. You're my seventh survivor. What do you weigh? Seven, eight stone? Boys like you didn't stand a chance.'

Fred's teeth were chattering too much for him to reply. It was the shock, he supposed, since he was warm enough stuffed up against his saviour's chest.

After some minutes – or hours – Fred found himself lowered on to his feet like a toddler.

'Stand, can you? My mates will take over.'

Fred *could* stand. The ambulance man tapped him approvingly on the shoulder. 'A cup of tea is all you need, mate. If I were you, I'd head for that fire over there.'

Fred saw the red glow in the distance, automatically wondered about Johnny Turk seeing it, but went along anyway.

Dawn lit up a new Gallipoli. The torrential rain had smashed everything in its path, carving out rivers, smoothing out trenches, turning shell holes into lakes. Now it gushed out into the sea where the continuing swells caused the big ships to tug out their anchors. At the shoreline, smaller boats were already beginning their daily cat and mouse with the shells. Except as yet there were no shells.

Fred looked down sleepily and wondered whatever would come his way next.

'It'll be bleeding dig, dig, dig,' grumbled a Tommy bundled up near Fred's feet.

He was right. Digging out corpses, digging graves, digging new trenches, water everywhere. The sodden men who returned to their corporals found it was business as usual with a whole army needing to be put to rights before the enemy got there first. But at least the sun was out.

Fred didn't mind digging. It kept him warm. Then at midday the sky became covered with low grey clouds and the wind turned round again to the north-east, bringing a menacing Black Sea bite. Fred found it hard to grip his shovel and the ground became stiff and resistant.

Later in the afternoon, he looked up, eyes red and tired, and saw snow falling, white against the ever-darkening sky. He ended the day once more in the front line, returning the usual potshots from across the way. His lieutenant suggested a foray across the lines assuming the enemy were unprepared, but the sergeant wasn't keen and the cold was becoming intense.

'Hey, Sarge, my trigger's gone solid!' called out one man. It was Joe Dingle, keeping away from Fred after accusing him of leaving him to drown. Silly bugger! As if he'd had a choice.

The nights were always cruel now but this was altogether different. There was something hostile in the air, worse even than before the deluge. No one spoke but huddled down into their overcoats. Those designated for guard duty buried their heads. Could they really be expected to sit up in this angry night? Of course they could. Wars don't take account of weather. Fred, who was not on duty, piled himself with anything he could find, under as well as above. He'd never known such a sharp drop in the temperature; the water in the bottom of the trench had actually begun to freeze.

Fred watched several men, including the still sulking Joe, pull out old biscuit tins, pile themselves with blankets and sit down. Fred wanted to point out that their boots were still in the icy water but suspected Joe would take no notice. He was beginning to think the only way to survive the night was to get up and walk around.

Sometime in the early hours an officer with a sergeant came round and tried to make them do exactly that.

'Come on, lads. If you don't want to be black lumps in the morning, you'd better get moving.'

Nobody stirred.

The sergeant had a go: 'Get up, you lazy sods, do what the lieutenant says. Or are you afraid of Johnny Turk? I tell you they're as frozen stiff as you!'

When there was still no reaction, officer and NCO began kicking the men up. Fred joined in for the exercise. This was a bit more successful: a few men stood but most slumped back the minute the boot passed, too miserable to care what happened to them.

More hours passed. The strangest thing of this bitter night was the utter silence compared to the usual level of activity carried out under cover of darkness. No mules came up the paths, no guns fired, no boats chugged in or away from the piers. Fred, swaying on his feet, head spinning, watched the snow turn to freezing rain and back again to snow. He knew he was hallucinating when he stood outside his body and saw he had changed into an Old Testament prophet with long robes and jutting beard, back braced forward against God's challenges.

Daylight was marked by an uncanny wailing as men woke and found their feet and hands black and swollen. Two sentries at their posts were found frozen all the way through. Tarpaulins were stiff like metal. Men cried, tears freezing on their faces, as their numbed limbs came back to life.

Joe was one of them. He was astonished at what had happened to his feet. Fred obliged by cutting off his boots.

'They're not mine,' Joe muttered dazedly, rubbing on the black misshapen stumps.

Guiltily, Fred took his arm. 'We'd better get to the ambulance station.'

Joe began to walk before shrieking. 'I can't walk on those. It's like knives piercing through.'

Other men had found the same and, dropping to their hands and knees, began to crawl out of the trenches. No one bothered about the enemy.

Outside the trench, they had a view of a new white glistening world. The hillside shone with ice. Upright men couldn't walk, they slid. Mud from the deluge had frozen on their overcoats which were solid like wood. A man in front of Fred and Joe cracked down heavily and they heard his thigh bone snap.

'Lucky bugger,' commented Fred unsympathetically. 'He'll be on one of those hospital ships sitting up in bed with a cup of tea while we're still defending king and country on this benighted rock.' Not that Joe was likely to be doing much of anything, thought Fred looking down at his struggling, moaning friend who he was alternately carrying and towing like a toboggan.

The ambulance station was completely overwhelmed. Men lying on the hard ground raised their blackened hands piteously like souls in hell. Many had blackened faces too.

After delivering Joe, Fred wandered round a bit noting the different ways men can suffer until he spotted the giant orderly who had saved him from slipping into the ravine. He'd just say his thanks.

But the giant was too preoccupied to listen. 'You know what I've found? Ten men frozen solid in the bushes. You know the reason? They'd been given some rum or got hold of some rum and made themselves so drunk they didn't even bother with overcoats. Come to help, have you, mate? No way we can dig graves till the thaw but I don't like to leave them there, stupid fuckers.'

Fred followed him. He didn't think there'd be much army discipline to worry him on that day.

The giant turned out to be loquacious. Fred used the word to himself with pleasure. It suited the expanse of the man. As they walked, or rather slid, he began to tell Fred how lucky he'd been not to be fighting at Suvla. 'A boat came down from there this morning and the skipper told me there were hundreds out there on the ridges, swept over by a minus twenty wind and nowhere to hide. Anzac was as bad, I'd reckon. So high up, they are.'

Fred thought about last night and Joe and the others. It was lucky, he supposed, to lose fingers and toes, ears and noses rather than your life.

'You're Australian, aren't you?'

'Emigrated there five years ago. I was visiting family when the war started so I joined up with you lot. Bad decision.' The giant forged ahead, pulling aside white bushes from which icicles dangled like decorations. 'Take a dekko at this! Apocalypse here and now!'

The men had frozen into drunken poses, one tipped back on his heels, one sprawled out backwards, another bent forward over crossed legs. Most of them had mugs in their hands now frozen to their fingertips. 'Hope it was a good party,' said Fred.

The giant lifted up a man whose arm was outstretched.

'What'll we do with them?' asked Fred, who was wondering why they couldn't be left in peace.

'We'll put them in a heap, ready for burial when they thaw.' It was the giant's job to make things orderly, Fred understood.

When they'd gathered them together, they threw a tarpaulin over them. It didn't do a very good job of disguising the leg hoisted in the air or the back bent like a hairpin. Fred found himself wondering about rigor mortis.

'They'll thaw soon enough,' said the giant, in his voice the satisfaction of a job well done.

Slipping and sliding on the ice which showed no sign of melting, Fred followed the giant back to the ambulance station.

Arthur was trying to chop up a chair but he was smashing it more than chopping it. This was because the axe that he'd bought for a few Ottoman liras (too many all the same) was blunt and useless. He was turning the chair into firewood because it was more important to keep warm than sit on a chair. It was intensely cold in the small courtyard where he stood, although the exercise had warmed him a little, probably as much as the fire would later. All he needed was enough warmth to start on the first volume of Gibbon's *Decline and Fall of the Roman Empire* which had arrived from Sylvia the day previously. At last the Red Cross had discovered them. The letter that had accompanied the book described Gussie's marriage and said that her mother still hoped the Colonel would reappear. Arthur found it hard to concentrate on either subject: Gussie's fate seemed unimportant and the probably fate of the Colonel too painful to contemplate. Sylvia had said very little about herself.

'How are you doing?' Trebble stood at the door to the small house where eight officers were quartered. The houses used like this had previously belonged to Armenians who had been driven from their homes and killed or starved to death in the deserts. Arthur was in the narrow yard attached to the house. Snow was piled high in one corner.

They had arrived at the Afion Kara Hissar camp in late October. Nothing had been prepared for them, no furniture, no food, no glass in the windows, but, despite the unhappy history of the place, they had been glad to be settled. From their top windows, they could see the great vertical mountain of rock that rose out of the flat Anatolian plain and gave its name to the camp.

'It won't make much of a blaze.' Arthur indicated the remains of the chair. He smiled at Trebble who was wearing a towel turban and an eiderdown over his uniform. 'It's lucky we don't salute each other any more.'

'It's you army chaps who go in for all that stuff. The navy knows its own worth without being reminded. I say, you don't think we should chop up our bedsteads?'

'Not with this axe, you wouldn't. Even Suleiman couldn't get through a loaf of bread with it.' Suleiman, who'd sold them the axe, was their guard who liked drawing attention to his spectacular muscles. 'We can't dispose of even one bed after the endless negotiations to get them.'

'You're probably right,' agreed Trebble crossly.

The common idea was that danger brought out a man's true nature but Arthur had decided captivity brought it out better, particularly if you were incarcerated with the same group of men and had very few occupations. Trebble, who had at first seemed a simple, goodhearted fellow, now was prone to dangerous mood swings and struggled to control a fierce anger. Arthur himself, on arrival the perfect (if sick) soldier and officer, had quickly reverted to the scholarly self he had almost forgotten. Books and study was all he cared about. He thought wistfully and almost unbelieving about the commander who would have died for his men. He supposed, regretfully, that he'd reverted to type. In fact, many of the officers, when not engaged in keeping themselves alive, turned to study – languages (including Turkish) or history were the favourites, but Standley wrote poetry.

He wondered how would they all manage if the Turks were defeated and they were sent back to fight again. Of course there were some who were longing to take up arms once more. They were the escapers, always plotting imaginative new plans.

'Can't stand the cold another second,' said Trebble. 'How about kicking a ball?' The ball was a new acquisition made of a turban stuffed with rags.

'Sorry. Got the fire to make. Then I'm booked for a game of chess with Lacey.'

Trebble went in and slammed the door.

Arthur bent to collect the piles of wood. He suspected Trebble would do better if there was an outside danger – apart from the cold. Some of the guards were bullies and the commandant of the camp liked to make regulations to show his power. Last week it had been roll-call of all officers at dawn; the temperature had been below freezing and the guard in charge, as angry as them, seemed unable to count, so they stood shaking with cold for two hours.

After a few days, with no further announcement, it just stopped happening.

The would-be escapees *were* in danger, of course. The hiding places for their maps became more and more elaborate. If they were found they would be shot. Perhaps that thought gave them the energy to carry on.

Arthur nudged the door open with his pile of wood and saw a bent figure standing just inside.

'On for the game, are you?' This was Captain Lacey, Arthur's chess opponent and a New Zealand medical officer. Generally a mild-mannered man, he'd arrived three nights ago in such a state of fury that he couldn't eat or talk. Next day he explained that he'd managed to wheedle his way into the men's section of the camp where conditions were appalling: filthy and vermin-infested, the men were given inedible food and most were still dressed in light clothing, often without boots. Unsurprisingly, half of them were sick. Even so they were due to be marched across the icy plain to some hard manual labour, probably building a new railway. He'd emptied his packets of the few medical supplies he'd been able to keep before making a protest to the commandant who couldn't understand a word of English and waved him off in a hurry.

'He was medieval,' the MO had pronounced repeatedly. 'Medieval, as if modern medicine and modern codes of behaviour didn't exist.'

Arthur had decided it was not the moment to discuss the differences between the educated members of the Ottoman Empire and the louts who ran their lives in the camp. The doctor's hands shook uncontrollably and he had a tic in his right eye.

'I'm on for a game,' Arthur told him now. 'Once I've got this fire going.'

After a game of chess, particularly if the doctor won as he usually did, he opened up more. He had been taken at Lone Pine in the Anzac sector where he'd been tending Australian wounded near the front line. 'Some of the doctors waited back at the base but I liked to be up there with the lads. In some cases half an hour can make all the difference between life and death. Have you seen what happens if a main artery in the leg starts haemorrhaging?'

When the doctor told medical horror stories, Arthur felt that he'd had it easier as a soldier. He was ordered to fight and enjoyed the exultation of battle. Of course he had suffered keenly for those men who were wounded or died but he didn't have to see their injuries close up, hour after hour, day after day.

Born in Kent, trained in London, Lacey had emigrated to New Zealand with his wife and young baby. When war was declared, he'd joined up immediately. 'I wanted to save lives,' he told Arthur, 'and what better place than a battlefield. Besides, I'm so proud of my new home as one of the furthest points of the great empire.'

It was obvious, too, that he had been an immensely brave, effective doctor. It was only his capture and his sight of the desperate conditions endured by the Tommies that had so un-manned him. 'I feel humiliated,' he had confessed late one night. 'It is as if my honour has been taken from me. All those poor sick creatures so close and I can do nothing to alleviate their suffering.'

Arthur had tried to help him by pointing out that no other doctor had even managed to get near them. But Lacey merely frowned and brooded. He had not yet had any letters from home and seemed to think he never would. Once he'd said, 'You're lucky with your fiancée' and Arthur had surprised himself by replying, 'I never feel my engagement with Sylvia is quite real. Not how the world works. Not my world anyway. I learnt how to be alone when I was ten and my parents died. Now I'm back there again.'

The fire, built in a makeshift fireplace, brought everyone out of their rooms. They were a ramshackle lot, very thin, dressed in any extra clothing they could get hold of, including a flowered woman's dress. Standley had managed to buy a fur hat he wore night and day. Those who had been there since Arthur had arrived no longer included Captain Lipcock, who had died of a heart attack in his sleep. Dr Lacey chalked that up against himself too.

The chess game drew onlookers for want of anything better to do. One of them, Lieutenant Moon, had the record for the highest number of wounds when he was captured. The nearest thing to a cabaret was Moon's calling out his wounds with accompanying actions.

'Go on, Moon, old man! Give us your wounds!' shouted someone and off he went, acting out his twenty-one wounds plus accompanying gestures and sound effects. 'Ping!' 'Wizz!' 'Oooh' 'Bullets to the body.' 'Yok! Aargh!' – bayonet in the hand – 'Yavol'

'Oooh!' – bayonet to the shoulder – 'Grrh!' 'Moan moan . . .' The climax came with the spade to the head: 'Wham! Bam! Am I dead!?' After which he lay unmoving. He was a perky young fellow from the Isle of Wight – and even Lacey and Arthur stopped to watch the performance.

'Which was the worst, Moon, old fellow?' asked Trebble as he gave him a hand up.

'In the stomach, Trebbers. Made a nasty sucking sound when the bugger pulled the bayonet out. In truth, the spade to the head came as a relief.'

As the men began joking about the relative nature of wounds – no one had avoided some injury or other – Arthur thought that sometimes they behaved as if their captivity was a bad farce. Maybe it was the English way.

Lately, groups of Russian prisoners had appeared in other houses and, judging by their fierce countenance, he couldn't see them playing silly games. A new commandant of the camp had been announced, Maslum Bey, and already rumours were circulating about his violent and sadistic behaviour. Perhaps Trebble would have something to fight against.

'Check,' said Lacey in an expressionless voice.

Arthur looked down at the board. He hadn't been attending and his king was menaced on three sides. 'Damn!'

'Where's your fighting spirit?' asked the doctor.

Arthur smiled wryly. Where indeed?

Twenty-Five

In December, 1915, the endless rumours finally became reality. Gallipoli was to be evacuated, probably at the end of the month. But then that turned out not to be quite true: Suvla and Anzac were to be evacuated. Some politician or other had decided they should hang on to Helles. Nobody was supposed to know anything because if the Turks found out there'd be a massacre when it came down to the last few thousand remaining. But everybody knew something, or thought they did.

Fred had even heard that General Hamilton had informed the War Office that an evacuation would cost 50 per cent of the Allied forces. Fred wasn't too worried, figuring that since the general had been wrong about everything else on Gallipoli, he was sure to be wrong about this. On the other hand, he didn't see how you could get a hundred thousand or more men off a battlefield without the enemy knowing.

'It's just not feasible,' he told his new friend, Fluffy. Fluffy, a completely bald Liverpudlian, had taken the place of Joe Dingle whose frostbitten feet had earned him the ride to Imbros.

'What's feasible? Free and easy?' Fluffy was more interested in Fred's point of view than Joe but often found his choice of words testing. Fred continued imperturbably.

'You get half the forces off with almost no trouble, although their spotter planes might notice the increase in lighters coming and going, but what next? You can't suddenly start firing half as much, else they'd surely get the drift.'

'If we're not leaving . . .' Fluffy paused to light a new cigarette from his old. He smoked so much that Fred said he was like a round-topped chimney. 'Then I don't know why you're bothered.' But he was egging on Fred. He liked the way his friend shook a new idea like a terrier with a rat.

'You know what, we'll have to change our habits. Go quiet for a couple of hours, that sort of thing. Get them used to it so we can sneak away.'

'So you think we'll be off?'

'Sooner or later.' Fred looked thoughtful. They sat with reasonable comfort in the second line of trenches where only the very random shot would reach them. 'Of course, Johnny Turk and his German bosses would never imagine the British running away.'

'It's not running away,' objected Fluffy. 'It's called a tactical something.'

'Withdrawal,' supplied Fred. 'They won't expect us to beat a retreat. Whatever you call it, the proud British Empire isn't expected to give up. A bad show. We don't do bad show.'

'They say half the French are gone already. I miss their big guns out there on our right.'

'They left their guns behind,' pointed out Fred. He was thinking that when the generals got round to Helles he wouldn't mind being with the last man off.

'Bloody frightening being the last man off,' commented Fluffy, as if reading his thoughts.

'I'd volunteer for it, if I got the chance.'

Fluffy considered this while absent-mindedly lighting another cigarette so that he had two in his mouth. He liked to explain that he had to make up for their stints in the front line when it was forbidden to smoke at night. Fred had never been much of a smoker and often gave him his ration just to see how many he'd get through in a day.

'Want to get your last minutes with your stiffs, do you?' said Fluffy, mockingly. He had once caught Fred on a nocturnal visit to the little groups of roughly marked graves. 'You'll be writing bloody mournful hymns next,' he'd told him. In answer Fred had quoted, ' "Blessed is the one / who does not walk in step with the wicked / or stand in the way that sinners take / or sit in the company of mockers, / but whose delight is in the law of the Lord, / and who meditates on his law day and night. / That person is like a tree planted by streams of water . . ." '

He'd only stopped when Fluffy's dirty hand closed round his mouth.

'Going last would be exciting,' said Fred, knowing it sounded like little boy talk.

'Exciting like ten bayonets in your guts?'

'Exciting like giving the Turks a bloody nose.'

'A bloody nose when you're running away?'

'Cheating them of their prey. That's all we are. Prey. With them sitting up there.'

'They can't move no more than we.'

'Why should they? It's their land, isn't it.'

Fluffy decided to change the subject, 'How about a lice offensive?'

'Take off our clothes in this cold?' Fred turned away.

'Funny the way them bloody insects survive the cold. Even when we were frozen stiff we were crawling with them.'

'I'm writing to Lil.'

Fluffy puffed a cigarette and watched his friend take out paper and pencil.

'Going to write in the dark, are you?'

'I don't need to see what I'm writing.' Fred bent his head.

He was an odd sort of bloke altogether, Fluffy thought, brave as a lion but wayward. More what you'd expect from a city boy than a country lad. With nothing else to think about, Fluffy wondered how he'd turn out – if he survived, that is. There were plenty of ways to die yet. A shell had killed outright four men only that morning. But he'd give odds on Fred surviving. Been out here from the beginning, that was something. Take his approach to lice: 'Live and let live,' is what he said, or, 'They'll be off on their own good time,' or, 'God's creatures need a home.' He was joking, probably, but he was that dry, you never knew.

Fluffy put out his cigarette and settled himself down to sleep. He'd bet Fred wasn't joking about volunteering to be last man off. What was it he'd quoted the other day? *A coward dies one thousand times, a brave man dies only once.* Or something like. The things he had in his head!

Fred wrote on blindly.

It won't be long now, sis. In my humble view, that is. You won't know your little brother. I've become a bookworm. Like a worm too, thin and brown and wriggly. You know I've taken to learning enough to surprise even myself. I sometimes think of being a schoolteacher. Help out boys like me . . . nothing to write about here . . . Tell the kids I've got a whole bagful of bullets for them – Turkish as well as ours . . .

Fred put down his pen and stared up at the cold, starlit sky. It wouldn't look so different in Dorset.

Sylvia frowned over the latest letter from Arthur. She wished it made her happy but it didn't. Happiness was what Gussie felt with her great bulging tummy and her pink cheeks and her dashing husband at the front who had now become the love of her life.

Her mother wasn't happy, of course, but she had a perfectly good reason with her truly beloved husband missing and, as she must soon admit, dead. Sylvia had just discovered that her mother was still writing regularly to her father, which she found piteous to the extreme. Sylvia, sitting at a small desk in her bedroom, allowed herself to think nostalgically of her kind, sensible father; he would have helped her to set her thoughts straight. Even her mother had satisfaction, if not happiness, from helping other officers' wives whose husbands were missing, and with all that was involved in overseeing the house and estate.

Sometimes Sylvia felt that Arthur, the brilliant, decisive Arthur that she had loved, was gone for ever. In his place there was a sober stranger, set far away in a kind of no man's land. His letters tried to drag her there too with his instructions of how to send parcels: *Use a 4lb biscuit tin, pack in sacking, then sew round with canvas. We like cheese, bacon, butter, marmalade, roast beef, all in tins supplied by Crosse & Blackwell for Travellers Abroad.*

The 'Travellers Abroad' should have touched her heart but somehow it didn't. She supposed she still loved him but if she did, why did she feel so much reluctance? Had she so little strength of mind that she could not bear their separation? It was her mind that seemed to be the problem. Her efforts to start up studies again with Gussie's father-in-law, Mr Gisburne, had foundered on her inability to concentrate. 'Your mind is elsewhere,' the rector had commented sympathetically. But *where* was it?

Her only relief was in writing to Hilda whose letters to her aroused all the eager expectation she couldn't feel for Arthur's.

My dear child,
Your spirit is worn out, Hilda wrote. *Do you remember how you forced yourself to work at Camberwell? I used to tell you how you were fighting against the grain. And then you rushed off to Egypt in a passion of love and duty. I've always been a sensible soul but you were not brought up like that, or perhaps it is your nature. From what you tell me, your sister is a practical sort of woman.*

Sylvia paused at this – Gussie a practical woman? She had always seemed a silly girl. It was true she had got what she wanted, sliding through compromises without trouble. *I can't imagine exactly how it was for you in Cairo,* she read on, *with both your dear father, God bless him, and your fiancé with you but both waiting to go into battle. I dread to think of the effect that must have had on your nerves.*

Once again Sylvia put aside the letter. If only it was as easy to put aside her memories! Those hours with Prideaux still had the power to make her shiver with guilt. She even toyed with the idea that it was this disloyal love-making, so against everything she valued about herself, that had caused Arthur's capture. Perhaps Prideaux had told him, and he had allowed himself to be captured. Could that be the reason she could hardly bear to read his letters? Her only success was managing to separate the Captain Prideaux she had known in Cairo with the blind and sick man she had met with Hilda in Malta. They were as different as the brilliant Arthur she had known from the pedantic captive.

There was still another page of Hilda's letter:

Yet, despite everything, you nursed in Egypt too, still there, on your own, when news, first of your father and then of Lieutenant Lamb, came. Oh my dear, of course you are suffering. Your fatigue of mind and spirit is overwhelming. Allow yourself to rest – and wait.

We are quite unlike but in my own way I have been in your position – I was when I came to Camberwell. It was, you might say, my last shot at life. I was approaching thirty and had never left my family with all the narrowness and prejudices of a provincial town. I was so jealous of you but I loved you too. Despite the miseries of our work, what silly fun we had! And from

London I came to Malta and now – and now – you know you saw
it yourself – I have found love. Not conventional love. Captain
Prideaux will never think more of me than a kind heart and a
capable pair of hands. But I love him and I tend to him and that
is enough for me. I will never leave his side until he dies.

Oh my dear friend, how wonderful it is to love! How blessed!

At this point, Sylvia could take no more. Putting her face in her
hands, she burst into tears. It seemed to her that ordinary plain
Hilda understood more about love than she ever had or could. In
her misery, she thought that her mother also understood and even
Gussie – probably everyone in the world except her! Sobbing,
with wet trickles running down her neck, she became certain that
she had never truly loved Arthur. No wonder she had made love
with that horrible Prideaux (the first Prideaux, not the second); no
wonder she could hardly manage to read poor imprisoned Arthur's
letters!

There was a knock at the door. Gussie's serious and very pink
face appeared. 'I heard you crying – I knew you'd had a letter from
Arthur.' She took a hesitant step forward.

It was a measure of Sylvia's unhappiness that, instead of telling
Gussie that the letter was from Hilda, she threw herself on her
sister's expansive bosom. 'Oh, Gussie! Everything's so dreadfully
horrid!'

'There, there.' Gussie patted her back tenderly and, for a
moment, and despite everything, Sylvia imagined her as a good
mother.

'Oh, poor Sylvia. Come and sit with me.' Gussie led her to the
bed where they sat down, arms still round each other. 'It's so hard
for you. I feel for you, I truly do.'

Gradually, Sylvia became calmer. She separated herself from
Gussie, went to a drawer, removed a handkerchief and wiped her
face.

'Have *you* heard any news of Reggie?'

'Yes. Oh, yes. He's quite well. Not in the fighting at the moment.
At least, he wasn't when he wrote.' She suddenly frowned and put
her hand on her stomach before recovering herself. 'Would you
like to feel baby? He's bounding about. I think he's going to be
just like Reggie, probably growing a moustache at this moment.'

Sylvia didn't want to touch Gussie's round taut tummy but her sister's proud face couldn't be disappointed. 'Golly! It's heaving about like a . . . I don't know what.'

'A baby,' supplied Gussie with a clear, happy laugh.

Beatrice continued to find out everything she could about the Allies' presence on the peninsula. She imagined how it must be in winter, the freezing nights and even snow, she'd read, although there were very few reports in *The Times* now. Her news came through the army grapevine which she'd never been much interested in before but now valued highly. She thought it had been summer with temperatures up to forty degrees when Bingo had arrived there and soon it would be Christmas.

Although in the day she continued to believe in the Colonel's existence and still wrote him letters, at night she only dreamed of him dead. Sometimes he was naked, his beautiful strong body splayed open like a Christ figure. Sometimes, he was in bloodstained rags, huddled and broken. Her worst nightmare was of a great black rat with long yellow teeth who tore at his flesh, even though his eyes were open. She always woke, screaming, but no one heard her in the big house and she would lie awake, alone, till morning.

She did not confide in her daughters. Gussie was preoccupied with motherhood and Sylvia seemed totally distant, presumably her thoughts far away in a Turkish prison camp. Under Beatrice's command, she had sent all the Colonel's regimental details to poor Arthur, asking him to spread the word. But Sylvia's big eyes had looked at her mother with a questioning kind of sympathy. Beatrice hadn't cared. She would look everywhere in the world for Bingo!

The person she saw most of was Lily Chaffey. The two women started the day together meeting on the dark winter mornings in the Colonel's study, Beatrice behind the desk, Lily in front of her on an upright chair. No detail of planning escaped them. After an hour, Mr Block the estate manager came to report. At first this had been a formality but after a while Beatrice began to ask difficult questions if he failed to bring the details. The head gardener and many of the men had gone to war.

'At least we still have a priest and a doctor,' remarked Beatrice one morning when cold rain dribbled at the windows.

'But not a schoolmaster after next week,' replied Lily.

'Surely old Badger couldn't lift a rifle. He's looked like Methuselah for the last thirty years.'

'Not Badger. It's young Will Gould who does all the work.'

Beatrice sighed. 'When will it stop!'

'We've got to build up Kitchener's new army,' said Lily with what might have been irony. Fred's latest letter was slipped between the sheets of her notepad. 'At least they'll be off Gallipoli by all accounts.'

Beatrice went pale and a look of irritation and distress passed over her face before being rigidly suppressed. 'I believe so.'

'I'm sorry, milady. That was thoughtless of me. It's just that my brother . . .' She stopped, realising she was only making matters worse.

Beatrice stood up and went to the window. 'I dislike bad weather extremely.' She was picturing a wounded man, not necessarily Bingo, crawling painfully up a hillside of slippery mud while rain sluiced over him.

Lily stood too. 'Will that be all?'

Beatrice turned back and stared at her housekeeper. 'Maybe your brother will be back with us soon.'

Lily looked startled. 'I don't know. He says once they're off, they'll get sent to another front. I think he suggested where but the censor blanked out the rest.'

'When he does come back, there'll always be work for him here. We've grown to appreciate our labourers.'

'Thank you, milady.' Lily gave her usual little dip of the head and went out of the room. As she crossed the dark hall towards the big drawing room where she could hear the recovering officers playing a noisy game of racing demon, she thought that she couldn't quite imagine the new Fred as a labourer.

The explosion was so vast, echoing and reverberating in the air, that for a full second every soldier on Helles stopped whatever they were doing and became rigid. They were used to levels of noise far beyond the normal: shelling from the ships at sea, cannons, artillery, machine gun, small arms; sometimes all together, like an orchestra gone mad. But this was different: a single enormous explosion. Those who were near enough saw the earth rise up like a volcano, and earth and stones and some human forms or parts of human forms fly into the air before tumbling back down in an uproarious clatter.

Some officers had been told it was coming but even they were surprised. 'Those sappers!' they exclaimed to each other. 'They certainly know their business.' The most senior officers understood that this violent event, prelude to the fiercest attack they'd mounted for months, was all about what was happening on Suvla and Anzac. It was a mere diversion as the twenty thousand men remaining crept away from their trenches and softly, softly made their way down to the beaches.

All Fred knew was that he was going up the gully ravine somewhere he'd hoped never to see again in his life. Other men were advancing up the Krithia Nullah which was, if anything, even a tougher climb. It was when they were halfway up that the explosions stopped them dead – well, only a few of them actually dead dead.

'That's Border Barricade,' muttered Fred, identifying the place where the sappers had placed their men as somewhere between the two front lines. Unsurprisingly, since shell fragments and rifle fire were pelting down like hail, nobody heard.

Fred had become ever keener to understand the plans of campaign, recognising names of the jagged ridges they climbed along, trying to identify their objective. Was it Achi Baba again – that mocking and seemingly unobtainable hill that had shimmered with scarlet poppies when he first arrived and now stood grim and bleak?

In the event Fred found his whole regiment was directed to hold the still smoking crater which had been linked up to an already existing crater in the Gully Ravine sector.

Night was falling as the men climbed down into a hole which must have been fifty feet deep. Even then there was no rest.

'I know you think you deserve a night off,' shouted their sergeant, who Fred approved of because he told them more than most, 'but Johnny Turk isn't going to give up this ground without a fight so I want every bloody man of you in the line, either

357

shooting or throwing those bloody little bombs of yours. Count yourself lucky. A few months ago it was bayonets and nothing else!'

It was true that most men had some kind of grenade now which was better than bully beef cans and fuses but there was no throwing them from the depths of the blasted hole. Soon they were back in the trenches which had been partially collapsed by the explosion but provided some cover.

After an hour or two, sappers joined them and Fred was sent out with them as bayonet man. It was a clear, moonlit night and he'd already spent a couple of hours watching one Turkish attack after another. He'd thrown so many grenades that his arm ached. Once, a line of soldiers dressed in blue had appeared and the lieutenant had shouted as if at a tourist sight, 'Look, there! Bulgarians!'

Bloody hell, Fred had thought, and how big is Bulgaria, I wonder. So he was keen enough to try something new. Besides, he admired the sappers, dark, hard-working men from Wales who seemed to have nerves of iron. Being buried alive was not Fred's idea of fun but they seemed to take tunnelling as natural.

'Hey, you. If you're the bloody bayonet man, then get it bloody fixed.'

Fred obeyed. He was looking down when a Turkish sniper, presumably spotting the entrance to the sap, let off three or four shots in quick succession.

Fred went down on his back. The moon spun above his head and he was filled with terrible rage. He wasn't supposed to die like this. He wasn't supposed to die at all. He'd been too long in this fucking stupid place to die.

'You hit?'

The moon righted itself. A sapper bent over him. He seemed more angry than concerned.

Fred put his hand up to his head. (So he could move his arm.) His helmet had been blown off and he felt blood. 'In my head.'

The sapper shouted 'Stretcher-bearer!', cursed a bit and went away.

Fred began to suspect he was only concussed but felt no inclination to move. He remembered sitting beside a dying man who was happy to go. 'They've got me downstairs, mate,' he'd said,

'No more fun for old Billy.' Well, they'd got him upstairs and it was just as well because he hadn't even started on downstairs yet.

The moon wavered, then contracted at its sides as if a giant hand was squeezing. The resulting sausage made Fred feel sick and he shut his eyes. The stunning noise of battle, so ordinary to him, receded.

'Walk, can you?' He opened his eyes to a white armband with a red cross.

'It's my head.' But all the same his legs wouldn't take him. 'Where is that Aussie giant?' he asked, thinking of his friend who'd saved him from the deluge. How comfortable he'd been in his arms!

'No Aussies here, mate. Not many there, either.'

Fred saw the moon had gone and a fresh dawn was coming up over the hills. All was quiet. Presumably the Turks had been thrown back without his help.

Sylvia was met at Filchester Halt, where she had required the conductor to stop the train, by a chauffeur wearing a cap adorned by a coat of arms, with a fur rug over his arm. He led her to a shining black Daimler. The train had been full of soldiers and she was glad none of them had got off to see her entering such luxury.

'Is your maid, behind, miss? And your bags?'

She saw the man was old and his hands shook. 'I have no maid and this is my case.' She indicated the small case at her feet. Inside it was Prideaux's letter which she had promised to deliver to his parents. After her return to England, she had managed to forget about it for several weeks but, as Christmas approached, guilt pricked her into action. Guilt also made her accept the invitation to stay at Filchester Hall for a night. 'It will make everything so much more civilised,' Lady Filchester had written graciously.

Sylvia did not believe it but, in her weary sense of living in a no man's land, nothing mattered very much. So she came.

Her spirits were raised by the sight of Filchester Hall. Ironically, with its golden stone and colonnade of pillars beneath a classical pediment, it reminded her of Bighi hospital, Malta, where Hilda and Captain Prideaux passed their days. She wondered, as she had done quite frequently on the journey, what was in Prideaux's letter. Loving wishes? It seemed likely to be less heart-warming, judging by the way he had spoken of his family and his class. Perhaps she would be thrown out on the principle of shooting the messenger, the croaking raven who brings unwelcome news.

A young liveried footman met the car. Having bowed out Sylvia, he addressed the driver in a piping voice. 'Mr Pither, sir, her ladyship will give tea in the library.'

Sylvia remembered Rupert's instructions to hand the letter to his father. 'Is his lordship at home?'

'At home? Or in residence?' asked Pither as he led her up the steps to the house.

'Either,' answered Sylvia. She decided that Pither must be a butler, forced by wartime exigencies to act as a chauffeur which was why he was being so pompous. The only other household she knew still possessing a butler was her grandmother's. But she had not been there for ages

'In residence but not at home,' said Pither.

Tea in the library, although the setting was magnificent, started badly.

'You were so quick,' said her ladyship, making it clear that she had expected her guest to change into more elegant clothing.

'I'm used to travelling,' replied Sylvia.

Lady Filchester was fair and handsome like her son, with good bones and a slim figure. She poured the tea and handed a cup to Sylvia. 'That is very enterprising of you. My son spent much of his time travelling.' Again Sylvia sensed disapproval.

'He is very knowledgeable about the East.'

'About the East? The East, you say. Unfortunately, he is an eldest son.'

'I understand you have several sons?'

'I had five sons. One is dead, killed at Ypres on 22nd April, one is in France, two are still at Eton. Perhaps they, too, will go to war. You know most about the other.'

This did not sound like an invitation to share her knowledge. 'He is being well looked after,' she said.

'I have been to Malta several times. Sir Ian Hamilton was governor on the last occasion. Such a gay and gallant man, although best avoided on the dance floor – too much hopping to feel one's toes safe. He and dear Jean, Lady Hamilton, entertained us at San

Antonio, their country house. Such a garden, like Kubla Khan, as Sir Ian commented. Bougainvillea, flowering pomegranates and blossoming trees of every colour. Dear Winston was there too, already First Sea Lord, but I'm afraid he wasn't very pleased with the navy. There was a special gunnery practice laid on and he discovered afterwards there had not been one hit. The admiral explained to him, "Well, First Lord, the shells seem either to have fallen short of the target or else gone just a *little* beyond it." You can imagine Winston's face!' Lady Filchester went off into a flurry of hard tinkling laughter.

Sylvia could not laugh or even smile. She decided that an evening with this woman was out of the question and that she must find an excuse to leave.

'And now,' said Lady Filchester, 'Sir Ian is in disgrace, Winston is sacked and my beloved son is dead.' Her elegant features suddenly took on the face of a drooping clown before just as quickly returning to upright. 'You are not married, I understand?'

'No,' agreed Sylvia, blushing. 'My fiancé is a prisoner of war in Turkey.'

'Is that so. Ah!' Her ladyship looked towards the door. 'My husband. Luckily, he prefers cold tea.'

Lord Filchester was a thin, stooping man, but he grasped Sylvia's hand firmly. He was dressed in plus fours and brought a feeling of cold winter into the room. 'I've been shooting, you know. Dark by four. Long dark evenings, you know.'

Sylvia thought he seemed kind but could think of nothing to say. He drank his tea quickly, standing with his back to the fire. 'Like tea cold, you know. Like dunking biscuits, too. Bad habits from my nanny. Good woman, though.'

He was trying to put her at ease, Sylvia guessed, perhaps making up for his wife's brittleness.

'You've seen Prideaux then? Blind, is he, poor fellow? Always got himself into trouble.'

'He's very brave.'

'Brave, you say?'

Sylvia saw Lady Filchester pursed her lips. 'About being blind.'

'Tremendous little chap he was. Like a lion.' Lord Filchester poured himself another cup of tea and downed it in one gulp.

'He asked me to give you a letter.' Sylvia took the envelope out of her bag.

'He wrote me a letter?' The earl looked stunned.

'He dictated it to a nurse. He's very well looked after,' repeated Sylvia who was fighting a distracted urge to run from the room.

'Good. Good. So that's why you're here. Personal delivery. Very kind. Trains all right?'

'Yes, thank you.' She stood and, under Lady Filchester's watchful eyes, handed over the letter.

'Good man.' The earl took it gingerly. 'Can't say I've had a letter from him since he was a boy. Only wrote when he wanted money, you know. Don't suppose he needs much of that where he is.' He turned the letter round in his hand. 'Better to be alive than dead, that's what I say.'

Lady Filchester moved on her chair so that she was staring out to the dark windows, still uncurtained. 'They say he will not live long.' Her voice was toneless.

'Mustn't say that, dear. Bad luck.'

'Bad luck? Is that what it is?' Lady Filchester pursed her lips and after that there was a long silence.

Fred watched the doctor make his way down the rows of men squeezed into the tent. He'd been there two days and knew there was not much wrong with him. He was trying to make up his mind whether he'd rather be back on duty or lying surrounded by disgusting sights and sounds. How men groaned and moaned and sighed and occasionally screamed! And the stink! At least the wounded in the trenches, now it was winter, didn't smell.

The MO, a cadaverous man with a blood-spattered uniform (there had been plenty to keep him busy after the last offensive) bent over Fred. 'You'll have a fine scar to show your sweetheart,' he commented approvingly. 'I hope she admires my needlework.'

'Thank you, sir,' said Fred wearily. 'Am I in the lines again?'

The doctor peered at him with startling pale eyes. 'I've seen you around, haven't I?'

'Since April, sir.'

'Amazing! We must be the only two who share that distinction.'

'Sir.' Fred was surprised by his own lassitude. Maybe the bullet had done more than give him a pretty scar. Or maybe it was that sausage moon.

'Your chaplain's looking for a new lad to set up his table, that sort of thing. Last one got blown sky high. Quite an intrepid fellow, your chaplain. Want me to fix it with your sergeant? Us old-timers must stick together.'

'Thank you, sir.' A stirring of his old curiosity made him ask, 'What kind of padre, sir?'

'Kind! Kind? You don't ask what kind of doctor, do you? The sort that cures your soul just as I cure your body.'

Fred fell back. 'Yes, sir.'

The MO, on his way to his next patient whose groans had increased in volume as the MO's conversation had increased in length, glanced over his shoulder. 'It won't be for long anyway, with Suvla and Anzac already on their way home.'

At once Fred was fully awake. 'Are we off then? Soon? How many made it?'

But the MO, with a grave face, was unravelling his next patient from a multitude of malodorous bandages. Fred pinched his nose shut. He wondered whether the doctor, with all the good intentions in the world, would remember about the chaplain. It was his brief confrontation with death, he supposed, that had caused his unusual lack of energy. Previously, he had been instinctively brave but now his body or mind had taught him death was possible so things were more complicated. I am eighteen and I am old, he thought.

'Hey, Nurse!' he shouted.

'And a hey nonny no to you,' answered a passing nurse who was carrying a bowl of used dressings so disgusting that Fred almost wished he hadn't stopped him.

'Heard anything about the evacuation plans? The MO says Anzac and Suvla are off?'

The nurse, who had a pale face and a round red nose, gave a loud sniff which Fred thought, under the circumstances, a mistake. 'I know two things for sure: they're still killing people here and I won't get any presents for Christmas. But they say we didn't lose one man, every one of them lucky sods off and laughing.'

It was true, then. So what would happen now?

What happened was that everything went on as usual, except

that the Turks' German commanders, deprived of part of their prey, brought up some new very big German guns to wipe out the rest of them.

Fred, assigned to the chaplain (known generally as Padre Pious for his earnest devotions), was not as safe as he'd hoped. Padre Pious had an unerring instinct for choosing the most dangerous locations for his services. If he set up at dawn near the beach, shells came in from the Asiatic side, and if he set up at dusk on a nice plateau, they came roaring in from Khilid Bahr.

In Fred's view the only reasonable explanation for this extraordinary knack was that he was determined to meet his just reward in heaven sooner rather than later – an ambition Fred didn't share. However, the odd thing was that, despite his fears when lying in the hospital tent, he found himself perfectly well able to operate under fire, even when the majority of the worshippers were either lying flat or fleeing for cover.

Eventually, he suggested to Padre Pious that he, Fred, help him to find locations more suited to his congregations. 'I've been here for months, Padre, Know every bit of land.'

'My aim, Chaffey,' said the Padre, a tough little man who'd been a boxer before receiving the call, 'is to bring God to the men wherever they might be, however dangerous. I've seen too many chaplains who never go up the line at all.'

'Yes, sir. But there's no use bringing God to men who are running in the other direction.'

Padre Pious was a humble sort of holy man, so after that he allowed Fred to choose their locations and the services became more tranquil and better attended.

Fred wrote about them to Lily.

I've never thought much about God as you know but you'd need a heart of stone not to be moved by our services. Dusk is the preferred time, the table set up in a shattered olive grove with candles lit if it's not too windy and Padre Pious all in white and the men muffled up against the cold and sometimes a red wintry glow over the sea and sometimes a mule train going by or a messenger on a horse and often enough there're graves nearby, on one side or the other or all round. They've enough of them, with their dark wooden crosses to take a hundred years of praying. Ah, Lil, the things I'll have to tell you. I wasn't so good a while back but I'm fine again now.

Lily brought the letter to Beatrice in the study.

'I just wondered, milady, if, when you go up to London, you hear any news about Gallipoli? It's not like Fred to admit to any weakness.'

Beatrice looked at Lily. It was so unusual for her perfect house-keeper to express any personal wishes. 'I believe the campaign is drawing to a close,' she said carefully. 'When is the letter dated?'

'Before Christmas, I believe.'

'Oh, poor things! Christmas in a heathen place!' Beatrice pictured the Colonel lying on hard ground, in the bleak midwinter, snow on snow . . .

'Fred is helping a priest, he writes.'

'Well, the letter hasn't taken long to arrive. That must mean ships are moving easily. I *hate* those submarines,' she added inconsequentially. Christmas had already gone and now New Year would come. How terrible this season was without Bingo! Beatrice passed her hand over her eyes. 'I'll let you know if I hear anything.'

'Thank you, m'lady.'

Beatrice made an effort to be kinder. 'From everything you have told me, Lily, your brother sounds like a survivor.' She thought fiercely: Survival, survival, survival. What else matters?

Twenty-Six

Fred was back with his regiment. Padre Pious, much to his righteous indignation, had been shipped out in the first wave of equipment and people that were considered inessential.

'Well, Chaffey,' he'd said as they both packed up their kit, 'we'll meet again in this world or the next.'

Fred had thought this a bit weak, although he supposed it was a compliment, so he quoted, ' "To them who seek by patient continuance in well doing, glory and honour and immortality, eternal life." St Paul's letters to the Romans, Chapter two, verse seven.'

Fluffy welcomed him back. Although nobody could totally believe they were leaving Gallipoli, everybody acted on the assumption. It had become a kind of game. 'I can't decide whether to show Johnny Turk how civilised the British Tommy is – in which case I'll set up a nice welcoming meal in a clean dugout or give him a wallop on the nose with a booby trap at the entrance and bully beef poisoned with petrol on the table.'

'You could leave him your poisonous cigarettes,' suggested Fred.

'Give away my Christmas cigarette parcel?'

'*Your* parcel!' Fred gave Fluffy a prod with his rifle butt. 'When I found it the address said Lieutenant Horsington.'

'And what use did he have for it, buried and prayed over by your Padre Pious? You shouldn't give things if you don't mean it.'

Sometimes Fluffy got on Fred's nerves but he was his mate so there was nothing to be done about it. He put it down to the strange atmosphere. Everyone was on edge, nervous, irritable, unsure whether to look forward to a better future or dread the unknown.

Men who'd been on the peninsula for months, who'd survived wounds, sickness, drowning and ice, had established a way of living which made each day bearable. They knew the good officers and the bad officers; they had learned how far they could stretch the rules without getting into trouble. Some of them, particularly the French, as was discovered when they left, had an understanding with the front-line Turks about when they would shoot and when they'd hold fire.

They were like prisoners who longed for their captivity to end but feared they might find themselves out of the frying pan into the void. As usual they were told very little and men started bringing their questions to Fred who was gaining a reputation of knowing more than the sergeant.

Where next? was what it usually boiled down to.

One boy, with lice jumping all over him, buttonholed Fred as they buried a man shot in one of those unlucky random snipings that still went on.

'Where next?' repeated Fred, leaning on his shovel – it was a clear, mild day and there was no need to be too energetic. 'It depends whether you fancy a hundred degree heat in the desert, or mud and slime in the trenches.'

'Which do you fancy, Chaff?'

Fred moved back. 'Keep your distance, mate. I don't want one of those gymnasts thinking I'm the parallel bars. Let's see, the trenches in France are nearer home, of course, and I hear all kinds of delights go on behind the lines.'

'Oh, I'm not that sort, Chaff. My mam brought me up to respect the ladies.'

'What did you think I was talking about? It's proper English ladies behind a tea urn and a stack of sandwiches.'

'It's just that some of the lads . . .'

'You worry too much, Sid.' The boy's name was Sid Blossom and he'd only been on Gallipoli a month. 'With those vermin all over you, no loose woman's going to give you a second thought. It's your mother's Praetorian Guard.' Fred had just been given a book about early Rome.

'Eh?'

'All things considered, I think you'd be better off in the desert. There's only one problem.'

'What's that?' Sid had large, short-sighted eyes that strained to see his mentor.

'You won't get a choice.'

Sid seemed astonished. 'But all the lads are talking about where they're going next!'

'No harm in that.'

'But what . . .' Sid gave up and, muttering 'desert' several times, picked up his shovel. They'd been digging for several minutes when he paused again. 'Where's this desert?'

'Wherever the army wants it to be,' answered Fred promptly.

They both stopped to watch a heavily laden mule train go up past them. 'You know something, those boxes are completely empty,' said Fred.

'Empty!' exclaimed Sid with his infinite capacity for astonishment.

'It's all part of the game,' explained Fred, 'to make Johnny Turk believe it's business as usual. Down on the piers, ships are coming in and out, even bringing men but they all go out again at night. The beach looks normal but in truth everything's on the way out. Food, horses, mules, ammunition, explosives. It's all got to go out under the enemy's nose.'

'You could have fooled me!'

'Let's hope Johnny Turk feels the same. Otherwise you won't need to worry where you're going next.'

Soon they'd finished digging and lowered down the poor chap. Fred stood staring at the grave. 'Pity he can't have a prayer or two with the padre gone.'

'Maybe you could say one?'

Fred had reached, '. . . which are departed hence from us with the sign of faith' when their corporal came to find them.

'Thought you'd gone in the bloody grave with him, poor bugger,' he grumbled. 'You've missed the news and all.'

'What's that?' asked Fred, instantly abandoning his priestly duties.

'We're the chosen ones. First to come, last to go.'

There were thirty-five thousand men still on Helles and they would be part of the second seventeen thousand to go in the final evacuation planned for 8th January – at least that was the date Fred got out of an RAMC man who'd overheard a staff officer talking to an MO. They were expecting – or preparing for – thousands

368

of casualties. 'How could the Turks be fooled three times?' as everyone tried not to say.

On the following afternoon, Fred and several dozen experienced men were introduced to the joys of the 'self-firing rifle'. Their sergeant was disdainful.

'Some bloody fool Tommy invented this so you've only your bleeding selves to blame!'

The men sat round him on the cold ground; they were well behind the lines and, although a wind blew from the north, there was no rain or snow, so it counted as a holiday. Most men smoked till the corporal got them on their feet and banned tobacco.

'We stand the rifles up on bleeding sandbags, see, with two tins filled with sand tied to the trigger. The sand in the top tin leaks out into the bottom bleeding one. When that's full, it pulls the trigger. Kills old Abdul without a blessed Tommy in sight. You, Chaffey, give us a demo.'

While the demonstration was carried out with doubtful results as the wind kept blowing away the sand, the sergeant turned his back, occasionally prodding the hard ground with his stick. Fred didn't share his impatience – anything new interested him. It would work well enough in the protection of the trenches, as apparently it had at Anzac, although they'd used water instead of sand.

'Now sand can do our job, we'll be off to Blighty!' sniggered one wit.

'I'll have you home in irons!' bellowed the sergeant, finally losing his patience. Silly tricks and creeping away in the night wasn't the proud British Army he knew. He continued bellowing, 'You won't find it so humorous when you're the only man left along a trench running for five hundred yards and you've got fifty thousand Turks baying for your blood one hundred yards in front of you!'

Everybody could see this was a bad prospect but somehow unimaginable. The trenches were their homes; they knew every bit of their section, every wriggle and hump, every weak and every strong spot in the sandbag wall. Some were dug so deep now that you needed to climb up to the firing step. It was impossible to imagine them empty.

Fred discovered that it was the sappers who'd really be the last men off; they'd be the ones to block and booby-trap the abandoned trenches and the routes down to the sea. Spotting a party of them at work on a path the other side of a gully, he scrambled across to them.

'Are you blocking that path?'

'Don't you silly buggers know we always unroll barbed wire on a Thursday!'

The conversation might have ended there except that Fred recognised they were the same group that he'd been assigned to as bayonet man. He pointed to his forehead where the scar was still a livid red. 'See what I got last time I was with you.'

The sapper let a coil of wire ping back. 'You, was it now. Thought you were up with the angels. Dai!' He called to a friend and said something in Welsh. The other man came over.

'You're a lucky fellow. We could do with a bit of luck the jobs we're doing. Care to take up your old role and join the Royal Engineers?'

'Gets boring writing love letters for Johnny Turk,' admitted Fred.

The second sapper laughed. He had very white teeth amid black stubble, an orange rag tied under his helmet.

'I've promised one officer to booby-trap his dugout, every item in it: desk, chair, typewriter, logbook, gramophone, pencil case. Boom! Boom!'

'Cushy life,' commented Fred jealously. 'Got a mahogany bookcase too?'

The sapper only laughed again. Fred had heard the Welsh tended to the mournful and broke into song every second sentence. But this man seemed cheerful as a (non-singing) cricket.

'You want me to put in a request for you? We'll be laying out surprises behind the men going down. There won't be anyone left to save us. We could do with a lucky bayonet man, though. We keep losing them.'

'I'd like the job,' said Fred, adding quickly as the conversation seemed to be getting doleful with all those dead bayonet men, 'How do we find the right paths, now you're closing so many?' He indicated the first sapper and all the others who had returned to laying tangled lumps of barbed wire or hacking great holes in the ground.

'Trails of white flour on the night, man. For now, just keep your eyes skinned. What's your sergeant called?'

'Sergeant Libby. He's not bad.'

'I'll start with him, then.'

So at the beginning of January, Fred was called out to join the Royal Engineers. Fluffy was unimpressed. 'You'll do anything to be different, that's a fact.'

Fred was collecting his kit together in neat piles and didn't say anything because he thought Fluffy had got it about right.

A lot of Tommies were sorting out their kit the same time he was. In Fred's view they chose the oddest keepsakes. Bullets and badges was fair enough, that was the language of the battlefield. But one man had a Turkish soldier's jacket – 'I killed him, didn't I?' And another a tortoise shell and another a page with Turkish writing on – 'Proves I fought Johnny Turk, doesn't it?' When Fred pointed out it looked like a bit of Allied propaganda material, he was unmoved. 'We wouldn't send it to the bleeding Germans, would we?'

'With the lot who run the war, I'm not too sure,' said Fred to raise a laugh. At least the bit of paper didn't weigh anything. Fluffy had somehow acquired a German officer's overcoat which was strictly illegal and very heavy.

'How do you think you'll climb a ladder up the side of a destroyer with that in your pack?' teased Fred.

'He wants to strut around Weston-super-Mare in it,' jeered someone else.

'What do you mean, heavy? I hear they're giving away all sorts on the beach sooner than let them fall into Johnny Turk's dirty hands: thigh boots, bedding, chairs and even bicycles. How do you take a bicycle up the side of a ship? But that's what they say.'

There were enough stories about handouts on the beach to make those departing last suffer acute anxiety lest there be no loot left for them. Fred had planned a little visit the following day on his way to take up his position with the sappers. Well, not exactly on his way.

With only three more days to the departure day, the atmosphere changed. After darkness fell, the men still on duty could hear the muffled sound of soldiers with sandbags over their boots winding their way down to the beach, four miles from front line to sea.

The initial anxiety gave way to a kind of frantic, just subdued, unacknowledged panic. Even the bravest feared being killed now, right at the end.

Routine, which had sustained them, making the extraordinary and horrific ordinary and bearable, no longer applied. Sometimes terrible new tasks were asked of them. That morning the corporal had chosen two men including Fluffy, all big men, and taken them off. Two hours later the corporal returned and disappeared silently, which was unusual, into his dugout. Some hours later, the men, pale and haggard trickled back.

'What is it?' said their mates.

'Don't ask!'

But they did and Fluffy told them. 'We were taken to the vet; he gave us pistols and told us how to do it: pretend there's a line from each eye to the opposite ear and shoot where the line crosses.' Although it was cold, Fluffy was sweating, droplets running off his bald head and down his face like tears. 'There were twenty horses and three mules, lovely trusting animals with gentle eyes and soft noses. We led them to one of those little gullies and the captain who'd come with us, said, "I'll go first" and he looked worse than if he had to go over the top. I'd have felt sorry for him if it wasn't my turn next. The first four or five weren't too bad but then the rest got the wind up and started rearing and screaming. That's when the corporal left saying he was injured which he bloody well wasn't.' Fluffy put a hand up and wiped his face and head, looking surprised at the wet. 'So we finished the job somehow; two or three shots for some of them.'

Nobody spoke at first but a mug with brandy was passed along.

'I thought they were taking the animals off,' said Fred. 'Like the men. It's not as if there're many horses.'

'Run out of space on the ships.' Fluffy seemed to be recovering. 'At least we didn't have to cut their throats, like they do where it's got to be kept quiet.'

Fred had said nothing more but as night came down, he began to imagine all the dead that would be left behind on Gallipoli. He no longer visited the sad little graves but he didn't want to forget them.

The silent hours, instigated to fool the Turks when there would be no one in the trenches to shoot and only the self-firing rifles to give a bang now and again, encouraged strange imaginings. Men saw non-existent Turks attacking, as they had when they first arrived and were green and jittery. Always restless, Fred volunteered to go out on patrol in no man's land. He was aware it was almost certainly his last night in the trenches and wanted to mark it in some way.

'I'll say my goodbyes to Johnny Turk, sir,' he told the young lieutenant who'd come for volunteers.

'Not on my watch.' The lieutenant seemed to be taking Fred seriously. 'We're just about half strength now and half our guns and artillery on the sea somewhere between here and Lemnos.'

'Haven't you heard about the bully beef tin, sir? Thrown over as a New Year's treat for Johnny Turk and came back a few days ago filled with mud and stones plus a message written in good English, "We are sorry you are leaving, we'll meet you again at Suez".'

The lieutenant came closer and even in the darkness, Fred could see his angry grimace. 'It's no joking matter.'

But it wasn't a joke. There really had been a bully beef tin which came back with the message Fred had quoted. He thought about it as he wriggled his way out of a sap into no man's land. It was a moonless night but stars flashed between streaky clouds. Everything was very quiet, so quiet that a wind, blowing the clouds along and shuffling through the mess that covered much of the ground, sounded loud and aggressive.

In fact, thought Fred, as he followed the lieutenant to within a few yards of the Turkish lines, if the Turks didn't get them, the weather still might. He'd heard the piers would be swept away with any level of wind, let alone a storm or thousands of men with their equipment traipsing across them. V Beach wasn't so bad with dear old SS *River Clyde* sitting there as solid as a rock. It'd be good to go out the same way he came in. But who knew where those sappers would lead him? W Beach was supposed to have some very flimsy piers with an old boat or two lashed up to them, and Gully Beach even worse. Yes, V Beach was the one for him.

Fred stopped moving abruptly. His body was so used to this kind of patrol when a sentry in the wrong place, a bright star, or a twanging wire could be his undoing, that he stopped before he had consciously seen the upraised hand.

Now he could hear why: a conversation was taking place in

the trench to his left. The soft Arabic was utterly un-warlike, relaxed as two men outside a pub. Fred waited for the lieutenant to signal their return. They'd accomplished their mission: no one was attacking on this front and, by the sound of it, or the lack of sound of it, not on any other front either.

But the lieutenant seemed to have different ideas and had started in the direction of the talking. Fred hesitated; the two men behind him, including Sid Blossom who'd taken to following him wherever he went, were quieter than mice. The lieutenant hadn't waved him forward. Perhaps he wanted to get a medal at the last ditch. There were men who liked to get as close as possible to a Turkish trench, throw two or three grenades and run. Fred had never thought it much of a sport, like throwing a brick into a hornet's nest. He'd liked the sound of those two men talking and killing wasn't what their patrol was about. Maybe his bully beef tin message had been taken by the lieutenant as a challenge.

So Fred stayed where he was and so did the men close behind him. The wind was flying over their prone bodies. It seemed darker so the clouds had probably closed up, obliterating the starlight. He couldn't see where the lieutenant was now and the conversation had stopped. Everything was quiet except for the wind.

He'd been in no man's land often before but never felt this eerie sense of nothingness and tension. Some men wouldn't go there at all, which was why it was generally a volunteer patrol. He made up his mind. He signalled a return to the men behind.

Movement, the need to thread the way carefully, immediately dispelled his odd mood. The lieutenant could look after himself.

They were nearly into the sap when two cans rolled together, clanging like a cymbal. Immediately a shot came from their own front line. Blossom gave a strange grunting burble. Fred went to him and pulled him into the sap. Even in the dark he could see that the single random shot had smashed into his mouth.

A few desultory shots came from the Turks. Where was the lieutenant?

He and the other man half dragged Blossom down the sap; he continued to make revolting noises of agony.

When they came out the other end and started for the dressing station, Fred suddenly saw the lieutenant.

'Where were you?' he said, staring at the three men. 'I called you back.'

Fred knew he hadn't. 'Blossom's hit,' he said. 'Sir.' He thought, if they hadn't hung around waiting for the lieutenant, Blossom wouldn't have kicked the cans together and lost half his face. But he knew it was no good thinking like that. Once you start, where do you stop? That Tommy who'd fired. What about him? They all knew there was a patrol out. He hoped it hadn't been Curly; he tended to the trigger-happy.

'We're taking him to the dressing station.' He paused. 'Sir.' The lieutenant seemed all right. Poor old Blossom. No sunny days in the desert for him. He felt glad he was going to join the sappers – tough little men, not clumsy like poor old Sid Blossom.

The next morning the black clouds had increased and would have hung heavily except that the wind had increased too and shunted them around the sky. Somewhere in his mind, Fred had imprinted still the beauty of May on Gallipoli, the bright flowers, the gilding sunrises, the slow rainbow sunsets.

He was determined to go down to the beach and walked as quickly as he could, although his pack slowed him down. Once he'd cleared the dangerous ridges and passes, he looked about him and became aware how empty the whole place was. Low plateaux where there'd been overpopulated trenches or camps of a hundred tents were now deserted, although the round bell tents were still in place.

He loitered, peered in a trench where everything remaining had been smashed, and then into a perfectly orderly tent. It must have belonged to an officer because there was a table and chair. It still smelled of pipe smoke. Fred sat in the chair and imagined himself, pipe in one hand and a sheaf of important papers in the other. Then he pictured what it would be like if a Turkish soldier came in after the evacuation. He had killed a good many of them, knew how poorly dressed they were, some almost in rags. Would they be impressed by the table and chair? Or perhaps Turks didn't sit on chairs.

Oppressed by the emptiness of the land and his gloomy thoughts, Fred was glad when he reached the end of a spur and found himself looking down on V Beach. The seemed to be as much activity as usual, if not more, boats coming and going, men and mules crossing to climb up the steep paths, crates of ammunition being loaded on carts or humped across the beach. He supposed it was mostly for show and wondered what was really going on. On the edge of the sea the great hulk of the *Clyde* sat unmoved.

As he watched, a bugle sounded from a cliff towards the Dardanelles and everyone who could dived for cover. It was the signal for a shell coming over from Asiatic Annie. This was real enough. Following its hysterical shrieking, the shell dropped harmlessly into the sea without exploding.

Fred scrambled down and made his way to the biggest supply depot where a crowd of soldiers and several harassed officers were gathered.

'I don't know what you men are lining up for!' A major came, banging his stick angrily on the ground. 'I've told you, no one gets anything until you're embarking out of here!' The sight of Fred's lone figure seemed to enrage him even further. 'What are you up to, Private? Where's your company?'

'Sir. Reporting for bayonet duty Royal Engineers. Sir!' Fred decided discretion was the better part of valour. A cold drizzle had begun and most of the men began to drift away. Fred had never seen the army in such disorder.

At that moment a full general, accompanied by several men, strolled up. Fred hung about watching as he took the major into the depot. Five minutes later, he re-emerged, the men loaded with boxes. The major had a deflated air; there was no way he could stop a general determined on looting.

Fred walked away as the bugle sounded again. The men carrying the boxes dropped them and ran for the cliffs. The general followed.

Just for the fun of it and because he'd given up worrying about shells, Fred picked up one of the boxes and walked in the other direction. This time the shell exploded, hitting a group of Indian drivers sitting cross-legged by their mules. Fred walked more quickly.

By chance, he came across a team of sappers, although not his friends, dismantling communication equipment. Rolls of cable were lying all around.

'Anything worth having in that box?' called one.

'Don't know.' Fred put the box down and took his knife out of his belt. The sappers gathered round.

'If it's alcohol, you'll be in trouble. The quartermaster's determined to smash the lot and let it run into the sea.'

Fred forced off the top of the box and found twenty or thirty pairs of leather gloves, tightly packed. The sapper began to laugh. 'I'm not saying they're not useful. We'll each have a pair, if you don't mind,' he added, taking one for himself.

'I wonder why the general wanted them,' said Fred.

'The general?' questioned the first sapper on his way back to the cable, gloves tucked into his waistband.

Fred shut up then. The appropriated gloves in the box seemed typical of his experiences on Gallipoli: unexplained, incomprehensible and pointless. Remembering why he was on the beach, he asked where the team which he was supposed to join was working.

The answer turned out to be W Beach. 'They're fixing up for some nice big bangs when we're all off.'

W Beach would be another longish trek, some of it in range from the new big guns on Achi Baba. It was past lunchtime and they'd been brewing up in the trenches. Fred took out a packet of biscuits.

'Eating dog biscuits, are you?' The sapper looked scornful. 'On the beach here there's Fortnum and Mason Paris biscuits. Tins and tins of them.'

Fred finished his dog biscuits. 'If your teeth can bite them, your stomach can digest them,' he said mildly. He set off walking again. At least it had stopped raining.

By the time he arrived at W Beach, his pack felt like a load of rocks. The scene, shrouded by a darkening afternoon, was even more confused than on V Beach. The main activity centred round the couple of piers which were under reconstruction. Here there was no *Clyde* through which the men could file on to the boats, just flimsy wooden piers plus a few old boats lashed up to them. It looked as if a couple of big waves would sweep the whole ramshackle lot out to sea. Once more Fred determined to make his exit via V Beach.

It was not difficult to find the Royal Engineers. Everyone pointed him to a long deep cavern set under the cliffs.

Dai welcomed Fred warmly once he'd remembered who he was. 'Our bit of luck, aren't you? We need it working in here. Want a tour?'

Fred wanted to sit down and have a cup of tea but tried to seem interested.

'We've got gun cotton, shells, SAA' – it was obvious Dai needed no encouragement – 'grenades, limbers full of shell . . . explosives of great power and beauty.'

'Power and beauty,' repeated Fred, glancing nervously at a man with a cigarette in his lips.

'We'll have them timed to go off at four a.m., half an hour after the last soldier's off.'

'Isn't that a little precise?' asked Fred.

Dai stared. 'We're trained to be precise.' He turned and said something in Welsh.

'What's my job?' asked Fred.

Dai turned back, surprised. 'That's up to you, man.'

Fred found an empty case, sat down on it, ate some biscuits and drank some water. Outside the cavern, it was drizzling again. Men ran to and fro on the beach, small figures from where he sat. In the distance on a promontory were the little white dots of hospital tents. He could see the Red Cross flags, drooping in the rain. He thought of going there for the company but this wasn't his section of Helles, he wouldn't know any of the medics and they'd wonder what he was doing away from his regiment. So did he, if it came to that. It had seemed a good idea at the time.

Behind him, the men were still working. The Welsh must see in the dark, he thought, all that mining underground. Without warning some shells landed on the beach from inland. He hadn't jumped at a shell for months but now he did. There came shouting, screaming. To distract himself, Fred rummaged in his bag and found by chance a small book Captain Prideaux had given him. It was poetry but he couldn't make out any of the words where he sat in the shadows. He wondered whether the captain had survived. He had played life by his own rules. Perhaps you could do that if you were born rich and grand. After what seemed a long time when the beach was shrouded in darkness and cloud and the cavern, to Fred's eyes, quite black, the sappers came out.

They were cheery now. One, apparently called Morgan, clapped Fred on the shoulder.

'How's our guardian angel?'

'Hungry,' said Fred.

'Did you see those big guns dragged across the beach?' asked Dai.

'Yes,' said Fred, who'd been a little surprised to see big guns being brought up at this stage in the game. 'Bit late for guns, isn't it?'

'Tree trunks!' Dai and Morgan both laughed.

Fred decided he'd spend this night where he was, then rejoin his regiment. Better the devil you know.

On the morning of 7th January at about eleven o'clock the Turks launched a heavy bombardment in the Fusilier Bluff and Gully Ravine area. Everybody heard it and everybody knew that, although the front-line trenches were mostly still manned, the support trenches were empty. Fred was approaching Gully Ravine and found fire coming in on both sides of it. Dumping his pack, he ran for a dugout. He forced his way into it through barbed wire, only at the last minute realising it might easily be booby-trapped by his friends, the sappers.

'I am a survivor.' Fred spoke out loud lying on the cold earth floor, littered with cigarette butts, cans and wires. It had that trench smell of blood and faeces, vomit and sweat, which his visit to the sea had briefly cleared from his nostrils. Once upon a time it must have been a front-line trench

A mouse rushed out of a hole and, when it saw the large figure in its path, stopped abruptly, bright eyes staring, whiskers quivering.

'I won't hurt you. All right, don't believe me. I wouldn't if I were you.'

Fred watched as it dashed back whence it came. He thought lying in the dugout listening to the bombardment was like all the times as a child he'd taken shelter from the rain, waiting for it to stop. Ninety per cent of the time a bombardment as heavy as this was the prelude to an attack, just what they most feared in the present circumstances. He didn't think he was scared but it was strange being under no one's command. Men didn't move without a command, a whistle blown, an arm raised. The chain of command, they called it, and he and his mates were the last link. Another strange thing: although they did most of the fighting and therefore took most of the casualties, they had least say in what they were up to. They couldn't all be stupid. He wasn't stupid.

Fred stood up and immediately realised that he was in a communications trench which would take him quite a way up to the front if the sappers hadn't blocked it off. He picked up his rifle and set off.

It was still light enough and the front-line trenches were close enough for the occupants to see the Turks coming out of their trenches and then falling back again after a pace or two, despite the urgings of their officers.

'Their hearts aren't in it,' commented Fluffy who stood on the fire step, cigarette in mouth. It wasn't their place to attack; they were the defenders.

'Maybe they know we're leaving?' said Fred. In fact there'd been hard fighting when he'd first arrived. Without a machine gun that had been hastily set up, there might not have been so many Turkish bodies in no man's land and they might have been keener to advance now.

'Deserter,' said Fluffy over his shoulder. The shooting was sporadic enough for an exchange of insults.

'I'm volunteering for the firing squad.' Fred thought it was good to be back with his mate and was wondering what had possessed him to abandon his pack when there was a fast volley of shots and Fluffy, head turned to Fred, fell back. In a split second, Fred saw that a Turkish officer had forced his men forward at pistol point and one of them had loosed a lucky shot. Unlucky for Fluffy, who wasn't dead, however, since he was swearing loudly.

Fred crouched over him at which he stopped swearing and pointed to his mouth. But blood was pouring from his shoulder, not his mouth. He began coughing and swearing by turns then struggled up and bent forward. One big cough and a cigarette popped out of his mouth. Immediately he bellowed, 'Get the stretcher!'

'I've never seen a man choke on his own cigarette before,' said Fred. After all, Fluffy had called him a deserter.

'Get me a bleeding medic,' yelled Fluffy even louder.

The small attack that wounded Fluffy turned out to be the last that day. Night came again and with it the silent period. If General von Sanders had ordered an advance to question his enemy's situation, then he had a firm answer: the Allies were still determined to hold on to their positions.

Now even the final seventeen thousand soldiers truly believed they would be leaving. The morning broke with an orgy of destruction. Anything they couldn't carry and might be useful to the Turks, they smashed: carts, bits of furniture, harnesses and what was left of the food supplies. Men seemed to enjoy the task as if it released all their anger and frustration. Fred noticed how some lay about them with wild laughter, others with ferocious yells. He himself acted with cool precision, unwilling to lose control. Now and again he looked up to the sky, where loose navy blue clouds were buffeted by a strong wind. He remembered the makeshift piers on W Beach and felt uneasy.

Instructions were given about how they were to creep away that evening: anything that might jingle or clang or tinkle or bang was stripped from them, including their bayonet holders, entrenching tools and water bottles. Each man had two sandbags to go over his boots; the hard surfaces of the front-line trenches were lined with old rags and uniforms.

The excited chatter, the strange preparations of the morning and early afternoon, gradually came to a standstill as everyone waited for dusk.

There was still firing and some loud explosions as large guns were blown up in the French sector, luckily sounding as if they had been fired rather than destroyed. Men felt naked and unprotected and no longer even whispered to each other. What if the Turks attacked now?

At about three o'clock Fred and three other privates were summoned by their corporal to join two lieutenants, a major and a lieutenant colonel who were in charge of counting out the men.

Lieutenant Colonel Proudfoot sat on an upturned crate while they stood round him; he was filled with energy and enthusiasm.

'Our job is to get groups of a hundred on the beach, not more not less. We gather the first two thousand at quarter to six and move off by six fifteen, which doesn't give us much time. They'll range from your own unit to the medical unit and some of the Royal Engineers when I need to even up the numbers.'

The colonel jumped to his feet and pointed to his left. They all looked. It seemed a spot like anywhere else on Gallipoli now: empty dugouts and shattered trees, in a flat plain at the end of a spur.

'You can't see from here but there's a small bridge that marks the place. The road's narrow unfortunately, but we'll manage.'

Fred was impressed by his confidence. It was like the early days of the campaign, except that now he was organising for a defeat not a victory. He recalled Lieutenant Colonel Doughty-Wylie who had rallied the troops so valiantly before courting a hero's death. Which had won him his VC: the brave charge or the tragic death? Proudfoot, despite his name, seemed sensible rather than heroic – but then his aim was to save lives rather than expend them.

In the next two hours, Fred was given permission to go in search of his kit. It soon turned into a farewell tour. Here among the stumps of apple trees and broken vines he'd fought his first battle, here were the rubble-filled streets of Krithia, the crumpled walls and piles of fragmented tiles. He scrambled down the gullies and remembered how the smell of wild thyme had mixed with the stink of rotting corpses. He passed little groups of crosses. A group of four or five were marked by a pine tree which had somehow survived the artillery fire. For one final time, he bent to read the names but there was nobody he recognised.

The wind hissed through the pine needles above his head. Fred looked up and saw an army of black clouds racing across the purple sky. It was time he went to the meeting place.

Twenty-Seven

A line of men filed silently past Lieutenant Colonel Proudfoot. Formed into groups of a hundred, they walked so fast that he was heard to mutter, after studying his watch. 'This beats all army records for moving infantry.'

It was dark but, despite their heavy packs and the difficult ground, nobody stumbled or fell. There was nothing for Fred to do so he watched the sky and the clouds and eventually saw a sparkling crescent moon emerge. He nudged the man next to him. 'They're flying a Turkish flag in the sky now.'

The man nodded without bothering to look up. That was the way on Gallipoli. Nothing surprised you any more. Earlier he'd told Fred that his wife, Mary, was expecting their first baby any day and that he was so excited about the possibility of going home and seeing the baby, even though he knew it was unlikely, that he'd begun to hold his breath when he prayed. 'Makes me closer to Him, see.'

Fred decided they were mostly mad. The hours passed slowly. Men came from Krithia and beyond. By ten o'clock the second wave was forming up. Despite their sheltered position, a cold wind found them out. Men moved from leg to leg – quietly. Any shot, even if they knew it was probably from a self-firing rifle, made them shudder and turn away.

Once Fred imagined he saw a whole view of Turks on the skyline, even picturing a German general in command. It was the absence of noise which made him realise they were advancing only in his mind.

The colonel, satisfied at the progress, left for the beach and the major took over command. At midnight, he called over Fred. He had an air of scarcely suppressed excitement. His pale moustache quivered as he handed over a note to Fred.

'Good chap. Chaffey, isn't it? No communication lines any more and the Colonel wants General Maude informed of our progress. Good progress, ha!'

'Sir!' agreed Fred.

'So you just nip down with this note. It tells him there're no hold-ups and we're on schedule.'

'Sir. Where to, sir?'

'Gully Beach.' The major seem surprised he didn't know. He tapped the note on Fred's hand. 'Major General Maude. He's being picked up by a lighter at two thirty. Off you go then.'

Fred thought of the long lonely walk, the rising wind, the paths blocked by wires and booby traps. He'd have to take the marked tracks as much as possible. Then he began to feel that old itch of curiosity and excitement.

'Good luck.' The major turned away to watch once more the men passing softly by.

'Sir!' Fred saluted and set off. At first he went the same way as the troops, their footfalls marking a slower cadence to his own faster pace. He wouldn't be able to keep it up but it was good to cover ground while his energy was high.

A few stars had joined the crescent moon, giving just enough light to see sudden turns or drops. After an hour, he turned off right, sliding down to a river bed he'd often followed. If he was lucky, it would take him all the way down to Gully Beach. He was surprised the general was going from there; they must be planning to pick him up straight off the shore, not easy if the wind built up the seas.

Fred slowed his progress; stones rolled uncomfortably under his boots. His pack dragged at his back. Several times he came across corpses of men or beasts. Some had obviously been tumbled out of their graves by the flood of water in November. There was no life. If he'd been out in an English night, there would have been badgers, hedgehogs – no, they'd be hibernating – foxes, deer, owls, otters, woodcock, nightingales, nightjars, boars – there had once been a family of boars living in the forest. A wave of nostalgia took Fred far into the English countryside. Time passed quickly. He was brought up short by a solid wall of barbed wire crossing his way. It was above his head and made up of thick strands tangled together, quite probably lovingly put there by the team of sappers who'd entertained him briefly. With no clippers on him, he'd just have to hope they hadn't done their job perfectly.

He walked along the wire slowly. It had come after a rise in the land and he suspected it was the final barricade before the slope down to the beach. He even imagined he could hear voices and after a while he was sure he heard the crash of waves on shingle. The wind was gusting in towards him, tugging at his helmet which eventually he threw off. If the Turks came now they could blast his head off and finish him quick. It seemed more likely he'd be barred for ever behind this wall of thorns, hearing but not being able to reach the tramp of men going down to shore, the hoot as the ship left in triumph.

Lily had told him a story when he was little about a prince who'd been after a princess asleep behind a briar hedge. He'd thought it stupid but now he tried to remember how the silly bugger with a feather in his hat had won through. Climbed it? If there was no break that was the only way. Climb to the top, throw his pack off first and then himself. At least he was wearing thick gloves – that box he'd stolen had been useful, after all.

Damn to hell Dai and Morgan and all the other sappers! There was no break. The best Fred could find was a yard or two when the wire was pulled tight instead of being in layers of springy coils. He began to climb.

Without feeling the slashes across his thighs, legs and face, Fred followed his pack over the top with all the propulsion he could muster. He landed awkwardly on something bulky and slid to the ground. He found himself staring at a huge eye. When he realised what it was, he leapt to his feet and began running, before coming back for his pack. He had fallen among rows of thirty or more dead horses, lying with their throats cut.

Shingle under his feet brought him to his senses. He saw there were a hundred or so men trooping in an orderly manner towards a lighter. He followed them, still feeling nothing from his gashes. He found a corporal and asked him for Major General Maude.

The man waved his arm. 'You'll catch him before he gets on board if you hurry.'

General Maude was watching as his staff officers organised piles of kit down the lighter. It was not easy with the ship continually turning sideways, despite efforts by all ranks of its crew.

'Message from Lieutenant Colonel Proudfoot, General Maude, sir.' Fred saluted and handed over the bit of paper. The general seemed remarkably calm, despite the last-ditch nature of the situation. He read the message, having first put a monocle in his right eye.

'Good show.' He looked up at Fred. 'This is the sort of thing the army is good at, you know, snatching victory out of defeat.'

'Yes, sir,' agreed Fred.

'Quite a trek to get here?'

'Had to climb the barbed wire, sir.'

'Thought you seemed a bit ragged. Better come on board with us.'

Fred thought he'd better too if he didn't want to be bombed to perdition when the Turks finally realised what the enemy was up to. Not that he liked the look of the ship one bit. He'd always known V Beach was the best place to get off. For a flash he thought about the murderous landing there, but only for a flash.

Despite the wind howling about their heads and the waves lashing the beach from all directions, somehow everybody got into the bucking lighter, one hundred and sixty men, as the corporal he'd spoken to earlier told him, plus officers, all squashed in like peas in a pod.

'You'd have been better off staying with your mates,' the corporal commented to Fred lugubriously. Under his helmet, he had a long face like a sad spaniel. 'Like I would have been better training men in Doncaster which is what I was doing till Christmas. Whoa!' The corporal grabbed the rail as the lighter gave a strange slippery motion, tipped slightly and fixed. The seamen yelled swear words, many of which seem particular to their profession.

'We're stuck!' exclaimed the corporal. 'Bleeding well stuck. Now all we need is shells crashing in from one side and men charging from the other and we'll say goodbye, Blighty, hello, crabs and fishes.'

It was true: they had grounded, still inside the shallow bay. Engines revved, men jumped in the water, men cursed, shouted, threw ropes, heaved ropes but nothing would move the boat.

Fred saw the general, looking as calm as ever, talking to the skipper of the boat.

Soon they were being disembarked, wading back to the shore

in the cold and angry sea. The General came too with his staff carrying kit from headquarters.

The men began to sing softly.

> *Take me back to Blighty*
> *Put me on the train from London town*
> *Take me over there*

Their voices were mostly smothered by the roar of the wind but Fred thought they'd be a friendly lot to perish with.

They all screwed up their eyes in the darkness to try and see how the lighter was getting on. Without any passengers, it soon got off the ground and, after a circle round, tried to run in at the shore. But the wind swept it forward in such a ferocious burst that it was obvious it would soon be grounded even with only a few men aboard.

The men stopped singing and watched nervously as the lighter gave up the hopeless task and headed out to sea. One lone voice tried ' "What's the use of worrying",' but was hushed quickly. If they weren't getting off in the boat then they wouldn't like Johnny Turk to know where they were.

A lieutenant from General Maude's came over and conferred with the NCOs. A quiet announcement was made: they were to walk to W Beach and catch the final line of boats departing from there.

Fred looked at the moon to estimate the time but it was hidden by clouds. A lieutenant passed by and he asked him, 'Sir, do you know the time, sir?'

The lieutenant stopped. Fred decided to be honest, 'The explosives are set to go off at W Beach at four o'clock, sir, so I was interested in what time it was now.'

'Are you sure?' The lieutenant looked at his watch. 'It's five to three. How do you know about the time?'

'I was with the sappers who were setting it up. They told me. "Precisely" is what they said.'

The lieutenant surveyed him critically. 'You look a bit the worse for wear.'

'Barbed wire, that's all. I came down from Gully Spur.'

'If you're really not hurt, I need a strong man to help with the staff kit. It's too heavy to carry, the horses are *hors de combat*, so we've found some stretcher vehicles. Heavy to drag.'

Fred cursed himself for asking the time.

As the men began to plod with admirable if understandable speed along the edge of the shore, he was sent up to the flat land where he'd found the *hors de combat* horses. Several stretchers on wheels were being piled with all kinds of equipment. Fred added his pack.

'Three pushing at the front,' said the general, who seemed to like being personally in command, 'two pushing at the back. Now those navy chappies have let us down, let's show them what the army is made of.'

He wasn't doing the work though. Fred found himself at the front. His gashes had begun to sting and his boots felt stuck to the ground. He kept going, though, like they all did, officers too.

After about half an hour, the general, who'd been sauntering about making encouraging remarks, became noticeably more attentive. He was heard to ask, 'Seen a big brown suitcase, have you? More of a trunk, initials on the top?'

No one had. The cavalcade stopped; men wiped their faces on their sleeves. The exertion on the rough ground had made them sweat, despite the wind and cool night air. Fred began to feel the horses were happier dead.

General Maude's servant, a small nervous man with a long thin moustache like a Chinaman, suddenly remembered seeing the trunk on the edge of the sea. So that was that, thought Fred, one more tiny loss among the unaccountable billion losses of the war.

But the general felt differently. 'I'm going back for it. I'll be damned if I'll let the Turks rifle through my possessions.'

Fred began to feel that the general's lack of urgency was not altogether healthy. He decided again that everybody was mad. It became personal when the general picked three men to go with him: his servant, the lieutenant and Fred. 'Don't worry,' the general assured them, smiling with big yellow teeth. 'We'll go back along the beach and beat these stretcher fellows to it.'

The trouble was they had to get back to the beach first, then find the trunk and only then hit the trail. Fred tried not to count the seconds with the movement of his boots.

The large trunk lay within a foot of the bounding waves which had respectfully declined even to splash it. Fred presumed that General Maude was extraordinarily brave under fire. They set out on the trudge to W Beach. Fred went ahead with the excuse of finding the way, the lieutenant and the servant carried the case while the general, swinging his stick, walked beside them.

Fred resisted asking the lieutenant the time but found himself continually picturing the cavern with its vast store of potential death. He had seen big shells explode and knew how the land bursts open and men fly up in pieces.

The wind became so violent that it blew in spray from the sea and nearly toppled them sideways. Fred pictured the piers on W Beach. How would the flimsy structures he had seen withstand the force of waves whipped into a frenzy? For the second time in his life he knew fear, his heart pounding too fast, his breath in little gasps. He turned round. Behind him, the servant and the lieutenant were struggling with the trunk. He went to them.

'My turn.' Thankfully, they handed it over and he put it on his back, strapping it with his belt and coat. He walked firmly forward. The fear which had only lasted a few minutes, gave place to a fierce determination.

It was a quarter to four when they arrived at W Beach, sliding down the incline amid a jumble of discarded tins. The lieutenant told Fred the time without being asked. They were spotted immediately by the captain of the lighter and three seamen came running towards them. Behind them, the lighter with small sparkling lights at bow and stern crashed impatiently against the pier. At least it hadn't splintered yet. Fred could just make out the rows of pale faces staring in their direction.

Without speaking, two of the seamen took the trunk from Fred and began running with it along the shingle. The new arrivals followed, the captain escorting the general who patted his arm while saying genially, 'We didn't get ahead of the stretcher-wallahs, then?'

The captain agreed courteously while urging the general onward. Fred overtook them; he kept his eyes turned away from the cavern of death, like a child who believes what he doesn't see doesn't exist. Was it possible, he wondered, that no one had told the general of the explosion's timing? Or was it that the general's wish for his belongings overrode considerations of general safety? This was the British Army, after all.

They reached the pier and gingerly crossed lashed-together planks that danced rebelliously under their boots. Nimble seamen took their arms and guided them towards the lighter. Waves of tension from the men waiting inside as well as real waves, cold and vicious, reached towards them.

At last they were in! The boat had seemed already full but it expanded to allow the general and his staff to progress through to the front. One of them, Fred noticed, was reciting something under his breath. Fred squeezed in at the stern. He wanted to see the last of Gallipoli. A few faces turned towards him but most seemed too exhausted to be curious and many had their eyes shut, sleeping on their feet.

Fred felt the engines take on the sea and, yard by yard, they moved away from the pier. And out into the open water.

Now Fred dared look back at the bay and pick out the black hole where the sappers had worked. But the wind hadn't given up. A great gust caught hold of the boat so that it could make no headway and actually began to drift back towards the shore. To Fred's horror, they were soon only fifty yards from the shore and exactly opposite the explosive-filled cavern. He remembered the soldier who held his breath when he was praying to God and found he was doing the same. 'Oh Lord, let the wind loose its hold! O merciful Lord let us leave this place of destruction!'

Slowly, the engines took a grip again and the skipper succeeded in getting the ship's nose facing the right way. Once more they were moving steadily, if slowly, out to sea, Fred was unable to take his eyes from the land.

The first hint of what was to follow came with flames spouting up like scarlet and purple trees on the beach. They were still only two hundred yards out when the explosion came, so magnificent and awful a sight that Fred found tears in his eyes. It felt as if it might blow them out of the water but the lighter, although tossed about on the waves, ploughed on. Great plumes of coloured smoke curled amongst the inferno and suddenly the lighter was enveloped by debris tossed out and falling from the sky.

Fred could see it crashing down by the ton: rock, shell cases, wheels, bars, boxes, tins, clods of earth. Most of the soldiers cowered down, putting their arms over their head. But by some miracle, everything fell round the boat, throwing up fountains of water, sometimes hissing, sometimes cracking or breaking the impact. Men, scrabbling in the wet bottom of the boat, pulled anything they could find over themselves. Fred stayed where he was.

He thought he would never again look on anything more beautiful. A wild exhilaration took hold of him. It seemed to him he was watching a vast funeral pyre for all those men who had died on the peninsula. Even the white foam of the waves bursting on the shore was reflected red, as red as the bloodstained water when they'd landed first at V Beach.

Fred watched. The lighter moved further away and two more explosions shrieked furiously into the sky. He began to scream out the names of the dead. The wind sent his words flying towards the land. He shook his fist at the fates who had allowed him to survive and so many good men to die. Again debris began to fall but this time a torrent of rubble clattered on the deck, as if their further removal was making them more under threat. The seamen cursed and even they crouched down.

Eyes still riveted to the ever-changing scene on shore, to the crimson heart of the show, to the dangerous fireworks of blue, orange and acid green, Fred felt a sharp blow to his right arm. He had been holding on to the rail with it. The pain came immediately, a violent, vengeful agony.

He remained conscious long enough to think, 'Now I won't be able to give Gallipoli the V sign.'

But you're left-handed, his brain added, before he slid to the deck.

PART FOUR

June 1916

⁂

'Few memories are sadder than the memory of lost opportunities and few failures more poignant than those which, viewed in retrospect, were surely avoidable and ought to have been avoided. The story of the Dardanelles is a memory such as these.'

Brigadier-General C.F. Aspinall-Oglander
– Military Operations – Gallipoli – Based on
Official Documents by Direction of the Historical
Section Committee of Imperial Defence

Twenty-Eight

It was a London society funeral. Large black cars and some carriages drew up slowly in front of the elegant, bow-fronted church. A small crowd gathered to watch, perhaps even admire, how the rich celebrated death. Most of the men were in uniform and all the women in deepest black, many wearing veils, sometimes trailing down their backs like a parody of a wedding veil. The day was bright, an early summer freshness in the air which gave an unreality to the gloomy scene. Not that everyone was gloomy.

Sylvia, escorting her mother, overheard two generals in animated conversation as they entered the church.

'Fine soldier, Fitzpaine,' said one.

'Stunning piece of staff work,' said the other, 'getting them off Gallipoli. Not a man lost, don't you know.'

'Pity Fitzpaine couldn't have hung on.'

'Those yeomanry were never quite the thing, what.'

Sylvia wondered if the lack of a coffin had lowered their sense of respect. He had been a fine man as well as 'a fine soldier' whose yeomanry weren't 'quite the thing'. In truth it was a memorial. But there were many funerals without corpses in this war, Sylvia added to herself with a touch of savagery.

On Beatrice's other side was her brother, the Earl of Deverill, one of the few men not in uniform. Behind them was his mother, the Dowager Countess of Deverill, on the arm of some general so old, decrepit and decorated with medals, that it seemed their weight might drag him to the ground. Every now and again he gave audible grunts as if urging a horse over a jump.

A few yards back, Gussie followed proudly on the arm of Reggie Gisburne who had his cap under his other arm, his Military Cross on his chest. He was limping, although he tried to disguise it.

Gussie was slim again because her baby, a girl, had been born two months earlier. Reggie had been wounded just before the birth and, after some time in a London hospital had joined Gussie, baby, the nurse and the maid in the Deverills' London home – the very place where little Artemis had been conceived.

Lady Deverill, to her own surprise, found a kindred spirit in her lively granddaughter. She proclaimed to her bachelor son, 'I don't know how poor dear Beatrice and Bingo produced such a spirited girl' – she pronounced it 'gel'. Deverill didn't answer at the time, or later, because he never listened to a word his magnificent mama pronounced. In fact he was so selfish that he seldom listened to a word anyone said (apart from his valet and butler) for fear they asked him to do something disagreeable. But he was a perfectly amenable fellow and could rise to an occasion.

He was aware, for example, that he was doing his duty by leading his sister into the church, and pleased by his behaviour. Even though Bingo had made little impression, he realised, with an unprecedented leap of the imagination, that the last time he'd led Beatrice into this very same church was on her wedding day, twenty-five years earlier – their father having died young. He squeezed her arm a little and hoped her tears wouldn't become gulps. Gulping, which led to heaving, was so unbecoming to a woman.

Sylvia was also wondering about her mother's state of mind. She knew, because Beatrice still wrote letters to her father, that she had not given up hope of his emerging from some hospital or prisoner-of-war camp, despite even the War Office now telling her he was dead. This decision was the reason for this memorial. Yet a month ago there had been a second reported sighting in Alexandria. Oh the cruelty of it! In her mother's diary, which Sylvia felt it proper to read now and again, she had written, *I am very low. Because I know it must not be true. But I cannot bear to give up hope.* She'd added, with conscious or unconscious symbolism, *Today an unseasonable storm blew the big ash tree down. It was quite an ordinary tree but I miss it.*

Sylvia thought of such things as they walked up to the front pew amid the standing congregation. An organist played a lugubrious tune she didn't know. Her mother had shown no interest in the service which, she'd confided in her daughter, was only to placate her grandmother. Her mother would have preferred to hold it in the Tollorum church. Then when it came to the choice of hymns, she'd suddenly announced she wanted 'Within the Churchyard.' 'But Mama . . .,' Sylvia had begun before losing her nerve. 'I know what you're thinking, my dear,' Beatrice had looked at her daughter with great seriousness. 'However you must not worry because I am composing a final more appropriate verse.'

This verse had been added and duly printed in the order of service, apparently giving Beatrice some satisfaction. On the evening before, she had read it to Sylvia who had found it very hard to stop her tears.

> *And those who die away from home.*
> *Their graves we may not see*
> *But we believe God keeps their souls*
> *Where ere their bodies be.*

It seemed that Beatrice could imagine her husband both dead and alive. Sylvia glanced sideways at her mother but she was too heavily veiled for any expression to be visible.

A London clergyman called Mr Percival took the service; Beatrice had not invited Mr Gisburne because she was still cross with him. Sylvia thought that, under the circumstances, she could do what she liked but felt relieved when the rector revealed that he dreaded going to London above all things. 'Do you remember how God promises to save Sodom for even ten just men?' Sylvia, not remembering, had encouraged him to continue. In the last few months, she had found herself able to study again and saw the rector every day. 'Well, I'm ashamed to admit, I would not save London for a *thousand* just men.'

Mr Percival was a very different kind of priest. For one thing he was wearing Eton blue socks which, since his trousers were rather short under his vestment, were mesmerisingly visible – at least to Sylvia. For another, he conducted the service at great speed, bustling about the altar as if afraid to bore his congregation. Perhaps fashionable London churchgoers were easily bored, Sylvia pondered.

She knew these petty thoughts were all a way of avoiding

mourning the death of her father but she knew he would forgive her, wherever he was.

There was no sermon but Lord Deverill and the ancient general both read lessons. This provided undeniable drama because, despite an usher on either side, it seemed unlikely that the general would make it up to the pulpit, or having reached the top, make it down again. There was an audible sigh of relief from the pews when he achieved it. Reading in strangely accented rushes of soft words, neither man was comprehensible at any point. Again, Sylvia wondered if this was the custom in order to avoid disturbing the fashionable from their important ruminations.

In scarcely more than half an hour they had reached the final hymn, 'Within the Churchyard'. Sylvia turned to smile in a sorrowful way at her mother and saw that Gussie had collapsed in a passion of tears, quite unconsoled, it seemed, by Reggie's encircling arm. For a moment, Sylvia felt impatient, the Colonel had been so much closer to her than to Gussie. But then in a sudden switch of emotion, she felt acutely jealous. Why was it that, despite her unhappiness, she could not lose herself in sobs, while Gussie, who had so much joy in her life, could fully live the tragic moment? Was it always to be like this now?

Outside the church, Lady Deverill held court while Beatrice stood by a pillar as if she would rather be behind it. Unlike most of the other women, she kept her veil down. If she had lifted it for any of her well-wishers who came to greet her, they would have seen a pale, sad but determined face, with no tear stains. She still had not let Bingo go.

Beside another pillar, the two generals, noticed disapprovingly by Sylvia, were once more in animated conversation. It seemed to be a continuation of their previous conversation:

'It was always a sideshow, what.'

'Did for Churchill.'

'Is he back from the front, do you know?'

'Never was at the *front*. But he's back, I'm told.'

Sylvia, looking at the two soldiers with their white moustaches, wondered where they were when Gallipoli was being planned. Frightened by the strength of her anger, she moved quickly on. So her father died for a *sideshow* whereas the *real* war was always being fought in Europe and thousands if not millions would die or be maimed but at least they'd know they'd died or lost their limbs *usefully*!

After the service, a family lunch had been arranged in the dark Mayfair house. Servants, brought up from the Deverills' country house, waited on them in pre-war style. The atmosphere was formal and might have been silent except that Lady Deverill entertained them with a list of those who had come to the memorial and those who had stayed away.

'It's the war,' she informed the company, magnanimously. 'Too many funerals and memorials – usually memorials. People can't keep up.'

There was a pause before Mr Percival, who had been invited to lunch at the last minute, remarked, 'So true, Your Ladyship. Recently, I held three services on one day. It is all very sad and wearisome.' He sighed.

That explained his speed, thought Sylvia. He had endured a great deal of practice.

'I did have Winston on the list,' continued Lady Deverill, 'after all, he is an old family friend, but Beatrice wouldn't hear of it. Not because he crossed the floor but because Beatrice sees him as the architect of the Gallipoli disaster, even the *murderer* of her husband, God rest his soul. I had never thought of you as political before!' The old lady gave a gay little laugh in the direction of her daughter. When Beatrice remained silent, her mother added, 'And she says she wouldn't go into a drawing room where Winston was invited.'

'Neither would I, Grandmama!' cried Sylvia, near tears at the sight of her mother's suffering face.

'Oh, my dear!' Lady Deverill stared at her granddaughter with surprise while her son, who had concentrated on his food and drink up till now, muttered in disapproval.

Sylvia subsided and there was another much longer pause before Lady Deverill turned again to Sylvia with a new idea. 'My dear, I have been invited to join the Central Prisoners-of-War Committee being formed by Lady Grant Duff. But I propose to submit your name instead. The Duchess of Bedford tells me some POWs are expected from Turkey. Not for some months, I fear.'

Sylvia put down her knife and fork and sat up straighter.

'They will come into Waterloo Station where members of the

committee will distribute the King's message of welcome.' Lady Deverill gazed at Sylvia with bright energetic eyes.

Sylvia looked down and said nothing. Since childhood she had found silence the best policy when confronted with one of her grandmama's ideas.

'Of course we cannot expect your dear Captain Lamb to be one of them since they are only repatriated when unfit for further service and I understand *he* is quite well. But I'm sure you will find the work interesting. Lord Sandwich is very involved.'

'Yes, Grandmama,' said Sylvia.

Gussie, who had sat quietly till then, turned to her sister. 'Just think if Arthur came off that train and you were standing there with a bunch of roses!'

'He won't,' said Sylvia.

'I fear not,' agreed Lady Deverill, 'but the welcoming party will take flowers on to the station. Such an imaginative thought for men who are starved of loveliness.'

'Oh, *yes!*' enthused Gussie.

After lunch was finished, baby Artemis was brought downstairs by the nurse. Everyone agreed that she looked exactly like Gussie with her big blue eyes and dark hair but Sylvia was reminded by her red cheeks and enthusiastic chortles of Reggie.

'We plan to have troops of children!' exclaimed Gussie, giving Reggie a longing look.

He responded, with only a slight sense of harassment, that he was needed on army matters and, regretfully, must depart.

Later, when the Deverills had left for the country and their mother had gone to her bedroom, the two sisters sat together in the drawing room.

'Oh, I'm glad that's over!' cried Gussie, throwing herself on the sofa. 'I do so hate to be unhappy!'

Sylvia looked at her curiously. 'You love your husband and your baby, don't you?'

'Of course I do. And living in London. And meeting people. And even doing good. I do have my committees, you know.'

'I'm sure you do,' said Sylvia quickly and kindly.

'It's so hard for you and Mama in that dreary house in the country and everything reminding you of dear Papa. Even those wounded officers.'

'I have my studies.'

'You're so clever. As clever as Reggie's papa, I wouldn't be surprised. During my sad time, he saved my life, but he did keep quoting things.'

Sylvia wondered if she enjoyed being likened to Mr Gisburne but she smiled all the same. 'Do you really want masses of children? It seems such a terrible world to bring them up in.'

'The war will end. Reggie says there's the biggest push ever being planned. Anyway, we can't stop the babies coming, can we? Not really. He says our nights together are the only thing he'll miss at the front. Oh, Sylvia, I do like being married, if you know what I mean, and I feel so sorry for you not having a man in your best years!'

'Thank you, dear,' said Sylvia, smiling again. There was something about her sister's happiness and warmth that took the offensiveness out of her remarks.

'Although I know,' continued Gussie, laughing, 'that I shouldn't talk like this to an unmarried young lady.'

The next day Sylvia and her mother returned to the country by train, both very thankful to be doing so. The same afternoon, Sylvia went to see Mr Gisburne with an essay she'd written on the Peloponnese war. He welcomed her warmly as always, commanding tea from his bad-tempered daughter, but Sylvia could see he was unsettled. He did not even glance at her essay.

The moment Gwen had retired, banging the door, he put on what Sylvia recognised as his sermon face. 'I have a dilemma, a fundamentally Christian dilemma. There has come to my acquaintance a young man who is displaying all the worst elements of the prodigal son. You remember that unfortunate creature?'

Sylvia admitted she did.

'Licentiousness of every kind,' continued the rector before pausing as if shocked by his words, although, thought Sylvia, they were common enough in his sermons.

'Who is he?' she asked. 'And what is it to do with me?'

'He is a young man,' the rector suddenly sat down and leant forward to Sylvia earnestly, 'about your age who fought gallantly as a volunteer soldier, even heroically, and for his pains has earned himself not a medal like my dear Reggie but a missing arm.'

'A missing arm,' repeated Sylvia, a little bewildered.

'He has lost his right arm above the elbow. It was crushed and could not be saved. He returned to England, somewhat surprisingly, with a shipload of wounded Australians to Weymouth. There he recuperated but already the signs of licentiousness were evident. He drank, he refused to obey orders necessary for the running of an efficient camp. So he was sent home. Not quite well. This was in early March.'

'Where is home?'

'Tollorum,' answered the rector, 'but he has no real home. That is part of the problem. When he came back his behaviour grew even wilder. Out of pity, I assume, the men bought him drinks at the pub and ladies who were not ladies gave him things that should have been sacred. One night, a month or two ago, I found him unconscious in my potting shed. Unconscious because of alcohol. It had been a stormy night and he was still wet through. I invited him into the kitchen and looked out some dry clothes while Gwen, doing her Christian duty, gave him breakfast. He begged me to let him sleep in the shed. He said that he had become used to sleeping rough on Gallipoli and this would be luxury.'

'Gallipoli,' said Sylvia, the word falling like lead in her heart.

'Yes. From start to finish. He told me he was the sole casualty of the evacuation. I asked him how he knew. He said from *The Times*. "But can you read?" I asked – you have to understand he looked like a wild man, dirty, unshaven, as if, like the prodigal son, he'd slept with the pigs.

' "I learnt on Gallipoli," he said. So I took him into the study – Gwen was not pleased – and handed him the Bible. He read it perfectly. I asked him what it meant and he answered with great intelligence. I was more than surprised. Then he said, "I can remember it too," and he told it all back to me, word for word. So I realised he was one of those remarkable people who have complete recall, probably based on a visual memory. I asked him if he liked books because I noticed his eyes kept straying to my bookshelves.

' "Yes," he answered, with great feeling.

' "If you are to borrow my books," I said, "you will have to clean up."

' "I was planning to steal some," he said, and we both smiled. Did I mention he's a very good-looking fellow?'

'No,' said Sylvia. 'I thought you said he was disabled?'

'Oh, yes. That, of course, is a terrible disadvantage for a boy destined to be a labourer on the estate.'

'The Tollorum estate?'

'Did I not say so? He is called Fred Chaffey and grew up in one of the cottages. Both his parents died young but his sister did her best to replace them. Then she married and her husband died.'

'Lily?' said Sylvia. 'You are talking of Lily who lives at the manor with her two children. My mother could not do without her.'

'You would not wish him there,' said the rector soberly. 'I'm afraid, despite his reading, his habits have not changed much for the better.'

'I'm sorry,' said Sylvia, realising that this lengthy preamble was leading to some request but unable to imagine what.

'However, I have discovered that he not only finds enjoyment in the printed word but has a true thirst for learning and, like yourself, has a serious interest in classical times, perhaps encouraged by the battleground where he found himself in such dangerous circumstances. Such things can impress on a man's thinking.'

'Yes.' Sylvia thought of the copy of *The Iliad* that she had sent to Arthur. Where was that now?

'I have started giving Chaffey a few lessons,' Gisburne continued. 'He is exceedingly quick. His concentration and of course his retention of information is superb. But still he does not change his ways. A week or two back he was found cut and bruised and once more unconscious with drink. He says he was tired and fell from his horse but I believe he was in a fight.'

'I thought he only had one arm.'

Mr Gisburne, looking surprised at Sylvia's unsympathetic tone, said, 'Yes, one hand and half an arm short. Doubtless that is the reason he gets into trouble. Humiliation often leads to aggression. Incidentally, he is left-handed and, fortunately, lost his right. Nevertheless, he is not so proficient at writing as reading yet but it will not take long. He never misses a lesson.'

'And I expect,' suggested Sylvia, 'his sister is a great help to him.'

'She tried to be but was perhaps too critical of him, not altogether appreciating the parable of the prodigal son who was welcomed, as you remember, with open arms. I am aware, however, that what Chaffey most needs is a civilising influence.'

'He has you.'

'Indeed. As I was at my night prayers, the Lord felt fit to put an idea in my head which I now propose to you.' The rector stood again and wrapped his thin arms around himself. 'I would like this unfortunate sinner to join our lessons. He shall not speak, unless with respectful questions, and he is much to learn about respect, but he will learn from you, the books, the tutorial system.' Stopping abruptly, he peered hopefully at Sylvia.

Sylvia looked at the carpet. She did not want a companion in her studies, particularly not a one-armed licentious soldier who would remind her of Arthur and her father every time she saw him. Mr Gisburne's study had been her sanctuary from what she saw as a woeful life.

'You meant when you first spoke,' she said in a constricted voice, 'that the Christian dilemma is mine. *You* have made up your mind.'

'Perhaps he need not come to every class,' said the rector.

Later in the afternoon, Sylvia found Lily where she was teaching the kitchen maids, there being no cook, how to slice a runner bean. The kitchen was light and airy, unlike in grander houses where most were put in the basement.

'I hear your brother's back, Lily,' said Sylvia, trying to sound nonchalant.

Lily frowned and took her into the scullery. 'The rector's told you, has he, Miss Sylvia? It is a big worry to me. He was always a wild boy and I'm afraid now his affliction has turned him absolutely bad. He will not even speak to me. I can see you, Betty,' she interrupted herself to call through the door. 'Practice makes perfect and you won't get that through gawping out of the window!'

Sylvia saw that Lily's difficult life had taught her the virtues of determination and hard work but not the gentler approach.

Simultaneously, both women gave a sigh. 'The letters he wrote from Gallipoli, miss,' said Lily gently, as if to contradict Sylvia's thought, 'were so thoughtful. But for a young man to lose an arm ... well, it changes everything.'

'Yes,' agreed Sylvia. 'Mr Gisburne has hopes of him.'

'I'm glad, miss.' Lily went back to the kitchen.

On the following morning, Sylvia dressed carefully. Although the garden was filled with exuberant blossom, she chose a dark skirt and a plain white shirt. She wanted to look like a blue-stocking, on the path to university.

She crossed the garden with her straw basket of books. A soft patter of rain accompanied her and the smell of fresh flowers and grass was very sweet.

Gwen opened the door to the rectory, looking more than ordinarily grim. 'He's in there,' she said. 'Like a cuckoo.'

'You mean Mr Chaffey.' Sylvia swept past her.

'Ah, Miss Fitzpaine. You are not overly damp, I hope, the dew of heaven falling too generously.'

Even for the rector, this was absurd. Sylvia realised he was nervous.

'Good morning, Mr Gisburne.'

'And this is Mr Chaffey.'

A slim figure came forward. He was about her height, dressed in dark shirt and trousers, with black hair, a sunburnt face and startling blue eyes. There was a pale scar on his forehead. Suddenly Sylvia recalled how the rector had called him very good-looking. He was staring at her curiously.

Fred stared at Miss Sylvia Fitzpaine and thought that she was thin and pale, that her bobbed hair was shocking, and that she looked unhappy, as well she might with her father dead and her fiancé a POW. Then he wondered why she had taken such trouble to look stern and mannish, so he smiled.

'Good morning, miss.' It was the ladies who had told Fred he had a lovely smile with his white even teeth and wide mouth, and he had got into the habit of using it when necessary. Women were teaching Fred a lot about the joys of life.

Obviously disconcerted, Sylvia held out a hand to shake his before realising there was no hand, at least no right hand, to shake. His face had taken all her attention. Blushing, she retreated.

Taking pity, Fred held out his left hand. They shook before Sylvia scurried to her usual chair. She wasn't prepared for a handsome confident man in the room; she was expecting a dissolute cripple who in a surly way would be grateful for her kindness. Even though Fred took a chair in the corner, she was acutely conscious of him.

Mr Gisburne didn't sit but began to talk, addressing, it appeared, the door which was situated roughly between Fred and Sylvia.

'As you both know, the Peloponnesian War 431 to 404, before Christ, marked a dramatic end to the golden age of Greece. Athens, the stronger city state in Greece prior to the war, was reduced to a state of near subjection while Sparta became the leading power in Greece . . .'

Sylvia heard the words without understanding, in much the same way as she heard the touch of the rain on the window. Out of the corner of her eye, she could see Chaffey studiously taking notes with his left hand. The right arm ended after six inches or so with a knot in the shirt. She couldn't understand how she'd failed to notice it at first. As a nurse, she became used to all sorts of disabilities, far more horrific than this, but there was something about its presence in the rector's study that made it disturbing. And yet there were men at Tollorum with limbs missing and she found nothing odd in that. Reluctantly, she came to the conclusion that it must be something about the man himself. He seemed so alive, so *unresigned*.

' "The growth of the power of Athens, and the alarm which this inspired in Lacedaemon, made war inevitable",' the rector quoted and looked up questioningly.

'Thucydides in his history of the same period,' responded Fred.

The rector nodded approvingly and glanced towards Sylvia. 'Your essay dealt very well with Thucydides' writing and his more warlike contributions. I shall read out a small portion.'

Fred listened carefully to a rather long portion of the essay. He admired the graceful sentences in which words seemed to balance each other without ever jarring. He understood that knowledge and understanding was not enough. But how to gain such fluency!

At the end of the session, he took books and paper, said polite farewells and went to the potting shed. He noticed it was leaking in one corner; a bit of corrugated on the roof would fix it easily enough. He changed out of the black clothing, lent by Mr Gisburne, and put on old jodhpurs and an army shirt. He was quick and adept in all movements, using his shortened arm when necessary. The shed was very tidy, although it had an earth floor and no glass in the window which, since it was much overhung by the roof outside let in no rain, although little light either. There was a small pallet bed in one corner, a stool and a bench which still had flower pots on one end. Nearby a row of spent bullets, some long and thin, others shorter and rounder, stood sentinel. Behind them was a set of teeth which might have been either glaring or smiling.

Fred put his books and papers away in a wooden box with a lid as protection against mice and went out to the garden privy. As he came out he saw Sylvia dawdling back to the manor across the garden. The rector must have kept her behind, talking about the new student, no doubt. Fred would have preferred to continue his lessons on his own but the rector had insisted. 'You will learn from each other,' he'd said, which was polite but a lie. What could she learn from him? Fred hurried down a track in the opposite direction.

Half an hour later, he went by the rectory again, this time on horseback. The horse was an ugly beast, struggling to free himself from the bit by throwing his heavy head up and down continually. Fred was no great rider even if he'd had both hands but in the end his will was stronger than the horse's. They set off on the cross-country track to Dorchester at a sharp trot which soon turned into a more comfortable canter.

Sylvia found a letter waiting for her in the hall. It was from Hilda. She took it to her room but waited till after lunch to read it.

Dearest friend,
This letter will surprise you extremely. Captain Prideaux and I are married and living on Gozo. Where is Gozo? you may ask. Although that is possibly not your first question! It is a very small, primitive island, a boat ride from Malta. It is all quite shocking but I have never been so happy in my life, nor expected to be. We are not man and wife in the normal way because the exertion would be too much for Prideaux's poor head but we are very tender

to each other – or at least he allows me to be tender to him – and I am, believe it or not, Lady Prideaux. He likes to say he can disinherit himself from his house and estates but not from his title. Every day is a lark. I would have been quite content to be his nurse for as long as he lived but he said that he detested self-sacrifice above everything. Then, when I got up my nerve and protested it was love not self-sacrifice, he said that was far far worse and a marriage of convenience was the only answer. So he summoned a Maltese priest he seemed to know called Father Lombardi and the deed was done.

Of course, they'd never have let him out of hospital without a nurse, even though the doctors can do nothing more than wait for him to die which he can do perfectly well on his own – or now with me. In fact I think he chose Gozo because he thought the journey here would kill him. He says he remembers it from past visits as the most remote place in the world and filled with happy laughing peasants. Quite untrue: they are black and fierce and their language is as impenetrable as their rocky land. But there is a glowing cathedral, in the golden heart of the main city, known as the Citadel. Oh, how I wish you could visit! But the war has flung all of us far apart: Malta, England, Turkey (your poor Lieutenant Lamb) and Gussie's husband in France, so you told me. Has the baby come yet?

Sylvia stopped reading and looked at the date of the letter. April. Somehow Hilda's news didn't surprise her particularly, perhaps because nothing stirred her emotions. She was pleased for her friend because she was happy, that was all. She picked up the letter again.

A few weeks back while we were still at the hospital, we heard the news that Gallipoli had been totally evacuated. It was a bad time. Prideaux, Rupert, became very bitter and withdrawn. From the few words he spoke I understood that it had brought back his furious anger over the campaign. I dared to point out that not every campaign could be successful and that to take the Dardanelles and Constantinople would have been a magnificent coup. Then he screamed out so loud that I feared for his head, 'Stupid woman! It could never have happened! It was annoyance *and foolishness! Children playing games about which they knew nothing! Lives were thrown away with no sensible hope of success! They were murderers!'*

It was terrible. He went on and on, ranting about the army, the politicians, even the navy who I thought had behaved quite well. We were inside because there had been a thunderstorm, and his passionate cries drew a crowd of patients and nurses. In truth, I thought he would die and I knew it would all be my fault for saying a few silly words. Luckily, Matron came and brought the doctor who gave the poor dear creature a sedative.

Oh, Sylvia, the things he has in his head, the things he has seen, made worse for not being able to fight because of his hand and believing all along it would end in failure. There's no wonder his brain hurts, even without the effect of a lump of shell. I do wonder how those other soldiers manage. Your unfortunate Lamb, for example. But then it's so much better if you take the line 'My country right or wrong.'

Oh dear, I've just read back and feel ashamed I have let all this out when you have so much to bear and I was bringing good news. Yet it was Rupert's outburst, I believe, that determined him to take his chances and leave the hospital. He could never travel back to England and would not want to. So here we are Lord and Lady Prideaux on a rocky island in the middle of nowhere and I read him books, often Dickens from an English library in Valletta – he says he is frightfully badly educated – and I describe what goes on around us. I am on the trail of a musician who will play to us – tambourines seem to be the local instrument! It cannot last, but for now I am blissfully happy. Remind me I wrote that when I am a lonely widow. At least I shall never have to think of myself as a dreary old spinster again.

Once again Sylvia put aside the letter, although there were only a few lines more. She realised she *did* think of herself as a dreary old spinster and that in some deep sense she did not believe that she and Arthur could ever be joined in marriage and happiness as Rupert and Hilda were, in an unlikely way and Gussie and Reggie were, and even her parents had been. But as soon as she had this thought, she put it aside as disloyal to Arthur. Now she must work, work and make herself the well-educated woman he had wanted.

Fred always stopped at the top of the hill where the sea came into view, blue or green or grey, according to the weather. The headstrong animal he rode was tired after the journey and content to stand still. Fred let the reins go and soon the horse ducked his head to crop the grass. The sea had got into his blood, Fred supposed, because it had so often been part of the view on Gallipoli. He had noted its moods as he had learnt the moods of the countryside before he left England.

'Come up, you brute!' The Tollorum farm manager only lent him the horse because it was considered unmanageable. In a time when horses were rare, most with the army overseas, he had been acquired to pull the plough but no one could get a harness on him.

'Downhill now.' The sea was not why Fred came this way. Below him was the town of Weymouth, surrounded by several waves of green hills. On one of these, about two or three miles out, spread rows of wooden huts, the homes of recuperating Australian soldiers. Others were in hospital in the town. These were the men who Fred had travelled with from Gallipoli to England.

Fred had found a mate on the journey: Robbie Gant. Fred sometimes wondered why he bothered since so many mates were blown out of his life one way or another. Robbie had all his limbs but only part of his brain. He was big and awkward, not unlike the horse, Fred sometimes noticed. He liked both. So he came to visit Robbie and they went into Weymouth and got drunk and found the ladies. Who was to stop them?

He arrived at the camp and tethered the horse. He had it all well organised. Fred liked that about himself. He slipped a few coins to a quiet boy who watched the horse and gave him hay and water. At dawn he'd ride it back again. He had christened his obstinate mount 'Gallipoli'.

Robbie and Fred enjoyed the walk to town. It strung them up. Robbie was a country boy too, and he liked the buzzards that mewed above, 'Just as if they're kittens, not killers,' he said, in one of his few remarks. In general, Robbie was not a talker. Fred liked that about him too.

There was a routine about Fred and Robbie's visits to Weymouth. They always visited the same pubs in the same sequence and at the last they met the ladies. By then they'd consumed enough local ale to make the world a very rosy place indeed. Even Fred had very little to say and the ladies who, with their quick eyes and slow voices, reminded him he was home, put an arm through their soldier boy and led him away. They knew the men had money, the Australians more, but it was the glamour of their fighting far away among the heathens that enthralled them. They were not virtuous women but they were not bad either and told Fred, 'There're worse things than missing one arm, love. Why do you think God took the trouble to give you two?' Robbie was more popular all the same, until he became too boisterous.

As they walked back to the camp in the grey blankness just before sunrise, ale sinking away from their heads, bodies satisfied and weary, Fred and Robbie talked about Gallipoli. They didn't bother to listen to each other; the birds, rousing themselves in ferocious chorus didn't listen either. They described assaults, bombardments, night raids, bad officers, good officers, vile deaths, foul disfigurements, friendships, loyalty, sickness, starvation.

At the camp, they nodded to each other and parted. Then Fred mounted Gallipoli who, half-asleep himself, took his nodding rider back to his stable where both of them spent the rest of the night.

When the sun or rain or farm manager disturbed him, Fred rose from the straw, patted the horse, before going to sluice himself under the stable pump. Then he went up to the rectory to prepare for his lesson.

The morning that Sylvia left for her second lesson with Fred, Beatrice received a parcel. With dire premonition, she took it to the Colonel's study. It was a smallish box wrapped in brown paper and tied with string, the knots fixed with sealing wax. She placed it on the desk and stood over it. A mark proclaimed it sent from the War Office.

Realising her heart was beating too fast, she went for support. But Sylvia had left for the rectory and Lily was seeing off an officer who had to be returned to hospital. Listening for a moment, Beatrice noticed how her voice was beginning to lose its country drawl for more clipped tones. She went back to the study and the box was still sitting there. She heard the ambulance which had come to collect the officer drive away. She turned over the idea, not for the first time, that Bingo's disappearance was part of a past campaign, soon to be forgotten. This made her so angry that she attacked the string and paper and threw open the box.

Inside were two envelopes and below them a book. It was bound in dark, dimpled leather, rather battered at the edges. She recognised it at once: it was Bingo's Bible. She lifted it up and clasped it to herself. Then she dropped it down abruptly and ran to the annexe where until last week the Colonel's bronzes had stood. She had decided they gave her more pain than comfort and ordered them to be cleared away. But now the Bible had come and it seemed like a terrible reproach. She brushed her fingers along the empty shelves and then returning to the study, snatched up the Bible again and took it to the armchair.

She noticed it was more worn than it had been and that it showed signs of water damage. With trembling hands, she opened the first pages and saw Bingo's signature. It had been given him by a bachelor uncle who had had it from his father. It was all recorded there but smudged from the effects of water. Was this the Aegean, the sea of dreams and heroes, whose shores had led him to his death? So much better if he'd stayed in Egypt and charged on horseback across the desert, instead of walking, heavy-footed, to his death!

Head filled with violent images of war, Beatrice put aside the Bible and returned to the box. There were the two envelopes. Still standing, she opened the first: the paper was black-edged – how she hated that – the printed heading: *Turf Club, Cairo*, crossed out and *Royal Bucks Hussars*, Aboosia written in with the date *Aug 29/15*. So very long ago! Only two days after that fatal wire from the War Office.

Dear Lady Beatrice,
I know nothing that I can write can help you to bear your loss,
but if there is any comfort I know it is shared by every officer
and every man in the brigade where he was beloved by all; you
should have heard the genuine feelings of regret which every man
expressed to me yesterday: 'The best gentleman and a soldier
whom we would follow anywhere.' I am only a junior captain in

his brigade and was very disappointed at not being able to go with the brigade but was unfit for service. I am afraid the brigade lost heavily, but what they accomplished (according to one eyewitness who saw it all) was wonderful . . .

Unaware up to now of tears pouring down her face, Beatrice dropped the letter, found a handkerchief and dried her face. It was now almost a year since the letter had been written. Where had it been? How hollow, even cruel, sounded the officer's consolation of wonderful accomplishments achieved when everybody now admitted that the 21st August attack had been totally pointless and accomplished nothing! She picked up the second letter.

This was a typed report from a Sergeant Mitchell headed: *re. Brigadier-General Fitzpaine* and dated *February 1916.*

Sir,

I was present in the final charge upon the Turkish position at Scimitar Hill on 21st August, 1915. Just before the charge I was standing quite near the brigadier above-mentioned. Another staff officer was with him at the time and I heard the latter address the brigadier and say: 'Do you think we can take the position, sir?" The brigadier turned and grasped him by the hand and said: 'We can but try if we die.' With those words upon his lips he dashed forward into the open towards the Turkish position calling upon the men to charge. Then it was hell. I did not see the brigadier again. But in the retreat that followed I rallied about three hundred men and held the position until ordered to withdraw at dawn the next morning. During the night men kept on asking me who was the brigadier that led the charge. I replied that I did not know his name. I enquired of them why they wanted to know. And they all without exception replied he was the bravest man they ever saw. All of those who saw the brigadier fall were of the opinion he was mortally wounded. Several attempts were made during the night to find him, and some of my men were wounded in the attempt. But all attempts were unsuccessful, owing to the deadly rifle and machine gun fire kept up by the enemy.

Signed J. Mitchell, Sgt.
S. W. Borderers Western Command Depot

Beatrice did not cry at this letter nor was she angry. Its very simplicity in stating the facts as this sergeant knew them was utterly convincing. She went back to the chair and sat down.

After a while she opened the drawer of the desk and took out the book in which she wrote her journal. She noted the day's date at the top of the page and then screwed on the top of her pen again. There seemed no words to express her feelings or, if there were, she didn't want to see them written down.

After quite five minutes she unscrewed the top of the pen and drew a black cross below the date. Then she closed the book and put it away in the drawer.

Twenty-Nine

The man, a Russian called Constantine, was tied upside down in the middle of the largest courtyard. Arthur could see him through the window. It was another of Maslum Bey's excesses. For at least an hour the soldiers had been taking it in turns to whip the Russian's feet. The sound of his groans, Russian curses, and the whips descending was awful. Inside the room, the British officers, sitting on boxes with books or idly standing, were silenced by hatred. It was very hot.

Arthur glanced out of the window again as there came a pause in the rhythm of beating and saw that Maslum Bey himself was approaching. Strutting, as if proud that eyes were upon him, he began to kick and beat Constantine all over his body, spitting to complete the humiliation. Constantine's only crime or folly was to put up a defensive arm when Maslum Bey had struck him.

Arthur looked away in disgust, although it was necessary to witness. During Maslum Bey's months as commandant of Afion Kara Hissar, the list of his atrocities had grown long: he had flogged British and Russians, he had imprisoned officers in filthy holes for little or no reason, he had lied, swindled and grown rich. But these were not the worst of his offences. Not even the treatment of Constantine whose torture was ended as he was dragged, unconscious, to some prison hole.

'We must add this to the latest letter,' said Arthur. The letters contained a code, devised by Arthur, in which they had been gradually unfolding Maslum Bey's iniquities. There were four young fair-headed men in the camp who had caught the commandant's eyes. They were taken by Turkish NCOs, threatened with beatings and imprisonment which was near enough to death, then passed on to Maslum Bey. They were from the West Country, scarcely more than boys, scared witless. Nobody blamed them but the revulsion for their torturer grew.

There were international rules about such behaviour. The Turkish government would not like Maslum Bey's excesses to become known. Arthur had already sent letters to his uncle who was quick-witted and knew his nephew well. He would understand and send them to the appropriate channel. It might take weeks but he was certain they would eventually get rid of the oppressor.

It was ironic that this task had saved Arthur from a depression which had overwhelmed him for the whole of April and May. It had been set off by the death of his New Zealand friend, Dr Lacey, in late March, and heightened by the anniversary of his landing at Gallipoli on 25th April. One of his housemates had been sent a copy of Rupert Brooke's poems. It was a thoughtless present and, in a moment of self-flagellation, Arthur picked it up. The patriotic fervour and ecstatic joy of the young soldier who never lived to fight moved Arthur to a multitude of contradictory emotions: recognition and wistfulness for the feelings he had once known himself; derision that Brooke had never known the reality; anger at how false and lying was the romance of his poetry; pride that he himself had faced the reality and fought bravely. But in the end it only magnified his sense of loss and failure. He would have been better dead, falling on his sword like an honourable soldier. The doctor had died of typhus, or so he self-diagnosed, and had himself quarantined in a shack attached to their house. Arthur believed that he had died because he was forbidden to look after the men who needed him. It had taken away his reason for living.

The image of Sylvia often came before Arthur in those terrible weeks but instead of being the strong independent woman he had known and made love to in Cairo, she had become again the child-like acolyte he had first met at a chaperoned tea party in Oxford. He had painted out her short fluffy hair and brought back long smooth coils set at the back of her head. Once he had tried to write to her about his feelings, but the thought of Turkish translators in Istanbul poring over it made him tear up the letter.

He was also affected by the atmosphere of the camp, at least among the British, which dictated a need to protect loved ones back home from unnecessary anxiety. Many letters contained the same information and requests: *I pray you are not worrying. We are perfectly all right and there are ten delightful fellows in the house; We spend the day sitting in the sun reading. This is a queer life but we are quite used to it now. The Russians sing expressively sometimes . . .; Got a dramatic society going now and have had several good shows . . .; Please number letters so I know if they've arrived. Send more photos . . .; We often play leapfrog and even knucklebones . . .; I shall be like a wound-up mainspring let loose when I return . . .*

Most of the writers assumed their captivity would be over by Easter, by summer, by Christmas, depending on the season. They knew very little of the actual progress of the war since they were only told about Turkish victories. Sometimes, they were able to judge for themselves as new prisoners came from Mesopotamia and the agonising defeat at Kut.

For two months Arthur didn't write at all and looked at his uncle's and Sylvia's letters with a blank eye. But the code, begun as a desultory scribble, became an obsession, and forced him into words. The key was the Greek letter *pi* with a value of 3.14159. To decode you took the third word of the first line, the first of the second line, the fourth of the third, and so on right through the letter following *pi*. In Arthur's simple letter to his uncle, military information, such as the movements of Turkish divisions could be inserted. And now information to bring about Maslum Bey's downfall. It might not be soon enough for the four boys from the West Country. One had been seen vomiting and crying but they all had faith it would happen. At another level, it lessened the feeling of powerlessness.

It did not help with writing to Sylvia. After Constantine had been taken away, Arthur went into the small exercise yard with a paper and pencil. Before Maslum Bey's regime had fully taken hold, they had been allowed out on occasional walks. Arthur had seen the granite mountain of Kara Hissar which rose perpendicularly out of the town and beyond the fields of white poppies. Sitting against a wall as far out of the sun as possible he wrote:

The white poppy fields grown for opium spread around the black crag of Kara Hissar, like crinoline skirts below a taut black bodice.

He looked at the words. What could Sylvia make of such nonsense? Since returning to relative sanity, he had been reading *The Mill on the Floss*, sent in to a fellow officer. He had read few novels in his life and the story of Victorian England struck him with as much force as when he'd first read *The Odyssey* as a ten-year-old boy. It amazed him that he should be so affected by Maggie Tulliver. Having been brought up alone from an early age, with no sister or feminine company, this intimate portrait of an ordinary young woman made him realise that there was a whole other race which he only knew to admire or avoid. For some reason he thought of Gussie's enormous vitality and how strange it seemed that she was now a wife and mother.

These new questionings made his letter-writing to Sylvia even harder. He became self-conscious and could scarcely be confident about more than a request for jam and sardines. Yet this was the woman he'd made love to – almost the only woman (there had been a married lady in Oxford, and an unmarried barmaid in Burford) – and expected to marry.

Arthur started another letter. The fierce sun had crept round and was grilling his outstretched legs.

My dear Sylvia,
It would give me great peace of mind if you would consider yourself free from any ties of engagement while I'm held here in Turkey. My feelings for you haven't changed.

This wasn't precisely true but his present emotions were far too complex to explain.

I have no idea how long the war will keep us apart but it may be a long time.

This suddenly came to Arthur as a certainty.

And we are both young, still learning about so much in this troubled world. Sadly, we cannot help each other grow in understanding. Rather than rely on the past to hold us together, I would like us to meet whenever that time comes, not as lovers nor as strangers but as people who have loved each other and may love again.
How portentous I sound! But it is hard not to become serious in a place like this. What I dread most is a falseness growing

418

in our love which neither of us dare admit for fear of hurting
the other. Oh, my dear friend – for I will never relinquish that
claim – please still think of me lovingly. There are those who
would consider me mad to write such a letter but I believe you will
understand.

Arthur laid down his pencil. His head and face were burning.
He put up his hand to the beard he'd grown during his depression.
It prickled with heat and sweat. Yet he had an airy, light-headed
feeling. The letter had been unplanned but it seemed to have freed
him of a burden which previously he had assumed a comfort. Already he felt nostalgic for those months at war when Sylvia had
been his shining moon, his gentle inspiration. Everything was
different now. His needs were different.

He did not consider what effect the letter might have on Sylvia.
That was beyond him. He stood slowly and went to a tap in the
corner of the yard. He watched brackish water trickle out along
with several crumpled insects, and smeared it over his face. The
smell of drains from the town beyond the walls floated over on
the dusty air. He picked up the pages of writing and went inside.

The torture of the Russian had quietened everyone and yet
made them restless and unable to take up the usual occupations.
When the sun had gone behind the black mass of Hara Kissar and
the streaks of scarlet had faded to the palest apricot, Arthur went
up to his bedroom which was empty of the three men who shared
it, and found his paper and pencil again.

Sylvia and Fred left the rectory together. It had been hot in the
small study and both of them were flushed. Fred's heightened
colour made the brilliance of his eyes even more startling. Sylvia
looked away uncomfortably.

'Is that *The Times*?' Fred indicated a paper sticking out from the
basket in which Sylvia carried her books. Quite soon he'd decided
Sylvia was too tall and thin to be attractive as a woman which
made him relaxed in her presence. Her short hair, too, put him off,
and her mournful lack of vitality. What he liked was the comments
she made which showed a more thoughtful grasp compared to his
own quick, intuitive reactions.

'I haven't read it yet.' They were walking side by side. Above them on this first day of July, the sky was a radiant blue. Beside them a crowd of bees and butterflies danced over the marigolds and lavender. Now and again a bird swept by, on the way to hedge or tree.

'They say there's something big going on across the Channel. But you won't read any truth in the paper.'

They left the rectory garden, passing Fred's shed, at which Sylvia averted her eyes, although not before she'd seen a shirt drying on its roof. They entered Tollorum's grounds. Fred had elected to take in hand the walled vegetable garden which had become overgrown and almost derelict with only one lad to tend it. Fred said everything had gone in too late but soon he'd be picking beans and peas and in another week or so he'd be pulling carrots and potatoes.

Enjoying the sunshine, Sylvia followed him idly through the gate in the walls. 'Do you mind?' she asked as she settled herself on a bench beside a bed of asparagus gone to seed and rising in a high froth.

Fred didn't answer but went to a shed, reappearing with a hoe which he took off to the far end of the garden. He became a small figure bent over a row of green shoots. There was not the slightest breeze where Sylvia sat and the stillness, apart from the fluttering cabbage whites which were in great profusion, and a faint constant singing of insects gave the atmosphere a dreamlike quality. Random thoughts floated in and out of her mind: her grandmother had rung this morning for Gussie; Gussie and her baby and the baby's nurse were spending the summer at Tollorum. Apparently, Grandmama could hear the guns from France in their house in Kent. She had told Gussie, 'Your dear husband will be winning more glory for himself,' and Gussie had repeated it proudly, not thinking of Arthur's circumstances. There would be more patients for them, although they usually received only the lightest wounded or the recuperating. Sylvia thought these men inhabited a closed world of their own, reliving where they had come from and knowing they must go back there. The look in their eyes made her stay away from them as much as possible. Gussie felt quite differently and already had several friends, one from Reggie's regiment.

Sylvia was attracted by a movement and saw that Fred was standing upright and staring in her direction. It was difficult to believe that their joint tutorials were supposed to be saving him from dissolution and damnation. One morning he'd appeared looking very strange, it was true, and he'd smelled unpleasant. But usually he was sharp in his understanding and remembering, particularly with the Greek language which she found hard. If he'd been anyone else she'd have thought him cleverer than her. Yet he was just passing time while he decided a way to earn his living with one arm while she was working her way towards Oxford, although that now seemed an unlikely ambition. But then her whole life – and not just hers – had been unlikely ever since war was declared nearly two years ago.

'Did I say I met Lieutenant Lamb out there?'

She must have closed her eyes because Chaffey stood quite close in front of her.

'Captain Lamb,' she said, flustered.

'*Captain* Lamb. Is that so?'

'He was promoted but he never fought as a captain.'

Fred resumed. 'He saved my bacon more than once. One time he picked me up from no man's land. A good soldier and officer.'

'He was a scholar.' Why was she contradicting Chaffey like this? Was it because she had been thinking of him and now he stood quite close and his sleeves were rolled and she could smell his sweat? But she knew that men sweated. Perhaps it was because she could see the scarred pink tip of his missing arm.

'I saw him nearly killed once. A boulder rolled down as we climbed a cliff.'

'Did you save his life as he saved yours?' Sylvia flapped at a fly to hide her sudden intensity.

'Lady Luck did that with no help from me. It bounced right over his head. Probably kept bouncing till it came to rest on the bottom of the Aegean. It stuck with me. Death coming out of the sky.'

'But it didn't come.'

'You can never know. That's the point. It's in the Bible. "Watch therefore for you know neither the time nor the hour." More true in war. That boulder should have killed him but it didn't. I've seen officers who thought they were safe if they stayed in their bunker and then the whole lot goes up in some freak shell. Trouble was, I forgot the lesson. I'd been safe for so long. Then I got this.' He waggled his stump in a way Sylvia suddenly found obscene. She blushed violently, little knowing that Fred spoke to her more as he might a mate than a young woman.

He took a step back. 'Sorry. Just wanted to tell you that the lieutenant, the captain, was a good soldier.'

'*Is*,' said Sylvia. 'But thank you.' She opened *The Times*, before looking up again. 'They can hear the big guns in Kent.'

Fred nodded as if he knew this already and walked away.

Sylvia turned her eyes firmly on to the paper. START OF A GREAT ATTACK, she read. FIERCE BATTLES IN THE SOMME, A 25-MILE FRONT, STRONG GERMAN POSTS TAKEN, 9,500 PRISONERS. Then in small print, WAR: SECOND YEAR: 335th DAY. She thought that her father had been killed and Arthur captured on the 17th day of the second year. She noted a few other headlines: A FAIR BATTLEGROUND and EVERYTHING HAS GONE WELL. That made her read a little further:

> Long awaited news of a great British offensive reached London on Saturday morning in a terse report from Headquarters. An attack had been launched north of the River Somme at 7.30 that morning; British troops had broken into the German forward system of defences on a front of 16 miles, and a French attack on our right was proceeding equally satisfactorily.

As she finished this first paragraph, she heard Gussie's confident cry from the direction of the house. 'Syl-vi-a!'

For a moment everything felt normal. 'I'm in the wa-alled garden,' she called back. But then she thought that Reggie was part of this new big push and hastily stuffed *The Times* under the bench.

Gussie appeared, pushing a large pram energetically. She looked impossibly pretty, wearing a white dress and a straw hat. No mourning rules for her.

'Where's Nurse?' asked Sylvia, after peering admiringly at the sleeping baby.

'Poor dear, she's just heard her youngest brother is killed. Not in any big show either. She says he was her mother's favourite so I told her to take some time off and write to her mama.'

'Perhaps she should go home,' said Sylvia doubtfully.

Gussy looked shocked. 'If everyone went home when they lost a brother or father, there'd be no work done at all. We have to *carry on*, you know. It's not just the fighting man that has a duty. Anyway, Nurse has four sisters.' Gussie sat down and took Sylvia's hand. 'I don't mean to sound hard but the war demands sacrifices from everyone. I have to live knowing that dearest Reggie is quite likely not to come back one of these days, particularly now with this great attack Grandmama can hear. I have to be strong for Artemis.'

'Yes, you do and you are.' Sylvia tried to sound warm and approving. She suspected that Gussie would have read *The Times* with equanimity, proud that her husband was part of such a grand affair. She, after all, had not seen the horrific wounds that shrapnel caused, tearing skin and bones, eyes and entrails. Sylvia had been frightened of nursing in Camberwell and filled with zeal in Cairo. Now she wondered if she could do it again. Hilda had always said she thought too much.

'I came to tell you it's lunchtime,' said Gussie. She screwed up her eyes because the sun had come round and shone in their faces. 'Is that Chaffey?'

'Yes,' said Sylvia, looking too.

'It must be strange having lessons with a man like that. I think Mr Gisburne is a little eccentric. He hardly lectured me at all when I told him I was going to have a baby.'

'He is very tolerant for a parson,' agreed Sylvia. She pondered a little. 'Perhaps he is trying to be a true Christian. Hate the sin and love the sinner.'

'I never felt much of a sinner. Just cross to begin with and afraid.' Gussie waved in the direction of Fred. 'He doesn't look much like one either.'

'Apparently his soul was in danger. Still is, I believe. He goes into Weymouth. He's awfully clever, though. Quick. Much quicker than me.'

'A dog can be quick.' Gussie stood up and peered into the pram. 'Don't you think she's the most beautiful baby in the whole world?'

'Definitely,' said Sylvia, smiling.

*

Arthur, lying awake on his string bed, leant over, found matches and lit a candle. He pulled paper from under the bed and began to write. It wasn't easy because he wore gloves but he persevered. He knew the story by heart:

Then Hermes went searching for King Odysseus but he did not find him in the cave which was his home while held captive by the goddess Calypso. Instead he was sitting disconsolate on the shore, his accustomed place, tormenting himself with tears and sighs and heartache and looking across the barren sea with streaming eyes.

Calypso saw this and decided to be merciful. She smiled at him. 'My unhappy friend, as far as I'm concerned, there is no need for you to prolong your miseries or waste any more of your life on this island.' She stroked his hand gently, 'For I, after all, have some sense of what is fair: my heart is not a block of iron. But it is strange that you want to leave when I am far more beautiful than Penelope, your wife, and can give you immortality. Nor can you imagine how much you must endure before you reach your homeland.'

Odysseus retorted without hesitation, his eyes bright, 'It is my never failing wish to return home. What if the gods above do wreck me on the wine-dark sea? My heart is steeled to suffering, for I have had many bitter and shattering experiences of war and on the stormy seas. So let any new disaster come. It is only one more.'

This narrative, first written 2,700 years ago, had a soothing effect on Arthur. Unlike his story with Sylvia, or even *The Mill on the Floss*, it did not ask for his involvement. He blew out the candle, rolled over and went to sleep.

Thirty

After the two sisters had walked away, one pink and buxom, the other tall and straight, Fred went over to the bench, retrieved *The Times*, and sat down.

He was going down to Weymouth later and he wanted to be up to date with the war news. He liked to instruct Robbie about the progress or lack of progress of the war. Unlike Sylvia, he read the various reports thoroughly, noting the distances and terrain, checking the names out on the map provided. It was so much simpler than Gallipoli, he decided: no sea, no proper hills, no deep gullies. It would be just a slogging match, he guessed, men getting out of trenches and running forward, forward and back, by day and by night, day after day. Even *The Times* hinted it wouldn't be a quick battle and the price would be high.

Fred left the paper and went down to the farm to pick up Gallipoli, the horse. Even such a brute recognised him now, nudging his ungainly head for the bread Fred brought. The perfect sky had clouded as they set off; banks of grey clouds tinged with purple rolled in. Rain-bearing, thought Fred and his mind went back to the storms of rain he'd known on Gallipoli. Rain had no terrors for him.

From the hill above Weymouth he could see the thick cloud beating its way along the dark sea. The rain hadn't reached him yet and for a few seconds he was lit by a hard shaft of sun. Then he saw something else: columns of men were leaving the rows of wooden huts and moving in the direction of the town. From so far away, they looked like ants, purposeful and unstoppable. Fred knew at once what was happening and kicked Gallipoli's solid sides until they were cantering down the slope.

As he clung to the horse's mane, Fred thought of the time he'd gone to war, the raucous jokes covering anxiety about the unknown, the excitement at leaving behind their families, many for the first time, the thrill of finding out they were going to sea and to a place far beyond their wildest imaginings. They were young, a fair few younger than they said, and it was all a great adventure. Training was over – thanks be, they agreed – and now they could get stuck into being real soldiers. They'd show the NCO bullies what they were effing made of. They were men all of a sudden, not boys.

Those Anzacs down there would have felt just the same, whatever distant town or station they started off from. But now it was different: they'd been through Gallipoli, they'd been wounded, they'd seen death,. they'd *heard* men dying, whimpering for a stretcher only a few yards into no man's land. They'd watched men caught in barbed wire where no help could reach them and their bodies disintegrated so fast that only their clothes were left like washing on a line. They *knew* about war. But there they marched below him: no questions, no answers.

Fred reached the town as the second column came in. He made his missing arm conspicuous and asked a corporal where they were headed. 'The station, mate,' he answered, peering upwards. 'That is the ugliest bleeding animal I've ever seen.'

'His name's Gallipoli. Where's the train going?'

'Want to come too? Lose your other bleeding arm? Where do you think, mate?'

'Southampton.'

'I didn't tell you. And don't ask me why we're not going from Weymouth.'

As they spoke, the men passed by. A crowd was gathering, some waving flags, some with posies of flowers, daisies, poppies and cornflowers.

'The Union Jack,' said Fred. 'Don't they know you're Australians?'

'What do I want with flowers,' grumbled the corporal, adding, 'We're part of the Empire, aren't we?'

'White for peace, blue for the sky, red for blood,' murmured Fred.

The rain came down, a deluge bouncing on the dusty road. The crowd, except for a valiant few, splintered and disappeared, Gallipoli snorted irritably, stamping his giant feet. But the men marched on, the corporal going with them, a tall, broad-shouldered man, his slouch hat, off which the waters sluiced, tipped at an angle. Fred followed them. He had a desperate longing to be part of this band of men, despite everything, because of everything.

Gallipoli became almost unmanageable, half rearing and threatening to knock out Fred's teeth with his heaving head. Fred spotted a strong lad, about fifteen or sixteen, watching the men longingly. The rain plastered down his hair.

'Hold this horse and I'll give you a sixpence.' He pressed the money on him. 'And another to come.'

'Hey, mister,' protested the boy. Gallipoli, disobliging as ever, dumped balls of dung at his feet.

Fred went, following the soldiers, marching now along the front. Rain smashed the waves flat, turning the sea into a silver sheet. The station was only one hundred yards from the front, built when royalty came to take the air. It was dark inside, the crowds of big khaki-clad men with their heavy packs, although no guns yet, filling every space. Steam rose from their wet clothes and from two trains ready to leave. Men were already aboard and here the well-wishers had appeared again, ruddy-faced and cheerful, giving good-luck slaps or kisses.

Fred found Robbie wielding a pack on either shoulder. 'Taking the family silver?'

Robbie showed no surprise at Fred's arrival. 'Lou's, isn't it.' He indicated a much smaller man at his side. 'Weak as a kitten. Fooled the medical board.'

'How can he fight?'

'He can walk. Can't you, Lou? Didn't want to be left behind.' Robbie prepared to go.

Fred thought, you can't fool the medical board with an arm gone, even if the ability to walk qualified you for death by machine gun. He couldn't understand how he could both want to go with them and be disgusted and angry at what they had to face. It crossed his mind to get on the train and go to Southampton.

'Put your stump to good use then,' said Robbie, winking lewdly over his shoulder.

Elbowing men out of his way both with his good arm and his stump, Fred left the station. He turned away from the sea and

427

walked quickly to the King's Arms, the first pub Robbie and he always visited. He didn't miss him there; it was the ale he came for, the sighing sense of relaxation as he poured glass after glass down his throat. When he went outside to take a piss, the sky had cleared to a pale lemon colour. He moved on to the next pub without having noticed who was in the first or even who had served him.

The second pub, the Rising Sun, was full and noisy but it made no difference to Fred. As there was no table free, he stood at the bar and tipped down the ale. One or two regulars, mostly old men, tried to talk to him or buy him a drink but his soldier's pension gave him enough to buy his own. He ignored them. The fog of pipe and cigarette smoke – he never smoked now – drove him out for air. He stayed, leaning against the red brick wall for a long time, until all colour had drained out of the sky. He thought that the Anzacs would be at Southampton now.

He skipped the third pub because he'd drunk enough already and went to the fourth, the Tippling Philosopher, where Robbie and he usually found their ladies. His regular now was called Pansy Pethermen, her eyes as pretty as the flower. Pethermen was her married name and her husband was at the front. 'We'd only been joined for five days,' she'd told Fred when they first met, 'so I don't feel very married. Besides, I sometimes think he just wanted a body to look after his poor old ma.' Old Mrs Pethermen was deaf and lived in the front room of a small cottage up a lane behind the town. She didn't appear to mind the four of them (Robbie's was a widow called Susan Flower) using the top floor. Once she made them a cup of tea. 'You're nicer than *he*,' meaning her son, 'ever was.' Since all Fred ever did was call out, 'Good evening, Ma' and once left her a bag of biscuits, he had a poor estimate of the man he was cuckolding.

This evening, Fred went straight up to Pansy who was standing beside Susan, both laughing, both with a cigarette in one hand and a drink in the other. 'Robbie's gone,' he said. He wanted a bit of sympathy, a wailing and gnashing of teeth – that was what women were good at, weren't they? Instead, they stared at him, eyes popping, almost aghast.

'What are you, then?' said a tall thin man, standing behind them.

428

'No one you know.' Normally quick-witted, Fred's alcoholic intake had slowed his thinking process to a standstill. Even so, he noted the man's tones were threatening. 'Pansy!' he appealed.

'Out!' bellowed a voice from the bar. 'All of you. Ladies too.'

Fred found himself propelled outside the pub, still confused about what was happening.

'It's *him*,' whispered Pansy in his ear.

'You leave the fucking bleeder alone. I'll deal with him!' menaced the tall, thin man. Big fists were raised.

'Oh, Tom. Just look at him, poor fellow,' wheedled Pansy in silvery tones. 'He's only got one arm. How could you suspect I'd go with a cripple like him, me who was courted by the whole of Weymouth and chose you?'

Unfortunately Fred's mind reactivated at the word 'cripple' and he realised only too clearly what was going on. Good sense, however remained absent. 'I know who *you* are and just watch out for this cripple!' He launched himself at the surprised man's midriff with such force that he fell to the ground, at which Fred began pummelling him with all the muscles of his strong left arm. Even whacked him over the head a few times with his stump.

Pansy and Susan shrieked piercingly and in a few seconds the pub emptied outside to watch the sport.

Meanwhile Tom Pethermen gathered his wits and began to hit back, the two men rolling over and over on the wet ground while the ladies continued to shriek. Since Tom was taller and had two hands, he soon began to get the better of Fred and the crowd quickly took sides.

'Shame on you, Tom Pethermen, hitting a soldier disabled while defending his country!' was the theme of one side.

'Go on, Tom, give the cocky bastard what's coming to him!' summed up the other. This faction, however, divided among itself, arguing whether losing a hand in war was better or worse than in a threshing accident or indeed whether losing a hand was bad at all, when compared to men with their faces smashed in or nothing left downstairs. If Pansy had wanted him, there was nothing wrong in that direction.

But Fred himself was feeling happier than he had all evening. He wasn't particularly keen on fights in general – a foolish waste of time – but bashing Pansy's husband was giving him enormous pleasure. It didn't worry him that he was getting hit too. That was a pleasure in its own way. *Thwack!* He could feel the man's ribs as he thumped in a good one.

But like all good things it had to end, and Tom, exasperated by his homecoming, picked up Fred's head in both hands and cracked it against the pub's wall. Fred slid down and lay still.

'He asked for it,' said Tom, defiantly, to the crowd. No one took him up on it. Grasping Pansy by the arm, he led her back inside.

The following morning Mr Chaffey did not appear for his lesson. Since Mr Gisburne did not refer to his absence, Sylvia said nothing either. It was a rainy morning and the two hours passed slowly. The next day the rector met her at the door to his house and led her carefully to the study. 'I have something to discuss with you.'

He stood leaning against the mantel as if in a pulpit. 'It is about Mr Chaffey.'

'Are you losing the fight for his soul?' asked Sylvia lightly. She would not submit to a sermon.

'Not just his soul, I'm afraid.' The rector joined his pale fingers. 'Our friend is very unwell.'

Sylvia stopped smiling but she felt annoyed and restless. The rector seemed to catch her mood and became less confident. All the same he ploughed on. 'The horse he rides came back without him early yesterday morning.' He looked up. 'It is extraordinary how a dull animal will always find its way to its stable.'

Sylvia refused to nod.

'This morning Chaffey was discovered in hospital in Weymouth. They are not pleased to have him. In fact they plan to discharge him tomorrow.'

'How did he become unwell?' Sylvia was curious enough to ask.

'Let us draw a veil. Suffice to say, he has an injury to his head.'

'I see,' said Sylvia, not seeing but imagining.

'The problem is, where should he recuperate?' Mr Gisburne came to his chair and sat for a moment, head bowed.

Sylvia didn't know why this whole conversation was annoying. Something about Chaffey, she suspected, but couldn't tell exactly why.

'He cannot improve his health in my potting shed. Nor will Gwen allow him in this house. Gwen is a charitable woman – the children hang on her every word in Sunday school – but she has her limits. And it transpires Chaffey is one of them.'

He's disturbing, that's why, thought Sylvia, and understood her own feelings. All she wanted was a dull calm in which she could lick her wounds. 'He is disturbing,' she said out loud.

'Ha!' responded the rector, as if it were a joke. 'Our scholar disturbing? Yes. Yes. Well, the good Lord often disturbed his followers.'

'What about the peace that passeth all understanding?' asked Sylvia in a vain effort to divert the conversation from what must assuredly lead to her own involvement.

'So I have talked to his sister,' continued the vicar, as if the last lines of conversation had not existed.

'You want him to come to the manor,' said Sylvia, giving up hope.

'He would not be looked after with the officers, of course.' The rector's face was already pink with relief. 'A small room. His sister to nurse him.'

'There's the butler's room,' said Sylvia.

'The butler's room,' exclaimed Mr Gisburne as if he'd seen a miraculous vision.

'Gussie will visit him with your granddaughter, I have no doubt,' added Sylvia with a viciousness that Gisburne chose to ignore.

'And Lady Beatrice . . . ?'

'My mother is the soul of generosity.'

'May you be rewarded in a better place.'

With this devout wish, they turned with relief to their books and for the next two hours were diverted by Tacitus's revolting descriptions of tortured Christian martyrs.

The room in which Fred recuperated was very small and, as with most butlers' quarters, lay at the command point of the kitchen, the back staircase, the door to the front of the house and the back door to outside. It was a noisy place, where pans clattered, girls whispered and doors slammed.

Lily found her brother's presence there oppressive. Her day was so busy that she would forget about him for hours at a time and then suddenly see the closed door with a weight of guilt and uncertainty. There was love, too, of course, but Lily found it difficult to deal with things or people she didn't understand and Fred seemed beyond her reach. When he had first returned and began his trips to Weymouth, she had thought him merely an adult extension of the naughty little boy she'd brought up like a mother.

She had tried to shame him into better behaviour or threaten him, until, eventually, he refused to see her. Instead, he'd moved into Mr Gisburne's potting shed. To spite her, as she thought. But then he began his lessons and caring for the vegetables. Lily still wouldn't let her children near him, but she realised he was very different from the boy who had left for the war or even the man who had written to her with his first words on paper. She had no time however, to do more than recognise the difference. But now he was in the middle of her life, made ill by a self-destructive act. Lily could not pity him so she saw that he was cared for and, after the first day, left him alone.

Fred had no wish for visitors. The head wound seemed to have encouraged all kind of ghostly visitations from Gallipoli which he would rather have stayed away. At night, in particular, he fought old battles, defending his mates who had long since died. His worst remembrance, often repeated, although before this time he had never thought of it, was shovelling the rotting and putrid Turkish and British corpses into a mass grave during the amnesty organised by Captain Prideaux. He would go to lift a bloated body and the arm or leg would come off in his hand. Then he would become aware that he was being watched and realise with horror that the soldier's eyes were wide open and staring at him and that he was alive, even though his whole body had turned to mush.

One morning there was a knock at the door. Fred said nothing but Sylvia came in anyway. Her nervous expression softened him.

'I've brought you some books.' There was no chair in the room so she remained standing. She seemed to be avoiding looking at him. 'What a lot of cobwebs!' she exclaimed.

Fred thought, with the things in his head, what would he mind about a few spiders. 'Spiders are clean,' he said, and it was the first time he'd spoken for days (apart from in his sleep when he wasn't aware of it).

'Are they? I bet you know what they are in Latin and Greek.

That's what I've brought you, Latin and Greek grammars because you find them so easy and you wouldn't want to tax your brain.' Sylvia flushed, with the sort of pink stain that carries on down the neck.

Fred thought the colour improved her appearance. 'Thank you,' he said.

'Aren't you lonely?' asked Sylvia, then gulped.

Fred nearly smiled. It was obvious that it had struck her that a man who chose to live in a potting shed was not likely to suffer from loneliness. 'No,' he said. 'It's good of you to have me at the manor. I'll be better soon.'

'I expect so.' Sylvia went to the door, before half turning. 'My sister's longing to visit you. She loves succouring the sick. Up to now I've kept her away.'

'Miss Augusta has a good deal of vitality,' said Fred seriously.

'That's what I thought,' said Sylvia, half out of the room before realising she was still holding the books. 'How stupid!' She came back and carefully placed them on the table by Fred's bed. He was only wearing a vest but she made a point of not averting her eyes from his exposed stump.

'I'd rather *you* visited me,' said Fred, surprising himself as much as Sylvia.

She fiddled with his water glass. The flush bloomed again. 'I will then. Now and again. Keep you up to date with the wicked happening of the fifth century BC.'

'That's what I thought,' agreed Fred, although he hadn't been thinking that at all. He'd just suddenly wanted her to come back, to bend over him gracefully, smelling of lavender.

Thirty-One

In March 1917, Beatrice received a telephone call from her mother:

'My dear, did you know that the Commission of Inquiry into the Dardanelles set up by dear old Asquith has finally been published? Of course it's typically absurd to call it the Dardanelles when once they'd lost a few battleships, they never got anywhere near the straits. Gallipoli is where the battle was fought and where poor Bingo met his fate.'

Beatrice, sitting in her husband's study, calmly waited for her mother to continue. Once she had accepted Bingo's death, the worst agony gradually passed. He was always present in her thoughts, however, because her aim was to please him in ways she hadn't needed to when he was alive. Then she had only needed his love.

'Is there anything new in it, Mama?'

'If you consider old men defending their positions new. Of course I haven't read it for myself but that wicked new young cripple Rigby-Smith at the War Office has given me a good idea. Apparently Godley – you know that Lieutenant general who commanded the Australians – sent his report to dear beleaguered Hamilton with a note advising the general that he'd tried to say as little as possible. You can see his point. After all, Asquith only commissioned the inquiry as a sop to public disquiet, and he's not even prime minister any more. When you consider those endless months of slaughter at the Somme last year and the war no nearer ending, it's scarcely surprising that no one cares to face the truth about Gallipoli. Men are like that. Politicians doubly so. They live in the present and damn the consequences. Even that dear rascal Winston, so Rigby-Smith tells me, comes out of it without real criticism.'

At this Beatrice's calm began to fray. 'I have asked you not to talk of that man.'

'But it's so unreasonable of you, my dear,' began Lady Deverill before thinking better of it.

Beatrice wondered that her mother, now aged seventy-five, still had such an appetite for political gossip. Surely she was affected by the ever rising death toll – with the young men who had been schoolboys when the war started, now going to the slaughter. Of course she wasn't in disagreement with most of what her mother said, it was the *tone* that upset her, the worldly *cynicism*. Bingo had never been like that. He couldn't have fought so heroically if he had.

'How is my dearest Gussie?' asked Lady Deverill, changing the subject with a new warm note in her voice.

Gussie was pregnant again. Reggie had fought all through the Battle of the Somme with no injury worse than a sprained ankle. This had been caused in December when he'd jumped off the train while it was still moving into Waterloo Station. 'I couldn't wait one more moment to clasp Gussie in my arms,' he'd explained later.

'She's very well,' sighed Beatrice, 'although I think she'll return to London very soon. She's always restless in the country.'

'It's her nature,' agreed Lady Deverill, with satisfaction. 'This war is very hard for young wives. Unlike the Boer war, their husbands are only over the Channel. Quite able to drop home for leave. *Most* unsettling. And they know more of what's going on. No chance of out of sight out of mind.'

Beatrice thought that the remnants of the Colonel's regiment had gone on to Mesopotamia. She said, 'This is a world war, Mama.' She thought it had made things no better for her that her husband had died so far away. How she would have loved one last look at him, one embrace, before he had been killed! Most soldiers who'd fought on Gallipoli were permitted only a couple of weeks on Lemnos or Imbros before being spread round the globe. There was never a chance of them coming back to England or Scotland or Australia or wherever their home was before re-entering the war. Beatrice's work helping the wives of officers whose place of death or disappearance was unknown had made her painfully aware of the sprawl of the army.

As Beatrice thought that the war enveloped absolutely everything, her mother continued to talk about Gussie. 'It is a pity, one must admit, she has saddled herself with a parson's son, but we can never know what the future holds, although the dear boy seems to survive quite miraculously. But Gussie's looks and her animation will take her anywhere. The minute this war is over I shall make sure that she meets all the right people...'

Beatrice stopped listening. It was this kind of talk which had ensured her brother had remained a bachelor and she had chosen dearest Bingo. The oldest son of a country family with a large estate would have seemed quite a catch to most people. But to her mother, his mundane army career, steady nature and lack of a title made him beyond the pale. I married him for love, thought Beatrice and a warm glow spread round her heart. Not even his death could take that away from her. This made her think of Sylvia.

'Sylvia will be taking her Oxford examination very soon,' she said with a brightness she did not feel. Sylvia was beyond her understanding, she'd decided.

'Ah, Sylvia,' said the countess in the tones of someone hearing about a war casualty.

Beatrice wondered why she had introduced the subject. 'Today she's in London with Adeline, the Duchess of Bedford, meeting those poor POWs from Turkey.'

But even this pandering to her mother's snobbery did not have the desired effect. 'Frankly, my dear, Gussie would be better suited to that committee,' she said waspishly. 'I've told Lady Bedford all about her.'

'Gussie is so busy with her baby, Mama,' Beatrice protested. 'Besides, you asked Sylvia at the beginning and her own fiancé is a prisoner of war in Turkey.' Beatrice looked at her watch. She'd never known her mother make such a long telephone call.

'Hasn't Captain Lamb escaped yet?' said the countess.

Sylvia, with Fred at her side, arrived at the station before the rest of the committee. Fred wore quite a smart tweed suit offered him by Mr Gisburne when he began helping out at the village school – a role surprising everyone. He held *The Times* under the remains of his right arm and carried a brown leather suitcase in his left.

Earlier, when Sylvia had asked whatever the rest of the reception committee would make of him, he'd answered gravely, 'They'll think, correctly, I am your bag carrier.'

'You mean like an officer's servant?'.

'Precisely.'

'But that's not true.'

'No.'

Over the months and without understanding how it had happened, Sylvia began to depend on Fred – not to be there all the time; his mysterious absences continued – but to be part of her life. When he was there, in Mr Gisburne's study or in the garden or in the school where she had visited him once or twice, she felt more present herself. Vaguely, she had decided that he released her from expected behaviour. Not that she was anything except drearily conventional but at least in her thoughts she felt free, and could express them to Fred, as she sometimes called him, although he always called her Miss Fitzpaine. Now and again she wondered if he might be mocking her.

Sylvia's pride in her brain power had increased over the last year as she worked hard and understood more, but her confidence in her manner and appearance was lower than ever. She knew she was too thin and that her bobbed hair made her look spinsterish, instead of gay and independent as it had originally. She took no interest in her clothes which were of dull colours and shapeless, and quite often wore small round glasses for which she had no real need but which gave her a sense of protection.

Her only social life came from the Central Prisoners of War Committee and its linked publication, named, with little inspiration, *The British Prisoner of War*. There were copies of it in the case carried by Fred which she was going to distribute to the returning soldiers. Cards printed with *The King's Message of Welcome* were also inside the case. They would be distributed by the Dowager Duchess of Bedford and Lord Sandwich.

'How many are there?' Fred had put down the suitcase and stood nonchalantly looking at her. It was a bright morning and the sun streamed down on to him through the glass roof.

'Forty-nine.' She had never got used to Fred's good looks – even more striking now he was well-fed and healthy. He seemed to have grown taller too. 'Fourteen stretcher cases,' she added.

As she spoke, a procession of ambulances drove on to the station forecourt.

'I'll get us cups of tea,' said Fred.

Sylvia watched him as he walked over to the canteen being set up by other members of the committee. She didn't know why he came up with her when she went to London, although she wanted to believe he liked her company as she did his. He usually stayed for a while before disappearing off on his own, returning to Tollorum on some train much later than hers, or so she assumed. He never gave her any explanation for his behaviour. Sometimes he seemed as much a mystery as when she'd read to him the year before during his recuperation at the manor. She'd enjoyed sitting there quietly with his blue eyes fixed on her face. Sometimes she felt as close to him as anyone.

'Guess what!' Fred came back to her quickly without the tea. 'Miss Wyke told me.'

'The train's been delayed by five hours.' Sylvia was surprised by his agitated expression. Normally he controlled his emotions.

'She heard it from her father who's in the government or something. Maybe it's in *The Times*.'

'What?' asked Sylvia, watching as Fred pulled open the paper.

'The Commission of Inquiry into the Dardanelles, as they like to call Gallipoli.'

'Are you expecting to learn something from it?' asked Sylvia.

'Not bloody likely.'

'Then why are you so excited?' He wore the same eager determined look on his face when he was questioning an interpretation at one of their shared tutorials. Then she admired it; now it scared her.

'One can hope. As Euripides said, "No one who lives in error is free." '

Sylvia flinched. She knew that quotation. It was one used fairly often by Arthur before he'd gone away. Once or twice before, Fred had come up with classical quotations that echoed from the past and it always unsettled her.

Fred refolded the paper in disgust and put it on top of the suitcase. 'Nothing!' Sylvia could see he was preparing to leave.

'Nothing *yet*,' she corrected him. 'Aren't you going to wait to see the men arrive?'

'Not in the mood. Poor blighters. What are they coming back to?'

'You might meet someone you served with,' persisted Sylvia – foolishly, she knew.

'Among three or four hundred thousand on Gallipoli. Anyway, everyone I knew was killed.'

'You knew Captain Lamb,' said Sylvia. 'He's not dead.' But he might as well be, she added to herself with a sharp pang. Why was she trying to keep Fred at her side? She had become acutely aware of his moods and knew that bitter anger, usually more repressed than on this occasion, preceded long absence. Perhaps she was trying to save him from himself.

'Here come your friends,' he said, moving away as a large black car drove beside the ambulances and parked in front of them. Quite a crowd of civilians and soldiers were arriving now, friends and relatives of the prisoners or just the curious. With the sun and the flags carried by many of them, the scene had a cheerful festive air. Sylvia was glad; the men deserved that.

'Miss Fitzpaine!' The boot of the car had been opened to reveal fifty bunches of daffodils.

'Coming!' Picking up the suitcase, Sylvia went over to help Mrs. Alexander, a stalwart lady who had lost her two sons to the war. She wondered for a moment what she would feel if Arthur had been one of the returning prisoners. It would mean he was sick or injured, of course, so it wouldn't be the best kind of homecoming.

'We should divide them into ten groups of five bunches each,' said Mrs Alexander.

They both looked up at the sound of an approaching steam engine. Sylvia felt herself flush with the thrill of it. She supposed that the thrill of it would have carried her through if Arthur had been on the train. She knew he wasn't because she'd seen the list of names. Besides, there was that letter he'd written to her from his camp. Cradling five bunches of daffodils, Sylvia went quickly to the barrier. A group of other women followed. The ambulances inched closer. An enormous sense of joyous anticipation made everyone laugh and cheer even before the train stopped. Some women were crying, mopping their tears, then waving hand-kerchiefs. Children escaped their mothers and ran about shriek-ing. Even the solemn procession of the Duchess of Bedford and

Lord Sandwich, the King's message now in their hands, made no impression on their celebrations.

Sylvia, standing just behind them, knew that the men had taken nearly a year to cross Europe, in many different trains, stopping at neutral countries, burying some men. Again, she thought about Arthur, wondering if this dark, smoky train made some sort of link between them.

A first door opened. Suddenly, apart from the engine which was still puffing out smoke every few seconds, there was silence. A leg, then a crutch appeared. Without waiting for the whole man, the crowd burst into cheers and frantic flag-waving.

Daffodils in hand, Sylvia went forward smiling.

Fred walked up Piccadilly towards Soho. But then, changing his mind, turned right down the Haymarket towards Trafalgar Square. It was a hot day and the rector's tweed suit was far too heavy. He took the jacket off and hung it over his right shoulder. He knew he should buy himself clothes; he had the money since he'd supplemented his army pension by working at the village school and also was more formally employed in the Tollorum garden. But then there were a lot of things he should do, starting by moving out of his shed. Fred smiled and swung his coat. How his living like a tramp annoyed Lil! Recently he'd extended the shed, adding a nice lean-to with a chimney and a gas ring for his kitchen. He loved his wooden home, the creatures that burrowed their way through the earth floor, the creatures that flew round his head, even the bat in the roof, the hedgehog that had curled up in a corner last winter. A veritable St Francis was he! That is until he took the Colonel's gun (lent by Miss Fitzpaine) and killed the pigeons and rooks and squirrels and rabbits. It's amazing what you can do with one and a half arms if your eye's true, Fred thought. The army had missed a trick there. They could have a whole regiment of cripples and knocked the Bosch for six without losing one able-bodied man.

Fred stopped walking, pushed his cap back on his head, and looked up at Nelson's column. Nelson had only one arm, didn't he, and an eye short as well, a great English hero, no less. It was too hot, that was the trouble. Not Gallipoli hot – no over-fed flies, no reek of death – but still too hot.

He was no longer sure why he travelled up on these trips to London with Miss Sylvia Fitzpaine. By now she'd be at a tea at Brown's Hotel for relatives of the officers held captive at Afion Kira Hissar. The first few times he'd come up he had known the reason why: to find a woman – which wasn't hard. They were willing which was what they were paid to be. But, in different ways, they'd annoyed him – particularly about his stump. Either they were over-sympathetic, wanting to know how it happened, or they barely hid their distaste, or they made lewd jokes, which was better than the others. The girls were what it was all about after all and the reason he didn't come back on the same train as Miss Fitzpaine.

But today, for example, he just couldn't be bothered. Those Weymouth girls had been the thing but he hadn't been welcome there after his fight and the other alternative, Dorchester, was too close to home. He had managed to track down Joe Dingle's family, thinking there might be a future there, but Joe, he eventually discovered, had been killed or died anyway, and his girlfriend, Margie, showed no wish to see him.

His most immediate need was a cup of tea and there, the other side of Trafalgar Square, was a Lyons Corner House. Who said there wasn't a God?

Mr Gisburne occasionally tried to broach the subject. Last time was when he was offering him the job at the Tollorum school. Surprised, Fred had objected, 'But I've got no certificates.'

'But you do believe in God.'

' "They who wait for the Lord shall restore their strength; they shall mount up like eagles . . ." ' Fred had quoted.

They had been sitting in the shed on a warm spring evening and Gisburne had given a sudden bleat and a little upward spring at Fred's words. 'We must have a thorough theological discussion.'

Sometimes Fred suspected the rector of having a taste for the sherry. Nevertheless he was a guest in his shed so he merely answered, 'I wouldn't trouble God with what I think.'

The Lyons Corner House was very big and half empty. Fred chose a table in a dim corner and ordered tea, bread and jam. He was waited on by an old chap whose shaking hands scarcely kept a grip on the tray. Fred breathed with relief when it finally made a rattling landing on the table. The whole world, he thought, is inhabited by old men, women and cripples. And soldiers, he added to himself as he noticed a fair young man in uniform sitting alone on the other side of the room.

Sometimes the train he and Miss Fitzpaine took was jam-packed with soldiers. On these occasions, she didn't join him, proceeding instead to the first class carriages. It was strange, he supposed, that she ever came to third class, but her clothes and demeanour were so modest as not to look out of place. He wondered that she didn't make more of herself. Lily was better dressed than she was.

When they sat together and if they were alone, they talked about all kinds of things. It was different to being at Tollorum, or the rectory, as if being on neutral ground they could be freer. Not no man's land, mind you, where the air throbbed with the terrified hearts of men desperate to evade death. Fred wondered whether the images of war would ever leave him. He still remembered fearfully the nights when he'd stayed at Tollorum Manor. Perhaps the Colonel's ghost had been haunting him. Sylvia's presence calmed him then and calmed him now.

Today on the train, Sylvia (he slipped into her name) had said to him, 'There are no men in our house.'

She was clearly not thinking of the recovering officers so he'd said, 'When Captain Lamb comes back, there'll be a man.'

Her face had gone rigid so that at first he thought she was shocked by the personal nature of the remark but then she recovered, saying in distant tones, 'Captain Lamb won't want to live at Tollorum. He plans to work at his uncle's bank.' Then she had faltered. 'Although he may be very much changed.' She had paused again. 'Following one very strange letter, I haven't heard from him for five weeks.' Her big eyes had looked as appealing as a child's and Fred felt sorry for her. His first impression that she didn't want Lamb at Tollorum was forgotten.

'You can't rely on the post.' Fred couldn't help thinking that there were fates worse for a woman than knowing her man is no longer risking death on a daily basis. Everybody's lives were altered for the worse by the war. The soldier opposite him, for example, had he killed already? Was he about to learn how to? Something about the steady way he sat told Fred it was the latter. But the question preoccupied him until he suddenly stood up and went over to him.

'Mind if I join you?'

The soldier, who had mild brown eyes and well-brushed short hair, did not seem too worried. He indicated the other chair. 'Be my guest.'

Fred went back and brought his cup of tea with him. The soldier's voice was educated and he was older than he'd first thought, perhaps as much as thirty.

'You're out of it now, I suppose.' He glanced at Fred's arm.

'And you're just starting?'

'I was in an exempted profession but then my number came up.'

'Funny that. Me younger and been through it and you, older and just starting.'

'Where did you fight?'

Fred realised that was it, why he'd come over, he wanted to talk about Gallipoli and not only to the vermin in the shed. 'Gallipoli. From first day to last.'

The soldier leaned forward as if truly interested. 'That finished over a year ago, didn't it?'

'Not for me it didn't.'

'No. I suppose not. It was Winston Churchill's show, wasn't it?'

'He had the bright idea. But there were plenty of others who went along.'

'I heard a funny story about that. At the very beginning when Churchill was pushing the Dardanelles to the War Council, one of the people he had to carry with him was Lord Fisher, the seventy-three-year-old First Sea Lord. He was convinced that Churchill, forty years younger, was a *genius*! Kept telling everyone so. But he also believed that trying to force the straits was a dreadful idea. Said privately that you'd need surprise and two hundred thousand soldiers for the whole campaign to succeed. Trouble was he couldn't stand up to Churchill – not in his presence, owing to his aforesaid "genius" and charisma. So – this is the funny bit – he did a runner and hid in the Charing Cross Hotel. Nobody could find him for ages.'

'And they went ahead with the campaign,' said Fred, not smiling.

'I'm afraid so. Fisher resigned officially in the end.' The soldier picked up his teacup.

Fred debated whether he wanted to go on with the conversation before deciding he did. 'Were you in politics?'

'I was a teacher. Then I got involved with something called the WEA – Workers' Educational Association. Maybe you've heard of it.'

'I live in the country.'

'Oh, we go all over the place. Helping men and women who were never given the chance of an education.'

As he explained further about a system in which people, ordinary working people, could sign up for three year courses in all kinds of subjects and entirely free, Fred thought how strange it was that he was doing exactly that same kind of thing with Mr Gisburne. He wasn't planning to tell that to a stranger, even if he did feel drawn to him.

'I'm afraid once I get going on the WEA, I'm unstoppable,' apologised the soldier.

'That's all right,' said Fred.

'It's a bit of a wrench leaving the country, you see. We're supposed to leave tomorrow, but I'm scared stiff it'll be pulled back to tonight.'

'Why is that?' asked Fred, curious at this calm man's sudden display of nerves.

'There's a big meeting at the Central Hall, Westminster. I've been working for ages on a project suggesting the school leaving age is raised to fifteen. I really want to know if the conference accepts it. That's where I'm going now. In my last hours of leave. Then I have to check in.' He looked at his watch. 'In fact I'd better be off now.'

'Care for a companion?' Fred felt a fool as he spoke but the soldier smiled at him.

'Of course. We love new recruits.' He held out a hand and when he was confronted by Fred's stump merely moved on to his left hand. 'I'm Colin Gledhill, Second Lieutenant Colin Gledhill.' He smiled again.

It's certainly different to looking for a tart, thought Fred, probably cheaper too. 'Fred Chaffey,' he said. 'Never made it beyond private and left school when I was eight.'

Gledhill laughed and they left the café together.

*

Sylvia recognised Mrs Twigg-Smith with the warmth felt for someone who has shared extraordinary experiences. How long ago seemed that morning when they'd arrived together off the ship at Alexandria! Arthur had been waiting on the dock for her and neither of them had recognised the other.

Mrs Twigg-Smith stood in the foyer of Brown's Hotel, waving her hand at Sylvia.

'Dear Mrs Twigg-Smith! When did you return?'

'Last year. I came home to die but, despite the best efforts of my sister with whom I live in Eastbourne, I'm still here. My experience of doctors should have taught me never to believe a word they say.'

'I'm so glad you haven't changed!' Sylvia found herself laughing in a way that was probably quite inappropriate. The POW meeting had been sad with too many good women competing, whereas Mrs Twigg-Smith linked her to a world where she'd been so *alive*, even if surrounded by desperate happenings.

'Are you so against change, dear Miss Fitzpaine? This calls for a glass of sherry.'

Following Mrs Twigg-Smith to the lounge, Sylvia noticed that she *had* changed, in appearance at least; she was thin like someone ill and bent like someone old. She still wore a veil on her hat, as if a dangerous sun might be round the corner.

Settled on two spongy chairs with sherry and biscuits at hand, Mrs Twigg-Smith began her usual interrogation. 'First, what are you doing in this elderly watering place?' She nodded briskly as Sylvia explained. 'And most of the ladies are mothers or wives?'

'They do such good work, sharing their experiences and giving helpful tips over parcels and censorship and that sort of thing. There's even a newsletter in which interesting points in the letters are printed for everyone to read. They're really wonderful people!' exclaimed Sylvia, although unable to avoid a frown.

'I see.' Mrs Twigg-Smith finished her glass of sherry and ordered another. Two round pink spots decorated her pale face. 'I expect Arthur thinks it's rotten luck being out of the war. Such a waste of time.' She looked at Sylvia questioningly.

'I suppose so.' Sylvia's voice verged on sullen.

'Of course he has the resources. I mean from what I saw of him and what you told me he is a very bookish sort of fellow. Not like either of my dear Twigg-Smiths, senior or junior; they would have *died* in a prisoner of war camp.' She paused briefly. 'Of course they died anyway outside a camp.'

Sylvia assumed she wasn't trying to make a joke. 'Actually, Arthur has broken off our engagement and since that letter, I've heard nothing for weeks.' To her horror, she burst into tears, sobbing uncontrollably. 'It's the sherry,' she gulped.

'Oh really?' Mrs Twigg-Smith surveyed her second empty glass. 'Personally, I find it a great consolation but then I *am* dying – if I'm to believe the doctors.' She patted Sylvia's hand but less in sympathy than to get her attention. 'When you've finished crying, dear, you can first tell me more, then I'll have some advice for you.'

Sylvia stopped quite quickly. Gussie had volunteered advice. When, in desperation, she'd shown her sister Arthur's letter, Gussie had been definite: 'Haven't you noticed yet how men are so noble and self-sacrificing? Arthur's written like this to save you pain. Reggie would do just the same. He doesn't mean it in his *heart*. Take no notice, Syl, that's my advice.'

Mrs Twigg-Smith sat back a little and surveyed Sylvia. 'So you are no longer engaged? Is that why you were weeping? Or is it something else? You might as well be honest with me.'

'I don't know!' began Sylvia, before seeing Mrs Twigg-Smith's beady eye. 'Don't know' would never be good enough for her. 'It started before his letter came,' she said softly. 'I began to feel that we'd just be playing at being in love. Compared to everything that was going on . . .'

'The war, you mean,' interrupted Mrs Twigg-Smith. 'Try and speak a little louder, dear. My hearing's not what it was.'

'I suppose he felt the same which is why he wrote the letter. He wrote about being friends.'

'Very sensible too. There's too much talk of love, particularly among young women. I think it's time for my advice. You must concentrate on finding your own way in life. Women have been taught to follow, which may work quite nicely for a few good ladies running their husbands' home as a price for a comfortable life. Already, though, before the war, this attitude was being questioned and now everything is speeded up.'

'I didn't know you were a suffragette!' Sylvia, who had been staring down gloomily, looked up, startled.

'Captain Lamb is not the answer to your life,' continued Mrs Twigg-Smith, ignoring Sylvia's cry. 'So what *are* you doing with your time when you're not agonising about one man whose life is so remote as to be incomprehensible and may or not be there in the future?'

'I'm studying,' said Sylvia defensively and explained about Oxford and Mr Gisburne and in the course of it Fred Chaffey's name came up. To her annoyance, she felt herself blushing.

'So who is this Mr Chaffey? Another man you're planning to follow?'

'Oh, no!' exclaimed Sylvia, before trying to explain Chaffey. In the end she compromised with, 'He comes from Tollorum village and fought as a private on Gallipoli where he lost an arm.'

The word 'private' was enough for Mrs Twigg-Smith to get the point. She said no more but rose to go. 'My best wishes to Lady Beatrice. Your father was an admirable man and a great loss. But women can be just as great and admirable when they're given the chance.'

The glow remained on Mrs Twigg-Smith's cheeks but, as they parted, Sylvia noticed once more her almost skeletal thinness and suspected they might not meet again.

Fred, cap on his lap, sat next to Colin Gledhill at the back of the Central Hall. The meeting hadn't started yet.

'I like sitting here,' said Gledhill loudly enough to rise above the noise of six or seven hundred lively voices. 'Usually I'm at the front with notes and things but from here I can really appreciate the excitement of so many people supporting our work. We've only been going fourteen years and just look at the turnout!' His eyes shone with pride and belief.

Fred took a breath. It was very hot and he could feel sweat breaking out under the rector's tweed. He looked round and saw, despite the presence of many ladies, most of the men had their jackets off. He studied their faces. They were all sorts: old, young, weather-beaten like labourers, smooth and pale like clerks. 'All this for education,' he murmured. 'And women too.'

Gledhill smiled broadly. 'So you'd leave out one half of human-kind?'

'Not me,' said Fred, thinking of Sylvia, but somehow he couldn't see her fitting in here. 'I had a mate on Gallipoli,' he said, 'Ernie Wilkes. Schoolteacher type, wanted to know everything, teach everything.'

'Helped you, did he? You'll have to get him involved. Where does he live?'

'I saw his brains spread over the ground.'

There was a pause before Gledhill said firmly, 'We mustn't let this bloody war interfere with our work.'

'What about you, then?' Fred stared bitterly at Gledhill's uniform. 'Interfering with you, isn't it?'

Gledhill's expression remained the same. 'I'm one man. There're people joining the movement all the time. People like you.'

Fred still hadn't decided what to answer when the hall became abruptly silent and the speakers came on to the stage.

Just before the chairman opened the proceedings, Gledhill leant over to Fred and whispered, 'There have to be changes, don't you see?'

Thirty-Two

'You've got very nice skin, you know, Hilda Horridge.'

Rupert and Hilda lay side by side on a wide day bed. Even behind the thick stone walls of their little house, the heat lay over them in an immense oppressive wave. Rupert wore loose cotton trousers and Hilda a sleeveless cotton shift. He was stroking her arm.

'Thank you,' said Hilda, holding up her other arm. She added in an objective tone of voice, 'They're quite brown now, I'm afraid. Sometimes I think of Birmingham and can't resist the sun.'

'Quite right and proper. Why don't you take off your dress so I can feel the skin hidden from the sun and see if it's a different texture. Blind people have very sensitive fingertips. I could feel the smallest mole.'

'Oh, Rupert!' Sometimes Hilda's love was so great that her heart felt as if it was expanding to a glowing mass. She sat up and slowly lifted off her dress. They had played this game before, although always carefully regulating themselves so that Rupert's excitement would not go too far.

'Ah,' he sighed contentedly. His fingers moved over the warm mound of her belly, her firm, strong thighs. They had been together a year on Gozo and often he thought it the happiest time of his life – perhaps the only happy time. 'I wish I could remember the Song of Solomon.'

'It's fearfully unflattering: "all thy hair is as a flock of goats, thy teeth are like a flock of sheep, thy neck is like the tower of David, thy nose is as the tower of Lebanon, thine eyes like the fish pools in Heshbou..."'

'Stop,' said Rupert, putting his hand over her mouth. 'I never knew you were a Bible-basher.' Rupert liked everything about Hilda: her generous size, her generous nature, her habit of speaking straightforwardly, her care for him. The problem about this strong liking that he did not dare to call love, was that he was beginning to worry about Hilda's future. Over the last two months, there had been several days when he had been completely incapacitated with shattering headaches worse even than when he had been first wounded. What would happen to her when he died?

'Put your hand on me,' he told Hilda.

Oh, what a loving hand! Would her touch send him to heaven? He gasped and she moved her hand away.

'No. Put it back. Ah, Hilda, I'm so well today. Open your legs. There. There. Do you know how perfect you are?'

'Rupert. Please.' Her voice so small, so scared, trembling, not at all her usual voice.

'I can roll over so quietly, so carefully. Neither of us will hardly know . . .'

There was no fan in the room because there was no electricity, only a whispering wind from the small window and the sound of two people breathing in unison.

Three Allied officers had escaped from Afion Kara Hissar: two British, one Australian. They had been hiding small amounts of supplies, food and clothing on their weekly walks into town. They needed to head off in the spring when good weather was ahead. There was nowhere to go but the sea and that meant crossing several mountain ranges. The men were strong – they'd been playing football and eating Marmite and Oxo, tinned bacon and suet pudding sent from England. But it was not clear how they'd feed themselves for weeks or even months. Nor whether there would be any boats if they did reach the sea.

Owing to the irregularity and sloppiness of the roll call, the three men's absence was not noted for two days. The rejoicing of those still in the camp, although heartfelt, was tempered by the knowledge that reprisals for the escape were certain.

Once before, several men had escaped and all the officers – British, French, Russian, Australian, New Zealand – had been locked into a disused Armenian church. It had been dark, airless, with minimal sanitation or outside space. Each man had lived and slept within a few feet of his neighbour.

The unhealthy conditions had caused Arthur's dysentery to return and he felt jealous of an officer who slept during the day and smoked opium during the night. Some men were permanently drunk. The only moments of release from these miserable surroundings came when the Russian choir sang, their magnificent bass voices telling of loves lost long ago – or so Arthur assumed. The British had played games and read books.

'It's lucky we've got rid of Maslum Bey,' Arthur remarked to Trebble. Two months earlier, the commandant had been tried and sentenced to five and a half months' imprisonment – six months would have seen his removal from the army and the authorities did not deem his behaviour bad enough for that.

'You can never predict a bloody thing with this lot,' said Trebble balefully. He was an unnerving sight. Six months ago he'd bet the war would be over by March. To show he was serious, he'd sworn not to shave while the fighting continued. Now it was June. He'd been hoping to go with the escapers but a septic toe tied him to the house.

'True enough.'

Two days passed with no reprisals, although word got out that the new commandant of the camp, in order to defend his position, had told the authorities that the escaping officers were on parole. This was quite untrue and meant that, if captured, they could be shot.

Anger, the sharp corrosive within every prisoner of war because it could have no useful outlet, made men foolish, feverish, sullen. The temperature, permanently in the eighties and nineties, intensified the smells of rotting food and other waste from the town situated close around the walls of their camp. Tempers became dangerously volatile. Many men wore nothing but shorts and boots, their naked skin peeling under the scorching sun.

Arthur put aside *Middlemarch* and turned back to the classics. It would soon be two years since his capture. Amongst the books Sylvia had sent him before he broke off their engagement was Ovid's collection of poems, *Ars amatoria*, borrowed, as she'd explained, from Mr Gisburne's bookshelves. Perhaps the opening lines were a reproach:

Siquis in hoc artem populo non novit amandi
Hoc legat et lecto carmine, doctus amet

Should anyone here not know the art of love,
Read this and learn by reading how to love.

For some reason, he had never read this famous work before and studied the many verses of advice with surprise. Ovid spoke so simply and directly that Arthur felt encouraged to try his hand at writing some poetry in Latin. He still practised the code in letters to his uncle when there was information to pass on, but writing poetry used another part of his brain. On hot evenings, he could spend hours over the choice of the right Latin word.

A week passed since the escape had become known and the prisoners began to relax. Then an unexpected roll call was announced to be held at mid-day. Conscious of their dignity, the officers put on their uniforms or what remained of them. The commandant kept them standing on the baked-hard ground for two hours and then delivered a long ranting speech, translated now and again into French. Up till then, he had seemed a reasonable man. At Christmas he'd come to share their celebration brandy and toasted the 'one God who looks down on all his creatures' followed by a toast to King George V which he certainly hadn't understood. The rant was out of character.

When he'd finished and various sickly men had fainted in the heat, he walked between the lines. At the first line, he tapped a man with a stick who was immediately brought out and held by guards. The same happened at the second and third lines until he reached the fourth line where Arthur stood impassively. He didn't particular mind the heat and the verses, *as many loves as . . . birds in the hidden branches . . . fronde tegunter aves* were whirling productively in his brain. When the stick tapped his shoulder and the guards gripped his arms, firmly but not brutally, he was astonished. He had given up the idea of his war being anything more than a dreary interruption in his life.

The four men were brought together and another long speech made and translated. It seemed they were to be taken to Constantinople and imprisoned there. Immediately the senior British officer strode forward and objected, reeling off the rights of prisoners of war. The commandant listened for a few minutes and then turned away.

The guards became more aggressive and hustled the men out

of the compound, down a steep cobbled street and into a filthy ground floor room with a shutter nailed over the only window. None of the four men lived in the same house, although they knew each other by sight. Two of them, Captain Langton and Major Tarrant, had come after the terrible defeat and march from Kut. The other, whose name Arthur didn't know, had arrived quite recently from Mesopotamia. So far none of them had spoken.

Then Langton, who was older than the rest of them, said gruffly, 'Captain Langton.' And then, after a pause, 'Bloody bad show.' Arthur wondered how often he'd used those words at Kut; at least he'd emerged alive.

'Captain Lamb,' Arthur said into the darkness.

'Lieutenant Wolf,' said the man by the door, adding, 'I think we're near the railway station.'

They all knew Afion lay at the centre of a network of railway lines. Arthur's hope that this was only theatre and they would find themselves back in camp after a day or two, diminished.

'Major Tarrant,' said the fourth man. 'Bloody bad luck. What we need most is water.'

Sylvia came out from the rectory. The garden was changing colour: the lavender was more grey than blue and tall yellow daisies and golden rod were thrusting upwards. She had just told Mr Gisburne that Lady Margaret Hall had accepted her to read English.

He had responded in waspish tones, 'I always suspected you were sunk by the Archidamian War.'

'There were so many wars in classical times,' she had apologised.

'And is it so different now?' He knocked his pipe crossly on the mantelpiece before turning back to her. 'I am sorry. My congratulations, Miss Fitzpaine. Now I've lost both my students. No wonder I am in a bad humour. Mr Chaffey is soon to live in London. Of course it's all most commendable. Reverend Temple is a brilliant and high-minded individual.' Sylvia hadn't known what he was talking about.

She lifted away a small bee which had become enmeshed in her woollen jacket. She hadn't seen Fred for weeks. Walking further into the garden, she saw the sun reflected in the little window of his shed. There seemed to be some movement behind it. She went over briskly and, feeling a little silly, knocked at the door. One doesn't usually knock at the door of a potting shed.

Fred opened it, his body filling the narrow doorway.

'I've come to tell you I'm going up to Oxford but I've switched to reading English, not Classics. Dear old Gisburne is quite put out.' She realised she was speaking in a rush out of nervousness. She had never penetrated Fred's domain before.

'Come in.' He pushed the door wider. 'Sit down.' He indicated a stool by a desk of wooden planks under the window. 'I wanted to say goodbye myself.'

'The rector said you were going to London.' Sylvia sat down. She noticed her hands were trembling and hid them in the folds of her skirt. All the space was covered with piles of books, some of which she recognised from the rectory library. There was a large trunk on the bed. 'I think he hoped you'd become the village schoolmaster.'

'Education is the only thing that matters. But I have to go out into the world.'

Sylvia felt confused. It was partly the rich earthy smell that filled the air and partly the new kind of confidence she sensed in Fred. 'Gisburne mentioned a Reverend Temple.'

Fred, who was still standing, raised his good arm in a kind of salute. 'He's our president. The WEA. The Workers' Educational Association. That's why I'm going to London. I can't explain what it means to me.' His voice rose. 'It's the only thing that means anything since I left Gallipoli. It's the only thing that can replace Gallipoli in my head!'

Sylvia stared; he looked like someone transfigured, a preacher, a prophet. 'What is the Workers' Educational Association?'

'We want to change everything. All those men and women who've never had a chance. We want to give them a way forward beyond the endless drudgery of work. Why shouldn't they have higher aspirations just because they were born in humble circumstances!'

'You're a Bolshevik, a communist!' Sylvia tried not to sound shocked. Why should it matter to her what he believed?

'This isn't about politics. The WEA is open to men and women from all sides.' He suddenly smiled, looking directly at Sylvia, and she felt herself flushing. She put a hand to her face. 'People do ask, though. Temple is the King's chaplain and he arranged for the president to go to Buckingham Palace and convince the King we were not Bolsheviks. Just last week, that was. Now the King wants to become a subscriber. Men must be educated.'

As Fred explained more: about R.H. Tawney from Balliol College, Oxford, who had inspired him with one of his talks; about his own minor role in the office in Red Lion Square – 'voluntary, really, but with enough money to fund lodgings with one of their friends' – Sylvia found herself unable to concentrate on his words. Instead she heard the agitated throb of her heart.

But she understood now why he had wanted to say goodbye and with that came the realisation that she would never see him again. Almost unconsciously, she put out her hand.

Fred stopped talking and looked at her. 'I'm sorry. You want to leave? I can't blame you.'

'No. I want to stay.' She took his hand and immediately felt a great sense of relief. His fingers were warm and firm and gripped hers. She looked into his face.

'Do you mean you want me to take the trunk off the bed?' His hot eyes stared at her.

'Yes.' She watched as he bent over the small bed and used both arms to swing the box on to the floor.

'Take off your clothes.' The sun had gone from the window now. She paused before slipping obediently out of her white shoes, her woollen jacket, her skirt, her blouse, her petticoat, her underwear. It seemed to take a long time. Fred watched seriously until she stood naked with her arms across her breasts.

Then he asked, 'Do you want me to undress too?'

Sylvia was surprised. 'Don't you want to?'

'Yes.'

Together, both naked, they went to the bed. Despite his arousal, Sylvia felt Fred's wariness. As they lay down side by side she remembered her two previous love-makings: the quick pledging of their troth with Arthur, the leisurely love-making with Rupert which had later made her so ashamed.

'I suppose when your fiancé comes back you will be able to forget this happened,' said Fred, stroking her body.

'I have no fiancé,' said Sylvia.

'You don't mind my arm?'

'No,' said Sylvia.

'I hadn't expected your body to be beautiful,' murmured Fred.

'I'm too thin.' Sylvia shut her eyes.

'I thought so but you're not.' He touched her breasts and her inner thighs. 'You won't regret this? You won't scream so that Mr Gisburne comes running?'

'No.' For a second, Sylvia pictured Gussie's swollen belly, her languorous voice when she talked of Reggie.

'I won't be able to stop soon,' said Fred.

'I don't want you to,' said Sylvia.

Afterwards, Fred sat on the bed where Sylvia still lay half asleep. 'You remember I'm going away.'

Sylvia was too lazy to answer.

'Perhaps that was why you wanted me, knowing you'd never see me again,' continued Fred. 'So it's safe.'

Sylvia still didn't answer so he went on again. 'I'll be in London and you'll be in Oxford. Not so far as the crow flies but they might as well be different worlds.'

Sylvia turned over and put her hand on his back. 'I thought your work was all about bringing the two worlds together. R.H. Tawney's in Oxford.'

Fred twisted round so he could see her. 'Join the WEA where the labourer gets to fuck the lady. That sort of thing?'

Sylvia wasn't certain if he was joking. 'I was thinking more about books,' she said. No one had ever said the word 'fuck' in her presence before. Why had he said it? 'We've read books to-gether – for a year now.' Her skin suddenly felt cold.

He crouched down beside the bed. 'I'm sorry about what I just said.' Sylvia realised she had tears in her eyes but only when he wiped them away. 'I lost my head. Not surprising with you there looking like an angel. Can I lie beside you again?'

The room had become dim but a bird was scratching on the roof, reminding Sylvia of the garden outside, and the manor's garden and all the rest of her life. 'We can still meet,' she said.

'There must be books we haven't read.' This time she knew he was joking because his hand was on her body again, more urgent than before. 'Or we could meet here in my foxhole.'

'Don't talk.'

'You've got the softest, whitest body I've ever seen.'

'Don't talk.'

*

The single line of cello that had accompanied Arthur at his first landing on Gallipoli had returned. It sang through his brain, blotting out the darkness of the cell, his hunger, his fever, his fear, the vermin, filth and stench, even his three companions. He thought, when he thought at all, that the music which he had never identified was his angel in time of greatest need and that on Gallipoli it had given him time to survive and become a soldier. He suspected he was half mad. But it gave him hope that he would survive this abominable place too. He did not think of Sylvia but sometimes allowed Greek heroes to take over his mind:

> *I have wrought a monument more lasting than bronze*
> *and higher than the pyramids of Kings*
> *which neither biting rain, nor angry wind can destroy*
> *nor the uncountable ranks of years, nor the flights of time.*

PART FIVE

1919

❧

'A leaf on the grey sand-path
Fallen and fair with rime!
A yellow leaf, a scarlet leaf,
And a green leaf ere its time.

Days rolled in blood, days torn,
Days innocent, days burnt black,
What is it the wind is sighing
As the leaves float, swift or slack?

The year's pale spectre is crying
For beauty invisibly shed,
For the things that never were told
And were killed in the minds of the dead.'

Laurence Binyon

Thirty-Three

The First World War ended on 11th November, 1918. By the beginning of 1919 Beatrice had already written many letters in an attempt to locate the Colonel's body. Her dreams, which in the last years had followed more normal channels, returned to Gallipoli. She imagined herself bent over a naked man whose hazel eyes stared back at her. She knew it was her husband's last appeal. This picture was accompanied by the sound of the sea and small birds twittering in a bright blue sky. There were no sign nor sound of fighting for which she was grateful.

At first she wrote generally for information, listing the names of other officers lost on the same day, 21st August, 1915, and whose bodies had never been found. Their families suffered as she did. They told each other, 'Now that the war is over, surely they can find their bodies and identify them.' They talked about 'bodies', although all of them were perfectly aware that, after three and a half years, they would be skeletons.

Beatrice's letters were humble and unemotional but, after she had only received polite responses, citing the many difficulties facing the soldiers now in charge of Gallipoli, she wrote more personally, asking for details. She was unable to disguise a sense of desperation:

Dear Major Stopford,
I have not sent the details about Brigadier-General Fitzpaine because I'm not quite sure what details are wanted. He was very heavily tattooed on the chest and I think sometimes the pigment is a preservation, but over three years is so long. He also wore a gold ring with a glass face containing strands of hair and a black metal wristwatch with his name scratched into the back.

I thought if you did not mind I would rather call, perhaps

Monday afternoon. Do you think you could inquire if among those identified are any of his brigade?

Beatrice paused to find the list of missing officers which she then copied out before continuing:

If most of these were found it would be less likely my husband would be now. Also I should be very interested to know about the others, as for some of them, like Captain Gardner, no evidence at all was ever forthcoming.

After this Beatrice laid down her pen and did not have the heart to continue until the following morning when another anguished night spurred her forward.

She heard nothing, however, for several weeks when a short letter, ignoring her plea for a meeting, informed her that any items belonging to the Brigadier-General would be returned to her but that none had been found and that it was extremely unlikely at this stage any would be.

More dreadful nights occurred while she imagined faceless Turks robbing Bingo of his clothes and his possessions. Once again, as he had in the early months of his disappearance, he looked at her in mute appeal.

So, after the lapse of a few days, she wrote another letter, asking if it was the practice of the Turks 'to strip the bodies of the fallen'. This received no response but only, eventually, an acknowledgement.

A week later, Sylvia came back for the Easter vacation. Beatrice's spirits rose a little. 'My dearest, you look so elegant!' This wasn't quite true; Sylvia's clothes were not fashionable. But since going to Oxford they fitted her better; she favoured smart caps and she had given up the unnecessary spectacles.

'It's lovely to be back at good old Tollorum.' Sylvia kissed her mother and looked around her. 'Nothing changes.'

'Oh, but it has! Our final patients left yesterday and now we're wondering how we can fill all those empty rooms.' Beatrice said this cheerfully but it sobered them both all the same. Neither said any more as they went together up the stairs to Sylvia's bedroom.

'This will always be the loveliest room in the world to me.'

Something in her voice made Beatrice realise she was speaking out of nostalgia, looking back to a past. 'I'm glad,' she said, mechanically.

'Where's Gussie? Her brood will fill a few rooms.'

'Gussie lives in London all the time now. She and Grandmama are inseparable. I sometimes wonder what will happen when Reggie comes out of the army.'

'They'll have ten more children,' Sylvia laughed, then went to the window. She spoke again while looking out. 'Don't worry, Mama. Reggie will never leave the army. He's found his niche.'

Beatrice sat on the bed. 'I expect you're right.' She thought of the Colonel. He had been a good soldier, yet so different from Reggie. Reggie was so . . . so . . . she tried to find the right word without being uncharitable, 'forthcoming'. He had won his award early on and then fought through the worst of the war, managing to survive until the end. *That* deserved an award. And in fact he had won another.

Bingo had been mentioned in a dispatch by General Hamilton in December 1915. The citation was signed by the then Secretary of State for War, Winston Churchill. Beatrice had put it away at once – so little recognition for the Colonel and given by two men who, between them, had destroyed his life. Of course Bingo himself would not have looked at it like that. Perhaps he had been discriminated against because he had left the regular army to run the estate and be with his family. Or perhaps by the time he died, Gallipoli was already a lost cause and no one wanted to remember it.

'I've had a letter from Arthur,' said Sylvia suddenly turning round, although she spoke in her usual quiet tones.

'A letter! Oh, my dear.' Beatrice felt discomfited that, while thinking about Bingo, she'd failed to ask about Arthur.

'Yes. It's quite disjointed, almost incoherent, written from different places at different times. But for the last two months or so he has been living in Istanbul.'

'Istanbul! In Turkey?'

'Oh, Mother.' Sylvia spoke a little impatiently. 'Of course in Turkey. How many Istanbuls are there? The city that the navy were aiming for before a few mines put them off. The city which seemed to get further from our poor soldiers every day they fought.'

'That's what I mean,' said Beatrice in a dignified voice. 'Arthur used to call it Constantinople. So did we all.'

Sylvia came and sat down on the bed beside her mother. 'Well, he's there now.' She looked at her mother's strained face. 'I'm sorry I shouted.'

'Why is he there?' asked Beatrice. 'Is the army employing him? Is he part of the occupying forces?'

'Yes. He seems to go to an office with some English major. He writes that Saint Sophia is wonderful. Somewhere else he says that he can't face England – or words to that effect.'

'Is he sick? Or hurt?'

'He doesn't say so.' Sylvia sounded doubtful. She took off her hat and shook out her hair. 'Apparently two of the three men who were with him in an Istanbul prison died there.'

'Surely that makes it even odder his wanting to be in that city.'

'I suppose he didn't see much of it.' Sylvia smiled. 'It was romantic Byzantium to him, not even Constantinople.'

'That's a long time ago,' said Beatrice restlessly. It had just struck her that Arthur was near enough to visit Gallipoli, the place she pictured night and day.

'I'm not sure he has the same sense of time as we do. After six months in prison he was sent back to Afion Kara Hissar. I think time has slowed down for him. At least that's what Fred thinks.' The name slipped out. Sylvia flushed.

'Fred?' repeated Beatrice but she wasn't really concentrating. Could Arthur possibly be persuaded to return to Gallipoli and search for Bingo? She put her hand to her mouth and flushed more brightly than her daughter.

'A friend,' said Sylvia. 'Isn't it time for lunch?'

During the next few days, Beatrice couldn't get her new idea out of her head. All attempts at gathering information about the Colonel had come to nothing. What she needed was a man on the spot. But would Arthur ever consent or, indeed, be allowed to go to Gallipoli? Already, there was talk of a widows' cruise to the peninsula, stopping in at Egypt and Malta, but that was in the future, not *now*. Besides, she didn't think she could bear to go herself, with chattering young women, planning to start a new life, bands playing on deck, dancing after dinner. She could imagine it would be just like the cruises she'd taken with Bingo. Oh, the horror!

For consolation, she turned to the bronzes, restored to their shelves and lovingly cared for. Yet still her mind whirled with plans, with problems. Arthur was not well, that was clear, otherwise he'd have rushed back to Sylvia, even if he had written that letter breaking off their engagement. Beatrice, like Gussie, found it hard to take that seriously. No, he was not well. So what chance was there he'd want to return to Gallipoli? After all, Bingo was not his father.

The garden was irresistible. Sylvia was taking a break from her work, although studying the Romantic poets, Wordsworth, Keats, Shelley, scarcely felt like work. She wondered what Arthur would think about her abandonment of the classics. Judging by his letter, he was not thinking of her at all. In his varied ramblings, philosophical, theological and even a little political, he never found space to enquire how she was or what she was doing. Not that she blamed him. How could you blame someone who'd been through so much? One of his ramblings had informed her that 'despair was the nearest he'd felt to happiness'. What could she make of *that*?

Sylvia looked up at the sky. It was a clear sharp day. Soon the air would warm and spring would come. She found herself moved by the sight of the tightly furled leaves. She touched a bud on a lilac tree and imagined it uncurling its pale leaves and heavy mauve flowers. Then she remembered it was a pink lilac and, smiling, adjusted her image.

A gardener passed with a wheelbarrow, clippers and shears. Men were beginning to drift back from the army and suddenly it was not difficult to find help in the garden.

'Morning, miss.' He tipped his cap.

'Lovely morning!' She didn't know him but that wouldn't stop her telling him about the WEA, when he'd been around a bit longer. Besides, the south-west wasn't well-organised yet. Bristol was the nearest WEA centre. But there could be reading and discussion circles. Perhaps she could persuade Fred to visit Tollorum and suggest her mother start a circle. She'd been so bookish before the war. Now she seemed feverish and inactive

– if you can be both together – where, before, she'd been languid and capable. Fairly capable, anyway. Sylvia wondered briefly whether she should talk to Lily about her before deciding against. She could not quite come to terms with the fact that her mother's housekeeper was Fred's sister. She supposed it was because the Fred in London seemed so different to the Fred in Dorset. Not that she met him often, she reminded herself, firmly. But she *did* meet him in Oxford and London.

Reluctantly, Sylvia turned away from the freshness of the garden and went inside to her books.

Beatrice shivered and buttoned up her coat. Her hands trembled but not enough to rock the cup on the saucer. She passed it to Sylvia. 'It's much too cold for tea in the garden,' she said.

'I just wanted to be outside.' Sylvia took the cup. She had spotted a first swallow under the eaves. 'And the war's over.' She looked at her mother with a challenging expression.

Beatrice stirred her tea. 'Have you thought of going to Arthur in Turkey?'

'No!' exclaimed Sylvia, scarcely understanding. 'What a strange idea! If he wanted to see me, he'd come here. I expect he's recovering on his own and he *does* have a job there.'

'There's masses to look at in Constantinople,' said Beatrice tenaciously.

'Mother! What *is* the matter?'

To Sylvia's horror, Beatrice burst into tears and, between sobs, explained herself. 'It is the thought of your papa, undiscovered, unburied, alone . . . it tortures me. I've been writing to all the right people but nobody admits to knowing anything. I thought if someone could actually go there. It's quite safe. In our hands and the Australians. At some point, relatives of the fallen will organise visits there, I'm assured, but I can't wait. I can't sleep. And when you told me that Arthur was still in Turkey and so close, I just thought . . . but why should he go . . . although Bingo was so fond of him and I believe Arthur too . . . then I thought . . . Oh, darling . . .'

Sylvia held her mother in her arms and remembered that day, four years ago, when she'd comforted her before. Then it was the premonition of the Colonel's death. She wondered whatever she

466

could do. For every possible reason, her mother's plan was crazy. 'Dearest Mama, I'm so sorry. So very sorry.'

Beatrice clutched at her daughter's hands. 'You will try, won't you, darling?' She looked up at her hopefully.

Sylvia sat in the Deverills' Mayfair drawing room. Despite Gussie's almost constant presence it was still as grandly old-fashioned as ever. Gussie was far too busy with her babies and her committees and her smart new friends to bother with minor points like the decor. Perhaps she even liked it. But Sylvia wondered what Fred would make of the heavy chandeliers, dark mahogany and Victorian level of decoration. He would arrive for tea at any minute.

That morning Gussie had departed to stay in the country with their grandmother. 'It's a real house party,' Gussie had sighed happily, between shouting at the nurse and Lady Deverill's new chauffeur who had come to fetch them but was rough with the cases. 'And Reggie will be with us on Sunday. Oh, Sylvia, I'm so lucky!'

Beyond lucky, Sylvia had thought wryly, when flu swept away returning soldiers and women were thrown out from the jobs they'd claimed in the war. Yet, within her privileged sphere, Gussie had made her own luck, recognising Reggie's heroic qualities, seducing their self-centred grandmother with her sheer vitality. Maybe her role in their grandmother's committee Children's Happy Evenings Association meant she did have some sort of social conscience. She'd probably have been even happier with their grandmother's favourite charity of which she'd been vice-president. The Women's National Anti-Suffrage League, thought Sylvia critically. But that had been disbanded early in 1918 when women, or at least some of them, had won the vote. On the other hand, the nearest she herself came to good works was hanging on to the coat-tails of Fred's Workers' Educational Association.

There was a knock on the door and the young manservant who had recently come begging for a job showed in Fred.

Sylvia sat where she was and watched him cross the room. He'd finally abandoned Mr Gisburne's suits and now he wore corduroy trousers and a jacket, with a scarf knotted loosely. It seemed to her a combination of working man, artist and, perhaps intellectual, although Arthur, who she'd always considered an intellectual, had looked nothing like this. It was four years since she'd last seen Arthur.

'Why are you staring at me like that?' Fred took a chair opposite her. 'Am I being interviewed for the post of third footman?'

Sylvia still had not mastered the difference in their class and smiled uneasily. 'You're changed every time I see you.'

'Then we must meet more often,' said Fred cheerily. 'I'm coming to Oxford in a couple of weeks, to help out with a discussion on whether the pure arts or vocational education should be the WEA policy. Everybody feels very strongly one way or the other.'

'Where do you stand?'

'All the real working men are against training men for slavery. Education should be about training the mind. But the trade unions see it differently.' He paused and looked up. 'I can never believe you're really interested.'

'Why not?'

'I wouldn't be if I were you. You've got everything already.'

'You want me to cut myself off from the rest of the world?'

Fred shrugged. 'The world?' He gazed round at the opulent room. 'When you have this?'

'You think I'm utterly selfish, don't you?'

'Not you. Everybody.' He held his hand up, a new habit. His shortened arm rested at his side. 'Correction. There are people in the organisation I admire greatly.'

They stared at each other. Fred tapped the side of his chair. 'I just saw Colin Gledhill, the man who introduced me to the WEA. He's in hospital. He was gassed in France, then got flu on his way home. He looks like a ghost but he still wants to hear every detail of the organisation's work. I told him we'd opened twenty more centres this year and he began to look almost human. That's the sort of man I admire.'

Sylvia looked at him gravely. 'I can see why.' There was a pause before she asked tentatively, 'Would you like some tea?'

He leant forward. 'Very much.' His eyes staring into hers made Sylvia blush and turn away, yet long to be closer. 'Can't we sit somewhere less like a mausoleum?'

'I knew you wouldn't like it.' Sylvia stood and Fred followed her to the door. He put his hand on her waist. She leant backwards against him.

'There's the breakfast room.'

'Your hair smells of camomile.'

'Or perhaps we could sneak upstairs.'

This was the fourth time Sylvia and Fred had made love. Once in a potting shed, once in Fred's rented room while listening nervously for the landlady, once in a field near Oxford, and now in an unused servant's bedroom where Sylvia had chosen to sleep. They did not tell each other why they came together but talked instead of their work.

On this afternoon, Sylvia began to talk about her mother. She was afraid of Fred's mockery so she said carefully, 'I know my mother is very fortunate with a lovely house and no money worries, but now that Gussie and I are always so much away . . .'

Fred lay back and listened to her voice. It was one of her most attractive features. Recently, he had been taken to his first ever concert and he'd found himself thinking about Sylvia as he listened to the piano. Beethoven, it was. He had so much to learn. He had never heard of Ludwig van Beethoven until that concert.

'So I know that it's utterly ridiculous but how can I convince her without terribly upsetting her?'

'What?' asked Fred lazily.

'You haven't been listening!'

'I have. To your voice. Not the sense.' He touched the side of her breast where it curved so gracefully upwards.

Sylvia sat up and stared angrily at the still recumbent Fred. 'My mother wants me to go to Istanbul where as you know my fiancé (ex) resides and persuade him to search Gallipoli for the bones of my dead father!'

'Utterly ridiculous,' said Fred. 'Why would any soldier who'd fought on Gallipoli want to go back there?' He spoke calmly but the mention of Gallipoli had dreadfully disturbed his mood. He, too, sat up. Sylvia had already begun dressing. He watched her long white body, graceful as she bent to pull on her stockings. 'I'm sorry. I love the sound of your voice. That's my only excuse. I'm truly sorry.'

Sylvia paused, then dragged her slip over her head. 'I don't know why I should think it was your business.'

Fred was sad to see her breasts covered. Then he realised he wanted to try and explain. 'The last time I saw Gallipoli was in January 1916 when it was going up like a pile of fireworks. Shortly afterwards, some of it came down and smashed my arm. And that's just the final five minutes of my time there. I shouldn't think Captain Lamb thinks much more highly of it.'

'No.' Sylvia stood up and carried on dressing. But after a few moments, she turned to Fred. 'I was being a fool.'

'A good daughter, maybe.'

'I didn't raise her hopes.' She looked at Fred, still naked on the bed. 'Are you just going to lie there?'

'Sit down a minute.' He knew she wouldn't resist him. When she was by him, he took her hand. 'Men don't talk about fighting once it's over because whatever we said you couldn't understand without having been there. What if I said, "I lay all day on a beach with men around me dead and the wounded moaning, not able to move a muscle for the snipers", or "The stink of the black and swollen bodies in no man's land made healthy men spew up their bully beef", or "I saw men with dysentery so bad it dripped out of their trouser legs but they still had to fight," or "I saw a man run ten strides with his head bouncing along behind him", or "A man whose feet had been blown off running along on the bloody stumps".'

'Stop,' begged Sylvia.

'And what was it all for?' continued Fred, inexorable. 'A foolish whim! A purpose that had no chance of success. The Turks should never have been in the war in the first place.' He stopped abruptly and flung himself back on the bed. 'But now I have something that makes sense and I don't even want to *think* about Gallipoli.'

Both were silent then. Fred could see Sylvia's bowed head, the delicate pale threads of her hair.

'There were such magical sunsets there,' said Fred suddenly. 'And sunrises too and when we first arrived the wild flowers filled the valleys and rose up the gullies in great waves of colour. There were vineyards and olive groves – I'd never seen either before. And the sea all around us as if we were on an island. I'm a country boy, I liked the ground to sleep on, the stars above my head. I never lost the feeling I was a survivor. Almost never. Everybody felt something different about Gallipoli. But it didn't matter what we felt. It was never ours for the taking. If I saw a Turk tomorrow, I'd shake his hand and say "Well done". If I saw one of those generals or politicians who imagined himself a victor, I'd spit in his face.'

There was another silence.

Sylvia, in her dress, lay down beside Fred. When he had been ill at Tollorum, she'd heard him talk like this, but she knew he didn't remember. She hadn't asked *him* to go back to Gallipoli. She hadn't even thought of it. But now that idea was in her head too.

Arthur sat outside a small café in Istanbul. The table was wooden and shared by two old men smoking a hookah. They were dressed in what would have been generously considered rags. Turkey's involvement in the war had reduced the country to extreme poverty. Even the rich were poor. Arthur didn't know why he lingered in the city. He was comfortable enough, living in a once grand house overlooking the Bosphorus. There were other Allied officers, including a French man and an Australian. None of them had fought at Gallipoli. He had been a POW for so long that he felt like Rip Van Winkle, asleep while the world went on around him, other wars, other failures and successes, the world quite changed when he woke.

Sometimes he walked down to the main quay and watched the Turkish soldiers who'd crossed the water from the railway station of Haidar Pasha. When he'd first arrived, it had been still freezing cold, bitter winds and snow. He'd come into the same station, a freed prisoner of war, sick and battered as they were, but part of the victorious army. Perhaps that was why he stayed on, trying to convince himself that he belonged to the conquering West. At first he'd imagined he might recognise some of his oppressors: Maslum Bey from Afion, or his vicious captors in Istanbul.

But the end of the war had changed everything. He had walked round the outside of his prison walls and felt unable to connect with the man who'd spent six months inside and watched two of his fellow captives die there. Maybe this was a sign that he wanted to move forward or maybe it was an unhealthy denial.

On a cold morning in late February, he'd noticed a few British soldiers lining the main street down to the quay. One of them told him that General Allenby was coming. 'He defeated the Turks in Palestine and Syria,' the soldier who was a Glaswegian, added proudly and almost incomprehensibly. Arthur felt even more like Rip Van Winkle but, since he was in his uniform, on sick leave but not discharged from the army, he had stayed to watch.

Two black cars came past. Allenby, big jutting face and small, clipped moustache, stared out of the window.

Arthur and the Scottish soldier had saluted. Arthur had felt a surge of pride. He remembered the feeling with pleasure. Eventually the army had caught up with him and advised him to regularise his position: clearly he was not sick any more, or not in his body. But he wasn't ready to leave Istanbul. *Stamboul*, that what they'd called it in prison.

Often he spent an hour or two at the magnificent church of Saint Sophia, now a mosque, but once the centre of Christendom. Under the whitewash he could see the wings of seraphims, the cross, the Virgin Mary. He was standing under the famous dome when another British soldier joined him, staring upwards in the same awe and wonderment. A major.

As they walked out, he said, 'I think you come here nearly as much as I do.'

Arthur had not noticed him before but nodded and muttered something ending with 'Sir.' He didn't think you saluted in a church – or mosque.

At the vestibule where Turkish soldiers were camped the major smiled, 'Keeping out the Greeks, I expect. How they'd love to take it back!'

'War makes many things possible,' said Arthur. 'But not that. Yet we set off with that dream.'

'You fought at Gallipoli?'

'Yes.'

'I was in France, then Egypt. I was on my way to Gallipoli but an old wound flared up.'

They had gone together to the officers' rest house, once the German Teutonia Club. Arthur had never been there before and admired the large grounds, even though the myrtle and bay tended to overrun the roses and oleander.

'I see you like the wild and romantic,' said the major.

'I like the peace.'

It turned out Major Guy Rockbourne had been a painter before the war, was married and had a baby that he'd never seen. He longed to be with them among the hop fields of Kent (he described their house with emotion) and found Arthur's wish to stay in Istanbul difficult to understand. Nevertheless he was a kind man and had seen much he didn't understand during his long war so he offered Arthur a job in his office. 'I can fix it easily. In theory the French are running this bit of the show but we seem to be doing the work. You didn't see Desperate Frankey coming into town the other day?'

'I'm afraid I've no idea what you're talking about.'

'The street was lined with French soldiers, buttons on their blue coats gleaming. Above their heads Greek maidens – I've never seen so many Greek girls since I got here – prepared to throw flower petals below their blue and white flags. Then up rides General Franchet d'Espèrey, Allied commander in Turkey, as fat and pompous as the bay cob he sits upon, one hand in his waistcoat like Napoleon. The petals floated down. David, Napoleon's painter, would have made such a picture!'

'It sounds as if Rowlandson would have done better.'

'Not that I have anything against the French as fighters. They were brave and pragmatic. No stupid heroics.'

'They held the most dangerous position on Gallipoli,' Arthur had agreed. When he was with Guy it felt as if he was been drawn back into life and the feeling was not unpleasant. He'd accepted the job, if not with eagerness then with a sense of inevitability. He didn't want to go back to England in irons. He'd bought a little more time.

So each day he breakfasted in the humble café with the old men and sometimes a destitute soldier or two, then proceeded to his office in an old Ottoman palace. He pushed paper around and watched the map of the East being redrawn. It seemed to him that for all the good intentions, the result pleased nobody. But he'd begun to believe that was the nature of life and turned back with relief to the ancient stories of the Greeks where everything could be found and everything understood.

He made plans to visit the ancient site of Troy. He remembered how its closeness had excited his imagination when he'd first arrived on Gallipoli. Eventually, it had become lost in the enemy land of Asia from where shells brought sudden and grisly death. He planned to go most weeks but still hadn't made the journey as the cruel winter gave way to a gentler spring.

Sylvia sat at her desk in her college room. Usually, its air of learning was enough to make her calm but at the moment her thoughts were disturbed by anxiety about her mother. She had seemed quite distraught in her last letter, still harping on about the Colonel's body.

Sylvia rose quickly and, black gown flying like wings behind her, dashed down two flights of stairs and across a quad to the porter's lodge.

'Morning, Miss Fitzpaine.' The porter, an old soldier, prided himself on knowing every student's name.

'Any letters, Brumble?'

There was a letter but not from Lady Beatrice. Sylvia took it back to her room. The stamp was black, with a dramatic picture of a haloed man surviving a shipwreck: St Paul on Malta. Hilda. It had been a year or more since she'd heard from her old friend, although Sylvia had written to tell of her new life at Oxford.

She sat back at her desk and opened the letter. The oak panelling around her shone in the June sunshine.

Dearest friend,

And what a bad friend I am to you. But perhaps when you hear my story you will forgive me. As you see, I am still in Malta, or to be more precise on Gozo where I have moved into the principal town. It was named Victoria in 1887 in honour of the Queen's Diamond Jubilee but everyone round here still calls it Rabat. Why ever do you need to know such things!

Where shall I start? Rupert is dead. My beloved Captain Prideaux is dead. So long ago it seems now. It was peaceful; he died in his sleep. He often had pain but it had been no worse than before. Or, if it was, he didn't tell me. He was happy. I'd never thought to see him so happy and certainly not something so unlooked for, so surprising. You see, dearest Sylvia, I have a son – Rupert, of course. His father knew him for six months before he died. That was why I made no contact. I was jealous of every moment. How strange – you were always the dreamer yet I have lived in a kind of dream ever since I met Rupert in the Bighi Hospital. I expected so little and yet I ended up with far more than the most fortunate woman.

Perhaps, after your shock, you'll wonder why I'm still on Gozo, why, now that the war is properly over, I have not come back to you in England bearing my prize. But nothing is quite easy. Before Rupert died – although asleep, he was in my arms – he received a letter from his father. Lord Filchester told him that all his brothers, save the youngest who was still in school, had been killed in France. This was a plea for Rupert to return home which, of course, even if he had wanted to, he couldn't do. But it made him face up to something else which caused him much soul-searching. Our little boy is the Filchester heir. You know Rupert's views on his family. If they knew that their heir was living on a faraway island with the daughter of a Birmingham businessman – they would demand him back at once to be brought up a proper little Englishman, rather than as a savage amongst popish infidels. I sympathised with Rupert's alienation and the long and the short of it is that we had not told the family of little Rupert's birth at the time of his father's death. And now, and now, well I am telling you. You met the family, you will understand my reluctance. Rupert didn't hate his parents but he hated their way of life.

Oh, Sylvia, our son is the most beautiful boy imaginable! I don't think he has an iota of my dull genes. His hair is as thick and golden as Rupert's, his nose as straight, his manner as charming, although with all the questing naughtiness you would expect. He is affectionate in a way his father was never allowed to be from an early age. In short, he is perfection. How could I ever give him up?

But I am not a selfish person – my happiness has always lain in making others happy – so I must do what is right for little Rupert. Certainly he cannot live on Gozo for ever. Tell me, dear friend, what shall I do? What is for the best? If only we were not separated by hundreds of miles of land and sea. But if I come to England, I could never keep Rupert's presence secret and then I run the risk of losing him for ever . . .

Sylvia put away the letter and went downstairs into the bright sunshine.

She walked, as she often did, towards the meadows where the River Cherwell moved slowly through green grass and silver willows. It was a place where she came to think through any difficulties and now she was deeply shaken by Hilda's extreme happiness and extreme unhappiness. Her dilemma was clear enough to Sylvia and she saw no obvious answer. The woman she had visited in her stately home, now bereft of all her sons except the last, would certainly snatch at the young Rupert. Nor could she see Hilda fitting into the surroundings. Yet Lord Filchester had been kind enough and it was possible his wife had been softened by so much grief.

Sylvia stood staring down at her reflection in the water. How alone she looked! Although the trees, pollarded so that leaves sprang from the heads of their sturdy trunks, had a rather human air. She stepped back to stand beside one and almost collided with a man coming up behind her.

'I'm so sorry.'

'I've been looking for you. The man on the door who seems to know everything sent me out here.'

Sylvia saw Fred with a sense of joy and relief. 'What are you doing here?'

'Sent here for a meeting. I told you.' He looked round. 'It's nearly as pretty as the countryside.'

'I was desperate to speak to someone.'

'Don't you have friends?'

'Yes, yes.' They began to walk together. Their hands dangled side by side and curled as if to clasp something or someone.

Incoherently, Sylvia began to explain about Hilda and Rupert which somehow turned into a retelling of her mother's ever more desperate demands.

After a while Fred stopped and turned her to face him. His hand on her shoulder seemed to give her strength. 'Why are you here?' she asked as she had before.

'I suppose I've missed you. But I do have a meeting at six p.m.'

'Tell me what you think.'

'Well, it's obvious, isn't it? Hilda wants you in Malta, Lady Beatrice wants you in Gallipoli and your fiancé is in Istanbul.'

Sylvia looked down. 'I've missed you too. He's not my fiancé.' She stared out at the summery scene. More people were around

476

now, mothers with prams, old people, young men, a few couples. 'Would you come with me?'

Fred showed no particular surprise but answered firmly, 'I'm busy, aren't I?'

'I don't think I could do it on my own.'

'There's plenty of folk who'd fancy some foreign travel, all expenses paid.' He seemed to be putting on his thickest West Country accent.

'But I want *you*.'

'I described to you how I left the place.'

'But Captain Prideaux taught you how to read.' Sylvia knew that about him now. 'You owe his widow something.'

'He just taught me some tricks when the trenches got too boring. You've travelled on your own before. You went out to Egypt when the war was still on. There'll be no torpedoes to frighten you.'

'I wasn't frightened of torpedoes.'

'There you are.' They walked on again.

When they reached a bench, Sylvia sat down purposefully. She hadn't given up. Fred sat easily, his good arm along the back of the bench but without touching her.

'You're not wearing a hat.' His fingers found her earlobe and stroked it lightly. Sylvia held her breath.

'Do you think you'll stick with the WEA?' She was trying a different tack.

'Of course.' His fingers moved to her cheek. 'How can you leave university and go travelling?'

'You were the one who told me to go.'

'I said it was the obvious answer.'

'I can go in the summer vac. It's months long.'

'So spoiled, you academics. And the working man using his few days off to find learning.'

'There's no need to mock me, Fred. You know I believe in what you're doing. More than I believe in what I'm doing, as a matter of fact. I should become political. I know I should.'

'You look very pretty when you're earnest.' Fred put his finger on her lips. 'I've told you the WEA isn't political.' He took his finger away and Sylvia felt the coolness.

'I will pay for you to come with me but no one else.'

'Can't we find somewhere to be private?'

It was impossible, they both knew it. But they sat hand in hand, close together, hot cheek to hot cheek.

Thirty-Four

Small fields, the grass dried to white, bounded by piled grey stones, spread down one side of the hill. Now and again there were a few goats or sheep and a cluster of stone houses. On the other side, uncultivated land, the rocks showing through scrub, dropped to a deep blue sea.

'I can see why you buried him here,' said Sylvia to Hilda. They were standing by a cairn of stones. Both wore wide-brimmed straw hats against the sun.

'It was terribly difficult. We tried three different spots before the men could dig. It makes you admire those ancient inhabitants. They carved out whole burial chambers underground.'

'We saw a group on Malta.' Sylvia took off her hat and wiped her face.

'When Rupert was well enough, we rode up in an oxen cart. I was terrified the jolting would kill him but he loved it here.'

'Even though he couldn't see.'

'He said he could feel it. You do feel air and space.' Hilda gently waved her hands while turning slowly about.' That's what he did.'

Sylvia went closer to the grave. 'Shall I add a few stones?'

'Yes, do. There's no shortage.' Hilda watched as Sylvia collected the stones and placed them carefully one by one. 'One of the hardest things will be leaving Rupert's grave.'

'So you've decided.'

'I just pretended there was a choice. There never was really. Seeing you here made it even more obvious. I'll leave before the winter storms. At least I'll be glad to see *my* parents.'

'Do you wish you'd known him earlier?'

'His blindness brought us together.'

Sylvia suddenly recalled Hilda's remark when they were at

the hospital in Camberwell. 'Do you remember how you once proclaimed when I was in self-sacrificing mode that you would never marry an incapacitated man since he'd have all the usual male aggravation and none of the bonuses?'

'How foolish I was!' Hilda smiled. 'Can you imagine the glamorous Captain Prideaux looking in the direction of plain old Hilda Horridge?'

Guiltily, Sylvia remembered that Rupert had looked in her direction. She changed the subject back to their original one. 'It's strange, you hating the thought of abandoning your husband's grave and my mother desperate to find a grave. Well, a grave with my father in it.'

'I suppose when you lose someone you love very much you trick yourself into believing something will make it easier: a grave, being near a grave. But of course nothing can.'

'I think my mother *will* feel calmer if we find my father in a grave somewhere.'

'And will you? Find him, I mean.'

'I don't know. I'm trying to be hopeful. Fred thinks it's impossible, although he himself didn't fight in the area where my father disappeared.'

'Ah, Fred,' said Hilda.

Both women looked up at the sound of high-pitched cries. Running towards them was a small, chubby figure.

'He's escaped me!' shouted Fred, following behind and waving a child's white Panama hat.

Hilda opened wide her arms and Rupert flung himself into them.

'He's bored with chasing skinny chickens,' said Fred. He plonked the hat over the boy's white-blond hair.

'We're about to leave,' said Hilda, rearranging the hat on her son's head.

Fred walked over to the cairn and, like Sylvia, bent to pick up a stone. 'Do locals add to it?'

'I think so.' Hilda and Sylvia moved closer.

'No name?' Fred asked.

'I expect there'll be grander memorials elsewhere.' Hilda didn't stop to watch him place it at the bottom of the pile. After he had finished, he stood back to attention. He had not imagined Prideaux ending up in such a solitary place. But perhaps it suited him.

Sylvia followed Hilda down the hill and thought that her friend wanted to keep Rupert's grave all to herself. Even Rupert Brooke, buried on the Greek island of Skyros, had been given a cross with a name.

Fred caught up with her and she glanced sideways. What did he think of Captain Prideaux's last resting place? Although they'd been together now for ten days and she felt closer to him than ever before, he still kept most of his feelings hidden from her. He'd told her without warning, 'I will come with you to Gallipoli.' But he hadn't explained why he'd changed his mind.

Arthur pettishly threw his cap on to his desk. 'Damn! Damn!'

'What is it?' Major Rockbourne looked up from where he sat on the other side of the room.

'Why do people want to come to Gallipoli? Isn't the world big enough?'

'What people?' Rockbourne stretched and came over. 'It's still off-limits, isn't it?'

'I don't know. I know I shouldn't be in Turkey if this is what we can expect.'

'Whatever's the matter, old man?'

Arthur had been about to sit down but instead picked up his cap again. 'Let's go for a drink.'

'You've only just got in,' pointed out Rockbourne. Arthur's behaviour was so untypical it made him curious. 'It's only eleven o'clock.'

'Well I'm going.'

The two men went out into the blasting heat of the streets. There was nothing compelling to hold them in their office. Soon they'd both be gone altogether. Turkey would find its own way to the future. Rockbourne wrote to his wife every other day. Their child, who'd been born when he was in Egypt, would be going to school soon.

The Teutonia's fans whirled in the empty bar. The shutters were already closed against the sun but thin streaks of light pierced the gloom.

'I'm sure the Germans never drank so early,' grumbled Rockbourne.

'And the Muslims don't drink at all, my dear Guy,' said Arthur settling at the bar. 'But it didn't help the Turks to win the war. We'll have two ouzos.' The Greek barman rolled down his shirtsleeves politely. 'On Gallipoli there was one stupid colonel who gave his men their rum ration after they'd fought, instead of before. The men joked it made it cheaper but he said it was wrong to lead befuddled men to their deaths.'

Arthur poured a small amount of water into his glass and took two large gulps.

Rockbourne pushed his aside. 'I've never heard you talk about your time on Gallipoli.'

'Failures are never very interesting.'

'I thought the British loved glorious defeats. Anyway, we won in the end, as you just pointed out. There was a report, wasn't there?'

Arthur didn't answer this. He was thinking about the need for heroes. He'd even longed to become one himself. If he hadn't been captured, he might have won a medal. Glory, glory, hallelujah. But men must die for their country. He took another swig of ouzo, then pushed the empty glass to the Greek who poured another.

Rockbourne took a sip from his. 'I'm hoping to get a home posting in the next month or two.' He remembered Arthur's earlier words. 'Who wants to come to Gallipoli?'

'No *want* about it. She's already halfway here, on Malta. Saw an opera called *Fedora* in Valletta. Visited a friend on Gozo. She wrote and told me all about it. The letter arrived this morning. She'll be here in a few days.' Arthur heard the panic in his voice.

'Who's "she"?' asked Rockbourne, patiently.

'My fiancée. My ex-fiancée. Miss Sylvia Fitzpaine. Her father was a Brigadier-General, killed at Suvla Bay. She wants to find out what happened to him. Apparently her mother's making herself ill with imagining. Sylvia's taken up the challenge.'

'She sounds very determined,' suggested Rockbourne carefully.

'I don't know why she thinks she'd be allowed on the peninsula.'

The major considered. He remembered a striking English girl in a post office in Cairo, during a rainstorm. They'd had a drink together at Shepheard's. He'd later discovered she was

Brigadier-General Fitzpaine's daughter. He decided to say nothing about it. 'I expect we can arrange something. The Imperial War Graves Commission has taken over from the army but there're plenty of our men out there doing the digging or whatever else is needed.'

Arthur turned from the bar to face his companion. 'Have *you* been there?'

'No. It sounded pretty nasty when they first arrived. No Allies had been buried since the end of the war, and all the crosses where there *had* been graves, burnt for firewood. Not that I blame the Turkish peasants. Winters here are bloody awful as you and I know well.'

'So you think she might be allowed onto the peninsula? She's travelling with some man from her family's estate. She didn't say his name.'

'You'd go with them, I assume. After all, Arthur, you have an official role out here. Between us we should be able to arrange it. Might give the workers a lift to see a pretty young woman among all that death. It'd be very hot, of course.'

'Yes.' Arthur studied his glass which was again empty. 'How did you know she's pretty?'

'I just assumed it!' Rockbourne smiled.

Arthur didn't smile back. 'They'd have to stay at Chanak and take a ferry over. They'd be landing in an area that was behind the Turkish lines. I was taken there when I was captured, not that I was in much of a state to appreciate it. A furious soldier had hit me over the head and my dysentery was starting up again. Not very heroic. But I met Liman von Sanders. It was quite unreal. Actually, now I come to think of it, it wasn't me who met him but a fellow captive who told me about it. Von Sanders assured him that we'd got it all wrong at Suvla. Hadn't given ourselves a chance. Well, we hadn't.'

'Nobody met Mr Mustafa Kemal?'

'Not that I recall.' Arthur slipped off the bar stool. 'You've been kind to pander to me, Guy. I haven't seen Sylvia since Cairo 1915 and I freed her from our engagement two years ago. Perhaps that's why I'm still in Turkey. Fleeing involvement.'

'Difficult times,' said Rockbourne gruffly. He watched as Arthur signed the chit for the barman.

'You'll be all right, old thing,' he said, clapping Arthur on the shoulder in a fatherly way.

Arthur looked a little surprised. He'd come to think of himself as at least as old as Guy Rockbourne. They went to the door, putting on their hats, just as two incoming officers took off theirs.

'To salute or not to salute?' muttered Rockbourne.

But Arthur had already slipped by. As they walked back to their offices, briskly despite the heat, he turned to the major. 'May I invite you to dinner with Miss Fitzpaine? I'd be so grateful. There's this chap too, although I've no idea if he eats with us.'

Sylvia and Hilda didn't talk about Fred till they were about to part. They stood on Gozo's dilapidated jetty, Rupert asleep in Hilda's arms. Fred was twenty yards away, arguing in sign language about their luggage. The boat, spinning across the waves to collect them, looked very small.

'However will you fit in?' said Hilda anxiously. 'This wind won't help.'

'Oh, Fred will arrange something.' Sylvia shaded her eyes against the sun. The wind had blown off her hat so she held it in one hand.

'You trust him with everything, do you?' Hilda smiled but Sylvia knew what she was asking.

'He certainly can't calm the waves. But I do need him. Although I don't know if he needs me, more than now and again, anyway.'

'He came with you.'

'Yes. But I don't know why. Perhaps he needed to see Gallipoli again.'

Hilda looked down at her son. 'I liked seeing him play with Rupert.'

'He has a nephew and niece at Tollorum but I didn't see him play with them. He did teach at the little school for a while but he never seemed very interested.'

'I can't see him as a village schoolmaster. I expect he doesn't know what he is yet. Do people in England understand what the war did to men?'

'Fred's arm is visible enough.'

'I don't mean that.'

'No. Well, you can't keep licking your wounds. Then there's

all the men who did plenty for the war effort but didn't fight. They get fed up with hearing about the soldiers' sacrifices. It's complicated.'

'Fred seems to be finding a way. This workers association he talks about.'

'So what do *you* think of him?' Sylvia, looking out to sea, watched the boat get suddenly bigger and come closer. She thought, I am about to part with the only person I can ask that question.

'I like him. But what does your mother think? Or your grandmother?'

'Oh, Hilda! Of course they don't know!'

'Do you remember that old bat at the hospital who got so excited over your lineage, recited it all by heart?'

'We're not getting married!' Sylvia frowned crossly.

'Not ever?'

'I don't *know*. My mother thinks I'll come back arm in arm with Arthur.'

'Perhaps you will. You so admired him. Look how you rushed out to nurse him.'

Both women turned to find Fred, his footsteps blown away by the wind, standing a couple of paces away.

'The luggage question is sorted out. One man fewer will come over with us. They'll want to leave quickly before the wind turns round in a more dangerous direction.' Suddenly the boat arrived and banged hard against the jetty.

Aroused by the noise, Rupert opened wide his crystal blue eyes, stared unfocused for a second, then fixed them on the boat, knocking and straining against its ties. Flinging his weight in its direction so that Hilda nearly lost hold of him, he cried, 'Bo'!'

Recovering him, Hilda walked towards the jetty, while murmuring to Sylvia over a shoulder, 'See? Men are born adventurers.'

Arthur allowed himself to be picked up by a veiled woman in the street. It was not exactly an impulsive act because he had followed the woman through several streets until he was sure she was leading him on. There were safer women for sex but it seemed that this anonymous depravity was what his libido demanded.

The encounter took place in a small room thinly portioned from a much larger, once grand space. The couch was clean, the woman, plump and soft-skinned, obliging. As she crouched over him, he felt a surge of excitement he hadn't known for years and images of Hector exploded in his brain. At his climax, he screamed out, frightening the woman who put her small hand over his mouth. Arthur was aware enough to smell cinnamon and another musky fragrance.

She allowed him to lie by her for a few moments and, in his happiness, he would have stayed for ever. But soon she brought a cloth with water and then his clothes.

Sitting half-dressed on the edge of the couch, his happiness changed to include a huge sorrow that this young woman had to earn her bread in this way. Her plump belly might even indicate she was pregnant. He reached into his pocket and gave her all the money he had. At that moment he felt more for her than for anyone in the world. He began to weep, tears pouring down his face

She was already veiled and the money disappeared under the black material. She waited patiently, not looking at him. But his pity was engulfing him. The tears were unstoppable. Holding his head in his hands, he gradually realised that he was not weeping over the fate of this poor woman, nor generally over the cruelty of the world. He was weeping for himself, for his own degraded life. He remembered the words of the French officer with whom he'd been captive. He'd told him that the French called orgasm *le petit mort*. Was it death he was seeking?

The woman came over and lightly touched his arm. She pointed to the door. Her face expressed no curiosity.

He dressed himself hurriedly, his fingers stumbling over the uniform buttons.

While they were still on the steps leading outside, he took her hand. 'Again?'

The black eyes looked at him seriously but he could read neither yes nor no. She gently pushed him into the street.

Sylvia and Fred had already spent two days in Valletta on their way to Gozo. It was then Sylvia had sent her letter to Arthur. Now they must spend another two days before their steamer, *Princess Eno*, left for Istanbul. They stayed in a palace newly converted into a hotel, in Castille Square. From their high up, side by side rooms, they could stare out at the golden walls of the city and the dark blue sea beyond. Sylvia began to suffer from the heat and spent most of the first day in the cathedral which she had visited four years ago with Hilda. There the sun couldn't follow her except to glimmer mysteriously on gilded saints and cascading chandeliers. She didn't revisit the lurid painting of Salome and St. John the Baptist's severed head.

'Do you pray?' Fred asked when they met in the evening. The forty degree heat seemed to suit him and he had spent the day walking and climbing, first round the city and then further out to small fishing villages hidden among the promontories. His face, already suntanned, was, apart from the scar on his forehead, as dark as any Maltese peasant.

Sylvia tried not to stare at him too obviously. 'Sometimes, I pray,' she said, answering his question. 'But I seem to need time to sit quietly. So different from you.'

Fred ordered a bottle of Maltese red wine and looked round at the restaurant which, although it was early, was already filling up, mostly with men in dark suits. It was the same one where Sylvia had come with Hilda.

Sometimes, lately, Fred and Sylvia found it difficult to be in each other's company.

'I went to see some cemeteries today,' said Fred, abruptly. 'So many nationalities buried on this island: British, Australian, Indian, French, New Zealanders. I suppose I'm getting in training for Gallipoli.' He smiled.

'You look so well,' said Sylvia enviously.

'What about you? Have you lost your nerve?' He didn't speak kindly but in a hectoring way.

'No. I don't know.' Sylvia sipped her wine. Of course he was right. She had lost her nerve. That's what it was all about. She had never minded heat in Cairo.

'I went down to the docks this morning. The *Princess Eno* puts in at Lemnos before it travels up the Dardanelles. Perhaps that will be near enough for you? I've been wondering whether a woman will ever be let on to Gallipoli.'

'You think it's a men-only place, do you?' Sylvia found a sustaining spark of anger. 'It's *my* father we're looking for.'

Fred sat back in his chair and looked at Sylvia. She had flushed but still her face was pale in the glowing light of the restaurant. She looked fragile, almost ethereal. 'There were never any women on Gallipoli. Not even nurses.'

'I know.' Sylvia glared. 'But before you soldiers landed, there were farmers there and men who tended the vineyards and the olive groves and I would expect, maybe I'm wrong, that they had wives, in other words, women.'

'There were always rumours,' said Fred, not rising to her anger, 'of women snipers on the Turkish side . . .'

'So perhaps my father was killed by a woman!' interrupted Sylvia, wanting to shout, although her voice was still low, and even glad to be ridiculous. It was better than silence between them.

'It was all fantastic. There were no women on Gallipoli.'

'Well, now there will be!'

'That's cleared up that then. You won't stay on Lemnos. Dreary place anyway, although I found it exciting at the time.'

Sylvia did not ask him about this excitement but began to pick at her food, a dish of stewed rabbit, which had just arrived. She thought more soberly that between Fred's memories of Gallipoli and hers of Arthur, it was no wonder that communication had become difficult.

Fred lay awake on the too-soft bed. After seeing Sylvia back to the hotel, he'd found a bar and drunk brandy till he was sent away. Visiting the cemeteries had not been a good idea. He had tried to guess by the dates on the gravestones what engagements the men had fought in. They had all died of wounds, brought from the hospitals on the island, so it was not an exact science. In fact, as some may have first waited on Gallipoli itself, Lemnos, Imbros or even the hospital ships, they could have died months after they'd first been wounded. But he'd persisted all the same, even looking for names he could recognise: Joe Dingle who'd been wounded once and then again, or Curly Wyke or Lennie or Silas Oakes or Charlie Tuck from Anzac. So many, many names. Naturally, he'd found none of them but the memories that had mostly left him in peace since throwing himself into work at the WEA returned with brutal intensity.

Leaving the shade of the pine trees that overhung much of the cemetery, he'd struck out for the cliffs and shoreline, eventually finding a little cove with a group of stone houses above and fishing boats pulled up on the pebbles. It calmed him to see a working place where men, however poor, lived in some kind of harmony with the world.

In the middle of the afternoon, finding himself alone on an isolated beach, he'd taken off his clothes, piled them neatly, and splashed into the water. It had relieved the heat but not helped to escape his memories; he'd seen too much death in the waters around Gallipoli. Tears mixed with sea water on his face.

Now, awake in his small bed, he thought wryly that he had accused Sylvia of losing her nerve when he was just as shaky. Why didn't he go to her room now, take her in his arms and suggest they stayed on Malta? They could tell her mother that they'd been forbidden access to Gallipoli; that they would never find her father's body anyway.

But it seemed that Gallipoli, and a Gallipoli that contained Captain Lamb, had become a condition of their friendship, of their love affair.

Fred sat up in an effort to order his thoughts. Strangely, his stump, which seldom hurt, had in the last few days had become painful with a heavy throbbing as if it had developed a pulse. He tried massage but it would not be soothed. He stood and went over to the window. Pushing open the shutters, at first he saw only darkness before his eyes began to pick out small lights from the ships in the harbour. Stars sprayed across the sky above. It was a tranquil scene; the air gentle and warm. Perhaps revisiting Gallipoli would be far easier than he imagined, even an anti-climax, a stretch of land now returned to its steady agricultural ways.

Fred stared out, but now unseeing, and realised that this outcome would be the most unbearable of all. The agony of Gallipoli must not be forgotten.

'I've discovered Miss Fitzpaine's steamer puts in at Chanak on its way to Istanbul. There's no reason for her to come to Istanbul at all.'

Major Rockbourne looked at Arthur, hunched over his drink in the bar, and thought he should get out more. His face was the colour of his ouzo. 'But surely she'll want to come. Byzantium and all that?'

'I could meet her at Chanak,' said Arthur, ignoring Rockbourne's comment. 'Arrange a hotel.'

'We can do that anyway.'

'I suppose, as the years pass, the place will be crawling with widows.'

'Really, Arthur!'

'Sorry.'

Arthur sent a telegram to Lemnos. SUGGEST DISEMBARK CHANAK STOP NEAREST POINT GALLIPOLI STOP WILL MEET PRINCESS ENO STOP. As he wrote it, he thought of Sylvia's arrival off the boat at Alexandria. She'd dashed, gay and boyish, into her father's arms.

Thirty-Five

The ferry that took Arthur, Sylvia and Fred from Chanak to the Gallipoli Peninsula was one of the 'beetle' landing crafts that had taken soldiers from the big ships to the beaches at Suvla Bay. Arthur recognised it at once but didn't try to relive the past. Besides, they would be landing on the eastern coast.

Sylvia was sitting at the front of the boat with her back towards the rest of them: Arthur and Fred, three soldiers, two members of the War Graves Commission. She held herself very straight, staring intently forward. She wore a long pale cotton coat and a floppy hat, tied on with a mauve scarf whose ends flew behind her. Arthur knew he had made her beautiful in his imagination but the reality amazed him. Then she had been a girl – he remembered, with a little shame, how he had patronised her, told her she could be a clever wife if she studied. Now she was a woman.

It was a very hot, menacing day, the clouds low and a liverish purple, as if the sun was forcing out from behind. There could be a storm.

Arthur turned round to face the small town they'd just left on the Asiatic side of the Dardanelles. It looked like an Italian seaside resort from where he sat: flimsy fretwork villas washed in pale colours, some with stone piers. More had survived the war than he would have thought possible. Even more remarkably, the massive white fortress nearby had only one shell hole where the Allied bombardment had hit its target. The stone fortress had been built 450 years ago, only nine years after the Turks took Constantinople. Its mirror image stood the other side of the narrows where they were heading – the white teeth through which any invading navy had to pass. Through which the British and French ships had failed to pass.

The night before they had dined at the Red Lion, as the Allied

491

armies officers' mess was known. It was in the centre of town which had been mostly destroyed by shelling and fires. Arthur was relieved, although somewhat surprised when Mr Chaffey came along too. It meant that he and Sylvia could not talk about personal matters. He should have recognised the name and the connection with Dorset immediately but there seemed no link between the chirpy boy he'd met, and indeed commanded on Gallipoli, and the handsome man who, as Sylvia had explained, worked for the WEA (an organisation Arthur knew nothing about) but had come along to help with arrangements.

Arthur looked at him now, seated at the third point of the triangle with Sylvia. He stared out as keenly as she did, but now and again made some comment to a soldier near him who pointed and once laughed. Arthur wondered whatever they could find to laugh about.

Arrangements was what they'd talked about over dinner: this ferry, the need to hire a boat to take them up the coast to Suvla, the possibility for camping on Gallipoli to save time, the essential meeting with the officer in charge of documenting all the bodies and planning the location of cemeteries.

Arthur had said to Sylvia, 'I suppose in an ideal world you would only want to go to Suvla where the Colonel died, but the chap we need to meet is based on Helles.'

When Sylvia merely agreed with a murmured 'yes', Chaffey, who had spoken very little, asked, 'Isn't Suvla where you were captured?' Adding, 'I never went there.'

Arthur had frowned at his chicken. Why did Chaffey know this? Did he have to answer? He had glanced at Sylvia who seemed not to be listening. 'On the evening of the twenty-first,' he admitted reluctantly and saw how Sylvia frowned at the date, the same date her father had died.

They had returned to the neutral ground of arrangements and by general agreement the evening had ended early and they'd walked back to the seafront villa where they were staying.

It felt as if neither Arthur himself nor Sylvia were able to confront their past. Perhaps it was not only the absence of Chaffey they needed but time to adjust and feel more daring.

At five the next morning, Arthur had been woken by an awareness of change. He'd sat up quickly and found his small grey room, with its dark bedstead and wardrobe, flushed with one of those ravishing dawns that everybody who'd fought on Gallipoli remembered. Going to the window, he'd looked out and seen Chaffey striding back from the direction of the town centre. It seemed obvious that he'd not been to bed. Suddenly, his face turned upwards and he waved. Arthur, with no inclination to wave back, guessed his peering face had been in the spotlight of the rising sun.

Neither of them had mentioned this little incident over breakfast, nor as they'd waited for the ferry to arrive with the two privates and the two soldiers from the War Graves Commission. In fact, they had scarcely spoken to each other.

Fred looked down at the churning green water, up at the threatening sky, so different from the promising dawn, then at the land ahead. He was acutely aware that it was the part of Gallipoli that the Allies had never reached, that it contained the mythical hill, Achi Baba, and all the promontories and high points from which the Turks had attacked them over eight months. He had the emotions of a child suddenly able to step through a locked door into a forbidden world. They would be landing at Khilid Bahr, below the great plateau of that name and north of Achi Baba. They were already close enough to see the landscape, burnt brown by summer sun, a jetty and a row of huts. A little over to the right stood the white fortress, pair to the one at Chanak. Beyond, the land sloped steeply upwards.

The beetle slowed abruptly, lowered itself in the water and rocked gently towards the jetty.

'I trust you brought your waterproofs?' One of the privates, a big Ulster man called Docherty, swept his hand at the clouds.

As the Turk at the helm jumped off the boat with a mooring rope, the first drops fell.

'Beware the deluge!' shouted Lamb, almost as if he was pleased. Sylvia took the hand of the Turk and stepped on to the jetty. He pointed her in the direction of one of the huts and she went there quickly without waiting for them.

'Might cool things down,' said the Ulster man. 'It's hard work going up and down those gullies.'

'Worse with the rain,' said Fred.

The two War Graves Commission men, Crankshaw and Fox, buttoned themselves into capes with hoods and strode away.

Fred didn't mind the rain. Already it was clearing away the clouds. Lamb didn't appear to mind either. The two of them got off the boat together.

'Gallipoli giving its usual friendly welcome,' said Fred.

They both stared to the dark plateau, brightness emerging behind to give it a ragged silhouette.

Out of the murk approached a sight that Fred first thought conjured up by his over-heated imagination: three horsemen, leading three more horses. There had been so few horses on Gallipoli, even Lord Kitchener had walked or climbed up the promontories.

'Do you see what I see?' he said to Lamb.

'They must be for us,' Arthur answered indifferently. 'I was expecting to be met.' He thought that the quickly advancing horsemen, with their capes flying, would have looked the same from 440 BC onwards. He stood waiting for them to arrive.

'Captain Lamb, sir.' The lead horseman slipped off his horse and saluted Arthur.

Fred watched. Although he was in civilian clothes, it brought back all the times he'd seen Lieutenant Lamb, as he then was, being saluted and saluting while he'd stood by, an unimportant soldier who was trained to obey – not that he had, particularly. Fred smiled.

'I'm Lieutenant Smalley. Major Strangeways sent me to give you any assistance. Shall we go under cover?' Behind him his shaggy horse, more a pony, shook himself so that the stirrups jingled and raindrops flew.

'It's not too bad.' Arthur indicated Fred. 'This is Chaffey. Mr Chaffey.' The two men shook hands.

'And there's a third in your party?' Smalley looked enquiringly.

'Miss Fitzpaine has taken cover.'

Smalley's face, expressive, rather monkey-like, crinkled in disbelief. '*Miss* Fitzpaine?'

'Why don't we find her?' suggested Arthur. 'It's on her account or her father's account we're here.'

At this moment Sylvia came out of the hut. A streak of sun came out of the clouds to join her. She waved and started towards them. The gap in the clouds closed again but the rain didn't return and it became even hotter than before.

'Major Strangeways left in a hurry at dawn. He only mentioned a Brigadier-General Fitzpaine,' explained Smalley, still discomposed.

'Have the farmers brought their wives back?' asked Fred, remembering Sylvia's irritation when he'd said there were no women on Gallipoli.

'I haven't seen any. Why do you ask? The villages are mostly smashed. In fact only a few farmers have come back: Turks and Greeks. The Turkish army occupied the place till the end of the war. They were the ones who burnt the crosses and failed to care for the cemeteries. You'll see all that for yourselves. It's just a pity the major got called off to Suvla.'

'But that's where we want to go,' explained Arthur.

'He's riding, walking, climbing and camping. Going to Anzac on the way.' He paused and eyed Arthur and Fred assessingly. 'I doubt you've time for that.'

'I expect we'll find him at Suvla,' said Arthur. He had been on the verge of informing Smalley that both he and Chaffey knew a great deal about Gallipoli's terrain, before thinking better of it. They were here only as Sylvia's escorts.

'Who will we find at Suvla?' Sylvia seemed a little out of breath and spoke brightly as if she were at a cocktail party.

'Major Strangeways,' said Arthur. 'Lieutenant Smalley has come in his place.'

'Good morning, Lieutenant.' Sylvia went over to the nearest pony and stroked his nose. 'And you brought us horses?'

'On this part of the peninsula there are areas which are fairly flat. It helps cover the distances.'

'My father left his horses in Egypt. A big black called Balaam – notoriously bad-tempered – was the one he loved best. I suppose they were reunited with his regiment. Those soldiers that survived went to Palestine when they came off Gallipoli. I've never had the heart to enquire about the horses, although I've thought of them now and again. Our stables are still mostly empty. Not that I care about that. I've never been very keen on riding.' Sylvia turned away from the pony she'd been petting and addressed the lieutenant. 'I don't think I'll accompany you on this expedition.

In the few days my father was on Gallipoli he never came here so there's no reason for me to look around. Besides, I'm not dressed for riding.'

All three men were silent for a moment. Sylvia had never altered her breezy manner and now had reverted to stroking the pony who blew down his nostrils and shook his head.

'We could walk,' suggested Fred.

'What will you do?' asked Arthur.

Sylvia left the pony and came towards them. 'That nice Docherty says the ferry will go back in an hour or two. I'll just potter about till then.'

'If that's what you want,' said Arthur.

Lieutenant Smalley still said nothing. He couldn't really think what this group was doing on Gallipoli anyway. Someone must have pulled strings.

'Now we're here I would like to look around,' said Arthur in a manner that seemed both detached and determined.

Fred went over to one of the ponies that had been led. It had a Roman nose and, although far smaller, it reminded him of his horse, Gallipoli.

'We'll leave you Docherty,' Arthur told Sylvia. 'You're probably doing the right thing. The weather is very unsettled. Of course, we'll pass on any information the lieutenant gives us. Get Docherty to take you to the Red Lion.'

'Yes.' She and Arthur were a little apart from the others and she suddenly took hold of his arm and said passionately, 'I can't bear the thought of being a tourist! My father would hate it. It's so . . . so . . .,' she hesitated, 'so *vulgar!*'

Arthur was only a little surprised. It *was* a bit strange, if not 'vulgar' to go traipsing round the scene of so much death.

'Do you feel none of us should go?'

'No! No! You and Fred, Mr Chaffey, are part of it. It's your *history*.' She still spoke intensely, although now distracted by a group of flies that were buzzing round her face. 'You go! I *want* you to go. More important, you *want* to go.'

Fred looking across at them, absent-mindedly rubbing his stump. It was hurting again. He wanted to be on horseback and seeing what there was to see. Sylvia was right. She shouldn't come

496

with them. It would have no meaning for her. She would be separated from them by her lack of understanding.

The lieutenant strolled over. 'Did you fight here?'

'Yes,' said Fred. 'From first to last.'

'And the captain?'

'Till August, then he was captured. And you?'

'No, thank God.'

'How could you tell we'd been here?'

'I'm not sure. Something about the way you trod the ground.'

'We know it well, although naturally not this part.'

Arthur came over. He had a stick that Fred hadn't noticed before, he swung it energetically. 'All fixed.'

Fred looked back and saw Sylvia was walking to the jetty, as if keen to get as far from Gallipoli as possible.

Once there she turned and looked back at them.

The men mounted and trotted away.

Sylvia watched them. She reflected that Gallipoli was more important to both of them than she was.

Then, almost out of sight, Fred turned in his saddle and waved. She lifted her hand in response and her scarf fluttered out.

They rode directly up to the plateau, the ponies puffing crossly, the men looking around constantly, occasionally wiping their faces as the sweat rolled into their eyes. A halo of flies formed around their ponies' heads. But they were ordinary small black flies, not the bloated ones that had tortured them during the fighting. Now and again they saw Turkish cemeteries, rows of grey wooden monuments, like small totem poles, marked by a few thin cypress trees.

'Three thousand Turks buried there,' shouted Smalley, pointing to one such cemetery, 'and three German military engineers; you can see their crosses.'

There was little of note otherwise and Arthur decided his enforced march from Suvla must have taken him further east and north. He was glad they were riding and pleased the hardy ponies got them up most of the way to the Khilid Bahr plateau. When the ground became steep and their hooves caught in the low, but dense, prickly scrub, they dismounted and led them. They had already passed Turkish trenches, some solidly reinforced with stone and, as they reached the top, they could see many more behind Achi Baba, on either side and up the slopes of other smaller hills. It was like a ghost habitation, as if left through plague or famine.

It reminded Fred of Helles as the evacuation had emptied the lines. He turned to Arthur. He had taken off his cap and stood frowning into the sun which had nearly won the fight with the clouds. 'They left victorious while we left in defeat.'

'Yes. I missed all that. The army believes it was a triumph of organisation. I suppose it was – at least, a great escape.' Arthur turned to face Fred. 'How did you feel about it?'

'We hated it. We didn't want to stay. We didn't want to go. Well, we did want to go but we still hated it. So many dead. So many left behind. Even the stupidest felt depressed.'

'But then anyone who could had to fight on somewhere else?'

'Yes. Tommy is a resilient chap.'

'I wasn't only thinking of the Tommies.'

Fred shrugged. 'What else do I know?'

Arthur thought Chaffey knew a lot more than how the Tommies felt. He had given that impression even during the fighting.

Lieutenant Smalley, who had been talking to the accompanying soldiers, came over and looked curiously at the two men. He decided to be direct. 'I suppose you'll recognise the ground as we get further along?' Arthur looked surprised so Smalley added, 'Mr Chaffey told me, sir.'

'Yes. We both fought down there,' said Fred. 'Slept on its earth, ate its flies, drank its contaminated water, watched sunsets, killed there, were wounded there, became ill there.'

'We did more than that,' said Arthur mildly.

'Captain Lamb commanded me, off and on,' said Fred.

Smalley nodded. So that was it: a regimental bond between officer and private. Yet there was no warmth between them, more wariness, as if they either didn't know each very well or were distrustful. But perhaps that was their natures, or even the effects of the war. Disabled soldiers were often bitter, in the lieutenant's experience, although Chaffey's ability to ride, walk and climb seemed unaffected by his missing limb.

'More off than on,' said Arthur. 'You were always an unusual soldier.'

Fred was unfazed. 'I was in Anzac for a while. Part of the time with the intelligence officer who arranged the day-long armistice in June. Captain Prideaux. Captain Lamb knew him too. We buried the dead. The putrid dead.'

'The general allowed that?' asked Smalley. 'Hamilton, wasn't it?'

'He was talked round.' Fred frowned and moved to face north. 'I suppose we could get to the place from here but I wouldn't care to revisit. My nose still recalls the stink.'

'We couldn't do it there and back in a day.' Smalley took a step towards Arthur. 'Where do you want to go from here, sir?'

'I'd like to stand on Achi Baba!' called out Fred. 'Stamp on its complacent head.'

Smalley waited for Arthur to speak.

'Could we get down to V Beach?' asked Arthur, after a pause.

'We can manage Achi Baba. As you can see it's not actually a hill but the continuation of a smaller plateau pointed towards Helles. But V Beach is quite a few miles with some steep climbs. We might be able to pick up the Krithia road, although even that's rough going. We'd still be pushed to get back before dark. It'd be easier to land at the beach from the sea.'

Fred thought that he could show them the quickest way on foot from the Allied front lines to V Beach with no trouble at all. The soldiers could ride back and arrange for a boat to pick them up. He wondered if he wanted to revisit V Beach any more than the terrible no man's land at Anzac. He remembered Carrots, the ginger-haired Irish soldier who'd accompanied him on a not very successful mission of mercy. Innocent days! The boy had died so speedily he'd never known his real name.

'Does Krithia village survive?' asked Arthur.

'More or less rubble,' answered Smalley. 'You'll see it clearly from Achi.'

'We'll start there then.'

Sylvia was back on the ferry. Docherty, the Ulster man with his big red face, was with her and several other soldiers on their way back for a day's leave at Chanak. The men talked excitedly.

Sylvia faced away from Gallipoli. The further it slipped behind, the more her spirits lifted. She couldn't remember what passionate words she'd delivered back there but she knew it was a dreadful place, a cursed place and that its natural beauty made things worse. Men had created the horror, all men, politicians or soldiers, so men would have to clear it up. There was no place for a woman there, not because she was weak or needed protecting, but because she'd played no part in the whole ghastly charade. Oh, men were brave too, even heroes, but she couldn't help wondering if that wasn't the whole point of war: to turn ordinary men into heroes.

She was glad she had left them to it. Perhaps she wouldn't even land at Suvla Bay, although she supposed she owed that to her parents. Sylvia put her chin on her hand and watched the line of Chanak's villas and the white fort come into focus. The Red Lion, she'd noticed, had a garden shaded by cypresses. She'd sit there and read de Quincey's *Confessions of an English Opium-Eater*. That should take her mind from one form of madness to another.

Arthur and Fred stood on the top of Achi Baba. Both felt pierced by the tragedy that had been enacted below them. Smalley, perhaps in an attempt to cover for their unmanly emotion, was pointing out and naming places of interest, as if leading a guided tour – which in a way he was.

'Directly below us is what remains of Krithia. You can see the Turkish trenches and, not much further on, the French and British. The Australians fought down there in May. You can also see the vineyard where there was heavy fighting in June. You might even be able to spot Lieutenant Colonel Doughty-Wylie's grave. His widow was here earlier this year and persuaded the major to leave his alone. Of course he was a VC.' Smalley warmed to his theme. 'There was talk she also visited it in '15 but some say it was his mistress, Gertrude Bell. Whoever, she was the only woman on Gallipoli during the fighting. There're rumours now that he'd enough of his complicated life, that he was suicidal. Don't believe it, myself. A soldier like that.'

Fred, who was stubbing his foot at the ground instead of looking out, said, 'These pit-holes are from our naval guns, I suppose. Never did more than scare the tortoises. Where are all the tortoises, incidentally?'

'You'll see plenty of them at Suvla,' said Smalley. 'If we'd camped you'd have heard the jackals too.'

'Jackals?' Fred straightened up.

'Yes. No one seems to have heard them during the campaign – perhaps the guns scared them away – but there're several packs now.'

Fred, following an unpleasant train of thought, was about to ask whether any of the dead still lay unburied, when Arthur, who was facing the way they'd come, exclaimed in a shocked voice, 'But you can't see the Dardanelles from here! The view's blocked by the plateau. We'd have had to fight the whole length of Khilid Bahr.'

Smalley frowned. 'Yes. That was quite a shock for a lot of people.'

Fred said nothing. It was a glorious day now, about one o'clock, the sky a pure blue and, very high above, the trill of larks. He thought that there had been larks when the army first arrived on Gallipoli.

Arthur swung round again and stared at the vineyard and the rubble of the little village he and Fred had fought through in April. He remembered the cat feeding on the dead Turk's brain. It had upset him at the time but later he had become used to far worse atrocities.

Fred joined in. He pointed. 'I think that's the piece of cliff we climbed and I watched the hand of God, in the shape of a boulder, bounce clean over your head.'

'I'd forgotten,' said Arthur stiffly. He supposed at some point he must try and work out what this man was doing here with Sylvia. He certainly didn't behave like a servant.

'We can even see V Beach,' said Fred. He walked forward to where the soldiers stood holding the ponies. 'Is that the *River Clyde*?' he asked of no one in particular. The great hulk, painted in its unfinished camouflage, was unmistakable.

'I went down there a few days ago,' said one of the soldiers. 'She's stripped of all her fittings. Every broken hull in the bay is stripped bare.'

For a moment, Fred thought of Sylvia. Whoever took the fittings of an old coaler would certainly not hesitate to strip the watch or ring off the corpse of a brigadier-general.

'We're still burying bones down there,' continued the same soldier. 'In some places the earth is white with bones. Those who fell between the lines. Bones and skulls. At one point I'd collected a whole heap of skulls, prior to burial, you understand, and someone took a photograph. Not very sensitive, I'd say.' He paused and gave Fred a friendly nudge. 'You can tell the race of a man by the shape of his skull, you know. We've experts. The Turks are different to Europeans, flatter at the back.'

Fred wondered what it was about him that made the soldier confide such things. Was it because he didn't look like an officer? Or was it his missing arm? 'You won't have found my hand there,' he said. 'It went down to the bottom of the ocean.'

Both soldiers laughed. Then the first, the cockiest, sounding as if he came from the north-east said, 'We were betting that you'd come here looking for it, complete with gold ring and all.'

Fred smiled. He supposed this was graveyard humour. 'No gold ring,' he said.

'Pity.' The first soldier looked thoughtful and turned to his mate. 'What was it that gave us the heebie-jeebies yesterday?'

'Teeth,' answered the other, 'grinning down at us from the stump of an olive tree.'

'Like the Cheshire cat,' suggested Fred, although he was thinking of the teeth that had clamped onto his thigh. He decided that he didn't need any more anecdotes. Both soldiers looked mystified.

'I don't know about cats but we've about had enough,' said the first. 'Been months with the bones, collecting, sorting, digging, burying. We've asked to be transferred to roads. Building them. Less depressing.'

'I can see that. Have either of you been at Suvla?'

'Not us.'

'So you don't know how they're getting on with the burying there.'

'No idea, mate. Sir. But it'll be the same story: bones everywhere you look. Bits and pieces of uniform. Bullets, mugs and water bottles. Nothing valuable.'

'Even worse next spring once they get ploughing. Turn up all sorts.'

'At least *we* won't be here.' As the soldier finished speaking, he nodded at his mate and the two men led the ponies away.

Lieutenant Smalley appeared beside Fred. Fred nodded towards the retreating men. 'Gruesome work for them?'

'Yes. We thought they'd like a day off, escorting us. We're trying to clear this section before the weather worsens.'

'Good idea.' Fred pictured the storm and floods when he'd hung on to a tree stump while corpses, or perhaps just one, washed by him. 'Storms can be fierce in a month or two,' he said mildly. 'Are we going down?'

'Captain Lamb is not sure. I suggested we show him some of the new cemeteries we're making. We're quite proud of them. In some places we have to begin by dismantling the fake graves marked out in 1917 to impress an inspection set up by the Pope. But the captain only grimaced and said, "That's quite an invitation." I suppose I've got used to the place and have a job of work to do.'

Fred realised Smalley was put out. 'Captain Lamb was a prisoner of war for three years. He has bad memories.'

'Well, perhaps he'll be more interested at Suvla where he was captured.'

'Perhaps.'

'He'll have Major Strangeways to talk to.'

'There is that.'

'So what'll we do?' Smalley took off his cap and wiped his forehead. 'As a matter of fact I'll be as glad to get out of here as the men. Earlier in the year we had an Australian journalist fellow here. Bean, he was called. Went all over the place, taking notes, mostly on Anzac but at Helles too. Trying to work out from where the bodies had fallen or the bullets or a hat or a boot just how the fighting had gone. He'd been here himself. I admired him. He helped us too. He seemed really pleased to get all the information to take back home. Like me, he had a job to do, that's the thing. Writing the official Australian history, so he told me.'

'I'll ask Captain Lamb what he wants.'

Arthur watched Chaffey coming towards them. He'd been talking to everybody. Arthur admired that, although it irritated him too. Far away memories stirred on when he'd preached socialism and the equality of men.

'What do you think?' said Fred. 'It's some view. Although I'd like to have come up in spring with the poppies. I'll never forget them waving up there like red flags of defiance. Do you want to carry on?'

'If you'd really like to know,' replied Arthur in a low intense voice, 'I can't imagine what we're doing in this charnel house! And that's not a question.'

'Let's go then.'

Arthur looked closely at his companion's face which seemed almost cheerful. 'You don't want to retrace old routes, old graves? Old memories? You dug Doughty-Wylie's grave, didn't you?'

'I've got better things in my head now. And Miss Fitzpaine's waiting.' Fred whistled a little between his teeth, surprising both of them. It was not his habit.

'Miss Fitzpaine,' repeated Arthur and then, wanting to be angry at something, tried to swat a horse-fly with his stick. 'Damned insects. I don't know how I allowed Miss Fitzpaine to persuade me into this damn fool expedition!'

'I didn't plan to come either.' The two men looked at each other. Despite Arthur's mistrust and Fred's assumed nonchalance, the solidarity which they had felt as they trotted away from Sylvia, reasserted itself.

Arthur tucked his stick under his arm. 'I'll tell Smalley. After all, we can always put in at V Beach on the way to Suvla.'

Thirty-Six

Sylvia was in the bar of the Red Lion when Arthur and Fred returned. Her hair was fluffed up and her cheeks were pink as if she'd rouged. She wore a light summer dress, pale yellow with frills on the sleeves and the neckline threaded with white ribbon. A string of jade beads reached nearly to her waist.

Both men stopped to look at her. They had come straight from the boat and were hot and dirty, their hair lank with sweat.

'They said I could wait for you here!' Sylvia called gaily. 'I'm sure it's against all the regulations.'

'We're filthy,' said Arthur. 'Can you wait a little longer while we clean up?'

'Don't worry about me. I'm going to do a little exploring.' Fred smiled at Sylvia, making contact without coming any closer. Both Arthur and Sylvia, for different reasons, felt uneasy.

'Can't you even keep me company while Captain Lamb's making himself presentable?' said Sylvia in the same bright manner.

Fred glanced at Arthur. 'No. I don't think so. I have a date. I'll see you in the morning.' He went out. The last rays of the sun glowed red through the open door.

Arthur came closer to Sylvia. 'You look very lovely.'

'Thank you.' Sylvia put up a hand to her beads and Arthur noticed it was trembling. 'Will you order me a drink before you go?'

'Of course.'

Once Arthur had left, Sylvia sipped her drink slowly and told herself that under the extraordinary circumstances any one of them must be allowed to behave as they thought fit. She, herself, had turned and fled from Helles.

*

Sylvia and Arthur sat at a table under the cypresses in the Red Lion garden. Insects, attracted by lights from the building behind them and a flaming torch in the actual garden, whirled noisily. The strong medicinal smell of the trees mixed with the cigarettes smoked by a group of soldiers at another table nearby.

'Are you being bitten?' asked Arthur.

This was the most personal remark he had made all evening. Over dinner they had talked about international post-war politics and then, rather more briefly about her mother, and Gussie's new life. There had been a tenderness in his voice as he asked the question which made her heart beat faster. He had even leant forward as if he might touch her hand.

'I picked up some citrine oil in Malta. Heaven knows what filth it's made of but it works wonderfully.' Actually, Fred had discovered the oil but she found herself unwilling to pronounce his name.

'Malta.' Arthur frowned. The dim light softened the taut lines of his face and he looked more as Sylvia remembered him from before the war. 'You wrote to me from there.'

'I was visiting my friend, Hilda, Captain Prideaux's widow. I'm sure I told you.'

Arthur curled his long fingers round his glass of brandy. He swirled the amber liquid reflectively. 'Captain Prideaux was a difficult sort of chap. But then I only met him in difficult circumstances.'

Sylvia stared at her own still full glass. 'Difficult' was, she suspected, an understatement of both the man and the circumstances.

Arthur looked up at her, suddenly animated. 'At the time I never could decide if he was rebellious just for the sake of it. But as it turned out, he'd got it about right.' He returned to his brandy.

Sylvia had been about to describe Prideaux's history following Arthur's capture but then realised that he did not want to know more. Arthur's interest and his mourning only went as far as his last sentence.

There was a silence between them in which the voices and laughter of the men at the next table seemed unnaturally boisterous. What secrets were they disguising? Sylvia wondered. She felt for the smooth beads of her necklace. She knew that if anything important was to be discussed, she must be the one to bring it up.

She tried to see Arthur's face. The darkness allowed her to look at him and think about him in a way she hadn't dared in the glare of the day. Had he become a complete stranger? Was he only helping her onto Gallipoli out of a duty to the past, more for her mother and father than herself?

But they had loved each other! They had exchanged passionate vows. They had planned to live their lives together. She realised, with a little surprise, that she wanted there to be something left. She wanted at very least that tenderness she had felt from him when they first sat down. She wanted to find him again, if only for these few minutes while they talked in this garden far away from everything.

'I don't think I did very well with my letter-writing to you,' she said.

He gave a start, then, when he'd understood what she'd said, a half-smile. 'You couldn't have done any better. Right from the time I landed on Gallipoli, I couldn't tell you the truth for all kinds of reasons – some due to my own weakness. You were kind. That was enough.'

The word 'kind' horrified Sylvia. 'But I loved you!' she protested.

The half-smile returned. 'Oh, yes. We loved each other. I'm glad of that, aren't you? We had such eager, happy times. I won't say "innocent" because I don't much believe in that sort of thing any more. Let's say we were filled with good intentions.'

But Sylvia was not prepared to give in yet. 'Do you remember when I came to you in Cairo? When you were sick?'

'I remember. You were like a boy, with your bobbed hair. I was shocked.' His tone was indulgent, as a father might reminisce about the antics of a child.

'We made love!'

'I know we did. I said already that we loved each other. It was that same night that I heard I was to be made a captain. I was so proud. The important general who told me while we were both dining with your father could quite easily be blamed for his death. One of the guilty men, anyway. I don't want to think these things, Sylvia, but they are true.'

'So being made a captain was as important as our making love!' Sylvia could hardly believe that she was saying, almost shouting, such a ridiculous accusation. It was even more ridiculous considering that she had made love with Prideaux only a few days after Arthur returned to Gallipoli.

But he would not rise again. Another silence fell. Sylvia took out a small bottle from her handbag and rubbed oil on her hands and neck. She put it away and clicked the brass clasp of the bag. 'I'm sorry. That was childish.' She leant across and gave Arthur her hand.

'I'm sorry too.' He held her hand for a moment before laying it gently back on the table. 'I suppose I'll come back to England eventually. To Oxford, if they'll have me. I'd be a frightfully bad banker,' he added. 'Probably cause a market crash. Much more suited to ancient history.'

Sylvia looked at him with surprise. Had he forgotten that she was studying at Oxford? She had certainly written and told him. 'I might be still there,' she said.

'Oh, yes.' He paused. 'I'm glad.'

He *had* forgotten. Was he glad that she had gone to university or that she might still be there when he arrived? If he arrived.

The soldiers at the next table got up. As they passed, they said, 'Good-night, sir.' Arthur nodded politely.

'Are you cold?' he asked Sylvia.

She took a cream shawl from the arm of the chair and wrapped it round her shoulders. She had thought he would ask her about Fred and she hadn't known how she would answer. But now it seemed that Fred was not to be mentioned. Perhaps it was the war that had taught them secrecy. Or perhaps the English were a cowardly race when it came to the emotions.

She could tell Arthur that she was having a love affair with Fred, even that she loved Fred. But at this moment she was not sure that was true. She must feel that Fred loved her.

Sylvia stood up and Arthur came round to pull back her chair. He was tall as he stood behind her, inches taller than Fred. She remembered how proud she'd been to be with him, how he'd dazzled her country girl's ignorance. How grateful she'd felt to him.

She spoke impulsively. 'Put your arm round me.'

Obediently, he put his arm around her waist.

'Thank you,' she murmured.

He leant forward and she felt his lips pressed briefly against her cheek. 'So beautiful,' he whispered.

She felt tears in her eyes. His lips had been cool.

They walked towards the clubhouse together but when they reached the door, Sylvia put his arm aside.

Thirty-Seven

The sky was clear over Gallipoli as Sylvia, Arthur and Fred stood on the narrow jetty at Chanak waiting for the boat they'd hired. They stayed a little apart from each other, breathing the fresh air of a radiant morning.

Arthur looked at his watch, then hitched up a leather satchel he wore over his shoulder. 'He promised seven o'clock. We've got a long day ahead.'

'I think I see a boat, sir,' said Docherty, staring upstream. Lieutenant Smalley was no longer with them. 'God knows where it's come from but it's being swept down by a four-knot current.'

Everybody peered in that direction and Sylvia held her bag a little closer. It was a soft bag which might have contained needlework and silks. Sylvia had chosen it carefully and placed pouches inside it in case something should be found – she didn't try to imagine what – and a notepad and pencil because she intended to jot down anything of interest said by Major Strangeways. She was vaguely aware that she was using the bag and its contents as a shield against emotion. Yesterday, at Helles, she had told Arthur and Fred, that it was *their* history. Today it was hers.

She hadn't seen Fred since he'd looked in at the Red Lion and announced he wasn't joining them.

The boat arrived, clean but old, crewed by two Turks. Fred helped Sylvia to step down to it. His hand, gripping hers, made her flush. She wanted to sit by him and feel his warmth hip to hip but he went forward and began to talk in some kind of pidgin English to one of the Turks. The two of them, with their dark, sunburned skin, flashed and gesticulated at each other.

They set off. Though the wind was not as strong as the day before, the swell was heavy and now and again the small boat slid sideways.

Arthur shouted to Sylvia. 'We'll hug the coast. At least if the boat breaks down we can swim to shore. You can swim, can't you?'

'Yes,' answered Sylvia. She thought it was as if they were strangers again.

Fred came back and sat near her. She felt grateful but looked at him warily. 'It'll be a long journey,' he said, frowning, 'Three or four hours at least in this tub.'

'You know I like boats,' said Sylvia. On Gozo they'd hired a boat to look at a grotto where the water was a startling turquoise.

'Yes. I know.' He smiled at her.

Suddenly Sylvia knew that he wanted to put his arm round her. Perhaps kiss her. She smiled.

'What do you think about stopping at V Beach?' shouted Arthur.

'We should push on!' shouted Fred.

Sylvia didn't mind the two men shouting at each other. She knew that soon they would be passing the beach where they had landed and would probably see reminders of their experiences there.

'I agree. We might drop in on the way back!' shouted Arthur.

The coast came up on their right, steep yellow cliffs, illuminated by the rising sun, a side view of where Fred and Arthur had walked the day before.

'There's the French trenches,' said Fred. 'Poor buggers. They had it from both sides.'

Sylvia made out dark circular lines above the cliffs. Arthur hadn't heard Fred's comment.

The boat, rocked and buffeted by the waves as the second Turk tried to force more from the engine, still processed slowly. Now and again a wave splashed over the side.

'It'll be more like five or six hours,' muttered Fred.

The first Turk poured out tea from a flask into a tin mug the size of an eggcup and offered it round. It was sweet but refreshing. As the sun rose higher and became hotter, Sylvia pulled the scarf tighter round her hat so that the brims narrowed her view. It was more restful like that. She put her hands, which were beginning to burn, in the pockets of her skirt.

A long bay, with a pale sandy beach, opened out. 'Morto Bay,' said Fred. 'The fort at Sedd el Bahr is at the end of it, then, round the headland, we reach V Beach.' He screwed round to face the other way. 'That's Kum Kale on the Asian side. It may seem distant to you but it seemed close to us when they started firing their big guns from there.' He seemed excited, invigorated.

'Troy!' shouted Arthur suddenly. He half stood up, rocking the boat.

'Sit down, you fool,' said Fred under his breath. Then to Sylvia, 'It's not as if we can see it.'

'I like to *know*,' said Sylvia, defending Arthur. But it was true she could see nothing but a misty brown sensation of land, of the vast expanse of Asia, of the Ottoman Empire that had held Arthur captive for three years. The empire had gone, yet he still cried 'Troy!'

The boat slowed as they passed the majestic ruins of the fort, white grass springing up among its fallen walls and towers. Then they were opposite V Beach, at the point of the peninsula. *So small*, thought Fred. Without the *Clyde* and the relics of other ships and boats, it would be just another little beach of shingle and shells. Bones now too, doubtless. Lots of them. The boat came in quite close, close enough to swim to shore. If he could swim, which he couldn't. Fred imagined splashing out of the clear blue water and strolling up the beach under a calm blue sky, just as he had on Malta. Would a replay like that cancel out some of his memories? He doubted it. He could see quite clearly the little shelf of land under which he'd sheltered on that first day. It was even lower than he remembered, offering scarcely any protection, but he didn't remember being scared, just fed up.

He turned away. He'd seen enough now. He wanted to get to Suvla, do whatever Sylvia felt necessary, and return to real life. Gallipoli was at best an aberration. He glanced at Sylvia but her hat obscured her face. He knew she'd have been upset by his absence the night before. But she had to deal with that. Actually, she had to deal with Arthur. Perhaps she had. They seemed no closer this morning than they had the day before. His 'date' had been a walk to the fort by the last rays of the sunset. He'd found an Australian soldier on a day's leave, studying a great round shell hole.

'Well at least our chaps hit something,' Fred had commented dourly.

'You were here?'

'Obvious, is it?'

'In your voice, mate.' They had smiled at each other, told each other their regiments and later found a bar well supplied with rum. Probably inherited army rations, they had agreed.

Fred tried to make himself more comfortable in the boat. The trip had become interminable. They had to round Cape Helles and pass W Beach where he'd made his final exit and X Beach and Gully beach and Y Beach and still there'd be Anzac Cove. They'd never make Suvla in time to see anything. What had Arthur and he been thinking? Of course, if soldiers did travel between the different beaches, which was unusual, they'd been on proper ships, linking the campaign fronts in the only possible way.

Now it struck him what was so different about the scene: apart from their own boat, a couple of fishing boats further out to sea, and all the wrecked hulks, there was nothing else floating on the blue waves. Back then, there'd been battleships, destroyers, lighters, tugs, steamers, even yachts, and of course the hospital ships which had tortured him with the thought of their clean security. How lavish is war!

'It's going to take us all day to get there!' shouted Fred to Arthur.

'I know!' shouted Arthur.

They passed W Beach and Fred peered forward, trying to pick out the cavern from which the explosives had burst. What lunatic exhilaration he'd felt as he'd watched its fireworks from the departing lighter! But, although the sun had followed them round the peninsula so that it still lit up every wrinkle and gully of the coastal cliffs, he could identify no gaping black hole. In the four years since their leaving, nature had the time to obliterate man's extravagances.

'Is it picnic time?' Fred said to Sylvia in a rough voice.

'If you like. Ask Docherty to get the basket.'

Fred lost interest in eating. He listened to the waves banging on the bottom of the boat. No one talked, not even the Turks. The wind was stronger as they headed up north. Sometimes he caught a glimpse of a new road on the peninsula or an indication of men working near tethered horses. Once or twice he saw new

513

cemeteries, no crosses on them, just the tablets of stone. Eventually, he shut his eyes and fell into an uncomfortable doze.

'Look at that!' Arthur was shouting in his ear.

A smart launch was bouncing over the waves towards them. Its chrome gleamed amid the white spray. A soldier with a loudhailer called to them. 'Major Strangeways invites you to lunch.'

'Saved,' exclaimed Fred and he touched Sylvia's arm.

'We accept!' shouted Arthur.

A picnic lunch had been laid out with army neatness on a plateau overlooking the beach. There were chairs for everybody and a canopy rigged against the sun.

As they walked towards it, Sylvia looked up at the rising cliffs and gasped in awe at the layers of dugouts where men had made their homes. They were all there, untouched, even the sandbags still in place. 'Our soldiers lived there like nesting birds,' commented Captain Brockman, an Australian who'd joined them on the quay. 'And in the end they flew away.'

'It's not often we get visitors,' said Major Strangeways, welcoming them. 'My only worry was that you'd shoot by.'

'Not in that tub,' said Arthur.

Brockman laughed. 'There was only one direction you were going to in it. Next stop Melbourne.'

'We're not usually as luxurious as this. It's the diggers' influence. They know how to make themselves comfortable.' The major indicated the cliff-side homes. 'We'll take you on to Suvla,' he continued. 'Then you can borrow the launch for your return to Chanak. I'll pay off your crew.'

Sylvia undid her scarf and took off her hat. She felt the air round her neck with relief. She fluffed up her damp hair.

The major was watching her and pulled out a wooden chair beside him. 'I met your father at Suvla,' he said when they were both sitting down. 'Just before I was wounded. I'm afraid he led a very desperate attack.'

'So we understand,' said Sylvia a little primly. But the major's words had made her heart beat faster. 'My mother finds it hard to come to terms with his death. So far away. So little known of how he died. That's why I've come here.'

The major nodded sympathetically. 'Yes. We hope the

514

memorials and cemeteries we're constructing will help relatives find peace. Even if it's only a photograph of a gravestone.'

Sylvia glanced at Fred and Arthur who were talking to the Australian, and swallowed a forkful of beans, before saying, 'My mother believes we'll find something to indicate where my father died.'

'I see. I will take you to the area where he was last seen. But I warn you, it is not a happy sight.'

'His was not a happy ending.'

'True enough.' The major paused before continuing. 'I thought we could walk in his footsteps. It won't take much more than a couple of hours, if that, from Lala Baba to Scimitar Hill. We can probably even cross the salt lake as he did.' Since Sylvia seemed unable to speak, he added in sombre tones, 'If I had my way, I'd make this part of the peninsula a memorial. A memorial park.'

Lunch didn't last long. In less than an hour they were on the launch, this time ploughing speedily through the waves. The day was still luminously beautiful, the sun still following round behind them.

Sylvia stayed at the side of the major. As they approached the wide sweep of Suvla Bay, he explained, 'Brigadier-General Fitzpaine could have landed at one of several beaches but we'll get as near to Lala Baba as we can. That's where he would have waited before setting out across the dry salt lake in the late afternoon. You see it there.' He pointed.

'You mean that little knoll?' Sylvia had read about the hill and imagined it far grander. She looked up as Fred shifted along to join them.

'It's much more open than I expected,' he commented. 'I suppose that long high ridge to the left, ending in a drop to the sea, is Kiretch Tepe?'

The major nodded. 'Our men got up there all right. We're still collecting skeletons.' He glanced at Sylvia. 'Sorry.'

Sylvia hadn't heard. She was concentrating on the view now directly ahead as the launch made for the shore. 'And beyond the flat stretch, the lake, I suppose, is that Chocolate Hill?'

'Yes. The Turkish troops held the higher ground behind that. They overlooked the whole area.'

Arthur only came to join them as they drew alongside a small newly built jetty.

'Our men are camped here. Not so many insects by the sea,' explained the major. 'A cemetery is being constructed over to our right but most of the work is further inland.'

They started walking at once, the major frowning at the position of the sun. He, Sylvia and Fred followed the soldiers who banged at the ground now and again with sticks they'd picked up, presumably to scare away anything unwanted, although the grass and scrub was dry and thin.

'Would it have been as hot as this?' asked Sylvia. Now they were off the boat and with no cover, they could feel the full force of the sun.

'Oh, yes. Forty degrees or more,' said the major. 'The soldiers working here drink pints of water – which is more than can be said for those poor chaps in '15. They'd come out of their trenches with tongues black and swollen. Early on, they had to be kept from the water tankers with guns. Even so, they cut holes.'

Arthur walked some way back on his own. There was a sound in his ears which after a while he identified as the mouth organ which had led them across the salt lake. He quickened his stride until he was beside Sylvia.

'I wasn't with General Fitzpaine,' he said loudly enough for them all to hear. 'I never saw him after Lala Baba but we took the same route as far as Chocolate Hill, which the English held, although not safely. The brigade I was with was ahead of his. From there, Fitzpaine attacked to the left and I to the right. If you don't mind, once we've crossed the lake, I'll follow my own route. I won't be long. I'll find you out. As you can see, it's fairly easy walking.'

'Oh, Arthur.' Sylvia turned to him but he wouldn't look at her.

It took them less than an hour to cross the white expanse. The salty dust puffed around their legs.

'It must have felt longer,' said Fred as they reached Chocolate Hill and stared back towards the glittering sea, 'with shrapnel dropping all around you.'

Arthur said, 'It wasn't too heavy.' Then he set off away from them, walking, Sylvia thought, as if he had some destination in mind.

The major said to Sylvia, 'We can't be sure of the general's route from here, although there were men watching from the top of the hill, but the smoke was very thick, plus there was an unusual mist. Unlucky that. Perhaps you read Ashmead-Bartlett's description in *The Times*. Someone sent it to me months later. He was a brave reporter but not altogether loyal, I sometimes thought.'

Sylvia said nothing. She was watching Fred who was scooping out something from under a thorny shrub. He showed her a tortoise at least a foot long. 'Want a pet?'

'I had a tortoise once. He was very boring. I didn't even know if he was a he.'

'English soldiers kept them as pets and French soldiers ate them.'

Sylvia didn't mind that Fred was trying to lighten the mood. But it wouldn't change anything. She imagined her sweet-tempered, middle-aged father leading his men across the open stretch of land to this relatively sheltered spot. 'I thought you'd found something to do with the battle.'

'Not likely to be much round here. The Red Cross carts would follow behind and pick up the injured and the dead.'

Sylvia saw that the soldiers and the major had carried on some way up a dusty track. She followed, not waiting while Fred carefully laid back the tortoise. A few wild roses appeared among a tangled mass of briars. She looked closer and saw that they were growing out of what must be a trench. She realised there was another further up. As she understood it, her father had never had the opportunity to shelter in a trench.

Fred caught up with her and they walked side by side. The major seemed worried about the time, setting a fast pace as the track became more rutted and steeper. When it turned into a field with the stalks of some kind of thinly planted crop, he waited for them. 'Later we'll go to a cemetery. We've called it Green Hill – a nice restful name. But we'll keep climbing up to Scimitar Hill, if you're game for it. There's quite a view from there.' He paused, coughed embarrassedly. 'Although I appreciate that it isn't exactly the point.'

'That's all right,' said Sylvia. She pointed to the edge of the field where a pile of stones topped by corrugated iron surrounded by a crude fence seemed to indicate some kind of dwelling.

'An old man lives there. He says this land is his. To prove the point, he got some relative down here to plough land and sow the field in the spring. He's done another one further along. Who knows if it's true but he's surrounded by enough ferocious dogs and smelly goats to earn respect.'

'How old?' asked Sylvia. They were standing in the shade of a holm oak tree which had grown beyond the stunted specimens all around. She thought if she were her mother, she'd imagine that old man as Brigadier-General Fitzpaine, Dorset landowner, memory lost and looking for a home.

'No way of telling.' The major answered her question cheerfully. 'They're all equally bent and brown and wrinkled.'

They began to walk across the field. The irregular ploughed ground and the crumbly earth made it difficult to keep their footing. Sylvia felt her legs shaking. 'Do you want an arm?' Fred came up beside her. 'Have to be my left.'

'Thank you.' Sylvia stared at him. His blue eyes were half shut against the glare. When he steadied her, his body felt strong and hard. She looked up and saw the whole surface of the field was decorated with white stones as if they'd been sprayed from above. She was about to point them out. Then she looked down and saw they were bones.

'Yes,' said Fred. 'I suppose it's a bit much to expect every last fibula and tibia to be picked up and tagged. I think the major wants us to go on.' He tried to see Sylvia's face under her hat. 'Your father didn't die here.'

They carried on, Sylvia stumbling, but trying not to peer too closely at the ground. The major waited again and when they reached him, Sylvia asked, 'Would it have looked like this when my father came?'

The major surveyed the scene round them. 'They'd been fighting round here for weeks before he arrived. The vegetation and trees that were burnt have grown up again. Before the war, it was quite a little Garden of Eden: vineyards, olive groves, wheat and barley.'

They went on again, climbing now over rough ground where Sylvia could pick out the sun-dried skeletons of wildflowers, rock roses, cornflowers, lavender, thyme, the occasional ear of barley and some clumps of flowering heather. Lavender, sage and lots of thyme were still flourishing. The vegetation made their progress even slower but now and again, Sylvia bent to pick a sprig. Perhaps she would take it home for her mother. At least they disguised the bones, although she had been shocked to trip on the remains of a boot. Occasionally, her attention was caught by a shining button or a bright flash of material. Resolutely, she followed the major.

'Nearly there!' he called encouragingly from above them. Like a parent to his children, thought Sylvia. He was a nice man and for a ghastly moment he reminded her of her father.

Then they were on the flat top of a small curving hill. It was covered by fronds of silvery grass. Sylvia stared round her, listened to her heavy breathing in the silence. Fred had dropped behind. You needed two hands to climb the last bit easily.

Sylvia brushed her skirt down and looked out. The major was right. The view was dazzling, right across the white salt lake to Lala Baba on the left and the long, high ridge on the right and between them both the endless shimmer of the aquamarine sea and china blue sky. She wondered if her father could have seen the same view, knowing, really, that it was impossible. He was in the forefront of an attack. The whole place was submerged under the smoke of battle, the burning undergrowth and the unexpected mist. He would have seen nothing.

'The sun would have been setting over the sea by the time they arrived.' The major and Fred stood on either side of her. 'But by all accounts those brave men didn't linger long but carried the attack forward over the hill. Are you ready?' They were all solicitous of her, thought Sylvia, perhaps the major felt guilty he hadn't died in this battle. 'The Turks were up there shooting down,' he waved his hand.

They moved down from the hill into a field as big and roughly ploughed as the other. The sea still shone far away to their left.

'This is where we think General Fitzpaine fell,' said Major Strangeways. In a modest but formal gesture, he took off his hat and held it against his chest. The two soldiers with him did the same. Fred gazed round at the wide field and then took off his hat too.

Arthur, walking the other side of Chocolate Hill, marvelled at how changed everything seemed. He remembered the savagery of the fighting but in a distanced impersonal way. When he saw a group of men, perhaps Greeks or Turks, clearing some areas of thick scrub and bramble, he went over to watch them. A British soldier approached him and saluted.

'What are they looking for?' Arthur asked.

'We're trying to work out the lines but it's all very higgledy-piggledy around here.'

'Yes. It was,' said Arthur casually.

The soldier eyed him curiously before saying, 'We're trying to find the Turkish front lines. We lost a lot of brave men there. But, judging by the bits of webbing and insignias we're picking up round about, we're not there yet.'

'I see.' Arthur didn't tell the soldier he was searching for the same place. He walked on, occasionally crossing a track or having to skirt impenetrable undergrowth. All the same, he felt certain he was heading in the right direction.

He'd already been on his own for over an hour.

In the end he fell into the trench, almost as he had before. It was very deep, as he'd remembered, and quite clear of vegetation. One part of it was roughly roofed with canvas and a sheet of corrugated iron. An old tin bucket lay on its side. It was surprisingly dark, the top of the trench just level with Arthur's head. It must have been above the heads of the Turks. He sniffed but there was none of the revolting odour of death, only a dank mustiness of earth which never saw the sun. He suspected someone was or had been living there.

After a moment, he slipped the satchel off his shoulder and unbuckled it. He put in his hand slowly and took out a pistol. It was an option he'd given himself before he'd left Constantinople. He could take his own life which had been taken from him four years ago in this very trench. Possibly this very trench. But he had left himself a choice. Death held no terrors for him. *A human being is only breath and shadow.* No one would hear the shot and some time, sooner or later, the soldier from the War Graves Commission would find his body. Perhaps the man would understand and wish he could put him under one of the neat little gravestones that were springing up over Gallipoli. Really, he deserved a memorial.

Sylvia hesitated at the edge of the field. Then eyes down, she began to pick her way slowly across it. The bones were no longer so shocking to her; now she noticed bullets and pieces of shrapnel.

The two men stayed behind, watching her. The major consulted his watch. 'I'm not sure we'll have time to visit the cemetery.'

Fred looked up at the sky. The sun was still blazing but at quite an angle. 'I wonder what's happened to Captain Lamb.'

Sylvia picked up two bullets, one short and fat, the other longer and slimmer. She thought of the bullets lined up by Fred in his potting shed. She felt painfully moved and also abandoned, lost. The field was big, no crop left and, among the bones and bullets, stones. What was she doing here? The idea of a treasure hunt was both ridiculous and even repugnant. The sky weighed heavily above her. At first she heard only silence but, as she stood still, the air seemed filled with a humming rising from the ground.

On the edge of the field, Fred said to the major, 'Do you hear it? The buzzing coming up from the earth?'

'I don't know,' said the major, 'I try not to hear things like that.'

'I expect it's insects,' said Fred consolingly.

Sylvia had been standing stock-still in the middle of the field for some minutes. Fred watched as she began to move again, faster, with her head down.

It was something glittering but she could not tell what. It seemed to be invisible. Then she saw the flash again, a few feet away; she moved quickly towards it. Expecting a button, a tin mug, an object, she saw a large dragonfly, the sunlight lighting up its translucent wings. It moved again, fluttering almost at ground level and she followed again. She was not prepared for beauty. Tears sprang into her eyes.

The dragonfly hovered at each stop, over a stone, a bit of dried stalk, a bone. Sylvia had a strange sense she was being led somewhere and yet the sight of the dragonfly was enough in itself. She was filled with rapture.

Five times the dragonfly paused, hovered, and each time Sylvia, mesmerised, followed its fast-beating, gossamer wings and elegant dark-striped body. On the sixth time, she'd just caught up again when the dragonfly darted away so quickly that she lost sight of it. For a second she didn't realise that it had left the ground and flown directly up into the sunshine. She shielded her eyes and stared upward. But she was too late: it had vanished. Blinking away tears, she crouched over the spot where the dragonfly had last landed. Something gleamed, half-buried in the earth.

Fred, still watching Sylvia, wondered what she was doing. He started walking towards her, followed, but not immediately, by Major Strangeways. The two soldiers stayed where they were.

Sylvia looked up as Fred's shadow reached towards her. 'I found something,' she said. 'Nothing much, I expect.' She held out her open hand.

'An insignia,' said Fred. 'A badge of rank.' He saw she'd been crying.

'It might be anyone's or it might be my father's.' She didn't tell him about the dragonfly.

Fred took the badge. He didn't know whether he wanted it to be a brigadier-general's or not. It was all too unlikely. 'It could be,' he said. 'It's been battered by something. A shell or a plough.'

The major joined them. He glanced at the badge. 'We find plenty of those.'

'Can you tell the rank?' asked Fred.

'Oh, I see.' The major was embarrassed. 'It could be a brigadier-general,' he said, as Fred had.

'It could be.' Sylvia took the badge and put it into her bag. She wasn't stupid but 'it could be' was enough for her.

Major Strangeways looked at the sun over the sea. The blue was slightly tinged with gold. 'If you would like to visit Green Hill Cemetery, we should go now. I'm sorry to rush you.' He began to walk away.

Fred realised Sylvia could hardly bear to leave the place where she stood. He came closer to her and put his good arm round her.

She spoke into his chest. 'It's not just my father. It's everything about the war. It's you. It's Hilda, Prideaux, Arthur. Nothing can ever be the same.'

'No.' Fred kissed her gently. She was right to mourn. She smelled of the sun, the soil, the dried grasses. He held her until

522

she wiped her face, and looked up at him more hopefully. Then he stepped back a little. 'Where *is* Arthur?'

They both stared across the field.

Arthur, coming out from behind a patch of tangled bushes, saw Fred and Sylvia and that they were holding hands. He stared for a moment more, then he walked over to join Major Strangeways.

The major looked relieved to see him. 'Did you find what you wanted, Captain?'

'Just about. A dangerous business, going back.'

'I should say so. That's the idea of cemeteries, you know. Helps people look forward. The problem here is we're faced with at least fifty per cent unidentified bodies. Gives one some difficult choices. The basic rule is you shouldn't have a named gravestone without a body. The rest go on a memorial, in a list. A bit sad, when you come to think of it.'

'Yes,' agreed Arthur who wasn't interested in the major's problems. He was wondering whether the sight of Sylvia and Fred hand in hand – they were walking towards him now – should upset him more.

'Now Miss Fitzpaine thinks she's found her father's badge. Frightfully unlikely, of course. But we did pick up the skeletons of officers in this area. That's why I brought her here. So it's not *impossible*. My question is, should I give Fitzpaine his own grave?'

'What?' said Arthur.

'It'll say "Believed to be buried in this cemetery" – quite vague really. Then his name, rank, dates, regiment and the line we've agreed on for everyone, officers and men. We're very democratic, you know.'

'What is the line?' asked Arthur, who'd begun to listen.

' *"Their glory shall not be blotted out."* So do you think I should give Fitzpaine his own headstone?'

'Why ever not?' exclaimed Arthur. Sylvia and Fred were only a few yards away.

'Why ever not,' repeated Major Strangeways, thoughtfully. 'It's not as if anyone can be sure about any identification under the circumstances. Thank you.'

'I wonder who chose the word "glory",' murmured Arthur almost to himself.

'You mean there's nothing very glorious about war.' The major smiled. 'People expect words like glory. I do myself.'

'Oh, I'm not against it. There were glorious deeds performed.'

Fred came up close to Arthur and said seriously, 'Glad you're with us, Captain.'

Arthur stared at him. What had he suspected to offer him such a welcome? Chaffey could not have known where he'd gone or why, the choice he'd given himself, yet he felt the man had some kind of intuition. So, he'd decided to live. People did that every day. 'Yes. I'm here.' He saw that Sylvia's eyes were bright. She smiled at him. 'Major Strangeways was telling me about the gravestones to be erected.'

'I had hoped to take you to Green Hill,' said the major, yet again consulting his watch. 'It's a lovely spot. A few pine trees already growing and we're planting more. I've always liked the sound of the wind singing through pine needles. There's a white stone wall and a memorial under construction, with the named graves, of which, of course, your father will be one, running on either side of it. I'm sure you can imagine . . .'

'Oh, yes,' said Sylvia. 'You're so very kind. We've seen far more than I ever expected.'

'Not at all. You must come back when the cemetery's finished. When Brigadier-General Fitzpaine's headstone is carved. Perhaps even Lady Beatrice will wish to visit.'

'Perhaps,' agreed Sylvia politely.

The major began walking quite fast in the general direction of the sea, taking a different route from their original one. The soldiers moved ahead, beating at the ground as they had earlier.

They were crossing a line of rushes on a dried river bed when the major approached Sylvia. She had taken off her hat and the lowering sun gave her hair and face a rich glow.

'I wondered whether you'd like me to arrange for the burial of the badge you found, in your father's grave?'

Sylvia stared at him, then smiled. 'You are so thoughtful. But you see while I was standing in the field I felt so strongly the spirit of my father and all the men who died there that I didn't want to take anything from them. So I dropped the badge down where I found it. Where he fell.' She paused before adding, 'I'm glad he has a grave, of course. My mother will be pleased. And even if

524

she doesn't want to come herself, I shall tell her about the wind singing a lullaby in the pines, and the white walls.'

The major nodded but also seemed a little surprised. She had been so downcast all day and now seemed almost exhilarated. Had finding her father's place of death meant so much?

They both began walking again, this time skirting the salt lake which now had a yellowish tint.

'It might have been different.' Arthur walked in step with Fred.

'Yes.' He remembered how glad he'd been of Lieutenant Lamb's attention. They'd known much of the same misery and euphoria. He glanced sideways. Lamb was still handsome, long face, straight nose, high brow with a lock of hair. He was staring at him now but passively. How he despised passive! Sylvia deserved better than that. He said deliberately, with an edge of malice, 'Everything at any time might be different.'

'You know what I'm talking about.' It was a statement, made without rancour or passion.

Yes. Fred knew what Arthur was talking about. But it was all bollocks. Childish nostalgia. If he wanted to complain he should go into politics and seek out those who'd created Gallipoli. Make sure such a bloody catastrophe never happened again.

Arthur saw his anger and stepped away. It was a pointless conversation. Perhaps Fred was right and he and Sylvia could never have made a life together. It felt like that. There was no going back. He'd given up Sylvia years ago, in a camp in Turkey. Their talk the night before had made that clear to both of them. The war had taken what little gift for love he'd had.

He wondered if Fred and he could be friends. Didn't Gallipoli make them friends? When they met in London or Oxford, would they be friends? What was the point of raging? He had not thought of Sylvia when he'd held a pistol to his head. Nor when he'd put it back in his satchel.

Arthur fell behind and watched as Fred and Sylvia joined hands again. He studied their attitudes. It was clear that they were lovers. It seemed Fred could love. He looked for jealousy and bitterness but instead he felt peace.

Fred let go of Sylvia's hand and came back to where Arthur

walked, head down. 'I'm sorry.' Arthur stopped and looked up. 'You're right. The war has made everything different.'

Arthur thought for a moment. 'Do you know what they're putting on the gravestones? "Their glory shall not be blotted out." Homer could have written that.'

Fred remembered the quotation. It came from the Bible: Ecclesiasticus 44: 13. 'Yes,' he said, 'it sounds like Homer.'

One by one or two by two, they reached Lala Baba and the jetty where the launch waited with its crew. Across the sea, the misty shape of Samothrace rose on the horizon. Nearer, Imbros showed its dark bulk. The launch rolled on the swell. The strong current flowing all the way down the Dardanelles from Constantinople had petered out here. The earlier wind had disappeared. They could have been travellers standing on the shores of an enchanted island.

They seemed unwilling to leave, staring around them in silence, to the hills, the dried lake, the distant promontories, then back to the sandy beach with its sprinkling of shells, the occasional seaweed draped over a stone, a block of wood, a rusty fragment of iron, tin or steel.

After all, this was a place of human habitation; there was no Calypso to beguile an Odysseus with her singing and weave him into her magic web. Under the waves lay the remains of army packs, boots, helmets, guns, boats, ships, the skeletons of men who had travelled here to serve their country and never left.

As the launch sped off to the open sea, the water turned from blue to bronze and a few white birds flew overhead.

Select Bibliography

Memoirs/Autobiographies

E. Ashmead-Bartlett, *The Uncensored Dardanelles*, Hutchinson 1928

C.E.W. Bean, *Gallipoli Mission*, Australian War Memorial 1948

C.E.W. Bean, *Gallipoli Correspondent*, selected and annotated by Kevin Fewster, George Allen & Unwin 1983

Chaplain Kenneth Best ed Gavin Roynan, *A Prayer for Gallipoli*, Simon & Schuster 2011

Violet Bonham Carter, *Winston Churchill – An Intimate Portrait*, Harcourt, Brace and World 1965

Edmund Blunden, *Undertones of War*, Richard Cobden-Sanderson 1928

Vera Brittain, *Testament of Youth*, Gollancz 1933

A.B. Facey, *A Fortunate Life*, Penguin (revised) 2005

Henry Hanna, KC, *The Pals at Suvla Bay*, E. Ponsonby 1916

Aubrey Herbert, *Mons, Anzac and Kut*, Hutchinson 1919

Compton Mackenzie, *Gallipoli Memories*, Cassell 1929

John Masefield, *Gallipoli*, William Heinemann 1916

Joseph Murray, *Gallipoli as I saw it*, William Kimber 1965

Ronald Skirth ed Duncan Barrett, *The Reluctant Tommy*, Pan 2010

Guy Slater (ed.), *My Warrior Sons –The Borton Family Diary*, Peter Davies 1973

John Still, *A Prisoner in Turkey*, BiblioLife (originally Bodley Head) 2009

Captain O. Teichman, DSO, MC *The Diary of a Yeomanry MO*, T. Fisher Unwin 1921

Biographies

Margaret Fitzherbert, *The Man who was Greenmantle – A Biography of Aubrey Herbert*, John Murray 1983

Christopher Hassall, *Rupert Brooke*, Faber & Faber 1964

Miles Jebb, *Patrick Shaw Stewart – An Edwardian Meteor*, The Dovecote Press 2010

Christopher Robbins, *The Empress of Ireland*, Scribner 2004

History

Brigadier-General C.F. Aspinall-Oglander, *Gallipoli Military Operations Based on Official Documents by Direction of the Historical Section, Committee of Imperial Defence, Vol I & II*, Heinemann 1929

Stephen Chambers, *Suvla, Gully Ravine, Anzac The Landing* (3 vols), Pen & Sword 2011/2003/2008

Peter Hart, *Gallipoli*, Profile Books 2011

Alan Moorehead, *Gallipoli*, Hamish Hamilton 1956

Huw and Jill Rodge, *Helles Landing*, Pen & Sword 2003

Stephen Snelling, *Gallipoli – VCs of the First World War*, The History Press 1995

Nigel Steele, *The Battlefields of Gallipoli*, Leo Cooper 1991

Nigel Steele and Peter Hart, *Defeat at Gallipoli*, Macmillan 1994

Richard Van Emden, *The Quick and the Dead – Fallen Soldiers and their Families in the Great War*, Bloomsbury 2011

Anthony Zarb-Dimech, *Malta during the First World War*, Veritas Press 2004

Fiction

A.P. Herbert, *The Secret Battle*, Methuen 1919

Ford Madox Ford, *Parade's End*, Alfred A. Knopf 1928

Irene Rathbone, *We that were Young*, Chatto & Windus 1932

Ernest Raymond, *Tell England*, George H. Doran Co 1922

Acknowledgements

The geography of the Gallipoli peninsula and the Dardanelles is an essential part of the story of the calamitous 1915 campaign. In June 2012 my husband and I joined a walking tour of the battlefields led by historian, Peter Hart. We swam on beaches where hundreds of soldiers had died, struggled up the same cliffs where soldiers under fire had carried up 70 lb packs, cut the brambles in trenches hardly changed after a hundred years, balanced along terrifying ridges, stumbled through gulleys where winter storms raged, and crossed fields still littered with bullets and bones. As well as thanking Peter and the trip's organiser, Roger Chapman, for this indispensable week of discovery, I also owe him a debt of gratitude for his book *Gallipoli* and his earlier book *Defeat at Gallipoli* written with Nigel Steele. Both books place great emphasis on the voice of the soldier. Other books that have been particularly useful are listed under the select bibliography.

Glory has three young soldiers and a young woman at the heart of the story but my interest in the subject arose from my grandfather's involvement. Brigadier-General the Earl of Longford was killed at Gallipoli on August 21st 1915 at the age of fifty. His military experience, culminating in a courageous and pointless death, forms the basis for the experiences of my invented character, Brigadier-General Fitzpaine. I would like to thank my brother, Thomas Pakenham, and his wife, Valerie, for inviting me to consult the family archive at Tullynally in Ireland and their daughter, Eliza Chisholm, who helped me sort through the boxes. My knowledge of officers captured on Gallipoli started out of a chance meeting with Sylvia Wingfield Digby whose grandfather, Captain Douglas Pass, was captured in the same action in which my grandfather died. Sylvia very kindly showed me her family archives of Captain Pass's years as a POW in Turkey. She drew my attention to a memoir by John Still, published online as *A Prisoner in Turkey* which was also an important source of information.

Biographer and military historian, Jonathan Walker, read an early manuscript and gave me some basic and much-needed advice on specific military detail. Any errors are my own. Grateful thanks to Nicholas Wingfield Digby for sharing his knowledge of the Classics, Greek and Roman, and to Dr Simon Cave for sharing his medical knowledge. Historian Linda Kelly passed on some fascinating nuggets of research.

My agent, Andrew Gordon, together with Marigold Atkey, has pushed forward this project enthusiastically from the start. At Orion, Deputy Publisher, Jon Wood, and editor, Laura Gerrard, have shown enormous interest and encouragement throughout the writing of the book while Deputy Publicity Director, Gaby Young, has put out the flags. Belinda Wingfield Digby gave the impression that she waited eagerly to type the next chapter of my handwritten manuscript which helped still my nerves in such a big work.

As always, my family have been enormously supportive. Particular thanks to my daughter, Rose Gaete, who brought her professional editor's eye to bear on the manuscript, and to Chloe and Hannah Billington who also read an early copy and made positive suggestions. Finally, my husband Kevin Billington has trodden with me the paths of Gallipoli both literally and metaphorically. His commitment to the project and his political and historical knowledge has made my own progress more confident.

Writing about a disastrous campaign which caused so much suffering, including to my own close relatives, has been an emotional business. It is ironic that Winston Churchill, one of Britain's greatest war heroes must bear a good part of the blame. My widowed grandmother refused to enter a drawing-room where Churchill or even his wife was expected. I hope by turning the story of Gallipoli into a novel I have lost nothing of the truth of the matter and made it easier for readers to appreciate the impact on those who took part in it both in the field and at home.